D0065068

WELCOME!

Inside this volume you'll find murder and mayhem presented by some of the world's greatest crime writers— ·

John Dickson Carr gives Dr. Gideon Fell the problem of the woman found strangled on a beach, where the sand is unmarked by footprints.

Ngaio Marsh has Inspector Roderick Alleyn solve a murder in a locked dressing room.

Bill Pronzini assigns his nameless private eye to shadow an automobile until its occupant suddenly vanishes into thin air.

Edward D. Hoch presents a spy story featuring murder in a locked automobile.

Anthony Boucher shows how to commit the perfect crime—with a time machine.

Frederic Brown tells a cockeyed tale of a ghoul who wants to get into—not out of—a locked morgue.

Ellery Queen examines the many facets of an impossible disappearance of priceless diamonds.

Clayton Rawson, with the help of the Great Merlini, demonstrates how to disappear from a telephone booth surrounded by witnesses.

L. Frank Baum, who would later send Dorothy and Toto on the Yellow Brick Road to Oz, dispatches a money-lender in an entirely different fashion.

Wilkie Collins will keep you awake with the case of a murderous bedroom.

Cornell Woolrich checks in with a story of a hotel room that kills.

Lillian de la Torre recreates the first true historical locked-room mystery.

And another ten tantalizingly teasing tales to taunt and terrify you in this collection of the greatest locked-room murders and impossible crimes.

DEATH LOCKED IN

Edited by
Douglas G. Greene and
Robert C.S. Adey

AN ANTHOLOGY OF LOCKED ROOM STORIES

INTERNATIONAL POLYGONICS, LTD.
New York

DEDICATION
For my brothers, David L. Greene and Paul E. Greene—DGG

For my parents, Ronald and Elsie Adey—RCSA

DEATH LOCKED IN
An original publication.

©Copyright 1987 by Douglas G. Greene.
Cover: Copyright© 1987 by International Polygonics, Ltd.

Library of Congress Card Catalog No. 87-82449
ISBN 0-930330-75-7

Printed and manufactured in the United States of America by
Guinn Printing, New York.
First IPL printing October 1987.
10 9 8 7 6 5 4 3 2 1

ACKNOWLEDGMENTS

I am grateful to Edward D. Hoch, Francis M. Nevins, Jr., Derek Smith and Dennis McMillan for helping to obtain stories, and to Lillian de la Torre for allowing us to appropriate (well, almost) the title of one of her short stories, "Murder Lock'd In." Thanks also go to Hugh Abramson, publisher of International Polygonics, who suggested this anthology, encouraged its completion, and watched over it every step of the way. I owe much to my co-editor, Robert C. S. Adey, who chose and introduced several of the stories and whose definitive work, *Locked Room Murders and Other Impossible Crimes,* is a guide to anyone interested in miracle problems.

—DGG

CONTENTS

INTRODUCTION

Detective stories come in all shapes and sizes, penny plain and twopenny colored. They can be slow-moving cerebral exercises or fast-paced thrillers or just about anything in-between, and fictional detectives investigate all manner of crimes, from the kidnapping of pet poodles to the loss of nuclear bombs. Sleuths constantly happen on corpses—in airplanes and on ships, in country houses and in slums, in forests and on football fields, in the White House and the jailhouse.

And in locked rooms.

It is *ingenuity* that ties together the stories in *Death Locked In*. John Dickson Carr, the greatest exponent of the seemingly impossible crime, wrote that "though this quality of ingenuity is not necessary to the detective story as such, you will never find the great masterpiece without it. Ingenuity lifts the thing up; it is triumphant; it blazes, like a diabolical lightning flash, from beginning to end. . . . When . . . we find ourselves flumdiddled by some master stroke of ingenuity which has turned our suspicions legitimately in the wrong direction, we can only salute the author and close the book with a kind of admiring curse." Readers of tales of miracle crimes want to know not only "whodunit" but also "how on earth could it have been done." *How can* a person be murdered while alone in a locked, indeed a hermetically sealed, room? *How can* a murderer strangle his victim who is sitting alone on a beach, and yet leave no footprints? *How*

9

can someone disappear from a house or, even more daringly, from an automobile that is constantly under observation? *How can* a man be killed by a pistol that is sealed in an envelope at the moment of the crime?

How can? That's the key question which locked-room readers approach a story of an impossible crime. Other fans of fictional mayhem may enjoy a supercharged spy thriller, or a naturalistic trip down mean streets, or the angst of a policeman who is just as worried about his digestion or his sex life as he is about the case he is more or less investigating; but true locked-room fans want something more. They want to be puzzled, to be challenged, even to be fooled. One type of reader, in the words of G. K. Chesterton, "not only desires to be gulled, but even desires to be gullible." Others, more active types, hope to reach the solution ahead of the detective; they work out timetables and re-read each word watching for the hidden clue, the disguised motive, the carefully placed red-herring, the true explanation of the locked room or the miraculous disappearance.

Locked-room murders and other seemingly impossible crimes—called by aficionados "miracle problems"—have a long history. For example, a brief undeveloped episode in Chretien de Troyes's twelfth-century romance, LANCELOT OR THE KNIGHT OF THE CART, is similar to the plot of Wilkie Collin's classic tale of a murderous room, "A Terribly Strange Bed." Many of the Gothic novels from the 1790s to the 1830s feature apparently supernatural events that are explained, not always persuasively, at the denoument. Mrs. Radcliffe's *Mysteries of Udolpho* (1794) has among many other ghostly events, a disappearance from a locked room. Perhaps the most interesting predecessor of the locked-room story is E.T.A. Hoffman's early nineteenth-century novella, "Mademoiselle de Scuderi, A Tale of the Times of Louis XIV," about a series of mysterious robberies and murders on the streets of Paris. When the murderer was pursued, he "sprang aside into the shade and disappeared through the wall." A policeman explained:

> We lighted the torches and sounded the wall backwards and forwards—not an indication of a door or a window

or an opening. It was a strong stone wall bounding a yard, and was joined on to a house in which live people against whom there has never risen the slightest suspicion. Today I have again taken a careful survey of the whole place. It must be the Devil himself who is mystifying us.

Later in the story, a man was discovered stabbed to death within a locked house. Sadly for locked-room fans, these scenes are only a small part of Hoffman's 30,000-word tale, and the explanation, involving a secret passage, makes one question the competence of those who "sounded the wall backwards and forwards."

Joseph Sheridan Le Fanu's "Passage in the Secret History of an Irish Countess" (1838) is probably the first "genuine" locked-room story, that is, one in which the apparent impossibility is a major plot element and which does not depend on such unfair devices as secret passages. Le Fanu's tale did not need a detective to explain it, but with the growth of interest in detection, both real and fictional, during the rest of the 19th century it became common to have a sleuth unravel miracle crimes. Eventually, almost every great detective solved a locked-room or an impossible disappearance during his or her career, and several specialized in such situations—The Thinking Machine, Father Brown, Dr. Gideon Fell, Rolf Le Roux, The Great Merlini, Senator Brooks U. Banner and others. In recent years, these amateur sleuths have been joined by private eyes and secret agents in explaining tricks and impossibilities.

The stories in *Death Locked In* challenge the impossible. The gates of the unknown are opened, devils fly, ghosts walk, and witches's curses are real. Crimes are committed that can have no rational, human explanation. Or so it seems. . . . We invite you to be challenged by the most ingenious of detective stories.

DOUGLAS G. GREENE
May 1987

THE FIRST LOCKED ROOM

By Lillian de la Torre (1902-   )

Occasionally unimaginative critics will state that locked-room murders do not occur in real life. That is, of course, demonstrably false. Evidence about a locked-room crime was presented to a law court as early as 1733. The case is recounted by Lillian de la Torre, the mistress of what she calls "histo-detection." De la Torre has devised new solutions to the classic mysteries of Elizabeth Canning (Eliz-abeth is Missing), the Douglas claimant (The Heir of Doug-las) and Belle Gunness (The Truth about Belle Gunness), and she had edited a collection of articles about seven-teenth- and eighteenth-century highwaymen, cut-purses and other wrong 'uns (Villainy Detected). She is best known for her four volumes of short stories featuring the eigh-teenth-century Great Cham of Literature, Dr. Samuel John-son, acting as a "detector," with Boswell in the role of Watson. "The First Locked Room," de la Torre explains, "is all true; according to my custom I have not even put words into people's mouths unless I found the words in the old accounts."

THEY were all dead in their beds. The two old women lay strangled. The young maid had fought for her life; she lay in a welter of blood, with her hair tossed about her.

The outside windows were four stories above Tanfield Court and the staircase windows were barred. They had locked them all, not against intrusion, but against the infection of the night vapors.

The front door was locked and bolted.

None of the gaping London crowd had ever heard of such a state of affairs; three women lying murdered in a place that was locked and barred. It was the year 1733. There were no detective stories, then, and no detectives either; no Scotland Yard, no Metropolitan Police, not even a single Bow Street runner. There was a justice of the peace in Bow Street, one Thomas De Veil, dispensing law and order strictly for cash; but his writ did not run in Tanfield Court. Tanfield Court was part of the Inner Temple. The lawyers who resorted there were too deep in their torts and mortauncestries to take cognizance of a real flesh-and-blood crime. The dignity of the law in Tanfield Court fell to be upheld by the Inner Temple watch.

That worthy stood about helplessly, all dubiety from his antique round hat to his buckled shoes. In spite of the panoply of his authority, the broad leathern belt about his middle and the staff of office in his hand, he was at a loss. He wondered what to do.

The center of an excited group of neighbors, Mistress Ann Love was telling how she came to make the gruesome discovery on this quiet winter Sunday. Her cap-muslin vibrated and the lawn kerchief upon her bosom rose and fell with agitation as she remembered her awful experience.

Mrs. Lydia Duncomb had been known to her for thirty years. The old lady, now bed-ridden, was a woman with a fortune; it consisted of a silver tankard and a green purse of gold moidores and broad pieces. She lived alone in the highest lodging in Tanfield Court with her old serving-woman Betty. When Betty grew too old for service, kind Mrs. Duncomb kept her on, and hired others to work for them both. For a while she depended on the regular charwomen of the Temple; but shortly before Christmas she had hired young Ann Price to live in and be always at hand.

"I was bidden to dine," agitated Mrs. Love told the neighbors. "At exactly one o'clock I came to the chamber-door. I knocked and waited a considerable time, but nobody answered."

Upon this, alarm had risen in the visitor's soul. She ran up and down the narrow stairs seeking assistance. A couple of charwomen were standing about. One of them, an impudent Irish wench in a blue riding-hood, Sarah Malcolm by name, was well known to Mrs. Love as a former charwoman of Mrs. Duncomb's.

Mrs. Love accosted her:

"Pritheee, Sarah, go and fetch the smith to open the door."

"I will go with all speed," said the Irish wench, and sauntered off.

She came back, which in itself is curious, and suggests that she knew no more than Mrs. Love what lay behind that bolted door. She came back without the smith.

"Oh!" says Mrs. Love to the other charwoman, with whom she was on more ceremonious terms, "Mistress Oliphant, I believe they are all dead, and the smith is not come. What shall we do to get in?"

"My master Grisly's chambers, you know," replied the resourceful Oliphant promptly, "are opposite to Mrs. Duncomb's. He went away last Tuesday and left the keys with me. Now, I will see if I cannot get out of his chamber-window into the gutter, and so into Mrs. Duncomb's apartment."

The intrepid charwoman carried out this program without mishap. Those waiting faintly heard the tinkle as the window-glass broke when Mrs. Oliphant effected her entry, and in another minute they distinctly heard the bolt inside the door grate back. Mrs. Love pressed in, and Sarah Malcolm followed. The first sight that met their eyes was the young maid on her pallet in the passage, wallowing in her blood. In the inner room the old serving-woman in her press bed lay strangled, and in the inmost room, on the best bed, Mrs. Duncomb was found strangled too.

The mob seemed to spring from nowhere. They pressed

into the murder chamber so thick that now the surgeon bending over the bedside was in danger of having his shanks snapped. He scanted his examination a little; but it was plain as a pike-staff; three were dead, and no one of them had done it.

The mob buzzed with excitement. They looked at the bolted door, and the barred window, and the murdered women, and shook their heads. It must have been a murdering ghost, or the Devil himself in person, to do that bloody work and then walk out through a bolted door.

The only thing was, what did the Devil want with the silver tankard and the green purse of gold? For the black strong-box had been rifled of Mrs. Duncomb's whole fortune.

The three-pair-of-stairs lodgers met in Tanfield Court. Mr. John Kerrel, advocate, was on his way back from Commons. He stared at his friend Mr. Gehagan, and both stared at the mob about their lodging. A writer of their acquaintance was among the mob.

"What's the matter?" they called to him.

"Murder's the matter," said he. "Mrs. Duncomb is dead by foul play." And he added to Kerrel, "That's your laundress' acquaintance."

The three-pair-of-stairs lodgers stepped over to a coffee-house in nearby Covent Garden. The place was agog over the murders. It was the general opinion that the murderer was some charwoman who was acquainted with the chambers. This made Mr. Kerrel mighty uneasy. Charwoman Sarah Malcolm had his key.

To minister to his malaise, Gehagan and Kerrel adjourned to the Horseshoe and Magpie in Essex Street. What potations they imbibed is not recorded. They returned to Tanfield Court at one in the morning, in a very unlikely condition to break this mysterious case; but break it they did.

As they stumbled up the dark stair, they saw a light in Mr. Kerrel's lodging. The door was open; the fire blazed in the grate; the candles burned in the scones; and by the fireside stood Sarah Malcolm. It gave Mr. Kerrel quite a turn.

"So, Sarah," says he nervously, "are you here at this time of night?"

This Sarah Malcolm could not deny.

"You knew Mrs. Duncomb," Kerrel went on, "have you heard of anybody that is taken up for the murders?"

"No," says she, "but a gentleman who had chambers under her has been absent two or three days, and he is suspected."

"Well!" says Mr. Kerrel. "I'll have nobody here that was acquainted with Mrs. Duncomb, till the murderer is found out; and therefore look up your things, and go away."

Mr. Gehagan thought it was time to call the watch. Down he went, and wrestled with the great front door, but he was in no condition to open it; he had to fetch Mr. Kerrel. It was Mr. Kerrel who finally wrenched the door open and bawled: "*Watch!*"

The two watchmen had taken refuge from the inclemency of the weather in the near-by watch-house. When they heard Mr. Kerrel's outcry, they reluctantly took up their staves and their square lanthorns, and came. Presumably they were sober, but they were of little more use than the two crapulous men of the law.

The four men found Sarah Malcolm obeying Mr. Kerrel's behest to look up her things. Mr. Kerrel was not so fuddled but he thought he ought to check his possessions. He soon proved to have been wise.

"Where are my waistcoats?" he demanded.

"Give me a word in private," says bold Sarah.

"No," says Mr. Kerrel, "I have no business with you that needs be made a secret of."

"I pawned them," confessed Sarah, "for two guineas."

Mr. Kerrel was angry.

"Why," cried he, "did you not ask me for money?"—a question which, taken with the presence of Sarah's "things" in the three-pair-of-stairs lodging, suggests that to Mr. Kerrel Sarah was more than a charwoman.

Mr. Kerrel's search continued.

"What's this?" he demanded kicking a bundle on the closet floor.

"An old gown," replied the Irish wench, "with a shift and apron in it; but pray do not look in it, for it is an indecent sight for a man to see."

Mr. Kerrel put it down again, and gave Sarah into the custody of the watch.

"Watch," says he, "take care of her, and do not let her go."

So down she went with the watchmen, and they did the exact opposite. They instructed her to return at ten in the morning, and shooed her off. She went as far as Tanfield Court Arch, and stopped. She turned back.

" 'Tis late," she whined, "and I live as far as Shoreditch, and therefore I had rather sit up with you in the watch-house all night than go home."

"No," said the obdurate watch, "you shall not sit up in the watch-house, and therefore go about your business, and be here again at ten o'clock."

Sarah Malcolm went off. Upstairs, Mr. Kerrel and Mr. Gehagan were too agitated to seek repose. What with their potations, and perhaps the thought of the bloody devil upstairs that could walk through a bolted door, they could not rest. Mr. Kerrel looked under the bed.

"Zounds," says he, "here's another bundle of linen that she has left behind her."

Upon this discovery he looked into another likely hiding-place, the close-stool, and there he found more linen, and a silver tankard with blood on it. The thing began to look thoroughly sinister. The two lawyers pelted down the stairs after the watch.

"Where's the woman?" they demanded.

"We let her go; for we found nothing upon her, and we were not regularly charged with her before a constable—"

"You dog," says Mr. Kerrel, "go and find her, or I'll send you to Newgate."

The frightened watchman made off. He was in luck. Sarah had found a pair of more complaisant watchmen at Temple Gate; she was sitting cosily with them. They haled her back. Pot-valiant Mr. Gehagan rated her in a fit of inebrious moral indignation.

"You bloody murdering bitch!" says he. "Was it not enough to rob the people, and be damned to you, but you must murder them too? I'll see you hanged, you bitch! You bloody bitch you!"

He showed her the tankard. She hastily began to wipe the handle with her apron.

"No, you bloody bitch," said Mr. Gehagan, repeating himself with more feeling than variety, "you shan't wipe it off."

" 'Tis my mother's," said Sarah, desisting, "I have but just fetched it out of pawn, I had thirty shillings for it."

"You bloody bitch you," says monotonous Mr. Gehagan, "your mother was never worth such a tankard."

"And the blood is my own," said Sarah; she showed the watchman where she had cut her finger.

The watch carried Sarah to the Compter, a prison for lesser malefactors. In the dirty common room she met an old acquaintance named Bridgewater, with a fetter on. They exchanged courtesies.

"Pray give me a dram," said Bridgewater, "for I have been a great while in prison."

Sarah was flush of money. She gave him a shilling and a farthing, and called for half a quartern of rum to make him drink.

Money bought everything in the prisons of 1733. It is likely that Bridgewater lay on the floor; but Sarah had a room to herself, and a bed with curtains. As she was walking pensively about this palatial chamber, she was surprised to hear her name called from the head of the bed. She pulled back the draperies, and there was the grateful Bridgewater peering in through a hole in the wall.

"Have you sent for any friends?" asked he.

"No," said Sarah.

"I'll do what I can for you," said he, and made off.

Shortly he was back.

"Here's a friend," said he, and presented a typical specimen of Newgate lawyer. Sarah knew him.

"Is that Will Gibbs?" said she. He owned that it was.

"And how," said Sarah, asking after some particular friends, "are Tom and James Alexander?"

Mr. Gibbs said they were well. Then he began to interrogate her. The question of the locked room was not raised. Mr. Gibbs was more interested in other matters.

"Who is there to swear against you?"

"My two masters will be the chief witnesses."

"And what can they charge you with?"

"The tankard is the only thing that can hurt me."

"Never fear then," says Gibbs with brisk confidence, "we'll

do well enough; we will get them that will rap (swear) the tankard was your grandmother's, and that you was in Shoreditch the night the murder was committed; and we'll have two men that shall shoot your two masters."

This program appealed to Sarah, especially the alibi, so dear to Mr. Tony Weller in after days.

"You must get someone to swear that I was at their house."

"It must be a woman," said Mr. Gibbs with nice regard for a lady's reputation, "and she won't swear under four guineas; but the four men will swear for two guineas apiece."

Sarah thought this a bargain. She produced twelve guineas, which Mr. Gibbs seized, promising to deliver the whole package of perjury at the Bull's-head in Bread-street when called for on the morrow.

On the morrow they carried her before the alderman to be charged. She was permitted to stop off at the Bull's head, but there was nobody there. Mr. Gibbs was doubtless drinking up his easy twelve guineas in some other house of resort.

Left on her own, Sarah Malcolm had to change her whole plan of campaign. She went before the alderman and offered to confess everything. She said that she did not murder the three women; but she knew who did. She named the villains: the two boys named Alexander, and a bold grenadier of a woman who had followed the troops, one Mary Tracey.

Mary Tracey and Sarah Malcolm, by Sarah's confession, were two of a kind. They planned to rob old Mrs. Duncomb, and called in the boys to help. On the Saturday night at eight o'clock, Sarah paid the household a visit and made a preliminary survey; she found the old serving woman very ill. At ten o'clock Mary Tracey arrived at Tanfield Court with the two young bullies. She was in a hurry, but Sarah said it was too soon. Tracey pressed her. Before eleven Sarah went upstairs, and her accomplices followed her. On the stair they met the young serving-wench with a blue jug in her hand; she was going for some milk to make a sack-posset. She looked at the accomplices suspiciously, and asked her friend Sarah who they were? Sarah said they were just some people going to call on Mr. Knight on the floor below. As soon as Ann Price was gone, Sarah gave her orders.

"Now," said she to Mary Tracey, "do you and Tom Alexander go down. I know the door is left ajar, because the old maid is ill, and can't get up to let the young maid in when she comes back. James shall slip in and hide himself under the bed."

Accordingly the others made themselves scarce, and James did as he was bidden. The young maid returned and made her sack-posset; the door was bolted, and silence fell upon Tanfield Court. It was a very stormy night. The watchmen kept up close in the comfortable watch-house, except just when they cried the hour. "Two o'clock of a very stormy night, and all's well," they cried; while James Alexander lay under the old woman's bed, and his accomplices waited upon the stair.

"Soon after this," Sarah confessed to the alderman, "I heard Mrs. Duncomb's door open; James Alexander came out, and said, 'Now is the time.' Then Mary Tracey and Thomas Alexander went in, but I stayed upon the stairs to watch. I told them where Mrs. Duncan's box stood; they came out between four and five, and one of them called me softly, and said *'Hip! How shall I shut the door?'* Says I, *'Tis a spring lock; pull it to, and it will be fast;'* and so one of them did."

They said nothing to Sarah about murder; they said they had been forced to gag the people. Sarah cared little for that.

The alderman asked nothing, and Sarah volunteered nothing, of how they had managed to shoot the bolt on the inside. The law was more interested in the loot. They came out with it, Sarah said, and would have shared it then and there, upon the stairs, but Sarah wanted to be further off. So they went under the arch in Figtree Court, where there was a lamp. There in that little pool of brightness in the stormy night they shared the swag. Sarah had the tankard with what money was in it, and those linens that disturbed Mr. Kerrel, for her whack. They advised her to be cunning; they told her, in their immemorial thieves' cant, to *plant* the *kale* under ground, and not be seen to be *flush*, "for if you be seen to be flush of *cole*, you will be suspected; and on Monday, be sure, about 3 or 4 o'clock, you come to the Pewter Platter on Holbourn-bridge."

Sarah Malcolm failed that rendezvous at the Pewter Platter. She was otherwise occupied, for the alderman sent her to Newgate.

She went with foreboding. As she entered the old stone keep over the pointed arch of the city gate that was new so many hundreds of years ago, she cried out in despair. "I am a dead woman!" cried she.

Her apprehensions were well grounded. Of those who went in at that door, many would rot with the gaol fever, and more would lie fettered a short while, and then come out to the hangman's cart.

Once inside, Sarah Malcolm recovered her equanimity. She went into the tap-house among the felons on the Common Side. As she pulled off her blue riding-hood, sharp eyes marked her. The eyes were sharper than the mind. The observer, too stupid to see how he might turn his observations to account, went and blabbed to another prisoner, one Roger Johnson:

"I observe that the wench's hair bulges behind; she has certainly money hid in her hair."

Roger Johnson knew Sarah; she had been in the habit of coming to Newgate in former days, to visit another Johnson, an Irishman, who had been jailed for stealing a Scotch peddler's pack. He was therefore in a favorable position for taking advantage of her. He called for a torch, and conducted her into the cellars.

"Child," said he familiarly, "there is reason to suspect that you are guilty of this murder, and therefore I have orders to search you" (which was a bare-faced lie).

Thereupon this impudent felon allowed his hands to stray familiarly over Sarah's buxom person. This little comedy over, he took the money from her hair, where it lay ill hid under the muslin cap.

"Aha!" said he, "I find the cole's planted in your hair; pray how did you come by it?"

"Mr. Johnson," said the desperate girl, "I'll make you a present of it, if you will but keep it to yourself, and let nobody know anything of the matter, for the other things that are against me are nothing but circumstances, and I shall come off well enough, and therefore I'll only desire you to let me have three-pence or six-pence a day till the sessions is over, and then I shall be at liberty to shift for myself."

"My dear," says Mr. Johnson, "I would not secrete the money for the world."

Mr. Johnson knew a trick worth two of that. He figured that with this bit of luck he could buy his way out of Newgate. He locked Sarah in, and went for an official of the jail.

After a while he fetched Sarah.

"What have you done with the bag?" asked he.

"I have it," said Sarah, "but what would you advise me to do with it?"

"Why," says he, "you might have thrown it down the necessary house, or have burnt it, but give it me, and I'll take care of it."

Sarah produced the green purse, and this petty Judas of Newgate took it. Then forth from a dark corner stepped the jailer, who had been planted there for a witness, and Sarah knew that her life was gone. They took her to the shadowy stone condemned hole, and I suppose fettered her with the long X-shaped wrist-to-ankle fetters they used for murderers. I am happy to say that Mr. Roger Johnson for all his sharpness stayed in Newgate.

Let no one take the adventures of Sarah with the watch, and among the prisoners, for romancing. They are typical of the slackness and venality of officialdom in the eighteenth century world of crime. Anything could happen in Newgate. Drunkenness and debauchery, extortion and petty thieving, bullying and fighting, were common among the prisoners herded into the dirty, nasty halls, and the jailers took part in all with gusto. Anything went, short of breaking jail, and for a price a man could do that too, for a brief vacation now and then.

Mary Tracey and the Alexanders were soon laid by the heels. Inefficient as the law was, it did not fail to make the Pewter Platter rendezvous.

Sarah Malcolm smiled with satisfaction to hear it. "I shall die now with pleasure," said she, "since the murderers are taken."

When confronted with them, she identified them at once:

"Ay, these are the persons that committed the murder."

She looked Mary Tracey in the eye with a boldness which surprised all the spectators.

"So, Mary," burst out her erstwhile friend bitterly, "see what you have brought me to; it is through you and the two Alexanders that I am brought to this shame, and must die for it; you all promised me you would do no murder, but to my great surprise I found the contrary."

They took the trio away. I hope they lodged them out of Sarah's sight.

Sarah's time in Newgate was short. In barely two weeks they haled her to the Sessions House in the Old Bailey, and set her in the dock. She was indicted for making an assault upon seventeen-year-old Ann Price, "with a knife made of iron and steel, of the value of three-pence, which she, the said Sarah Malcolm, then and there in her right hand held." I cannot say what difference the material and monetary value of the weapon could make; but both were always carefully specified in indictments.

Sarah Malcolm was a Tartar in the dock. The chaplain of Newgate had already noted with regret that she was of a most bold, daring, boisterous, and wilful spirit. These qualities now stood her in good stead, for in those days a murderer in the dock stood entirely alone. He was allowed no legal counsel, but must speak for himself as he had the wit and the courage. Many a culprit stood mum before the court and went mum to the gallows; but not Sarah Malcolm. She heckled every witness.

Mr. Kerrel and Mr. Gehagan led off. They told how she had been taken up. Mr. Gehagan repeated his monotonous profanity with modest pride; he had much ado, he told the court, to keep his hands off the bitch. The watchmen, in more moderate terms, told their story of her taking-up. Sarah Malcolm cross-questioned them all.

Then Mrs. Love and Mrs. Oliphant were called to repeat how they had made that gruesome discovery.

Mrs. Oliphant added a piquant detail. She had visited Mrs. Duncomb the night before the murders, and had heard foreboding talk. Mrs. Duncomb was sorry Mr. Grisly had left, because it was so lonesome. Sarah Malcolm was sitting by the fire with the old serving-woman. "My mistress talks of dying," said the old servant, "and would have me die with her." The court thrilled at this specimen of prophecy. Counsel disregarded it. He proceeded to treat Mrs. Oliphant as a locked-room expert, doubtless in view of her prowess in getting one open.

"You say you opened the casement, and found the door locked and bolted; how do you think the persons who did the murder could get out?"

"I don't know," said Oliphant. "I heard somebody say, they must get down the chimney, it is a large kitchen chimney."

"Is there any way for a person to get out and leave the door bolted?"

"I know of none."

"Mr. Grisly's chambers have been empty, you say, ever since Tuesday, could they not get into his chambers, and so into hers?"

"I don't know: there is a silly lock to his door, and I believe it may be easily picked."

This left the puzzle of the locked room still unsolved. Sarah Malcolm thought it a good point, and pressed it in her heckling. She only succeeded in drawing a sharp remark from the bench:

"Somebody did get in and out too, that is plain to a demonstration," said the judge, plying his nosegay of herbs against the gaol infection.

The prosecuting counsel was ready to demonstrate.

"My lord, we shall now shew that it was practicable for the door to be bolted withinside by a person who was without."

The prosecutor put his investigator on the stand, and the classic string trick was exposed in court for the first time:

"There being a difficulty started how the door could be bolted with inside, I took Mr. Farlow, porter of the Temple, with me; he put a string about the neck of the bolt, and then I shut him out, and he pulled the bolt to by both ends of the string, and then letting go one end, he pulled the string out."

Sarah Malcolm closed the proceedings with an eloquent speech in her own defence; but she marred all with the impudence of her closing remark:

"My lord," said Sarah Malcolm coolly to the judge, "as there was more money found upon me than belonged to Mrs.

Duncomb, I hope your lordship will be so good as to order what was my own to be returned to me."

His lordship did no such thing. He listened to the jury's verdict of guilty, and sentenced her to be hanged by the neck until dead.

This closed the matter of Mrs. Lydia Duncomb, as far as the law was concerned. The Alexanders were held a while, and then let go. After a little indecision the law took them up again, and then they faded from public gaze. They must have got off, for they figure in none of the black lists of the hanged. It is odd no one of the three turned King's Evidence.

Meanwhile they took Sarah Malcolm back to Newgate. She had two weeks of life left.

The chaplain of Newgate could make nothing of her. She declined to confess herself a murderess. She declared herself a Romanist. "She is a most obdur'd, impenitent sinner!" ejaculated the good man in despair.

William Hogarth came down to Newgate and painted her picture, which subsequently adorned the wall of Horace Walpole's gingerbread castle at Strawberry Hill. There she sits on her plain gown and kerchief, with her apron looped up and the fear of death on her face, the lips compressed, the nostrils dilated, the eyes slewed slidewise. She might have been hearing already the awful admonition of the bellman of St. Sepulchre's, fee'd by some dead worthy to chant outside the condemned cell his lugubrious reminder:

"All you that in the condemned hold do lie,
Prepare you, for tomorrow you shall die.
Watch all, and pray, the hour is drawing near,
That you before the Almighty must appear.
Examine well yourselves, in time repent,
That you may not t'eternal flames be sent.
And when St. Sepulchre's bell tomorrow tolls,
The Lord above have mercy on your souls!
Past twelve o'clock!"

But even that solemn admonition, reverberating on the cold spring night, could not quite quench Sarah Malcolm's spirit.

"D'ye hear, Mr. Bellman," she called from her cell when the chant was done, "call for a pint of wine, and I will throw you a shilling to pay for it," and down went the shilling accordingly.

They hanged her in Fleet Street, before Mitre Court, near the Inner Temple, "because of the atrociousness of her crimes, and for terror to other wickedly disposed people." She went to her death neatly dressed in a crepe mourning gown, holding up her head in the cart with an air, and her color was so high that spectators did not scruple to allege that she was painted.

They ran the cart under the gallows, and put the noose about her neck. Just before the cart drew away she looked towards the Temple, and cried out:

"Oh! My master, my master! I wish I could see him!"

Mr. Kerrel was nowhere to be seen. But perhaps he came to her later, for the *Gentleman's Magazine* reported:

"Her Corpse was carried to an Undertaker upon Snow Hill where Multitudes of People resorted, and gave Money to see it; among the rest a Gentleman in deep new Mourning, who kiss'd her . . ."

Who killed the women of Tanfield Court?

That question is bound up with the Locked Room puzzle: who left the door bolted on the inside and why, and how was it done?

It was not Sarah Malcolm. She didn't know how it was done, or even that it was done. The best information she could give the examining alderman was something about a spring lock.

It was not her three accomplices. If we accept Sarah Malcolm's story, it exonerates them. She sat within earshot, for when they "hipped" softly to attract her attention, she replied at once. She told them to pull the spring lock to, and she heard them do it. If they had fiddled around doing the string trick, she would have known it. More, sitting within earshot, she heard not a sound of Ann Price's bitter struggle for her life. The robbers came out and told her they had left their victims gagged; nothing the lookout had heard caused her to disbelieve them.

Then who killed those three women, and left the door bolted on the inside, and why, and how was it done?

A piece of the puzzle has vanished, here and there, with

the lapse of time, notably the big piece labeled "Motive"; but enough pieces remain, and I have faithfully recorded them here, to delineate the face of the murderer.

Suppose.

Suppose you hated, with a half-insane hate, the girl called Ann Price. Suppose you looked out of a window, early Sunday morning, and saw in the room across the court Ann Price's mistress, bound and gagged on her bed. It would occur to you in a flash, here is this household delivered into my hands. You would get out at the window with your case-knife. It is easy to go around the roof by the gutters; it will be done again tomorrow. You go around. Mrs. Duncomb's casement is locked, but you break the glass, put your hand in, and lift the latch. The old woman is quickly strangled. In the next room the sick old servant goes as easily. In the next room, nearest the door, you know your enemy lies. You enter stealthily.

Ann Price is asleep; bound, and gagged, and asleep.

Suppose an idea of refined cruelty enters your half-insane mind. You will not kill Ann Price. You will leave her alive in a locked house with the two dead women. The law will do the rest, with all the appurtenances of lingering shame and terror. You step to the outer door and shoot the bolt. Now you have only to loose the sleeping girl's bonds, and escape the way you came. You turn from the bolted door.

Ann Price is awake and looking at you. Now you will have to kill her. She breaks out of her bonds in the extreme of her terror, and the fight is bloody; but at last she lies still with the blood on her hair. You do not tarry to unbolt the door, but flee in haste over the roof, the way you came. You hope no one heard the struggle, and in fact no one did, for Mr. Knight and Mr. Grisly are gone away, and Mr. Kerrel and Mr. Gehagan have been making a night of it.

Are you safe? Not as long as a broken window points the way to the empty chambers across the court. There is only one way to be safe: *you* must be the one to break into the apparently locked dwelling.

So you hang around. You hang around until the dinner guest comes knocking at the bolted door. There is an ugly moment when the locksmith is sent for; but your luck holds;

he doesn't come. *You* suggest a way in: you will enter Mr. Grisly's chambers, for you have the key, and work your way around by the gutters, and enter by the window. No other woman has stomach for such airy peregrinations, and there is no man there to dispute the errand with you. So off you go, once more, out at the window and around the dizzy gutters. Once more you smash the smashed pane, and enter the apartment. Now there will be no one, ever, to say that the pane was smashed the night before. Didn't Mrs. Love hear the tinkle of breaking glass? You draw back the bolt and let them in, Mrs. Love and Sarah Malcolm and half the world besides.

Ann Oliphant must have laughed loud and long when they hanged Sarah Malcolm.

PASSAGE IN THE SECRET HISTORY OF AN IRISH COUNTESS

By Joseph Sheridan Le Fanu (1814-1873)

Le Fanu, an Irishman of Huguenot descent, was, in the words of the great ghost-story writer M. R. James, one of the best story-tellers of the nineteenth century. When he was almost fifty years old and by this time a widower and a recluse, Le Fanu published The House by the Churchyard, *the first of a series of wonderfully atmospheric novels of mystery and intrigue. A number of these novels had their origins in short stories that Le Fanu had written and published many years before, and the basic story-lines often went through a variety of incarnations before emerging as full-length novels.* Uncle Silas *(1864), with its truly malevolent villainness and her quite unforgettable comeuppance, is perhaps the best of them all and in the view of many commentators the outstanding mystery novel of the nineteenth century. It too had its roots in earlier, shorter versions, "The Murdered Cousin" in 1851 and originally in 1838 in the following story.*

THE following paper is written in a female hand, and was no doubt communicated to my much-regretted friend by the lady whose early history it serves to illustrate, the Countess D——. She is no more—she long since died, a childless and a widowed wife, and, as her letter sadly predicts, none survive to whom the publication of this narrative can prove "injurious, or even painful." Strange! two powerful and wealthy families, that in which she was born, and that into which she had married, have ceased to be—they are utterly extinct.

To those who know anything of the history of Irish families, as they were less than a century ago, the facts which immediately follow will at once suggest *the names* of the principal actors; and to others their publication would be useless—to us, possibly, if not probably, injurious. I have, therefore, altered such of the names as might, if stated, get us into difficulty; others, belonging to minor characters in the strange story, I have left untouched.

My dear friend,—You have asked me to furnish you with a detail of the strange events which marked my early history, and I have, without hesitation, applied myself to the task, knowing that, while I live, a kind consideration for my feelings will prevent your giving publicity to the statement; and conscious that, when I am no more, there will not survive one to whom the narrative can prove injurious, or even painful.

My mother died when I was quite an infant, and of her I have no recollection, even the faintest. By her death, my education and habits were left solely to the guidance of my surviving parent; and, as far as a stern attention to my religious instruction, and an active anxiety evinced by his procuring for me the best masters to perfect me in those accomplishments which my station and wealth might seem to require, could avail, he amply discharged the task.

My father was what is called an oddity, and his treatment of me, though uniformly kind, flowed less from affection and tenderness than from a sense of obligation and duty. Indeed, I seldom even spoke to him except at meal-times, and then his manner was silent and abrupt; his leisure hours, which were many, were passed either in his study or in solitary walks; in short, he seemed to take no further interest in my happiness or improvement than a conscientious regard to the discharge of his own duty would seem to claim.

Shortly before my birth a circumstance had occurred which had contributed much to form and to confirm my father's secluded habits—it was the fact that a suspicion of *murder* had fallen upon his younger brother, though not sufficiently definite to lead to an indictment, yet strong enough to ruin him in public opinion.

This disgraceful and dreadful doubt cast upon the family name, my father felt deeply and bitterly, and not the less so that he himself was thoroughly convinced of his brother's innocence. The sincerity and strength of this impression he shortly afterwards proved in a manner which produced the dark events which follow. Before, however, I enter upon the statement of them, I ought to relate the circumstances which had awakened the suspicion; inasmuch as they are in themselves somewhat curious, and, in their effects, most intimately connected with my after-history.

My uncle, Sir Arthur T——n, was a gay and extravagant man, and, among other vices, was ruinously addicted to gaming; this unfortunate propensity, even after his fortune had suffered so severely as to render inevitable a reduction in his expenses by no means inconsiderable, nevertheless continued to actuate him, nearly to the exclusion of all other pursuits; he was, however, a proud, or rather a vain man, and could not bear to make the diminution of his income a matter of gratulation and triumph to those with whom he had hitherto competed, and the consequence was, that he frequented no longer the expensive haunts of dissipation, and retired from the gay world, leaving his coterie to discover his reasons as best they might.

He did not, however, forego his favourite vice, for, though he could not worship his great divinity in the costly temples where it was formerly his wont to take his stand, yet he found it very possible to bring about him a sufficient number of the votaries of chance to answer all his ends. The consequence was, that Carrickleigh, which was the name of my uncle's residence, was never without one or more of such visitors as I have described.

It happened that upon one occasion he was visited by one Hugh Tisdall, a gentleman of loose habits, but of considerable wealth, and who had, in early youth, travelled with my uncle upon the Continent; the period of his visit was winter, and, consequently, the house was nearly deserted excepting by its regular inmates; it was therefore highly acceptable, particularly as my uncle was aware that his visitor's tastes accorded exactly with his own.

Both parties seemed determined to avail themselves of their suitability during the brief stay which Mr. Tisdall had promised; the consequence was, that they shut themselves up in Sir Arthur's private room for nearly all the day and the greater part of the night, during the space of nearly a week, at the end of which the servant having one morning, as usual, knocked at Mr. Tisdall's bedroom door repeatedly, received no answer, and, upon attempting to enter, found that it was locked; this appeared suspicious, and, the inmates of the house having been alarmed, the door was forced open, and, on proceeding to the bed, they found the body of its occupant perfectly lifeless, and hanging half-way out, the head downwards, and near the floor. One deep wound had been inflicted upon the temple, apparently with some blunt instrument which had penetrated the brain; and another blow, less effective, probably the first aimed, had grazed the head, removing some of the scalp, but leaving the skull untouched. The door had been double-locked upon the *inside*, in evidence of which the key still lay where it had been placed in the lock.

The window, though not secured on the interior, was closed—a circumstance not a little puzzling, as it afforded the only other mode of escape from the room. It looked out, too, upon a kind of courtyard, round which the old buildings stood, formerly accessible by a narrow doorway and passage lying in the oldest side of the quadrangle, but which had since been built up, so as to preclude all ingress or egress; the room was also upon the second story, and the height of the window considerable. Near the bed were found a pair of razors belonging to the murdered man, one of them upon the ground, and both of them open. The weapon which had inflicted the mortal wound was not to be found in the room, nor were any footsteps or other traces of the murderer discoverable.

At the suggestion of Sir Arthur himself, a coroner was instantly summoned to attend, and an inquest was held; nothing, however, in any degree conclusive was elicited; the walls, ceiling, and floor of the room were carefully examined, in order to ascertain whether they contained a trap-door or other concealed mode of entrance—but no such thing appeared.

Such was the minuteness of investigation employed, that, although the grate had contained a large fire during the night, they proceeded to examine even the very chimney, in order to discover whether escape by it were possible; but this attempt, too, was fruitless, for the chimney, built in the old fashion, rose in a perfectly perpendicular line from the hearth to a height of nearly fourteen feet above the roof, affording in its interior scarcely the possiblity of ascent, the flue being smoothly plastered, and sloping towards the top like an inverted funnel, promising, too, even if the summit were attained, owing to its great height, but a precarious descent upon the sharp and steep-ridged roof; the ashes, too, which lay in the grate, and the soot, as far as it could be seen, were undisturbed, a circumstance almost conclusive of the question.

Sir Arthur was of course examined; his evidence was given with clearness and unreserve, which seemed calculated to silence all suspicion. He stated that, up to the day and night immediately preceding the catastrophe, he had lost to a heavy amount, but that, at their last sitting, he had not only won back his original loss, but upwards of four thousand pounds in addition; in evidence of which he produced an acknowledgment of debt to that amount in the handwriting of the deceased, and bearing the date of the fatal night. He had mentioned the circumstance to his lady, and in presence of some of the domestics; which statement was supported by *their* respective evidence.

One of the jury shrewdly observed, that the circumstance

of Mr. Tisdall's having sustained so heavy a loss might have suggested to some ill-minded persons accidentally hearing it, the plan of robbing him, after having murdered him in such a manner as might make it appear that he had committed suicide; a supposition which was strongly supported by the razors having been found thus displaced, and removed from their case. Two persons had probably been engaged in the attempt, one watching by the sleeping man, and ready to strike him in case of his awakening suddenly, while the other was procuring the razors and employed in inflicting the fatal gash, so as to make it appear to have been the act of the murdered man himself. It was said that while the juror was making this suggestion Sir Arthur changed colour.

Nothing, however, like legal evidence appeared against him, and the consequence was that the verdict was found against a person or persons unknown; and for some time the matter was suffered to rest, until, after about five months, my father received a letter from a person signing himself Andrew Collis, and representing himself to be the cousin of the deceased. This letter stated that Sir Arthur was likely to incur not merely suspicion, but personal risk, unless he could account for certain circumstances connected with the recent murder, and contained a copy of a letter written by the deceased, and bearing date, the day of the week, and of the month, upon the night of which the deed of blood had been perpetrated. Tisdall's note ran as follows:

"DEAR COLLIS,

"I have had sharp work with Sir Arthur; he tried some of his stale tricks, but soon found that *I* was Yorkshire too: it would not do—you understand me. We went to the work like good ones, head, heart and soul; and, in fact, since I came here, I have lost no time. I am rather fagged, but I am sure to be well paid for my hardship; I never want sleep so long as I can have the music of a dice-box, and wherewithal to pay the piper. As I told you, he tried some of his queer turns, but I foiled him like a man, and, in return, gave him more than he could relish of the genuine *dead knowledge*.

"In short, I have plucked the old baronet as never baronet was plucked before; I have scarce left him the stump of a quill; I have got promissory notes in his hand to the amount of—if you like round numbers, say, thirty thousand pounds, safely deposited in my portable strongbox, alias double-clasped pocket-book. I leave this ruinous old rat-hole early on tomorrow, for two reasons—first, I do not want to play with Sir Arthur deeper than I think his security, that is, his money, or his money's worth, would warrant; and, secondly, because I am safer a hundred miles from Sir Arthur than in the house with him. Look you, my worthy, I tell you this between ourselves—I may be wrong, but, by G—, I am as sure as that I am now living, that Sir A—— attempted to poison me last night; so much for old friendship on both sides.

"When I won the last stake, a heavy one enough, my friend leant his forehead upon his hands, and you'll laugh when I tell you that his head literally smoked like a hot dumpling. I do not know whether his agitation was produced by the plan which he had against me, or by his having lost so heavily—though it must be allowed that he had reason to be a little funked, whichever way his thoughts went; but he pulled the bell, and ordered two bottles of champagne. While the fellow was bringing them he drew out a promissory note to the full amount, which he signed, and, as the man came in with the bottles and glasses, he desired him to be off; he filled out a glass for me, and, while he thought my eyes were off, for I was putting up his note at the time, he dropped something slyly into it, no doubt to sweeten it; but I saw it all, and, when he handed it to me, I said, with an emphasis which he might or might not understand:

" 'There is some sediment in this; I'll not drink it.'

" 'Is there?' said he, and at the same time snatched it from my hand and threw it into the fire. What do you think of that? have I not a tender chicken to manage? Win or lose, I will not play beyond five thousand to-night, and tomorrow sees me safe out of the reach of Sir Arthur's champagne. So, all things considered, I think you must allow that you are not the last who have found a knowing boy in

"Yours to command,
'HUGH TISDALL."

Of the authenticity of this document I never heard my father express a doubt; and I am satisfied that, owing to his strong conviction in favour of his brother, he would not have admitted it without sufficient injury, inasmuch as it tended to confirm the suspicions which already existed to his prejudice.

Now, the only point in this letter which made strongly against my uncle, was the mention of the "double-clasped pocket-book" as the receptacle of the papers likely to involve him, for this pocket-book was not forthcoming, nor anywhere to be found, nor had any papers referring to his gaming transactions been found upon the dead man. However, whatever might have been the original intention of this Collis, neither my uncle nor my father ever heard more of him; but he published the letter in Faulkner's newspaper, which was shortly afterwards made the vehicle of a much more mysterious attack. The passage in that periodical to which I allude, occurred about four years afterwards, and while the fatal occurrence was still fresh in public recollection. It commenced by a rambling preface, stating that "a *certain person* whom *certain* persons thought to be dead, was not so, but living, and in full possession of his memory, and moreover ready and able to make *great* delinquents tremble." It then went on to describe the murder, without, however, mentioning names; and in doing so, it entered into minute and circumstantial particulars of which none but an *eye-witness* could have been possessed, and by implications almost too unequivocal to be regarded in the light of insinuation, to involve the "*titled gambler*" in the guilt of the transaction.

My father at once urged Sir Arthur to proceed against the paper in an action of libel; but he would not hear of it, nor consent to my father's taking any legal steps whatever in the matter. My father, however, wrote in a threatening tone to Faulkner, demanding a surrender of the author of the obnoxious article. The answer to this application is still in my possession, and is penned in an apologetic tone: it states that the manuscript had been handed in, paid for, and inserted as an advertisement, without sufficient inquiry, or any knowledge as to whom it referred.

No step, however, was taken to clear my uncle's character in the judgment of the public; and as he immediately sold a small property, the application of the proceeds of which was known to none, he was said to have disposed of it to enable himself to buy off the threatened information. However the truth might have been, it is certain that no charges respecting the mysterious murder were afterwards publicly made against my uncle, and, as far as external disturbances were concerned, he enjoyed henceforward perfect security and quiet.

A deep and lasting impression, however, had been made upon the public mind, and Sir Arthur T— —n was no longer visited or noticed by the gentry and aristocracy of the country, whose attention and courtesies he had hitherto received. He accordingly affected to despise these enjoyments which he could not procure, and shunned even that society which he might have commanded.

This is all that I need recapitulate of my uncle's history, and I now recur to my own. Although my father had never, within my recollection, visited, or been visited by, my uncle, each being of sedentary, procrastinating, and secluded habits, and their respective residences being very far apart—the one lying in the county of Galway, the other in that of Cork— he was strongly attached to his brother, and evinced his affection by an active correspondence, and by deeply and proudly resenting that neglect which had marked Sir Arthur as unfit to mix in society.

When I was about eighteen years of age, my father, whose health had been gradually declining, died, leaving me in heart wretched and desolate, and, owing to his previous seclusion, with few acquaintances, and almost no friends.

The provisions of his will were curious, and when I had sufficiently come to myself to listen to or comprehend them, surprised me not a little: all his vast property was left to me, and to the heirs of my body, for ever; and, in default of such heirs, it was to go after my death to my uncle, Sir Arthur, without any entail.

At the same time, the will appointed him my guardian, desiring that I might be received within his house, and reside with his family, and under his care, during the term of my minority; and in consideration of the increased expense consequent upon such an arrangement, a handsome annuity was allotted to him during the term of my proposed residence.

The object of this last provision I at once understood: my father desired, by making it the direct, apparent interest of Sir Arthur that I should die without issue, while at the same time he placed me wholly in his power, to prove to the world how great and unshaken was his confidence in his brother's innocence and honour, and also to afford him an opportunity of showing that this mark of confidence was not unworthily bestowed.

It was a strange, perhaps an idle scheme; but as I had been always brought up in the habit of considering my uncle as a deeply-injured man, and had been taught, almost as a part of my religion, to regard him as the very soul of honour, I felt no further uneasiness respecting the arrangement than that likely to result to a timid girl, of secluded habits, from the immediate prospect of taking up her abode for the first time in her life among total strangers. Previous to leaving my home, which I felt I should do with a heavy heart, I received a most tender and affectionate letter from my uncle, calculated, if anything could do so, to remove the bitterness of parting from scenes familiar and dear from my earliest childhood, and in some degree to reconcile me to the measure.

It was during a fine autumn that I approached the old domain of Carrickleigh. I shall not soon forget the impression of sadness and of gloom which all that I saw produced upon my mind; the sunbeams were falling with a rich and melancholy tint upon the fine old trees, which stood in lordly groups, casting their long, sweeping shadows over rock and sward. There was an air of neglect and decay about the spot, which amounted almost to desolation; the symptoms of this increased in number as we approached the building itself, near which the ground had been originally more artificially and carefully cultivated than elsewhere, and whose neglect consequently more immediately and strikingly betrayed itself.

As we proceeded, the road wound near the beds of what

had been formally two fish-ponds, which were now nothing more than stagnant swamps, overgrown with rank weeds, and here and there encroached upon by the straggling underwood; the avenue itself was much broken, and in many places the stones were almost concealed by grass and nettles; the loose stone walls which had here and there intersected the broad park were, in many places, broken down, so as no longer to answer their original purpose as fences; piers were now and then to be seen, but the gates were gone; and, to add to the general air of dilapidation, some huge trunks were lying scattered through the venerable old trees, either the work of the winter storms, or perhaps the victims of some extensive but desultory scheme of denudation, which the projector had not capital or perseverance to carry into full effect.

After the carriage had travelled a mile of this avenue, we reached the summit of rather an abrupt eminence, one of the many which added to the picturesqueness, if not to the convenience of this rude passage. From the top of this ridge the grey walls of Carrickleigh were visible, rising at a small distance in front, and darkened by the hoary wood which crowded around them. It was a quadrangular building of considerable extent, and the front which lay towards us, and in which the great entrance was placed, bore unequivocal marks of antiquity; the time-worn, solemn aspect of the old building, the ruinous and deserted appearance of the whole place, and the associations which connected it with a dark page in the history of my family, combined to depress spirits already predisposed for the reception of sombre and dejecting impressions.

When the carriage drew up in the grassgrown court yard before the hall-door, two lazy-looking men, whose appearance well accorded with that of the place which they tenanted, alarmed by the obstreperous barking of a great chained dog, ran out from some half-ruinous out-houses, and took charge of the horses; the hall-door stood open, and I entered a gloomy and imperfectly lighted apartment, and found no one within. However, I had not long to wait in this awkward predicament, for before my luggage had been deposited in the house, indeed, before I had well removed my cloak and other wraps, so as to enable me to look around, a young girl ran lightly into the hall, and kissing me heartily, and somewhat boisterously, exclaimed:

"My dear cousin, my dear Margaret—I am so delighted—so out of breath. We did not expect you till ten o'clock; my father is somewhere about the place, he must be close at hand. James—Corney—run out and tell your master—my brother is seldom at home, at least at any reasonable hour—you must be so tired—so fatigued—let me show you to your room—see that Lady Margaret's luggage is all brought up—you must lie down and rest yourself—Deborah, bring some coffee—up these stairs; we are so delighted to see you—you cannot think how lonely I have been—how steep these stairs are, are not they? I am so glad you are come—I could hardly bring myself to believe that you were really coming—how good of you, dear Lady Margaret."

There was real good-nature and delight in my cousin's greeting, and a kind of constitutional confidence of manner which placed me at once at ease, and made me feel immediately upon terms of intimacy with her. The room into which she ushered me, although partaking in the general air of decay which pervaded the mansion and all about it, had nevertheless been fitted up with evident attention to comfort, and even with some dingy attempt at luxury; but what pleased me most was that it opened, by a second door, upon a lobby which communicated with my fair cousin's apartment; a circumstance which divested the room, in my eyes, of the air of solitude and sadness which would otherwise have characterised it, to a degree almost painful to one so dejected in spirits as I was.

After such arrangements as I found necessary were completed, we both went down to the parlour, a large wainscoted room, hung round with grim old portraits, and, as I was not sorry to see, containing in its ample grate a large and cheerful fire. Here my cousin had leisure to talk more at her ease; and from her I learned something of the manners and the habits of the two remaining members of her family, whom I had not yet seen.

On my arrival I had known nothing of the family among whom I was come to reside, except that it consisted of three individuals, my uncle, and his son and daughter, Lady T——n having been long dead. In addition to this very scanty stock of information, I shortly learned from my communicative companion that my uncle was, as I had suspected, completely retired in his habits, and besides that, having been so far back as she could well recollect, always rather strict, as reformed rakes frequently become, he had latterly been growing more gloomily and sternly religious than heretofore.

Her account of her brother was far less favourable, though she did not say anything directly to his disadvantage. From all that I could gather from her, I was led to suppose that he was a specimen of the idle, coarse-mannered, profligate, low-minded "*squirearchy*"—a result which might naturally have flowed from the circumstance of his being, as it were, outlawed from society, and driven for companionship to grades below his own—enjoying, too, the dangerous prerogative of spending much money.

However, you may easily suppose that I found nothing in my cousin's communication fully to bear me out in so very decided a conclusion.

I awaited the arrival of my uncle, which was every moment to be expected, with feelings half of alarm, half of curiosity—a sensation which I have often since experienced, though to a less degree, when upon the point of standing for the first time in the presence of one of whom I have long been in the habit of hearing or thinking with interest.

It was, therefore, with some little perturbation that I heard, first a slight bustle at the outer door, then a slow step traverse the hall, and finally witnessed the door open, and my uncle enter the room. He was a striking-looking man; from peculiarities both of person and of garb, the whole effect of his appearance amounted to extreme singularity. He was tall, and when young his figure must have been strikingly elegant; as it was, however, its effect was marred by a very decided stoop. His dress was of a sober colour, and in fashion anterior to anything which I could remember. It was, however, handsome, and by no means carelessly put on; but what completed the singularity of his appearance was his uncut, white hair, which hung in long, but not at all neglected curls, even so far as his shoulders, and which combined with his regularly classic features, and fine dark eyes, to bestow upon him an air of venerable dignity and pride, which I have never seen equalled elsewhere. I rose as he entered, and met him about the middle of the room; he kissed my cheek and both my hands, saying:

"You are most welcome, dear child, as welcome as the command of this poor place and all that it contains can make you. I am most rejoiced to see you—truly rejoiced. I trust that you are not much fatigued—pray be seated again." He led me to my chair, and continued: "I am glad to perceive you have made acquaintance with Emily already; I see, in your being thus brought together, the foundation of a lasting friendship. You are both innocent, and both young. God bless you—God bless you, and make you all that I could wish."

He raised his eyes, and remained for a few moments silent, as if in secret prayer. I felt that it was impossible that this man, with feelings so quick, so warm, so tender, could be the wretch that public opinion had represented him to be. I was more than ever convinced of his innocence.

His manner was, or appeared to me, most fascinating; there was a mingled kindness and courtesy in it which seemed to speak benevolence itself. It was a manner which I felt cold art could never have taught; it owned most of its charm to its appearing to emanate directly from the heart; it must be a genuine index of the owner's mind. So I thought.

My uncle having given me fully to understand that I was most welcome, and might command whatever was his own, pressed me to take some refreshment; and on my refusing, he observed that previously to bidding me good-night, he had one duty further to perform, one in whose observance he was convinced I would cheerfully acquiesce.

He then proceeded to read a chapter from the Bible; after which he took his leave with the same affectionate kindness with which he had greeted me, having repeated his desire that I should consider everything in his house as altogether at my disposal. It is needless to say that I was much pleased with my uncle—it was impossible to avoid being so; and I could not help saying to myself, if such a man as this is not safe from the assaults of slander, who is? I felt much happier than I had done since my father's death, and enjoyed that night the first refreshing sleep which had visited me since that event.

My curiosity respecting my male cousin did not long remain unsatisfied—he appeared the next day at dinner. His manners, though not so coarse as I had expected, were exceedingly disagreeable; there was an assurance and a forwardness for which I was not prepared; there was less of the vulgarity of manner, and almost more of that of the mind, than I had anticipated. I felt quite uncomfortable in his presence; there was just that confidence in his look and tone which would read encouragement even in mere toleration; and I felt more disgusted and annoyed at the coarse and extravagant compliments which he was pleased from time to time to pay me, than perhaps the extent of the atrocity might fully have warranted. It was, however, one consolation that he did not often appear, being much engrossed by pursuits about which I neither knew nor cared anything; but when he did appear, his attentions, either with a view of his amusement or to some more serious advantage, were so obviously and perseveringly directed to me, that young and inexperienced as I was, even *I* could not be ignorant of his preference. I felt more provoked by this odious persecution that I can express, and discouraged him with so much vigour, that I employed even rudeness to convince him that his assiduities were unwelcome; but all in vain.

This had gone on for nearly a twelvemonth, to my infinite annoyance, when one day as I was sitting at some needlework with my companion Emily, as was my habit, in the parlour, the door opened, and my cousin Edward entered the room. There was something, I thought, odd in his manner—a kind of struggle between shame and impudence—a kind of flurry and ambiguity which made him appear, if possible, more than ordinarily disagreeable.

"Your servant, ladies," he said, seating himself at the same time; "sorry to spoil your *tête-à-tête*, but never mind, I'll only take Emily's place for a minute or two; and then we part for a while, fair cousin. Emily, my father wants you in the corner turret. No shilly-shally; he's in a hurry." She hesitated. "Be off—tramp, march!" he exclaimed, in a tone which the poor girl dared not disobey.

She left the room, and Edward followed her to the door. He stood there for a minute or two, as if reflecting what he should say, perhaps satisfying himself that no one was within hearing in the hall.

At length he turned about, having closed the door, as if carelessly, with his foot; and advancing slowly, as if in deep thought, he took his seat at the side of the table opposite to mine.

There was a brief interval of silence, after which he said:

"I imagine that you have a shrewd suspicion of the object of my early visit; but I suppose I must go into particulars. Must I?"

"I have no conception," I replied, "what your object may be."

"Well, well," said he, becoming more at his ease as he proceeded, "it may be told in a few words. You know that it is totally impossible—quite out of the question—that an off-hand young fellow like me, and a good-looking girl like yourself, could meet continually, as you and I have done, without an attachment—a liking growing up on one side or other; in short, I think I have let you know as plain as if I spoke it, that I have been in love with you almost from the first time I saw you."

He paused; but I was too much horrified to speak. He interpreted my silence favourably.

"I can tell you," he continued, "I'm reckoned rather hard to please, and very hard to *hit*. I can't say when I was taken with a girl before; so you see fortune reserved me— —"

Here the odious wretch wound his arm round my waist. The action at once restored me to utterance, and with the most indignant vehemence I released myself from his hold, and at the same time said:

"I have not been insensible, sir, of your most disagreeable attentions—they have long been a source of much annoyance to me; and you must be aware that I have marked my disapprobation—my disgust—as unequivocally as I possibly could, without actual indelicacy."

I paused, almost out of breath from the rapidity with

which I had spoken; and without giving him time to renew the conversation, I hastily quitted the room, leaving him in a paroxysm of rage and mortification. As I ascended the stairs, I heard him open the parlour-door with violence, and take two or three rapid strides in the direction in which I was moving. I was now much frightened, and ran the whole way until I reached my room; and having locked the door, I listened breathlessly, but heard no sound. This relieved me for the present; but so much had I been overcome by the agitation and annoyance attendant upon the scene which I had just gone through, that when my cousin Emily knocked at my door, I was weeping in strong hysterics.

You will readily conceive my distress, when you reflect upon my strong dislike to my cousin Edward, combined with my youth and extreme inexperience. Any proposal of such a nature must have agitated me; but that it should have come from the man whom of all others I most loathed and abhorred, and to whom I had, as clearly as manner could do it, expressed the state of my feelings, was almost too overwhelming to be borne. It was a calamity, too, in which I could not claim the sympathy of my cousin Emily, which had always been extended to me in my minor grievances. Still I hoped that it might not be unattended with good; for I thought that one inevitable and most welcome consequence would result from this painful *eclaircissement*, in the discontinuance of my cousin's odious persecution.

When I arose next morning, it was with the fervent hope that I might never again behold the face, or even hear the name, of my cousin Edward; but such a consummation, though devoutly to be wished, was hardly likely to occur. The painful impressions of yesterday were too vivid to be at once erased; and I could not help feeling some dim foreboding of coming annoyance and evil.

To expect on my cousin's part anything like delicacy or consideration for me, was out of the question. I saw that he had set his heart upon my property, and that he was not likely easily to forego such an acquisition—possessing what might have been considered opportunities and facilities almost to compel my compliance.

I now keenly felt the unreasonableness of my father's conduct in placing me to reside with a family of all whose members, with one exception, he was wholly ignorant, and I bitterly felt the helplessness of my situation. I determined, however, in case of my cousin's persevering in his addresses, to lay all the particulars before my uncle, although he had never in kindness or intimacy gone a step beyond our first interview, and to throw myself upon his hospitality and his sense of honour for protection against a repetition of such scenes.

My cousin's conduct may appear to have been an inadequate cause for such serious uneasiness; but my alarm was caused neither by his acts nor words, but entirely by his manner, which was strange and even intimidating to excess. At the beginning of the yesterday's interview there was a sort of bullying swagger in his air, which towards the end gave place to the brutal vehemence of an undisguised ruffian—a transition which had tempted me into a belief that he might seek even forcibly to extort from me a consent to his wishes, or by means still more horrible, of which I scarcely dared to trust myself to think, to possess himself of my property.

I was early next day summoned to attend my uncle in his private room, which lay in a corner turret of the old building; and thither I accordingly went, wondering all the way what this unusual measure might prelude. When I entered the room, he did not rise in his usual courteous way to greet me, but simply pointed to a chair opposite to his own. This boded nothing agreeable. I sat down, however, silently waiting until he should open the conversation.

"Lady Margaret," at length he said, in a tone of greater sternness than I thought him capable of using, "I have hitherto spoken to you as a friend, but I have not forgotten that I am also your guardian, and that my authority as such gives me a right to control your conduct. I shall put a question to you, and I expect and will demand a plain, direct answer. Have I rightly been informed that you have contemptuously rejected the suit and hand of my son Edward?"

I stammered forth with a good deal of trepidation:

"I believe—that is, I have, sir, rejected my cousin's proposals; and my coldness and discouragement might have convinced him that I had determined to do so."

"Madam," replied he, with suppressed, but, as it appeared

to me, intense anger, "I have lived long enough to know that *coldness* and discouragement, and such terms, form the common cant of a worthless coquette. You know to the full, as well as I, that *coldness and discouragement* may be so exhibited as to convince their object that he is neither distasteful or indifferent to the person who wears this manner. You know, too, none better, that an affected neglect, when skillfully managed, is amongst the most formidable of the engines which artful beauty can employ. I tell you, madam, that having, without one word spoken in discouragement, permitted my son's most marked attentions for a twelvemonth or more, you have no right to dismiss him with no further explanation that demurely telling him that you had always looked coldy upon him; and neither your wealth nor your *ladyship*" (there was an emphasis of scorn on the word, which would have become Sir Giles Overreach himself) "can warrant you in treating with contempt the affectionate regard of an honest heart."

I was too much shocked at this undisguised attempt to bully me into an acquiescence in the interested and unprincipled plan for their own aggrandisement, which I now perceived my uncle and his son to have deliberately entered into, at once to find strength or collectedness to frame an answer to what he had said. At length I replied, with some firmness:

"In all that you have just now said, sir, you have grossly misstated my conduct and motives. Your information must have been most incorrect as far as it regards my conduct towards my cousin; my manner towards him could have conveyed nothing but dislike; and if anything could have added to the strong aversion which I have long felt towards him, it would be his attempting thus to trick and frighten me into a marriage which he knows to be revolting to me, and which is sought by him only as a means for securing to himself whatever property is mine."

As I said this, I fixed my eyes upon those of my uncle, but he was too old in the world's ways to falter beneath the gaze of more searching eyes than mine; he simply said:

"Are you acquainted with the provisions of your father's will?"

I answered in the affirmative; and he continued:

"Then you must be aware that if my son Edward were— which God forbid—the unprincipled, reckless man you pretend to think him"—(here he spoke very slowly, as if he intended that every word which escaped him should be registered in my memory, while at the same time the expression of his countenance underwent a gradual but horrible change, and the eyes which he fixed upon me became so darkly vivid, that I almost lost sight of everything else)—"if he were what you have described him, think you, girl, he could find no briefer means than wedding contracts to gain his ends? 'twas but to gripe your slender neck until the breath had stopped, and lands, and lakes, and all were his."

I stood staring at him for many minutes after he had ceased to speak, fascinated by the terrible serpent-like gaze, until he continued with a welcome change of countenance:

"I will not speak again to you upon this topic until one month has passed. You shall have time to consider the relative advantages of the two courses which are open to you. I should be sorry to hurry you to a decision. I am satisfied with having stated my feelings upon the subject, and pointed out to you the path of duty. Remember this day month—not one word sooner."

He then rose, and I left the room, much agitated and exhausted.

This interview, all the circumstances attending it, but most particularly the formidable expression of my uncle's countenance while he talked, though hypothetically, of *murder*, combined to arouse all my worst suspicions of him. I dreaded to look upon the face that had so recently worn the appalling livery of guilt and malignity. I regarded it with the mingled fear and loathing with which one looks upon an object which has tortured them in a nightmare.

In a few days after the interview, the particulars of which I have just related, I found a note upon my toilet-table, and on opening it I read as follows:

"MY DEAR LADY MARGARET,

"You will be perhaps surprised to see a strange face in your room to-day. I have dismissed your Irish maid, and

secured a French one to wait upon you—a step rendered
necessary by my proposing shortly to visit the Continent,
with all my family.

"Your faithful guardian,
ARTHUR T——N."

On inquiry, I found that my faithful attendant was actually gone, and far on her way to the town of Galway; and in
her stead there appeared a tall, raw-boned, ill-looking, elderly Frenchwoman, whose sullen and presuming manners
seemed to imply that her vocation had never before been that
of a lady's-maid. I could not help regarding her as a creature
of my uncle's, and therefore to be dreaded, even had she been
in no other way suspicious.

Days and weeks passed away without any, even a momentary doubt upon my part, as to the course to be pursued by
me. The allotted period had at length elapsed; the day arrived on which I was to communicate my decision to my
uncle. Although my resolution had never for a moment
wavered, I could not shake off the dread of the approaching
colloquy; and my heart sunk within me as I heard the
expected summons.

I had not seen my cousin Edward since the occurrence of
the grand *eclaircissement*; he must have studiously avoided
me—I suppose from policy, it could not have been from
delicacy. I was prepared for a terrific burst of fury from my
uncle, as soon as I should make known my determination;
and I not unreasonably feared that some act of violence or of
intimidation would next be resorted to.

Filled with these dreary forebodings, I fearfully opened
the study door, and the next minute I stood in my uncle's
presence. He received me with a politeness which I dreaded,
as arguing a favourable anticipation respecting the answer
which I was to give; and after some slight delay, he began by
saying:

"It will be a relief to both of us, I believe, to bring this
conversation as soon as possible to an issue. You will excuse
me, then, my dear niece, for speaking with an abruptness
which, under other circumstances, would be unpardonable.
You have, I am certain, given the subject of our last interview

fair and serious consideration; and I trust that you are now prepared with candour to lay your answer before me. A few words will suffice—we perfectly understand one another."

He paused, and I, though feeling that I stood upon a mine which might in an instant explode, nevertheless answered with perfect composure:

"I must now, sir, make the same reply which I did upon the last occasion, and I reiterate the declaration which I then made, that I never can nor will, while life and reason remain, consent to a union with my cousin Edward."

This announcement wrought no apparent change in Sir Arthur, except that he became deadly, almost lividly pale. He seemed lost in dark thought for a minute, and then with a slight effort said:

"You have answered me honestly and directly; and you say your resolution is unchangeable. Well, would it had been otherwise—would it had been otherwise—but be it as it is—I am satisfied."

He gave me his hand—it was cold and damp as death; under an assumed calmness, it was evident that he was fearfully agitated. He continued to hold my hand with an almost painful pressure, while, as if unconsciously, seeming to forget my presence, he muttered:

"Strange, strange, strange, indeed! fatuity, helpless fatuity!" there was here a long pause. "Madness *indeed* to strain a cable that is rotten to the very heart—it must break—and then—all goes."

There was again a pause of some minutes, after which, suddenly changing his voice and manner to one of wakeful alacrity, he exclaimed:

"Margaret, my son Edward shall plague you no more. He leaves this country on to-morrow for France—he shall speak no more upon this subject—never, never more—whatever events depended upon your answer must now take their own course; but, as for this fruitless proposal, it has been tried enough; it can be repeated no more."

At these words he coldly suffered my hand to drop, as if to express his total abandonment of all his projected schemes of alliance; and certainly the action, with the accompanying words, produced upon my mind a more solemn and depressing effect than I believed possible to have been caused by the course which I had determined to pursue; it struck upon my heart with an awe and heaviness which *will* accompany the accomplishment of an important and irrevocable act, even though no doubt or scruple remains to make it possible that the agent should wish it undone.

"Well," said my uncle, after a little time, "we now cease to speak upon this topic, never to resume it again. Remember you shall have no farther uneasiness from Edward; he leaves Ireland for France on to-morrow; this will be a relief to you. May I depend upon your *honour* that no word touching the subject of this interview shall ever escape you?"

I gave him the desired assurance; he said:

"It is well—I am satisfied—we have nothing more, I believe, to say upon either side, and my presence must be a restraint upon you, I shall therefore bid you farewell."

I then left the apartment, scarcely knowing what to think of the strange interview which had just taken place.

On the next day my uncle took occasion to tell me that Edward had actually sailed, if his intention had not been interfered with by adverse circumstances; and two days subsequently he actually produced a letter from his son, written, as it said, *on board*, and despatched while the ship was getting under weigh. This was a great satisfaction to me, and as being likely to prove so, it was no doubt communicated to me by Sir Arthur.

During all this trying period, I had found infinite consolation in the society and sympathy of my dear cousin Emily. I never in after-life formed a friendship so close, so fervent, and upon which, in all its progress, I could look back with feelings of such unalloyed pleasure, upon whose termination I must ever dwell with so deep, yet so unembittered regret. In cheerful converse with her I soon recovered my spirits considerably, and passed my time agreeably enough, although still in the strictest seclusion.

Matters went on sufficiently smooth, although I could not help sometimes feeling a momentary, but horrible uncertainty respecting my uncle's character; which was not altogether unwarranted by the circumstances of the two trying interviews whose particulars I have just detailed. The un-

pleasant impression which these conferences were calculated to leave upon my mind, was fast wearing away, when
there occurred a circumstance, slight indeed in itself, but
calculated irresistibly to awaken all my worst suspicions,
and to overwhelm me again with anxiety and terror.

I had one day left the house with my cousin Emily, in order
to take a ramble of considerable length, for the purpose of
sketching some favourite views, and we had walked about
half a mile when I perceived that we had forgotten our
drawing materials, the absence of which would have defeated the object of our walk. Laughing at our own thought-
lessness, we returned to the house, and leaving Emily
without, I ran upstairs to procure the drawing-books and
pencils, which lay in my bedroom.

As I ran up the stairs was met by the tall, ill-looking
Frenchwoman, evidently a good deal flurried.

"Que veut, madame?" said she, with a more decided effort
to be polite than I had ever known her make before.

"No, no—no matter," said I, hastily running by her in the
direction of my room.

"Madame," cried she, in a high key, "restez ici, s'il vous
plait; votre chambre n'est pas faite—your room is not ready
for your reception yet."

I continued to move on without heeding her. She was
some way behind me, and feeling that she could not otherwise prevent my entrance, for I was now upon the very lobby,
she made a desperate attempt to seize hold of my person: she
succeeded in grasping the end of my shawl, which she drew
from my shoulders; but slipping at the same time upon the
polished oak floor, she fell at full length upon the boards.

A little frightened as well as angry at the rudeness of this
strange woman, I hastily pushed open the door of my room,
at which I now stood, in order to escape from her; but great
was my amazement on entering to find the apartment
preoccupied.

The window was open, and beside it stood two male
figures; they appeared to be examining the fastenings of the
casement, and their backs were turned towards the door.
One of them was my uncle; they both turned on my entrance,
as if startled. The stranger was booted and cloaked, and

wore a heavy broad-leafed hat over his brows. He turned but for a moment, and averted his face; but I had seen enough to convince me that he was no other than my cousin Edward. My uncle had some iron instrument in his hand, which he hastily concealed behind his back; and coming towards me, said something as if in an explanatory tone; but I was too much shocked and confounded to understand what it might be. He said something about "*repairs*—window-frames—cold, and safety."

I did not wait, however, to ask or to receive explanations, but hastily left the room. As I went down the stairs I thought I heard the voice of the Frenchwoman in all the shrill volubility of excuse, which was met, however, by suppressed but vehement imprecations, or what seemed to me to be such, in which the voice of my cousin Edward distinctly mingled.

I joined my cousin Emily quite out of breath. I need not say that my head was too full of other things to think much of drawing for that day. I imparted to her frankly the cause of my alarms, but at the same time as gently as I could; and with tears she promised vigilance, and devotion, and love. I never had reason for a moment to repent the unreserved confidence which I then reposed in her. She was no less surprised than I at the unexpected appearance of Edward, whose departure for France neither of us had for a moment doubted, but which was now proved by his actual presence to be nothing more than an imposture, practised, I feared, for no good end.

The situation in which I had found my uncle had removed completely all my doubts as to his designs. I magnified suspicions into certainties, and dreaded night after night that I should be murdered in my bed. The nervousness produced by sleepless nights and days of anxious fears increased the horrors of my situation to such a degree, that I at length wrote a letter to a Mr. Jefferies, an old and faithful friend of my father's, and perfectly acquainted with all his affairs, praying him, for God's sake, to relieve me from my present terrible situation, and communicating without reserve the nature and grounds of my suspicions.

This letter I kept sealed and directed for two or three days always about my person, for discovery would have been ruinous, in expectation of an opportunity which might be safely trusted, whereby to have it placed in the post-office. As neither Emily nor I were permitted to pass beyond the precincts of the demesne itself, which was surrounded by high walls formed of dry stone, the difficulty of procuring such an opportunity was greatly enhanced.

At this time Emily had a short conversation with her father, which she reported to me instantly.

After some indifferent matter, he had asked her whether she and I were upon good terms, and whether I was unreserved in my disposition. She answered in the affirmative; and he then inquired whether I had been much surprised to find him in my chamber on the other day. She answered that I had been both surprised and amused.

"And what did she think of George Wilson's appearance?"

"Who?" inquired she.

"Oh, the architect," he answered, "who is to contract for the repairs of the house; he is accounted a handsome fellow."

"She could not see his face," said Emily, "and she was in such a hurry to escape that she scarcely noticed him."

Sir Arthur appeared satisfied, and the conversation ended.

This slight conversation, repeated accurately to me by Emily, had the effect of confirming, if indeed anything was required to do so, all that I had before believed as to Edward's actual presence; and I naturally became, if possible, more anxious than ever to despatch the letter to Mr. Jefferies. An opportunity at length occurred.

As Emily and I were walking one day near the gate of the demesne, a lad from the village happened to be passing down the avenue from the house; the spot was secluded, and as this person was not connected by service with those whose observation I dreaded, I committed the letter to his keeping, with strict injunctions that he should put it without delay into the receiver of the town post-office; at the same time I added a suitable gratuity, and the man having made many protestations of punctuality, was soon out of sight.

He was hardly gone when I began to doubt my discretion in having trusted this person; but I had no better or safer means of despatching the letter, and I was not warranted in suspecting him of such wanton dishonesty as an inclination to tamper with it; but I could not be quite satisfied of its safety until I had received an answer, which could not arrive for a few days. Before I did, however, an event occurred which a little surprised me.

I was sitting in my bedroom early in the day, reading by myself, when I heard a knock at the door.

"Come in," said I; and my uncle entered the room.

"Will you excuse me?" said he. "I sought you in the parlour, and thence I have come here. I desired to say a word with you. I trust that you have hitherto found my conduct to you such as that of a guardian towards his ward should be."

I dared not withhold my consent.

"And," he continued, "I trust that you have not found me harsh or unjust, and that you have perceived, my dear niece, that I have sought to make this poor place as agreeable to you as may be."

I assented again; and he put his hand in his pocket, whence he drew a folded paper, and dashing it upon the table with startling emphasis, he said:

"Did you write that letter?"

The sudden and fearful alteration of his voice, manner, and face, but, more than all, the unexpected production of my letter to Mr. Jefferies, which I at once recognised, so confounded and terrified me, that I felt almost choking.

I could not utter a word.

"Did you write that letter?" he repeated with slow and intense emphasis. "You did, liar and hypocrite! You dared to write this foul and infamous libel; but it shall be your last. Men will universally believe you mad, if I choose to call for an inquiry. I can make you appear so. The suspicions expressed in this letter are the hallucinations and alarms of moping lunacy. I have defeated your first attempt, madam; and by the holy God, if ever you make another, chains, straw, darkness, and the keeper's whip shall be your lasting portion!"

With these astounding words he left the room, leaving me almost fainting.

I was now almost reduced to despair; my last cast had failed; I had no course left but that of eloping secretly from the castle, and placing myself under the protection of the nearest magistrate. I felt if this were not done, and speedily, that I should be *murdered*.

No one, from mere description, can have an idea of the unmitigated horror of my situation—a helpless, weak, inexperienced girl, placed under the power and wholly at the mercy of evil men, and feeling that she had it not in her power to escape for a moment from the malignant influences under which she was probably fated to fall; and with a consciousness that if violence, if murder were designed, her dying shriek would be lost in void space; no human being would be near to aid her, no human interposition could deliver her.

I had seen Edward but once during his visit, and as I did not meet with him again, I began to think that he must have taken his departure—a conviction which was to a certain degree satisfactory, as I regarded his absence as indicating the removal of immediate danger.

Emily also arrived circuitously at the same conclusion, and not without good grounds, for she managed indirectly to learn that Edward's black horse had actually been for a day and part of a night in the castle stables, just at the time of her brother's supposed visit. The horse had gone, and, as she argued, the rider must have departed with it.

This point being so far settled, I felt a little less uncomfortable; when being one day alone in my bedroom, I happened to look out from the window, and, to my unutterable horror, I beheld, peering through an opposite casement, my cousin Edward's face. Had I seen the evil one himself in bodily shape, I could not have experienced a more sickening revulsion.

I was too much appalled to move at once from the window, but I did so soon enough to avoid his eye. He was looking fixedly into the narrow quadrangle upon which the window opened. I shrank back unperceived, to pass the rest of the day in terror and despair. I went to my room early that night, but I was too miserable to sleep.

At about twelve o'clock, feeling very nervous, I determined to call my cousin Emily, who slept, you will remember, in the next room, which communicated with mine by a second door. By this private entrance I found my way into her chamber, and without difficulty persuaded her to return to my room and sleep with me. We accordingly lay down together, she undressed, and I with my clothes on, for I was every moment walking up and down the room, and felt too nervous and miserable to think of rest or comfort.

Emily was soon fast asleep, and I lay awake, fervently longing for the first pale gleam of morning, reckoning every stroke of the old clock with an impatience which made every hour appear like six.

It must have been about one o'clock when I thought I heard a slight noise at the partition-door between Emily's room and mine, as if caused by somebody's turning the key in the lock. I held my breath, and the same sound was repeated at the second door of my room—that which opened upon the lobby—the sound was here distinctly caused by the revolution of the bolt in the lock, and it was followed by a slight pressure upon the door itself, as if to ascertain the security of the lock.

The person, whoever it might be, was probably satisfied, for I heard the old boards of the lobby creak and strain, as if under the weight of somebody moving cautiously over them. My sense of hearing became unnaturally, almost painfully acute. I suppose the imagination added distinctness to sounds vague in themselves. I thought that I could actually hear the breathing of the person who was slowly returning down the lobby. At the head of the staircase there appeared to occur a pause; and I could distinctly hear two or three sentences hastily whispered; the steps then descended the stairs with apparently less caution. I now ventured to walk quickly and lightly to the lobby door, and attempted to open it; it was indeed fast locked upon the outside, as was also the other.

I now felt that the dreadful hour was come; but one desperate expedient remained—it was to awaken Emily, and by our united strength to attempt to force the partition-door, which was slighter than the other, and though this to pass to the lower part of the house, whence it might be possible to escape to the grounds, and forth to the village.

I returned to the bedside and shook Emily, but in vain. Nothing that I could do availed to produce from her more than a few incoherent words—it was a death-like sleep. She had certainly drank of some narcotic, as had I probably also, spite of all the caution with which I had examined everything presented to us to eat or drink.

I now attempted, with as little noise as possible, to force first one door, then the other—but all in vain. I believe no strength could have effected my object, for both doors opened inwards. I therefore collected whatever movables I could carry thither, and piled them against the doors, so as to assist me in whatever attempts I should make to resist the entrance of those without. I then returned to the bed and endeavoured again, but fruitlessly, to awaken my cousin. It was not sleep, it was torpor, lethargy, death. I knelt down and prayed with an agony of earnestness; and then seating myself upon the bed, I awaited my fate with a kind of terrible tranquillity.

I heard a faint clanking sound from the narrow court which I have already mentioned, as if caused by the scraping of some iron instrument against stones or rubbish. I at first determined not to disturb the calmness which I now felt, by uselessly watching the proceedings of those who sought my life; but as the sounds continued, the horrible curiosity which I felt overcame every other emotion, and I determined, at all hazards, to gratify it. I therefore crawled upon my knees to the window, so as to let the smallest portion of my head appear above the sill.

The moon was shining with an uncertain radiance upon the antique grey buildings, and obliquely upon the narrow court beneath, one side of which was therefore clearly illuminated, while the other was lost in obscurity, the sharp outlines of the old gables, with their nodding clusters of ivy, being at first alone visible.

Whoever or whatever occasioned the noise which had excited my curiosity, was concealed under the shadow of the dark side of the quadrangle. I placed my hand over my eyes to shade them from the moonlight, which was so bright as to be almost dazzling, and, peering into the darkness, I first dimly, but afterwards gradually, almost with full distinctness, beheld the form of a man engaged in digging what appeared to be a rude hole close under the wall. Some implements, probably a shovel and pickaxe, lay beside him, and to these he every now and then applied himself as the nature of the ground required. He pursued his task rapidly, and with as little noise as possible.

"So," thought I, as, shovelful after shovelful, the dislodged rubbish mounted into a heap, "they are digging the grave in which, before two hours pass, I must lie, a cold, mangled corpse. I am *theirs*—I cannot escape."

I felt as if my reason was leaving me. I started to my feet, and in mere despair I applied myself again to each of the two doors alternately. I strained every nerve and sinew, but I might was well have attempted, with my single strength, to force the building itself from its foundation. I threw myself madly upon the ground, and clasped my hands over my eyes as if to shut out the horrible images which crowded upon me.

The paroxysm passed away. I prayed once more, with the bitter, agonised fervour of one who feels that the hour of death is present and inevitable. When I arose, I went once more to the window and looked out, just in time to see a shadowy figure glide stealthily along the wall. The task was finished. The catastrophe of the tragedy must soon be accomplished.

I determined now to defend my life to the last; and that I might be able to do so with some effect, I searched the room for something which might serve as a weapon; but either through accident, or from an anticipation of such a possibility, everything which might have been made available for such a purpose had been carefully removed. I must then die tamely and without an effort to defend myself.

A thought suddenly struck me—might it not be possible to escape through the door, which the assassin must open in order to enter the room? I resolved to make the attempt. I felt assured that the door through which ingress to the room would be effected, was that which opened upon the lobby. It was the more direct way, besides being, for obvious reasons, less liable to interruption than the other. I resolved, then, to place myself behind a projection of the wall, whose shadow would serve fully to conceal me, and when the door should be opened, and before they should have discovered the identity of the occupant of the bed, to creep noiselessly from the room, and then to trust to Providence for escape.

In order to facilitate this scheme, I removed all the lumber which I had heaped against the door; and I had nearly completed my arrangements, when I perceived the room suddenly darkened by the close approach of some shadowy object to the window. On turning my eyes in that direction, I observed at the top of the casement, as if suspended from above, first the feet, then the legs, then the body, and at length the whole figure of a man present himself. It was Edward T——n.

He appeared to be guiding his descent so as to bring his feet upon the centre of the stone block which occupied the lower part of the window; and, having secured his footing upon this, he kneeled down and began to gaze into the room. As the room was gleaming into the chamber, and the bed-curtains were drawn, he was able to distinguish the bed itself and its contents. He appeared satisfied with is scrutiny, for he looked up and made a sign with his hand, upon which the rope by which his descent had been effected was slackened from above, and he proceeded to disengage it from his waist; this accomplished, he applied his hands to the window-frame, which must have been ingeniously contrived for the purpose, for, with apparently no resistance, the whole frame, containing casement and all, slipped from its position in the wall, and was by him lowered into the room.

The cold night wind waved the bed-curtains, and he paused for a moment—all was still again—and he stepped in upon the floor of the room. He held in his hand what appeared to be a steel instrument, shaped something like a hammer, but larger and sharper at the extremities. This he held rather behind him, while, with three long, tip-toe strides, he brought himself to the bedside.

I felt that the discovery must now be made, and held my breath in momentary expectation of the execration in which he would vent his surprise and disappointment. I closed my eyes—there was a pause, but it was a short one. I heard two dull blows, given in rapid succession: a quivering sigh, and the long-drawn, heavy breathing of the sleeper was for ever suspended. I unclosed my eyes, and saw the murderer fling the quilt across the head of his victim: he then, with the instrument of death still in his hand, proceeded to the lobby-door, upon which he tapped sharply twice or thrice. A quick step was then heard approaching, and a voice whispered something from without. Edward answered, with a kind of chuckle, "Her ladyship is past complaining; unlock the door, in the devil's name, unless you're afraid to come in, and help me lift the body out of the window."

The key was turned in the lock—the door opened—and my uncle entered the room.

I have told you already that I had placed myself under the shade of a projection of the wall, close to the door. I had instinctively shrunk down, cowering towards the ground on the entrance of Edward through the window. When my uncle entered the room he and his son both stood so very close to me that his hand was every moment upon the point of touching my face. I held my breath, and remained motion-less as death.

"You had no interruption from the next room?" said my uncle.

"No," was the brief reply.

"Secure the jewels, Ned; the French harpy must not lay her claws upon them. You're a steady hand, by G— —! not much blood—eh?"

"Not twenty drops," replied his son, "and those on the quilt."

"I'm glad it's over," whispered my uncle again. "We must lift the—the *thing* through the window, and lay the rubbish over it."

They then turned to the bedside, and, winding the bed-clothes round the body, carried it between them slowly to the window, and, exchanging a few brief words with some one below, they shoved it over the window-sill, and I heard it fall heavily on the ground underneath.

"I'll take the jewels," said my uncle; "there are two caskets in the lower drawer."

He proceeded, with an accuracy which, had I been more at ease, would have furnished me with matter of astonish-ment, to lay his hand upon the very spot where my jewels lay; and having possessed himself of them, he called to his son:

"Is the rope made fast above?"

"I'm not a fool—to be sure it is," replied he.

They then lowered themselves from the window. I now rose lightly and cautiously, scarcely daring to breathe, from my place of concealment, and was creeping towards the door, when I heard my cousin's voice, in a sharp whisper, exclaim: "Scramble up again! G—d d— —n you, you've forgot to lock the room-door!" and I perceived, by the straining of the rope which hung from above, that the mandate was instantly obeyed.

Not a second was to be lost. I passed through the door, which was only closed, and moved as rapidly as I could, consistently with stillness, along the lobby. Before I had gone many yards, I heard the door through which I had just passed double-locked on the inside. I glided down the stairs in terror, lest, at every corner, I should meet the murderer or one of his accomplices.

I reached the hall, and listened for a moment to ascertain whether all was silent around; no sound was audible. The parlour windows opened on the park, and through one of them I might, I thought, easily effect my escape. Accordingly, I hastily entered; but, to my consternation, a candle was burning in the room, and by its light I saw a figure seated at the dinner-table, upon which lay glasses, bottles, and the other accompaniments of a drinking-party. Two or three chairs were placed about the table irregularly, as if hastily abandoned by their occupants.

A single glance satisfied me that the figure was that of my French attendant. She was fast asleep, having probably drank deeply. There was something malignant and ghastly in the calmness of this bad woman's features, dimly illuminated as they were by the flickering blaze of the candle. A knife lay upon the table, and the terrible thought struck me—"Should I kill this sleeping accomplice in the guilt of the murderer, and thus secure my retreat?"

Nothing could be easier—it was but to draw the blade across her throat—the work of a second. An instant's pause, however, corrected me. "No," thought I, "the God who has conducted me thus far through the valley of the shadow of death, will not abandon me now. I will fall into their hands, or I will escape hence, but it shall be free from the stain of blood. His will be done."

I felt a confidence arising from this reflection, an assurance of protection which I cannot describe. There was no other means of escape, so I advanced, with a firm step and collected mind, to the window. I noiselessly withdrew the bars and unclosed the shutters—I pushed open the casement, and, without waiting to look behind me, I ran with my utmost speed, scarcely feeling the ground under me, down the avenue, taking care to keep upon the grass which bordered it.

I did not for a moment slack my speed, and I had now gained the centre point between the park-gate and the mansion-house. Here the avenue made a wider circuit, and in order to avoid delay, I directed my way across the smooth sward round which the pathway wound, intending, at the opposite side of the flat, at a point which I distinguished by a group of old birch-trees, to enter again upon the beaten track, which was from thence tolerably direct to the gate.

I had, with my utmost speed, got about half way across this broad flat, when the rapid treading of a horse's hoofs struck upon my ear. My heart swelled in my bosom as though I would smother. The clattering of galloping hoofs approached—I was pursued—they were now upon the sward on which I was running—there was not a bush or a bramble to shelter me—and, as if to render escape altogether desperate, the moon, which had hitherto been obscured, at this moment shone forth which a broad clear light, which made every object distinctly visible.

The sounds were now close behind me. I felt my knees bending under me, with the sensation which torments one in dreams. I reeled—I stumbled—I fell—and at the same instant the cause of my alarm wheeled past me at full gallop. It was one of the young fillies which pastured loose about the park, whose frolics had thus all but maddened me with terror. I scrambled to my feet, and rushed on with weak but rapid steps, my sportive companion still galloping round and round me with many a frisk and fling, until, at length, more dead than alive, I reached the avenue-gate and crossed the stile, I scarce knew how.

I ran through the village, in which all was silent as the grave, until my progress was arrested by the hoarse voice of a sentinel, who cried: "Who goes there?" I felt that I was now safe. I turned in the direction of the voice, and fell fainting at the soldier's feet. When I came to myself, I was sitting in a miserable hovel, surrounded by strange faces, all bespeaking curiosity and compassion.

Many soldiers were in it also; indeed, as I afterwards found, it was employed as a guard-room by a detachment of troops quartered for that night in the town. In a few words I informed their officer of the circumstances which had occurred, describing also the appearance of the persons engaged in the murder; and he, without loss of time, proceeded to the mansion-house of Carrickleigh, taking with him a party of his men. But the villains had discovered their mistake, and had effected their escape before the arrival of the military.

The Frenchwoman was, however, arrested in the neighbourhood upon the next day. She was tried and condemned upon the ensuing assizes; and previous to her execution, confessed the "*she had a hand in making Hugh Tisdall's bed.*" She had been a housekeeper in the castle at the time, and a kind of *chère amie* of my uncle's. She was, in reality, able to speak English like a native, but had exclusively used the French language, I suppose to facilitate her disguise. She died the same hardened wretch which she had lived, confessing her crimes only, as she alleged, that her doing so might involve Sir Arthur T——n, the great author of her guilt and misery, and whom she now regarded with unmitigated destestation.

With the particulars of Sir Arthur's and his son's escape, as far as they are known, you are acquainted. You are also in possession of their after fate—the terrible, the tremendous retribution which, after long delays of many years, finally overtook and crushed them. Wonderful and inscrutable are the dealings of God with His creatures.

Deep and fervent as must always be my gratitude to heaven for my deliverance, effected by a chain of providential occurrences, the failing of a single link of which must have ensured my destruction, I was long before I could look back upon it with other feelings than those of bitterness, almost of agony.

The only being that had ever really loved me, my nearest and dearest friend, ever ready to sympathise, to counsel, and to assist—the gayest, the gentlest, the warmest heart— the only creature on earth that cared for me—*her* life had been the price of my deliverance; and I then uttered the wish, which no event of my long and sorrowful life has taught me to recall, that she had been spared, and that, in her stead, *I* were mouldering in the grave, forgotten and at rest.

I CAN FIND MY WAY OUT

By Ngaio Marsh (1899-1982)

"I Can Find My Way Out," one of the rare short stories about Inspector Roderick Alleyn, is a contrast to Le Fanu's tale in everything except quality. Marsh's story is a comedy of manners rather than exercise in suspense, and the impossibility is underplayed. Just before he neatly explains how to gas someone in a locked room, Alleyn says, "Don't let us have any nonsense about sealed rooms." Like Marsh's novels it is a quietly satisfying story based on a milieu she knew well—the theater and the tensions among actors and playwright. At her death in 1982 at the age of 83, New Zealand author Ngaio Marsh was one of the most honored of modern mystery writers, having become a Dame of the British Empire and recognized as a Grand Master by the Mystery Writers of America.

AT half-past six on the night in question, Anthony Gill, unable to eat, keep still, think, speak or act coherently, walked from his rooms to the Jupiter Theatre. He knew that there would be nobody backstage, that there was nothing for him to do in the theatre, that he ought to stay quietly in his rooms and presently dress, dine and arrive at, say, a quarter to eight. But it was as if something shoved him into his clothes, thrust him into the street and compelled him to hurry through the West End to the Jupiter. His mind was overlaid with a thin film of inertia. Odd lines from the play occurred to him, but without any particular significance. He found himself busily reiterating a completely irrelevant sentence: "She has a way of laughing that would make a man's heart turn over."

Piccadilly, Shaftesbury Avenue. "Here I go," he thought, turning into Hawke Street, "towards my play. It's one hour and twenty-nine minutes away. A step a second. It's rushing towards me. Tony's first play. Poor young Tony Gill. Never mind. Try again."

The Jupiter. Neon lights: I CAN FIND MY WAY OUT—*by Anthony Gill*. And in the entrance the bills and photographs. *Coralie Bourne with H. J. Bannington, Barry George and Canning Cumberland.*

Canning Cumberland. The film across his mind split and there was the Thing itself and he would have to think about it. How bad would Canning Cumberland be if he came down drunk? Brilliantly bad, they said. He would bring out all the tricks. Clever actor stuff, scoring off everybody, making a fool of the dramatic balance. "In Mr. Canning Cumberland's hands indifferent dialogue and unconvincing situations seemed almost real." What can you do with a drunken actor?

He stood in the entrance feeling his heart pound and his inside deflate and sicken.

Because, of course, it was a bad play. He was at this moment and for the first time really convinced of it. It was terrible. Only one virtue in it and that was not his doing. It had been suggested to him by Coralie Bourne: "I don't think the play you have sent me will do as it is but it has occurred to me—" It was a brilliant idea. He had rewritten the play round it and almost immediately and quite innocently he had begun to think of it as his own although he had said shyly to

Coralie Bourne: "You should appear as joint author." She had quickly, over-emphatically, refused. "It was nothing at all," she said. "If you're to become a dramatist you will learn to get ideas from everywhere. A single situation is nothing. Think of Shakespeare," she added lightly. "Entire plots! Don't be silly." She had said later, and still with the same hurried, nervous air: "Don't go talking to everyone about it. They will think there is more, instead of less, than meets the eye in my small suggestion. Please promise." He promised, thinking he'd made an error in taste when he suggested that Coralie Bourne, so famous an actress, should appear as joint author with an unknown youth. And how right she was, he thought, because, of course, it's going to be a ghastly flop. She'll be sorry she consented to play in it.

Standing in front of the theatre he contemplated nightmare possibilities. What did audiences do when a first play flopped? Did they clap a little, enough to let the curtain rise and quickly fall again on a discomforted group of players? How scanty must the applause be for them to let him off his own appearance? And they were to go on to the Chelsea Arts Ball. A hideous prospect. Thinking he would give anything in the world if he could stop his play, he turned into the foyer. There were lights in the offices and he paused, irresolute, before a board of photographs. Among them, much smaller than the leading players, was Dendra Gay with the eyes looking straight into his. *She had a way of laughing that would make a man's heart turn over.* "Well," he thought, "so I'm in love with her." He turned away from the photograph. A man came out of the office. "Mr. Gill? Telegrams for you."

Anthony took them and as he went out he heard the man call after him: "Very good luck for tonight, sir."

There were queues of people waiting in the side street for the early doors.

At six-thirty Coralie Bourne dialed Canning Cumberland's number and waited.

She heard his voice. "It's me," she said.

"O, God! darling, I've been thinking about you." He spoke rapidly, too loudly. "Coral, I've been thinking about Ben. You oughtn't to have given that situation to the boy."

"We've been over it a dozen times, Cann. Why not give it to

Tony? Ben will never know." She waited and then said nervously, "Ben's gone, Cann. We'll never see him again."

"I've got a 'Thing' about it. After all, he's your husband."

"No, Cann, no."

"Suppose he turns up. It'd be like him to turn up."

"He won't turn up."

She heard him laugh. "I'm sick of all this," she thought suddenly. "I've had it once too often. I can't stand any more. . . . Cann," she said into the telephone. But he had hung up.

At twenty to seven, Barry George looked at himself in his bathroom mirror. "I've got a better appearance," he thought, "than Cann Cumberland. My head's a good shape, my eyes are bigger and my jaw line's cleaner. I never let a show down. I don't drink. I'm a better actor." He turned his head a little, slewing his eyes to watch the effect. "In the big scene," he thought, "I'm the star. He's the feed. That's the way it's been produced and that's what the author wants. I ought to get the notices."

Past notices came up in his memory. He saw the print, the size of the paragraphs; a long paragraph about Canning Cumberland, a line tacked on the end of it. "Is it unkind to add that Mr. Barry George trotted in the wake of Mr. Cumberland's virtuosity with an air of breathless dependability?" And again: "It is a little hard on Mr. Barry George that he should be obliged to act as foil to this brilliant performance." Worst of all: "Mr. Barry George succeeded in looking tolerably unlike a stooge, an achievement that evidently exhausted his resources."

"Monstrous!" he said loudly to his own image, watching the fine glow of indignation in the eyes. Alcohol, he told himself, did two things to Cann Cumberland. He raised his finger. Nice, expressive hand. An actor's hand. Alcohol destroyed Cumberland's artistic integrity. It also invested him with devilish cunning. Drunk, he would burst the seams of a play, destroy its balance, ruin its form and himself emerge blazing with a showmanship that the audience mistook for genius. "While I," he said aloud, "merely pay my author the compliment of faithful interpretation. Psha!"

He returned to his bedroom, completed his dressing and

pulled his hat to the right angle. Once more he thrust his face close to the mirror and looked searchingly at its image. "By God!" he told himself, "he's done it once too often, old boy. Tonight we'll even the score, won't we? By God, we will."

Partly satisfied, and partly ashamed, for the scene, after all, had smacked a little of ham, he took his stick in one hand and a case holding his costume for the Arts Ball in the other, and went down to the theatre.

At ten minutes to seven, H. J. Bannington passed through the gallery queue on his way to the stage door alley, raising his hat and saying: "Thanks so much," to the gratified ladies who let him through. He heard them murmur his name. He walked briskly along the alley, greeted the stage-doorkeeper, passed under a dingy lamp, through an entry and so to the stage. Only working lights were up. The walls of an interior set rose dimly into shadow. Bob Reynolds, the stage-manager, came out through the prompt-entrance. "Hello, old boy," he said, "I've changed the dressing-rooms. You're third on the right: they've moved your things in. Suit you?"

"Better, at least, than a black-hole the size of a W.C. but without its appointments," H.J. said acidly. "I suppose the great Mr. Cumberland still has the star-room?"

"Well, yes, old boy."

"And who pray, is next to him? In the room with the other gas fire?"

"We've put Barry George there, old boy. You know what he's like."

"Only too well, old boy, and the public, I fear, is beginning to find out." H.J. turned into the dressing-room passage. The stage-manager returned to the set where he encountered his assistant. "What's biting *him?*" asked the assistant. "He wanted a dressing-room with a fire." "Only natural," said the A.S.M. nastily. "He started life reading gas meters."

On the right and left of the passage, nearest the stage end, were two doors, each with its star in tarnished paint. The door on the left was open. H.J. looked in and was greeted with the smell of greasepaint, powder, wet-white, and flowers. A gas fire droned comfortably. Coralie Bourne's dresser was spreading out towels. "Good evening, Katie, my jewel," said H.J. "La Belle not down yet?" "We're on our way," she said.

H.J. hummed stylishly: *"Bella filia del amore,"* and returned to the passage. The star-room on the right was closed but he could hear Cumberland's dresser moving about inside. He went on to the next door, paused, read the card, "Mr. Barry George," warbled a high derisive note, turned in at the third door and switched on the light.

Definitely not a second lead's room. No fire. A wash-basin, however, and opposite mirrors. A stack of telegrams had been placed on the dressing-table. Still singing he reached for them, disclosing a number of bills that had been tactfully laid underneath and a letter, addressed in a flamboyant script.

His voice might have been mechanically produced and arbitrarily switched off, so abruptly did his song end in the middle of a roulade. He let the telegrams fall on the table, took up the letter and tore it open. His face, wretchedly pale, was reflected and endlessly re-reflected in the mirrors.

At nine o'clock the telephone rang. Roderick Alleyn answered it. "This is Sloane 84405. No, you're on the wrong number. *No.*" He hung up and returned to his wife and guest. "That's the fifth time in two hours."

"Do let's ask for a new number."

"We might get next door to something worse."

The telephone rang again. "This is not 84406," Alleyn warned it. "No, I cannot take three large trunks to Victoria Station. No, I am not the Instant All Night Delivery. No."

"They're 84406," Mrs. Alleyn explained to Lord Michael Lamprey. "I suppose it's just faulty dialing, but you can't imagine how angry everyone gets. Why do you want to be a policeman?"

"It's a dull hard job, you know—" Alleyn began.

"Oh," Lord Mike said, stretching his legs and looking critically at his shoes, "I don't for a moment imagine I'll leap immediately into false whiskers and plainclothes. No, no. But I'm revoltingly healthy, sir. Strong as a horse. And I don't think I'm as stupid as you might feel inclined to imagine—"

The telephone rang.

"I say, do let me answer it," Mike suggested and did so.

"Hullo?" he said winningly. He listened, smiling at his hostess. "I'm afraid—" he began. "Here, wait a bit— Yes, but—" His expression became blank and complacent. "May I," he said presently, "repeat your order, sir? Can't be too sure, can we? Call at 11 Harrow Gardens, Sloane Square, for one suitcase to be delivered immediately at the Jupiter Theatre to Mr. Anthony Gill. Very good, sir. Thank you, sir. Collect. Quite."

He replaced the receiver and beamed at the Alleyns.

"What the devil have you been up to?" Alleyn said.

"He just simply wouldn't listen to reason. I tried to tell him."

"But it may be urgent," Mrs. Alleyn ejaculated.

"It couldn't be more urgent, really. It's a suitcase for Tony Gill at the Jupiter."

"Well, then—"

"I was at Eton with the chap," said Mike reminiscently. "He's four years older than I am so of course he was madly important while I was less than the dust. This'll larn him."

"I think you'd better put that order through at once," said Alleyn firmly.

"I rather thought of executing it myself, do you know, sir. It'd be a frightfully neat way of gate-crashing the show, wouldn't it? I did try to get a ticket but the house was sold out."

"If you're going to deliver this case you'd better get a bend on."

"It's clearly an occasion for dressing up though, isn't it? I say," said Mike modestly, "would you think it most frightful cheek if I—well I'd promise to come back and return everything. I mean—"

"Are you suggesting that my clothes look more like a vanman's than yours?"

"I thought you'd have things—"

"For Heaven's sake, Rory," said Mrs. Alleyn, "dress him up and let him go. The great thing is to get that wretched man's suitcase to him."

"I know," said Mike earnestly. "It's most frightfully sweet of you. That's how I feel about it."

Alleyn took him away and shoved him into an old and

• begrimed raincoat, a cloth cap and a muffler. "You wouldn't deceive a village idiot in a total eclipse," he said, "but out you go."

He watched Mike drive away and returned to his wife.

"What'll happen?" she asked.

"Knowing Mike, I should say he will end up in the front stalls and go on to supper with the leading lady. She, by the way, is Coralie Bourne. Very lovely and twenty years his senior so he'll probably fall in love with her." Alleyn reached for his tobacco jar and paused. "I wonder what's happened to her husband," he said.

"Who was he?"

"An extraordinary chap. Benjamin Vlasnoff. Violent temper. Looked like a bandit. Wrote two very good plays and got run in three times for common assault. She tried to divorce him but it didn't go through. I think he afterwards lit off to Russia." Alleyn yawned. "I believe she had a hell of a time with him," he said.

"All Night Delivery," said Mike in a hoarse voice, touching his cap. "Suitcase. One." "Here you are," said the woman who had answered the door. "Carry it carefully, now, it's not locked and the catch springs out."

"Fanks," said Mike. "Much obliged. Chilly, ain't it?"

He took the suitcase out to the car.

It was a fresh spring night. Sloane Square was threaded with mist and all the lamps had halos round them. It was the kind of night when individual sounds separate themselves from the conglomerate voice of London; hollow sirens spoke imperatively down on the river and a bugle rang out over in Chelsea Barracks; a night, Mike thought, for adventure.

He opened the rear door of the car and heaved the case in. The catch flew open, the lid dropped back and the contents fell out. "Damn!" said Mike and switched on the inside light.

Lying on the floor of the car was a false beard.

It was flaming red and bushy and was mounted on a chin-piece. With it was incorporated a stiffened mustache. There were wire hooks to attach the whole thing behind the ears. Mike laid it carefully on the seat. Next he picked up a wide black hat, then a vast overcoat with a fur collar, finally a pair of black gloves.

Mike whistled meditatively and thrust his hands into the pockets of Alleyn's mackintosh. His right-hand fingers closed on a card. He pulled it out. "Chief Detective-Inspector Alleyn," he read, "C.I.D. New Scotland Yard."

"Honestly," thought Mike exultantly, "this is a gift."

Ten minutes later a car pulled into the curb at the nearest parking place to the Jupiter Theatre. From it emerged a figure carrying a suitcase. It strode rapidly along Hawke Street and turned into the stage-door alley. As it passed under the dirty lamp it paused, and thus murkily lit, resembled an illustration from some Edwardian spy-story. The face was completely shadowed, a black cavern from which there projected a square of scarlet beard, which was the only note of color.

The doorkeeper who was taking the air with a member of stage-staff, moved forward, peering at the stranger.

"Was you wanting something?"

"I'm taking this case in for Mr. Gill."

"He's in front. You can leave it with me."

"I'm so sorry," said the voice behind the beard, "but I promised I'd leave it backstage myself."

"So you will be leaving it. Sorry, sir, but no one's admitted be'ind without a card."

"A card? Very well. Here is a card."

He held it out in his black-gloved hand. The stage-door-keeper, unwillingly removing his gaze from the beard, took the card and examined it under the light. "Coo!" he said, "what's up, governor?"

"No matter. Say nothing of this."

The figure waved its hand and passed through the door. " 'Ere!" said the doorkeeper excitedly to the stage-hand, "take a slant at this. That's a plainclothes flattie, that was."

"*Plain* clothes!" said the stage-hand. "Them!"

" 'E's disguised," said the doorkeeper. "That's what it is. 'E's disguised 'isself."

" 'E's bloody well lorst 'isself be'ind them whiskers if you arst me."

Out on the stage someone was saying in a pitched and beautifully articulate voice: "*I've always loathed the view from these windows. However if that's the sort of thing you admire. Turn off the lights, damn you. Look at it.*"

"Watch it, now, watch it," whispered a voice so close to Mike that he jumped. "O.K.," said a second voice somewhere above his head. The lights on the set turned blue. "Kill that working light." "Working light gone."

Curtains in the set were wrenched aside and a window flung open. An actor appeared, leaning out quite close to Mike, seeming to look into his face and saying very distinctly: "God: it's frightful!" Mike backed away towards a passage, lit only from an open door. A great volume of sound broke out beyond the stage. "House lights," said the sharp voice. Mike turned into the passage. As he did so, someone came through the door. He found himself face to face with Coralie Bourne, beautifully dressed and heavily painted.

For a moment she stood quite still; then she made a curious gesture with her right hand, gave a small breathy sound and fell forward at his feet.

Anthony was tearing his program into long strips and dropping them on the floor of the O.P. box. On his right hand, above and below, was the audience; sometimes laughing, sometimes still, sometimes as one corporate being, raising its hands and striking them together. As now; when down on the stage, Canning Cumberland, using a strange voice, and inspired by some inward devil, flung back the window and said: "God: it's frightful!"

"Wrong! Wrong!" Anthony cried inwardly, hating Cumberland, hating Barry George because he let one speech of three words over-ride him, hating the audience because they liked it. The curtain descended with a long sigh on the second act and a sound like heavy rain filled the theatre, swelled prodigiously and continued after the house-lights welled up.

"They seem," said a voice behind him, "to be liking your play."

It was Gosset, who owned the Jupiter and had backed the show. Anthony turned on him stammering: "He's destroying it. It should be the other man's scene. He's stealing."

"My boy," said Gosset, "he's an actor."

"He's drunk. It's intolerable."

He felt Gosset's hand on his shoulder.

"People are watching us. You're on show. This is a big

thing for you; a first play, and going enormously. Come and have a drink, old boy. I want to introduce you—"

Anthony got up and Gosset, with his arm across his shoulders, flashing smiles, patting him, led him to the back of the box.

"I'm sorry," Anthony said. "I can't. Please let me off. I'm going backstage."

"Much better not, old son." The hand tightened on his shoulder. "Listen, old son—" But Anthony had freed himself and slipped through the pass-door from the box to the stage.

At the foot of the breakneck stairs Dendra Gay stood waiting. "I thought you'd come," she said.

Anthony said: "He's drunk. He's murdering the play."

"It's only one scene, Tony. He finishes early in the next act. It's going colossally."

"But don't you understand—"

"I do. You *know* I do. But you're success, Tony darling! You can hear it and smell it and feel it in your bones."

"Dendra—" he said uncertainly.

Someone came up and shook his hand and went on shaking it. Flats were being laced together with a slap of rope on canvas. A chandelier ascended into darkness. "Lights," said the stage-manager, and the set was flooded with them. A distant voice began chanting. "Last act, please. Last act."

"Miss Bourne all right?" the stage-manager suddenly demanded.

"She'll be all right. She's not on for ten minutes," said a woman's voice.

"What's the matter with Miss Bourne?" Anthony asked.

"Tony, I must go and so must you. Tony, it's going to be grand. *Please* think so. *Please*."

"Dendra—" Tony began, but she had gone.

Beyond the curtain, horns and flutes announced the last act.

"Clear please."

The stage hands came off.

"House lights."

"House lights gone."

"Stand by."

And while Anthony still hesitated in the O.P. corner, the

curtain rose. Canning Cumberland and H. J. Bannington opened the last act.

As Mike knelt by Coralie Bourne he heard someone enter the passage behind him. He turned and saw, silhouetted against the lighted stage, the actor who had looked at him through a window in the set. The silhouette seemed to repeat the gesture Coralie Bourne had used, and to flatten itself against the wall.

A woman in an apron came out of the open door.

"I say—here!" Mike said.

Three things happened almost simultaneously. The woman cried out and knelt beside him. The man disappeared through a door on the right.

The woman, holding Coralie Bourne in her arms, said violently: "Why have you come back?" Then the passage lights came on. Mike said: "Look here, I'm most frightfully sorry," and took off the broad black hat. The dresser gaped at him, Coralie Bourne made a crescendo sound in her throat and opened her eyes. "Katie?" she said.

"It's all right, my lamb. It's not him, dear. You're all right." The dresser jerked her head at Mike: "Get out of it," she said.

"Yes, of course, I'm most frightfully—" He backed out of the passage, colliding with a youth who said: "Five minutes, please." The dresser called out: "Tell them she's not well. Tell them to hold the curtain."

"No," said Coralie Bourne strongly. "I'm all right, Katie. Don't say anything. Katie, what was it?"

They disappeared into the room on the left.

Mike stood in the shadow of a stack of scenic flats by the entry into the passage. There was great activity on the stage. He caught a glimpse of Anthony Gill on the far side talking to a girl. The call-boy was speaking to the stage-manager who now shouted into space: "Miss Bourne all right?" The dresser came into the passage and called: "She'll be all right. She's not on for ten minutes." The youth began chanting: "Last act, please." The stage-manager gave a series of orders. A man with an eyeglass and a florid beard came from further down the passage and stood outside the set, bracing his figure and giving little tweaks to his clothes. There was a sound of horns and flutes. Canning Cumberland emerged from the room on the right and on his way to the stage, passed close to Mike, leaving a strong smell of alcohol behind him. The curtain rose.

Behind his shelter, Mike stealthily removed his beard and stuffed it into the pocket of his overcoat.

A group of stage-hands stood nearby. One of them said in a hoarse whisper: " 'E's squiffy." "Garn, 'e's going good." "So 'e may be going good. And for why? *Becos* 'e's squiffy."

Ten minutes passed. Mike thought: "This affair has definitely not gone according to plan." He listened. Some kind of tension seemd to be building up on the stage. Canning Cumberland's voice rose on a loud but blurred note. A door in the set opened. "Don't bother to come," Cumberland said. "Goodbye. I can find my way out." The door slammed. Cumberland was standing near Mike. Then, very close, there was a loud explosion. The scenic flats vibrated, Mike's flesh leapt on his bones and Cumberland went into his dressing-rooms. Mike heard the key turn in the door. The smell of alcohol mingled with the smell of gunpowder. A stage-hand moved to a trestle table and laid a pistol on it. The actor with the eyeglass made an exit. He spoke for a moment to the stage-manager, passed Mike and disappeared in the passage.

Smells. There were all sorts of smells. Subconsciously, still listening to the play, he began to sort them out. Glue. Canvas. Greasepaint. The call-boy tapped on the doors. "Mr. George, please." "Miss Bourne, please." They came out, Coralie Bourne with her dresser. Mike heard her turn a door handle and say something. An indistinguishable voice answered her. Then she and her dresser passed him. The others spoke to her and she nodded and then seemed to withdraw into herself, waiting with her head bent, ready to make her entrance. Presently she drew back, walked swiftly to the door in the set, flung it open and swept on, followed a minute later by Barry George.

Smells. Dust, stale paint, cloth. Gas. Increasingly, the smell of gas.

The group of stage-hands moved away behind the set to the side of the stage. Mike edged out of cover. He could see the prompt-corner. The stage-manager stood there with folded arms, watching the action. Behind him were grouped the players who were not on. Two dressers stood apart, watching. The light from the set caught their faces. Coralie Bourne's voice sent phrases flying like birds into the auditorium.

Mike began peering at the floor. Had he kicked some gas fitting adrift? The call-boy passed him, stared at him over his shoulder and went down the passage, tapping. "Five minutes to the curtain, please. Five minutes." The actor with the elderly make-up followed the call boy out. "God, what a stink of gas," he whispered. "Chronic, ain't it?" said the call-boy. They stared at Mike and then crossed to the waiting group. The man said something to the stage-manager who tipped his head up, sniffing. He made an impatient gesture and turned back to the prompt-box, reaching over the prompter's head. A bell rang somewhere up in the flies and Mike saw a stage-hand climb to the curtain platform.

The little group near the prompt corner was agitated. They looked back towards the passage entrance. The call-boy nodded and came running back. He knocked on the first door on the right. *"Mr. Cumberland! Mr. Cumberland! You're on for the call."* He rattled the door handle. *"Mr. Cumberland! You're on."*

Mike ran into the passage. The call-boy coughed retchingly and jerked his hand at the door. "Gas!"

"Break it in."

"I'll get Mr. Reynolds."

He was gone. It was a narrow passage. From halfway across the opposite room Mike took a run, head down, shoulder forward, at the door. It gave a little and a sickening increase in the smell caught him in the lungs. A vast storm of noise had broken out and as he took another run he thought: "It's hailing outside."

"Just a minute if *you* please, sir."

It was a stage-hand. He'd got a hammer and screwdriver. He wedged the point of the screwdriver between the lock and the doorpost, drove it home and wrenched. The screws squeaked, the wood splintered and gas poured into the passage. "No winders," coughed the stage-hand.

Mike wound Alleyn's scarf over his mouth and nose. Half-forgotten instructions from anti-gas drill occurred to him. The room looked queer but he could see the man slumped down in the chair quite clearly. He stooped low and ran in.

He was knocking against things as he backed out, lugging the dead weight. His arms tingled. A high insistent voice hummed in his brain. He floated a short distance and came to earth on a concrete floor among several pairs of legs. A long way off, someone said loudly: "I can only thank you for being so kind to what I know, too well, is a very imperfect play." Then the sound of hail began again. There was a heavenly stream of clear air flowing into his mouth and nostrils. "I could eat it," he thought and sat up.

The telephone rang. "Suppose," Mrs. Alleyn suggested, "that this time you ignore it."

"It might be the Yard," Alleyn said, and answered it.

"Is that Chief Detective-Inspector Alleyn's flat? I'm speaking from the Jupiter Theatre. I've rung up to say that the Chief Inspector is here and that he's had a slight mishap. He's all right, but I think it might be as well for someone to drive him home. No need to worry."

"What sort of mishap?" Alleyn asked.

"Er—well—er, he's been a bit gassed."

"*Gassed!* All right. Thanks, I'll come."

"*What* a bore for you darling," said Mrs. Alleyn. "What sort of case is it? Suicide?"

"Masquerading within the meaning of the act, by the sound of it. Mike's in trouble."

"What trouble, for Heaven's sake?"

"Got himself gassed. He's all right. Good-night darling. Don't wait up."

When he reached the theatre, the front of the house was in darkness. He made his way down the side alley to the stage-door where he was held up.

"Yard," he said, and produced his official card.

"'Ere," said the stage-doorkeeper, "'ow many more of you?"

"The man inside was working for me," said Alleyn and walked in. The doorkeeper followed, protesting.

To the right of the entrance was a large scenic dock from which the double doors had been rolled back. Here Mike was sitting in an armchair, very white about the lips. Three men and two women, all with painted faces, stood near him and behind them a group of stage-hands with Reynolds, the stage-manager, and, apart from these, three men in evening dress. The men looked woodenly shocked. The women had been weeping.

"I'm most frightfully sorry, sir," Mike said. "I've tried to explain. This," he added generally, "is Inspector Alleyn."

"I can't understand all this," said the oldest of the men in evening dress irritably. He turned on the doorkeeper. "You said—"

"I seen 'is card—"

"I know," said Mike, "but you see—"

"This is Lord Michael Lamprey," Alleyn said. "A recruit to the Police Department. What's happened here?"

"Doctor Rankin, would you—?"

The second of the men in evening dress came forward. "All right, Gosset. It's a bad business, Inspector. I've just been saying the police would have to be informed. If you'll come with me—"

Alleyn followed him through a door onto the stage proper. It was dimly lit. A trestle table had been set up in the centre and on it, covered with a sheet, was an unmistakable shape. The smell of gas, strong everywhere, hung heavily about the table.

"Who is it?"

"Canning Cumberland. He'd locked the door of his dressing-room. There's a gas fire. Your young friend dragged him out, very pluckily, but it was no go. I was in front. Gosset, the manager, had asked me to supper. It's a perfectly clear case of suicide as you'll see."

"I'd better look at the room. Anybody been in?"

"God, no. It was a job to clear it. They turned the gas off at the main. There's no window. They had to open the double doors at the back of the stage and a small outside door at the end of the passage. It may be possible to get in now."

He led the way to the dressing-room passage. "Pretty thick, still," he said. "It's the first room on the right. They burst the lock. You'd better keep down near the floor."

The powerful lights over the mirror were on and the room still had its look of occupation. The gas fire was against the left hand wall. Alleyn squatted down by it. The tap was still turned on, its face lying parallel with the floor. The top of the heater, the tap itself, and the carpet near it, were covered with a creamish powder. On the end of the dressing-table shelf nearest to the stove was a box of this powder. Further along the shelf, greasepaints were set out in a row beneath the mirror. Then came a wash basin and in front of this an overturned chair. Alleyn could see the track of heels, across the pile of the carpet, to the door immediately opposite. Beside the wash basin was a quart bottle of whiskey, three parts empty, and a tumbler. Alleyn had had about enough and returned to the passage.

"Perfectly clear," the hovering doctor said again, "Isn't it?"

"I'll see the other rooms, I think."

The one next to Cumberland's was like his in reverse, but smaller. The heater was back to back with Cumberland's. The dressing-shelf was set out with much the same assortment of greasepaints. The tap of this heater, too, was turned on. It was of precisely the same make as the other and Alleyn, less embarrassed here by fumes, was able to make a longer examination. It was a common enough type of gas fire. The lead-in was from a pipe through a flexible metallic tube with a rubber connection. There were two taps, one in the pipe and one at the junction of the tube with the heater itself. Alleyn disconnected the tube and examined the connection. It was perfectly sound, a close fit and stained red at the end. Alleyn noticed a wiry thread of some reddish stuff resembling packing that still clung to it. The nozzle and tap were brass, the tap pulling over when it was turned on, to lie in a parallel plane with the floor. No powder had been scattered about here.

He glanced round the room, returned to the door and read the card: "Mr. Barry George."

The doctor followed him into the rooms opposite these, on the left-hand side of the passage. They were a repetition in design of the two he had already seen but were hung with women's clothes and had a more elaborate assortment of grease paint and cosmetics.

There was a mass of flowers in the star room. Alleyn read

the cards. One in particular caught his eye: "From Anthony
Gill to say a most inadequate 'thank you' for the great idea." A
vase of red roses stood before the mirror: "To your greatest
triumph, Coralie darling. C.C." In Miss Gay's room there
were only two bouquets, one from the management and one
"from Anthony, with love."

Again in each room he pulled off the lead-in to the heater
and looked at the connection.

"All right, aren't they?" said the doctor.

"Quite all right. Tight fit. Good solid grey rubber."

"Well, then—"

Next on the left was an unused room, and opposite it, "Mr.
H. J. Bannington." Neither of these rooms had gas fires. Mr.
Bannington's dressing-table was littered with the usual
array of greasepaint, the materials for his beard, a number
of telegrams and letters, and several bills.

"About the body," the doctor began.

"We'll get a mortuary van from the Yard."

"But—Surely in a case of suicide—"

"I don't think this is suicide."

"But, good God!—D'you mean there's been an accident?"

"No accident," said Alleyn.

At midnight, the dressing-room lights in the Jupiter Theatre were brilliant, and men were busy there with the tools of
their trade. A constable stood at the stage-door and a van
waited in the yard. The front of the house was dimly lit and
there, among the shrouded stalls, sat Coralie Bourne, Basil
Gosset, H. J. Bannington, Dendra Gay, Anthony Gill, Reynolds, Katie the dresser, and the call-boy. A constable sat
behind them and another stood by the doors into the foyer.
They stared across the backs of seats at the fire curtain.
Spirals of smoke rose from their cigarettes and about their
feet were discarded programs. "Basil Gosset presents I CAN
FIND MY WAY OUT by Anthony Gill."

In the manager's office Alleyn said: "You're sure of your
facts, Mike?"

"Yes, sir. Honestly. I was right up against the entrance into
the passage. They didn't see me because I was in the shadow.
It was very dark offstage."

"You'll have to swear to it."

"I know."

"Good. All right, Thompson. Miss Gay and Mr. Gosset may go home. Ask Miss Bourne to come in."

When Sergeant Thompson had gone Mike said: "I haven't had a chance to say I know I've made a perfect fool of myself. Using your card and everything."

"Irresponsible gaiety doesn't go down very well in the service, Mike. You behaved like a clown."

"I *am* a fool," said Mike wretchedly.

The red beard was lying in front of Alleyn on Gosset's desk. He picked it up and held it out. "Put it on," he said.

"She might do another faint."

"I think not. Now the hat: yes—yes, I see. Come in."

Sergeant Thompson showed Coralie Bourne in and then sat at the end of the desk with his notebook.

Tears had traced their course through the powder on her face, carrying black cosmetic with them and leaving the greasepaint shining like snail-tracks. She stood near the doorway looking dully at Michael. "Is he back in England?" she said. "Did he tell you to do this?" She made an impatient movement. "Do take it off," she said, "it's a very bad beard. If Cann had only looked—" Her lips trembled. "Who told you to do it?"

"Nobody," Mike stammered, pocketing the beard. "I mean— As a matter of fact, Tony Gill—"

"*Tony?* But *he* didn't know. Tony wouldn't do it. Unless—"

"Unless?" Alleyn said.

She said frowning: "Tony didn't want Cann to play the part that way. He was furious."

"He says it was his dress for the Chelsea Arts Ball," Mike mumbled. "I brought it here. I just though I'd put it on—it was idiotic, I know—for fun. I'd no idea you and Mr. Cumberland would mind."

"Ask Mr. Gill to come in," Alleyn said.

Anthony was white and seemed bewildered and helpless. "I've told Mike," he said. "It was my dress for the ball. They sent it round from the costume-hiring place this afternoon but I forgot it. Dendra reminded me and rang up the Delivery people—or Mike, as it turns out—in the interval."

"Why," Alleyn asked, "did you choose that particular disguise?"

"I didn't. I didn't know what to wear and I was too rattled to think. They said they were hiring things for themselves and would get something for me. They said we'd all be characters out of a Russian melodrama."

"Who said this?"

"Well—well, it was Barry George, actually."

"*Barry,*" Coralie Bourne said. "*It was Barry.*"

"I don't understand," Anthony said. "Why should a fancy dress upset everybody?"

"It happened," Alleyn said, "to be a replica of the dress usually worn by Miss Bourne's husband who also had a red beard. That was it, wasn't it Miss Bourne? I remember seeing him—"

"Oh, yes," she said, "you would. He was known to the police." Suddenly she broke down completely. She was in an armchair near the desk but out of the range of its shaded lamp. She twisted and writhed, beating her hand against the padded arm of the chair. Sergeant Thompson sat with his head bent and his hand over his notes. Mike, after an agonized glance at Alleyn, turned his back. Anthony Gill leant over her: "Don't," he said violently. "Don't! For God's sake, stop."

She twisted away from him and gripping the edge of the desk, began to speak to Alleyn; little by little gaining mastery of herself. "I want to tell you. I want you to understand. Listen." Her husband had been fantastically cruel, she said. "It was a kind of slavery." But when she sued for divorce he brought evidence of adultery with Cumberland. They had thought he knew nothing. "There was an abominable scene. He told us he was going away. He said he'd keep track of us and if I tried again for divorce, he'd come home. He was very friendly with Barry in those days." He had left behind him the first draft of a play he had meant to write for her and Cumberland. It had a wonderful scene for them. "And now you will never have it," he had said, "because there is no other playwright who could make this play for you but I." He was, she said, a melodramatic man but he was never ridiculous. He returned to the Ukraine where he was born and they had heard no more of him. In a little while she would have been able to presume death. But years of waiting did not agree with Canning Cumberland. He drank consistently and at his worst used to imagine her husband was about to return. "He was really terrified of Ben," she said. "He seemed like a creature in a nightmare."

Anthony Gill said: "This play—was it—?"

"Yes. There was an extraordinary similarity between your play and his. I saw at once that Ben's central scene would enormously strengthen your piece. Cann didn't want me to give it to you. Barry knew. He said: 'Why not?' He wanted Cann's part and was furious when he didn't get it. So you see, when he suggested you should dress and make-up like Ben—" She turned to Alleyn. "You see?"

"What did Cumberland do when he saw you?" Alleyn asked Mike.

"He made a queer movement with his hands as if—well, as if he expected me to go for him. Then he just bolted into his room."

"He thought Ben had come back," she said.

"Were you alone at any time after you fainted?" Alleyn asked.

"I? No. No, I wasn't. Katie took me into my dressing-room and stayed with me until I went on for the last scene."

"One other question. Can you, by any chance, remember if the heater in your room behaved at all oddly?"

She looked wearily at him. "Yes, it did give a sort of plop, I think. It made me jump. I was nervy."

"You went straight from your room to the stage?"

"Yes. With Katie. I wanted to go to Cann. I tried the door when we came out. It was locked. He said: 'Don't come in.' I said: 'It's all right. It wasn't Ben,' and went on to the stage."

"I heard Miss Bourne," Mike said.

"He must have made up his mind by then. He was terribly drunk when he played his last scene." She pushed her hair back from her forehead. "May I go?" she asked Alleyn.

"I've sent for a taxi, Mr. Gill, will you see if it's there? In the meantime, Miss Bourne, would you like to wait in the foyer?"

"May I take Katie home with me?"

"Certainly. Thompson will find her. Is there anyone else we can get?"

"No, thank you. Just old Katie."

Alleyn opened the door for her and watched her walk into the foyer. "Check up with the dresser, Thompson," he murmured, "and get Mr. H. J. Bannington."

He saw Coralie Bourne sit on the lower step of the dress-circle stairway and lean her head against the wall. Nearby, on a gilt easel, a huge photograph of Canning Cumberland smiled handsomely at her.

H. J. Bannington looked pretty ghastly. He had rubbed his hand across his face and smeared his makeup. Florid red paint from his lips had stained the crêpe hair that had been gummed on and shaped into a beard. His monocle was still in his left eye and gave him an extraordinarily rakish look. "See here," he complained, "I've about *had* this party. When do we go home?"

Alleyn uttered placatory phrases and got him to sit down. He checked over H.J.'s movements after Cumberland left the stage and found that his account tallied with Mike's. He asked if H.J. had visited any of the other dressing-rooms and was told acidly that H.J. knew his place in the company. "I remained in my unheated and squalid kennel, thank you very much."

"Do you know if Mr. Barry George followed your example?"

"Couldn't say, old boy. He didn't come near *me*."

"Have you any theories at all about this unhappy business, Mr. Bannington?"

"Do you mean, why did Cann do it? Well, speak no ill of the dead, but I'd have thought it was pretty obvious he was morbid-drunk. Tight as an owl when we finished the second act. Ask the great Mr. Barry George. Cann took the big scene away from Barry with both hands and left him looking pathetic. All wrong artistically, but that's how Cann was in his cups." H.J.'s wicked little eyes narrowed. "The great Mr. George," he said, "must be feeling very unpleasant by now. You might say he'd got a suicide on his mind, mightn't you? Or don't you know about that?"

"It was not suicide."

The glass dropped form H.J.'s eye. "God!" he said. "God, I told Bob Reynolds! I toid him the whole plant wanted overhauling."

"The gas plant, you mean?"

"Certainly. I was in the gas business years ago. Might say I'm in it still with a difference, ha-ha!"

"Ha-ha!" Alleyn agreed politely. He leaned forward. "Look here," he said: "We can't dig up a gas man at this time of night and may very likely need an expert opinion. You can help us."

"Well, old boy, I was rather pining for a spot of shut-eye. But, of course—"

"I shan't keep you very long."

"God, I hope not!" said H.J. earnestly.

Barry George had been made up pale for the last act. Colorless lips and shadows under his cheek bones and eyes had skilfully underlined his character as a repatriated but broken prisoner-of-war. Now, in the glare of the office lamp, he looked like a grossly exaggerated figure of mourning. He began at once to tell Alleyn how grieved and horrified he was. Everybody, he said, had their faults, and poor old Cann was no exception but wasn't it terrible to think what could happen to a man who let himself go downhill? He, Barry George, was abnormally sensitive and he didn't think he'd ever really get over the awful shock this had been to him. What, he wondered, could be at the bottom of it? Why had poor old Cann decided to end it all?

"Miss Bourne's theory," Alleyn began. Mr. George laughed. "Coralie?" he said. "So she's got a theory! Oh, well. Never mind."

"Her theory is this. Cumberland saw a man whom he mistook for her husband and, having a morbid dread of his return, drank the greater part of a bottle of whiskey and gassed himself. The clothes and beard that deceived him had, I understand, been ordered by you for Mr. Anthony Gill."

This statement produced startling results. Barry George broke into a spate of expostulation and apology. There had been no thought in his mind or resurrecting poor old Ben, who was no doubt dead but had been, mind you, in many ways one of the best. They were all to go to the Ball as exaggerated characters from melodrama. Not for the world—he gesticulated and protested. A line of sweat broke out along the margin of his hair. "I don't know what you're getting at," he shouted. "What are you suggesting?"

"I'm suggesting, among other things, that Cumberland was murdered."

"You're mad! He'd locked himself in. They had to break down the door. There's no window. You're crazy!"

"Don't," Alleyn said wearily, "let us have any nonsense about sealed rooms. Now, Mr. George, you knew Benjamin Vlasnoff pretty well. Are you going to tell us that when you suggested Mr. Gill should wear a coat with a fur collar, a black sombrero, black gloves and a red beard, it never occurred to you that his appearance might be a shock to Miss Bourne and to Cumberland?"

"I wasn't the only one," he blustered. "H.J. knew. And if it had scared him off, *she* wouldn't have been so sorry. She'd had about enough of him. Anyway if this is murder, the costume's got nothing to do with it."

"That," Alleyn said, getting up, "is what we hope to find out."

In Barry George's room, Detective Sergeant Bailey, a fingerprint expert, stood by the gas heater. Sergeant Gibson, a police photographer, and a uniformed constable were near the door. In the centre of the room stood Barry George, looking from one man to another and picking at his lips.

"I don't know why he wants me to watch all this," he said. "I'm exhausted. I'm emotionally used up. What's he doing? Where is he?"

Alleyn was next door in Cumberland's dressing-room, with H.J., Mike and Sergeant Thompson. It was pretty clear now of fumes and the gas fire was burning comfortably. Sergeant Thompson sprawled in the armchair near the heater, his head sunk and his eyes shut.

"This is the theory, Mr. Bannington," Alleyn said. "You and Cumberland have made your final exits; Miss Bourne and Mr. George and Miss Gay are all on the stage. Lord Michael is standing just outside the entrance to the passage. The dressers and stage-staff are watching the play from the side. Cumberland has locked himself in this room. There he is, dead drunk and sound asleep. The gas fire is burning, full pressure. Earlier in the evening he powdered himself and a thick layer of the powder lies undisturbed on the tap. Now."

He tapped on the wall.

The fire blew out with a sharp explosion. This was followed by the hiss of escaping gas. Alleyn turned the taps off. "You see," he said, "I've left an excellent print on the powdered surface. Now, come next door."

Next door, Barry George appealed to him stammering: "But I didn't know. I don't know anything about it. I don't *know*."

"Just show Mr. Bannington, will you, Bailey?"

Bailey knelt down. The lead-in was disconnected from the tap on the heater. He turned on the tap in the pipe and blew down the tube.

"An air lock, you see. It works perfectly."

H.J. was staring at Barry George. "But I don't know about gas, H.J., H.J., tell them—"

"One moment." Alleyn removed the towels that had been spread over the dressing-shelf, revealing a sheet of clean paper on which lay the rubber push-on connection.

"Will you take this lens, Bannington, and look at it. You'll see that it's stained a florid red. It's a very slight stain but it's unmistakably greasepaint. And just above the stain you'll see a wiry hair. Rather like some sort of packing material, but it's not that. It's crêpe hair, isn't it?"

The lens wavered above the paper.

"Let me hold it for you," Alleyn said. He put his hand over H.J.'s shoulder and, with a swift movement, plucked a tuft from his false moustache and dropped it on the paper. "Identical, you see. Ginger. It seems to be stuck to the connection with spirit-gum."

The lens fell. H.J. twisted round, faced Alleyn for a second, and then struck him full in the face. He was a small man but it took three of them to hold him.

"In a way, sir, it's handy when they have a smack at you," said Detective Sergeant Thompson half an hour later. "You can pull them in nice and straightforward without any 'will you come to the station and make a statement' business."

"Quite," said Alleyn, nursing his jaw.

Mike said: "He must have gone to the room after Barry George and Miss Bourne were called."

"That's it. He had to be quick. The call-boy would be round in a minute and he had to be back in his own room."

"But look here—what about motive?"

"That, my good Mike, is precisely why, at half-past one in the morning, we're still in this miserable theatre. You're getting a view of the duller aspect of homicide. Want to go home?"

"No. Give me another job."

"Very well. About ten feet from the prompt-entrance, there's a sort of garbage tin. Go through it."

At seventeen minutes to two, when the dressing-rooms and passage had been combed clean and Alleyn had called a spell, Mike came to him with filthy hands. "*Eureka,*" he said, "I hope."

They all went into Bannington's room. Alleyn spread out on the dressing-table the fragments of paper that Mike had given him.

"They'd been pushed down to the bottom of the tin," Mike said.

Alleyn moved the fragments about. Thompson whistled through his teeth. Bailey and Gibson mumbled together.

"There you are," Alleyn said at last.

They collected round him. The letter that H. J. Bannington had opened at this same table six hours and forty-five minutes earlier, was pieced together like a jig-saw puzzle.

"Dear H.J.

Having seen the monthly statement of my account, I called at my bank this morning and was shown a check that is undoubtedly a forgery. Your histrionic versatility, my dear H.J., is only equalled by your audacity as a calligraphist. But fame has its disadvantages. The teller has recognized you. I propose to take action."

"Unsigned," said Bailey.

"Look at the card on the red roses in Miss Bourne's room, signed C.C. It's a very distinctive hand." Alleyn turned to Mike. "Do you still want to be a policeman?"

"Yes."

"Lord help you. Come and talk to me at the office tomorrow."

"Thank you, sir."

They went out, leaving a constable on duty. It was a cold morning. Mike looked up at the façade of the Jupiter. He could just make out the shape of the neon sign: I CAN FIND MY WAY OUT *by Anthony Gill.*

THE SUICIDE OF KIAROS

By L. Frank Baum (1856-1919)

Before he wrote The Wonderful Wizard of Oz *and other classic fairy tales for children, Lyman Frank Baum contributed short stories to adult periodicals. "The Suicide of Kiaros," which appeared in an 1896 issue of the now obscure magazine* The White Elephant, *is a cleanly told murder story without the sentimentality that permeated many other stories of the period. And unexpectedly it foreshadows some of the Oz books:* The Lost Princess of Oz *and* Glinda of Oz *come close to being detective stories, and the unmasking of the Wizard in the first Oz book is similar to the solutions of many locked-room murders in which the seemingly magical turns out to be humbug. It is not surprising that two masters of the impossible crime, Ellery Queen and John Dickson Carr, grew up reading the Oz books.*

I

MR. FELIX MARSTON, cashier for the great mercantile firm of Van Alsteyne & Traynor, sat in his little private office with a balance-sheet before him and a frown upon his handsome face. At times he nervously ran his slim fingers through the mass of dark hair that clustered over his forehead, and the growing expression of annoyance upon his features fully revealed his disquietude.

The world knew and admired Mr. Marston, and a casual onlooker would certainly have decided that something had gone wrong with the firm's financial transactions; but Mr. Marston knew himself better than the world did, and grimly realized that although something had gone wrong indeed, it affected himself in an unpleasantly personal way.

The world's knowledge of the popular young cashier included the following items: He had entered the firm's employ years before in an inferior position, and by energy, intelligence and business ability, had worked his way up until he reached the post he now occupied, and became his employers' most trusted servant. His manner was grave, earnest and dignified; his judgment, in business matters, clear and discerning. He had no intimate friends, but was courteous and affable to all he met, and his private life, so far as it was known, was beyond all reproach. Mr. Van Alsteyne, the head of the firm, conceived a warm liking for Mr. Marston, and finally invited him to dine at his house. It was there the young man first met Gertrude Van Alsteyne, his employer's only child, a beautiful girl and an acknowledged leader in society. Attracted by the man's handsome face and gentlemanly bearing, the heiress encouraged him to repeat his visit, and Marston followed up his advantage so skillfully that within a year she had consented to become his wife. Mr. Van Alsteyne did not object to the match. His admiration for the young man deepened, and he vowed that upon the wedding day he would transfer one-half his interest in the firm to his son-in-law.

Therefore the world, knowing all this, looked upon Mr. Marston as one of fortune's favorites, and predicted a great future for him. But Mr. Marston, as I said, knew himself more intimately than did the world, and now, as he sat looking upon that fatal trial balance, he muttered in an undertone:

"Oh, you fool—you fool!"

Clear-headed, intelligent man of the world though he was, one vice had mastered him. A few of the most secret, but most dangerous gambling dens knew his face well. His ambition was unbounded, and before he had even dreamed of being able to win Miss Van Alsteyne as his bride, he had figured out several ingenious methods of winning a fortune at the green table. Two years ago he had found it necessary to "borrow" a sum of money from the firm to enable him to carry out these clever methods. Having, through some unforeseen calamity, lost the money, another sum had to be abstracted to allow him to win back enough to even the accounts. Other men have attempted this before; their experiences are usually the same. By a neat juggling of figures, the books of the firm had so far been made to conceal his thefts, but now it seemed as if fortune, in pushing him forward, was about to hurl him down a precipice.

His marriage to Gertrude Van Alsteyne was to take place in two weeks, and as Mr. Van Alsteyne insisted upon keeping his promise to give Marston an interest in the business, the change in the firm would necessitate a thorough overhauling of the accounts, which meant discovery and ruin to the man who was about to grasp a fortune and a high social position—all that his highest ambition had ever dreamed of attaining.

It is no wonder that Mr. Marston, brought face to face with his critical position, denounced himself for his past folly, and realized his helplessness to avoid the catastrophe that was about to crush him.

A voice outside interrupted his musings and arrested his attention.

"It is Mr. Marston I wish to see."

The cashier thrust the sheet of figures within a drawer of the desk, hastily composed his features and opened the glass door beside him.

"Show Mr. Kiaros this way," he called, after a glance at his visitor. He had frequently met the person who now entered his office, but he could not resist a curious glance as the

THE SUICIDE OF KIAROS   97

man sat down upon a chair and spread his hands over his
knees. He was short and thick-set in form, and both oddly
and carelessly dressed, but his head and face were most
venerable in appearance. Flowing locks of pure white graced
a forehead whose height and symmetry denoted unusual
intelligence, and a full beard of the same purity reached full
to his waist. The eyes were full and dark, but not piercing in
character, rather conveying in their frank glance kindness
and benevolence. A round cap of some dark material was
worn upon his head, and this he deferentially removed as he
seated himself, and said:

"For me a package of value was consigned to you, I
believe?"

Marston nodded gravely.

"Mr. Williamson left it with me," he replied.

"I will take it," announced the Greek, calmly; "twelve
thousand dollars it contains."

Marston started.

"I knew it was money," he said, "but was not aware of the
amount. This is it, I think." He took from the huge safe a
packet, corded and sealed, and handed it to his visitor.
Kiaros took a pen-knife from his pocket, cut the cords and
removed the wrapper, after which he proceeded to count the
contents.

Marston listlessly watched him. Twelve thousand dollars.
That would be more than enough to save him from ruin, if
only it belonged to him instead of this Greek money-lender.

"The amount, it is right," declared the old man, re-wrap-
ping the parcel of notes; "you have my thanks, sir. Good-
afternoon," and he rose to go.

"Pardon me, sir," said Marston, with a sudden thought, "it
is after banking hours. Will it be safe to carry this money
with you until morning?"

"Perfectly," replied Kiaros; "I am never molested, for I am
old, and few know my business. My safe at home large sums
often contains. The money I like to have near me, to accom-
modate my clients."

He buttoned his coat tightly over the packet, and then in
turn paused to look at the cashier.

"Lately you have not come to me for favors," he said.

"No," answered Marston, arousing from a slight reverie; "I have not needed to. Still, I may be obliged to visit you again soon."

"Your servant I am pleased to be," said Kiaros, with a smile, and turning abruptly he left the office.

Marston glanced at his watch. He was engaged to dine with his betrothed that evening, and it was nearly time to return to his lodgings to dress. He attended to one or two matters in his usual methodical way, and then left the office for the night, relinquishing any further duties to his assistant. As he passed throught the various business offices on his way out, he was greeted respectfully by his fellow employees, who already regarded him a member of the firm.

II

Almost for the first time during their courtship, Miss Van Alsteyne was tender and demonstrative that evening, and seemed loath to allow him to leave the house when he pleaded a business engagement and arose to go. She was a stately beauty, and little given to emotional ways, therefore her new mood affected him greatly, and as he walked away he realized, with a sigh, how much it would cost him to lose so dainty and charming a bride.

At the first corner he paused and examined his watch by the light of the street lamp. It was nine o'clock. Hailing the first passing cab, he directed the man to drive him to the lower end of the city, and leaning back upon the cushions, he became occupied in earnest thought.

The jolting of the cab over a rough pavement finally aroused him, and looking out he signaled the driver to stop.

"Shall I wait, sir?" asked the man, as Marston alighted and paid his fare.

"No."

The cab rattled away, and the cashier retraced his way a few blocks and then walked down a side street that seemed nearly deserted, so far as he could see in the dim light. Keeping track of the house numbers, which were infrequent and often nearly obliterated, he finally paused before a tall, brick building, the lower floors of which seemed occupied as a warehouse.

"Two eighty-six," he murmured; "this must be the place. If I remember right there should be a stairway at the left—ah, here it is."

There was no light at the entrance, but having visited the place before, under similar circumstances, Marston did not hesitate, but began mounting the stairs, guiding himself in the darkness by keeping one hand upon the narrow rail. One flight—two—three—four!

"His room should be straight before me," he thought, pausing to regain his breath; "yes, I think there is a light shining under the door."

He advanced softly, knocked, and then listened. There was a faint sound from within, and then a slide in the upper panel of the door was pushed aside, permitting a strong ray of lamp-light to strike Marston full in the face.

"Oho!" said a calm voice, "Mr. Marston has honored me. To enter I entreat you."

The door was thrown open and Kiaros stood before him, with a smile upon his face, gracefully motioning him to advance. Marston returned the old man's courteous bow, and entering the room, took a seat near the table, at the same time glancing at his surroundings.

The room was plainly but substantially furnished. A small safe stood in a corner at his right, and near it was the long table, used by Kiaros as a desk. It was littered with papers and writing material, and behind it was a high-backed, padded easychair, evidently the favorite seat of the Greek, for after closing the door he walked around the table and sat within the big chair, facing his visitor.

The other end of the room boasted a fire-place, with an old-fashioned mantel bearing an array of curiosities. Above it was a large clock, and at one side stood a small book-case containing a number of volumes printed in the Greek language. A small alcove, containing a couch, occupied the remaining side of the small apartment, and it was evident these cramped quarters constituted Kiaros' combined office and living rooms.

"So soon as this I did not expect you," said the old man, in his grave voice.

"I am in need of money," replied Marston, abruptly, "and

my interview with you this afternoon reminded me that you have sometimes granted me an occasional loan. Therefore, I have come to negotiate with you."

Kiaros nodded, and studied with his dark eyes the composed features of the cashier.

"A satisfactory debtor you have ever proved," said he, "and to pay me with promptness never failed. How much do you require?"

"Twelve thousand dollars."

In spite of his self-control, Kiaros started as the young man coolly stated this sum.

"Impossible!" he ejaculated, moving uneasily in his chair.

"Why is it impossible?" demanded Marston. "I know you have the money."

"True; I deny it not," returned Kiaros, dropping his gaze before the other's earnest scrutiny; "also to lend money is my business. But see—I will be frank with you Mr. Marston—I cannot take the risk. You are cashier for hire; you have no property; security for so large a sum you cannot give. Twelve thousand dollars! It is impossible!"

"You loaned Williamson twelve thousand," persisted Marston, doggedly.

"Mr. Williamson secured me."

Marston rose from his chair and began slowly pacing up and down before the table, his hands clasped tightly behind him and an impatient frown contracting his features. The Greek watched him calmly.

"Perhaps you have not heard, Mr. Kiaros," he said, at length, "that within two weeks I am to be married to Mr. Van Alsteyne's only daughter."

"I had not heard."

"And at the same time I am to receive a large interest in the business as a wedding gift from my father-in-law."

"To my congratulations you are surely entitled."

"Therefore my need is only temporary. I shall be able to return the money within thirty days, and I am willing to pay you well for the accommodation."

"A Jew I am not," returned Kiaros, with a slight shrug, "and where I lend I do not rob. But so great a chance I cannot undertake. You are not yet married, a partner in the firm not yet. To die, to quarrel with the lady, to lose Mr. Van Alsteyne's confidence, would leave me to collect the sum wholly unable. I might a small amount risk—the large amount is impossible."

Marston suddenly became calm, and resumed his chair with a quiet air, to Kiaros' evident satisfaction.

"You have gambled?" asked the Greek, after a pause.

"Not lately. I shall never gamble again. I owe no gambling debts; this money is required for another purpose."

"Can you not do with less?" asked Kiaros; "an advance I will make of one thousand dollars; not more. That sum is also a risk, but you are a man of discretion; in your ability I have confidence."

Marston did not reply at once. He leaned back in his chair, and seemed to be considering the money-lender's offer. In reality there passed before his mind the fate that confronted him, the scene in which he posed as a convicted felon; he saw the collapse of his great ambitions, the ruin of those schemes he had almost brought to fruition. Already he felt the reproaches of the man he had robbed, the scorn of the proud woman who had been ready to give him her hand, the cold sneers of those who gloated over his downfall. And then he bethought himself, and drove the vision away, and thought of other things.

Kiaros rested his elbow upon the table, and toyed with a curious-looking paper-cutter. It was made of pure silver, in the shape of a dagger; the blade was exquisitely chased, and bore a Greek motto. After a time Kiaros looked up and saw his guest regarding the paper-cutter.

"It is a relic most curious," said he, "from the ruins of Missolonghi rescued, and by a friend sent to me. All that is Greek I love. Soon to my country I shall return, and that is why I cannot risk the money I have in a lifetime earned."

Still Marston did not reply, but sat looking thoughtfully at the table. Kiaros was not impatient. He continued to play with the silver dagger, and poised it upon his finger while he awaited the young man's decision.

"I think I shall be able to get along with the thousand

dollars," said Marston at last, his collected tones showing no trace of the disappointment Kiaros had expected. "Can you let me have it now?"

"Yes. As you know, the money is in my safe. I will make out the note."

He quietly laid down the paper-cutter and drew a note-book from a drawer of the table. Dipping a pen in the inkwell, he rapidly filled up the note and pushed it across the table to Marston.

"Will you sign?" he asked, with his customary smile.

Marston drew his chair close to the table and examined the note.

"You said you would not rob me!" he demurred.

"The commission it is very little," replied Kiaros, coolly. "A Jew much more would have exacted."

Marston picked up the pen, dashed off his name, and tossed the paper towards Kiaros. The Greek inspected it carefully, and rising from his chair, walked to the safe and drew open the heavy door. He placed the note in one drawer, and from another removed an oblong tin box, which he brought to the table. Reseating himself, he opened this box and drew out a large packet of banknotes.

Marston watched him listlessly as he carefully counted out one thousand dollars.

"The amount is, I believe, correct," said Kiaros, after a second count; "if you will kindly verify it I shall be pleased."

Marston half arose and reached out his hand, but he did not take the money. Instead, his fingers closed over the handle of the silver-dagger, and with a swift, well-directed blow he plunged it to the hilt in the breast of the Greek. The old man lay back in his chair with a low moan, his form quivered once or twice and then became still, while a silence that suddenly seemed oppressive pervaded the little room.

III

Felix Marston sat down in his chair and stared at the form of Kiaros. The usually benevolent features of the Greek were horribly convulsed, and the dark eyes had caught and held a sudden look of terror. His right hand, resting upon the table, still grasped the bundle of bank-notes. The handle of the silver dagger glistened in the lamplight just above the heart, and a dark-colored fluid was slowly oozing outward and discoloring the old man's clothing and the point of his snowy beard.

Marston drew out his handkerchief and wiped the moisture from his forehead. Then he arose, and going to his victim, carefully opened the dead hand and removed the money. In the tin box was the remainder of the twelve thousand dollars the Greek had that day received. Marston wrapped it all in a paper and placed it in his breast pocket. Then he went to the safe, replaced the box in its drawer, and found the note he had just signed. This he folded and placed carefully in his pocket-book. Returning to the table, he stood looking down upon the dead man.

"He was a very good fellow, old Kiaros," he murmured; "I am sorry I had to kill him. But this is no time for regrets; I must try to cover all traces of my crime. The reason most murderers are discovered is because they become terrified, are anxious to get away, and so leave clues behind them. I have plenty of time. Probably no one knows of my visit here to-night, and as the old man lives quite alone, no one is likely to come here before morning."

He looked at his watch. It was a few minutes after ten o'clock.

"This ought to be a case of suicide," he continued, "and I shall try to make it look that way."

The expression of Kiaros' face first attracted his attention. That look of terror was incompatible with suicide. He drew a chair beside the old man and began to pass his hands over the dead face to smooth out the contracted lines. The body was still warm, and with a little perseverance, Marston succeeded in relaxing the drawn muscles until the face gradually resumed its calm and benevolent look.

The eyes, however, were more difficult to deal with, and it was only after repeated efforts that Marston was able to draw the lids over them, and hide their startled and horrified gaze. When this was accomplished, Kiaros looked as peaceful as if asleep, and the cashier was satisfied with his progress. He now lifted the Greek's right hand and attempted to clasp the fingers over the handle of the dagger, but they fell away limply.

"Rigor mortis had not yet set in," reflected Marston, "and I must fasten the hand in position until it does. Had the man himself dealt the blow, the tension of the nerves of the arm would probably have forced the fingers to retain their grip upon the weapon." He took his handkerchief and bound the fingers over the hilt of the dagger, at the same time altering the position of the head and body to better suit the asssumption of suicide.

"I shall have to wait some time for the body to cool," he told himself, and then he considered what might be done in the meantime.

A box of cigars stood upon the mantel. Marston selected one and lit it. Then he returned to the table, turned up the lamp a trifle, and began searching in the drawers for specimens of the Greek's handwriting. Having secured several of these he sat down and studied them for a few minutes, smoking collectedly the while, and taking care to drop the ashes in a little tray that Kiaros had used for that purpose. Finally he drew a sheet of paper towards him, and carefully imitating the Greek's sprawling chirography, wrote as follows:

"My money I have lost. To live longer I cannot. To die I am therefore resolved.   Kiaros."

"I think that will pass inspection," he muttered, looking at the paper approvingly, and comparing it again with the dead man's writing. "I must avoid all risks, but this forgery is by far too clever to be detected." He placed the paper upon the table before the body of the Greek, and then rearranged the papers as he had found them.

Slowly the hours passed away. Marston rose from his chair at intervals and examined the body. At one o'clock rigor mortis began to set in, and a half hour later Marston removed the handkerchief, and was pleased to find the hand retained its grasp upon the dagger. The position of the dead body was now very natural indeed, and the cashier congratulated himself upon his success.

There was but one task remaining for him to accomplish. The door must be found locked upon the inside. Marston searched until he found a piece of twine, one end of which he pinned lightly to the top of the table, a little to the left of the inkwell. The other end of the twine he carried to the door, and passed it through the slide in the panel. Withdrawing the key from the lock of the door, he now approached the table for the last time, taking a final look at the body, and laying the end of his cigar upon the tray. The theory of suicide had been excellently carried out; if only the key could be arranged for, he would be satisfied. Reflecting thus, he leaned over and blew out the light.

It was very dark, but he had carefully considered the distance beforehand, and in a moment he had reached the hallway and softly closed and locked the door behind him. Then he withdrew the key, found the end of the twine which projected through the panel, and running this through the ring of the key, he passed it inside the panel, and allowed the key to slide down the cord until a sharp click told him it rested upon the table within. A sudden jerk of the twine now unfastened the end which had been pinned to the table, and he drew it in and carefully placed it in his pocket. Before closing the door of the panel, Marston lighted a match, and satisfied himself the key was lying in the position he had wished. He breathed more freely then and closed the panel.

A few minutes later he had reached the street, and after a keen glance up and down, he stepped boldly from the doorway and walked away.

To his surprise, he now felt himself trembling with nervousness, and despite his endeavors to control himself, it required all of his four-mile walk home to enable him to regain his wonted composure.

He let himself in with his latch-key, and made his way noiselessly to his room. As he was a gentleman of regular habits, the landlady never bothered herself to keep awake watching for his return.

IV

Mr. Marston appeared at the office the next morning in an unusually good humor, and at once busied himself with the regular routine of duties.

As soon as he was able, he retired to his private office and began to revise the books and make out a new trial balance. The exact amount he had stolen from the firm was put into the safe, the false figures were replaced with correct ones, and by noon the new balance sheet proved that Mr. Marston's accounts were in perfect condition.

Just before he started for luncheon a clerk brought him the afternoon paper.

"What do you think, Mr. Marston?" he said. "Old Kiaros has committed suicide."

"Indeed! Do you mean the Kiaros who was here yesterday?" inquired Marston, as he put on his coat.

"The very same. It seems the old man lost his money in some unfortunate speculation, and so took his own life. The police found him in his room this morning, stabbed to the heart. Here is the paper, sir, if you wish to see it."

"Thank you," returned the cashier, in his usual quiet way. "I will buy one when I go out," and without further comment he went to luncheon.

But he purchased a paper, and while eating read carefully the account of Kiaros' suicide. The report was reassuring; no one seemed to dream the Greek was the victim of foul play.

The verdict of the coroner's jury completed his satisfaction. They found that Kiaros had committed suicide in a fit of despondency. The Greek was buried and forgotten, and soon the papers teemed with sensational accounts of the brilliant wedding of that estimable gentleman, Mr. Felix Marston, to the popular society belle, Miss Gertrude Van Alsteyne. The happy pair made a bridal trip to Europe, and upon their return Mr. Marston was installed as an active partner in the great firm of Van Alsteyne, Traynor & Marston.

*   *   *   *   *   *   *

This was twenty years ago. Mr. Marston to-day has an enviable record as an honorable and highly respected man of business, although some consider him a trifle too cold and calculating.

His wife, although, she early discovered the fact that he had married her to further his ambition, has found him reserved and undemonstrative, but always courteous and indulgent to both herself and her children.

He holds his head high and looks every man squarely in the eye, and he is very generally envied, since everything seems to prosper in his hands.

Kiaros and his suicide are long since forgotten by the police and the public. Perhaps Marston recalls the Greek at times. He told me this story when he lay upon what he supposed was his death-bed.

In writing it down I have only altered the names of the characters. I promised Marston that so long as he lived I would not denounce him, and he still lives.

T E SPHERICAL G OUL

By Fredric Brown (1906-1972)

Well-crafted impossible crime stories rarely appeared in the pulp magazines of the 1930s and the 1940s. The detective and mystery pulps, with their garish covers and luridly titled stories, usually hired authors who could supply plenty of corpses, not coherent plots. In the light of this editorial preference, it is surprising how many good writers produced good stories for the pulps. "The Spherical Ghoul," which appeared in 1943 in Thrilling Mystery, could have been written by no one other than Fredric Brown. Both in his science fiction and in his detective stories, Brown had an offbeat—"cockeyed" some critics have said—view of humanity that led to unusual protagonists in self-contained worlds: carnivals, asylums, morgues. The solution to this story may seem screwy, but it is apparently practical. And never repeatable. At least in fiction.

Murder Makes the Morgue Go

I HAD no premonition of horror to come. When I reported to work that evening I had not the faintest inkling that I faced anything more startling than another quiet night on a snap job.

It was seven o'clock, just getting dark outside, when I went into the coronor's office. I stood looking out the window into the gray dusk for a few minutes.

Out there, I could see all the tall buildings of the college, and right across the way was Kane Dormitory, where Jerry Grant was supposed to sleep. The same Grant being myself.

Yes, "supposed to" is right. I was working my way through the last year of an ethnology course by holding down a night job for the city, and I hadn't slept more than a five-hour stretch for weeks.

But that night shift in the coroner's department *was* a snap, all right. A few hours' easy work, and the rest of the time left over for study and work on my thesis. I owed my chance to finish out that final year and get my doctor's degree despite the fact that Dad had died, to the fact that I'd been able to get that job.

Behind me, I could hear Dr. Dwight Skibbine, the coroner, opening and closing drawers of his desk, getting ready to leave. I heard his swivel chair squeak as he shoved it back to stand up.

"Don't forget you're going to straighten out that card file tonight, Jerry," he said. "It's in a mess."

I turned away from the window and nodded. "Any customers around tonight?" I asked.

"Just one. In the display case, but I don't think you'll have anybody coming in to look at him. Keep an eye on that refrigeration unit, though. It's been acting up a bit."

"Thirty-two?" I asked just to make conversation, I guess, because we always keep the case at thirty-two degrees.

He nodded. "I'm going to be back later, for a little while. If Paton gets here before I get back tell him to wait."

He went out, and I went over to the card file and started to straighten it out. It was a simple enough file—just a record of possessions found on bodies that were brought into the morgue, and their disposal after the body was either identified and claimed, or buried in potter's field—but the clerks on the day shift managed to get the file tangled up periodically.

It took me a little while to dope out what had gummed it up this time. Before I finished it, I decided to go downstairs to the basement—the morgue proper—and be sure the refrigerating unit was still holding down Old Man Fahrenheit.

It was. The thermometer in the showcase read thirty-two degrees on the head. The body in the case was that of a man of about forty, a heavy-set, ugly-looking customer. Even as dead as a doornail and under glass, he looked mean.

Maybe you don't know exactly how morgues are run. It's simple, if they are all handled the way the Springdale one was. We had accommodations for seven customers, and six of them were compartments built back into the walls, for all the world like the sliding drawers of a file cabinet. Those compartments were arranged for refrigeration.

But the showcase was where we put unidentified bodies, so they could be shown easily and quickly to anybody who came in to look at them for identification purposes. It was like a big coffin mounted on a bier, except that it was made of glass on all sides except the bottom.

That made it easy to show the body to prospective identifiers, especially as we could click a switch that threw on lights right inside the display case itself, focused on the face of the corpse.

Everything was okay, so I went back upstairs. I decided I would study a while before I resumed work on the file. The night went more quickly and I got more studying done if I alternated the two. I could have had all my routine work over with in three hours and had the rest of the night to study, but it had never worked as well that way.

I used the coroner's secretary's desk for studying and had just got some books and papers spread out when Mr. Paton came in. Harold Paton is superintendent of the zoological gardens, although you would never guess it to look at him. He looked like a man who would be unemployed eleven months of the year because department store Santa Clauses were hired for only one month out of twelve. True, he would need a little padding and a beard, but not a spot of make-up otherwise.

"Hello Jerry," he said. "Dwight say when he was coming back?"

"Not exactly, Mr. Paton. Just said for you to wait."

The zoo director sighed and sat down.

"We're playing off the tie tonight," he said, "and I'm going to take him."

He was talking about chess, of course. Dr. Skibbine and Mr. Paton were both chess addicts of the first water, and about twice a week the coroner phoned his wife that he was going to be held up at the office and the two men would play a game that sometimes lasted well after midnight.

I picked up a volume of *The Golden Bough* and started to open it to my bookmark. I was interested in it, because *The Golden Bough* is the most complete account of the superstitions and early customs of mankind that has ever been compiled.

Mr. Paton's eyes twinkled a little as they took in the title of the volume in my hand.

"That part of the course you're taking?" he asked.

I shook my head. "I'm picking up data for my thesis from it. But I do think it ought to be in a course on ethnology."

"Jerry, Jerry," he said, "you take that thesis too seriously. Ghosts, ghouls, vampires, werewolves. If you ever find any, bring them around, and I'll have special cages built for them at the zoo. Or could you keep a werewolf in a cage?"

You couldn't get mad at Mr. Paton, no matter how he kidded you. That thesis was a bit of a sore point with me. I had taken considerable kidding because I had chosen as my subject, "The Origin and Partial Justification of Superstitions." When some people razzed me about it, I wanted to take a poke at them. But I grinned at Mr. Paton.

"You shouldn't have mentioned vampires in that category," I told him. "You've got them already. I saw a cageful the last time I was there."

"What? Oh, you mean the vampire bats."

"Sure, and you've got a unicorn too, or didn't you know that a rhinoceros is really a unicorn? Except that the medieval artists who drew pictures of it had never seen one and were guessing what it looked like."

"Of course, but—"

There were footsteps in the hallway, and he stopped talking as Dr. Skibbine came in.

"Hullo, Harold," he said to Mr. Paton, and to me: "Heard part of what you were saying, Jerry, and you're right. Don't let Paton kid you out of that thesis of yours."

He went over to his desk and got the chessmen out of the bottom drawer.

"I can't outtalk the two of you," Mr. Paton said, "But say, Jerry, how about ghouls? This ought to be a good place to catch them if there are any running loose around Springdale. Or is that one superstition you're not justifying?"

"Superstition?" I said. "What makes you think that's—"

Then the phone rang, and I went to answer it without finishing what I was going to say.

When I came away from the phone, the two men had the chess pieces set up. Dr. Skibbine had the whites and moved the pawn to king's fourth opening.

"Who was it, Jerry?" he asked.

"Just a man who wanted to know if he could come in to look at the body that was brought in this afternoon. His brother's late getting home."

Dr. Skibbine nodded and moved his king's knight in answer to Mr. Paton's opening move. Already both of them were completely lost in the game. Obviously, Mr. Paton had forgotten what he had asked me about ghouls, so I didn't butt in to finish what I had started to say.

I let *The Golden Bough* go, too, and went to look up the file folder on the unidentified body downstairs. If somebody was coming in to look at it, I wanted to have all the facts about it in mind.

There wasn't much in the folder. The man had been a tramp, judging from his clothes and the lack of money in his pockets and from the nature of the things he did have with him. There wasn't anything at all to indicate identification.

He had been killed on the Mill Road, presumably by a hit-run driver. A Mr. George Considine had found the body and he had also seen another car driving away. The other car had been too distant for him to get the license number or any description worth mentioning.

Of course, I thought, that car might or might not have been the car that had hit the man. Possibly the driver had seen and deliberately passed up the body, thinking it was a drunk.

But the former theory seemed more likely, because there was little traffic on the Mill Road. One end of it was blocked off for repairs, so the only people who used it were the few who lived along there, and there were not many of them. Probably only a few cars a day came along that particular stretch of the road.

Mr. Considine had got out of his car and found that the man was dead. He had driven on to the next house, half a mile beyond, and phoned the police from there, at four o'clock.

That's all there was in the files.

I had just finished reading it when Bill Drager came in. Bill is a lieutenant on the police force, and he and I had become pretty friendly during the time I had worked for the coroner. He was a pretty good friend of Dr. Skibbine too.

"Sorry to interrupt your game, Doc," he said, "but I just wanted to ask something."

"What, Bill?"

"Look—the stiff you got in today. You've examined it already?"

"Of course, why?"

"Just wondering. I don't know what makes me think so, but—well, I'm not satisfied all the way. *Was* it just an auto accident?"

Why the Dead Man Crossed the Road

Dr. Skibbine had a bishop in his hand, ready to move it, but he put it down on the side of the board instead.

"Just a minute, Harold," he said to Mr. Paton, then turned his chair around to stare at Bill Drager. "Not an auto accident?" he inquired. "The car wheels ran across the man's neck, Bill. What more do you want?"

"I don't know. Was that the sole cause of death, or were there some other marks?"

Dr. Skibbine leaned back in the swivel chair.

"I don't think being hit was the cause of death, exactly. His forehead struck the road when he fell, and he was probably dead when the wheels ran over him. It could have been, for that matter, that he fell when there wasn't even a car around and the car ran over him later."

"In broad daylight?"

"Um—yes, that does sound unlikely. But he could have fallen into the path of the car. He had been drinking plenty. He reeked of liquor."

"Suppose he was hit by a car," Bill said. "How would you reconstruct it? How he fell, I mean, and stuff like that."

"Let's see. I'd say he fell first and was down when the car first touched him. Say he started across the road in front of the car. Horn honked and he tried to turn around and fell flat instead, and the motorist couldn't stop in time and ran over him."

I had not said anything yet, but I put in a protest at that.

"If the man was as obviously drunk as that," I said, "why would the motorist have kept on going? He couldn't have thought he would be blamed if a drunk staggered in front of his car and fell, even before he was hit."

Drager shrugged. "That could happen, Jerry," he said. "For one thing, he may not have any witnesses to prove that it happened that way. And some guys get panicky when they hit a pedestrian, even if the pedestrian is to blame. And then again, the driver of the car might have had a drink or two himself and been afraid to stop because of that."

Dr. Skibbine's swivel chair creaked.

"Sure," he said, "or he might have been afraid because he had a reckless driving count against him already. But, Bill, the cause of death was the blow he got on the forehead when he hit the road. Not that the tires going over his neck wouldn't have finished him if the fall hadn't."

"We had a case like that here five years ago. Remember?"

Dr. Skibbine grunted. "I wasn't here five years ago. Remember?"

"Yes, I forgot that," said Bill Drager.

I had forgotten it, too. Dr. Skibbine was a Springdale man, but he had spent several years in South American countries doing research work on tropical diseases. Then he had come back and had been elected coroner. Coroner was an easy job in Springdale and gave a man more time for things like research and chess than a private practice would.

"Go on down and look at him, if you want," Dr. Skibbine told Bill. "Jerry'll take you down. It will get his mind off ghouls and goblins."

I took Bill Drager downstairs and flicked on the lights in the display case.

"I can take off the end and slide him out of there if you want me to," I said.

"I guess not," Drager said and leaned on the glass top to look closer at the body. The face was all you could see, of course, because a sheet covered the body up to the neck, and this time the sheet had been pulled a little higher than usual, probably to hide the unpleasant damage to the neck.

The face was bad enough. There was a big, ugly bruise on the forehead, and the lower part of the face was cut up a bit.

"The car ran over the back of his neck after he fell on his face, apparently," Bill Drager said. "Ground his face into the road a bit and took off skin. But—"

"But what?" I prompted when he lapsed into silence.

"I don't know," he said. "I was mostly wondering why he would have tried to cross the road at all out there. Right at that place there's nothing on one side of the road that isn't on the other."

He straightened up, and I switched off the showcase lights.

"Maybe you're just imagining things, Bill," I said. "How do you know he tried to cross at all? Doc said he'd been drinking, and maybe he just staggered from the edge of the road out toward the middle without any idea of crossing over."

"Yeah, there's that, of course. Come to think of it, you're probably right. When I got to wondering, I didn't know about the drinking part. Well, let's go back up."

We did, and I shut and locked the door at the head of the stairs. It is the only entrance to the morgue, and I don't know why it has to be kept locked, because it opens right into the coroner's office where I sit all night, and the key stays in the lock.

Anybody who could get past me could unlock it himself.
But it's just one of those rules. Those stairs, incidentally, are
absolutely the only way you can get down into the morgue
which is walled off from the rest of the basement of the
Municipal Building.

"Satisfied?" Dr. Skibbine asked Bill Drager, as we walked
into the office.

"Guess so," said Drager. "Say, the guy looks vaguely familiar. I can't place him, but I think I've seen him somewhere.
Nobody identified him yet?"

"Nope," said Doc. "But if he's a local resident, somebody
will. We'll have a lot of curiosity seekers in here tomorrow.
Always get them after a violent death."

Bill Drager said he was going home and went out. His shift
was over. He had just dropped in on his own time.

I stood around and watched the chess game for a few
minutes. Mr. Paton was getting licked this time. He was two
pieces down and on the defensive. Only a miracle could save
him.

Then Doc moved a knight and said, "Check," and it was all
over but the shouting. Mr. Paton could move out of check all
right, but the knight had forked his king and queen, and
with the queen gone, as it would be after the next move, the
situation was hopeless.

"You got me, Dwight," he said. "I'll resign. My mind must
be fuzzy tonight. Didn't see that knight coming."

"Shall we start another game? It's early."

"You'd beat me. Let's bowl a quick game, instead, and get
home early."

After they left, I finished up my work on the card file and
then did my trigonometry. It was almost midnight then. I
remembered the man who had phoned that he was coming
in and decided he had changed his mind. Probably his
brother had arrived home safely, after all.

I went downstairs to be sure the refrigerating unit was
okay. Finding that it was, I came back up and locked the door
again. Then I went out into the hall and locked the outer
door. It's supposed to be kept locked, too, and I really should
have locked it earlier.

After that, I read *The Golden Bough*, with a note-book in

front of me so I could jot down anything I found that would fit into my thesis.

I must have become deeply engrossed in my reading because when the night bell rang, I jumped inches out of my chair. I looked at the clock and saw it was two in the morning.

Ordinarily, I don't mind the place where I work at all. Being near dead bodies gives some people the willies, but not me. There isn't any nicer, quieter place for studying and reading than a morgue at night.

But I had a touch of the creeps then. I do get them once in a while. This time it was the result of being startled by the sudden ringing of that bell when I was so interested in something that I had forgotten where I was and why I was there.

I put down the book and went out into the long dark hallway. When I had put on the hall light, I felt a little better. I could see somebody standing outside the glass-paned door at the end of the hall. A tall thin man whom I didn't know. He wore glasses and was carrying a gold-headed cane.

"My name is Burke, Roger Burke," he said when I opened the door. "I phoned early this evening about my brother being missing. Uh—may I—"

"Of course," I told him. "Come this way. When you didn't come for so long, I thought you had located your brother."

"I thought I had," he said hesitantly. "A friend said he had seen him this evening, and I quit worrying for a while. But when it got after one o'clock and he wasn't home, I—"

We had reached the coroner's office by then, but I stopped and turned.

"There's only one unidentified body here," I told him, "and that was brought in this afternoon. If your brother was seen this evening, it couldn't be him."

The tall man said, "Oh," rather blankly and looked at me a moment. Then he said, "I hope that's right. But this friend said he saw him a distance, on a crowded street. He could have been mistaken. So as long as I'm here—"

"I guess you might as well," I said, "now that you're here. Then you'll be sure."

I led the way through thee office and unlocked the door.

I was glad, as we started down the stairs, that there seemed little likelihood of identification. I hate to be around when one is made. You always seem to share, vicariously, the emotion of the person who recognizes a friend or relative.

At the top of the stairs I pushed the button that put on the overhead lights downstairs in the morgue. The switch for the showcase was down below. I stopped to flick it as I reached the bottom of the stairs, and the tall man went on past me toward the case. Apparently he had been a visitor here before.

I had taken only a step or two after him when I heard him gasp. He stopped suddenly and took a step backward so quickly that I bumped into him and grabbed his arm to steady myself.

He turned around, and his face was a dull pasty gray that one seldom sees on the face of a living person.

"My God!" he said. "Why didn't you warn me that—"

It didn't make sense for him to say a thing like that. I've been with people before when they have identified relatives, but none of them had ever reacted just that way. Or had it been merely identification? He certainly looked as though he had seen something horrible.

I stepped a little to one side so that I could see past him. When I saw, it was as though a wave of cold started at the base of my spine and ran up along my body. I had never seen anything like it—and you get toughened when you work in a morgue.

The glass top of the display case had been broken in at the upper, the head, end, and the body inside the case was— well, I'll try to be as objective about it as I can. The best way to be objective is to put it bluntly. The flesh of the face had been eaten away, eaten away as though acid had been poured on it, or as though—

I got hold of myself and stepped up to the edge of the display case and looked down.

It had not been acid. Acid does not leave the marks of teeth.

Nauseated, I closed my eyes for an instant until I got over it. Behind me, I heard sounds as though the tall man, who had been the first to see it, was being sick. I didn't blame him.

"I don't—" I said, and stepped back. "Something's happened here."

Silly remark, but you can't think of the right thing to say in a spot like that.

"Come on," I told him. "I'll have to get the police."

The thought of the police steadied me. When the police got here, it would be all right. They would find out what had happened.

Facing Horror

As I reached the bottom of the stairs my mind started to work logically again. I could picture Bill Drager up in the office firing questions at me, asking me, "When did it happen? You can judge by the temperature, can't you?"

The tall man stumbled up the stairs past me as I paused. Most decidedly I didn't want to be down there alone, but I yelled to him:

"Wait up there. I'll be with you in a minute."

He would have to wait, of course, because I would have to unlock the outer door to let him out.

I turned back and looked at the thermometer in the broken case, trying not to look at anything else. It read sixty-three degrees, and that was only about ten degrees under the temperature of the rest of the room.

The glass had been broken, then, for some time. An hour, I'd say offhand, or maybe a little less. Upstairs, with the heavy door closed, I wouldn't have heard it break. Anyway, I hadn't heard it break.

I left the lights on in the morgue, all of them, when I ran up the stairs.

The tall man was standing in the middle of the office, looking around as though he were in a daze. His face still had that grayish tinge, and I was just as glad that I didn't have to look in a mirror just then, because my own face was likely as bad.

I picked up the telephone and found myself giving Bill Drager's home telephone number instead of asking for the police. I don't know why my thoughts ran so strongly to Bill Drager, except that he had been the one who had suspected that something more than met the eye had been behind the hit-run case from the Mill Road.

"Can—will you let me out of here?" the tall man said. "I— I—that wasn't my—"

"I'm afraid not," I told him. "Until the police get here. You—uh—witnessed—"

It sounded screwy, even to me. Certainly he could not have had anything to do with whatever had happened down there. He had preceded me into the morgue only by a second and hadn't even reached the case when I was beside him. But I knew what the police would say if I let him go before they had a chance to get his story.

Then Drager's voice was saying a sleepy, "Hullo," into my ear.

"Bill, I said, "you got to come down here. That corpse downstairs—it's—I—"

The sleepiness went out of Drager's voice.

"Calm down, Jerry," he said. "It can't be that bad. Now, what happened?"

I finally got it across.

"You phoned the department first, of course?" Drager asked.

"N-no. I thought of you first because—"

"Sit tight," he said. "I'll phone them and then come down. I'll have to dress first, so they'll get there ahead of me. Don't go down to the morgue again and don't touch anything."

He put the receiver on the hook, and I felt a little better. Somehow the worst seemed to be over, now that it was off my chest. Drager's offering to phone the police saved me from having to tell it again, over the phone.

The tall man—I remembered now that he had given the name Roger Burke—was leaning against the wall, weakly.

"Did—did I get from what you said on the phone that the body wasn't that way when—when they brought it in?" he asked.

I nodded. "It must have happened within the last hour," I said. "I was down there at midnight, and everything was all right then."

"But what—what happened?"

I opened my mouth and closed it again. Something happened down there, but what? There wasn't any entrance to the morgue other than the ventilator and the door that opened at the top of the stairs. And nobody—nothing—had gone through that door since my trip of inspection.

I thought back and thought hard. No, I hadn't left this

office for even a minute between midnight and the time the night bell had rung at two o'clock. I had left the office then, of course, to answer the door. But whatever had happened had not happened then. The thermometer downstairs proved that.

Burke was fumbling cigarettes out of his pocket. He held out the package with a shaky hand, and I took one and managed to strike a match and light both cigarettes.

The first drag made me feel nearly human. Apparently he felt better too, because he said:

"I—I'm afraid I didn't make identification one way or the other. You couldn't—with—" He shuddered. "Say, my brother had a small anchor tattooed on his left forearm. I forgot it or I could have asked you over the phone. Was there—"

I thought back to the file and shook my head.

"No," I said definitely. "It would have been on the record, and there wasn't anything about it. They make a special point of noting down things like that."

"That's swell," Burke said. "I mean—Say, if I'm going to have to wait, I'm going to sit down. I still feel awful."

Then I remembered that I had better phone Dr. Skibbine too, and give him the story first—hand before the police got here and called him. I went over to the phone.

The police got there first—Captain Quenlin and Sergeant Wilson and two other men I knew by sight but not by name. Bill Drager was only a few minutes later getting there, and around three o'clock Dr. Skibbine came.

By that time the police had questioned Burke and let him go, although one of them left to go home with him. They told him it was because they wanted to check on whether his brother had shown up yet, so the Missing Persons Bureau could handle it if he hadn't. But I guessed the real reason was that they wanted to check on his identity and place of residence.

Not that there seemed to be any way Burke could be involved in whatever had happened to the body, but when you don't know what has happened, you can't overlook angle. After all, he was a material witness.

Bill Drager had spent most of the time since he had been there downstairs, but he came up now.

"The place is tighter than a drum down there, except for

that ventilator," he said. "And I noticed something about it. One of the vanes in it is a little bent."

"How about rats?" Captain Quenlin asked.

Drager snorted. "Ever see rats break a sheet of glass?"

"The glass might have been broken some other way." Quenlin looked at me. "You're around here nights, Jerry Grant. Ever see any signs of rats or mice?"

I shook my head, and Bill Drager backed me up.

"I went over the whole place down there," he said. "There isn't a hole anywhere. Floor's tile set in cement. The walls are tile, in big close-set slabs, without a break. I went over them."

Dr. Skibbine was starting down the steps.

"Come on, Jerry," he said to me. "Show me where you and this Burke fellow were standing when he let out a yip."

I didn't much want to, but I followed him down. I showed him where I had been and where Burke had been and told him that Burke had not gone closer to the case than about five feet at any time. Also, I told him what I had already told the police about my looking at the thermometer in the case.

Dr. Skibbine went over and looked at it.

"Seventy-one now," he said. "I imagine that's as high as it's going. You say it was sixty-three when you saw it at two? Yes, I'd say the glass was broken between twelve-thirty and one-thirty."

Quenlin had followed us down the stairs. "When did you get home tonight, Dr. Skibbine?" he asked.

The coroner looked at him in surprise. "Around midnight. Good Lord, you don't think *I* had anything to do with this, do you, Quenlin?"

The captain shook his head. "Routine question. Look, Doc, why would anybody or anything do that?"

"I wouldn't know," Skibbine said slowly, "unless it was to prevent identification of the corpse. That's possible. The body will never be identified now unless the man has a criminal record and his prints are on file. But making that 'anything' instead of 'anybody' makes it easier, Cap. I'd say 'anything' was hungry, plenty hungry."

I leaned back against the wall at the bottom of the stairs, again fighting nausea that was almost worse than before.

Rats? Besides the fact that there weren't any rats, it would have taken a lot of them to do what had been done.

"Jerry," said Bill Drager, "you're sure you weren't out of the office up there for even a minute between midnight and two o'clock? Think hard. Didn't you maybe go to the washroom or something?"

"I'm positive," I told him.

Drager turned to the captain and pointed up to the ventilator.

"There are only two ways into this morgue, Cap," he said. "One's through the door Jerry says he sat in front of, and the other's up there."

My eyes followed his pointing finger, and I studied the ventilator and its position. It was a round opening in the wall, twelve or maybe thirteen inches across, and there was a wheel-like arrangement of vanes that revolved in it. It was turning slowly. It was set in the wall just under the high ceiling, maybe sixteen feet above the floor, and it was directly over the display case.

"Where's that open into?" Quenlin asked.

"Goes right through the wall," Dr. Skibbine told him. "Opens on the alley, just a foot or two above the ground. There's another wheel just like that one on the outside. A little electric motor turns them."

"Could the thing be dismantled from the outside?"

Dr. Skibbine shrugged. "Easiest way to find that out is to go out in the alley and try it. But nobody could get through there, even if you got the thing off. It's too narrow."

"A thin man might—"

"No, even a thin man is wider than twelve inches across the shoulders, and that's my guess on the width of that hole."

Quenlin shrugged.

"Got a flashlight, Drager?" he asked. "Go on out in the alley and take a look. Although if somebody did get that thing off, I don't see how the devil they could have—"

Then he looked down at the case and winced. "If everybody's through looking at this for the moment," he said, "for crying out loud put a sheet over it. It's giving me the willies. I'll dream about ghouls tonight."

The word hit me like a ton of bricks. Because it was then I remembered that we had talked about ghouls early that very evening. About—how had Mr. Paton put it?—"ghosts, ghouls, vampires, werewolves," and about a morgue being a good place for ghouls to hang around; and about—

Some of the others were looking at me, and I knew that Dr. Skibbine, at least, was remembering that conversation. Had he mentioned it to any of the others?

Sergeant Wilson was standing behind the other men and probably didn't know I could see him from where I stood, for he surreptitiously crossed himself.

"Ghouls, nuts!" he said in a voice a bit louder than necessary. "There ain't any such thing. Or is there?"

It was a weak but dramatic ending. Nobody answered him.

Me, I had had enough of that morgue for the moment. Nobody had put a sheet over the case because there was not one available downstairs.

"I'll get a sheet," I said and started up for the office. I stumbled on the bottom step.

"What's eating—" I heard Quenlin say, and then as though he regretted his choice of words, he started over again. "Something's wrong with the kid. Maybe you better send him home, Doc."

He probably didn't realize I could hear him. But by that time I was most of the way up, so I didn't hear the coroner's answer.

Wildest Talent

From the cabinet I got a sheet, and the others were coming up the steps when I got back with it. Quenlin handed it to Wilson.

"You put it on, Sarge," he said.

Wilson took it, and hesitated. I had seen his gesture downstairs and I knew he was scared stiff to go back down there alone. I was scared, too, but I did my Boy Scout act for the day and said:

"I'll go down with you, Sergeant. I want to take a look at that ventilator."

While he put the sheet over the broken case, I stared up at

the ventilator and saw the bent vane. As I watched, a hand reached through the slit between that vane and the next and bent it some more.

Then the hand, Bill Drager's hand, reached through the widened slit and groped for the nut on the center of the shaft on which the ventilator wheel revolved. Yes, the ventilator could be removed and replaced from the outside. The bent vane made it look as though that had been done.

But why? After the ventilator had been taken off, what then? The opening was too small for a man to get through and besides it was twelve feet above the glass display case.

Sergeant Wilson went past me up the stairs, and I followed him up. The conversation died abruptly as I went through the door, and I suspected that I had been the subject of the talk.

Dr. Skibbine was looking at me.

"The cap's right, Jerry," he said. "You don't look so well. We're going to be around here from now on, so you take the rest of the night off. Get some sleep."

Sleep, I thought. What's that? How could I sleep now? I felt dopy, I'll admit, from lack of it. But the mere thought of turning out a light and lying down alone in a dark room— huh-uh! I must have been a little lightheaded just then, for a goofy parody was running through my brain:

A ghoul hath murdered sleep, the innocent sleep, sleep that knits . . .

"Thanks, Dr. Skibbine," I said. "I—I guess it will do me good, at that."

It would get me out of here, somewhere where I could think without a lot of people talking. If I could get the unicorns and rhinoceros out of my mind, maybe I had the key. Maybe, but it didn't make sense yet.

I put on my hat and went outside and walked around the building into the dark alley.

Bill Drager's face was a dim patch in the light that came through the circular hole in the wall where the ventilator had been.

He saw me coming and called out sharply, "Who's that?"

and stood up. When he stood, he seemed to vanish, because it put him back in the darkness.

"It's me—Jerry Grant," I said. "Find out anything, Bill?"

"Just what you see. The ventilator comes out, from the outside. But it isn't a big enough hole for a man." He laughed a little offkey. "A ghoul, I don't know. How big is a ghoul, Jerry?"

"Can it, Bill," I said. "Did you do that in the dark? Didn't you bring a flashlight?"

"No. Look, whoever did it earlier in the night, if somebody did, wouldn't have dared use a light. They'd be too easy to see from either end of the alley. I wanted to see if it could be done in the dark."

"Yes," I said thoughtfully. "But the light from the inside shows."

"Was it on between midnight and two?"

"Um—no. I hadn't thought of that."

I stared at the hole in the wall. It was just about a foot in diameter. Large enough for a man to stick his head into, but not to crawl through.

Bill Drager was still standing back in the dark, but now that my eyes were used to the alley, I could make out the shadowy outline of his body.

"Jerry," he said, "you've been studying this superstition stuff. Just what is a ghoul?"

"Something in Eastern mythology, Bill. An imaginary creature that robs graves and feeds on corpses. The modern use of the word is confined to someone who robs graves, usually for jewelry that is sometimes interred with the bodies. Back in the early days of medicine, bodies were stolen and sold to the anatomists for purposes of dissection, too."

"The modern ones don't—uh—"

"There have been psychopathic cases, a few of them. One happened in Paris, in modern times. A man named Bertrand. Charles Fort tells about him in his book *Wild Talents*."

"*Wild Talents*, huh?" said Bill. "What happened?"

"Graves in a Paris cemetery were being dug up by something or someone who—" there in the dark alley, I couldn't say it plainly—"who—uh—acted like a ghoul. They couldn't catch him but they set up a blunderbuss trap. It got this man Bertrand, and he confessed."

Bill Drager didn't say anything, just stood there. Then, just as though I could read his mind, I got scared because I knew what he was thinking. If anything like that had happened here tonight, there was only one person it could possibly have been.

Me.

Bill Drager was standing there silently, staring at me, and wondering whether I—

Then I knew why the others had stopped talking when I had come up the stairs just a few minutes before, back at the morgue. No, there was not a shred of proof, unless you can call process of elimination proof. But there had been a faint unspoken suspicion that somehow seemed a thousand times worse than an accusation I could deny.

I knew, then, that unless this case was solved suspicion would follow me the rest of my life. Something too absurd for open accusation. But people would look at me and wonder, and the mere possibility would make them shudder. Every word I spoke would be weighed to see whether it might indicate an unbalanced mind.

Even Bill Drager, one of my best friends, was wondering about me now.

"Bill," I said, "for God's sake, you don't think—"

"Of course not, Jerry."

But the fact that he knew what I meant before I had finished the sentence, proved I had been right about what he had been thinking.

There was something else in his voice, too, although he had tried to keep it out. Fear. He was alone with me in a dark alley, and I realized now why he had stepped back out of the light so quickly. Bill Drager was a little afraid of me.

But this was no time or place to talk about it. The atmosphere was wrong. Anything I could say would make things worse.

So I merely said, "Well, so long, Bill," as I turned and walked toward the street.

Half a block up the street on the other side was an all-night restaurant, and I headed for it. Not to eat, for I felt as though I would never want to eat again. The very thought of food was sickening. But a cup of coffee might take away some of the numbness in my mind.

Hank Perry was on duty behind the counter, and he was alone.

"Hi, Jerry," he said, as I sat down on a stool at the counter. "Off early tonight?"

I nodded and let it go at that.

"Just a cup of black coffee, Hank," I told him, and forestalled any salestalk by adding, "I'm not hungry. Just ate."

Silly thing to say, I realized the minute I had said it. Suppose someone asked Hank later what I had said when I came in. They all knew, back there, that I had not brought a lunch to work and hadn't eaten. Would I, from now on, have to watch every word I said to avoid slips like that?

But whatever significance Hank or others might read into my words later, there was nothing odd about them now, as long as Hank didn't know what had happened at the morgue.

He brought my coffee. I stirred in sugar and waited for it to cool enough to drink.

"Nice night out," Hank said.

I hadn't noticed, but I said, "Yeah."

To me it was one terrible night out, but I couldn't tell him that without spilling the rest of the story.

"How was business tonight, Hank?" I asked.

"Pretty slow."

"How many customers," I asked, "did you have between midnight and two o'clock?"

"Hardly any. Why?"

"Hank," I said, "something happened then. Look, I can't tell you about it now, honestly. I don't know whether or not it's going to be given out to the newspapers. If it isn't, it would lose me my job even to mention it. But will you think hard if you saw anybody or anything out of the ordinary between twelve and two?"

"Um," said Hank, leaning against the counter thoughtfully. "That's a couple of hours ago. Must have had several customers in here during that time. But all I can remember are regulars. People on night shifts that come in regularly."

"When you're standing at that grill in the window frying

something, you can see out across the street," I said. "You ought to be able to see down as far as the alley, because this is a pretty wide street."

"Yeah, I can."

"Did you see anyone walk or drive in there?"

"Golly," said Hank. "Yeah, I did. I think it was around one o'clock. I happened to notice the guy on account of what he was carrying."

I felt my heart hammering with sudden excitement.

"What was he carrying? And what did he look like? "

"I didn't notice what he looked like," said Hank. "He was in shadow most of the time. But he was carrying a bowling ball."

"A bowling ball?"

Hank nodded. "That's what made me notice him. There aren't any alleys—I mean bowling alleys—right around here. I bowl myself so I wondered where this guy had been rolling."

"You mean he was carrying a bowling ball under his arm?"

I was still incredulous, even though Hank's voice showed me he was not kidding.

He looked at me contemptuously.

"No. Bowlers never carry 'em like that on the street. There's a sort of bag that's made for the purpose. A little bigger than the ball, some of them, so a guy can put in his bowling shoes and stuff."

I closed my eyes a moment to try to make sense out of it. Of all the things on this mad night, it seemed the maddest that a bowling ball had been carried into the alley by the morgue —or something the shape of a bowling ball. At just the right time, too. One o'clock.

It would be a devil of a coincidence if the man Hank had seen hadn't been the one.

"You're sure it was a bowling ball case?"

"Positive. I got one like it myself. And the way he carried it, it was just heavy enough to have the ball in it." He looked at me curiously. "Say, Jerry, I never thought of it before, but a case like that would be a handy thing to carry a bomb in. Did someone try to plant a bomb at the morgue?"

"No."

"Then if it wasn't a bowling ball—and you act like you think it wasn't—what would it have been?"

"I wish I knew," I told him. "I wish to high heaven I knew." I downed the rest of my coffee and stood up.

"Thanks a lot, Hank," I said. "Listen, you think it over and see if you can remember anything else about that case or the man who carried it. I'll see you later."

Horror in a Bowling Ball

What I needed was some fresh air, so I started walking. I didn't pay any attention to where I was going; I just walked.

My feet didn't take me in circles, but my mind did. A bowling ball! Why would a bowling ball, or something shaped like it, be carried into the alley back of the morgue? A bowling ball would fit into that ventilator hole, all right, and a dropped bowling ball would have broken the glass of the case.

But a bowling ball wouldn't have done—the rest of it.

I vaguely remembered some mention of bowling earlier in the evening and thought back to what it was. Oh yes. Dr. Skibbine and Mr. Paton had been going to bowl a game instead of playing a second game of chess. But neither of them had bowling balls along. Anyway, if Dr. Skibbine had told the truth, they had both been home by midnight.

If not a bowling ball, then what? A ghoul? A spherical ghoul?

The thought was so incongruously horrible that I wanted to stop, right there in the middle of the sidewalk and laugh like a maniac. Maybe I was near hysteria.

I thought of going back to the morgue and telling them about it, and laughing. Watching Quenlin's face and Wilson's when I told them that our guest had been a man-eating bowling ball. A spherical—

Then I stopped walking, because all of a sudden I knew what the bowling ball had been, and I had the most important part of the answer.

Somewhere a clock was striking half-past three, and I looked around to see where I was. Oak Street, only a few doors from Grant Parkway. That meant I had come fifteen or sixteen blocks from the morgue and that I was only a block and a half from the zoo. At the zoo, I could find out if I was right.

So I started walking again. A block and a half later I was across the street from the zoo right in front of Mr. Paton's house. Strangely, there was a light in one of the downstairs rooms.

I went up onto the porch and rang the bell. Mr. Paton came to answer it. He was wearing a dressing gown, but I could see shoes and the bottoms of his trouser legs under it.

He didn't look surprised at all when he opened the door.

"Yes, Jerry?" he said, almost as though he had been expecting me.

"I'm glad you're still up, Mr. Paton," I said. "Could you walk across with me and get me past the guard at the gate? I'd like to look at one of the cages and verify—something."

"You guessed then, Jerry?"

"Yes, Mr. Paton," I told him. Then I had a sudden thought that scared me a little. "You were seen going into the alley," I added quickly, "and the man who saw you knows I came here. He saw you carrying—"

He held up his hand and smiled.

"You needn't worry, Jerry," he said. "I know it's over—the minute anybody is smart enough to guess. And—well, I murdered a man all right, but I'm not the type to murder another to try to cover up, because I can see where that would lead. The man I did kill deserved it, and I gambled on—Well, never mind all that."

"Who was he?" I asked.

""His name was Mark Leedom. He was my assistant four years ago. I was foolish at that time—I'd lost money speculating and I stole some zoo funds. They were supposed to be used for the purchase of—Never mind the details. Mark Leedom found out and got proof.

"He made me turn over most of the money to him, and he—retired, and moved out of town. But he's been coming back periodically to keep shaking me down. He was a rat, Jerry, a worse crook than I ever thought of being. This time I couldn't pay so I killed him."

"You were going to make it look like an accident on the Mill Road?" I said. "You killed him here and took him—"

"Yes, I was going to have the car run over his head, so he wouldn't be identified. I missed by inches, but I couldn't try again because another car was coming, and I had to keep on driving away.

"Luckily, Doc Skibbine didn't know him. It was while Doc was in South America that Leedom worked for me. But there are lots of people around who did know him. Some curiosity seeker would have identified him in the week they hold an unidentified body and—well, once they knew who he was and traced things back, they'd have got to me eventually for the old business four years ago if not the fact that I killed him."

"So that's why you had to make him unidentifiable," I said. "I see. He looked familiar to Bill Drager, but Bill couldn't place him."

He nodded. "Bill was just a patrolman then. He probably had seen Leedom only a few times, but someone else—Well, Jerry, you go back and tell them about it. Tell them I'll be here."

"Gee, Mr. Paton, I'm sorry I got to," I said. "Isn't there anything—"

"No. Go and get them. I won't run away, I promise you. And tell Doc he wouldn't have beat me that chess game tonight if I hadn't let him. With what I had to do, I wanted to get out of there early. Good night, Jerry."

He eased me out onto the porch again before I quite realized why he had never had a chance to tell Dr. Skibbine himself. Yes, he meant for them to find him here when they came, but not alive.

I almost turned to the door again, to break my way in and stop him. Then I realized that everything would be easier for him if he did it his way.

Yes, he was dead by the time they sent men out to bring him in. Even though I had expected it, I guess I had a case of the jitters when they phoned in the news, and I must have showed it, because Bill Drager threw an arm across my shoulders.

"Jerry," he said, "this has been the devil of a night for you. You need a drink. Come on.

The drink made me feel better and so did the frank admiration in Drager's eyes. It was so completely different from what I had seen there back in the alley.

"Jerry," he told me, "you ought to get on the Force. Figuring out that—of all things—he had used an armadillo."

"But what else was possible? Look! All those ghoul legends trace back to beasts that are eaters of carrion. Like hyenas. A hyena could have done what was done back there in the morgue. But no one could have handled a hyena—pushed it through that ventilator hole with a rope on it to pull it up again.

"But an armadillo is an eater of corpses, too. It gets frightened when handled and curls up into a ball, like a bowling ball. It doesn't make any noise, and you could carry it in a bag like the one Hank described. It has an armored shell that would break the glass of the display case if Paton lowered it to within a few feet and let it drop the rest of the way. And of course he looked down with a flashlight to see—"

Bill Drager shuddered a little.

"Learning is a great thing if you like it," he said. "Studying origins of superstitions, I mean. But me, I want another drink. How about you?"

OUT OF HIS HEAD

By Thomas Bailey Aldrich (1836-1907)

Thomas Bailey Aldrich, the author of The Story of a Bad Boy, *wrote several books with elements of mystery and detection, including* Marjory Daw, The Stillwater Tragedy, *and his earliest prose work, an episodic novel called* Out of His Head. *Published in 1862, it was one of the first books by an American to follow Poe's lead in featuring an amateur detective. The discerning reader may not be surprised by the solution to the locked-room problem, which owes much to "The Murders in the Rue Morgue;" what is surprising is the character of Paul Lynde, Aldrich's detective, who narrates the story. Lynde is a mild lunatic who is working on a mysterious invention called the "Moon-Apparatus." And Lynde's motive in confronting the killer is, to say the least, out of the ordinary.*

The Danseuse

THE ensuing summer I returned North, and, turning my attention to mechanism, was successful in producing several wonderful pieces of work, among which may be mentioned a brass butterfly, made to flit so naturally in the air as to deceive the most acute observers. The motion of the toy, the soft down and gorgeous damask-stains on the pinions, were declared quite perfect. The thing is rusty and won't work now; I tried to set it going for Dr. Pendegrast, the other day.

A manikin musician, playing a few exquisite airs on a miniature piano, likewise excited much admiration. This figure bore such an absurd, unintentional resemblance to a gentleman who has since distinquished himself as a pianist, that I presented the trifle to a lady admirer of Gottschalk.

I also became a taxidermist, and stuffed a pet bird with springs and diminutive flutes, causing it to hop and carol, in its cage, with great glee. But my masterpiece was a nimble white mouse, with pink eyes, that could scamper up the walls, and masticate bits of cheese in an extraordinary style. My chambermaid shrieked, and jumped up on a chair, whenever I let the little fellow loose in her presence. One day, unhappily, the mouse, while nosing around after its favorite ailment, got snapt in a rat-trap that yawned in the closet, and I was never able to readjust the machinery.

Engaged in these useful inventions—useful, because no exercise of the human mind is ever in vain—my existence for two or three years was so placid and uneventful, I began to hope that the shadows which had followed on my path from childhood, making me unlike other men, had returned to that unknown world where they properly belong; but the Fates were only taking breath to work out more surely the problem of my destiny. I must keep nothing back. I must extenuate nothing.

I am about to lift the veil of mystery which, for nearly seven years, has shrouded the story of Mary Ware; and though I lay bare my own weakness, or folly, or what you will, I do not shrink from the unveiling.

No hand but mine can now perform the task. There was, indeed, a man who might have done this better than I. But he went his way in silence. I like a man who can hold his tongue.

On the corner of Clarke and Crandall streets, in New York, stands a dingy brown frame-house. It is a very old house, as its obsolete style of structure would tell you. It has a morose, unhappy look, though once it must have been a blythe mansion. I think that houses, like human beings, ultimately become dejected or cheerful, according to their experience. The very air of some front-doors tells their history.

This house, I repeat, has a morose, unhappy look, at present, and is tenanted by an incalculable number of Irish families, while a picturesque junk-shop is in full blast in the basement; but at the time of which I write, it was a second-rate boarding-place, of the more respectable sort, and rather largely patronized by poor, but honest, literary men, tragic-actors, members of the chorus, and such like gilt people.

My apartments on Crandall street were opposite this building, to which my attention was directed soon after taking possession of the rooms, by the discovery of the following facts:

First, that a charming lady lodged on the second-floor front, and sang like a canary every morning.

Second, that her name was Mary Ware.

Third, that Mary Ware was a danseuse, and had two lovers—only two.

Mary Ware was the leading lady at The Olympic. Night after night found me in the parquette. I can think of nothing with which to compare the airiness and utter abandon of her dancing. She seemed a part of the music. She was one of beauty's best thoughts, then. Her glossy gold hair reached down to her waist, shading one of those mobile faces which remind you of Guido's picture of Beatrix Cenci—there was something so fresh and enchanting in the mouth. Her luminous, almond eyes, looking out winningly from under their drooping fringes, were at once the delight and misery of young men.

Ah! you were distracting in your nights of triumph, when the bouquets nestled about your elastic ankles, and the kissing of your castanets made the pulses leap; but I remember when you lay on your cheerless bed, in the blank daylight, with the glory faded from your brow, and "none so poor as to do you reverence."

Then I stooped down and kissed you—but not till then.

Mary Ware was to me a finer study than her lovers. She had two, as I have said. One of them was commonplace enough—well-made, well-dressed, shallow, flaccid. Nature, when she gets out of patience with her best works, throws off such things by the gross, instead of swearing. He was a lieutenant, in the navy I think. The gilt button has charms to soothe the savage breast.

The other was a man of different mould, and interested me in a manner for which I could not then account. The first time I saw him did not seem like the first time. But this, perhaps, is an after-impression.

Every line of his countenance denoted character; a certain capability, I mean, but whether for good or evil was not so plain. I should have called him handsome, but for a noticeable scar which ran at right angles across his mouth, giving him a sardonic expression when he smiled.

His frame might have set an anatomist wild with delight—six feet two, deep-chested, knitted with tendons of steel. Not at all a fellow to amble on plush carpets.

"Some day," thought I, as I saw him stride by the house, "he will throw the little Lieutenant out of that second-story window."

I cannot tell, to this hour, which of those two men Mary Ware loved most—for I think she loved them both. A woman's heart was the insolvable charade with which the Sphinx nipt the Egyptians. I was never good at puzzles.

The flirtation, however, was food enough for the whole neighborhood. But faintly did the gossips dream of the strange drama that was being shaped out, as compactly as a tragedy of Sophocles, under their noses.

They were very industrious in tearing Mary Ware's good name to pieces. Some laughed at the gay Lieutenant, and some at Julius Kenneth; but they all amiably united in condemning Mary Ware.

This state of affairs had continued for five or six months, when it was reported that Julius Kenneth and Mary Ware were affianced. The Lieutenant was less frequently seen in

Crandall street, and Julius waited upon Mary's footsteps with the fidelity of a shadow.

Yet—though Mary went to the Sunday concerts with Julius Kenneth, she still wore the Lieutenant's roses in her bosom.

A Mystery

One drizzly November morning—how well I remember it!—I was awakened by a series of nervous raps on my bed-room door. The noise startled me from an unpleasant dream.

"O, sir!" cried the chambermaid on the landing, "There's been a dreadful time across the street. They've gone and killed Mary Ware!"

"Ah!"

That was all I could say. Cold drops of perspiration stood on my forehead.

I looked at my watch; it was eleven o'clock; I had over-slept myself, having sat up late the previous night.

I dressed hastily, and, without waiting for breakfast, pushed my way through the murky crowd that had collected in front of the house opposite, and passed up stairs, unquestioned.

When I entered the room, there were six people present: a thick-set gentleman, in black, with a bland professional air, a physician; two policemen; Adelaide Woods, an actress; Mrs. Marston, the landlady; and Julius Kenneth.

In the centre of the chamber, on the bed, lay the body of Mary Ware—as pale as Seneca's wife.

I shall never forget it. The corpse haunted me for years afterwards, the dark streaks under the eyes, and the wavy hair streaming over the pillow—the dead gold hair. I stood by her for a moment, and turned down the counterpane, which was drawn up closely to the chin.

"There was that across her throat
Which you had hardly cared to see."

At the head of the bed sat Julius Kenneth, bending over the icy hand which he held in his own. He was kissing it.

The gentleman in black was conversing in undertones with Mrs. Marston, who every now and then glanced furtively toward Mary Ware.

The two policemen were examining the doors, closets and windows of the apartment with, obviously, little success.

There was no fire in the air-tight stove, but the place was suffocatingly close. I opened a window, and leaned against the casement to get a breath of fresh air.

The physician approached me. I muttered something to him indistinctly, for I was partly sick with the peculiar mouldy smell that pervaded the room.

"Yes," he began, scrutinizing me, "the affair looks very perplexing, as you remark. Professional man, sir? No? Bless me!—beg pardon. Never in my life saw anything that looked so exceedingly like nothing. Thought, at first, 'twas a clear case of suicide—door locked, key on the inside, place undisturbed; but then we find no instrument with which the subject could have inflicted that wound on the neck. Queer. Party must have escaped up chimney. But how? Don't know. The windows are at least thirty feet from the ground. It would be impossible for a person to jump that far, even if he could clear the iron railing below. Which he couldn't. Disagreeable things to jump on, those spikes, sir. Must have been done with a sharp knife. Queer, very. Party meant to make sure work of it. The carotid neatly severed, upon my word."

The medical gentleman went on in this monologuic style for fifteen minutes, during which time Kenneth did not raise his lips from Mary's fingers.

Approaching the bed, I spoke to him; but he only shook his head in reply.

I understood his grief.

After regaining my chamber, I sat listlessly for three or four hours, gazing into the grate. The twilight flitted in from the street; but I did not heed it. A face among the coals fascinated me. It came and went and came. Now I saw a cavern hung with lurid stalactites; now a small Vesuvius vomiting smoke and flame; now a bridge spanning some tartarean gulf; then these crumbled, each in its turn, and from out the heated fragments peered the one inevitable face.

The *Evening Mirror*, of that day, gave the following detailed report of the inquest:

"This morning, at eight o'clock, Mary Ware, the celebrated

danseuse, was found dead in her chamber, at her late residence on the corner of Clarke and Crandall streets. The perfect order of the room, and the fact that the door was locked on the inside, have induced many to believe that the poor girl was the victim of her own rashness. But we cannot think so. That the door was fastened on the inner side, proves nothing except, indeed, that the murderer was hidden in the apartment. That the room gave no evidence of a struggle having taken place, is also an insignificant point. Two men, or even one, grappling suddenly with the deceased, who was a slight woman, would have prevented any great resistance. The deceased was dressed in a ballet-costume, and was, as we conjecture, murdered directly after her return from the theatre. On a chair near the bed, lay several fresh bouquets, and a water-proof cloak which she was in the habit of wearing over her dancing-dress, on coming home from the theatre at night. No weapon whatever was found on the premises. We give below all the material testimony elicited by the coroner. It explains little.

"*Josephine Marston* deposes: I keep a boarding house at No. 131 Crandall Street. Miss Ware has boarded with me for the past two years. Has always borne a good character as far as I know. I do not think she had many visitors; certainly no male visitors, excepting a Lieutenant King, and Mr. Kenneth to whom she was engaged. I do not know when King was last at the house; not within three days, I am confident. Deceased told me that he had gone away. I did not see her last night when she came home. The hall-door is never locked; each of the borders has a latchkey. The last time I saw Miss Ware was just before she went to the theatre, when she asked me to call her at eight o'clock (this morning) as she had promised to walk with 'Jules,' meaning Mr. Kenneth. I knocked at the door nine or ten times, but received no answer. Then I grew frightened and called one of the lady boarders, Miss Woods, who helped me to force the lock. The key fell on the floor inside as we pushed against the door. Mary Ware was lying on the bed, dressed. Some matches were scattered under the gas-burner by the bureau. The room presented the same appearance it does now.

"*Adelaide Woods* deposes: I am an actress by profession. I

occupy the room next to that of the deceased. Have known her twelve months. It was half-past eleven when she came home; she stopped in my chamber for perhaps three-quarters of an hour. The call-boy of The Olympic usually accompanies her home from the theatre when she is alone. I let her in. Deceased had misplaced her night-key. The partition between our rooms is of brick; but I do not sleep soundly, and should have heard any unusual noise. Two weeks ago, Miss Ware told me she was to be married to Mr. Kenneth in January next. The last time I saw them together was the day before yesterday. I assisted Mrs. Marston in breaking open the door. (Describes the position of the body, etc., etc.)

"Here the call-boy was summoned, and testified to accompanying the deceased home the night before. He came as far as the steps with her. The door was opened by a woman; could not swear it was Miss Woods, though he knows her by sight. The night was dark, and there was no lamp burning in the entry.

"*Julius Kenneth* deposes: I am a master-machinist. Reside at No.—Forsythe street. Miss Ware was my cousin. We were engaged to be married next—(Here the witness' voice failed him.) The last time I saw her was on Wednesday morning, on which occasion we walked out together. I did not leave my room last evening: was confined by a severe cold. A Lieutenant King used to visit my cousin frequently; it created considerable talk in the neighborhood: I did not like it, and requested her to break the acquaintance. She informed me, Wednesday, that King had been ordered to some foreign station, and would trouble me no more. Was excited at the time, hinted at being tired of living; then laughed, and was gayer than she had been for weeks. Deceased was subject to fits of depression. She had engaged to walk with me this morning at eight. When I reached Clark street I learned that she—(Here the witness, overcome by emotion, was allowed to retire.)

"*Dr. Wren* deposes: (This gentleman was very learned and voluble, and had to be suppressed several times by the coroner. We furnish a brief synopsis of his testimony.) I was called in to view the body of the deceased. A deep incision on the throat, two inches below the left ear, severing the left common carotid and the internal jugular vein, had been inflicted with some sharp instrument. Such a wound would, in my opinion, produce death almost instantaneously. The body bore no other signs of violence. A slight mark, almost indistinguishable, in fact, extended from the upper lip toward the right nostril—some hurt, I suppose, received in infancy. Deceased must have been dead a number of hours, the rigor mortis having already supervened, etc., etc.

"*Dr. Ceccarini* corroborated the above testimony.

"The night-watchman and seven other persons were then placed on the stand; but their statements threw no fresh light on the case.

"The situation of Julius Kenneth, the lover of the ill-fated girl, draws forth the deepest commiseration. Miss Ware was twenty-four years of age.

"Who the criminal is, and what could have led to the perpetration of the cruel act, are questions which, at present, threaten to baffle the sagacity of the police. If such deeds can be committed with impunity in a crowded city, like this, who is safe from the assassin's steel?"

Thou Art The Man

I could but smile on reading all this serious nonsense.

After breakfast, the next morning, I made my toilet with extreme care, and presented myself at the sheriff's office.

Two gentlemen who were sitting at a table, busy with papers, started nervously to their feet, as I announced myself. I bowed very calmly to the sheriff, and said, "*I am the person who murdered Mary Ware!*"

Of course I was instantly arrested; and that evening, in jail, I had the equivocal pleasure of reading these paragraphs among the police items of the *Mirror*:

"The individual who murdered the ballet-girl, in the night of the third inst., in a house on Crandall street, surrendered himself to the sheriff this forenoon.

"He gave his name as Paul Lynde, and resides opposite the place where the tragedy was enacted. He is a man of medium stature, has restless gray eyes, chestnut hair, and a supernaturally pale countenance. He seems a person of excellent address, is said to be wealthy, and nearly connected with an influential New England family. Notwithstanding his gentlemanly manner, there is that about him which would lead one to select him from out a thousand, as a man of cool and desperate character.

"Mr. Lynde's voluntary surrender is not the least astonishing feature of this affair; for, had he preserved silence he would, beyond a doubt, have escaped even suspicion. The murder was planned and executed with such deliberate skill, that there is little or no evidence to complicate him. In truth, there is *no* evidence against him, excepting his own confession, which is meagre and confusing enough. He freely acknowledges the crime, but stubbornly refuses to enter into any details. He expresses a desire to be hanged immediately!

"How Mr. Lynde entered the chamber, and by what means he left it, after committing the deed, and why he cruelly killed a lady with whom he had had (as we gather from the testimony) no previous acquaintance—are enigmas which still perplex the public mind, and will not let curiosity sleep. These facts, however, will probably be brought to light during the impending trial. In the meantime, we await the dénouement with interest."

Paul's Confession

On the afternoon following this disclosure, the door of my cell turned on its hinges, and Julius Kenneth entered.

In *his* presence I ought to have trembled; but I was calm and collected. He, feverish and dangerous.

"You received my note?"

"Yes; and have come here, as you requested."I waved him to a chair, which he refused to take. Stood leaning on the back of it.

"You of course know, Mr. Kenneth, that I have refused to reveal the circumstances connected with the death of Mary Ware? I wished to make the confession to you alone."

He regarded me for a moment from beneath his shaggy eyebrows.

"Well?"

"But even to you I will assign no reason for the course I pursued. It was necessary that Mary Ware should die."

"Well?"

"I decided that she should die in her chamber, and to that end I purloined her night-key.

Julius Kenneth looked through and through me, as I spoke.

"On Friday night after she had gone to the theatre, I entered the hall-door by means of the key, and stole unobserved to her room, where I secreted myself under the bed, or in that small clothes-press near the stove—I forget which. Sometime between eleven and twelve o'clock, Mary Ware returned. While she was in the act of lighting the gas, I pressed a handkerchief, saturated with chloroform, over her mouth. You know the effect of chloroform? I will, at this point spare you further detail, merely remarking that I threw my gloves and the handkerchief in the stove; but I'm afraid there was not fire enough to consume them."

Kenneth walked up and down the cell greatly agitated; then seated himself on the foot of the bed.

"Curse you!"

"Are you listening to me, Mr. Kenneth?"

"Yes!"

"I extinguished the light, and proceeded to make my escape from the room, which I did in a manner so simple that the detectives, through their desire to ferret out wonderful things, will never discover it, unless, indeed, *you* betray me. The night, you will recollect, was foggy; it was impossible to discern an object at four yards distance—this was fortunate for me. I raised the window-sash and let myself out cautiously, holding on by the sill, until my feet touched on the moulding which caps the window below. I then drew down the sash. By standing on the extreme left of the cornice, I was able to reach the tin water-spout of the adjacent building, and by that I descended to the sidewalk."

The man glowered at me like a tiger, his eyes green and golden with excitement: I have since wondered that he did not tear me to pieces.

"On gaining the street," I continued coolly, "I found that I had brought the knife with me. It should have been left in the chamber—it would have given the whole thing the aspect of suicide. It was too late to repair the blunder, so I threw the knife—"

"Into the river!" exclaimed Kenneth, involuntarily.

And then I smiled.

"How did you know it was I!" he shrieked.

"Hush! they will overhear you in the corridor. It was as plain as day. I knew it before I had been five minutes in the room. First, because you shrank instinctively from the corpse, though you seemed to be caressing it. Secondly, when I looked into the stove, I saw a glove and handkerchief, partly consumed; and then I instantly accounted for the faint close smell which had affected me before the room was ventilated. It was chloroform. Thirdly, when I went to open the window, I noticed that the paint was scraped off the brackets which held the spout to the next house. This conduit had been newly painted two days previously—I watched the man at work; the paint on the brackets was thicker than anywhere else, and had not dried. On looking at your feet, which I did critically, while speaking to you, I saw that the leather on the inner side of each boot was slightly chafed, paint-marked. It is a way of mine to put this and that together!"

"If you intend to betray me—"

"O, no, but I don't, or I should not be here—alone with you. I am, as you may allow, not quite a fool."

"Indeed, sir, you are as subtle as—"

"Yes, I wouldn't mention him."

"Who?"

"The devil."

Kenneth mused.

"May I ask, Mr. Lynde, what you intend to do?"

"Certainly—remain here."

"I don't understand you," said Kenneth with an air of perplexity.

"If you will listen patiently, you shall learn why *I* have acknowledged this deed, why *I* would bear the penalty. I believe there are vast, intense sensations from which we are excluded, by the conventional fear of a certain kind of death. Now, this pleasure, this ecstacy, this something, I don't know what, which I have striven for all my days, is known only to a privileged few—innocent men, who, through some oversight of the law, are *hanged by the neck!* How rich is

Nature in compensations! Some men are born to be hung, some have hanging thrust upon them, and some (as I hope to do) achieve hanging. It appears ages since I commenced watching for an opportunity like this. Worlds could not tempt me to divulge your guilt, nor could worlds have tempted me to commit your crime, for a man's conscience should be at ease to enjoy, to the utmost, this delicious death! Our interview is at an end, Mr. Kenneth. I held it my duty to say this much to you."

And I turned my back on him.

"One word, Mr. Lynde."

Kenneth came to my side, and laid a heavy hand on my shoulder, that red right hand, which all the tears of the angels cannot make white again.

"Did you send this to me last month?" asked Kenneth, holding up a slip of paper on which was scrawled, *Watch them*—in my handwriting.

"Yes," I answered.

Then it struck me that these few thoughtless words, which some sinister spirit had impelled me to write, were the indirect cause of the whole catastrophe.

"Thank you," he said hurriedly. "I watched them!" Then, after a pause, "I shall go far from here. I can not, I *will* not die yet. Mary was to have been my wife, so she would have hidden her shame—O cruel! she, my own cousin, and we the last two of our race! Life is not sweet to me, it is bitter, bitter; but I shall live until I stand front to front with *him*. And you? They will not harm you—*you* are a madman?"

Julius Kenneth was gone before I could reply.

The cell door shut him out forever—shut him out in the flesh. His spirit was not so easily exorcised.

After all, it was a wretched fiasco. Two officious friends of mine, who had played chess with me, at my lodgings, on the night of the 3rd, proved an alibi; and I was literally turned out of the Tombs; for I insisted on being executed.

Then it was maddening to have the newspapers call me a monomaniac.

I a monomaniac?

What was Pythagoras, Newton, Fulton? Have not the great

original lights of every age, been regarded as madmen? Science, like religion, has its martyrs.

Recent surgical discoveries have, I believe, sustained me in my theory; or, if not, they ought to have done so. There is said to be a pleasure in drowning. Why not in strangulation?

In another field of science, I shall probably have full justice awarded me—I now allude to the Moon-Apparatus, which is still in an unfinished state, but progressing.

MURDER BY PROXY

By M. McDonnell Bodkin (1850-1933)

The popularity of Sherlock Holmes's adventures in The
Strand *magazine, beginning in 1891, opened the great
age of the detective short story. Readers demanded tales
featuring detectives who used tiny clues to deduce the
solutions of bloodthirsty crimes, and thus were born such
sleuths as Arthur Morrison's Martin Hewitt, Baroness
Orczy's Old Man in the Corner, and McDonnell Bodkin's
Paul Beck. Bodkin, an Irish lawyer and Member of Par-
liament, created perhaps the earliest family of detectives.
He began with* Paul Beck, The Rule of Thumb Detective
(1898), followed by Dora Myrl, The Lady Detective *(1900).
Beck married Myrl in* The Capture of Paul Beck *(1909).
Their son was clearly quite precocious, for only two years
later the lad had begun his own detective career in* Young
Beck, a Chip off of the Old Block.

*Paul Beck is a contrast to the flamboyant Holmes and
other eccentric detectives of the era. His success is based
in part on the fact that he never appears to be intelligent: "I
just go by the rule of thumb," he explains, "and muddle
and puzzle out my cases as best I can." But the problems
that he investigates, including the following story from the
first volume of his adventures, are among the cleverest of
the turn-of-the century.*

AT two o'clock precisely on that sweltering 12th of August, Eric Neville, young, handsome, *débonnaire*, sauntered through the glass door down the wrought-iron staircase into the beautiful, old-fashioned garden of Berkly Manor, radiant in white flannel, with a broad-brimmed Panama hat perched lightly on his glossy black curls, for he had just come from lazing in his canoe along the shadiest stretches of the river, with a book for company.

The back of the Manor House was the south wall of the garden, which stretched away for nearly a mile, gay with blooming flowers and ripening fruit. The air, heavy with perfume, stole softly through all the windows, now standing wide open in the sunshine, as though the great house gasped for breath.

When Eric's trim, tan boot left the last step of the iron staircase it reached the broad gravelled walk of the garden. Fifty yards off the head gardener was tending his peaches, the smoke from his pipe hanging like a faint blue haze in the still air that seemed to quiver with the heat. Eric, as he reached him, held out a petitionary hand, too lazy to speak.

Without a word the gardener stretched for a huge peach that was striving to hide its red face from the sun under narrow ribbed leaves, plucked it as though he loved it, and put it softly in the young man's hand.

Eric stripped off the velvet coat, rose-coloured, green, and amber, till it hung round the fruit in tatters, and made his sharp, white teeth meet in the juicy flesh of the ripe peach.

BANG!

The sudden shock of sound close to their ears wrenched the nerves of the two men; one dropped his peach, and the other his pipe. Both stared about them in utter amazement.

"Look there, sir," whispered the gardener, pointing to a little cloud of smoke oozing lazily through a window almost directly over their head, while the pungent spice of gunpowder made itself felt in the hot air.

"My uncle's room," gasped Eric. "I left him only a moment ago fast asleep on the sofa."

He turned as he spoke, and ran like a deer along the garden walk, up the iron steps, and back through the glass door into the house, the old gardener following as swiftly as his rheumatism would allow.

Eric crossed the sitting-room on which the glass door opened, went up the broad, carpeted staircase four steps at a time, turned sharply to the right down a broad corridor, and burst straight through the open door of his uncle's study.

Fast as he had come, there was another before him. A tall, strong figure, dressed in light tweed, was bending over the sofa where, a few minutes before, Eric had seen his uncle asleep.

Eric recognised the broad back and brown hair at once.

"John," he cried—"John, what is it?"

His cousin turned to him a handsome, manly face, ghastly pale now even to the lips.

"Eric, my boy," he answered falteringly, "this is too awful. Uncle has been murdered—shot stone dead."

"No, no; it cannot be. It's not five minutes since I saw him quietly sleeping," Eric began. Then his eyes fell on the still figure on the sofa, and he broke off abruptly.

Squire Neville lay with his face to the wall, only the outline of his strong, hard features visible. The charge of shot had entered at the base of the skull, the grey hair was all dabbled with blood, and the heavy, warm drops still fell slowly on to the carpet.

"But who can have—" Eric gasped out, almost speechless with horror.

"It must have been his own gun," his cousin answered. "It was lying there on the table, to the right, barrel still smoking, when I came in."

"It wasn't suicide—was it?" asked Eric, in a frightened whisper.

"Quite impossible, I should say. You see where he is hit."

"But it was so sudden. I ran the moment I heard the shot, and you were before me. Did you see any one?"

"Not a soul. The room was empty."

"But how could the murderer escape?"

"Perhaps he leapt through the window. It was open when I came in."

"He couldn't do that, Master John." It was the voice of the gardener at the door. "Me and Master Eric was right under the window when the shot came."

"Then how in the devil's name did he disappear, Simpson?"

"It's not for me to say, sir."

John Neville searched the room with eager eyes. There was no cover in it for a cat. A bare, plain room, panelled with brown oak, on which hung some guns and fishing rods—old-fashioned for the most part, but of the finest workmanship and material. A small bookcase in the corner was the room's sole claim to be called "a study." The huge leather-covered sofa on which the corpse lay, a massive round table in the centre of the room, and a few heavy chairs completed the furniture. The dust lay thick on everything, the fierce sunshine streamed in a broad band across the room. The air was stifling with heat and the acrid smoke of gunpowder.

John Neville noticed how pale his young cousin was. He laid has hand on his shoulder with the protecting kindness of an elder brother.

"Come, Eric," he said softly, "we can do no good here."

"We had best look round first, hadn't we, for some clue?" asked Eric, and he stretched his hand towards the gun; but John stopped him.

"No, no," he cried hastily, "we must leave things just as we find them. I'll send a man to the village for Wardle and telegraph to London for a detective."

He drew his young cousin gently from the room, locked the door on the outside, and put the key in his pocket.

"Who shall I wire to?" John Neville called from his desk with pencil poised over the paper, to his cousin, who sat at the library table with his head buried in his hands. "It will need a sharp man—one who can give his whole time to it."

"I don't know any one. Yes, I do. That fellow with the queer name that found the Duke of Southern's opal—Beck. That's it. Thornton Crescent, W.C., will find him."

John Neville filled in the name and address to the telegram he had already written—

"Come at once. Case of murder. Expense no object. John Neville, Berkly Manor, Dorset."

Little did Eric guess that the filling in of that name was to him a matter of life or death.

John Neville had picked up a time-table and rustled through the leaves. "Hard lines, Eric," he said; "do his best, he cannot get here before midnight. But here's Wardle already, anyhow; that's quick work."

A shrewd, silent man was Wardle, the local constable, who now came briskly up the broad avenue; strong and active too, though well over fifty years of age.

John Neville met him at the door with the news. But the groom had already told of the murder.

"You did the right thing to lock the door, sir," said Wardle, as they passed into the library where Eric still sat apparently unconscious of their presence, "and you wired for a right good man. I've worked with this here Mr. Beck before now. A pleasant spoken man and a lucky one. 'No hurry, Mr. Wardle,' he says to me, 'and no fuss. Stir nothing. The things about the corpse have always a story of their own if they are let tell it, and I always like to have the first quiet little chat with them myself.'"

So the constable held his tongue and kept his hands quiet and used his eyes and ears, while the great house buzzed with gossip. There was a whisper here and a whisper there, and the whispers patched themselves into a story. By slow degrees dark suspicion settled down and closed like a cloud round John Neville.

Its influence seemed to pass in some strange fashion through the closed doors of the library. John began pacing the room restlessly from end to end.

After a little while the big room was not big enough to hold his impatience. He wandered out aimlessly, as it seemed, from one room to another; now down the iron steps to gaze vacantly at the window of his uncle's room, now past the locked door in the broad corridor.

With an elaborate pretence of carelessness Wardle kept him in sight through all his wanderings, but John Neville seemed too self-absorbed to notice it.

Presently he returned to the library. Eric was there, still sitting with his back to the door, only the top of his head showing over the high chair. He seemed absorbed in thought or sleep, he sat so still.

But he started up with a quick cry, showing a white, frightened face, when John touched him lightly on the arm.

"Come for a walk in the grounds, Eric?" he said. "This waiting and watching and doing nothing is killing work; I cannot stand it much longer."

"I'd rather not, if you don't mind," Eric answered wearily; "I feel completely knocked over."

"A mouthful of fresh air would do you good, my poor boy; you do look done up."

Eric shook his head.

"Well, I'm off," John said.

"If you leave me the key, I will give it to the detective, if he comes."

"Oh, he cannot be here before midnight, and I'll be back in an hour."

As John Neville walked rapidly down the avenue without looking back, Wardle stepped quietly after, keeping him well in view.

Presently Neville turned abruptly in amongst the woods, the constable still following cautiously. The trees stood tall and well apart, and the slanting sunshine made lanes of vivid green through the shade. As Wardle crossed between Neville and the sun his shadow fell long and black on the bright green.

John Neville saw the shadow move in front of him and turned sharp round and faced his pursuer.

The constable stood stock still and stared.

"Well, Wardle, what is it? Don't stand there like a fool fingering your baton! Speak out, man—what do you want of me?"

"You see how it is, Master John," the constable stammered out, "I don't believe it myself. I've known you twenty-one years—since you were born, I may say—and I don't believe it, not a blessed word of it. But duty is duty, and I must go through with it; and facts is facts, and you and he had words last night, and Master Eric found you first in the room when—"

John Neville listened, bewildered at first. Then suddenly, as it seemed to dawn on him for the first time that he *could* be suspected of this murder, he kindled a sudden hot blaze of anger.

He turned fiercely on the constable. Broad-chested, strong limbed, he towered over him, terrible in his wrath; his hands clenched, his muscles quivered, his strong white teeth shut tight as a rat-trap, and a reddish light shining at the back of his brown eyes.

"How dare you! how dare you!" he hissed out between his teeth, his passion choking him.

He looked dangerous, that roused young giant, but Wardle met his angry eyes without flinching.

"Where's the use, Master John?" he said soothingly. "It's main hard on you, I know. But the fault isn't mine, and you won't help yourself by taking it that way."

The gust of passion appeared to sweep by as suddenly as it arose. The handsome face cleared and there was no trace of anger in the frank voice that answered. "You are right, Wardle, quite right. What is to be done next? Am I to consider myself under arrest?"

"Better not, sir. You've got things to do a prisoner couldn't do handy, and I don't want to stand in the way of your doing them. If you give me your word it will be enough."

"My word for what?"

"That you'll be here when wanted."

"Why, man, you don't think I'd be fool enough—innocent or guilty—to run away. My God! run away from a charge of murder!"

"Don't take on like that, sir. There's a man coming from London that will set things straight, you'll see. Have I your word?"

"You have my word."

"Perhaps you'd better be getting back to the house, sir. There's a deal of talking going on amongst the servants. I'll keep out of the way, and no one will be the wiser for anything that has passed between us."

Half-way up the avenue a fast-driven dog-cart overtook John Neville, and pulled up so sharply that the horse's hoofs sent the coarse gravel flying. A stout, thick-set man, who up to that had been in close chat with the driver, leapt out more lightly than could have been expected from his figure.

"Mr. John Neville, I presume? My name is Beck—Mr. Paul Beck."

"Mr. Beck! Why, I thought you couldn't have got here before midnight."

"Special train," Mr. Beck answered pleasantly. "Your wire said 'Expense no object.' Well, time is an object, and comfort is an object too, more or less, in all these cases; so I took a special train, and here I am. With your permission, we will send the trap on and walk to the house together. This seems a bad business, Mr. Neville. Shot dead, the driver tells me. Any one suspected?"

"I'm suspected." The answer broke from John Neville's lips almost fiercely.

Mr. Beck looked at him for a minute with placid curiosity, without a touch of surprise in it.

"How do you know that?"

"Wardle, the local constable, has just told me so to my face. It was only by way of a special favour he refrained from arresting me then and there."

Mr. Beck walked on beside John Neville ten or fifteen paces before he spoke again.

"Do you mind," he said, in a very insinuating voice, "telling me exactly why you are suspected?"

"Not in the very least."

"Mind this," the detective went on quickly, "I give you no caution and make you no pledge. It's my business to find out the truth. If you think the truth will help you, then you ought to help me. This is very irregular, of course, but I don't mind that. When a man is charged with a crime there is, you see, Mr. Neville, always one witness who knows whether he is guilty or not. There is very often only that one. The first thing the British law does by way of discovering the truth is to close the mouth of the only witness that knows it. Well, that's not my way. I like to give an innocent man a chance to tell his own story, and I've no scruple in trapping a guilty man if I can."

He looked John Neville straight in the eyes as he spoke.

The look was steadily returned. "I think I understand. What do you want to know? Where shall I begin?"

"At the beginning. What did you quarrel with your uncle about yesterday?"

John Neville hesitated for a moment, and Mr. Beck took a mental note of his hesitation.

"I didn't quarrel with him. He quarrelled with me. It was this way: There was a bitter feud between my uncle and his neighbour, Colonel Peyton. The estates adjoin, and the quarrel was about some shooting. My uncle was very violent—he used to call Colonel Peyton 'a common poacher.' Well, I took no hand in the row. I was rather shy when I met the Colonel for the first time after it, for I knew my uncle had the wrong end of the stick. But the Colonel spoke to me in the kindest way. "No reason why you and I should cease to be friends, John," he said. "This is a foolish business. I would give the best covert on my estate to be out of it. Men cannot fight duels in these days, and gentlemen cannot scold like fish-wives. But I don't expect people will call me a coward because I hate a row."

"Not likely," I said.

"The Colonel, you must know, had distinguished himself in a dozen engagements, and has the Victoria Cross locked up in a drawer of his desk. Lucy once showed it to me. Lucy is his only daughter and he is devoted to her. Well, after that, of course, the Colonel and I kept on good terms, for I liked him, and I liked going there and all that. But our friendship angered my uncle. I had been going to the Grange pretty often of late, and my uncle heard of it. He spoke to me in a very rough fashion of Colonel Peyton and his daughter at dinner last night, and I stood up for them."

"By what right, you insolent puppy," he shouted, "do you take this upstart's part against me?"

"The Peytons are as good a family as our own, sir," I said—that was true—"and as for right, Miss Lucy Peyton has done me the honour of promising to be my wife."

"At that he exploded in a very tempest of rage. I cannot repeat his words about the Colonel and his daughter. Even now, though he lies dead yonder, I can hardly forgive them. He swore he would never see or speak to me again if I disgraced myself by such a marriage. "I cannot break the entail," he growled, "worse luck. But I can make you a beggar while I live, and I shall live forty years to spite you. The poacher can have you a bargain for all I care. Go, sell yourself as dearly as you can, and live on your wife's fortune as soon as you please."

"Then I lost my temper, and gave him a bit of my mind."

"Try and remember what you said; it's important."

"I told him that I cast his contempt back in his face; that I loved Lucy Peyton, and that I would live for her, and die for her, if need be."

"Did you say 'it was a comfort he could not live forever?' You see the story of your quarrel has travelled far and near. The driver told me of it. Try and remember—did you say that?"

"I think I did. I'm sure I did now, but I was so furious I hardly knew what I said. I certainly never meant—"

"Who was in the room when you quarrelled?"

"Only Cousin Eric and the butler."

"The butler, I suppose, spread the story?"

"I suppose so. I'm sure Cousin Eric never did. He was as much pained at the scene as myself. He tried to interfere at the time, but his interference only made my uncle more furious."

"What was your allowance from your uncle?"

"A thousand a year."

"He had power to cut it off, I suppose?"

"Certainly."

"But he had no power over the estate. You were heir-apparent under the entail, and at the present moment you are the owner of Berkly Manor?"

"That is so; but up to the moment you spoke I assure you I never even remembered—"

"Who comes next to you in the entail?"

"My first cousin, Eric. He is four years younger than I am."

"After him?"

"A distant cousin. I scarcely know him at all; but has a bad reputation, and I know my uncle and he hated each other cordially."

"How did your uncle and your cousin Eric hit it off?"

"Not too well. He hated Eric's father—his own youngest brother—and he was sometimes rough on Eric. He used to abuse the dead father in the son's presence, calling him cruel and treacherous, and all that. Poor Eric had often a hard time of it. Uncle was liberal to him so far as money went—as liberal as he was to me—had him to live at the Manor and denied him nothing. But now and again he would sting the poor lad by a passionate curse or a bitter sneer. In spite of all, Eric seemed fond of him."

"To come now to the murder; you saw your uncle no more that night, I suppose?"

"I never saw him alive again."

"Do you know what he did next day?"

"Only by hearsay."

"Hearsay evidence is often first-class evidence, though the law doesn't think so. What did you hear?"

"My uncle was mad about shooting. Did I tell you his quarrel with Colonel Peyton was about the shooting? He had a grouse moor rented about twelve miles from here, and he never missed the first day. He was off at cock-shout with the head gamekeeper, Lennox. I was to have gone with him, but I didn't, of course. Contrary to his custom he came back about noon and went straight to his study. I was writing in my own room and heard his heavy step go past the door. Later on Eric found him asleep on the great leather couch in his study. Five minutes after Eric left I heard the shot and rushed into his room."

"Did you examine the room after you found the body?"

"No. Eric wanted to, but I thought it better not. I simply locked the door and put the key in my pocket till you came."

"Could it have been suicide?"

"Impossible, I should say. He was shot through the back of the head."

"Had your uncle any enemies that you know of?"

"The poachers hated him. He was relentless with them. A fellow once shot at him, and my uncle shot back and shattered the man's leg. He had him sent to hospital first and cured, and then prosecuted him straight away, and got him two years."

"Then you think a poacher murdered him?" Mr. Beck said blandly.

"I don't well see how he could. I was in my own room on the same corridor. The only way to or from my uncle's room was past my door. I rushed out the instant I heard the shot, and saw no one."

"Perhaps the murderer leapt through the window?"

"Eric tells me that he and the gardener were in the garden almost under the window at the time."

"What's your theory, then, Mr. Neville?"

"I haven't got a theory."

"You parted with your uncle in anger last night?"

"That's so."

"Next day your uncle is shot, and you are found—I won't say caught—in his room the instant afterwards."

John Neville flushed crimson; but he held himself in and nodded without speaking.

The two walked on together in silence.

They were not a hundred yards from the great mansion—John Neville's house—standing high above the embowering trees in the glow of the twilight, when the detective spoke again.

"I'm bound to say, Mr. Neville, that things look very black against you, as they stand. I think that constable Wardle ought to have arrested you."

"It's not too late, yet," John Neville answered shortly, "I see him there at the corner of the house and I'll tell him you said so."

He turned on his heel, when Mr. Beck called quickly after him: "What about that key?"

John Neville handed it to him without a word. The detective took it as silently and walked on to the entrance and up the great stone steps alone, whistling softly.

Eric welcomed him at the door, for the driver had told of his coming.

"You have had no dinner, Mr. Beck?" he asked courteously.

"Business first; pleasure afterwards. I had a snack in the train. Can I see the gamekeeper, Lennox, for five minutes alone?"

"Certainly. I'll send him to you in a moment here in the library."

Lennox, the gamekeeper, a long-limbed, high-shouldered, elderly man, shambled shyly into the room, consumed by nervousness in the presence of a London detective.

"Sit down, Lennox—sit down," said Mr. Beck kindly. The very sound of his voice, homely and good-natured, put the man at his ease. "Now, tell me, why did you come home so soon from the grouse this morning?"

"Well, you see, sir, it was this ways. We were two hours hout when the Squire, 'e says to me, 'Lennox,' 'e says, 'I'm sick of this fooling. I'm going 'ome.'"

"No sport?"

"Birds wor as thick as blackberries, sir, and lay like larks."

"No sportsman, then?"

"Is it the Squire, sir?" cried Lennox, quite forgetting his shyness in his excitement at this slur on the Squire. "There wasn't a better sportsman in the county—no, nor as good. Real, old-fashioned style, 'e was. 'Hang your barnyard shooting,' 'e'd say when they'd ask him to go kill tame pheasants. 'E put up 'is own birds with 'is own dogs, 'e did. 'E'd as soon go shooting without a gun very near as without a dog any day. Aye and 'e stuck to 'is old 'Manton' muzzle-loader to the last. 'Old it steady, Lennox,' 'ed say to me oftentimes, 'and point it straight. It will hit harder and further than any of their telescopes, and it won't get marked with rust if you don't clean it every second shot.'"

"'Easy to load, Squire,'" the young men would say, cracking up their hammerless breech-loaders.

"'Aye,'" he'd answer them back, "'and spoil your dog's work. What's the good of a dog learning to "down shot," if you can drop in your cartridges as quick as a cock can pick corn.'

"A dead shot the Squire was, too, and no mistake, sir, if he wasn't flurried. Many a time I've seen him wipe the eyes of gents who thought no end of themselves with that same old muzzle-loader that shot hisself in the long run. Many a time I seen—"

"Why did he turn his back on good sport yesterday?" asked Mr. Beck, cutting short his reminiscences.

"Well, you see, it was scorching hot for one thing, but that wasn't it, for the infernal fire would not stop the Squire if he was on for sport. But he was in a blazing temper all the morning, and temper tells more than most anything on a man's shooting. When Flora sprung a pack—she's a young dog, and the fault wasn't hers either—for she came down the wind on them—but the Squire had the gun to his shoulder to shoot her. Five minutes after she found another pack and set like a stone. They got up as big as haycocks and as lazy as crows, and he missed right and left—never touched a feather—a thing I haven't seen him do since I was a boy.

"'It's myself I should shoot, not the dog,' he growled and he flung me the gun to load. When I'd got the caps on and had shaken the powder into the nipples, he ripped out an oath that 'e'd have no more of it. 'E walked right across country to where the trap was . The birds got up under his feet, but divil a shot he'd fire, but drove straight 'ome.

"When we got to the 'ouse I wanted to take the gun and fire it off, or draw the charges. But 'e told me to go to—, and carried it up loaded as it was to his study, where no one goes unless they're sent for special. It was better than an hour afterwards I heard the report of the 'Manton'; I'd know it in a thousand. I ran for the study as fast as—"

Eric Neville broke suddenly into the room, flushed and excited.

"Mr Beck," he cried, "a monstrous thing has happened. Wardle, the local constable, you know, has arrested my cousin on a charge of wilfull murder of my uncle."

Mr. Beck, with his eyes intent on the excited face, waved his big hand soothingly.

"Easy," he said, "take it easy, Mr. Neville. It's hurtful to your feelings, no doubt; but it cannot be helped. The constable has done no more than his duty. The evidence is very strong, as you know, and in such cases it's best for all parties to proceed regularly."

"You can go," he went on, speaking to Lennox, who stood dumfoundered at the news of John Neville's arrest, staring with eyes and mouth wide open.

Then turning again very quietly to Eric: "Now, Mr. Neville, I would like to see the room where the corpse is."

The perfect placidity of his manner had its effect upon the boy, for he was little more than a boy, calming his excitement as oil smooths troubled water.

"My cousin has the key," he said; "I will get it."

"There is no need," Mr. Beck called after him, for he was half-way out of the room on his errand: "I've got the key if you will be good enough to show me the room."

Mastering his surprise, Eric showed him upstairs, and along the corridor to the locked door. Half unconsciously, as it seemed, he was following the detective into the room, when Mr. Beck stopped him.

"I know you will kindly humour me, Mr. Neville," he said, "but I find that I can look closer and think clearer when I'm by myself. I'm not exactly shy you know, but it's a habit I've got."

He closed the door softly as he spoke, and locked it on the inside, leaving the key in the lock.

The mask of placidity fell from him the moment he found himself alone. His lips tightened, and his eyes sparkled, and his muscles seemed to grow rigid with excitement, like a sporting dog's when he is close upon the game.

One glance at the corpse showed him that it was not suicide. In this, at least, John Neville had spoken the truth.

The back of the head had literally been blown in by the charge of heavy shot at close quarters. The grey hair was clammy and matted, with little white angles of bone protruding. The dropping of the blood had made a black pool on the carpet, and the close air of the room was foetid with the smell of it.

The detective walked to the table where the gun, a handsome, old-fashioned muzzle-loader, lay, the muzzle still pointed at the corpse. But his attention was diverted by a water-bottle, a great globe of clear glass quite full, and perched on a book a little distance from the gun, and between it and the window. He took it from the table and tested the water with the tip of his tongue. It had a curious, insipid, parboiled taste, but he detected no foreign flavour in it. Though the room was full of dust there was almost none on the cover of the book where the water-bottle stood, and Mr. Beck noticed a gap in the third row of the bookcase where the book had been taken.

After a quick glance round the room Mr. Beck walked to the window. On a small table there he found a clear circle in the thick dust. He fitted the round bottom of the water-bottle to this circle and it covered it exactly. While he stood by the window he caught sight of some small scraps of paper crumbled up and thrown into a corner. Picking them up and smoothing them out he found they were curiously drilled with little burnt holes. Having examined the holes minutely with his magnifying glass, he slipped these scraps folded on each other into his waistcoat pocket.

From the window he went back to the gun. This time he examined it with the minutest care. The right barrel he found had been recently discharged, the left was still loaded. Then he made a startling discovery. *Both barrels were on halfcock.* The little bright copper cap twinkled on the nipple of the left barrel, from the right nipple the cap was gone.

How had the murderer fired the right barrel without a cap? How and why did he find time in the midst of his deadly work to put the cock back to safety?

Had Mr. Beck solved this problem? The grim smile deepened on his lips as he looked, and there was an ugly light in his eyes that boded ill for the unknown assassin. Finally he carried the gun to the window and examined it carefully through a magnifying glass. There was a thin dark line, as if traced with the point of a red-hot needle, running a little way along the wood of the stock and ending in the right nipple.

Mr. Beck put the gun back quietly on the table. The whole investigation had not taken ten minutes. He gave one look at the still figure on the couch, unlocked the door, locking it after him, and walked out through the corridor, the same cheerful, imperturbable Mr. Beck that had walked into it ten minutes before.

He found Eric waiting for him at the head of the stairs. "Well?" he said when he saw the detective.

"Well," replied Mr. Beck, ignoring the interrogation in his voice, "when is the inquest to be? That's the next thing to be thought of; the sooner the better."

"To-morrow, if you wish. My cousin John sent a messenger to Mr. Morgan, the coroner. He lives only five miles off, and he has promised to be here at twelve o'clock to-morrow. There will be no difficulty in getting a jury in the village."

"That's right, that's all right," said Mr. Beck, rubbing his hands; "the sooner and the quieter we get those preliminaries over the better."

"I have just sent to engage the local solicitor on behalf of my cousin. He's not particularly bright, I'm afraid, but he's the best to be had on a short notice."

"Very proper and thoughtful on your part—very thoughtful indeed. But solicitors cannot do much in such cases. It's the evidence we have to go by, and the evidence is only too plain, I'm afraid. Now, if you please," he went on more briskly, dismissing the disagreeable subject, as it were, with a wave of his big hand, "I'd be very glad of that supper you spoke about."

Mr. Beck supped very heartily on a brace of grouse—the last of the dead man's shooting—and a bottle of ripe Burgundy. He was in high good-humour, and across "the walnuts and the wine" he told Eric some startling episodes in his career, which seemed to divert the young fellow a little from his manifest grief for his uncle and anxiety for his cousin.

Meanwhile John Neville remained shut close in his own room, with the constable at the door.

The inquest was held at half-past twelve next day in the library.

The Coroner, a large, red-faced man, with a very affable manner, had got to his work promptly.

The jury "viewed the body" steadily, stolidly, with a kind of morose delectation in the grim spectacle.

In some unaccountable way Mr. Beck constituted himself a master of the ceremonies, a kind of assessor to the court.

"You had best take the gun down," he said to the Coroner as they were leaving the room.

"Certainly, certainly," replied the Coroner.

"And the water-bottle," added Mr. Beck.

"There is no suspicion of poison, is there?"

"It's best not to take anything for granted," replied Mr. Beck sententiously.

"By all means if you think so," replied the obsequious Coroner. "Constable, take that water-bottle down with you."

The large room was filled with people of the neighbourhood, mostly farmers from the Berkly estate and small shopkeepers from the neighbouring village.

A table had been wheeled to the top of the room for the Coroner, with a seat at it for the ubiquitous local newspaper correspondent. A double row of chairs was set at the right hand of the table for the jury.

The jury had just returned from viewing the body when the crunch of wheels and hoofs was heard on the gravel of the drive, and a two-horse phaeton pulled up sharp at the entrance.

A moment later there came into the room a handsome, soldier-like man, with a girl clinging to his arm, whom he supported with tender, protecting fondness that was very touching. The girl's face was pale, but wonderfully sweet and winsome; cheeks with the faint, pure flush of the wild rose, and eyes like a wild fawn's.

No need to tell Mr. Beck that here were Colonel Peyton and his daughter. He saw the look—shy, piteous, loving—that the girl gave John Neville as she passed close to the table where he sat with his head buried in his hands; and the detective's face darkened for a moment with a stern purpose, but the next moment it resumed its customary look of good-nature and good-humour.

The gardener, the gamekeeper, and the butler were briefly examined by the Coroner, and rather clumsily cross-examined by Mr. Waggles, the solicitor whom Eric had thoughtfully secured for his cousin's defence.

As the case against John Neville gradually darkened into grim certainty, the girl in the far corner of the room grew white as a lily, and would have fallen but for her father's support.

"Does Mr. John Neville offer himself for examination?" said the Coroner, as he finished writing the last words of the butler's deposition describing the quarrel of the night before.

"No, sir," said Mr. Waggles. "I appear for Mr. John Neville, the accused, and we reserve our defence."

"I really have nothing to say that hasn't been already said," added John Neville quietly.

"Mr. Neville," said Mr. Waggles pompously, "I must ask you to leave yourself entirely in my hands."

"Eric Neville!" called out the Coroner. "This is the last witness, I think."

Eric stepped in front of the table and took the Bible in his hand. He was pale, but quiet and composed, and there was an unaffected grief in the look of his dark eyes and in the tone of his soft voice that touched every heart—except one.

He told his story shortly and clearly. It was quite plain that he was most anxious to shield his cousin. But in spite of this, perhaps because of this, the evidence went horribly against John Neville.

The answers to questions criminating his cousin had to be literally dragged from him by the Coroner.

With manifest reluctance he described the quarrel at dinner the night before.

"Was your cousin very angry?" the Coroner asked.

"He would not be human if he were not angry at the language used."

"What did he say?"

"I cannot remember all he said."

"Did he say to your uncle: 'Well, you will not live for ever?' No answer.

"Come, Mr. Neville, remember you are sworn to tell the truth."

In an almost inaudible whisper came the words: "He did."

"I'm sorry to pain you, but I must do my duty.

"When you heard the shot you ran straight to your uncle's room, about fifty yards, I believe?"

"About that."

"Whom did you find there bending over the dead man?"

"My cousin. I am bound to say he appeared in the deepest grief."

"But you saw no one else?"

"No."

"Your cousin is, I believe, the heir to Squire Neville's property; the owner I should say now?"

"I believe so."

"That will do; you can stand down."

This interchange of question and answer, each one of which seemed to fit the rope tighter and tighter round John Neville's neck, was listened to with hushed eagerness by the room full of people.

There was a long, deep drawing-in of breath when it ended. The suspense seemed over, but not the excitement.

Mr. Beck rose as Eric turned from the table, quite as a matter of course, to question him.

"You say you *believe* your cousin was your uncle's heir— don't you *know* it?"

Then Mr. Waggles found his voice.

"Really, sir," he broke out, addressing the Coroner, "I must protest. This is grossly irregular. This person is not a professional gentleman. He represents no one. He has no *locus standi* in court at all.

No one knew better than Mr. Beck that technically he had no title to open his lips; but his look of quiet assurance, his calm assumption of unmistakable right, carried the day with the Coroner.

"Mr. Beck," he said, "has, I understand been brought down specially from London to take charge of this case, and I certainly shall not stop him in any question he may desire to ask."

"Thank you, sir," said Mr. Beck, in the tone of a man whose clear right has been allowed. Then again to the witness: "Didn't you know John Neville was next heir to Berkly Manor?"

"I know it, of course."

"And if John Neville is hanged you will be the owner?"

Every one was startled at the frank brutality of the question so blandly asked. Mr. Waggles bobbed up and down excitedly; but Eric answered, calmly as ever—"That's very coarsely and cruelly put."

"But it's true?"

"Yes, it's true."

"We will pass from that. When you came into the room after the murder, did you examine the gun?"

"I stretched out my hand to take it, but my cousin stopped me. I must be allowed to add that I believe he was actuated, as he said, by a desire to keep everything in the room untouched. He locked the door and carried off the key. I was not in the room afterwards."

"Did you look closely at the gun?"

"Not particularly."

"Did you notice that both barrels were at half cock?"

"No."

"Did you notice that there was no cap on the nipple of the right barrel that had just been fired?"

"Certainly not."

"That is to say you did not notice it?"

"Yes."

"Did you notice a little burnt line traced a short distance on the wood of the stock towards the right nipple?"

"No."

Mr. Beck put the gun into his hand.

"Look close. Do you notice it now?"

"I see it now for the first time."

"You cannot account for it, I suppose?"

"No."

"Sure?"

"Quite sure."

All present followed this strange, and apparently purposeless cross-examination with breathless interest, groping vainly for its meaning.

The answers were given calmly and clearly, but those that looked closely saw that Eric's nether lip quivered, and it was only by a strong effort of will that he held his calmness.

Through the blandness of Mr. Beck's voice and manner a subtle suggestion of hostility made itself felt, very trying to the nerves of the witness.

"We will pass from that," said Mr. Beck again. "When you went into your uncle's room before the shot why did you take a book from the shelf and put it on the table?"

"I really cannot remember anything about it."

"Why did you take the water-bottle from the window and stand it on the book?"

"I wanted a drink."

"But there was none of the water drunk."

"Then I suppose it was to take it out of the strong sun."

"But you set it in the strong sun on the table?"

"Really I cannot remember those trivialities." His self-control was breaking down at last.

"Then we will pass from that," said Mr. Beck a third time.

He took the little scraps of paper with the burnt holes through them from his waistcoat pocket, and handed them to the witness.

"Do you know anything about these?"

There was a pause of a second. Eric's lips tightened as if with a sudden spasm of pain. But the answer came clearly enough—

"Nothing whatever."

"Do you ever amuse yourself with a burning glass?"

This seeming simple question was snapped suddenly at the witness like a pistol-shot.

"Really, really," Mr. Waggles broke out, "this is mere trifling with the Court."

"That question does certainly seem a little irrelevant, Mr. Beck," mildly remonstrated the Coroner.

"Look at the witness, sir," retorted Mr. Beck sternly. "He does not think it irrelevant."

Every eye in court was turned on Eric's face and fixed there.

All colour had fled from his cheeks and lips; his mouth had fallen open, and he stared at Mr. Beck with eyes of abject terror.

Mr. Beck went on remorselessly: "Did you ever amuse yourself with a burning glass?"

No answer.

"Do you know that a water-bottle like this makes a capital burning glass?"

Still no answer.

"Do you know that a burning glass has been used before now to touch off a cannon or fire a gun?"

Then a voice broke from Eric at last, as it seemed in defiance of his will; a voice unlike his own—loud, harsh, hardly articulate; such a voice might have been heard in the torture chamber in the old days when the strain on the rack grew unbearable.

"You devilish bloodhound!" he shouted. "Curse you, curse you, you've caught me! I confess it—I was the murderer!" He fell on the ground in a fit.

"And you made the sun your accomplice!" remarked Mr. Beck, placid as ever.

OUT OF THIS WORLD

By Peter Godfrey (1917-   )

Peter Godfrey has written so many short stories that even he doesn't have a complete record of where and when they were all published. Many of these stories are of crime and mystery, and in Rolf Le Roux he has created one of the most thoughtful and intelligent of modern detectives. The cases he investigates include a number so bizarre and impossible that only the most ingenious of solutions will suffice. Godfrey's stories have long been favorites with magazine and anthology editors, but surprisingly only one volume of Le Roux's cases has ever appeared, Death Under the Table, published only in Godfrey's native South Africa in 1954 and now so scarce as to be virtually unobtainable. From that collection we present for the first time in the United States in its original form one of Oom Rolf's most challenging cases.

. . . One of the major attractions of a visit to Cape Town, is a trip to the summit of Table Mountain by aerial cableway. From the upper station glorious vistas of magnificent scenery, stretching for miles in every direction, delight the eye of the beholder . . . The lower station is readily accessible, being served by a feeder bus from the Kloof Nek terminus.
—Contemporary Guide Book.

AND that day, the last day of March, was the same as all the others. After the test run at 9:30 a.m. the passengers began to arrive, and every half-hour the driver in his cabin at the top of Table Mountain started the cableway in operation. The car at the upper station descended, and the lower car ascended. Passengers came up and passengers went down, gawking at the magnificent panorama over the head of the blasé conductor in each car.

No accelerations, decelerations or stoppages. Seven minutes to complete the journey. Seven minutes for those at the lower station to reach the top of the mountain, the same seven minutes for those at the top to get down. A normal day, like all the other days.

And all day the cars went up and down, and the engineer on the upper station chatted with the driver and checked his instruments and read and smoked. And the driver chatted with the engineer and sometimes with a conductor who happened to be on the top at the time, and he operated the motor, and read.

In the restaurant on the summit the proprietress worked and chatted and sold curios and buttered scones and made tea and coffee. In the box-office at the lower station the station-master sold his tickets, and chatted with the conductor who happened to be down at the time, and drank tea.

But, imperceptibly, the sun was crawling across the sky. At 5:30 p.m. the electric hooter moaned its warning that the last trip of the day was commencing, and into the upper car came the straggling sightseers, the engineer came, the proprietress of the restaurant, and, of course, the conductor. Then two bells rang, and they were on their way.

For the space of seven minutes there was nobody on top of the mountain except the driver and the Native labourer. Then the ascending car brought the conductor who would also spend the night on the summit.

The two white men did not smile or chat or joke; but this, too, was normal. They did not like each other. The Native also kept to himself.

And the sun extinguished itself in the ocean, and the lights of the city far below winked brazenly at the softer pinpoints in the sky.

The men at the top of the mountain ate their evening meal in silence, and then one went to bed with a book, but the other walked out to look at the stars. He found the planet for which he was searching, and while he watched it his thoughts circled his mind.

He thought of what he had told the others—of the Being from that planet whom he could see and talk to, but who was invisible to the other men. He wondered if he had done the right thing, talking about the Being; he wondered whether the listeners were beginning to believe.

And then he had other thoughts.

After a long while he went back to the upper station and undressed and climbed into bed. As he had climbed into bed on countless occasions in the past. The last action of a normal day. But to-morrow . . .

And the night grew blacker and then less black. the lights of heaven faded first, and then the lights of the city. The east changed colour. The sun rose.

Brander, the station-master at the lower station, came into the room which housed the landing platform, and peered myopically up along the giant stretch of steel rope. The old Native, Piet, was sweeping out the car which had remained overnight at the lower station—the right-hand car. He said: "Dag, Baas Brander," and let his eyes follow the white man's along the span of the cable.

"Dag, Piet," said Brander.

Two thousand feet above, the upper station looked like a doll's house, perched on the edge of the cliff. The outlines of Table Mountain stood deep-etched by the morning sun. On the flat top of the elevation there was no sign of cloud—the tablecloth, as people in Cape Town call it—and there was no stirring of the air.

Brander thought: "Good weather. No South-easter. We will be operating all day."

And he thought: "Here on the lower station you are on earth, and if you are on the upper station you are also on earth, but going from one to the other along that steel wire, you are neither on earth nor in heaven. You are between. You go from earth to earth, but while you journey you are out of this world."

And then he thought: "When you journey to Mars it must be like that, only there is no lower station and no upper station and no cable."

He mumbled: "Praise the Lord."

Piet started sweeping again, carefully poking the broom edgeways into the corners of the car. He saw Brander looking at him, and grinned. "Baas Dimble is the engineer to-day," he said. "The car must be very clean."

"That's right, Piet," said Brander. "It would be better if Baas Dimble found nothing to complain about here at the lower station. Make a good job. You still have twenty minutes."

In the upper station the driver, Clobber, settled himself in a chair in his cabin and opened the latest issue of *Planet Epics*. He just about had time, he reckoned, to finish the story "Vengeance on Venus" before the test run at 9:30.

Line by line his eyes swallowed words, phrases and sentences. He was just at the critical point when the earthman hero and his gamma-ray robot had been cornered by the evil Venerian Swamp-slugs, when he felt eyes behind him. Without looking he knew it was Heston who had come in, and he had an annoying mental image of thin lips contorting in a sardonic smile.

Only, when he turned, Heston's face was as serious as always. "Did I interrupt you?" he asked.

"Oh go to hell," said Clobber. He marked the place in his book and put it down. He asked: "Well?"

"I just wanted to talk to you," said Heston.

"Or pull my leg about the science fiction I read? I tell you, Heston, I'm getting pretty fed up with your attitude. I can take a joke as well as anybody, but the way you keep on about this man from Mars—well, it's getting a little too thick. I read the stuff because I like it, see—and I'm not the only one who does. This stunt of yours may have been funny to start with, but I'm damned if it's funny now. Cut it out, do you hear?"

Heston looked hurt.

"I don't know why you keep thinking I'm joking," he said. "I'm not smiling, am I? I know it sounds insane, but you must believe me because it's true. I thought you'd understand, just because you do read science fiction. Gha does exist. I can see him and talk to him even though you can't."

Clobber said: "Oh, my God!"

"But it's not about him I want to talk to you—at least, he only comes into it indirectly. It's more of a personal problem. Do you mind?"

"All right. Go ahead."

"I'm a bit worried about the trip down."

"Why? You know as well as I do that nothing can go wrong with the cable."

"No, it's not that. It's just . . . Look, Clobber, I don't want you to think I'm pulling your leg, because I'm really very serious. I don't think I'm going to get down alive. You see, yesterday was my birthday—I turned 31 and it was March 31—and I had to spend last night up here. Now, I'm not being superstitious or anything, but I've been warned that the day after my birthday I'd not be alive if my first trip was from the top to the bottom of the mountain. If I hadn't forgotten, I'd have changed shifts with someone, but as it is . . ."

"Look here, Heston, if you're not bluffing, you're the biggest damn fool—"

"I'm not bluffing, Clobber. I mean it. You see, I haven't got a relation in the world. If anything does happen. I'd like you to see that each of the men gets something of mine as a sort of keepsake. You can have my watch, Dimble gets my binoculars—"

"Sure, sure. And your million pound bank account goes to Little Orphan Annie. Don't be a damned fool. Who gave you this idiotic warning, anyway?"

"It was Gha."

"Get to hell out of here, you little rat! Coming here and—"

"But I mean it, Clobber—"

"Get out! It would be a damned good thing for all of us if you didn't reach the bottom alive—"

Dimble, neat and officious but friendly, arrived at the lower station in the station wagon, and with him came the conductor Skager, and Mrs. Orvin who owned and managed the restaurant on the top of the mountain.

Brander shuffled forward to meet them.

"Nice day," said Dimble. "What's your time, Brander? 9:25? Good. I see your watch agrees with mine. Nothing like accuracy, I say. Set my watch night and morning by the wireless. Everything ship-shape here? Good."

In the background Skager scratched a pimple on his neck. Mrs. Orvin said: "How's your hand, Mr. Brander?"

The station-master peered below his glasses at his left hand, which was neatly bound with fresh white bandages. "Getting better slowly, thanks. It's still a little painful. I can't use it much yet."

"Don't like that fellow Heston," said Dimble. "Seems all right at his work, but I don't like his attitude. Nasty trick he played on you, Brander."

"Perhaps it wasn't a trick, Mr. Dimble. Perhaps he didn't know the other end of the iron was hot."

"Nonsense," said Mrs. Orvin. "He probably heated it up specially. I can believe anything of him. Impertinent, that's what he is."

"Even if he did do it," said Brander. "I can't bear any hard feelings."

"You're a religious man, eh Brander? All right in its way, but too impractical. No good turning the other cheek to a chap like Heston. Doesn't appreciate decency, believe me. No, I'm different. If he'd done it to me, I'd have my knife into him." There was unexpected venom in Dimble's tones.

"He'll *get* a knife into him one of these days," said Skager. He hesitated. "He'll be coming down in the first car, won't he?"

"Yes," said Brander.

"And it's just about time," said Dimble. "We'd better get in the car. After you, Mrs. Orvin. So long, Brander."

"Goodbye, Mr. Dimble—Mrs. Orvin—Skager—"

Heston came through the door leading to the landing platform at the upper station. In the car, the Native Ben was still sweeping.

"Hurry up, you lazy black swine," said Heston. "What in hell have you been doing with yourself this morning? It's almost time to go and you're still messing about. Get out of my way."

The Native looked at him with a snarl. "You musn't talk to

me like that. I am not your dog. I have been twenty years with this company, and in all that time nobody has ever spoken to me like that—"

"Then it's time someone started. Go on—get out."

Ben muttered: "I would like to—"

"You'd like to what? Come up behind me when I'm not looking, I suppose? Well, you won't get much chance for that. And don't hang around—voetsak!"

From the driver's cabin they heard the two sharp bells that indicated that the lower car was ready to move. Ben stepped aside. As the upper car began to slide down and away, he went through the door, up the stairs and into the driver's cabin. He looked over Clobber's shoulder through the plate-glass window.

The upper car was then twenty of thirty yards from the station. Both men saw Heston lean out the side of the car and salute them with an exaggerated sweep of his right arm. Both men muttered under their breath.

As the seconds ticked by, the two cars approached each other in mid-air.

In the ascending car Dimble looked at the one that was descending with a critical eye. Suddenly he became annoyed. "That fool," he said. "Look how he's leaning out over the door. Dangerous—"

His voice trailed off. As the cars passed each other, he saw something protruding from Heston's back—something that gleamed sliver for an inch or two and was surmounted by a handle of bright scarlet. Dimble said: "God!"

He reached and jerked the emergency brake. Skager moaned: "He's not leaning." Mrs. Orvin gulped audibly.

"That's my knife," she said, "the one he said the Martian . . ."

The telephone bell in the car rang insistently. Dimble answered it.

"What's the trouble?" came Clobber's voice over the wire.

"It's Heston. He's slumped over the door of the car. There seems to be a knife in his back."

"A knife? Hell! He was alive when he left here, because he waved to me. Ben saw him too . . . What should we do?"

"Just hang on a second. Brander, are you on the other end? Have you heard this conversation?"

"Yes, Mr. Dimble."

"Well, Heston's car is nearer you now. We'll finish the journey. When the car arrives at your station, see if he's still alive. In any event, telephone us right away. Is that clear?"

"Yes, Mr. Dimble."

"All right, Clobber. I'm releasing the brake now. Speed it a little."

"Sure."

The cars moved again.

At the top, Dimble led the rush up the stairs to the driver's cabin, where Clobber's white face greeted them. They waited.

The telephone rang.

Clobber stretched out a tentative hand, but Dimble was ahead of him.

"I've seen him," said Brander's voice, queerly. "He's dead"

"Are you sure?"

"Yes. He's dead."

"Well, look here, Brander, don't touch anything. Get on the phone to the police right away. And let Piet stand guard over the body until they get here. All right?"

"It might be difficult to do that, Mr. Dimble. There are people here already for tickets, so I can't leave the box, and Piet is scared of bodies. He's said so. I've locked the door leading to the car—won't that be enough?"

"No. If anyone there is curious, they can climb round the side, and possibly spoil evidence. Let me speak to Piet."

"Here he is, Mr. Dimble."

"Hullo, Piet. Listen—this is Mr. Dimble here. I want you to go into the room with the car, and see nobody touches anything."

"No, Baas. Not me, Baas. Not with a dead body, Baas."

"Oh, dammit. All right, let me talk to Mr. Brander. Brander? Listen. This is the best plan. Don't sell any tickets—we won't be operating today, anyway. We'll start the cars and stop them halfway, so nobody will be able to get near them. In the meantime, you telephone the police. Do you understand that?"

"Yes, I will telephone the police."

"And give us a ring the moment they are here."

"Yes, Mr. Dimble."

The police came.

Inspector Dirk Joubert was in charge of the party, and with him was his uncle Rolf le Roux, the inevitable *krom-steel* protruding through the forest of his beard. Facetious Detective-Sergeant Johnson was there, serious Sergeant Botha, Doc McGregor with his black bag, and several uniformed men.

They all mounted the steps to the lower station building, and found Brander waiting for them.

"Where is the body?" asked Joubert.

Brander told them, walked out of the ticket office to point out the two cable cars opposite each other, high above, in the centre of the abyss.

"If you're going to examine the body today, Doc," said Johnson, "you'd better start walking the wire. Here, I'll give you a hand up."

Brander said: "Oh, no, the driver at the top can bring the car back to where we are standing."

Johnson grinned. "You don't say."

"Oh yes." He remembered: "I'm supposed to ring Mr. Dimble the engineer as soon as you had arrived. Would you like to speak to him?"

"Yes," said Joubert.

They walked back to the ticket office. Brander made the connection. "Hullo," he said, "hullo, Mr. Dimble. The police are here. They would like to talk to you."

Joubert took the instrument from his proffered hand. "Yes? Inspector Joubert talking. We'd like you to let the car with the body come down here. What's that? No. It'd be better if you people stayed on top of the mountain until I telephone you again. Hullo! Just one moment. While we're about it, you might give me an idea of what happened. I see. You went up in the right-hand car, and as you passed the left-hand car halfway you saw the knife sticking out of his back. And then? Yes. Yes. And why did you move the car with the body halfway back again? Mm. No, that's all right—it was quite a good idea. Well look, I'll get a full statement from you later. You'd better tell the driver to get the cars started. Goodbye now."

Almost as soon as he put the receiver down the cable began to whine.

They walked back to the room which housed the landing platform, and watched the approaching car. When it was still a fair distance away they could see the figure slumped over the gate, quite clearly, with the scarlet splash of the knife-handle protruding from its back.

"I can tell you one thing right now," said McGregor. "It's no' a suicide."

"It is the will of the Lord," said Brander.

The car jerked slightly to a stop.

"You men go to work," said Joubert. "I want to talk to Mr. Brander."

Rolf walked to one side with the two men.

"Look, Brander," said Joubert. "I know roughly what happened from Mr. Dimble, but I'd like your side of it. When the car came down, did you examine the body?"

"No."

"Why not?"

"He was dead. I could see that."

"And did anyone else come near the body before the driver hoisted it off? This Native, Piet?"

"No, not Piet. He is afraid of bodies. He would not go near the car. He stood at the door until the motors started, though, in case anyone else wanted to go through."

"Who else could have gone through?"

"Well, there was a man and two women here—passengers—but they left when I wouldn't sell them tickets."

Joubert started on a new track. "Heston was his name, wasn't it? Yes. Tell me, Brander, what sort of a man was he? Was there anyone working here who hated him?"

Brander hesitated. "I do not like to talk about him. He is dead now. What does it matter what he was like in life? Now he is a soul on Mars."

It was Rolf who queried the last word: "Mars?"

"Yes." Something almost like animation shone behind Brander's thick glasses. "I see you have not heard of Scientific Calvinism?"

"No," said Rolf. "What is it?"

"A religion. I am a Believer. Let me try and explain. We all know there is a heaven, the seat of the Almighty. Yet so few people have tried to find where heaven is. I don't want to go into long details, but Eremiah, the founder of Scientific Calvinism, has proved beyond any shadow of doubt that what we call heaven is in reality the planet Mars. If you are interested, I have some books—"

"Not just now," said Joubert. "I want you to answer my question. Is there anybody here who hated Heston?"

"He was not liked," said Brander, "but nobody here hated him enough to kill him."

"No? Someone stuck a knife in his back, all the same. Who could have done it?"

"The angel of death," said Brander. "The mighty messenger from Mars. It was the will of the Lord."

"And that is all you can tell me?"

"That is all I know."

Brander went back to the ticket office. Joubert walked out whistling. He came back a few seconds later, and behind him two uniformed attendants carried a long basket.

"Well, doc?" asked Joubert.

"One blow," said McGregor. "A verra clean swift blow. No mess. The murderer struck him from behind and above. Either the killer stood on something, or he was a verra tall man."

"Or woman?"

"Maybe. I canna say one way or another."

Johnson had evidently been eavesdropping on the examination of Brander. He asked: "Could it have been an angel, doc, or a Martian? You know one of those thin seven-foot monstrosities with no ears and pop-eyes?"

McGregor looked at him stolidly.

"Well," said Johnson, "at least the height seems to fit. And another thing: Martians don't have hands, do they? They have tentacles, satin-smooth and very pliable and strong as iron."

"What are you getting at the noo?" asked McGregor.

"Telling you something, doc. You see, this murderer didn't leave fingerprints."

Joubert said: "Cut out the nonsense, Johnson. So the man wore gloves. All right. Doc, you go back with the body and do the p.m. If anything else crops up, telephone me here. Let's go and talk to this Native, Piet."

But Piet knew nothing. He was old and superstitious and very afraid of death. He had not even looked at the body. The nearest he had come to it was to stand on guard on the other side of a closed door.

Brander telephoned Dimble, and handed the instrument to Joubert.

"We're coming up, Dimble. What is the signal for starting the car? Two bells—right. Some of my men will be on this station. No, I don't care about the rules about conductors on every trip. We're coming up without one, and the car at the top can come down without one too. All right—so it's irregular. I'll take the responsibility. Nobody on top must come down, do you hear? We'll want to interview you one at a time. Is there a room there we can use? The restaurant? Right. You'll hear the signal in a couple of minutes."

Joubert, Oom Rolf and Johnson. Four uniformed policemen. Going up in the car in which death had come down.

"I don't think we'll be long," said Joubert. "The solution's on top, obviously."

Rolf said: "How do you make that out?"

"When the cars reached the middle of the run, Heston already had the knife in his back. There was nobody with him in the car, or he'd have been seen. Therefore, Heston must have been killed before he left the top. One of the men stationed up there is the chap we're looking for."

"Maybe," said Johnson, grinning, "and maybe the Martian who did it was one of the invisible breed."

Rolf looked worried. He said to Joubert: "I hope you are right."

"Of course I am right. It's the only possible explanation."

"So what are you going to do? First question the men who were on top when the cars started this morning?"

"No. Let them stew in their own juice for a while. This Dimble seems a proper fuss pot—better get him over first."

Dimble.

"And so I told Brander to see the body was guarded, and when I found Piet was afraid, I told him—"

"Right. Mr. Dimble. We've got all that. Now, just let me get one thing clear. The two men, apart from Heston, who stayed on the mountain last night, were Clobber the driver and the Native Ben?"

"Yes."

"Did either of these two men have anything against Heston?"

"Probably. Heston wasn't a very likable chap, you know. But I don't think anyone would murder him."

Joubert said again: "Someone did. Now look, Dimble—to your knowledge did either Clobber or Ben have anything against Heston?"

"Not to my knowledge, no. They may have. For that matter we all disliked him. He was always doing something damned foolish. Like practical jokes—only there was malice behind them, and he never acted as though he was joking. Never could be sure. Nasty type."

Rolf interposed: "What sort of actions are you talking about Mr. Dimble?"

"Well, like putting an emetic in my sandwiches when I wasn't looking. Couldn't prove it was him, though. And burning Brander's hand."

Joubert said: "I noticed his left hand was in bandages. What happened?"

"Heston handed him a length of iron to hold, and it was all but red-hot."

"I see. So it would appear that both you and Brander had cause to hate the man?"

"Cause, yes, and I must admit I didn't like him. But Brander is different. We were talking about it this morning, and he didn't seem to bear any grudge. He's a religious type, you know."

"So I gathered," said Joubert, drily.

Dimble went on: "And that reminds me. Skager had it in for Heston, too. When I mentioned that if it had been my hand he had burned. I'd have my knife in for him. Skager said that one day someone *would* . . . Hey! That's ironic, isn't it?"

"Yes," said Joubert, "All right, Dimble. Let's have Skager."

A pasty, gangling man, who had not long left youth behind him, but still carried youth's pimples.

"I didn't mean anything by it, Inspector. It's just an expression. I didn't like him."

"So you didn't like him, and you just used an expression? Doesn't it strike you as strange that a few minutes later Heston did have a knife in his back?"

"I haven't thought about it."

"Well, think now. Skager, why did you hate Heston?"

"Look, Inspector, I had nothing to do with the murder. How could I have killed him?"

"How do you know how he was killed? I tell you, Skager, I'm prepared to arrest any man who attempts to hide his motives. Now, answer my question."

A slight pause of defiance, then—

"Well, I don't suppose it makes any difference. I've got a girl friend. Some time ago someone rang her up and told her not to go out with me because I had an incurable disease. It took me weeks before I could get near enough to convince her it was a lie."

"And you thought Heston made the phonc-call?"

"Yes."

"Why?"

"Well, I don't know. Maybe it was because he was always talking about my pimples. In any case, it was just the kind of thing he would do."

"So you hated him, eh Skager—hated him enough to kill him?"

"Why do you pick on me, Inspector? Honest, I don't know anything about the murder. Why don't you speak to Mrs. Orvin? She said the knife was hers—she said something about a Martian—"

Joubert asked, very distincly: "She said something about what?"

"A Martian."

Johnson grinned.

Mrs. Orvin said: "The knife was mine. My brother-in-law sent it to me from the Belgian Congo."

"What did you use it for?"

"Mainly as an ornament. It was kept on this shelf under the glass of the counter. I've used it once or twice as a paper knife."

"So anyone could have taken it while you were in the kitchen?"

"Yes. That's what must have happened."

"When did you find it was missing?"

"Last Tuesday."

"And when had you last seen it previous to that?"

"A few minutes before. You see, I had been using it to cut some string, and then I put it down to go into the kitchen—"

"Just a minute, Mrs. Orvin. Was there anyone else in the restaurant at the time?"

"Yes, quite a few people. There were four or five tourists and Heston and Clobber."

"Clobber was here?"

"Yes, having his tea. He sat at the far corner table."

"And Heston?"

"At first he was on the balcony, but when I came back from the kitchen he was sitting at this table."

"So when you missed the knife, what did you do?"

"I went to speak to Heston. You see, I was quite sure just where I had left it, and so—"

Heston looked up innocently at her. "Yes, Mrs. Orvin?"

"Mr. Heston, have you by any chance seen my knife?"

"You mean the big one with the red handle? Of course I have. You were using it a minute ago."

"Well, it's gone now. Did you see anyone take it?"

"No, I didn't see anyone take it, Mrs. Orvin, but I know who's got it all the same."

"Who?"

"Gha."

"What?"

"Gha. Oh, I'm sorry. You don't know about him, do you? Gha's a man from Mars, very tall and thin and strong, but you can't see him or hear him—only I can do that. He told me he needed a knife."

"Mr. Heston, if this is you idea of a joke, I don't think it's very funny. If you've got my knife, please give it to me."

"I haven't got your knife, Mrs. Orvin. And I'm not joking about Gha—it's perfectly true. Some of the other men at the station also know about him.

"Why don't you ask Clobber?"

"And did you ask Clobber, Mrs. Orvin?"

"Yes."

"What did he say?"

"He muttered something about liking to break Heston's neck."

"And about the knife?"

"He said he didn't know anything at all about that."

"Well, thanks. I think that will be all for now. Don't call anyone else for the moment, Mrs. Orvin. We'll let them know when we want them."

Mrs. Orvin left.

Rolf allowed a puff of smoke to billow through his beard. He said to Johnson: "Everywhere we go, we bump into your Martian."

"Martian, nothing," said Joubert. "This is murder, not fantasy. Someone wearing gloves killed Heston, and that person did it on top of the mountain. It can only be one of two men—the Native or Clobber. I fancy Clobber."

"And what will you say," asked Rolf, "if we find that Heston was alive when he left the upper station? Will you then believe in the Martian?"

"Not even then," said Joubert. "Heston couldn't have been alive—there is no possible way of stabbing a man suspended by himself two thousand feet above anything. All I would say is that the impression was given that Heston was alive when he left the mountain—that a clever alibi has been created. And no matter how good an alibi is, it can always be broken."

"I still have a feeling about this case," said Rolf.

"There are too many feelings altogether. What we need are a few facts. Let's get Clobber in."

One of the policemen went to call him.

Clobber's face was pale. He was still wearing the dirty dustcoat he used while driving. Joubert looked at something protruding from the pocket, and glanced significantly at Johnson and Rolf.

"Do you always wear cotton gloves?" he asked Clobber.

"Yes. They keep my hands clean."

"I see. They also have another very useful purpose. They don't leave fingerprints."

Clobber paled even more. "What are you getting at? I didn't kill Heston. He was alive when he left the summit."

"And dead when he passed the other car halfway down? Come off it, Clobber. He must have been killed up here. Either you or Ben are guilty."

Clobber said: "Neither of us did it. I tell you he was alive when he left."

"That's what you say. The point is, can you prove it?"

"Yes, I think so. After the car had started, when he was about twenty yards out, he leaned over the side of the car and waved to me. Ben had just come into my cabin. He saw him too."

"Where was Ben before that?"

"He was with Heston at the car."

A new gleam came into Joubert's eye. He leaned forward.

"Look, Clobber," he said, "what was there to prevent Ben stabbing Heston just as the car pulled away?"

"I suppose he could have. Only, as I've told you, Ben was with me when Heston waved."

"Think carefully now, Clobber. Are you sure it was a wave you saw? Couldn't it possible have been that the body was wedged upright, and you saw it as it slumped over the door?"

"No, definitely not. The arm moved up and down two or three times. He was alive. I'm sure of that."

Joubert flung up his hands in a gesture of impatience.

"All right then. Say he was alive. How do you explain the fact that halfway down the knife was in his back? Who could have done it?"

Clobber looked harassed. "I don't know. The only idea . . . It doesn't make sense. It can't be right."

"What idea?"

"Well, I'd better explain a bit. I had a talk with Heston this morning. He hold me he didn't expect to get to the bottom of the mountain alive."

Rolf echoed: "Didn't expect?"

"Yes. He said he'd been warned. His 31st birthday was yesterday—the 31st of the month—and he'd been told that if he spent last night on top of the mountain he'd never reach the bottom alive. I thought he was pulling my leg."

"Warned? Who warned him?"

"That was a queer thing. He used to claim that he could see and hear an invisible creature from Mars, called Gha. That's where he got the warning."

Joubert threw up the sponge. "Oh my God," he said.

Johnson grinned again, but Rolf's face was serious. "Tell me, Mr. Clobber," he said, "how long ago is it since Heston started talking about this man from Mars?"

"Oh, quite a while now. I took it as a sort of peculiar joke."

"Why? Did he laugh or wink about it?"

"No. He was always dead serious, but I thought it was a definite dig at me."

"Why?"

"Well, he knew I'm fond of reading science fiction magazines, and he was a queer sort of fellow. It seemed to me he turned the conversation to Gha the moment I came in. Or Brander—you know about his religion, of course?"

"Yes."

"I thought it was just a crude way of being sarcastic. Just a minute. Yes. I think I remember the first time he mentioned Gha."

"When was that?"

"About a month ago. You see, I'd just come off duty and I was hanging around at the lower station. Heston was there and Brander, and somehow or other the conversation led to the subject of death—"

Clobber said: "When a man dies, he leaves his body behind. Now, I don't believe that there's any spiritual worth in it—once you're gone, your body's just a mixture of chemicals. That's why I can't agree with all the hocus-pocus of funerals and holding the dead in awe. There should be a law compelling the use of bodies for practical purposes—making fertiliser, medical research, any-thing—but not hiding them in holes in the ground under fancy headstones."

Brander was shocked. "Oh, no, Clobber. You're wrong. You are wrong. Your body is not worth much while you are alive, because it only exists as a compartment for the human soul. Nothing can remove that soul from that body except the Lord or one of his angels, and when that is done, the body is automatically sanctified. It has received the holy touch of Mars. I have a pamphlet inside if you will wait a minute—"

"No, don't bother, Brander. I know about your religion. Remember that book you lent me? I read it. Really. I don't think the arguments are particularly scientific. You know, astronomers know quite a bit about Mars today, and we can say with quite a lot of certainty that there is no life such as we know it on earth—"

"But that is just the point, Mr. Clobber—of course the life on Mars is not like life on earth. It is a spiritual life, a life of the soul—"

Heston broke in suddenly: "You're both right—and both wrong. I know."

Clobber said: "What do you mean you know? What are you getting at?"

"I'll tell you some other time," said Heston. "Here's the station wagon, and I'm in a hurry. Remind me, won't you?"

Joubert said: "And so, when you reminded him, he told you about Gha?"

"Yes."

"And now you believe in him yourself?"

"I don't know what to believe."

Joubert rose. "Well, I do. There are no men from Mars, and nothing here except a cleverly planned murder. And God help you if you did it, Clobber—because I'm going to smash your alibi."

"You can't smash the truth," said Clobber. "In any case, why should I be the one under suspicion?"

"One of the reasons," said Joubert, "is that you wear gloves."

Clobber grinned for the first time. "Then you'll have to widen your suspect list. We all wear them up here. Dimble has a pair. Ben, too. And, yes, Mrs. Orvin generally carries kid gloves."

"All right," said Joubert, savagely. "That's enough for now. Tell Ben we want to see him."

Ben came, gave his evidence, and went.

"If I could prove that he and Clobber were collaborating." Joubert started, but Rolf stopped him with a shake of his head.

"No, Dirk. There is nothing between them. I could see that. You could see it, too.

Johnson asked, suddenly: "What price the Martian now?"

"All that talk," said Joubert, "is just a red herring. I'll admit I don't see how the murder could have been done, but it was—and not by a Martian. Someone has worked out a careful scheme. What one mind has thought of before, we can think of again."

"Another trouble," said Johnson, "is to work out whose mind did the thinking. You pays your penny and you takes your choice. On the surface of things, nobody could possibly have done it. We have searched the car pretty thoroughly, and there's no trace of any sort of apparatus that might explain the stabbing of a man in mid-air. The knife couldn't have been thrown, and the only way it could have been shot out of a weapon is from the sky—the wound came from above, remember—and a plane or balloon would certainly have been noticed. There's just no explanation—except the Martian."

Rolf le Roux took his pipe from his mouth.

"Seriously," he said, "there's more about this Gha than meets the eye."

Joubert snarled: "Now, Oom, don't tell me you believe —?"

Rolf's eyes twinkled. He asked: "What other explanation can you offer?"

"None. Not now, anyway. But even at this stage there are certain facts that stand out. First, this is a carefully premeditated crime. Second, it was done before the car left the summit—"

"No, Dirk. The most important facts in this case lie in what Heston told Clobber—that Gha had warned him he was to be killed—the significance of his last night on the mountain—his 31st birthday—"

"What are you getting at, Oom?"

"I think I know how and why he was killed, Dirk. It is only a theory now, and I do not like to talk until I have proof. But you can help me get that proof . . ."

The word went round. A reconstruction of the crime. Everyone must do exactly as he did when Heston was killed.

Whispers.

"Who's going to take Heston's place?"

"The elderly chap with the beard; Le Roux, I think his name is. The one they call Oom Rolf."

"Do you think they'll find out anything? Do you think—"

"We'll know soon enough, anyway."

On the lower station Joubert pressed the button which rang the signal for the reconstruction to start. Dimble, Mrs. Orvin and Skager went towards the bottom car. Sergeant Botha went, too.

Rolf Le Roux came through the door of the upper landing platform and looked at Ben sweeping out the empty car.

He said: "Baas Heston spoke to you, and you stopped sweeping?"

"Yes. And then I came out of the car like this."

"And then?"

"Then we talked."

"Where did Baas Heston stand?"

"He got into the car, and stood near the door. Yes, just about there." He paused. "Do you think you will find out who killed him?"

"It is possible."

"I hope not, Baas. This Heston was a bad man."

"All the same, it was not right that he should be killed. The murderer must be punished."

Two sharp bells rang in the driver's cabin. The car began to move. Ben went through the door up the stairs and stood in the cabin with Clobber and Johnson. They saw Rolf lean over and wave with an exaggerated gesture.

Clobber reached to lift a pair of binoculars, but Johnson gripped his arm. "Wait. Did you pick them up at this stage the first time?"

"No. I only used them after the emergency brake was applied."

"Then leave them alone now."

They watched the two cars crawling slowly across space towards each other.

In the ascending car Dimble peered approvingly at the one which was descending. "That's right," he said to Botha. "He's leaning over the door exactly as Heston—Good God!"

He pulled the emergency brake. Mrs. Orvin sobbed and then screamed.

The telephone rang. Botha clapped the instrument to his ear.

"Everything okay?" asked Johnson from above.

"No," said Botha, "no. Something's happened to Rolf. There's a knife sticking out of his back. It looks like the same knife . . ."

From the lower station Joubert cut in excitedly. "What are you saying, Botha? It's impossible."

"It's true, Inspector. I can see it quite clearly from here. And he's not moving . . ."

"What now?" asked Johnson.

"Get him down here," said Joubert. "Quick. He may still be alive."

The cars moved again.

In the driver's cabin Johnson looked through the powerful binoculars, watched the car with the sagging figure go down, down, losing sight of it only as it entered the lower station.

Joubert, with Brander, stood at the end of the room watching the approaching car. He felt suddenly lost and bewildered and angry. "Oom Rolf," he muttered.

Brander's eyes were sombre with awe. "The Lord has given," he said, "and the Lord has taken away. Blessed be the name of the Lord."

He stepped forward ahead of Joubert as the car bumped to a stop, walking with both hands raised, lips intoning a prayer. "You have sanctified this mortal with death, O Lord; you have taken his soul for your own to the golden fields of Mars . . ."

The head of the corpse with the knife in its back suddenly twisted, smiled, said gloatingly: "April Fool!"

Brander shivered into shocking action. With his bandaged left hand he gripped the hilt of the knife that had been held between Rolf's left arm and his body, and raised it high in a convulsive gesture. Rolf twisted away, but his movement was unnecessary. Joubert had acted, too.

Brander struggled, but only for a second. Then he stood meekly, peering in myopic surprise at the handcuffs clicking round his wrists.

"And that is how Heston was killed," said Rolf. "He died because last night on the mountain he remembered that today was April 1—All Fools Day—and because his was that type of mind, he thought of a joke, and he played it to the bitter end. A joke on Clobber, on the people in the ascending car, on Brander. And Brander, because he is the man he is, could not tolerate such blasphemy, and made the joke come true."

"It was the will of the Lord," said Brander.

"And that is also why there were no fingerprints on the knife. Brander is lefthanded—he reached for the hot iron with that hand, remember—and because he reached for the hot iron with that hand it was burnt, and so today it is bandaged. And because it was bandaged he could leave no fingerprints. The way Heston was stooping, too, explains the angle of the wound."

Joubert said, "So it was not premeditated after all." And then to Brander: " And why did you not tell the truth?"

Brander looked up in surprise. "But I did—I told you it was the Angel. Don't you see? My arm may have struck the blow, but it was not me who killed Heston. The Angel of Death did that. The Mighty Messenger from Mars entered my body the better to punish the evil one who scoffed at holy death . . ."

And he said suddenly: "On your knees, mortals! This spot is sanctified. The Messenger has been here—flashing through chaos from golden Mars to green earth, from green earth to golden Mars. And from this place he has taken a Soul."

And he mumbled, and his voice tailed off in the wake of his eyes, and his gaze saw far beyond the mountain and the blue of the sky.

THE MYSTERY OF THE HOTEL DE L'ORME

By M. M. B.

The Victorian era teemed with all manner of magazines. One of the most notable was London Society, "an illustrated magazine of light and amusing literature for the hours of relaxation." It offered, at a very affordable price, a 100-plus page mixture of prose and poetry, of fact and fiction, and all generously decorated with full-page engravings. The Christmas and Holiday numbers, well-stocked with ghosts and mysteries, are particulary interesting but the present tale, from the pen of the impenetrably initialled "M. M. B.," appeared in a standard issue of 1862, only the second year of the magazine's life. Whoever M. M. B. may have been, he or she combined melodramatic Victorian writing with a locked-room method worthy of the next century's classic puzzlers.

THE little town of St. Bignold was in a ferment when, early in the forenoon of the 8th of October, 1812, a report rang through it that a murder had been committed within its walls. Such a thing had not been heard of for years; not, at all events, since the Comte de l'Orme's marriage with the blackeyed daughter of Lopez, the moneylender—the event from which all the late great occurrences at St. Bignold were dated—and strangely enough the victim of the atrocious deed was Madame de l'Orme herself.

Every one at St. Bignold knew how ill that unequal marriage had turned out; indeed, could it be otherwise when it was only for her wealth that the young handsome comte had sold himself to the high-tempered, jealous heiress? Yet at the time all had admired his self-sacrifice, for it was well known that it was made not for his own sake alone, but for that of his orphan sisters and brother, who without it had been left portionless and uneducated. For them he sacrificed his liberty, for them he bound himself for life to one whose golden attractions far exceeded those of her person, and whose pride, self-will, and jealousy, rendered the first five years after their marriage one long-continued succession of disputes and discomforts. At the end of that time old Lopez died; and soon afterwards it was announced that the Comte de l'Orme had volunteered for the Russian campaign.

No one was astonished, and all were rejoiced to learn that he had discovered so glorious and exemplary a means of escaping from the thraldom in which he had hitherto been held; but they were amazed, indeed, when a week or two after his departure the comtesse broke up her establishment at the castle, and removed to the strange old house at St. Bignold, bequeathed to her by her father.

The reasons for this change it was difficult to discover, and no one had a right to question them. Yet, the "Hotel de l'Orme," as the neighbours had nicknamed old Lopez's dwelling-place on his daughter's marriage, was not the place likely to be selected as the abode of a woman so proud of her rank, and so resolute in resisting the slightest approach to familiarity from any one she chose to consider her inferior.

It is true that the comtesse had had the original entrance to the house built up, and a new approach made to it through a cul-de-sac opening almost directly into the better part of the town; and probably she imagined that by this precaution she had acquired an aristocratic retirement for her mansion, which certainly boasted of some apartments of good size. But to one really alive to the *bienséances* of life the situation of the house would have caused incessant annoyance, for the original front abutted on one of the worst streets of St. Bignold, inhabited by the very poorest of the people, whose windows completely commanded those of the hotel. One often sees such streets as the Rue Sylvaine in ancient walled towns, where the contracted space obliged the architects to make height take the place of breadth, where the gabled houses rise to an immense height, and each story overhangs the one beneath, until the uppermost ones almost meet in the centre, leaving between scarce one narrow strip of sky, and entirely shutting out the rays of the joyful, health-giving sun. Such was the case in the Rue Sylvaine; and of course the Hotel de l'Orme was as dark and dismal as possible, in spite of its carved windows and the really elegant balustrades which ran along the narrow ledge of the third floor, where madame's principal apartments were situated. The furniture and establishment of the hotel were more in keeping with the situation of the house than the rank of its owner. The ground floor was let off to a shoemaker, whose wife took charge of the apartment above in which Madame de l'Orme received the very few persons who visited her on business affairs—visitors of friendship there never were. A few stiff-backed chairs and spider-legged tables, with one or two tiny squares of carpet in the midst of the highly-waxed floors, composed the furniture of these desolate-looking rooms; nor was the private apartment of madame much more luxuriously furnished, except in one respect, and that oddly enough was in mirrors! The whole chamber seemed lined with them. Turn where you would your own face and figure met your gaze, and the room seemed filled to suffocation with the reflected reflections of it. On a stranger the effect at first was very startling. He seemed to find himself in a crowded room, and a moment or two elapsed ere he discovered that the ideal crowd was formed of repeated images of himself. There were, however, no strangers admitted there during Madame de l'Orme's life. After her death there were enough, heaven knows!

The small establishment of this dreary place consisted, besides Madeline the shoemaker's wife, of a coachman and footman, who only entered the house at stated hours to receive orders for the day, and Madame de l'Orme's maid, Julie, a young girl of twenty, the only member of the household of the chateau who had accompanied her mistress to St. Bignold.

To Julie alone were intrusted the mysteries of the sanctum on the third floor; no one else was permitted to cross the threshold of its iron-bound door, no one else was admitted to the slightest degree of confidence from her haughty mistress. The reason of this confidence in so young a girl it had hitherto been impossible to fathom, though many speculated on the strangeness of one in all respects so great a contrast to her mistress, being exempt from the harsh treatment every one else had to bear from Madame de l'Orme. But then, as some one wisely remarked, "Who knew what treatment she really did receive?" Old Madeline reported that Julie said Madame was very good to her; but that might or might not be; who could tell? It was certain that Julie always looked melancholy, and that betokened no very happy home!

Julie's history was a sad and simple one. Her parents had died of fever when she was a mere infant, and the Comte de l'Orme—he was the Comte Auguste then—had taken pity on the pretty homeless child, and had persuaded his mother to have her brought to the château, and educated under her own eye. Thus the little girl was in many things almost a lady, and hence perhaps arose her reserve to those of her own rank, and the few friendships she made among them. On the comte's marriage, Julie was transferred to the new comtesse's care, and had been retained in a confidential capacity near her person ever since. Indeed it was often said that if Madame de l'Orme cared for any one or trusted any one, it was Julie.

Scandal-mongers hinted that the watchful care she bestowed on the orphan might arise less from affection than jealousy; that she was clever enough to see that the best chance of discouraging Monsieur de l'Orme's evident partiality for the young girl was to keep her constantly under her own eye. But this was only scandal. It is true that in his lady's presence it was impossible for him to say even one kind word to the child whose life he had saved, and whom he had hitherto treated with brotherly kindness, but that was all. Yet every one remarked that when Monsieur de l'Orme and his valet left the castle little Julie looked very sad, and when some time afterwards it was certain that they had joined the fatal Russian expedition she looked sadder still. Then the news from the seat of war, how eagerly she listened to it! How pale her cheek grew when a report reached St. Bignold that the division in which Monsieur de l'Orme served had been exposed to great danger at the passage of the Niemen! How her pretty eyes filled with tears when, in spite of the official bulletins of success and victory, faint rumors reached France of the miseries the great army had endured from fatigue, famine and sickness! And how the colour glowed in her softly-rounded cheek when the so-called "glorious victory" of Borodino filled the public ear with delight! What was it to Julie that thousands had fallen on either side? Those in whom St. Bignold was interested were safe. Those? Nay, it was easy to see that Julie thought only of one. *He* was safe! But who was that he? The Comte de l'Orme?

The good news caused excitement even in Madame de l'Orme's cold bosom; and when the dignitaries of St. Bignold requested her to preside at a grand ball to be given in honour of the great event, she graciously acceded to their wishes, and for once, forsaking her usual habits of seclusion, appeared at the ball in a splendid dress and wearing her most magnificent jewels. More than this, she gave Julie permission to attend the civic ball which was to take place the succeeding evening at the Hotel de Ville, in celebration of the same great victory. Julie was charmed at the thought of going. "She had never been at a public ball before," she told Madeline, "and had not danced, actually not danced since— since monsieur left the château. But at this ball she should dance, and with a light heart too, for there would be no more battles, or famine, or misery now, would there? The road to Moscow was open, people said; the false Russians were already at our Emperor's feet, and so the army must return very soon. Ah yes! she should enjoy the ball so much!"

Such was Julie's confidence to her only friend, as, after madame's departure for the ball, she lingered a moment on the threshold of the heavy door of division ere closing it between herself and the outer world till her mistress's return.

Poor Julie! On the very night on which she had promised herself so much enjoyment she sat alone in a prison cell, accused of murdering her benefactress, and without the slightest hope of clearing herself from the imputation.

Chapter II

"Oh that I had one friend, one counsellor in my great need!" she exclaimed in the bitterness of her sorrow; "but I have none, not one. Would to God I had been the victim and not madame! It would have been a moment's pang and then peace. But this hopeless waiting—this shameful death! And Louis, even Louis will never know that I die innocent!"

This last thought was agony indeed. "Louis to believe her guilty of such a crime!" and burying her face in her clasped hands, she wept as if her heart were breaking.

A touch of the shoulder and the sound of a familiar voice roused her from her stupor of grief, and glancing up with a startled air at the speaker, she recognized the old priest who had known her from childhood.

"Take comfort, my daughter," he said, "and trust in God to help you. Remember that though a mother may forget her child, He never forsakes those who trust in Him."

Julie sank at the feet of the good old man.

"Oh mon père, I thank you for those blessed words. And yet there is so much against me that—that though God may know my innocence, and you also may believe it, those stern judges will not."

"Calm yourself, my child, and tell me how it all happened. I will do what I can to help you to prove your innocence, but to be able to do this you must have no concealments from me."

"Indeed, I shall tell you everything, for I have no real crime to confess, mon père, only one little fault; but oh! what misery that has brought!" and sobs checked her utterance.

The good old priest allowed her emotion to have its way for a time, and when she regained her composure she told him the whole truth.

After leaving Madeline and carefully closing the door of communication between herself and the under part of the house, Julie had re-entered the comtesse's apartment and availed herself of the few hours of leisure afforded by her absence to put the finishing touches to the simple white muslin dress she intended to wear at the civic ball. When the dress was complete an allowable vanity induced her to try it on; and as she marked the graceful folds in which it fell round her really elegant figure, the thought occurred to her that, perhaps, a very few weeks only might elapse before she should again wear a white dress along with her *couronne de mariée,* and should kneel with Louis before the altar in the dear old chapel at beautiful de l'Orme.

"With Louis, my daughter?" said Father Sylvestre, interrupting the naive relation.

"Ah, mon père, you must remember Louis, monsieur's own valet?" she said, quickly. "You cannot have forgotton my Louis? As children, we were always together, and afterwards we used to dance together on fête days. When he left de l'Orme with monsieur I thought my heart would break; but we both knew he ought to go, and he went."

"Ah, yes, I remember."

"I knew you could not forget him! she said, with eagerness. "He came back to see me, you know, one little hour before he went with monsieur to that terrible Russia; and since then he has written once or twice to poor Julie. It was not wrong to receive his letters, was it, mon père?" and she raised her pleading dovelike eyes to the old man's face.

"No, my daughter," he answered, gently, as he laid his tremulous hand on her head. "Go on. You thought of Louis and your bridal dress?"

"Yes. But by-and-by more sinful thoughts came into my mind; for my eyes chancing to fall on a beautiful cachemire madame had worn in the morning, I wondered how Louis would like to see such a pretty thing on my shoulders, and then I put it on to see how it would suit my white dress; and it looked so lovely that I turned from one mirror to another to

admire myself in it. And then I—I began to wish I were a rich
lady, and could wear cachemires every day. And when once
that thought took possession of me I went on. I took the
earrings madame had taken out when she made her grande
toilette, and fastened them in my ears; I hung her gold chain
round my neck and clasped her bracelets round my wrists;
and at the sight of every new ornament the wicked thought of
longing to be a lady got more and more hold of me, till at last I
laughed aloud at my delight. The sound seemed to echo on
the stillness of the room, and I almost believed that it was not
my own voice alone that had so strange an effect upon me. I
shuddered, I knew not why, and at last worked myself up to
such a pitch of terror, that, as I glanced uneasily at the
mirror before me, I almost fancied that I saw a man's face
peering at me from between the closed curtains of the
window behind me. I shudder still when I think how terrified I felt when I remembered how lonely and unprotected I
was. But the very excess of my terror checked my screams,
and I stood quite still before the mirror, trying to convince
myself that the momentary glimpse of that face was only a
phantom raised up by my conscience to punish my vanity.
And by-and-by I began to recollect how impossible it was
that any one could gain access to the room, whose only
entrance was through my own chamber, which was only
reached from the staircase with that heavy iron-bound door
always kept so carefully fastened. And as to the windows,
they were forty or fifty feet from the ground. As I reflected
thus, my fears became quieted, and hastily unfastening the
chain and bracelets, I replaced them in the trinket drawer. I
then took off the cachemire, folded it carefully, and put it
away, that I might no longer have my thoughts engrossed by
its lovely colour. And when this was done, I changed my
dress and took up the embroidery madame had left me to
finish. There was one thing, however, which I quite forgot—
the earrings! It was pure forgetfulness, mon père, leaving
them in my ears, but they will not believe that it was so, and
they found them there, and that you know was greatly
against me." She paused a moment and then continued her
history.

"Perhaps it was because these fatal rings were still in my

ears; perhaps, that I had real cause for my terror; but, in spite of every effort, I could not keep my thoughts quiet as I sat at my work. The mirrors seemed to reflect and reflect again the light of my little lamp as I had never seen them do before; strange ghostly lights and shadows appeared to flit through the room, and whenever I chanced to look up, I was haunted by the dread of again seeing the face I had imagined peering behind the window-curtains. At last, I could endure the uncertainty of no longer, and I forced myself to look behind every curtain in the room. It was very difficult to gain the necessary courage, but I did it, and found nothing—nothing; nothing but thick darkness."

"And then, my child?"

"Ah! then madame came home very tired and very—" she paused, then added ingenuously, "People are often a little irritable when they are tired, and madame complained that I hurt her in arranging her hair for the night; and perhaps I did, for I was very sleepy. But, thank God! she said 'Good night, God bless you, my child!' before I left her. That is such a comfort to me now!"

The rest of the story was more briefly told. Julie slept late the morning after the ball, and when she awoke she was surprised to find that the door of communication between her room and that of her mistress was still closed. Madame de l'Orme was in the habit of bolting it every night after Julie left her, but by an ingenious mechanical contrivance could, when she wished it, withdraw the bolt without rising from bed, and in the morning it was generally unfastened. When this was not the case a single tap at the door was enough to break the light sleep of the comtesse. But to-day it was not so. Again and again Julie repeated the summons without receiving an answer. Ten o'clock struck, half-past ten, and there was no sound in the chamber. Eleven came, and Julie, alarmed at the length of her mistress's slumbers. determined on a desperate step to relieve her anxiety; She could obtain no assistance from without, for the key of the staircase-door was in her mistress's possession. She was therefore a prisoner in her own room, from which there was but one mode of egress, and that so perilous that only her present circumstances could have induced her to attempt it.

Her window and those of the next room opened on a very narrow balcony, or rather ledge of stone, and along this ledge it was barely possible for her to creep, and by means of the key of her own window, which accident had previously taught her fitted the others also, make her way into Madame de l'Orme's chamber. It was a dangerous attempt; one too which, if successful, might draw down upon her her mistress's anger. Still she would willingly risk that, if she were sure that the balcony could bear her weight. How frail it looked! And so high from the ground that if she fell—! Her head grew giddy at the thought, but she was a brave, unselfish girl, and her anxiety on Madame de l'Orme's account nerved her to dare the perilous passage. As she stepped cautiously from the window she almost gave up the project in despair. The ledge was scarce two feet wide, the balustrade that guarded it only eighteen inches high; but she resolutely turned her eyes from the abyss beneath, and with the key in her hand reached the other window in safety. But the key was unnecessary, the window was open—! The start occasioned by this discovery almost caused her to overbalance herself, but the instinct of self-preservation taught her to clutch at the window-frame for support. She regained her equilibrium, thrust aside the closed curtain, and entered the room.

All was still as death; but as she glanced hastily round she perceived that the secretaire where Madame de l'Orme kept her money and valuable papers was open, and rifled of its contents; the jewel-casket left last night on the dressing-table was gone, and the wardrobes also were open, but apparently untouched. Could this have been done without rousing so light a sleeper as her mistress? A new fear fell upon her as she felt this was impossible, and with a tremulous step she advanced towards the bed. The curtains at its head were drawn as she was accustomed to find them in a morning, the bed-clothes were unruffled. Nothing in the whole aspect of the bed gave token of violence, and yet she hesitated to withdraw the drapery.

"Madame, it is very late," she whispered. There was no answer. She repeated the words in a louder tone, and at length ventured to touch the hand that lay placidly outside the coverlet. Its touch was sufficient—that chilling peculiar touch which nothing but Death can give. She tore the curtain aside—the sight paralyzed her.

Madame de l'Orme was murdered, foully murdered, as Hazael murdered his master. A thick towel, used by the comtesse in her morning bath, had been soaked in water and pressed down on the sleeper's face, so that suffocation had ensued, and that so suddenly, that she appeared to have passed from slumber to death without a struggle.

Julie removed the cloth and gazed with tearful eyes on the altered countenance. The generous feelings of youth forgot the faults of the dead, and remembered only that she had sheltered and protected her—an orphan. And now who would protect her? Protect her! ah! heavens, who would believe that she had no part in this great, this terrible crime? Like a flash of lightning, the full danger of her position darted across her mind. Every suspicion was against her, nothing was in her favour.

The result showed the truth of her fears. Every circumstance combined to prove her guilt. Even Madeline, the person first summoned to her aid, could only say that "It was a sad pity Mademoiselle Julie had been so imprudent. She might be innocent, but it was strange that she should have madame's earrings on; and one could not but confess that the mode of madame's death was one which could have been effected by a child. And Mademoiselle Julie was the only person in her mistress's confidence, and it must have required one who knew where her valuables were and where she kept her keys—under her pillow it seemed—to select only the valuables and jewels, and articles of small bulk, and leave all that was heavy and useless. True, these things were not found among Julie's little possessions, but a man in one of the opposite houses had seen her pass along the balcony, and she did it with such apparent ease that one could not but feel that what was done once might have been done fifty times."

In short, the mass of evidence was so conclusive against Julie, that the popular voice which had lately spoken of her as the victim of a high-tempered woman's harshness, now considered nothing bad enough for the ungrateful girl, and she might have been torn to pieces by the infuriated crowd had she not been rescued from them by the officers of justice.

Father Sylvestre listened to every particular with unflagging attention, and every now and then put pertinent questions to Julie, intended to shake her testimony in her own favour were it possible she had attempted to deceive him. But she never swerved from the simple unvarnished truth, and when she came to the end she said simply, "And now can you save me?"

He shook his head. "The evidence against you is strong," he said, gravely. "God alone can make you a way through his tangled thicket. But trust in Him whatever befalls you, remembering always that this life is not the end of all; that there is another world where righteous judgment is given; and there, if not here, you will be acquitted of this crime."

"Ah! mon père, I would bear all willingly but for my Louis. It will cause him such bitter grief to believe his Julie a criminal."

"I shall myself clear you to Louis if you are not acquitted by your judges, my daughter." And cheered by this promise and by the good old man's blessing, Julie laid her down on her prison couch and slept.

Through Father Sylvestre's influence the trial was delayed for many weeks, in the hope that the popular prejudice against Julie would pass away, or that some accident might offer a clue by which to trace out the real murderer.

The latter hope was disappointed, but the former was soon effected by the growing interest in the close of the fatal Russian campaign, and the return by twos and threes of the survivors. In these matters of public interest Julie had been almost forgotten by the inhabitants of St. Bignold, when a rumour arose that Monsieur de l'Orme had escaped the many dangers of the war, and was on the point of returning to the château. If such were the case, would it not be an insult to him to find that no steps had been taken to avenge his wife's murderer? The trial must be no longer delayed. It took place. Every one knows that in France such matters are very differently conducted from what they are with us. There no warning is given to the prisoner to beware lest he implicate himself by any confession. On the contrary, all means are employed by leading questions and cross-examinations to draw from the supposed criminal anything that may lead to his conviction, and poor Julie's artless answers served rather to fix than to remove the imputations against her.

The trial ended in her conviction.

All hope was over now; but Father Sylvestre's teaching had not been in vain, and though doomed to a shameful and undeserved death, Julie bore her fate so meekly yet so bravely, that even the stern officers of the Court gave way when they saw the look of patient resignation that rested on that sweet face. As for the populace, its mood had changed once more. They now regretted the fate they had invoked upon her, and crowded round the door by which she was to pass out to express their sympathy and commiseration. But for Father Sylvestre's aid, the efforts of the officials had scarcely availed to save her from the pressure of the fickle crowd. At last a passage was made for her amid their ranks, and she had almost reached the door of her prison, when a man rushed forward, and, flinging himself straight in her path, exclaimed, "Julie, my Julie!" in such accents of grief that it did not require her sudden paleness, or her agonized whisper of "Louis," to remind Father Sylvestre that the toil-worn soldier before him was the girl's lover.

Chapter III

The explanations that followed this terrible meeting, the sympathy of the crowd, the misery of Louis, may be imagined, but fortunately for both him and Julie neither his natural temper nor his late habits of life were of a kind to lead him to despair easily.

"Julie is innocent, and must be proved so," was his ready answer, when the old priest endeavoured to make him submit to his fate. "I shall save her even yet. I feel it—I am certain of it. Give me but three days more of that precious life and I shall save her."

The old man shook his head, but promised to do his utmost, and the boon was readily granted to the united prayers of the good father and of the gallant soldier, who had gone through that dreadful campaign. Louis, however, scarcely waited to hear that it was granted before he set energetically to work to track out the truth. He gained admission to the Hotel de l'Orme—he examined every part of it, as if still expecting to find traces of the murderer—he opened the windows one by one—he passed as Julie had done along the narrow ledge outside them, and paused as she had done at the open window of the mirrored boudoir.

"You have found something, my friend?" said the sergeant of police who had accompanied him in his search. "It does not, however, seem of much consequence," he added, as he returned the fragment of a small steel instrument which Louis had discovered still sticking in the back of the window. "She used it, I suppose, to force back the bolt. It looks like the sharp point of a pair of scissors."

"No," said Louis, quietly, "it is part of a graver's tool. Not a very likely instrument to be found in a woman's repository; and, trifling as it is, it may be a clue to what I want. Are there many engravers at St. Bignold's?"

"Let me see. Engravers? No, only one; Clement Lebrun by name."

"I seem to have heard of him before."

"Probably," replied the sergeant, drily. "It was he who saw Mademoiselle Julie pass along the balcony."

"Then he lives close by?"

"Yes, and no. It is a good quarter of a mile by the road to reach the Rue Sylvaine, and yet," pointing out of the window, "that is his house right opposite."

Louis gave a start as he said this, and leaned far out of the window, as if he longed to clear the narrow space between at a bound, then drawing back examined the balcony more minutely than before.

"You have an idea, my friend," again suggested the sergeant.

"I have."

"And I also."

Louis looked keenly at his companion, but could read nothing in his imperturbable countenance. "Let us seek this Lebrun," he said at last.

"He is not a man to be trifled with," said the sergeant.

"Nor am I," was the calm, decided answer.

After tracing several intricate winding streets they reached the Rue Sylvaine, and entered Lebrun's house, in everything a contrast to that they had just quitted. It was as much crowded with human beings as the Hotel de l'Orme was deserted; as full of life and sound as the other was empty of all but fearful memories.

Lebrun received them coldly but courteously, and learning from the sergeant that Louis was a friend of the de l'Orme family, and desirous to know all he could tell of the murder, he gave his story calmly and succinctly.

"All he knew," he said, "was that, when sitting at work the morning after the murder, he had been attracted by seeing a girl step out from the opposite window, and, walking along the narrow ledge, enter the one adjoining it. It had struck him at the time as peculiar, and on hearing of the murder he naturally mentioned what he had seen."

"And you could speak with authority," said the sergeant; "for, though Madame de l'Orme's house is some distance from this by the road, I should say that her windows were within thirty feet of yours. What say you, Monsieur Louis?"

"Thirty," said Louis, leaning out of the wide casement, to do which more easily he removed a pot of flowers which stood against the balustrade. "I should say twenty was nearer the mark."

"I never measured the distance," said the engraver, sullenly.

His change of tone struck both the sergeant and Louis, but neither spoke in return, although each devoted himself to a careful examination of Lebrun's premises; Louis by removing the flower-pots in the balcony one by one and examining the upper edge of the balustrade, the sergeant by scanning closely but unobtrusively the furniture of the workshop. There were only two things which seemed to either suspicious; but as they tallied with the idea that had occurred to both they observed them minutely. One was, that the plants in the window were far more valuable than seemed consistent with the poverty of the engraver; the other that, besides the various things essential to his trade, there was a very long plank of wood leaning against the wall in the darkest corner of the room. The sergeant also perceived that Lebrun's eyes furtively followed his as they rested inquisitively on the hidden plank.

"Have you any more questions to ask me, gentlemen?" the

engraver at last said, in a tone that had less of courtesy than the words he used, "for I am a poor man, and cannot afford to lose the daylight."

"Yes," said Louis, turning from the window. "I wish you to tell me what use you make of this?" selecting a particular tool from those that were lying on the table.

"It is a graver," said the man at once.

"I thought so; and this is one also, is it not?" and he took from his pocket the fragment he had found at the Hotel de l'Orme.

"It seems so," stammered Lebrun, growing suddenly pale; but added quickly, "Why do you ask me?"

"Because I wish to know whether it is yours?"

Before he could make up his mind how to answer the apparently simple, but evidently embarrassing question, the sergeant tapped him on the shoulder. "Mon ami," he said, "I have measured the plank in the corner of your chamber. I find it is twenty feet long. Will you permit me to remove one to two of your beautiful flowers, and, resting it on the part of the balustrade already broken, thrust it across the street towards the Hotel de l'Orme? It seems to me it will find a resting-place on the broken part of the balustrade opposite madame's chamber window. What think you, Monsieur Louis?"

. During this courteous address Lebrun's paleness changed to something still more ghastly—a grey hue, like that of death; and when, a moment afterwards, the sergeant, suddenly changing his tone, said, "Clement Lebrun, I arrest you as the murderer of Madame de l'Orme," he made no effort to refute the accusation, but with the calmness of despair permitted the arrest to take place. Little more was necessary to prove Lebrun's guilt and Julie's innocence. As Louis had said, the finding of the broken graver, though a trifle, was the clue to the whole mystery. The position of Lebrun's house, as respected the Hotel de l'Orme, naturally suggested to a military eye the possible means of passing from one to another, which the broken edge of the carved balustrade on either side confirmed. The rest was easy, and was made certain by the confession of the murderer. He had long resolved to possess himself of the jewels and money which Madame de l'Orme was said to keep in her own chamber, and had intended to secrete himself there during her absence at the ball and secure his booty at leisure. Julie's presence had prevented him. His was the face she had seen in the mirror; and her unconscious interference with his projects then had suggested to him afterwards the fiendish idea of turning the suspicion of the murder on her. His success had been more complete than he had dared to hope. But it is seldom indeed that, to use a Scotch expression, a murderer is not "so left to himself" as to leave one fatal clue to his crime where all else has been concealed with consummate ability. In Lebrun's case there were two—the broken tool and the plank of wood by which he had bridged over the abyss. But for this oversight on his part the innocent must have suffered for the guilty.

A month later and Julie's love dream was fulfilled. Kneeling in her white dress before the altar of the chapel of the château, the wreath of orange-flowers on her head, and Monsieur de l'Orme himself honouring the ceremony by his presence, she became the wife of her faithful Louis; and each was dearer to the other because each had, though in such different circumstances, stood face to face with the grim king of terrors, Death, and been rescued from him by an arm more mighty still, in whom both had trusted even when hope had almost become despair.

THE MAGIC BULLET

By Edward D. Hoch (1930-   )

Hoch is that most rara *of* avis, *someone who fits the cliche "a legend in his own lifetime." He is the only current crime writer who specializes in the short story. For some years it has been virtually impossible—Heaven be praised—to pick up a mystery magazine from the newsstand without finding Hoch's name prominent among the contributors. He has created some of the most memorable and best loved short-story detectives of all times—Simon Ark, who may or may not be 2000 years old; homicide detective Captain Leopold; Rand the counterspy; Nick Velvet of the bizarre taste in thefts; old-time Westerner Ben Snow, and so on and so forth. And let's not forget Dr. Sam Hawthorne, the retired physician who investigated innumerable impossible crimes in the twenties and thirties, and now reveals all with the help of "a small libation." But here's one of Hoch's puzzle-solvers you may not have heard of, mysterious Harry Ponder whose activities are so clandestine that only two cases, "The Magic Bullet" and "Siege Perilous," have been reported.*

I REALLY never believed in the magic bullet, even after I saw a man killed by it. But if it wasn't a magic bullet, it was the next best thing.

My name is Harry Ponder, and at the time of the trouble, I was attached to the United States Embassy staff at Beneu. It was a pleasant country, with perfect weather and a nice breeze off the nearby ocean. The work was easy and there were lots of girls. But then the Communists, too, decided it was a nice country. Though I was directly responsible to a somewhat shadowy Washington agency, I was nominally under the ambassador, a gruff balding man named Jason McTurk who'd gotten the job after a good many years with the State Department. Places like Beneu too often had ambassadors who'd been little more than ward heelers back home, but McTurk was a different breed entirely. I liked him. He plunged into things and got results.

I was in the library with Sam Kanton one morning when McTurk called me into his office. He'd just heard the news about the rebels. "What is this, Harry? Rebel armies at the outskirts of the city?"

"It's Rojo," I told him. The night-duty officer had awakened me with the news before dawn. "He's down from the hills with about two hundred followers. Not enough to take the city, but enough to make it damned embarrassing for Colonel Saks."

Rojo had been a key member of Saks's government until the previous year, when they'd had a falling-out. Colonel Saks had ordered Rojo arrested and Rojo had replied by killing a guard and fleeing to the hills with a handful of followers. Recently, stories had drifted back that the rebel was organizing a highly trained army, possibly with outside help, to return and oust Colonel Saks.

"Rojo! What's your information, Harry? Are the Communists behind him?"

"No more than the fascists are behind Saks. I won't swear he isn't armed with a few Communist weapons, but things like that happen."

Jason McTurk scooped up the phone and asked the operator to get him Colonel Saks. After a few moments' wait, he barked into the phone, "Colonel, this is Jason McTurk! What in hell's going on?"

He listened in silence, only grunting now and again to confirm his presence on the line. "All right," he rasped. "Do you think I should speak with Rojo? He knows me from the old days." A pause, and then, "I'll be in touch with Washington."

He hung up and I asked, "How bad is it?"

"Bad enough. Rojo's forces have occupied the east bank of the river. Saks is ready to blow up the bridge if they start across."

Only a quarter of the city's land was located east of the Beney River, and much of that was a rundown slum. Rojo's small force had met no resistance there, but crossing the single bridge to occupy our side of the city was another matter. We had the government buildings, police, troops, and citizens loyal to Colonel Saks.

I remembered another crossing, ten miles outside the city. "What about the South Bridge?"

"Saks had the army blow it up an hour ago. But he doesn't want to destroy the city bridge unless he's forced to."

"All right," I said. "What do we do?"

"Contact Washington. Explain the situation."

I nodded. "Were you serious about meeting Rojo?"

"If it would do any good."

I left his plush office and went down to the message room. It was always locked, with the only key on a ring in my pocket. I took it out now and opened the door, entering a tiny room jammed with electronic equipment. Within ten minutes, I'd encoded a message to Washington and sent it on our standard frequency. They acknowledged at once, but I knew it would be afternoon before we received a real reply.

As I opened the door to leave, I found Sam Kanton waiting for me. Sam was in his middle thirties, about my age, but he looked older. As our USIA man, he was in charge of the medium-sized library attached to the embassy. I liked him in small doses, but we'd never gotten really friendly. He has an odd way of staring at you with his pained eyes and, after a time, it could be unnerving.

"I just heard what's happening," he said. "Do you think he'll get this far? Wreck the library or anything?"

"No reason to think so," I told him. "Rojo is an enemy of

Colonel Saks, but not of the United States. In fact, it's to his advantage to stay friendly with us. Your library's safe."

"He doesn't have to cross the bridge," Sam Kanton pointed out. "There are plenty of boats."

"He has a small force. The government troops would slaughter them if they tried to cross by boat. If he's serious, he has to cross the bridge. But I'll bet he'll try to bargain."

"Rojo bargain? For what?"

I shrugged. "His old cabinet post, maybe."

"Things never go back to where they were," Kanton said.

"Maybe Rojo doesn't know that."

I drove downtown to see how the city was reacting to Rojo's threat. The palace was ten blocks from the embassy, a great old relic of the pseudo-colonial days. As I neared it, the crowds seemed to grow thicker. Perhaps they thought the palace of Colonel Saks was the safest place to be, though certainly it would be Rojo's prime target if and when he crossed the river.

Carol Lake was there, standing near the edge of the crowd by the gate. She was a blonde American girl who ran a gift shop in the lobby of Beneu's largest hotel, and I'd had an occasional drink with her. She was pretty and fairly intelligent, and I liked her.

"I thought you'd be down, Harry," she said. "What's the real story?"

"You probably know as much as I do. Rojo is across the river."

"Is he coming here?"

"With a couple of hundred men? I doubt that."

She stepped back from the crowd and lit a cigarette, beating me to it. "There's been talk, though, Harry. These people are still a superstitious lot, and they credit Rojo with magical powers."

I knew what she said was true. Rojo played upon men's ignorance and superstition. Perhaps that was why he'd chosen to attack the poorer section of the city first.

"I doubt if Colonel Saks is worried," I told her.

"Rojo talks of a magic bullet, one to seek out and kill Saks wherever he hides."

"And Saks has a lot of unmagic bullets, marked for Rojo."

We'd walked a bit away from the others, down a quiet side street.

"Some people say you're a CIA man assigned to the embassy."

"I hear those things," I told her, laughing it off.

"Are you?"

"Beneu isn't Moscow. There's no CIA man here."

She smiled and dropped the subject. "Had lunch yet?"

"No, but it's a damn good idea."

After lunch, I left her and went down to the bridge. There were two guards at our end, armed with Sten guns. I knew one of them, a youth named Marto. He was staring across the bridge at three ragged men at the far end, as if daring them to start across.

"Any trouble, Marto?" I asked.

"None, I am ready." He patted the gun. "We have armored cars in the next block, waiting. And the bridge is mined. They would never reach the middle."

I offered him a cigarette. "Has anyone crossed this morning?"

"No one. Orders of Colonel Saks."

That told me what I wanted to know. The ambassador would need permission of both sides to speak with Rojo. I headed back to the embassy under a cloudy sky.

"I'm going to see him," Jason McTurk said, slapping the desk with a newspaper. "Someone has to talk with Rojo."

I was standing against the wall, out of the way, while Colonel Saks himself paced the floor. It was the second time he'd set foot in the American embassy—the first visit since our Independence Day reception—and he was making a show of it. Saks was tall and just a bit overweight, with a broad chest suitable for medals. He was a minor-league tyrant, but he was the only game in town, and so we supported him. With Rojo, there was always the fear that he would become another Castro.

"I should talk with Rojo." Saks was insisting. "Not you."

"He'd kill you as soon as you crossed the bridge—and he wouldn't need any magic bullet for it, either."

Colonel Saks grunted. "I could bomb them to dust from the air."

The ambassador looked pained. "Your air force is made up entirely of American planes and American-trained pilots. We would not look favorably on their use in crushing Rojo, especially if some deal is still possible between you two."

"Very well," Saks said at last. "But will he see you?"

"I think so," McTurk told him. "If you'll write me a pass to get through your sentries on this side."

Colonel Saks sat at the desk and wrote a few words on a sheet of embassy stationery, signing with his familiar flourish. "Give this to my sentries."

McTurk turned to me for the first time in the meeting. "Contact Washington, Harry, and tell them what goes. Then have my car brought around. I'll drive."

"You're going now? And alone?"

"It'll be dark in an hour. I want to arrive while they can still see me coming and recognize the car."

"Washington won't be happy about that."

"Don't ask them, tell them."

But as I left the office, I confronted Sam Kanton. "All hell's breaking loose, Harry!" he said excitedly. "There's an American reporter in my library, and he wants to know the whole story!"

"Who is it?" I asked.

"Fellow named Cranston."

"Tell him there's nothing now."

I hurried past him to the message room. Kanton was in charge of information; surely he could find something to tell a wire-service reporter. Moving a bit too quickly, I yanked my key chain from its pocket and felt it snap. A half-dozen keys went flying. I picked up the message-center key first, then the almost identical key to my room and the rest of them. I dumped them in my pocket and threaded the message-room key back onto its ring, then inserted it into the waiting hole at the center of the doorknob. The door opened and I went in. The incident seemed nothing but a nuisance at the time.

I quickly encoded a message to Washington about the planned meeting. That would give them something to stew about. Then I left the room and went around to the back of the embassy where McTurk's driver—a black man named George—was already checking the car.

"That's all right," I told him. "He's driving himself."

Actually, I wasn't too worried about McTurk driving across that bridge alone. The official car was a big Caddy limousine complete with air-conditioning, power windows and a telephone link to the embassy. Best of all, the windows were of bullet-proof glass, installed a few years earlier when the Beneu situation had become dangerously fluid. I attached the small American flags to the fender posts to show that the ambassador would be inside and stepped back, feeling reasonably secure. Rojo wouldn't kill McTurk. And he just *might* talk to him.

Five minutes later, I drove the car out the embassy gate, with McTurk in the back seat with Colonel Saks. A slim young American yelled something that I couldn't hear through the thick glass, and I guessed him to be the reporter, Cranston.

We dropped Saks at the palace, and I let McTurk take my place in the driver's seat. "You're sure you don't want me along?"

"Not this trip, Harry. Thanks."

The bridge was only a few blocks away and I trotted through the back streets in time to see the Caddy slow down for the two guards with their Sten guns. Then it shot forward onto the wide bridge.

McTurk was about halfway across the bridge when it happened. There was a muffled sound, more like a cough than a shot, and the big car suddenly seemed to waver on the road. It twisted to the left and bounced over the curb to a halt, looking like a great dead beetle which would never move again. Then I was running, past Marto and the other guard, who shouted and waved their Sten guns at me. I was running because something had gone cold inside me and I was suddenly terrified. At the far end of the bridge, Rojo's men had sprung into action, and I knew at any moment I might be cut down by gunfire. But just then I didn't care.

I reached the car and tried the door on the driver's side. It was locked, and so were the others. The unbroken windows were all tightly closed. And Jason McTurk was slumped inside, alone, blood gushing from a jagged, horrible bullet wound in his left temple. Just at that moment, I began to believe in Rojo's magic bullet.

It was already dusk, and they had to focus a spotlight on us while we used rifle butts to batter open a window and unlock the car door. Then we carefully removed the body and I leaned inside, shining a flashlight over the interior. There seemed nothing out of the ordinary.

"What happened?" I asked Marto.

"Nothing, sir. He gave me this order signed by Colonel Saks, and we let him pass. He was all right then."

I turned to the police captain who'd appeared on the scene. "I'm going back with you. We'll take this car apart inch by inch, if necessary, to find the device that killed him."

"There are no powder burns," the officer pointed out. "He could not have been shot from inside the car."

"No. But he couldn't have been shot from outside, either."

I spent the next three hours convincing myself of the impossibility. McTurk was dead, murdered almost before my eyes. He'd been shot and killed instantly while alone inside a sealed car which no bullet had penetrated.

Finally Sam Kanton appeared at the palace where we'd taken the car. He seemed even more distraught than earlier. "Washington is going crazy, Harry! They finally called by overseas telephone. Said they'd been sending messages for hours. I heard the message-room bell ring, but I couldn't get in. The door was locked."

"It always is, Sam," I said with a sigh. I didn't bother to add that it was locked to keep people like Sam out.

"Cranston wired out the story of the killing." He was actually trembling as he spoke. "Washington wants details."

"I'll handle them. Calm down."

"But he's *dead*, Harry! The ambassador's *dead*!"

I knew our second in command was vacationing in Washington. That seemed to leave me in charge. "Secretaries?"

"Just George, the driver. It hit him hard."

"It hit us all hard."

I drove back with Sam because there was nothing more to be done with the car. For the next hour, I was busy on the phone to Washington, using the emergency scrambler. I told them all I knew, which wasn't much.

"Did Rojo do it?" a crackly official voice asked.

"I don't know. Maybe."

"If Rojo is responsible, we certainly can't support him.."

"You're not supporting him now," I reminded the voice. "Give me a day. Till tomorrow night."

"This is very serious."

"Murder usually is."

I hung up the scrambler and went out to see George. He was staring at the dark earth as if he'd lost his best friend. Maybe he had.

"Did you notice anyone fooling with the car, George?"

"No, sir! I was polishing it all afternoon. Nobody came near it."

I got out the other car and drove into the center of town. It was a little after midnight when I parked on a dark side street by Carol Lake's apartment. She met me at the door, not really surprised.

"I heard the news, Harry. I thought you'd come."

"I need a drink and I don't want to be seen in public. A reporter is dogging me."

She fixed me a taut scotch and curled up in the chair opposite, looking like a little girl. I told her what I knew, just to talk it out.

"He was a good man," she said. "He got things done."

I nodded. "And yet somebody wanted him dead." I smoked a cigarette in the near darkness, watching the glow from hers.

"Are you CIA, Harry?" she asked.

"That again? Does it matter?"

I couldn't see her face as she replied. "I like to know about the man I'm going to sleep with."

Reluctantly I got to my feet. "That's not an invitation I'd usually refuse, but I can't stay. Not tonight."

"Harry, I need somebody. It's like that weekend when Kennedy was killed."

I held her for a moment. "Another time. When we're both a little more human." Then I left her there, a glowing cigarette in the darkness.

There was another cigarette outside, waiting for me. It

belonged to the slender American I spotted earlier in the day. He was leaning against my car, waiting.

"I thought you might be good for the night," he said.

"I usually hit people for remarks like that."

"I'm Cranston, with the wire service."

"I know who you are."

"You've been avoiding me."

"Not too successfully. How'd you find me here?"

"The car has embassy plates. I knew it wasn't Sam Kanton. He's no ladies' man."

"What do you want?" I opened the car door.

"What's your reaction to Colonel Saks' statement?"

My hand froze on the door. "What statement?"

"He announced that his investigation shows Jason McTurk committed suicide. Could I quote your reaction?"

It was after one and I was tired, but not too tired to confront Colonel Saks in his office. He seemed to have aged ten years in the last few hours, and I had a fleeting sense of sorrow for the man. Only fleeting, though.

"Couldn't it have waited until morning?" he growled.

"No, it couldn't. What's this crap about McTurk killing himself? You know damned well there was no pistol in the car."

"Nevertheless . . ."

"Why would he kill himself on the way to see Rojo? And *how*?"

"You're excited. Tired."

"Damned right, I'm tired. But I'm not going to let you call McTurk's murder a suicide."

"Murder is impossible. It was a locked car, bulletproof."

"So maybe it was Rojo's magic bullet that did it."

Colonel Saks sighed. "I must tell you. Rojo contacted me tonight, after the killing. He is willing to talk peace. Under those circumstances, I can hardly have my people say he killed your ambassador with a magic bullet, can I?"

"How come he's so ready to talk peace?"

"McTurk's death, of course. He fears Washington will blame him and approve the use of bombing planes against his forces."

"But he denies the killing?"

"Of course. He says the Communists killed McTurk in an effort to widen the division here."

"That's possible," I admitted. "But then let's blame the Communists instead of calling it suicide."

"We will see what tomorrow brings." He rose from his desk. "But right now I must insist that you leave."

I left. I'm never one to push my luck.

I went back to the embassy and chatted with a sleepy Sam Kanton about the funeral arrangements. When I reached my room, I dug to the bottom of my pocket for the loose keys and fitted the right one into the lock. Nothing happened. It wouldn't turn. I took it out and looked at it, then took out my key chain with the almost identical message-room key. I'd always identified them by their positions on the key ring, but obviously I'd confused them when they dropped earlier. The key on the chain opened my door.

I was sitting on the edge of the bed, puzzling over the keys, when Carol Lake phoned. "I shouldn't even tell you this after the way you walked out on me," she said, "but I know how the ambassador could have been shot in a sealed car. It just came to me. Can you drive over?"

"This is no time for games, Carol. Tell me what you know."

She gave a long sigh of loneliness. "All right. Remember the telephone in the car? Suppose McTurk lifted the receiver to his ear, and a bullet was fired from it."

"I'll talk to you later," I said, hanging up. I had to check that car one more time.

It was the middle of the night and I was standing by the Caddy feeling like a damned fool. The car had been brought back to the embassy grounds, and it took me only a moment to establish that the telephone receiver was perfectly genuine. Of course, the police had checked it along with everything else, and besides, if Carol's theory were to hold water, you had to imagine McTurk reaching for the receiver with his right hand and placing it against his right ear. But the bullet had entered his left temple. No one driving a car and talking on the phone would ever twist it over to his left ear. Besides, there were no powder burns.

I turned from the car and started back to my room. I was

almost to the side door when the shadows suddenly seemed to come alive.

Then, in an instant, I was fighting for my life.

I hit the hard asphalt driveway and rolled over, trying to shake loose my attacker. Over and over we rolled, and I felt rather than saw the knife inches from my throat. He was clinging like a tiger, gradually getting the best of me.

Then there was a light from the doorway, and I had a blurred glimpse of Sam Kanton hurling himself at my attacker. That was the break I needed. I squirmed free, and between the two of us, we quickly overpowered and disarmed him.

"Who is it?" Kanton asked, shining a light on the twisted face beneath us.

"An old friend," I answered.

It was Marto, the guard from the bridge, with a knife this time, instead of his Sten gun.

All thought of sleep had vanished now, and I paced the floor like a caged beast while Marto slumped in a chair in my office.

"I must obey my colonel," Marto said, and that was all.

"He sent you here?" Sam Kanton asked. "To kill Harry?"

But Marto only shrugged and said no more.

We tried calling the palace, but Colonel Saks had retired and could not be disturbed. I bit my lip and wondered what to do.

"You're not going to release him?" Sam asked.

"No," I decided. "Let's lock him in the basement until morning. I've got to puzzle this thing out."

I went back to my room, still uneasy, and remembered the keys. Two keys—one for my room and one for the message center—almost alike. I'd confused them when my chain broke, and I'd tried to open the door to my room with the message-center key. It hadn't worked, of course. But then, how had I been able to open the message center earlier in the day with my room key?

I dozed, thinking about it, until the phone rang at just after eight. It was Colonel Saks himself, sounding disturbed. "I understand you have one of my men a prisoner."

"You might say that, Colonel. He tried to kill me."

"I'm sure not! Scare you, perhaps, but not kill you!"

"Then you did send him?"

"Mr. Ponder, you must stop trying to stir things up. This morning at ten o'clock, Rojo crosses the bridge to talk peace. Your ambassador's death has brought us together. Will you pull us apart with your murder investigation?"

"I just want to know who killed him. And how. It's my job."

"Go back to Washington, Mr. Ponder. While you can."

"Thanks very much for the advice."

I hung up and poured some coffee, then went out and talked to George, the driver, for a while. Sam Kanton had gone out somewhere, and none of the secretaries had come to work. The embassy was officially in mourning.

I remembered the keys and walked down the hall to the message room. I tried the correct key and the door opened. I tried the room key and the door opened. I tried my hand on the knob and the door opened. It wasn't locked.

Then I went out and opened the trunk of the second embassy car—the one I'd driven to Carol's place the night before. Beneath the spare tire, carefully wrapped in oiled rags, was a high-powered hunting rifle with a telescopic sight.

That was when I knew how Jason McTurk had been shot to death in his sealed car, and who had done it.

The word of Rojo's coming had spread quickly through the city, and a large crowd was already at the bridge awaiting his arrival. He came just five minutes after ten, in an open car surrounded by armed guards on the running boards and trunk.

"Everybody's here," a voice said, close to me. It was Cranston, the reporter, after one last story.

"Stick close," I said. "I might need you."

I pushed through a little closer, until I saw Colonel Saks himself come to talk peace. Then I saw Carol Lake, standing near the spot where Marto had been with his Sten gun the day before. I tried to edge closer, but the crowd was thick. Then there was cheering as Saks stepped forward to the car to shake Rojo's hand in a gesture of friendship. I saw Sam

Kanton at the edge of the crowd, standing on the roof of a car.

"Sam!" I shouted, but he didn't hear me above the roar. There was nothing else to do. He already had his gun out when I shot him twice in the legs and watched him tumble into the crowd.

Colonel Saks was unhappy. He paced the floor, smoking a thin cigar. "Tell me the whole thing," he commanded.

"Washington already has my report," I said. "Everything's in it, including your attempt to scare or kill me."

"Forget that!"

"I saved Rojo's life this morning. And probably yours, too."

"Will Sam Kanton live?"

I nodded. "He'll live. And tell us about his motive, I hope. We already know he was in the pay of the Communists, trying to start a civil war here. I imagine he killed McTurk just so Rojo would be blamed for it. When that didn't work, he tried to kill Rojo himself, hoping his followers would then kill you."

"But he is an American! An embassy employee!"

I shrugged. "We have all kinds."

"How did you know about him?"

I told Saks about the keys. "I never tried the knob of the message room, because it was always supposed to be locked. I just inserted the key and turned. So when the door was unlocked the last couple of days, I didn't even realize it. Of course, he slipped in and read the messages I sent to Washington. That was how he know McTurk was meeting Rojo"

"How did he unlock the door?"

"Old trick. He caught me as I was coming out the other day and stopped to chat with me. He just managed to turn the inside button to the unlocked position while we talked. His mistake was leaving the door unlocked for me to discover later."

"You knew he was the one who unlocked it?"

I nodded. "He told me later he heard the message bell ringing, but couldn't get in because the door was locked. Since the door was unlocked during this whole period, I realized he'd lied about that. And once I suspected him, I knew he must have taken the second embassy car and beaten us to the bridge yesterday. I found the murder weapon in the trunk. It was a high-powered rifle. He shot McTurk from our side of the river bank, down about fifty yards from the bridge."

"But the car! It was closed and bulletproof!"

"Yes, it was. But I remembered hearing the shot, and that told me a lot. With those thick windows closed, I couldn't even hear a voice yelling right next to the car. If the death shot had been fired inside by some device, I never would have heard it. Besides, there were no powder burns, and the jagged nature of the entrance wound hinted at a high-powered rifle bullet fired from a distance."

"But how did it enter the closed car?"

I lit a cigarette. "Simple. The car wasn't closed. McTurk slowed down and handed Marto your signed note giving permission to cross the bridge. To get the note out of the car, he had to open the window, of course. There was no other way. When he speeded up to cross the bridge, the window on the driver's side had to still be open, even though we couldn't see it. McTurk must have pressed the button for the power window and it started to close. It was almost completely closed when Sam Kanton's bullet passed through the opening and into McTurk's left temple. His finger was still on the power button, and the window closed completely by the time the finger fell away in death."

"How could Kanton know that would happen?"

"He couldn't. He was probably quite upset that it did, since he wanted the blame clearly attached to Rojo's snipers. He overheard our talk about the note of permission, so he guessed McTurk would open his bulletproof window as he started across, presenting a perfect target in the telescopic sight. He didn't know the window would close and leave us with an impossible crime."

"The gods of chance," Colonel Saks mumbled. "What can I report to Washington?"

"That there is peace between Rojo and me. For now, at least."

I nodded. Soon I left the palace and drove back to the

embassy. Later, I would go up to see Carol Lake, but just then I wanted to be alone. It hadn't been a magic bullet after all that killed Jason McTurk, but I still wondered if Rojo might not have some future magic for use on Colonel Saks.

A TERRIBLY STRANGE BED

By Wilkie Collins (1824-1889)

Wilkie Collins, born and bred a Londoner, was Charles Dickens's closest friend and the author of a string of novels of mystery and sensation including four, The Dead Secret, The Woman in White, Armadale *and* The Moonstone, *reckoned among the best of their kind. He was also a regular contributor of short stories to the periodicals of the day, and in the February 1852 issue of Dickens's* Household Words *appeared his "A Terribly Strange Bed." This chilling tale, the idea for which had been suggested to him by the artist, Herrick, proved to be so popular that many later authors (including Joseph Conrad) used the theme again—but none of them so effectively as Collins in the original version.*

SHORTLY after my education at college was finished, I happened to be staying at Paris with an English friend. We were both young men then, and lived, I am afraid, rather a wild life, in the delightful city of our sojourn. One night we were idling about the neighborhood of the Palais Royal, doubtful to what amusement we should next betake ourselves. My friend proposed a visit to Frascati's; but his suggestion was not to my taste. I knew Frascati's, as the French saying is, by heart; had lost and won plenty of five-franc pieces there, merely for amusement's sake, until it was amusement no longer, and was thoroughly tired, in fact, of all the ghastly respectabilities of such a social anomaly as a respectable gambling-house. "For Heaven's sake," said I to my friend, "let us go somewhere where we can see a little genuine, blackguard, poverty-stricken gaming, with no false gingerbread glitter thrown over it at all. Let us get away from fashionable Frascati's, to a house where they don't mind letting in a man with a ragged coat, or a man with no coat, ragged or otherwise." "Very well," said my friend, "we needn't go out of the Palais Royal to find the sort of company you want. Here's the place just before us; as blackguard a place, by all report, as you could possibly wish to see." In another minute we arrived at the door, and entered the house.

When we got upstairs, and had left our hats and sticks with the doorkeeper, we were admitted into the chief gambling-room. We did not find many people assembled there. But, few as the men were who looked up at us on our entrance, they were all types—lamentably true types—of their respective classes.

We have come to see blackguards; but these men were something worse. There is a comic side, more or less appreciable, in all blackguardism—here there was nothing but tragedy—mute, weird tragedy. The quiet in the room was horrible. The thin, haggard, long-haired young man, whose sunken eyes fiercely watched the turning up of the cards, never spoke; the flabby, fat-faced, pimply player, who pricked his piece of pasteboard perseveringly, to register how often black won, and how often red—never spoke; the dirty, wrinkled old man, with the vulture eyes and the darned greatcoat, who had lost his last *sou,* and still looked on desperately, after he could play no longer—never spoke. Even the voice of the croupier sounded as if it were strangely dulled and thickened in the atmosphere of the room. I had entered the place to laugh, but the spectacle before me was something to weep over. I soon found it necessary to take refuge in excitement from the depression of spirits which was fast stealing on me. Unfortunately I sought the nearest excitement, by going to the table and beginning to play. Still more unfortunately, as the event will show, I won—won prodigiously; won incredibly; won at such a rate that the regular players at the table crowded round me; and staring at my stakes with hungry, superstitious eyes, whispered to one another that the English stranger was going to break the bank.

The game was *Rouge et Noir.* I had played at it in every city in Europe, without, however, the care or the wish to study the Theory of Chances—that philosopher's stone of all gamblers! And a gambler, in the strict sense of the word, I had never been. I was heart-whole from the corroding passion for play. My gaming was a mere idle amusement. I never resorted to it by necessity, because I never knew what it was to want money. I never practiced it so incessantly as to lose more than I could afford, or to gain more than I could coolly pocket without being thrown off my balance by my good luck. In short, I had hitherto frequented gambling-tables— just as I frequented ballrooms and opera-houses—because they amused me, and because I had nothing to do with my leisure hours.

But on this occasion it was very different—now, for the first time in my life, I felt what the passion for play really was. My success first bewildered, and then, in the most literal meaning of the word, intoxicated me. Incredible as it may appear, it is nevertheless true, that I only lost when I attempted to estimate chances, and played according to previous calculation. If I left everything to luck, and staked without any care or consideration, I was sure to win—to win in the face of every recognized probability in favor of the bank. At first some of the men present ventured their money safely enough on my color; but I speedily increased my stakes to sums which they dared not risk. One after another they left off playing, and breathlessly looked on at my game.

Still, time after time, I staked higher and higher, and still won. The excitement in the room rose to fever pitch. The silence was interrupted by a deep-muttered chorus of oaths and exclamations in different languages, every time the gold was shoveled across to my side of the table—even the imperturbable croupier dashed his rake on the floor in a (French) fury of astonishment at my success. But one man present preserved his self-possession, and that man was my friend. He came to my side, and whispering in English, begged me to leave the place, satisfied with what I had already gained. I must do him the justice to say that he repeated his warnings and entreaties several times, and only left me and went away after I had rejected his advice (I was to all intents and purposes gambling drunk) in terms which rendered it impossible for him to address me again that night.

Shortly after he had gone, a hoarse voice behind me cried: "Permit me, my dear sir—permit me to restore to their proper place two napoleons which you have dropped. Wonderful luck, sir! I pledge you my word of honor, as an old soldier, in the course of my long experience in this sort of thing, I never saw such luck as yours—never! Go on, sir— *Sacré mille bombes!* Go on boldly, and break the bank!"

I turned round and saw, nodding and smiling at me with inveterate civility, a tall man, dressed in a frogged and braided surtout.

If I had been in my senses, I should have considered him, personally, as being rather a suspicious specimen of an old soldier. He had goggling, blood-shot eyes, mangy mustaches and a broken nose. His voice betrayed a barrack-room intonation of the worst order, and he had the dirtiest pair of hands I ever saw—even in France. These little personal peculiarities exercised, however, no repelling influence on me. In the mad excitement, the reckless triumph of that moment, I was ready to "fraternize" with anybody who encouraged me in my game. I accepted the old soldier's offered pinch of snuff; clapped him on the back, and swore he was the honestest fellow in the world—the most glorious relic of the Grand Army that I had ever met with. "Go on!" cried my military friend, snapping his fingers in ecstacy—"Go on, and win! Break the bank—*Mille tonnerres!* my gallant English comrade, break the bank!"

And I *did* go on—went on at such a rate, that in another quarter of an hour the croupier called out, "Gentlemen, the bank has discontinued for to-night." All the notes, and all the gold in that "bank," now lay in a heap under my hands; the whole floating capital of the gambling-house was waiting to pour into my pockets!

"Tie up the money in your pocket-handkerchief, my worthy sir," said the old soldier, as I wildly plunged my hands into my heap of gold. "Tie it up, as we used to tie up a bit of dinner in the Grand Army; your winnings are too heavy for any breeches-pockets that ever were sewed. There! that's it—shovel them in, notes and all! *Credié!* what luck! Stop! another napoleon on the floor! *Ah! sacré petit polisson de Napoleon!* have I found thee at last? Now then, sir—two tight double knots each way with your honorable permission, and the money's safe. Feel it! feel it, fortunate sir! hard and round as a cannon-ball—*Ah, bah!* if they had only fired such cannon-balls at us at Austerlitz—*nom d'une pipe!* if they only had! And now, as an ancient grenadier, as an ex-brave of the French army, what remains for me to do? I ask what? Simply this, to entreat my valued English friend to drink a bottle of Champagne with me, and toast the goddess Fortune in foaming goblets before we part!"

Excellent ex-brave! Convivial ancient grenadier! Champagne by all means! An English cheer for an old soldier! Hurra! hurra! Another English cheer for the goddess Fortune! Hurra! hurra! hurra!

"Bravo! the Englishman; the amiable, gracious Englishman, in whose veins circulates the vivacious blood of France! Another glass? *Ah, bah!*—the bottle is empty! Never mind! *Vive le vin!* I, the old soldier, order another bottle, and half a pound of *bonbons* with it!"

"No, no, ex-brave; never—ancient grenadier! *Your* bottle last time; *my* bottle this! Behold it! Toast away! The French Army! the great Napoleon! the present company! the croupier! the honest croupier's wife and daughters—if he has any! the Ladies generally! everybody in the world!"

By the time the second bottle of Champagne was emptied, I felt as if I had been drinking liquid fire—my brain seemed all aflame. No excess in wine had ever had this effect on me before in my life. Was it the result of a stimulant acting upon my system when I was in a highly excited state? Was my stomach in a particularly disordered condition? Or was the Champagne amazingly strong?

"Ex-brave of the French Army!" cried I, in a mad state of exhilaration, "*I* am on fire! how are *you?* You have set me on fire! Do you hear, my hero of Austerlitz? Let us have a third bottle of Champagne to put the flame out!"

The old soldier wagged his head, rolled his goggle-eyes, until I expected to see them slip out of their sockets; placed his dirty forefinger by the side of his broken nose; solemnly ejaculated "Coffee!" and immediately ran off into an inner room.

The word pronounced by the eccentric veteran seemed to have a magical effect on the rest of the company present. With one accord they all rose to depart. Probably they had expected to profit by my intoxication; but finding that my new friend was benevolently bent on preventing me from getting dead drunk, had now abandoned all hope of thriving pleasantly on my winnings. Whatever their motive might be, at any rate they went away in a body. When the old soldier returned, and sat down again opposite to me at the table, we had the room to ourselves. I could see the croupier, in a sort of vestibule which opened out of it, eating his supper in solitude. The silence was now deeper than ever.

A sudden change, too, had come over the "ex-brave." He assumed a portentously solemn look; and when he spoke to me again, his speech was ornamented by no oaths, enforced by no finger-snapping, enlivened by no apostrophes or exclamations.

"Listen, my dear sir," said he, in mysteriously confidential tones—"listen to an old soldier's advice. I have been to the mistress of the house (a very charming woman, with a genius for cookery!) to impress on her the necessity of making us some particularly strong and good coffee. You must drink this coffee in order to get rid of your little amiable exaltation of spirits before you think of going home—you *must*, my good and gracious friend! With all that money to take home to-night, it is a sacred duty to yourself to have your wits about you. You are known to be a winner to an enormous extent by several gentlemen present to-night, who, in a certain point of view, are very worthy and excellent fellows; but they are mortal men, my dear sir, and they have their amiable weaknesses! Need I say more? Ah, no, no! you understand me! Now, this is what you must do—send for a cabriolet when you feel quite well again—draw up all the windows when you get into it—and tell the driver to take you home only through the large and well-lighted thoroughfares. Do this; and you and your money will be safe. Do this; and to-morrow you will thank an old soldier for giving you a word of honest advice."

Just as the ex-brave ended his oration in very lachrymose tones, the coffee came in, ready poured out in two cups. My attentive friend handed me one of the cups with a bow. I was parched with thirst, and drank it off at a draught. Almost instantly afterward, I was seized with a fit of giddiness, and felt more completely intoxicated than ever. The room whirled round and round furiously; the old soldier seemed to be regularly bobbing up and down before me like the piston of a steam-engine. I was half deafened by a violent singing in my ears; a feeling of utter bewilderment, helplessness, idiocy, overcame me. I rose from my chair, holding on by the table to keep my balance; and stammered out that I felt dreadfully unwell—so unwell that I did not know how I was to get home.

"My dear friend," answered the old soldier—and even his voice seemed to be bobbing up and down as he spoke—"my dear friend, it would be madness to go home in *your* state; you would be sure to lose your money; you might be robbed and murdered with the greatest ease. *I* am going to sleep here; do *you* sleep here, too—they make up capital beds in this house—take one; sleep off the effects of the wine, and go home safely with your winnings to-morrow—to-morrow, in broad daylight."

I had but two ideas left; one, that I must never let go hold of my handkerchief full of money; the other, that I must lie down somewhere immediately, and fall off into a comfortable sleep. So I agreed to the proposal about the bed, and took the offered arm of the old soldier, carrying my money with my disengaged hand. Preceded by the croupier, we passed along some passages and up a flight of stairs into the bedroom which I was to occupy. The ex-brave shook me warmly by the hand, proposed that we should breakfast together, and then, followed by the croupier, left me for the night.

I ran to the wash-hand stand; drank some of the water in my jug; poured the rest out, and plunged my face into it; then sat down in a chair and tried to compose myself. I soon felt better. The change for my lungs, from the fetid atmosphere of the gambling-room to the cool air of the apartment I now occupied, the almost equally refreshing change for my eyes, from the glaring gaslights of the "salon" to the dim, quiet flicker of one bedroom-candle, aided wonderfully the restorative effects of cold water. The giddiness left me, and I began to feel a little like a reasonable being again. My first thought was of the risk of sleeping all night in a gambling-house; my second, of the still greater risk of trying to get out after the house was closed, and of going home alone at night through the streets of Paris with a large sum of money about me. I had slept in worse places than this on my travels; so I determined to lock, bolt, and barricade my door, and take my chance till the next morning.

Accordingly, I secured myself against all intrusion; looked under the bed, and into the cupboard; tried the fastening of the window; and then, satisfied that I had taken every proper precaution, pulled off my upper clothing, put my light, which was a dim one, on the hearth among a feathery litter of wood-ashes, and got into bed, with the handkerchief full of money under my pillow.

I soon felt not only that I could not go to sleep, but that I could not even close my eyes. I was wide awake, and in a high fever. Every nerve in my body trembled—every one of my senses seemed to be preternaturally sharpened. I tossed and rolled, and tried every kind of position, and perseveringly sought out the cold corners of the bed, and all to no purpose. Now I thrust my arms over the clothes; now I poked them under the clothes; now I violently shot my legs straight out down to the bottom of the bed; now I convulsively coiled

them up as near my chin as they would go; now I shook out
my crumpled pillow, changed it to the cool side, patted it flat,
and lay down quietly on my back; now I fiercely doubled it in
two, set it up on end, thrust it against the board of the bed,
and tried a sitting posture. Every effort was in vain; I
groaned with vexation as I felt that I was in for a sleepless
night.

What could I do? I had no book to read. And yet, unless I
found out some method of diverting my mind, I felt certain
that I was in the condition to imagine all sorts of horrors; to
rack my brain with forebodings of every possible and impossible danger; in short, to pass the night in suffering all
conceivable varieties of nervous terror.

I raised myself on my elbow, and looked about the room—
which was brightened by a lovely moonlight pouring
straight through the window—to see if it contained any
pictures or ornaments that I could at all clearly distinguish.
While my eyes wandered from wall to wall, a remembrance of
Le Maistre's delightful little book, *Voyage autour de ma
Chambre,* occurred to me. I resolved to imitate the French-
author, and find occupation and amusement enough to
relieve the tedium of my wakefulness, by making a mental
inventory of every article of furniture I could see, and by
following up to their sources the multitude of associations
which even a chair, a table, or a wash-hand stand may be
made to call forth.

In the nervous unsettled state of my mind at that moment,
I found it much easier to make my inventory than to make
my reflections, and thereupon soon gave up all hope of
thinking in Le Maistre's fanciful track—or, indeed, of thinking at all. I looked about the room at the different articles of
furniture, and did nothing more.

There was, first, the bed I was lying in; a four-post bed, of
all things in the world to meet with in Paris—yes, a
thorough clumsy British four-poster, with a regular top
lined with chintz—the regular fringed valance all round—
the regular stifling, unwholesome curtains, which I remembered having mechanically drawn back against the posts
without particularly noticing the bed when I first got into
the room. Then there was the marble-topped wash-hand

stand, from which the water I had spilled, in my hurry to pour it out, was still dripping, slowly and more slowly, on to the brick floor. Then two small chairs, with my coat, waistcoat, and trousers flung on them. Then a large elbow-chair covered with dirty-white dimity, with my cravat and shirt collar thrown over the back. Then a chest of drawers with two of the brass handles off, and a tawdry, broken china inkstand placed on it by way of ornament for the top. Then the dressing-table, adorned by a very small looking-glass, and a very large pincushion. Then the window—an unusually large window. Then a dark old picture, which the feeble candle dimly showed me. It was the picture of a fellow in a high Spanish hat, crowned with a plume of towering feathers. A swarthy, sinister ruffian, looking upward, shading his eyes with his hand, and looking intently upward—it might be at some tall gallows at which he was going to be hanged. At any rate, he had the appearance of thoroughly deserving it.

This picture put a kind of constraint upon me to look upward too—at the top of the bed. It was a gloomy and not an interesting object, and I looked back at the picture. I counted the feathers in the man's hat—they stood out in relief—three white, two green. I observed the crown of his hat, which was of a conical shape, according to the fashion supposed to have been favored by Guido Fawkes. I wondered what he was looking up at. It couldn't be at the stars; such a desperado was neither astrologer nor astronomer. It must be at the high gallows, and he was going to be hanged presently. Would the executioner come into possession of his conical crowned hat and plume of feathers? I counted the feathers again—three white, two green.

While I still lingered over this very improving and intellectual employment, my thoughts insensibly began to wander. The moonlight shining into the room reminded me of a certain moonlight night in England—the night after a picnic party in a Welsh valley. Every incident of the drive homeward, through lovely scenery, which the moonlight made lovelier than ever, came back to my remembrance, though I had never given the picnic a thought for years; though, if I had *tried* to recollect it, I could certainly have

recalled little or nothing of that scene long past. Of all the
wonderful faculties that help to tell us we are immortal,
which speaks the sublime truth more eloquently than memory? Here was I, in a strange house of the most suspicious
character, in a situation of uncertainty, and even of peril,
which might seem to make the cool exercise of my recollection almost out of the question; nevertheless, remembering,
quite involuntarily, places, people, conversations, minute
circumstances of every kind, which I had thought forgotten
forever; which I could not possibly have recalled at will, even
under the most favorable auspices. And what cause had
produced in a moment the whole of this strange, complicated, mysterious effect? Nothing but some rays of moonlight shining in at my bedroom window.

I was still thinking of the picnic—of our merriment on the
drive home—of the sentimental young lady who *would* quote
"Childe Harold" because it was moonlight. I was absorbed by
these past scenes and past amusements, when, in an instant, the thread on which my memories hung snapped
asunder; my attention immediately came back to present
things more vividly than ever, and I found myself, I neither
knew why nor wherefore, looking hard at the picture again.

Looking for what?

Good God! the man had pulled his hat down on his brows!
No! the hat itself was gone! Where was the conical crown?
Where the feathers—three white, two green? Not there! In
place of the hat and feathers, what dusky object was it that
now hid his forehead, his eyes, his shading hand?

Was the bed moving?

I turned on my back and looked up. Was I mad? drunk?
dreaming? giddy again? or was the top of the bed really
moving down—sinking slowly, regulary, silently, horribly,
right down throughout the whole of its length and breadth—
right down upon me, as I lay underneath?

My blood seemed to stand still. A deadly paralyzing coldness stole all over me as I turned my head round on the pillow
and determined to test whether the bed-top was really moving or not, by keeping my eye on the man in the picture.

The next look in that direction was enough. The dull,
black, frowzy outline of the valance above me was within an

inch of being parallel with his waist. I still looked breath-lessly. And steadily and slowly—very slowly—I saw the fig-ure, and the line of frame below the figure, vanish, as the valance moved down before it.

I am, constitutionally, anything but timid. I have been on more than one occasion in peril of my life, and have not lost my self-possession for an instant; but when the conviction first settled on my mind that the bed-top was really moving, was steadily and continuously sinking down upon me, I looked up shuddering, helpless, panic-striken, beneath the hideous machinery for murder, which was advancing closer and closer to suffocate me where I lay.

I looked up, motionless, speechless, breathless. The can-dle, fully spent, went out; but the moonlight still brightened the room. Down and down, without pausing and without sounding, came the bed-top, and still my panic terror seemed to bind me faster and faster to the mattress on which I lay-down and down it sank, till the dusty odor from the lining of the canopy came stealing into my nostrils.

At that final moment the instinct of self-preservation startled me out of my trance, and I moved at last. There was just room for me to roll myself sidewise off the bed. As I dropped noiselessly to the floor, the edge of the murderous canopy touched me on the shoulder.

Without stopping to draw my breath, without wiping the cold sweat from my face, I rose instantly on my knees to watch the bed-top. I was literally spell-bound by it. If I had heard footsteps behind me, I could not have turned round; if a means of escape had been miraculously provided for me, I could not have moved to take advantage of it. The whole life in me was, at that moment, concentrated in my eyes.

It descended—the whole canopy, with the fringe round it, came down—down—close down; so close that there was not room now to squeeze my finger between the bed-top and the bed. I felt at the sides, and discovered that what had appear-ed to me from beneath to be the ordinary light canopy of a four-post bed was in reality a thick, broad mattress, the substance of which was concealed by the valance and its fringe. I looked up and saw the four posts rising hideously bare. In the middle of the bed-top was a huge wooden screw that had evidently worked it down through a hole in the ceiling, just as ordinary presses are worked down on the substance selected for compression. The frightful apparatus moved without making the faintest noise. There had been no creaking as it came down; there was now not the faintest sound from the room above. Amid a dead and awful silence I beheld before me—in the nineteenth century, and in the civilized capital of France—such a machine for secret murder by suffocation as might have existed in the worst days of the Inquisition, in the lonely inns among the Hartz Mountains, in the mysterious tribunals of Westphalia! Still, as I looked on it, I could not move, I could hardly breathe, but I began to recover the power of thinking, and in a moment I discovered the murderous conspiracy framed against me in all its horror.

My cup of coffee had been drugged, and drugged too strongly. I had been saved from being smothered by having taken an overdose of some narcotic. How I had chafed and fretted at the fever fit which had preserved my life by keeping me awake! How recklessly I had confided myself to the two wretches who had led me into this room, determined, for the sake of my winnings, to kill me in my sleep by the surest and most horrible contrivance for secretly accomplishing my destruction! How many men, winners like me, had slept, as I had proposed to sleep, in that bed, and had never been seen or heard of more! I shuddered at the bare idea of it.

But ere long all thought was again suspended by the sight of the murderous canopy moving once more. After it had remained on the bed—as nearly as I could guess—about ten minutes, it began to move up again. The villains who worked it from above evidently believed that their purpose was now accomplished. Slowly and silently, as it had descended, that horrible bed-top rose toward its former place. When it reached the upper extremities of the four posts, it reached the ceiling, too. Neither hole nor screw could be seen; the bed became in appearance an ordinary bed again—the canopy an ordinary canopy—even to the most suspicious eyes.

Now, for the first time, I was able to move—to rise from my knees—to dress myself in my upper clothing—and to consider of how I should escape. If I betrayed by the smallest noise that the attempt to suffocate me had failed, I was certain to be murdered. Had I made any noise already? I listened intently, looking toward the door.

No! no footsteps in the passage outside—no sound of a tread, light or heavy, in the room above—absolute silence everywhere. Besides locking and bolting my door, I had moved an only wooden chest against it, which I had found under the bed. To remove this chest (my blood ran cold as I thought of what its contents *might* be!) without making some disturbance was impossible; and, moreover, to think of escaping through the house, now barred up for the night, was sheer insanity. Only one chance was left me—the window. I stole to it on tiptoe.

My bedroom was on the first floor, above an *entresol*, and looked into the back street. I raised my hand to open the window, knowing that on that action hung, by the merest hair-breadth, my chance of safety. They keep vigilant watch in a House of Murder. If any part of the frame cracked, if the hinge creaked, I was a lost man! It must have occupied me at least five minutes, reckoning by time—five *hours*, reckoning by suspense—to open that window. I succeeded in doing it silently—in doing it with all the dexterity of a house-breaker—and then looked down into the street. To leap the distance beneath me would be almost certain destruction! Next, I looked round at the sides of the house. Down the left side ran a thick water-pipe—it passed close by the outer edge of the window. The moment I saw the pipe I knew I was saved. My breath came and went freely for the first time since I had seen the canopy of the bed moving down upon me!

To some men the means of escape which I had discovered might have seemed difficult and dangerous enough—to *me* the prospect of slipping down the pipe into the street did not suggest even a thought of peril. I had always been accustomed, by the practice of gymnastics, to keep up my schoolboy powers as a daring and expert climber; and knew that my head, hands, and feet would serve me faithfully in any hazards of ascent or descent. I had already got one leg over the window-sill, when I remembered the handkerchief filled with money under my pillow. I could well have afforded to leave it behind me, but I was revengefully determined that the miscreants of the gambling-house should miss their plunder as well as their victim. So I went back to the bed and tied the heavy handkerchief at my back by my cravat.

Just as I had made it tight and fixed it in a comfortable place, I thought I heard a sound of breathing outside the door. The chill feeling of horror ran through me again as I listened. No! dead silence still in the passage—I had only heard the night air blowing softly into the room. The next moment I was on the window-sill—and the next I had a firm grip on the water-pipe with my hands and knees.

I slid down into the street easily and quietly, as I thought I should, and immediately set off at the top of my speed to a branch "Prefecture" of Police, which I knew was situated in the immediate neighborhood. A "Sub-prefect," and several picked men among his subordinates, happened to be up, maturing, I believe, some scheme for discovering the perpetrator of a mysterious murder which all Paris was talking of just then. When I began my story, in a breathless hurry and in very bad French, I could see that the Sub-prefect suspected me of being a drunken Englishman who had robbed somebody; but he soon altered his opinion as I went on, and before I had anything like concluded, he shoved all the papers before him into a drawer, put on his hat, supplied me with another (for I was bare-headed), ordered a file of soldiers, desired his expert followers to get ready all sorts of tools for breaking open doors and ripping up brick flooring, and took my arm, in the most friendly and familiar manner possible, to lead me with him out of the house. I will venture to say that when the Sub-prefect was a little boy, and was taken for the first time to the play, he was not half as much pleased as he was now at the job in prospect for him at the gambling-house!

Away we went through the streets, the Sub-prefect cross-examining and congratulating me in the same breath as we marched at the head of our formidable *posse comitatus*. Sentinels were placed at the back and front of the house the moment we got to it; a tremendous battery of knocks was directed against the door; a light appeared at a window; I was told to conceal myself behind the police—then came more knocks and a cry of "Open in the name of the law!" At that terrible summons bolts and locks gave way before an invisible hand, and the moment after the Sub-prefect was in the passage, confronting a waiter half-dressed and ghastly pale. This was the short dialogue which immediately took place:

"We want to see the Englishman who is sleeping in this house?"

"He went away hours ago."

"He did no such thing. His friend went away; *he* remained. Show us to his bedroom!"

"I swear to you, Monsieur le Sous-prefect, he is not here! he—"

"I swear to you, Monsieur le Garçon, he is. He slept here—he didn't find your bed comfortable—he came to us to complain of it—here he is among my men—and here am I ready to look for a flea or two in his bedstead. Renaudin! (calling to one of the subordinates, and pointing to the waiter) collar that man and tie his hands behind him. Now, then, gentlemen, let us walk upstairs!"

Every man and woman in the house was secured—the "Old Soldier" the first. Then I identified the bed in which I had slept, and then we went into the room above.

No object that was all extraordinary appeared in any part of it. The Sub-prefect looked round the place, commanded everybody to be silent, stamped twice on the floor, called for a candle, looked attentively at the spot he had stamped on, and ordered the flooring there to be carefully taken up. This was done in no time. Lights were produced, and we saw a deep raftered cavity between the floor of this room and the ceiling of the room beneath. Through this cavity there ran perpendicularly a sort of case of iron thickly greased; and inside the case appeared the screw, which communicated with the bed-top below. Extra lengths of screw, freshly oiled; levers covered with felt; all the complete upper works of a heavy press—constructed with infernal ingenuity so as to join the fixtures below, and when taken to pieces again to go into the smallest possible compass—were next discovered and pulled out on the floor. After some little difficulty the Sub-prefect succeeded in putting the machinery together, and, leaving his men to work it, descended with me to the bedroom. The smothering canopy was then lowered, but not so noiselessly as I had seen it lowered. When I mentioned this to the Sub-prefect, his answer, simple as it was, had a terrible significance. "My men," said he, "are working down the bed-top for the first time—the men whose money you won were in better practice."

We left the house in the sole possession of two police agents—every one of the inmates being removed to prison on the spot. The Sub-prefect, after taking down my "*procés verbal*" in his office, returned with me to my hotel to get my passport. "Do you think," I asked, as I gave it to him, "that any men have really been smothered in that bed, as they tried to smother *me*?"

"I have seen dozens of drowned men laid out at the Morgue," answered the Sub-prefect, "in whose pocketbooks were found letters stating that they had committed suicide in the Seine, because they had lost everything at the gaming-table. Do I know how many of those men entered the same gambling-house that *you* entered? won as *you* won? took that bed as *you* took it? slept in it? were smothered in it? and were privately thrown into the river, with a letter of explanation written by the murderers and placed in their pocketbooks? No man can say how many or how few have suffered the fate from which you have escaped. The people of the gambling-house kept their bedstead machinery a secret from *us*—even from the police! The dead kept the rest of the secret for them. Good-night, or rather good-morning, Monsieur Faulkner! Be at my office again at nine o'clock—in the meantime, *au revoir!*"

The rest of my story is soon told. I was examined and re-examined; the gambling-house was strickly searched all through from top to bottom; the prisoners were separately interrogated; and two of the less guilty among them made a confession. I discovered that the Old Soldier was the master of the gambling-house—*justice* discovered that he had been drummed out of the army as a vagabond years ago; that he had been guilty of all sorts of villainies since; that he was in possession of stolen property, which the owners identified; and that he, the croupier, another accomplice, and the woman who had made my cup of coffee, were all in the secret of the bedstead. There appeared some reason to doubt whether the inferior persons attached to the house knew anything of the suffocating machinery; and they received the benefit of that doubt, by being treated simply as thieves and vagabonds. As for the Old Soldier and his two head myrmidons, they went to the galleys; the woman who had drugged my coffee was imprisoned for I forget how many years; the regular attendants at the gambling-house were considered "suspicious" and placed under "surveillance"; and I became, for one whole week (which is a long time) the head "lion" in Parisian society. My adventure was dramatized by three illustrious play-makers, but never saw theatrical daylight; for the censorship forbade the introduction on the stage of a correct copy of the gambling-house bedstead.

One good result was produced by my adventure, which any censorship must have approved: it cured me of ever again trying *"Rouge et Noir"* as an amusement. The sight of a greencloth, with packs of cards and heaps of money on it, will henceforth be forever associated in my mind with the sight of a bed canopy descending to suffocate me in the silence and darkness of the night.

THE ROOM WITH SOMETHING WRONG

By Cornell Woolrich (1903-1968)

Cornell Woolrich was a tormented and haunted man who wrote about tormented and haunted people. His mastery of suspense in such novels as The Bride Wore Black *(1940) is based on his belief that darkness is always threatening to overwhelm us. Even his straight detective stories, such as "The Room with Something Wrong," from a 1938 pulp magazine, contain Woolrichian elements of irrationality in the motive of the murderer and the growing obsession of the detective. And few writers could equal Woolrich in capturing the despair of the Depression and its seedy hotels and often shabby characters. It is unexpected that two such different writers as Wilkie Collins and Cornell Woolrich are joined by the common theme of a murderous room. Which story is the more terrifying we leave to the reader to decide.*

THEY thought it was the Depression the first time it happened. The guy had checked in one night in the black March of '33, in the middle of the memorable bank holiday. He was well-dressed and respectable-looking. He had baggage with him, plenty of it, so he wasn't asked to pay in advance. Everyone was short of ready cash that week. Besides, he'd asked for the weekly rate.

He signed the register *James Hopper, Schenectady,* and Dennison, eyeing the red vacancy-tags in the pigeonholes, pulled out the one in 913 at random and gave him that. Not the vacancy-tag, the room. The guest went up, okayed the room, and George the bellhop was sent up with his bags. George came down and reported a dime without resentment; it was '33, after all.

Striker had sized him up, of course. That was part of his duties, and the house detective found nothing either for him or against him. Striker had been with the St. Anselm two years at that time. He'd had his salary cut in '31, and then again in '32, but so had everyone else on the staff. He didn't look much like a house dick, which was why he was good for the job. He was a tall, lean, casual-moving guy, without that annoying habit most hotel dicks have of staring people out of countenance. He used finesse about it; got the same results, but with sort of a blank, idle expression as though he were thinking of something else. He also lacked the usual paunch, in spite of his sedentary life, and never wore a hard hat. He had a little radio in his top-floor cubbyhole and a stack of vintage "fantastics," pulp magazines dealing with super-science and the supernatural, and that seemed to be all he asked of life.

The newcomer who had signed as Hopper came down again in about half an hour and asked Dennison if there were any good movies near by. The clerk recommended one and the guest went to it. This was about eight p.m. He came back at eleven, picked up his key, and went up to his room. Dennison and Striker both heard him whistling lightly under his breath as he stepped into the elevator. Nothing on his mind but a good night's rest, apparently.

Striker turned in himself at twelve. He was subject to call twenty-four hours a day. There was no one to relieve him.

The St. Anselm was on the downgrade, and had stopped having an assistant house dick about a year before.

He was still awake, reading in bed, about an hour later when the deskman rang him. "Better get down here quick, Strike! Nine-thirteen's just fallen out!" The clerk's voice was taut, frightened.

Striker threw on coat and pants over his pajamas and got down as fast as the creaky old-fashioned elevator would let him. He went out to the street, around to the side under the 13-line.

Hopper was lying there dead, the torn leg of his pajamas rippling in the bitter March night wind. There wasn't anyone else around at that hour except the night porter, the policeman he'd called, and who had called his precinct house in turn, and a taxi driver or two. Maxon, the midnight-to-morning clerk (Dennison went off at eleven-thirty), had to remain at his post for obvious reasons. They were just standing there waiting for the morgue ambulance; there wasn't anything they could do.

Bob, the night porter, was saying: "I thought it was a pillow someone drap out the window. I come up the basement way, see a thick white thing lying there, flappin' in th' wind. I go over, fix to kick it with my foot—" He broke off. "Golly, man!"

One of the drivers said, "I seen him comin' down." No one disputed the point, but he insisted, "No kidding, I seen him coming down! I was just cruisin' past, one block over, and I look this way, and I see—whisht *ungh*—like a pancake!"

The other cab driver, who hadn't seen him coming down, said: "I seen you head down this way, so I thought you spotted a fare, and I chased after you."

They got into a wrangle above the distorted form. "Yeah, you're always chiselin' in on my hails. Follyn' me around. Can't ye get none o' your own?"

Striker crossed the street, teeth chattering, and turned and looked up the face of the building. Half the French window of 913 was open, and the room was lit up. All the rest of the line was dark, from the top floor down.

He crossed back to where the little group stood shivering and stamping their feet miserably. "He sure picked a night for it!" winced the cop. The cab driver opened his mouth a couple of seconds ahead of saying something, which was his speed, and the cop turned on him irritably. "Yeah, we know! You seen him coming down. Go home, will ya!"

Striker went in, rode up, and used his passkey on 913. The light was on, as he had ascertained from the street. He stood there in the doorway and looked around. Each of the 13's, in the St. Anselm, was a small room with private bath. There was an opening on each of the four sides of these rooms: the tall, narrow, old-fashioned room door leading in from the hall; in the wall to the left of that, the door to the bath, of identical proportions; in the wall to the right of the hall door, a door giving into the clothes closet, again of similar measurements. These three panels were in the style of the Nineties, not your squat modern aperture. Directly opposite the room door was a pair of French windows looking out onto the street. Each of them matched the door measurements. Dark blue roller-shades covered the glass on the inside.

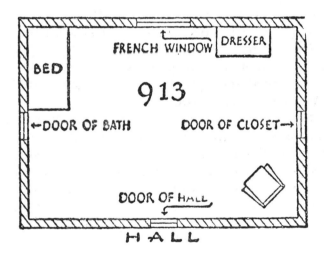

But Striker wasn't thinking about all that particularly, just then. He was interested only in what the condition of the room could tell him: whether it had been suicide or an accident. The only thing disturbed in the room was the bed, but that was not violently disturbed as by a struggle, simply normally disarranged as by someone sleeping. Striker, for some reason or other, tested the sheets with the back of his hand for a minute. They were still warm from recent occupancy. Hopper's trousers were neatly folded across the seat of a chair. His shirt and underclothes were draped over the back of it. His shoes stood under it, toe to toe and heel to heel. He was evidently a very neat person.

He had unpacked. He must have intended to occupy the room for the full week he had bargained for. In the closet, when Striker opened it, were his hat, overcoat, jacket and vest, the latter three on separate hangers. The dresser drawers held his shirts and other linen. On top of the dresser was a white-gold wristwatch, a handful of change, and two folded squares of paper. One was a glossy handbill from the show the guest had evidently attended only two hours ago. *Saturday through Tuesday—the laugh riot, funniest, most tuneful picture of the year, "Hips Hips Hooray!" Also "Popeye the Sailor."* Nothing in that to depress anyone.

The other was a note on hotel stationery—*Hotel Management: Sorry to do this here, but I had to do it somewhere.*

It was unsigned. So it was suicide after all. One of the two window halves, the one to the right stood inward to the room. The one he had gone through.

"You the houseman?" a voice asked from the doorway.

Striker turned and a precinct detective came in. You could tell he was that. He couldn't have looked at a dandelion without congenital suspicion or asked the time of day without making it a leading question. "Find anything?"

Striker handed over the note without comment.

Perry, the manager, had come up with him, in trousers and bathrobe. He was a stout, jovial-looking man ordinarily, but right now he was only stout. "He hadn't paid yet, either," he said ruefully to the empty room. He twisted the cord of his robe around one way, then he undid it and twisted it around the other way. He was very unhappy. He picked the wristwatch up gingerly by the end of its strap and dangled it close to his ear, as if to ascertain whether or not it had a good movement.

The precinct dick went to the window and looked down, opened the bath door and looked in, the closet door and looked in. He gave the impression of doing this just to give the customers their money's worth; in other words, as far as he was concerned, the note had clinched the case.

"It's the old suey, all right," he said and, bending over at the dresser, read aloud what he was jotting down. "James Hopper, Skun-Skunnect—"

Striker objected peevishly. "Why did he go to bed first, then get up and go do it? They don't usually do that. He took the room for a week, too."

The precinct man raised his voice, to show he was a police detective talking to a mere hotel dick, someone who in his estimation wasn't a detective at all. "I don't care if he took it for six months! He left this note and hit the sidewalk, didn't he? Whaddaya trying to do, make it into something it ain't?"

The manager said, "Ssh! if you don't mind," and eased the door to, to keep other guests from overhearing. He sided with the precinct man, the wish being father to the thought. If there's one thing that a hotel man likes less than a suicide, it's a murder. "I don't think there's any doubt of it."

The police dick stooped to reasoning with Striker. "You were the first one up here. Was there anything wrong with the door? Was it forced open or anything?"

Striker had to admit it had been properly shut; the late occupant's key lay on the dresser where it belonged, at that very moment.

The police dick spread his hands, as if to say: "There you are, what more do you want?"

He took a last look around, decided the room had nothing more to tell him. Nor could Striker argue with him on this point. The room had nothing more to tell anyone. The dick gathered up Hopper's watch, change and identification papers, to turn them over to the police property-clerk, until they were claimed by his nearest of kin. His baggage was left in there temporarily; the room was darkened and locked up.

Riding down to the lobby, the dick rubbed it in a little. "Here's how those things go," he said patronizingly. "No one got in there or went near him, so it wasn't murder. He left a note, so it wasn't an accident. The word they got for this is suicide. Now y'got it?"

Striker held his palm up and fluttered it slightly. "Teacher, can I leave the room?" he murmured poignantly.

The stout manager, Perry, had a distrait, slightly anticipatory expression on his moon face now; in his mind it was the next day, he had already sold the room to someone else, and had the two dollars in the till. Heaven, to him, was a houseful of full rooms.

The body had already been removed from the street outside. Somewhere, across a coffee counter, a cab driver was saying: "I seen him coming down."

The city dick took his departure from the hotel, with the magnanimous assurance: "It's the depresh. They're poppin' off like popcorn all over the country this week. *I* ain't been able to cash my paycheck since Monday."

Perry returned to his own quarters, with the typical managerial admonition, to Maxon and Striker, "Soft pedal, now, you two. Don't let this get around the house." He yawned with a sound like air brakes, going up in the elevator. You could still hear it echoing down the shaft after his feet had gone up out of sight.

"Just the same," Striker said finally, unasked, to the night clerk, "I don't care what that know-it-all says, Hopper didn't have suicide on his mind when he checked in here at seven-thirty. He saw a show that was full of laughs, and even came home whistling one of the tunes from it. We both heard him. He unpacked all his shirts and things into the bureau drawers. He intended staying. He went to bed first; I felt the covers, they were warm. Then he popped up all of a sudden and took this standing broad jump."

"Maybe he had a bad dream," Maxon suggested facetiously. His was a hard-boiled racket. He yawned, muscularly magnetized by his boss' recent gape, and opened a big ledger. "Some of 'em put on a fake front until the last minute—whistle, go to a show, too proud to take the world into their confidence, and then—bang—they've crumpled."

And on that note it ended. As Maxon said, there was no accounting for human nature. Striker caught the sleepiness from the other two, widened his jaws terrifyingly, brought them together again with a click. And yet somehow, to him, this suicide hadn't run true to form.

He went back up to his own room again with a vague feeling of dissatisfaction, that wasn't strong enough to do anything about, and yet that he couldn't altogether throw off. Like the feeling you get when you're working out a

THE ROOM WITH SOMETHING WRONG   251

crossword puzzle and one of the words fills up the space satisfactorily, but doesn't seem to have the required meaning called for in the solution.

The St. Anselm went back to sleep again, the small part of it that had been awake. The case was closed.

People came and went from 913 and the incident faded into the limbo of half-forgotten things. Then in the early fall of '34 the room came to specific attention again.

A young fellow in his early twenties, a college type, arrived in a roadster with just enough baggage for overnight. No reservation or anything. He signed in as Allan Hastings, Princeton, New Jersey. He didn't have to ask the desk if there were any shows. He knew his own way around. They were kind of full-up that weekend. The only red vacancy-tag in any of the pigeonholes was 913. Dennison gave him that— had no choice.

The guest admitted he'd been turned away from two hotels already. They all had the S.R.O. sign out. "It's the Big Game, I guess," he said.

"What Big Game?" Striker was incautious enought to ask.

"Where've you been all your life?" he grinned.

Some football game or other, the house dick supposed. Personally a crackling good super-science story still had the edge on twenty-two huskies squabbling over a pig's inflated hide, as far as he was concerned.

Hastings came back from the game still sober. Or if he'd had a drink it didn't show. "We lost," he said casually at the desk on his way up, but it didn't seem to depress him any. His phone, the operator reported later, rang six times in the next quarter of an hour, all feminine voices. He was apparently getting booked up solid for the rest of the weekend.

Two girls and a fellow, in evening clothes, called for him about nine. Striker saw them sitting waiting for him in the lobby, chirping and laughing their heads off. He came down in about five minutes, all rigged up for the merry-merry, even down to a white carnation in his lapel.

Striker watched them go, half-wistfully. "That's the life," he said to the man behind the desk.

"May as well enjoy it while you can," said Dennison philosophically. "Here today and gone tomorrow."

Hastings hadn't come back yet by the time Striker went up

and turned in. Not that Striker was thinking about him particularly, but he just hadn't seen him. He read a swell story about mermaids kidnapping a deep-sea diver, and dropped off to sleep.

The call came through to his room at about four-thirty in the morning. It took him a minute or two to come out of the deep sleep he'd been in.

"Hurry it up, will you, Strike?" Maxon was whining impatiently. "The young guy in nine-thirteen has taken a flier out his window."

Striker hung up, thinking blurredly, "Where've I heard that before—nine-thirteen?" Then he remembered—last year, from the very same room.

He filled the hollow of his hand with cold water from the washstand, dashed it into his eyes, shrugged into some clothing, and ran down the fire stairs at one side of the elevator shaft. That was quicker than waiting for the venerable mechanism to crawl up for him, then limp down again.

Maxon, who was a reformed drunk, gave him a look eloquent of disgust as Striker chased by the desk. "I'm getting off the wagon again if this keeps up—then I'll have some fun out of all these bum jolts."

There was more of a crowd this time. The weather was milder and there were more night owls in the vicinity to collect around him and gape morbidly. The kid had fallen farther out into the street than Hopper—he didn't weigh as much, maybe. He was lying there face down in the shape of a St. Andrew's cross. He hadn't undressed yet, either. Only his shoes and dinner jacket had been taken off. One strap of his black suspenders had torn off, due to the bodily contortion of the descent or from the impact itself. The white of his shirt was pretty badly changed by now, except the sleeves. He'd had a good-looking face; that was all gone too. They were turning him over as Striker came up.

The same cop was there. He was saying to a man who had been on his way home to read the after-midnight edition of the coming morning's newspaper: "Lemme have your paper, Mac, will you?"

The man demurred, "I ain't read it myself yet. I just now bought it."

The cop said, "You can buy another. We can't leave him lying like this."

The thing that had been Hastings was in pretty bad shape. The cop spread the paper, separating the sheets, and made a long paper-covered mound.

The same precinct dick showed up in answer to the routine notification that had been phoned in. His greeting to Striker was as to the dirt under his feet. "You still on the face of the earth?"

"Should I have asked your permission?" answered the hotel man drily.

Eddie Courlander—that, it seemed, was the police dick's tag—squatted down, looked under the pall of newspapers, shifted around, looked under from the other side.

"Peek-a-boo!" somebody in the small crowd said irreverently.

Courlander looked up threateningly. "Who said that? Gawan, get outa here, wise guys! If it happened to one of youse, you wouldn't feel so funny."

Somebody's night-bound coupé tried to get through, honked imperiously for clearance, not knowing what the obstruction was. The cop went up to it, said; "Get back! Take the next street over. There's a guy fell out of a window here."

The coupé drew over to the curb instead, and its occupants got out and joined the onlookers. One was a girl carrying a night-club favor, a long stick topped with paper streamers. She squealed, *"Ooou, ooou-ooou,"* in a way you couldn't tell if she was delighted or horrified.

Courlander straightened, nodded toward Striker. "What room'd he have? C'mon in."

He didn't remember that it was the same one. Striker could tell that by the startled way he said, "Oh, yeah, that's right too!" when he mentioned the coincidence to him.

Perry and the night porter were waiting outside the room door. "I wouldn't go in until you got here," the manager whispered virtuously to the cop, "I know you people don't like anything touched." Striker, however, had a hunch there was a little superstitious fear at the back of this as well, like a kid shying away from a dark room.

"You're thinking of murder cases," remarked Courlander contemptuously. "Open 'er up."

The light was on again, like the previous time. But there was a great difference in the condition of the room. Young Hastings obviously hadn't had Hopper's personal neatness. Or else he'd been slightly lit up when he came in. The daytime clothes he'd discarded after coming back from the game were still strewn around, some on chairs, some on the floor. The St. Anselm didn't employ maids to straighten the rooms after five in the evening. His patent-leathers lay yards apart as though they had been kicked off into the air and left lying where they had come down. His bat-wing tie was a black snake across the carpet. There was a depression and creases on the counterpane on top of the bed, but it hadn't been turned down. He had therefore lain down on the bed, but not in it.

On the dresser top stood a glittering little pouch, obviously a woman's evening bag. Also his carnation, in a glass of water. Under that was the note. Possibly one of the shortest suicide notes on record. Three words. *What's the use?*

Courlander read it, nodded, showed it to them. "Well," he said, "that tells the story."

He shrugged.

In the silence that followed the remark, the phone rang sharply, unexpectedly. They all jolted a little, even Courlander. Although there was no body in the room and never had been, it was a dead man's room. There was something macabre to the peal, like a desecration. The police dick halted Striker and the manager with a gesture.

"May be somebody for him," he said, and went over and took it. He said, "Hello?" in a wary, noncommittal voice. Then he changed to his own voice, said: "Oh. Have you told her yet? Well, send her up here. I'd like to talk to her."

He hung up, explained: "Girl he was out with tonight is down at the desk, came back to get her bag. He must have been carrying it for her. It has her latchkey in it and she couldn't get into her own home."

Perry turned almost unconsciously and looked into the dresser mirror to see if he needed a shave. Then he fastidiously narrowed the neck opening of his dressing gown and smoothed the hair around the back of his head.

The dick shoved Hastings' discarded clothes out of sight on the closet floor. This was definitely not a murder case, so there was no reason to shock the person he was about to question, by the presence of the clothes.

There was a short tense wait while she was coming up on the slow-motion elevator. Coming up to see someone that wasn't there at all. Striker said rebukingly, "This is giving it to her awful sudden, if she was at all fond of the guy."

Courlander unwittingly gave an insight into his own character when he said callously, "These girls nowadays can take it better than we can—don't worry."

The elevator panel ticked open, and then she came into the square of light thrown across the hall by the open doorway. She was a very pretty girl of about twenty-one or-two, tall and slim, with dark red hair, in a long white satin evening gown. Her eyes were wide with startled inquiry, at the sight of the three of them, but not frightened yet. Striker had seen her once before, when she was waiting for Hastings in the lobby earlier that evening. The other man of the original quartette had come up with her, no doubt for propriety's sake, and was standing behind her. They had evidently seen the second girl home before coming back here. And the side street where he had fallen was around the corner from the main entrance to the hotel.

She crossed the threshold, asked anxiously, "Is Allan—Is Mr. Hastings ill or something? The desk man said there's been a little trouble up here."

Courlander said gently, "Yes, there has." But he couldn't make anything sound gentle.

She looked around. She was starting to get frightened now. She said, "What's happened to him? Where is he?" Then she saw the right half of the window standing open. Striker, who was closest to it, raised his arm and pushed it slowly closed. Then he just looked at her.

She understood, and whimpered across her shoulder, "Oh, Marty!" and the man behind her put an arm around her shoulder to support her.

They sat down. She didn't cry much—just sat with her head bent looking over at the floor. Her escort stood behind her chair, hands on her shoulders, bucking her up.

Courlander gave her a minute or two to pull herself together, then he started questioning. He asked them who they were. She gave her name. The man with her was her brother; he was Hastings' classmate at Princeton.

He asked if Hastings had had much to drink.

"He had a few drinks," she admitted, "but he wasn't drunk. Mart and I had the same number he did, and we're not drunk." They obviously weren't.

"Do you know of any reason, either one of you, why he should have done this?"

The thing had swamped them with its inexplicability, it was easy to see that. They just shook their heads dazedly.

"Financial trouble?"

The girl's brother just laughed—mirthlessly. "He had a banking business to inherit, some day—if he'd lived."

"Ill health? Did he study too hard, maybe?"

He laughed again, dismally. "He was captain of the hockey team, he was on the baseball team, he was the bright hope of the swimming team. Why should he worry about studying? Star athletes are never allowed to flunk."

"Love affair?" the tactless flatfoot blundered on.

The brother flinched at that. This time it was the girl who answered. She raised her head in wounded pride, thrust out her left hand.

"He asked me to marry him tonight. He gave me this ring. That was the reason for the party. Am I so hard to take?"

The police dick got red. She stood up without waiting to ask whether she could go or not. "Take me home, Mart," she said in a muffled voice. "I've got some back crying to catch up on."

Striker called the brother back again for a minute, while she went on along toward the elevator; shoved the note before him. "Was that his handwriting?"

He pored over it. "I can't tell, just on the strength of those three words. I've never seen enough of it to know it very well. The only thing I'd know for sure would be his signature—he had a cockeyed way of ending it with a little pretzel twist—and that isn't on there." Over his shoulder, as he turned to go once more, he added: "That was a favorite catchword of his, though. 'What's the use?' I've often heard him use it. I guess it's him all right."

"We can check it by the register," Striker suggested after they'd gone.

The dick gave him a scathing look. "Is it your idea somebody else wrote his suicide note for him? That's what I'd call service!"

"Is it your idea he committed suicide the same night he got engaged to a production number like you just saw?"

"Is it your idea he didn't?"

"Ye-es," said Striker with heavy emphasis, "but I can't back it up."

The register showed a variation between the two specimens of handwriting, but not more than could be ascribed to the tension and nervous excitement of a man about to end his life. There wasn't enough to the note for a good handwriting expert to have got his teeth into with any degree of certainty.

"How long had he been in when it happened?" Striker asked Maxon.

"Not more than half an hour. Bob took him up a little before four."

"How'd he act? Down in the mouth, blue?"

"Blue nothing, he was tappin' out steps there on the mosaic, waitin' for the car to take him up."

Bob, the night man-of-all-work, put in his two cents' worth without being asked: "On the way up he said to me, "Think this thing'll last till we get up there? I'd hate to have it drop me now. I got engaged tonight."

Striker flashed the police dick a triumphant look. The latter just stood by with the air of one indulging a precocious child. "Now ya through, little boy?" he demanded. "Why don't you quit trying to make noise like a homicide dick and stick to your own little racket?"

"It's a suicide, see?" continued the police dick pugnaciously, as though by raising his voice he was deciding the argument. "I've cased the room, and I don't care if he stood on his head or did somersaults before he rode up." He waved a little black pocket-notebook under Striker's nose. "Here's my report, and if it don't suit you, why don't you take it up with the Mayor?"

Striker said in a humble, placating voice: "Mind if I ask you something personal?"

"What?" said the precinct man sourly.

"Are you a married man?"

"Sure I'm married. What's that to—?"

"Think hard. The night you became engaged, the night you first proposed to your wife, did you feel like taking your own life afterwards?"

The police dick went "Arrrr!" disgustedly, flung around on his heel, and stalked out, giving the revolving door an exasperated twirl that kept it going long after he was gone.

"They get sore, when you've got 'em pinned down," Striker remarked wryly.

Perry remonstrated impatiently, "Why are you always trying to make it out worse than it is? Isn't it bad enough without looking for trouble?"

"If there's something phony about his death, isn't it worse if it goes undetected than if it's brought·to light?"

Perry said, pointedly thumbing the still-turning door, "*That* was the police we just had with us."

"We were practically alone," muttered his disgruntled operative.

And so they couldn't blame it on the Depression this time. That was starting to clear up now. And besides, Allan Hastings had come from well-to-do people. They couldn't blame it on love either. Perry half-heartedly tried to suggest he hadn't loved the girl he was engaged to, had had somebody else under his skin maybe, so he'd taken this way to get out of it.

"That's a woman's reason, not a man's," Striker said disgustedly. "Men don't kill themselves for love; they go out and get tanked, and hop a train for some place else, instead!" The others both nodded, probing deep within their personal memories. So that wouldn't wash either.

In the end there wasn't anything they could blame it on but the room itself. "That room's jinxed," Maxon drawled slurringly. "That's two in a row we've had in there. I think it's the thirteen on it. You oughta change the number to nine-twelve and a half or nine-fourteen and a half or something, boss."

That was how the legend first got started.

Perry immediately jumped on him full-weight. "Now listen, I won't have any of that nonsense! There's nothing wrong with that room! First thing you know the whole hotel'll have a bad name, and then where are we? It's just a coincidence, I tell you, just a coincidence!"

Dennison sold the room the very second day after to a middle-aged couple on a visit to the city to see the sights. Striker and Maxon sort of held their breaths, without admitting it to each other. Striker even got up out of bed once or twice that first night and took a prowl past the door of nine-thirteen, stopping to listen carefully. All he could hear was a sonorous baritone snore and a silvery soprano one, in peaceful counterpoint.

The hayseed couple left three days later, perfectly unharmed and vowing they'd never enjoyed themselves as much in their lives.

"Looks like the spirits are lying low," commented the deskman, shoving the red vacancy-tag back into the pigeonhole.

"No," said Striker, "looks like it only happens to singles. When there's two in the room nothing ever happens."

"You never heard of anyone committing suicide in the presence of a second party, did you?" the clerk pointed out not unreasonably. "That's one thing they gotta have privacy for."

Maybe it had been, as Perry insisted, just a gruesome coincidence. "But if it happens a third time," Striker vowed to himself, "I'm going to get to the bottom of it if I gotta pull the whole place down brick by brick!"

The Legend, meanwhile, had blazed up, high and furious, with the employees; even the slowest-moving among them had a way of hurrying past Room 913 with sidelong glances and fetish mutterings when any duty called them to that particular hallway after dark. Perry raised hell about it, but he was up against the supernatural now; he and his threats of discharge didn't stack up at all against that. The penalty for repeating the rumor to a guest was instant dismissal if detected by the management. *If.*

Then just when the legend was languishing from lack of any further substantiation to feed upon, and was about to die down altogether, the room came through a third time!

The calendar read Friday, July 12th, 1935, and the thermometers all read 90-plus. He came in mopping his face like everyone else, but with a sort of professional good humor about him that no one else could muster just then. That was one thing that tipped Striker off he was a salesman. Another was the two bulky sample cases he was hauling with him until the bellboy took them over. A third was his ability to crack a joke when most people felt like eggs in a frying pan waiting to be turned over.

"Just rent me a bath without a room," he told Dennison. I'll sleep in the tub all night with the cold water running over me."

"I can give you a nice inside room on the fourth." There were enough vacancies at the moment to offer a choice, these being the dog days.

The newcomer held up his hand, palm outward. "No thanks, not this kind of weather. I'm willing to pay the difference."

"Well, I've got an outside on the sixth, and a couple on the ninth."

"The higher the better. More chance to get a little circulation into the air."

There were two on the ninth, 13 and 19. Dennison's hand paused before 13, strayed on past it to 19, hesitated, came back again. After all, the room had to be sold. This was business, not a kid's goblin story. Even Striker could see that. And it was nine months now since— There'd been singles in the room since then, too. And they'd lived to check out again.

He gave him 913. But after the man had gone up, he couldn't refrain from remarking to Striker: "Keep your fingers crossed. That's the one with the jinx on it." As though Striker didn't know that! "I'm going to do a little more than that," he promised himself privately.

He swung the register around toward him so he could read it. *Amos J. Dillberry, City,* was inscribed on it. Meaning this was the salesman's headquarters when he was not on the road, probably. Striker shifted it back again.

He saw the salesman in the hotel dining room at mealtime that evening. He came in freshly showered and laundered, and had a wisecrack for his waiter. That was the salesman in him. The heat certainly hadn't affected his appetite any, the way he stoked.

"If anything happens," thought Striker with gloomy foreboding, "that dick Courlander should show up later and try to tell me this guy was depressed or affected by the heat! He should just try!"

In the early part of the evening the salesman hung around the lobby a while, trying to drum up conversation with this and that sweltering fellow-guest. Striker was in there too, watching him covertly. For once he was not a hotel dick sizing somebody up hostilely, he was a hotel dick sizing somebody up protectively. Not finding anyone particularly receptive, Dillberry went out into the street about ten, in quest of a soulmate.

Striker stood up as soon as he'd gone, and took the opportunity of going up to 913 and inspecting it thoroughly. He went over every square inch of it; got down on his hands and knees and explored all along the baseboards of the walls; examined the electric outlets; held matches to such slight fissures as there were between the tiles in the bathroom; rolled back one half of the carpet at a time and inspected the floorboards thoroughly; even got up a chair and fiddled with the ceiling light fixture, to see if there was anything tricky about it. He couldn't find a thing wrong. He tested the windows exhaustively, working them back and forth until the hinges threatened to come off. There wasn't anything defective or balky about them, and on a scorching night like this the inmate was bound to leave them wide open and let it go at that, not fiddle around with them in any way during the middle of the night. There wasn't enough breeze, even this high up, to swing a cobweb.

He locked the room behind him, went downstairs again with a helpless dissatisfied feeling of having done everything that was humanly possible—and yet not having done anything at all, really. What was there he could do?

Dillberry reappeared a few minutes before twelve, with a package cradled in his arm that was unmistakably for refreshment purposes up in his room, and a conspiratorial expression on his face that told Striker's experienced eyes

what was coming next. The salesman obviously wasn't the
solitary drinker type.

Striker saw her drift in about ten minutes later, with the
air of a lady on her way to do a little constructive drinking.
He couldn't place her on the guest list, and she skipped the
desk entirely—so he bracketed her with Dillberry. He did
exactly nothing about it—turned his head away as though he
hadn't noticed her.

Maxon, who had just come on in time to get a load of this,
looked at Striker in surprise. "Aren't you going to do anything about that?" he murmured. "She's not one of our
regulars."

"I know what I'm doing," Striker assured him softly. "She
don't know it, but she's subbing for night watchman up
there. As long as he's not alone, nothing can happen to him."

"Oh, is that the angle? Using her for a chest protector, eh?
But that just postpones the showdown—don't solve it. If you
keep using a spare to ward it off, how you gonna know what
it is?"

"That," Striker had to admit, "is just the rub. But I hate
like the devil to find out at the expense of still another life."

But the precaution was frustrated before he had time to
see whether it would work or not. The car came down almost
immediately afterwards, and the blonde was still on it,
looking extremely annoyed and quenching her unsatisfied
thirst by chewing gum with a sound like castanets. Beside
her stood Manager Perry, pious determination transform-
ing his face.

"Good night," he said, politely ushering her off the car.

"Y'couldda at least let me have one quick one, neat, you big
overstuffed blimp!" quoth the departing lady indignantly.
"After I helped him pick out the brand!"

Perry came over to the desk and rebuked his houseman:
"Where are your eyes, Striker? How did you let that come
about? I happened to spot her out in the hall waiting to be let
in. You want to be on your toes, man."

"So it looks like he takes his own chances," murmured
Maxon, when the manager had gone up again.

"Then I'm elected, personally," sighed Striker. "Maybe it's
just as well. Even if something had happened with her up

there, she didn't look like she had brains enough to be able to tell what it was afterwards."

In the car, on the way to his room, he said, "Stop at nine a minute—and wait for me." This was about a quarter to one.

He listened outside 13. He heard a page rustle, knew the salesman wasn't asleep, so he knocked softly. Dillberry opened the door.

"Excuse me for disturbing you. I'm the hotel detective."

"I've been quarantined once tonight already," said the salesman, but his characteristic good humor got the better of him even now. "You can come in and look if you want to, but I know when I'm licked."

"No, it isn't about that." Striker wondered how to put it. In loyalty to his employer he couldn't very well frighten the man out of the place. "I just wanted to warn you to please be careful of those windows. The guard-rail outside them's pretty low, and—"

"No danger," the salesman chuckled. "I'm not subject to dizzy spells and I don't walk in my sleep."

Striker didn't smile back. "Just bear in mind what I said, though, will you?"

Dillberry was still chortling good-naturedly. "If he *did* lose his balance during the night and go out," thought Striker impatiently, "it would be like him still to keep on sniggering all the way down."

"What are you worried they'll do—creep up on me and bite me?" kidded the salesman.

"Maybe that's a little closer to the truth than you realize," Striker said to himself mordantly. Looking at the black, night-filled aperture across the lighted room from them, he visualized it for the first time as a hungry, predatory maw, with an evil active intelligence of its own, swallowing the living beings that lingered too long within its reach, sucking them through to destruction, like a diabolic vacuum cleaner. It looked like an upright, open black coffin there, against the cream-painted walls; all it needed was a silver handle at each end. Or like a symbolic Egyptian doorway to the land of the dead, with its severe proportions and pitch-black core and the hot, lazy air coming through it from the nether world.

He was beginning to hate it with a personal hate, because it baffled him, it had him licked, had him helpless, and it struck without warning—an unfair adversary.

Dillberry giggled, "You got a look on your face like you tasted poison! I got a bottle here hasn't been opened yet. How about rinsing it out?"

"No, thanks," said Striker, turning away. "And it's none of my business, I know, but just look out for those windows if you've got a little something under your belt later."

"No fear," the salesman called after him. "It's no fun drinking alone. Too hot for that, anyway."

Striker went on up to his own room and turned in. The night air had a heavy, stagnant expectancy to it, as if it were just waiting for something to happen. Probably the heat, and yet he could hardly breathe, the air was so leaden with menace and sinister tension.

He couldn't put his mind to the "fantastic" magazine he'd taken to bed with him—he flung it across the room finally. "You'd think I knew, ahead of time!" he told himself scoffingly. And yet deny it as he might, he did have a feeling that tonight was going to be one of those times. Heat jangling his nerves, probably. He put out his light—even the weak bulb gave too much warmth for comfort—and lay there in the dark, chainsmoking cigarettes until his tongue prickled.

An hour ticked off, like drops of molten lead. He heard the hour of three strike faintly somewhere in the distance, finally. He lay there, tossing and turning, his mind going around and around the problem. What *could* it have been but two suicides, by coincidence both from the one room? There had been no violence, no signs of anyone having got in from the outside.

He couldn't get the infernal room off his mind; it was driving him nutty. He sat up abruptly, decided to go down there and take soundings. Anything was better than lying there. He put on shirt and pants, groped his way to the door without bothering with the light—it was too hot for lights—opened the door and started down the hall. He left the door cracked open behind him, to save himself the trouble of having to work a key on it when he got back.

He'd already rounded the turn of the hall and was at the fire door giving onto the emergency stairs, when he heard a faint trill somewhere behind him. The ding-a-ling of a telephone bell. Could that be his? If it was—He tensed at the implication. It kept on sounding; it must be his, or it would have been answered by now.

He turned and ran back, shoved the door wide open. It was. It burst into full-bodied volume, almost seemed to explode in his face. He found the instrument in the dark, rasped, "Hello?"

"Strike?" There was fear in Maxon's voice now. "It's—it's happened again."

Striker drew in his breath, and that was cold too, in all the heat of the stuffy room. "Nine-thirteen?" he said hoarsely.

"Nine-thirteen!"

He hung up without another word. His feet beat a pulsing tattoo, racing down the hall. This time he went straight to the room, not down to the street. He'd seen too often what "they" looked like, down below, after they'd grounded. This time he wanted to see what that hell box, that four-walled coffin, that murder crate of a room looked like. Right after. Not five minutes or even two, but right after—as fast as it was humanly possible to get there. But maybe five minutes had passed, already; must have, by the time it was discovered, and he was summoned, and he got back and answered his phone. Why hadn't he stirred his stumps a few minutes sooner? He'd have been just in time, not only to prevent, but to see what it was—if there was anything to see.

He got down to the ninth, heat or no heat, in thirty seconds flat, and over to the side of the building the room was on. The door was yawning wide open, and the room light was out. "Caught you, have I?" flashed grimly through his mind. He rounded the jamb like a shot, poked the light switch on, stood crouched, ready to fling himself—

Nothing. No living thing, no disturbance.

No note either, this time. He didn't miss any bets. He looked into the closet, the bath, even got down and peered under the bed. He peered cautiously down from the lethal window embrasure, careful where he put his hands, careful where he put his weight.

He couldn't see the street, because the window was too high up, but he could hear voices down there.

He went back to the hall and stood there listening. But it was too late to expect to hear anything, and he knew it. The way he'd come galloping down like a war horse would have drowned out any sounds of surreptitious departure there might have been. And somehow, he couldn't help feeling there hadn't been any, anyway. The evil was implicit in this room itself—didn't come from outside, open door to the contrary.

He left the room just the way he'd found it, went below finally. Maxon straightened up from concealing something under the desk, drew the back of his hand recklessly across his mouth. "Bring on your heebie-jeebies," he said defiantly. "See if I care—now!"

Striker didn't blame him too much at that. He felt pretty shaken himself.

Perry came down one car-trip behind him. "I never heard of anything like it!" he was seething. "What kind of a merry-go-round is this anyway?"

Eddie Courlander had been sent over for the third time. Happened to be the only one on hand, maybe. The whole thing was just a monotonous repetition of the first two times, but too grisly—to Striker, anyway—to be amusing.

"This is getting to be a commutation trip for me," the police dick announced with macabre humor, stalking in. "The desk lieutenant only has to say, 'Suicide at a hotel,' and I say right away, 'The St. Anselm,' before he can tell me."

"Only it isn't," said Striker coldly. "There was no note."

"Are you going to start that again?" growled the city dick.

"It's the same room again, in case you're interested. Third time in a little over two years. Now, don't you think that's rubbing it in a little heavy?"

Courlander didn't answer, as though he *was* inclined to think that, but—if it meant siding with Striker—hated to have to admit it.

Even Perry's professional bias for suicide—if the alternative had to be murder, the *bête-noir* of hotel men—wavered in the face of this triple assault. "It does look kind of spooky," he faltered, polishing the center of his bald head. "All the rooms below, on that line, have those same floor-length windows, and it's never taken place in any of the others."

"Well, we're going to do it up brown this time and get to the bottom of it!" Courlander promised.

They got off at the ninth. "Found the door open like this, too," Striker pointed out. "I stopped off here on my way down."

Courlander just glanced at him, but still wouldn't commit himself. He went into the room, stopped dead center and stood there looking around, the other two just behind him. Then he went over to the bed, fumbled a little with the covers. Suddenly he spaded his hand under an edge of the pillow, drew it back again.

"I thought you said there was no note?" he said over his shoulder to Striker.

"You not only thought. I did say that."

"You still do, huh?" He shoved a piece of stationery at him. "What does this look like—a collar button?"

It was as laconic as the first two. *I'm going to hell, where it's cool!* Unsigned.

"That wasn't in here when I looked the place over the first time," Striker insisted with slow emphasis. "That was planted in here between then and now!"

Courlander flung his head disgustedly. "It's white, isn't it? The bedclothes are white too, ain't they? Why don't you admit you missed it?"

"Because I know I didn't! I had my face inches away from that bed, bending down looking under it."

"Aw, you came in half-asleep and couldn't even see straight, probably!"

"I've been awake all night, wider awake than you are right now!"

"And as for your open door—" Courlander jeered. He bent down, ran his thumbnail under the panel close in to the jamb, jerked something out. He stood up exhibiting a wedge made of a folded-over paper match-cover. "He did that himself, to try to get a little circulation into the air in here."

Striker contented himself with murmuring, "Funny no

one else's door was left open." But to himself he thought, ruefully, "It's trying its best to look natural all along the line, like the other times; which only proves it isn't."

The city dick answered, "Not funny at all. A woman alone in a room wouldn't leave her door open for obvious reasons; and a couple in a room wouldn't, because the wife would be nervous or modest about it. But why shouldn't a guy roomining by himself do it, once his light was out, and if he didn't have anything of value in here with him? That's why his was the only door open like that. The heat drove him wacky; and when he couldn't get any relief no matter what he did—"

"The heat did nothing of the kind. I spoke to him at twelve and he was cheerful as a robin."

"Yeah, but a guy's resistance gets worn down, it frays, and then suddenly it snaps." Courlander chuckled scornfully. "It's as plain as day before your eyes."

"Well," drawled Striker, "if this is your idea of getting to the bottom of a thing, baby, you're easily pleased! I'll admit it's a little more work to keep digging, than just to write down 'suicide' in your report and let it go at that," he added stingingly.

"I don't want any of your insinuations!" Courlander said hotly. "Trying to call me lazy, huh? All right," he said with the air of doing a big favor, "I'll play ball with you. We'll make the rounds giving off noises like a detective, if that's your idea."

"You'll empty my house for me," Perry whined.

"Your man here seems to think I'm laying down on the job." Courlander stalked out, hitched his head at them to follow.

"You've never played the numbers, have you?" Striker suggested stolidly. "No number ever comes up three times in a row. That's what they call the law of averages. Three suicides from one room doesn't conform to the law of averages. And when a thing don't conform to that law, it's phony."

"You forgot your lantern slides, perfessor," sneered the police dick. He went next door and knuckled 915, first gently, then resoundingly.

The door opened and a man stuck a sleep-puffed face out at them. He said, "What-d'ye want? It takes me half the night to work up a little sleep and then I gotta have it busted on me!" He wasn't just faking being asleep—it was the real article; anyone could see that. The light hurt his eyes; he kept blinking.

"Sorry, pal," Courlander overrode him with a businesslike air, "but we gotta ask a few questions. Can we come in and look around?"

"No, ya can't! My wife's in bed!"

"Have her put something over her, then, 'cause we're comin'!"

"I'm leaving the first thing in the morning!" the man threatened angrily. "You can't come into my room like this without a search warrant!" He thrust himself belligerently into the door opening.

"Just what have you got to hide, Mr. Morris?" suggested Striker mildly.

The remark had an almost magical effect on him. He blinked, digested the implication a moment, then abruptly swept the door wide open, stepped out of the way.

A woman was sitting up in bed struggling into a wrapper.

Courlander studied the wall a minute. "Did you hear any rise of any kind from the next room before you fell asleep?"

The man shook his head, said: "No."

"About how long ago did you fall asleep?"

"About an hour ago," said the man sulkily.

Courlander turned to the manager. "Go back in there a minute, will you, and knock on the wall with your fist from that side. Hit it good."

The four of them listened in silence; not a sound came through. Perry returned, blowing his breath on his stinging knuckles.

"That's all," Courlander said to the occupants. "Sorry to bother you." He and Striker went out again. Perry lingered a moment to try to smooth their ruffled plumage.

They went down to the other side of the death chamber and tried 911. "This witch," said Perry, joining them, "has got ears like a dictaphone. If there was anything to hear, she heard it all right! I don't care whether you disturb her or not. I've been trying to get rid of her for years."

She was hatchet-faced, beady-eyed, and had a cap with a

draw-string tied closely about her head. She seemed rather satisfied at finding herself an object of attention, even in the middle of the night, as though she couldn't get anyone to listen to her most of the time.

"Asleep?" she said almost boastfully. "I should say not! I haven't closed my eyes all night." And then, overriding Courlander's attempt at getting in a question, she went on: "Mr. Perry, I know it's late, but as long as you're here, I want to show you something!" She drew back into the center of the room, crooked her finger at him ominously. "You just come here!"

The three men advanced alertly and jockeyed into position from which they could see.

She swooped down, flung back a corner of the rug, and straightened up again, pointing dramatically. A thin film of dust marked the triangle of flooring that had just been bared. "What do you think of that?" she said accusingly. "Those maids of yours, instead of sweeping the dust *out* of the room, sweep it under the rug."

The manager threw his hands up over his head, turned, and went out. "The building could be burning," he fumed "and if we both landed in the same fireman's net, she'd still roll over and complain to me about the service!"

Striker lingered behind just long enough to ask her: "You say you've been awake all night. Did you hear anything from the room next door, nine-thirteen, during the past half-hour or so?"

"Why, no. Not a sound. Is there something wrong in there?" The avid way she asked it was proof enough of her good faith. He got out before she could start questioning him.

Courlander grinned. "I can find a better explanation even than the heat for him jumping, now," he remarked facetiously. "He musta seen *that* next door to him and got scared to death."

"That would be beautifully simple, wouldn't it?" Striker said cuttingly. "Let's give it one more spin," he suggested. "No one on either side of the room heard anything. Let's try the room directly underneath—eight-thirteen. The closet and bath arrangement makes for soundproof side-partitions, but the ceilings are pretty thin here."

Courlander gave the manager an amused look, as if to say, "Humor him!"

Perry, however, rolled his eyes in dismay. "Good heavens, are you trying to turn my house upside-down, Striker? Those are the Youngs, our star guests, and you know it!"

"D'you want to wait until it happens a fourth time?" Striker warned him. "It'll bring on a panic if it does."

They went down to the hallway below, stopped before 813. "These people are very wealthy," whispered the manager apprehensively. "They could afford much better quarters. I've considered myself lucky that they've stayed with us. Please be tactful. I don't want to lose them." He tapped apologetically, with just two fingernails.

Courlander sniffed and said, "What's that I smell?

"Incense," breathed the manager. "*Sh!* Don't you talk out of turn now."

There was a rustling sound behind the door, then it opened and a young Chinese in a silk robe stood looking out at them. Striker knew him, through staff gossip and his own observation, to be not only thoroughly Americanized in both speech and manner but an American by birth as well. He was Chinese only by descent. He was a lawyer and made huge sums looking after the interests of the Chinese businessmen down on Pell and Mott Streets—a considerable part of which he lost again betting on the wrong horses, a pursuit he was no luckier at than his average fellow-citizen. He was married to a radio singer. He wore horn-rimmed glasses.

"Hi!" he said briskly. "The Vigilantes! What's up, Perry?"

"I'm so sorry to annoy you like this," the manager began to whine.

"Skip it," said Young pleasantly. "Who could sleep on a night like this? We've been taking turns fanning each other in here. Come on in."

Even Striker had never been in the room before; the Youngs were quality folk, not to be intruded upon by a mere hotel detective. A doll-like creature was curled up on a sofa languidly fanning herself, and a scowling Pekinese nestled on her lap. The woman wore green silk pajamas. Striker took note of a tank containing tropical fish, also a lacquered Buddha on a table with a stick of sandalwood burning before it.

Striker and Courlander let Perry put the question, since being tactful was more in his line. "Have you people been disturbed by any sounds coming from over you?"

"Not a blessed thing," Mrs. Young averred. "Have we, babe? Only that false-alarm mutter of thunder that didn't live up to its promise. But that came from outside, of course."

"Thunder?" said Striker, puzzled. "What thunder? How long ago?"

"Oh, it wasn't a sharp clap," Young explained affably.

"Way off in the distance, low and rolling. You could hardly hear it all all. There was a flicker of sheet-lightning at the same time—that's how we knew what it was."

"But wait a minute," Striker said discontentedly. "I was lying awake in my room, and I didn't hear any thunder, at anytime tonight."

"There he goes again," Courlander slurred out of the corner of his mouth to Perry.

"But your room's located in a different part of the building," Perry interposed diplomatically. "It looks out on a shaft, and that might have muffled the sound."

"Thunder is thunder. You can hear it down in a cellar, when there is any to hear," Striker insisted.

The Chinese couple good-naturedly refused to take offense. "Well, it was very low, just a faint rolling. We probably wouldn't have noticed it ourselves, only at the same time there was this far-off gleam of lightning, and it seemed to stir up a temporary breeze out there, like when a storm's due to break. I must admit we didn't feel any current of air here inside the room, but we both saw a newspaper or rag of some kind go sailing down past the window just then."

"No, that wasn't a—" Striker stopped short, drew in his breath, as he understood what it was they must have seen.

Perry was frantically signaling him to shut up and get outside. Striker hung back long enough to ask one more question. "Did your dog bark or anything, about the time this—'promise of a storm' came up?"

"No, Shan's very well behaved," Mrs. Young said fondly.

"He whined, though," her husband remembered. "We thought it was the heat."

Striker narrowed his eyes speculatively. "Was it right at that same time?"

"Just about."

Perry and Courlander were both hitching their heads at him to come out, before he spilled the beans. When he had joined them finally, the city dick flared up: "What'd you mean by asking that last one? You trying to dig up spooks, maybe?—hinting that their dog could sense something? All it was is, the dog knew more than they did. It knew that wasn't a newspaper flicked down past their window. That's why it whined!"

Striker growled stubbornly. "There hasn't been any thunder or any lightning at any time tonight—I know what I'm saying! I was lying awake in my room, as awake as they were!"

Courlander eyed the manager maliciously. "Just like there wasn't any farewell note, until I dug it out from under the pillow."

Striker said challengingly, "You find me *one other person*, in this building or outside of it, that saw and heard that thunder and lightning' the same as they did, and we'll call it quits!"

"Fair enough. I'll take you up on that!" Courlander snapped. "It ought to be easy enough to prove to you that that wasn't a private preview run off in heaven for the special benefit of the Chinese couple."

"And when people pay two hundred a month, they don't lie," said Perry quaintly.

"We'll take that projecting wing that sticks out at right angles," said the dick. "It ought to have been twice as clear and loud out there as down on the eighth. Or am I stacking the cards?"

"You're not exactly dealing from a warm deck," Striker said. "If it was heard below, it could be heard out in the wing, and still have something to do with what went on in 913. Why not pick somebody who was out on the streets at the time and ask him? There's your real test."

"Take it or leave it. I'm not running around on the street this hour of the night, asking people 'Did you hear a growl of thunder thirty minutes ago?' I'd land in Bellevue in no time!"

"This is the bachelor wing," Perry explained as they rounded the turn of the hall. "All men. Even so, they're entitled to a night's rest as well as anyone else. Must you disturb *every-one* in the house?"

"Not my idea," Courlander rubbed it in. "That note is still enough for me. I'm giving this guy all the rope he needs, that's all."

They stopped outside 909. "Peter the Hermit," said Perry disgustedly. "Aw, don't take him. He won't be any help. He's nutty. He'll start telling you all about his gold mines up in Canada."

But Courlander had already knocked. "He's not too nutty to know thunder and lightning when he hears it, is he?"

Bedsprings creaked, there was a slither of bare feet, and the door opened.

He was about sixty, with a mane of snow-white hair that fell down to his shoulders, and a long white beard. He had mild blue eyes, with something trusting and childlike about them. You only had to look at them to understand how easy it must have been for the confidence men, or whoever it was, to have swindled him into buying those worthless shafts sunk into the ground up in the backwoods of Ontario.

Striker knew the story well; everyone in the hotel did. But others laughed, while Striker sort of understood—put two and two together. The man wasn't crazy, he was just disappointed in life. The long hair and the beard, Striker suspected, were not due to eccentricity but probably to stubborness; he'd taken a vow never to cut his hair or shave until those mines paid off. And the fact that he hugged his room day and night, never left it except just once a month to buy a stock of canned goods, was understandable too. He'd been "stung" once, so now he was leery of strangers, avoided people for fear of being "stung" again. And then ridicule probably had something to do with it too. The way that fool Courlander was all but laughing in his face right now, trying to cover it with his hand before his mouth, was characteristic.

The guest was down on the register as Atkinson, but no one ever called him anything but Peter the Hermit. At irregular intervals he left the hotel, to go "prospecting" up to his mine pits, see if there were any signs of ore. Then he'd come back again disappointed, but without having given up hope, to retire again for another six or eight months. He kept the same room while he was away, paying for it just as though he were in it.

"Can we come in, Pops?" the city dick asked, when he'd managed to straighten his face sufficiently.

"Not if you're going to try to sell me any more gold mines."

"Naw, we just want a weather report. You been asleep or awake?"

"I been awake all night, practickly."

"Good. Now tell me just one thing. Did you hear any thunder at all, see anything like heat-lightning flicker outside your window, little while back?"

"Heat-lightning don't go with thunder. You never have the two together," rebuked the patriarch.

"All right, all right," said Courlander wearily. "Any kind of lightning, plain or fancy, and any kind of thunder?"

"Sure did. Just once, though. Tiny speck of thunder and tiny mite of lightning, no more'n a flash in the pan. Stars were all out and around too. Darnedest thing I ever saw!"

Courlander gave the hotel dick a look that should have withered him. But Striker jumped in without waiting. "About this flicker of lightning. Which direction did it seem to come from? Are you sure it came from above and not"—he pointed meaningly downward—"from *below* your window?"

This time it was the Hermit who gave him the withering look. "Did you ever hear of lightning coming from below, son? Next thing you'll be trying to tell me rain falls up from the ground!" He went over to the open window, beckoned. "I'll show you right about where it panned out. I was standing here looking out at the time, just happened to catch it." He pointed in a northeasterly direction. "There. See that tall building up over thattaway? It come from over behind there—miles away, o'course—but from that part of the sky."

"Much obliged, Pops. That's all."

They withdrew just as the hermit was getting into his stride. He rested a finger alongside his nose, trying to hold their attention, said confidentially: "I'm going to be a rich man one of these days, you wait'n see. Those mines o'mine are going to turn into a bonanza." But they closed the door on him.

Riding down in the car, Courlander snarled at Striker: "Now, eat your words. You said if we found one other person heard and saw that thunder and sheet-lightning—"

"I know what I said," Striker answered dejectedly. "Funny—private thunder and lightning that some hear and others don't."

Courlander swelled with satisfaction. He took out his notebook, flourished it. "Well, here goes, ready or not! You can work yourself up into a lather about it by yourself from now on. I'm not wasting any more of the city's time—or my own—on anything as self-evident as this!"

"Self-evidence, like beauty," Striker reminded him, "is in the eye of the beholder. It's there for some, and not for others."

Courlander stopped by the desk, roughing out his report. Striker, meanwhile, was comparing the note with Dillberry's signature in the book. "Why, this scrawl isn't anything like his John Hancock in the ledger!" he exclaimed.

"You expect a guy gone out of his mind with the heat to sit down and write a nice copybook hand?" scoffed the police dick. "It was in his room, wasn't it?"

This brought up their former bone of contention. "Not the first time I looked."

"I only have your word for that."

"Are you calling me a liar?" flared Striker.

"No, but I think what's biting you is, you got a suppressed desire to be a detective."

"I think," said Striker with deadly irony, "you have too."

"Why, you—!"

Perry hurriedly got between them. "For heaven's sake," he pleaded wearily, "isn't it hot enough and messy enough, without having a fist fight over it?"

Courlander turned and stamped out into the suffocating before-dawn murk. Perry leaned over the desk, holding his head in both hands. "That room's a jinx," he groaned, "a voodoo."

"There's nothing the matter with the room—there can't possibly be," Striker pointed out. "That would be against nature and all natural laws. That room is just plaster and bricks and wooden boards, and they can't hurt anyone—in themselves. Whatever's behind this is some human agency, and I'm going to get to the bottom of it if I gotta sleep in there myself!" He waited a minute, let the idea sink in, take hold of him, then he straightened, snapped his fingers decisively. "That's the next step on the program! I'll be the guinea pig, the white mouse! That's the only way we can ever hope to clear it up."

Perry gave him a bleak look, as though such foolhardiness would have been totally foreign to his own nature, and he couldn't understand anyone being willing to take such an eerie risk.

"Because I've got a hunch," Striker went on grimly. "It's not over yet. It's going to happen again and yet again, if we don't hurry up and find out what it is."

Now that the official investigation was closed, and there was no outsider present to spread rumors that could give his hotel a bad name, Perry seemed willing enough to agree with Striker that it wasn't normal and natural. Or else the advanced hour of the night was working suggestively on his nerves. "B-but haven't you any idea at all, just as a starting point," he quavered, "as to what it could be—if it is anything? Isn't it better to have some kind of a theory? At least know what to look for, not just shut yourself up in there blindfolded?"

"I could have several, but I can't believe in them myself. It could be extramural hypnosis—that means through the walls, you know. Or it could be fumes that lower the vitality, depress, and bring on suicide mania—such as small quantities of monoxide will do. But this is summertime and there's certainly no heat in the pipes. No, there's only one way to get an idea, and that's to try it out on myself. I'm going to sleep in that room myself tomorrow night, to get the *feel* of it. Have I your okay?"

Perry just wiped his brow, in anticipatory horror. "Go ahead if you've got the nerve," he said limply. "You wouldn't catch me doing it!"

Striker smiled glumly. "I'm curious—that way."

Striker made arrangements as inconspicuously as possible the next day, since there was no telling at which point anonymity ended and hostile observation set in, whether up in the room itself or down at the registration desk, or somewhere midway between the two. He tried to cover all the externals by which occupancy of the room could be detected without at the same time revealing his identity. Dennison, the day clerk, was left out of it entirely. Outside of Perry himself, he took only Maxon into his confidence. No one else, not even the cleaning help. He waited until the night clerk came on duty at eleven-thirty before he made the final arrangements, so that there was no possibility of foreknowledge.

"When you're sure no one's looking—and not until then," he coached the night clerk, "I want you to take the red vacancy-tag out of the pigeonhole. And sign a phony entry in the register—John Brown, anything at all. We can erase it in the morning. That's in case the leak is down here at this end. I know the book is kept turned facing you, but there *is* a slight possibility someone could read it upside-down while stopping by here for their key. One other important thing: I may come up against something that's too much for me, whether it's physical or narcotic or magnetic. Keep your eye on that telephone switchboard in case I need help in a hurry. If nine-thirteen flashes, don't wait to answer. I mayn't be able to give a message. Just get up there in a hurry."

"That's gonna do you a lot of good," Maxon objected fearfully. "By the time anyone could get up there to the ninth on that squirrel-cage, it would be all over! Why don't you plant Bob or someone out of sight around the turn of the hall?"

"I can't. The hall may be watched. If it's anything external, and not just atmospheric or telepathic, it comes through the hall. It's got to. That's the only way it can get in. This has got to look *right*, wide open, unsuspecting, or whatever it is won't strike. No, the switchboard'll be my only means of communication. I'm packing a Little Friend with me, anyway, so I won't be exactly helpless up there. Now remember, 'Mr. John Brown' checked in here unseen by the human eye sometime during the evening. Whatever it is, it can't be watching the desk *all* the time, twenty-four hours a day. And for Pete's sake, don't take any nips tonight. Lock the bottle up in the safe. My life is in your hands. Don't drop it!"

"Good luck and here's hoping," said Maxon sepulchrally, as though he never expected to see Striker alive again.

Striker drifted back into the lounge and lolled conspicuously in his usual vantage-point until twelve struck and Bob
began to put the primary lights out. Then he strolled into
the hotel drug store and drank two cups of scalding black
coffee. Not that he was particularly afraid of not being able to
keep awake, tonight of all nights, but there was nothing like
making sure. There might be some soporific or sedative
substance to overcome, though how it could be adminis-
tered he failed to see.

He came into the lobby again and went around to the
elevator bank, without so much as a wink to Maxon. He gave
a carefully studied yawn, tapped his fingers over his mouth.
A moment later there was a whiff of some exotic scent behind
him and the Youngs had come in, presumably from Mrs.
Young's broadcasting station. She was wearing an embroidered silk shawl and holding the Peke in her arm.

Young said, "Hi, fella." She bowed slightly. The car door
opened.

Young said, "Oh, just a minute—my key," and stepped over
to the desk.

Striker's eyes followed him relentlessly. The register was
turned facing Maxon's way. The Chinese lawyer glanced
down at it, curved his head around slightly as if to read it
right side up, then took his key, came back again. They rode
up together. The Peke started to whine. Mrs. Young fondled
it, crooned: "*Sh, Shan,* be a good boy." She explained to
Striker, "It always makes him uneasy to ride up in an
elevator."

The couple got off at the eighth. She bowed again. Young
said, "G'night." Striker, of course, had no idea of getting off
at any but his usual floor, the top, even though he was alone
in the car. He said in a low voice to Bob: "Does that dog whine
other times when you ride it up?"

"No, sir," the elevator man answered. "It nevah seem' to
mind until tonight. Mus' be getting ritzy."

Striker just filed that detail away: it was such a tiny little
thing.

He let himself into his little hole-in-the-wall room. He
pulled down the shade, even though there was just a blank
wall across the shaft from his window. There was a roof ledge
farther up. He took his gun out of his valise and packed it in

his back pocket. That was all he was taking with him; no "fantastics" tonight. The fantasy was in real life, not on the printed page.

He took off his coat and necktie and hung them over the back of a chair. He took the pillow off his bed and forced it down under the bedclothes so that it made a longish mound. He'd brought a newspaper up with him. He opened this to double-page width and leaned it up against the head of the bed, as though someone were sitting up behind it reading it. It sagged a little, so he took a pin and fastened it to the woodwork. He turned on the shaded reading lamp at his bedside, turned out the room light, so that there was just a diffused glow. Then he edged up to the window sidewise and raised the shade again, but not all the way, just enough to give a view of the lower part of the bed if anyone were looking down from above—from the cornice, for instance. He always had his reading lamp going the first hour or two after he retired other nights. Tonight it was going to burn all night. This was the only feature of the arrangement Perry would have disapproved of, electricity bills being what they were.

That took care of things up here. He edged his door open, made sure the hallway was deserted, and sidled out in vest, trousers, and carrying the .38. He'd done everything humanly possible to make the thing foolproof, but it occurred to him, as he made his way noiselessly to the emergency staircase, that there was one thing all these precautions would be sterile against, if it was involved in any way, and that was mindreading. The thought itself was enough to send a shudder up his spine, make him want to give up before he'd even gone any further, so he resolutely put it from him. Personally he'd never been much of a believer in that sort of thing, so it wasn't hard for him to discount it. But disbelief in a thing is not always a guarantee that it does not exist or exert influence, and he would have been the first to admit that.

The safety stairs were cement and not carpeted like the hallways, but even so he managed to move down them with a minimum of sound once his senses had done all they could to assure him the whole shaft was empty of life from its top to its bottom.

He eased the hinged fire door on the ninth open a fraction of an inch, and reconnoitered the hall in both directions; forward through the slit before him, rearward through the seam between the hinges. This was the most important part of the undertaking. Everything depended on this step. It was vital to get into that room unseen. Even if he did not know what he was up against, there was no sense letting what he was up against know who he was.

He stood there for a long time like that, without moving, almost without breathing, narrowly studying each and every one of the inscrutably closed doors up and down the hall. Finally he broke for it.

He had his passkey ready before he left the shelter of the fire door. He stabbed it into the lock of 913, turned it, and opened the door with no more than two deft, quick, almost soundless movements. He had to work fast, to get in out of the open. He got behind the door once he was through, got the key out, closed the door—and left the room dark. The whole maneuver, he felt reasonably sure, could not have been accomplished more subtly by anything except a ghost or wraith.

He took a long deep breath behind the closed door and relaxed—a little. Leaving the room dark around him didn't make for very much peace of mind—there was always the thought that *It* might already be in here with him—but he was determined not to show his face even to the blank walls.

He was now, therefore, Mr. John Brown, Room 913, for the rest of the night, unsuspectingly waiting to be—whatever it was had happened to Hopper, Hastings, Dillberry. He had a slight edge on them because he had a gun in his pocket, but try to shoot a noxious vapor (for instance) with a .38 bullet!

First he made sure of the telephone, his one lifeline to the outside world. He carefully explored the wire in the dark, inch by inch from the base of the instrument down to the box against the wall, to make sure the wire wasn't cut or rendered useless in any way. Then he opened the closet door and examined the inside of that, by sense of touch alone. Nothing in there but a row of empty hangers. Then he cased the bath, still without the aid of light; tried the water faucets, the drains, even the medicine chest. Next he devoted his attention to the bed itself, explored the mattress and the springs, even got down and swept an arm back and forth under it, like an old maid about to retire for the night. The other furniture also got a health examination. He tested the rug with his foot for unevennesses. Finally there remained the window, that mouthway to doom. He didn't go close to it. He stayed well back within the gloom of the room, even though there was nothing, not even a rooftop or water tank, opposite, from which the interior of this room could be seen; the buildings all around were much lower. It couldn't tell him anything; it seemed to be just a window embrasure. If it was more than that, it was one up on him.

Finally he took out his gun, slipped the safety off, laid it down beside the phone on the nightstand. Then he lay back on the bed, shoes and all, crossed his ankles, folded his hands under his head, and lay staring up at the pool of blackness over him that was the ceiling. He couldn't hear a thing, after that, except the whisper of his breathing, and he had to listen close to get even that.

The minutes pulled themselves out into a quarter hour, a half, a whole one, like sticky taffy. All sorts of horrid possibilities occurred to him, lying there in the dark, and made his skin crawl. He remembered the Conan Doyle story, "The Speckled Band," in which a deadly snake had been lowered through a transom night after night in an effort to get it to bite the sleeper. That wouldn't fit this case. He'd come upon the scene too quickly each time. You couldn't juggle a deadly snake—had to take your time handling it. None of his three predecessors had been heard to scream, nor had their broken bodies shown anything but the impact of the fall itself. None of the discoloration or rigidity of snake venom. He'd looked at the bodies at the morgue.

But it was not as much consolation as it should have been, in the dark. He wished he'd been a little braver—one of these absolutely fearless guys. It didn't occur to him that he was being quite brave enough already for one guy, coming up here like this. He'd stretched himself out in here without any certainty he'd ever get up again alive.

He practiced reaching for the phone and for his gun, until he knew just where they both were by heart. They were close enough. He didn't even have to unlimber his elbow. He lit a cigarette, but shielded the match carefully, with his whole body turned toward the wall, so it wouldn't light up his face too much. John Brown could smoke in bed just as well as House Dick Striker.

He kept his eyes on the window more than anything else, almost as if he expected it to sprout a pair of long octopus arms that would reach out, grab him, and toss him through to destruction.

He asked himself fearfully: "Am I holding it off by lying here awake like this waiting for it? Can it *tell* whether I'm awake or asleep? Is it on me, whatever it is?" He couldn't help wincing at the implication of the supernatural this argued. A guy could go batty thinking things like that. Still, it couldn't be denied that the condition of the bed, each time before this, proved that the victims had been asleep and not awake just before it happened.

He thought, "I can pretend I'm asleep, at least, even if I don't actually go to sleep." Nothing must be overlooked in this battle of wits, no matter how inane, how childish it seemed at first sight.

He crushed his cigarette out, gave a stage yawn, meant to be heard if it couldn't be seen, threshed around a little like a man settling himself down for the night, counted ten, and then started to stage-manage his breathing, pumping it slower and heavier, like a real sleeper's. But under it all he was as alive as a third rail and his heart was ticking away under his ribs like a taximeter.

It was harder to lie waiting for it this way than it had been the other, just normally awake. The strain was almost unbearable. He wanted to leap up, swing out wildly around him in the dark, and yell: "Come on, you! Come on and get it over with!"

Suddenly he tensed more than he was already, if that was possible, and missed a breath. Missed two—forgot all about timing them. Something—what was it?—something was in the air; his nose was warning him, twitching, crinkling, almost like a retriever's. Sweet, foreign, subtle, something that didn't belong. He took a deep sniff, held it, while he tried to test the thing, analyze it, differentiate it, like a chemist without apparatus.

Then he got it. If he hadn't been so worked up in the first

place, he would have got it even sooner. Sandalwood. Sandalwood incense. That meant the Chinese couple, the
Youngs, the apartment below. They'd been burning it last
night when he was in there, a stick of it in front of that joss of
theirs. But how could it get up here? And how could it be
harmful, if they were right in the same room with it and it
didn't do anything to them?

How did he know they were in the same room with it? A
fantastic picture flashed before his mind of the two of them
down there right now, wearing gauze masks of filters over
their faces, like operating surgeons. Aw, that was ridiculous! They'd been in the room a full five minutes with the
stuff—he and Perry and Courlander—without masks and
nothing had happened to them.

But he wasn't forgetting how Young's head had swung
around a little to scan the reversed register when they came
in tonight—nor how their dog had whined, like it had
whined when Dillberry's body fell past their window, when—
Bob had said—it never whined at other times.

He sat up, pulled off his shoes, and started to move
noiselessly around, sniffing like a bloodhound, trying to
find out just how and where that odor was getting into the
room. It must be at some particular point more than another. It wasn't just *soaking* up through the floor. Maybe it was
nothing, then again maybe it was something. It didn't seem
to be doing anything to him so far. He could breathe all
right, he could think all right. But there was always the
possibility that it was simply a sort of smoke-screen or
carrier, used to conceal or transport some other gas that
was to follow. The sugar-coating for the poison!

He sniffed at the radiator, at the bathroom drains, at the
closet door, and in each of the four corners of the room. It
was faint, almost unnoticeable in all those places. Then he
stopped before the open window. It was much stronger here;
it was coming in here!

He edged warily forward, leaned out a little above the low
guard-rail, but careful not to shift his balance out of normal, for this very posture of curiosity might be the crux of
the whole thing, the incense a decoy to get them to lean out
the window. Sure, it was coming out of their open window,

traveling up the face of the building, and—some of it—drifting in through his. That was fairly natural, on a warm, still night like this, without much circulation to the air.

Nothing happened. The window didn't suddenly fold up and throw him or tilt him and pull him after it by sheer optical illusion (for he wasn't touching it in any way). He waited a little longer, tested it a little longer. No other result. It was, then, incense and nothing more.

He went back into the room again, stretched out on the bed once more, conscious for the first time of cold moisture on his brow, which he now wiped off. The aroma became less noticeable presently, as though the stick had burned down. Then finally it was gone. And he was just the way he'd been before.

"So it wasn't that," he dismissed it, and reasoned, "It's because they're Chinese that I was so ready to suspect them. They always seen sinister to the Occidental mind."

There was nothing else after that, just darkness and waiting. Then presently there was a gray line around the window enclosure, and next he could see his hands when he held them out before his face, and then the night bloomed into day and the death watch was over.

He didn't come down to the lobby for another hour, until the sun was up and there was not the slimmest possibility of anything happening any more—this time. He came out of the elevator looking haggard, and yet almost disappointed at the same time.

Maxon eyed him as though he'd never expected to see him again. "Anything?" he asked, unnecessarily.

"Nothing," Striker answered.

Maxon turned without another word, went back to the safe, brought a bottle out to him.

"Yeah, I could use some of that," was all the dick said.

"So I guess this shows," Maxon suggested hopefully, "that there's nothing to it after all. I mean about the room being—"

Striker took his time about answering. "It shows," he said finally, "that whoever it is, is smarter than we gave 'em credit for. Knew enough not to tip their mitts. Nothing happened because Someone knew I was in there, knew who I was, and knew *why* I was in there. And *that* shows it's somebody in this hotel who's at the bottom of it."

"You mean you're not through yet?"

"Through yet? I haven't even begun!"

"Well, what're you going to do next?"

"I'm going to catch up on a night's sleep, first off," Striker let him know. "And after that, I'm going to do a little clerical work. Then when that's through, I'm going to keep my own counsel. No offense, but"—he tapped himself on the forehead—"only this little fellow in here is going to be in on it, not you nor the manager nor anyone else."

He started his "clerical work" that very evening. Took the old ledgers for March, 1933, and October, 1934, out of the safe, and copied out the full roster of guests from the current one (July, 1935). Then he took the two bulky volumes and the list of present guests up to his room with him and went to work.

First he canceled out all the names on the current list that didn't appear on either of the former two rosters. That left him with exactly three guests who were residing in the building now and who also had been in it at the time of one of the first two "suicides." The three were Mr. and Mrs. Young, Atkinson (Peter the Hermit), and Miss Flobelle Heilbron (the cantankerous vixen in 911). Then he canceled those of the above that didn't appear on *both* of the former lists. There was only one name left uncanceled now. There was only one guest who had been in occupancy during *each and every one* of the three times that a "suicide" had taken place in 913. Atkinson and Miss Heilbron had been living in the hotel in March, 1933. The Youngs and Miss Heilbron had been living in the building in October, 1934. Atkinson (who must have been away the time before on one of his nomadic "prospecting trips"), the Youngs, and Miss Heilbron were all here now. The one name that recurred triply was Miss Flobelle Heilbron.

So much for his "clerical work." Now came a little research work.

She didn't hug her room quite as continuously and tenaciously as Peter the Hermit, but she never strayed very far from it nor stayed away very long at a time—was constantly popping in and out a dozen times a day to feed a cat she kept.

He had a word with Perry the following morning, and soon after lunch the manager, who received complimentary passes to a number of movie theaters in the vicinity, in return for giving them advertising space about his premises, presented her with a matinee pass for that afternoon. She was delighted at this unaccustomed mark of attention, and fell for it like a ton of bricks.

Striker saw her start out at two, and that gave him two full hours. He made a bee-line up there and passkeyed himself in. The cat was out in the middle of the room nibbling at a plate of liver which she'd thoughtfully left behind for it. He started going over the place. He didn't need two hours. He hit it within ten minutes after he'd come into the room, in one of her bureau drawers, all swathed up in intimate wearing apparel, as though she didn't want anyone to know she had it.

It was well worn, as though it had been used plenty—kept by her at nights and studied for years. It was entitled *Mesmerism, Self-Taught; How to Impose Your Will on Others.*

But something even more of a giveaway happened while he was standing there holding it in his hand. The cat raised its head from the saucer of liver, looked up at the book, evidently recognized it, and whisked under the bed, ears flat.

"So she's been practicing on you, has she?" Striker murmured. "And you don't like it. Well, I don't either. I wonder who else she's been trying it on?"

He opened the book and thumbed through it. One chapter heading, appropriately enough was, "Experiments at a Distance." He narrowed his eyes, read a few words. "In cases where the subject is out of sight, behind a door or on the other side of a wall, it is better to begin with simple commands, easily transferable. 1—Open the door. 2—Turn around," etc.

Well, "jump out of the window" was a simple enough command. Beautifully simple—and final. Was it possible that old crackpot was capable of—? She was domineering enough to be good at it, heaven knows. Perry'd wanted her out of the building years ago, but she was still in it today.

Striker had never believed in such balderdash, but suppose—through some fluke or other—it had worked out with
ghastly effect in just this one case?

He summoned the chambermaid and questioned her. She
was a lumpy, work-worn old woman, and had as little use for
the guest in question as anyone else, so she wasn't inclined
to be reticent. "Boss me?" she answered, "Man, she sure do!"

"I don't mean boss you out loud. Did she ever try to get you
to do her bidding without, uh, talking?"

She eyed him shrewdly, nodded. "Sure nuff. All the time.
How you fine out about it?" She cackled uproariously. "She
dippy, Mr. Striker, suh. I *mean!* She stand still like this, look
at me *hard,* like this." She placed one hand flat across her
forehead as if she had a headache. "So nothing happen', I just
mine my business. Then she say: "Whuffo you don't do what
I just tole you?' I say, 'You ain't tole me nothing yet.' She say,
'Ain't you got my message? My sum-conscious done tole you,
"Clean up good underneath that chair."'

"I say, 'Yo sum-conscious better talk a little louder, den,
cause I ain't heard a thing—and I got good ears!'"

He looked at her thoughtfully. "Did you ever *feel* anything
when she tried that stunt? Feel like doing the things she
wanted?"

"Yeah man!" she vigorously asserted. "But not what she
wanted! I feel like busting dis yere mop-handle on her haid,
dass what I feel!"

He went ahead investigating after he'd dismissed her, but
nothing else turned up. He was far from satisfied with what
he'd got on Miss Heilbron, incriminating as the book was. It
didn't *prove* anything. It wasn't strong enough evidence to
base an accusation on.

He cased the Youngs' apartment that same evening, while
they were at the wife's broadcasting studio. This, over Perry's
almost apoplectic protests. And there, as if to confuse the
issue still further, he turned up something that was at least
as suspicious in its way as the mesmerism handbook. It was
a terrifying grotesque mask of a demon, presumably a prop
from the Chinese theater down on Doyer Street. It was
hanging at the back of the clothes closet, along with an
embroidered Chinese ceremonial robe. It was limned in

some kind of luminous or phosphorescent paint that made it visible in the gloom in all its bestiality and horror. He nearly jumped out of his shoes himself at first sight of it. And that only went to show what conceivable effect it could have seeming to swim through the darkness in the middle of the night, for instance, toward the bed of a sleeper in the room above. That the victim would jump out of the window in frenzy would be distinctly possible.

Against this could be stacked the absolute lack of motive, the conclusive proof (two out of three times) that no one had been in the room with the victim, and the equally conclusive proof that the Youngs hadn't been in the building at all the first time, mask or no mask. In itself, of course, the object had as much right to be in their apartment as the mesmerism book had in Miss Heilbron's room. The wife was in theatrical business, liable to be interested in stage curios of that kind.

Boiled down, it amounted to this: that the Youngs were still very much in the running.

It was a good deal harder to gain access to Peter the Hermit's room without tipping his hand, since the eccentric lived up to his nickname to the fullest. However, he finally managed to work it two days later, with the help of Perry, the hotel exterminator, and a paperful of red ants. He emptied the contents of the latter outside the doorsill, then Perry and the exterminator forced their way in on the pretext of combating the invasion. It took all of Perry's cajolery and persuasiveness to draw the Hermit out of his habitat for even half an hour, but a professed eagerness to hear all about his "gold mines" finally turned the trick, and the old man was led around the turn of the hall. Striker jumped in as soon as the coast was clear and got busy.

It was certainly fuller of unaccountable things than either of the other two had been, but on the other hand there was nothing as glaringly suspicious as the mask or the hypnotism book. Pyramids of hoarded canned goods stacked in the closet, and quantities of tools and utensils used in mining operations: sieves, pans, short-handled picks, a hooded miner's lamp with a reflector, three fishing rods and an assortment of hooks ranging from the smallest to big triple-toothed monsters, plenty of tackle, hip boots, a shot-gun, a pair of scales (for assaying the gold that he had never found), little sacks of worthless ore, a mallet for breaking up the ore specimens, and the pair of heavy knapsacks that he took with him each time he set out on his heartbreaking expeditions. It all seemed legitimate enough. Striker wasn't enough of a mining expert to know for sure. But he was enough of a detective to know there wasn't anything there that could in itself cause the death of anyone two rooms over and at right angles to this.

He had, of necessity, to be rather hasty about it, for the old man could be heard regaling Perry with the story of his mines just out of sight around the turn of the hall the whole time Striker was in there. He cleared out just as the exter-minator finally got through killing the last of the "planted" ants.

To sum up: Flobelle Heilbron still had the edge on the other two as chief suspect, both because of the mesmerism hand-book and because of her occupancy record. The Chinese couple came next, because of the possibilities inherent in that mask, as well as the penetrative powers of their incense and the whining of their dog. Peter the Hermit ran the others a poor third. Had it not been for his personal eccen-tricity and the location of his room, Striker would have eliminated him altogether.

On the other hand, he had turned up no real proof yet, and the motive remained as unfathomable as ever. In short, he was really no further than before he'd started. He had tried to solve it circumstantially, by deduction, and that hadn't worked. He had tried to solve it first hand, by personal observation, and that hadn't worked. Only one possible way remained, to try to solve it at *second hand*, through the eyes of the next potential victim, who would at the same time be a material witness—if he survived. To do this it was necessary to anticipate it, *time* it, try to see if it had some sort of spacing or rhythm to it or was just hit-or-miss, in order to know more or less when to expect it to recur. The only way to do this was to take the three dates he had and average them.

Striker took the early part of that evening off. He didn't ask permission for it, just walked out without saying anything to anyone about it. He was determined not to take anyone into his confidence this time.

He hadn't been off the premises a night since he'd first been hired by the hotel, and this wasn't a night off. This was strictly business. He had seventy-five dollars with him that he'd taken out of his hard-earned savings at the bank that afternoon. He didn't go where the lights were bright. He went down to the Bowery.

He strolled around a while looking into various barrooms and "smoke houses" from the outside. Finally he saw something in one that seemed to suit his purpose, went in and ordered two beers.

"Two?" said the barman in surprise. "You mean one after the other?"

"I mean two right together at one time," Striker told him.

He carried them over to the table at the rear, at which he noticed a man slumped with his head in his arms. He wasn't asleep or in a drunken stupor. Striker had already seen him push a despairing hand through his hair once.

He sat down opposite the motionless figure, clinked the glasses together to attract the man's attention.

"This is for you," Striker said, pushing one toward him.

The man just nodded dazedly, as though incapable of thanks any more. Gratitude had rusted on him from lack of use.

"What're your prospects?" Striker asked him bluntly.

"None. Nowhere to go. Not a cent to my name. I've only got one friend left, and I was figgerin' on looking him up long about midnight. If I don't tonight, maybe I will tomorrow night. I surely will one of these nights, soon. His name is the East River."

"I've got a proposition for you. Want to hear it?"

"You're the boss."

"How would you like to have a good suit, a clean shirt on your back for a change? How would you like to sleep in a comfortable bed tonight? In a three dollar room, all to yourself, in a good hotel uptown?"

"Mister," said the man in a choked voice, "if I could do that once again, just once again, I wouldn't care if it was my last night on earth! What's the catch?"

"What you just said. It's liable to be." He talked for a while, told the man what there was to know, the little that he himself knew. "It's not certain, you understand. Maybe nothing'll happen at all. The odds are about fifty-fifty. If nothing does happen, you keep the clothes, the dough, and I'll even dig up a porter's job for you. You'll be that much ahead. Now I've given it to you straight from the shoulder. I'm not concealing anything from you, you know what to expect."

The man wet his lips reflectively. "Fifty-fifty—that's not so bad. Those are good enough odds. I used to be a gambler when I was young. And it can't hurt more than the river filling up your lungs. I'm weary of dragging out my days. What've I got to lose? Mister, you're on." He held out an unclean hand hesitantly. "I don't suppose you'd want to—"

Striker shook it as he stood up. "I never refuse to shake hands with a brave man. Come on, we've got a lot to do. We've got to find a barber shop, a men's clothing store if there are any still open, a luggage shop, and a restaurant."

An hour and a half later a taxi stopped on the corner diagonally opposite the St. Anselm, with Striker and a spruce, well-dressed individual seated in it side by side. On the floor at their feet were two shiny, brand-new valises, containing their linings and nothing else.

"Now there it is over there, on the other side," Striker said. "I'm going to get out here, and you go over in the cab and get out by yourself at the entrance. Count out what's left of the money I gave you."

His companion did so laboriously. "Forty-nine dollars and fifty cents."

"Don't spend another penny of it, get me? I've already paid the cabfare and tip. See that you carry your own bags in, so they don't notice how light they are. Remember, what's left is all yours if—"

"Yeah, I know," said the other man unabashedly. "If I'm alive in the morning."

"Got your instructions straight?"

"I want an outside room. I want a ninth floor outside room. No other floor will do. I want a ninth floor outside room with a bath."

"That'll get you the right one by elimination. I happen to

know it's vacant. You won't have to pay in advance. The two bags and the outfit'll take care of that. Tell him to sign Harry Kramer for you—that what you said your name was? Now this is your last chance to back out. You can still welsh on me if you want—I won't do anything to you."

"No," the man said doggedly. "This way I've got a chance at a job tomorrow. The other way I'll be back on the beach. I'm glad somebody finally found some use for me."

Striker averted his head, grasped the other's scrawny shoulder encouragingly. "Good luck, brother—and God forgive me for doing this, if I don't see you again." He swung out of the cab, opened a newspaper in front of his face, and narrowly watched over the top of it until the thin but well-dressed figure had alighted and carried the two bags up the steps and into a doorway from which he might never emerge alive.

He sauntered up to the desk a few minutes later himself, from the other direction, the coffee shop entrance. Maxon was still blotting the ink on the signature.

Striker read, *Harry Kramer, New York City—913*

He went up to his room at his usual time, but only to get out his gun. Then he came down to the lobby again. Maxon was the only one in sight. Striker stepped in behind the desk, made his way back to the telephone switchboard, which was screened from sight by the tiers of mailboxes. He sat down before the switchboard and shot his cuffs, like a wireless operator on a ship at sea waiting for an SOS. The St. Anselm didn't employ a night operator. The desk clerk attended to the calls himself after twelve.

"What's the idea?" Maxon wanted to know.

Striker wasn't confiding in anyone this time. "Can't sleep," he said noncommittally. "Why should you object if I give you a hand down here?"

Kramer was to knock the receiver off the hook at the first sign of danger, or even anything that he didn't understand or like the looks of. There was no other way to work it than this, roundabout as it was. Striker was convinced that if he lurked about the ninth floor corridor within sight or earshot of the room, he would simply be banishing the danger, postponing it. He didn't want that. He wanted to know what it was. If he waited in his own room he would be even more cut off. The danger signal would have to be relayed up to him from down here. The last three times had shown him how ineffective that was.

A desultory call or two came through the first hour he was at the board, mostly requests for morning calls. He meticulously jotted them down for the day operator. Nothing from 913.

About two o'clock Maxon finally started to catch on. "You going to work it all night?"

"Yeh," said Striker shortly. "Don't talk to me. Don't let on I'm behind here at all."

At two thirty-five there were footsteps in the lobby, a peculiar sobbing sound like an automobile tire deflating, and a whiff of sandalwood traveled back to Striker after the car had gone up. He called Maxon guardedly back to him.

"The Youngs?"

"Yeah, they just came in."

"Was that their dog whining?"

"Yeah, I guess it hadda see another dog about a man."

Maybe a dead man, thought Striker morosely. He raised the plug toward the socket of 913. He ought to call Kramer, make sure he stayed awake. That would be as big a give-away as pussyfooting around the hall up there, though. He let the plug drop back again.

About three o'clock more footsteps sounded. Heavy ones stamping in from the street. A man's voice sounded hoarsely."Hey, desk! One of your people just tumbled out, around on the side of the building!"

The switchboard stool went over with a crack, something blurred streaked across the lobby, and the elevator darted crazily upward. Striker nearly snapped the control lever out of its socket, the way he bore down on it. The car had never traveled so fast before, but he swore horribly all the way up. Too late again!

The door was closed. He needled his passkey at the lock, shouldered the door in. The light was on, the room was empty. The window was wide open, the guy was gone. The fifty-fifty odds had paid off—the wrong way.

Striker's face was twisted balefully. He got out his gun.

He was standing there like that, bitter, defeated, granite-eyed, the gun uselessly in his hand, when Perry and Courlander came. It would be Courlander again, too!

"Is he dead?" Striker asked grimly.

"That street ain't quilted," was the dick's dry answer. He eyed the gun scornfully. "What're you doing? Holding the fort against the Indians, sonny boy?"

"I suggest instead of standing there throwing bouquets," Striker said, "you phone your precinct house and have a dragnet thrown around this building." He reached for the phone. Courlander's arm quickly shot out and barred him. "Not so fast. What would I be doing that for?"

"Because this is murder!"

"Where've I heard that before?" He went over for the inevitable note. "What's this?" He read it aloud. *"Can't take it any more."*

"So you're still going to trip over those things!"

"And you're still going to try to hurdle it?"

"It's a fake like all the others were. I knew that all along. I couldn't prove it until now. This time I can! Finally."

"Yeah? How?"

"Because the guy couldn't write! Couldn't even write his own name! He even had to have the clerk sign the register for him downstairs. And if that isn't proof there's been somebody else in this room, have a look at that." He pointed to the money Kramer had left neatly piled on the dresser top. "Count that! Four-fifty. Four singles and a four-bit piece. He had forty-nine dollars and fifty cents on him when he came into this room, and he didn't leave the room. He's down there in his underwear now. Here's all his outer clothing up here. What became of that forty-five bucks?"

Courlander looked at him. "How do you know so much about it? How do you know he couldn't write, and just what dough he had?"

"Because I planted him up here myself!" Striker ground out exasperatedly. "It was a setup! I picked him up, outfitted him, staked him, and brought him in here. He ran away to sea at twelve, never even learned his alphabet. I tested him and found out he was telling the truth. He couldn't write a word, not even his own name! Are you gonna stand here all night or are you going to do something about it?

Courlander snatched up the phone, called his precinct house. "Courlander. Send over a detail, quick! St. Anselm. That suicide reported here has the earmarks of a murder."

"Earmarks!" scoffed Striker. "It's murder from head to foot, with a capital *M!*" He took the phone in turn. "Pardon me if I try to lock the stable door after the nag's been stolen. . . . H'lo, Maxon? Anyone left the building since this broke, anyone at all? Sure of that? Well, see that no one does. Call in that cop that's looking after the body. Lock up the secondary exit through the coffee shop. No one's to leave, no one at all, understand?" He threw the phone back at Courlander. "Confirm that for me, will you? Cops don't take orders from me. We've got them! They're still in the building some place! There's no way to get down from the roof. It's seven stories higher than any of the others around it."

But Courlander wasn't taking to cooperation very easily. "All this is based on your say-so that the guy couldn't write and had a certain amount of money on him when he came up here. So far so good. But something a little more definite than that better turn up. Did you mark the bills you gave him?"

"No, I didn't," Striker had to admit. "I wasn't figuring on robbery being the motive. I still don't think it's the primary one, I think it's only incidental. I don't think there is any consistent motive. I think we're up against a maniac."

"If they weren't marked, how do you expect us to trace them? Everyone in this place must have a good deal more than just forty-five dollars to their name! If you did plant somebody, why didn't you back him up, why didn't you look after him right? How did you expect to be able to help him if you stayed all the way downstairs, nine floors below?"

"I couldn't very well hang around outside the room. That would've been tipping my hand. I warned him, put him on his guard. He was to knock the phone over. That's all he had to do. Whatever it was, was too quick even for that."

Two members of the Homicide Squad appeared. "What's all the fuss and feathers? Where're the earmarks you spoke of, Courlander? The body's slated for an autopsy, but the examiner already says it don't look like anything but just the fall killed him."

"The house dick here," Courlander said, "insists the guy couldn't write and is short forty-five bucks. He planted him up here because he has an idea those other three cases—the ones I covered, you know—were murder."

They started to question Striker rigorously as though he himself were the culprit. "What gave you the idea it would happen tonight?"

"I didn't know it would happen tonight. I took a stab at it, that's all. I figured it was about due somewhere around now."

"Was the door open or locked when you got up here?"

"Locked."

"Where was the key?"

"Where it is now—over there on the dresser."

"Was the room disturbed in any way?"

"No, it was just like it is now."

They took a deep breath in unison, a breath that meant they were being very patient with an outsider. "Then what makes you think somebody besides himself was in here at the time?"

"Because that note is here, and he couldn't write! Because there's forty-five dollars—"

"One thing at a time. Can you prove he couldn't write?"

"He proved it to *me!*"

"Yes, but can you prove it to *us?*"

Striker caught a tuft of his own hair in his fist, dragged at it, let it go again. "No, because he's gone now."

The other one leaned forward, dangerously casual. "You say you warned him what to expect, and yet he was willing to go ahead and chance it, just for the sake of a meal, a suit of clothes, a bed. How do you explain that?"

"He was at the end of his rope. He was about ready to quit anyway."

Striker saw what was coming.

"Oh, he was? How do you know?"

"Because he told me so. He said he was—thinking of the river."

"*Before* you explained your proposition or after?"

"*Before*," Striker had to admit.

They blew out their breaths scornfully, eyed one another as though this man's stupidity was unbelievable. "He brings a guy up from the beach," one said to the other, "that's already told him *beforehand* he's got doing the Dutch on his mind, and then when the guy goes ahead and does it, he tries to make out he's been murdered."

Striker knocked his chair over, stood up in exasperation. "But can't you get it through your concrete domes? What was driving him to it? The simplest reason in the world! *Lack of shelter, lack of food, lack of comfort.* Suddenly he's given all that at one time. Is it reasonable to suppose he'll cut his own enjoyment of it short, put an end to it halfway through the night? Tomorrow night, yes, after he's out of here, back where he was again, after the letdown has set in. But not tonight."

"Very pretty, but it don't mean a thing. The swell surroundings only brought it on quicker. He wanted to die in comfort, in style, while he was about it. That's been known to happen too, don't forget. About his not being able to write, sorry, but"—they flirted the sheet of notepaper before his eyes—"this evidence shows he *was* able to write. He must have put one over on you. You probably tipped your mitt in giving him your writing test. He caught on you were looking for someone who didn't write, so he played 'possum. About the money—well, it musta gone out the window with him even if he *was* just in his underwear, and somebody down there snitched it before the cop came along. No evidence. The investigation's closed as far as we're concerned." They sauntered out into the hall.

"Damn it," Striker yelled after them, "you can't walk out of here! You're turning your backs on a murder!"

"We *are* walking out," came back from the hallway. "Put that in your pipe and smoke it!" The elevator door clicked mockingly shut.

Courlander said almost pityingly. "It looks like tonight wasn't your lucky night."

"It isn't yours either!" Striker bellowed. He swung his fist in a barrel-house right, connected with the city dick's lower jaw, and sent him volplaning back on his shoulders against the carpet.

Perry's moonface and bald head were white as an ostrich egg with long-nursed resentment. "Get out of here!" You're fired! Bring bums into my house so they can commit suicide on the premises, will you? You're through!"

"Fired?" Striker gave him a smouldering look that made Perry draw hastily back out of range. "I'm quitting, is what you mean! I wouldn't even finish the night out in a murder nest like this!" He stalked past the manager, clenched hands in pockets, and went up to his room to pack his belongings.

His chief problem was to avoid recognition by any of the staff, when he returned there nearly a year later. To achieve this after all the years he'd worked in the hotel, he checked in swiftly and inconspicuously. The mustache he had been growing for the past eight months and which now had attained full maturity, effectively changed the lower part of his face. The horn-rimmed glasses, with plain inserts instead of ground lenses, did as much for the upper part, provided his hat brim was tipped down far enough. If he stood around, of course, and let them stare, eventual recognition was a certainty, but he didn't. He put on a little added weight from the long months of idleness in the furnished room. He hadn't worked in the interval. He could no doubt have got another berth, but he considered that he was still on a job—even though he was no longer drawing pay for it—and he meant to see it through.

A lesser problem was to get the room itself. If he couldn't get it at once, he fully intended taking another for a day or two until he could, but this of course would add greatly to the risk of recognition. As far as he could tell, however, it was available right now. He'd walked through the side street bordering the hotel three nights in a row, after dark, and each time that particular window had been unlighted. The red tag would quickly tell him whether he was right or not.

Other than that, his choice of this one particular night for putting the long-premeditated move into effect was wholly arbitrary. The interval since the last time it had happened roughly approximated the previous intervals, and that was all he had to go by. One night, along about now, was as good as another.

He paid his bill at the rooming house and set out on foot, carrying just one bag with him. His radio and the rest of his belongings he left behind in the landlady's charge, to be called for later. It was about nine o'clock now. He wanted to get in before Maxon's shift. He'd been more intimate with Maxon than the other clerks, had practically no chance of getting past Maxon unidentified.

He stopped in at a hardware store on his way and bought two articles: a long section of stout hempen rope and a small sharp fruit, or kitchen, knife with a wooden handle. He inserted both objects in the bag with his clothing, right there in the shop, then set out once more. He bent his hat brim a little lower over his eyes as he neared the familiar hotel entrance, that was all. He went up the steps and inside unhesitatingly. One of the boys whom he knew by sight ducked for his bag without giving any sign of recognition. That was a good omen. He moved swiftly to the desk without looking around or giving anyone a chance to study him at leisure. There was a totally new man on now in Dennison's place, someone who didn't know him at all. That was the second good omen. And red was peering from the pigeonhole of 913.

His eye quickly traced a vertical axis through it. Not another one in a straight up-and-down line with it. It was easy to work it if you were familiar with the building layout, and who should be more familiar than he?

He said, "I want a single on the side street, where the traffic isn't so heavy." He got it the first shot out of the box!

He paid for it, signed *A. C. Sherman, New York,* and quickly stepped into the waiting car, with his head slightly lowered but not enough so to be conspicuously furtive.

A minute later the gauntlet had been successfully run. He gave the boy a dime, closed the door, and had gained his objective undetected. Nothing had been changed in it. It was the same as when he'd slept in it that first time, nearly two years ago now. It was hard to realize, looking around at it, that it had seen four men go to their deaths. He couldn't help wondering. "Will I be the fifth?" That didn't frighten him any. It just made him toughen up inside and promise, "Not without a lotta trouble, buddy, not without a lotta trouble!"

He unpacked his few belongings and put them away as casually as though he were what he seemed to be, an unsuspecting newcomer who had just checked into a hotel. The coiled rope he hid under the mattress of the bed for the time being; the fruit knife and his gun under the pillows.

He killed the next two hours, until the deadline was due; undressed, took a bath, then hung around in his pajamas reading a paper he'd brought up with him.

At twelve he made his final preparations. He put the room light out first of all. Then in the dark he removed the whole bedding, mattress and all, transferred it to the floor, laying bare the framework and bolted-down coils of the bed. He looped the rope around the bed's midsection from side to side, weaving it inextricably in and out of the coils. Then he knotted a free length to a degree that defied undoing, splicing the end for a counter-knot.

He coiled it three times around his own middle, again knotting it to a point of Houdini-like bafflement. In between there was a slack of a good eight or ten feet. More than enough, considering the ease with which the bed could be pulled about on its little rubber-tired casters, to give him a radius of action equal to the inside limits of the room. Should pursuit through the doorway become necessary, that was what the knife was for. He laid it on the nightstand, alongside his gun.

Then he replaced the bedding, concealing the rope fastened beneath it. He carefully kicked the loose length, escaping at one side, out of sight under the bed. He climbed in, covered up.

The spiny roughness and constriction of his improvised safety-belt bothered him a good deal at first, but he soon found that by lying still and not changing position too often, he could accustom himself to it, even forget about it.

An hour passed, growing more and more blurred as it neared its end. He didn't try to stay awake, in fact encouraged sleep, feeling that the rope would automatically give him more than a fighting chance, and that to remain awake and watchful might in some imponderable way ward off the very thing he was trying to come to grips with.

At the very last he was dimly conscious, through already

somnolent faculties, of a vague sweetness in the air, lulling him even further. Sandalwood incense. "So they're still here," he thought indistinctly. But the thought wasn't sufficient to rouse him to alertness; he wouldn't let it. His eyelids started to close of their own weight. He let them stay down.

Only once, after that, did his senses come to the surface. The scratchy roughness of the rope as he turned in his sleep. "Rope," he thought dimly, and placing what it was, dropped off into oblivion again.

The second awakening came hard. He fought against it stubbornly, but it slowly won out, dragging him against his will. It was twofold. Not dangerous or threatening, but mentally painful, like anything that pulls you out of deep sleep. Excruciatingly painful. He wanted to be let alone. Every nerve cried out for continued sleep, and these two spearheads—noise and glare—continued prodding at him, tormenting him.

Then suddenly they'd won out. *Thump!*—one last cruelly jolting impact of sound, and he'd opened his eyes. The glare now attacked him in turn; it was like needles boring into the pupils of his defenseless, blurred eyes. He tried to shield them from it with one protective hand, and it still found them out. He struggled dazedly upright in the bed. The noise had subsided, was gone, after that last successful bang. But the light—it beat into his brain.

It came pulsing from beyond the foot of the bed, so that meant it was coming through the open bathroom door. The bed was along the side wall, and the bathroom door should be just beyond its foot. He must have forgotten to put the light out in there. What a brilliance! He could see the light through the partly open door, swinging there on its loose, exposed electric-cord. That is to say, he could see the pulsing gleam and dazzle of it, but he couldn't get it into focus; it was like a sunburst. It was torture, it was burning his sleepy eyeballs out. Have to get up and snap it out. How'd that ever happen anyway? Maybe the switch was defective, current was escaping through it even after it had been turned off, and he was sure he had turned it off.

He struggled out of bed and groped toward it. The room

around him was just a blur, his senses swimming with the combination of pitch-blackness and almost solar brilliance they were being subjected to. But it was the bathroom door that was beyond the foot of the bed, that was one thing he was sure of, even in his sleep-fogged condition.

He reached the threshold, groped upward for the switch that was located above the bulb itself. To look upward at it was like staring a blast furnace in the face without dark glasses. It had seemed to be dangling there just past the half-open door, so accessible. And now it seemed to elude him, swing back a little out of reach. Or maybe it was just that his fumbling fingers had knocked the loose cord into that strange, evasive motion.

He went after it, like a moth after a flame. Took a step across the threshold, still straining upward after it, eyes as useless as though he were standing directly in a lighthouse beam.

Suddenly the doorsill seemed to rear. Instead of being just a flat strip of wood, partitioning the floor of one room from the other, it struck him sharply, stunningly, way up the legs, just under the kneecaps. He tripped, overbalanced, plunged forward. The rest was hallucination, catastrophe, destruction.

The light vanished as though it had wings. The fall didn't break; no tiled flooring came up to stop it. The room had suddenly melted into disembodied night. No walls, no floor, nothing at all. Cool air of out-of-doors was rushing upward into the vacuum where the bathroom apparently had been. His whole body was turning completely over, and then over again, and he was going down, down, down. He only had time for one despairing thought as he fell at a sickening speed: "I'm *outside* the building!"

Then there was a wrench that seemed to tear his insides out and snap his head off at his neck. The hurtling fall jarred short, and there was a sickening, swaying motion on an even keel. He was turning slowly like something on a spit, clawing helplessly at the nothingless around him. In the cylindrical blackness that kept wheeling about him he could make out the gray of the building wall, recurring now on this side, now on that, as he swiveled. He tried to get a grip on the wall with his fingertips, to steady himself, gain a fulcrum! Its sandpapery roughness held no indentation to which he could attach himself even by one wildly searching thumb.

He was hanging there between floors at the end of the rope which had saved his life. There was no other way but to try to climb back along its length, until he could regain that treacherous guard rail up there over his head. It could be done, it had to be. Fortunately the rope's grip around his waist was automatic. He was being held without having to exert himself, could use all his strength to lift himself hand over hand. That shouldn't be impossible. It was his only chance, at any rate.

The tall oblong of window overhead through which he had just been catapulted bloomed yellow. The room lights had been put on. Someone was in there. Someone was in there. Someone had arrived to help him. He arched his back, straining to look up into that terrifying vista of night sky overhead—but that now held the warm friendly yellow patch that meant his salvation.

"Grab that rope up there!" he bellowed hoarsely. "Pull me in! I'm hanging out here! Hurry! There isn't much time!"

Hands showed over the guard-rail. He could see them plainly, tinted yellow by the light behind them. Busy hands, helping hands, answering his plea, pulling him back to the safety of solid ground.

No, wait! Something flashed in them, flashed again. Sawing back and forth, slicing, biting into the rope that held him, just past the guard-rail. He could feel the vibration around his middle, carried down to him like the hum along a wire. Death-dealing hands, completing what had been started, sending him to his doom. With his own knife, that he'd left up there beside the bed!

The rope began to fritter. A little severed outer strand came twining loosely down the main column of it toward him, like a snake. Those hands, back and forth, like a demon fiddler drawing his bow across a single tautened violin string in hurried, frenzied funeral march that spelled Striker's doom!

"Help!" he shouted in a choked voice, and the empty night sky around seemed to give it mockingly back to him.

A face appeared above the hands and knife, a grinning derisive face peering down into the gloom. Vast mane of snow-white hair and long white beard. It was Peter the Hermit.

So now he knew at last—too late. Too late.

The face vanished again, but the hands, the knife, were busier then ever. There was a microscopic dip, a *give*, as another strand parted, forerunner of the hurtling, whistling drop to come, the hurtling drop that meant the painful, bone-crushing end of him.

He burst into a flurry of helpless, agonized motion, flailing out with arms and legs—at what, toward what? Like a tortured fly caught on a pin, from which he could never hope to escape.

Glass shattered somewhere around him; one foot seemed to puncture the solid stone wall, go all the way through it. A red-hot wire stroked across his instep and he jerked convulsively.

There was a second preliminary dip, and a wolf howl of joy from above. He was conscious of more yellow light, this time from below, not above. A horrified voice that was trying not to lose its self-control sounded just beneath him somewhere. "Grab this! Don't lose your head now! Grab hold of this and don't let go whatever happens!"

Wood, the wood of a chair back, nudged into him, held out into the open by its legs. He caught at it spasmodically with both hands, riveted them to it in a grip like rigor mortis. At the same time somebody seemed to be trying to pull his shoe off his foot, that one foot that had gone in through the wall and seemed to be cut off from the rest of him.

There was a nauseating plunging sensation that stopped as soon as it began. His back went over until he felt like he was breaking in two, then the chair back held, steadied, reversed, started slowly to draw him with it. The severed rope came hissing down on top of him. From above there was a shrill cackle, from closer at hand a woman's scream of pity and terror. Yellow closed around him, swallowed him completely, took him in to itself.

He was stretched out on the floor, a good solid floor—and it was over. He was still holding the chair in that viselike grip. Young, the Chinese lawyer, was still hanging onto it by the legs, face a pasty gray. Bob, the night porter, was still holding onto his one ankle, and blood was coming through the sock. Mrs. Young, in a sort of chain arrangement, was hugging the porter around the waist. There was broken glass around him on the floor, and a big pool of water with tropical fish floundering in it from the overturned tank. A dog was whining heartbreakingly somewhere in the room. Other than that, there was complete silence.

None of them could talk for a minute or two. Mrs. Young sat squarely down on the floor, hid her face in her hands, and had brief but high-powered hysterics. Striker rolled over and planted his lips devoutly to the dusty carpet, before he even took a stab at getting to his shaky and undependable feet.

"What the hell happened to *you?*" heaved the lawyer finally, mopping his forehead. "Flying around out there like a bat! You scared the daylights out of me."

"Come on up to the floor above and get all the details," Striker invited. He guided himself shakily out of the room, stiff-arming himself against the door frame as he went. His legs still felt like rubber, threatening to betray him.

The door of 913 stood open. In the hallway outside it he motioned them cautiously back. "I left my gun in there, and he's got a knife with him too, so take it easy." But he strode into the lighted opening as though a couple of little items like that weren't stopping him after what he'd just been through and nearly didn't survive.

Then he stopped dead. There wasn't anyone at all in the room—any more.

The bed, with the severed section of rope still wound securely around it, was upturned against the window opening, effectively blocking it. The entire bedding, mattress and all, had slid off it, down into the street below. It was easy to see what had happened. The weight of his body, dangling out there, had drawn it first out into line with the opening (and it moved so easily on those rubber-tired casters!), then tipped it over on its side. The mattress and all the encumbering clothes had spilled off it and gone out of their own weight, entangling, blinding, and carrying with them, like a linen avalanche, whatever and whoever stood in their way. It was a fitting finish for an ingenious, heartless murderer.

The criminal caught neatly in his own trap.

"He was too anxious to cut that rope and watch me fall at the same time," Striker said grimly. "He leaned too far out. A feather pillow was enough to push him over the sill!"

He sauntered over to the dresser, picked up a sheet of paper, smiled a little—not gaily. "My 'suicide note'!" He looked at Young. "Funny sensation, reading your own farewell note. I bet not many experience it! Let's see what I'm supposed to have said to myself. *I'm at the end of my rope.* Queer, how he hit the nail on the head that time! He made them short, always. So there wouldn't be enough to them to give the handwriting away. He never signed them, either. Because he didn't know their names. He didn't even know what they looked like."

Courlander's voice sounded outside, talking it over with someone as he came toward the room. ". . . mattress and all! But instead of him landing on it, which might have saved his life, *it* landed on *him*. Didn't do him a bit of good! He's gone forever."

Striker, leaning against the dresser, wasn't recognized at first.

"Say, wait a minute, where have I seen *you* before?" the city dick growled finally, after he'd given a preliminary look around the disordered room.

"What a detective you turned out to be!" grunted the shaken Striker rudely.

"Oh, it's you, is it? Do you haunt the place? What do you know about this?"

"A damn sight more than you!" was the uncomplimentary retort. "Sit down and learn some of it—or are you still afraid to face the real facts?"

Courlander sank back into a chair mechanically, mouth agape, staring at Striker.

"I'm not going to *tell* you about it," Striker went on. "I'm going to demonstrate. That's always the quickest way with kindergarten-age intelligences!" He caught at the overturned bed, righted it, rolled it almost effortlessly back into its original position against the side wall, *foot facing directly toward the bathroom door.*

"Notice that slight vibration, that humming the rubber-tired casters make across the floorboards? That's the 'distant thunder' the Youngs heard that night. I'll show you the lightning in just a minute. I'm going over there to his room now. Before I go, just let me point out one thing: the sleeper goes to bed in an unfamiliar room, and his last recollection is of the bathroom door being down there at the foot, the windows over here on this side. He wakes up dazedly in the middle of the night, starts to get out of bed, and comes up against the wall first of all. So then he gets out at the opposite side; but this has only succeeded in disorienting him, balling him up still further. All he's still sure of, now, is that the bathroom door is somewhere down there *at the foot of the bed!* Now just watch closely and you'll see the rest of it in pantomime. I'm going to show you just how it was done."

He went out and they sat tensely, without a word, all eyes on the open window.

Suddenly they all jolted nervously, in unison. A jumbo, triple-toothed fishhook had come into the room, through the window, on the end of three interlocked rods—a single line running through them from hook to reel. It came in diagonally, from the projecting wing. It inclined of its own extreme length, in a gentle arc that swept the triple-threat hook down to floor level. Almost immediately, as the unseen "fisherman" started to withdraw it, it snagged the lower right-hand foot of the bed. It would have been hard for it not to, with its three barbs pointing out in as many directions at once. The bed started to move slowly around after it, on those cushioned casters. There was not enough vibration or rapidity to the maneuver to disturb a heavy sleeper. The open window was at the foot of the bed, where the bathroom had been before the change.

The tension of the line was relaxed. The rod jockeyed a little until the hook had been dislodged from the bed's "ankle." The liberated rod was swiftly but carefully withdrawn, as unobtrusively as it had appeared a moment before.

There was a short wait, horrible to endure. Then a new object appeared before the window opening—flashing refracting light, so that it was hard to identify for a minute even though the room lights were on in this case and the subjects were fully awake. It was a lighted miner's lamp with an unusually high-powered reflector behind it. In addition to this, a black object of some kind, an old sweater or miner's shirt, was hooded around it so that it was almost invisible from the street or the windows on the floor below—all its rays beat inward to the room. It was suspended from the same trio of interlocked rods.

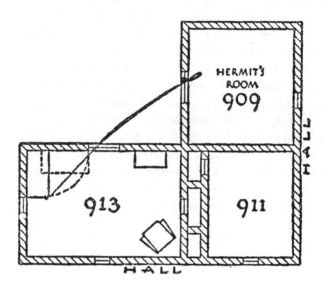

It swayed there motionless for a minute, a devil's beacon, an invitation to destruction. Then it nudged inward, knocked repeatedly against the edge of the window frame, as though to deliberately awaken whoever was within. Then the light coyly retreated a little farther out into the open, but very imperceptibly, as if trying to snare something into pursuit. Then the light suddenly whisked up and was gone, drawn up through space.

With unbelievable swiftness, far quicker than anybody could have come up from the street, the closed door flew back at the touch of Striker's passkey, he darted in, tossed the "suicide note" he was holding onto the dresser, then swiveled the bed back into its original position in the room, scooped up imaginary money.

He stepped out of character and spread his hands conclusively. "See? Horribly simple and—simply horrible."

The tension broke. Mrs. Young buried her face against her husband's chest.

"He was an expert fisherman. Must have done a lot of it up around those mines of his," Striker added. "Probably never failed to hook that bed first cast off the reel. This passkey, that let him in here at will, must have been mislaid years ago and he got hold of it in some way. He brooded and brooded over the way he'd been swindled; this was his way of getting even with the world, squaring things. Or maybe he actually thought these various people in here were spies who came to learn the location of his mines. I don't know, I'm no psychiatrist. The money was just secondary, the icing to his cake. It helped him pay for his room here, staked him to the supplies he took along on his 'prospecting' trips.

"A few things threw me off for a long time. He was away at the time young Hastings fell out. The only possible explanation is that that, alone of the four, was a genuine suicide. By a freak coincidence it occurred in the very room the Hermit had been using for his murders. And this in spite of the fact that Hastings had less reason than any of the others; he had just become engaged. I know it's hard to swallow, but we'll have to. I owe you an apology on that one suicide, Courlander."

"And I owe you an apology on the other three, and to show you I'm not bad loser, I'm willing to make it in front of the whole Homicide Squad of New York."

Young asked curiously, "Have you any idea of just where those mines of his that caused all the trouble are located? Ontario, isn't it? Because down at the station tonight a Press Radio news flash came through that oil had been discovered in some abandoned gold-mine pits up there, a gusher worth all kinds of money, and they're running around like mad trying to find out in whom the title to them is vested. I bet it's the same ones!"

Striker nodded sadly. "I wouldn't be surprised. That would be just like one of life's bum little jokes."

INVISIBLE HANDS

By John Dickson Carr (1906-1977)

"He can create atmosphere with an adjective," said Dorothy L. Sayers, "and alarm with an allusion." No one more effectively combined atmosphere with fairplay clueing than John Dickson Carr, and no one was a greater master of tricks and impossibilities. During a writing career of almost 50 years, Carr invented more than one hundred miracle crimes. In his tales, locks and bolts are no impediment to murder, rooms seem to disappear, coffins move of their own accord, invisible murderers seem to fly through the air, and people dive into swimming pools and vanish. Carr devised several solutions to one of the classic impossible situations in which a victim is found alone with only his own footprints on otherwise unmarked snow or sand. "Invisible Hands" is one of five short stories featuring Carr's "vast and beaming," harrumphing detective Dr. Gideon Fell.

HE could never understand afterward why he felt uneasiness, even to the point of fear, before he saw the beach at all.

Night and fancies? But how far can fancies go?

It was a steep track down to the beach. The road, however, was good, and he could rely on his car. And yet, halfway down, before he could even taste the sea-wind or hear the rustle of the sea, Dan Fraser felt sweat on his forehead. A nerve jerked in the calf of his leg over the foot brake.

"Look, this is damn silly!" he thought to himself. He thought it with a kind of surprise, as when he had first known fear in wartime long ago. But the fear had been real enough, no matter how well he concealed it, and they believed he never felt it.

A dazzle of lightning lifted ahead of him. The night was too hot. This enclosed road, bumping the springs of his car, seemed presssed down in an airless hollow.

After all, Dan Fraser decided, he had everything to be thankful for. He was going to see Brenda; he was the luckiest man in London. If she chose to spend weekends as far away as North Cornwall, he was glad to drag himself there—even a day late.

Brenda's image rose before him, as clearly as the flash of lightning. He always seemed to see her half laughing, half pouting, with light on her yellow hair. She was beautiful; she was desirable. It would only be disloyalty to think any trickiness underlay her intense, naive ways.

Brenda Lestrange always got what she wanted. And she had wanted him, though God alone knew why: he was no prize package at all. Again, in imagination, he saw her against the beat and shuffle of music in a night club. Brenda's shoulders rose from a low-cut silver gown, her eyes as blue and wide-spaced as the eternal Eve's.

You'd have thought she would have preferred a dasher, a roaring bloke like Toby Curtis, who had all the women after him. But that, as Joyce had intimated, might be the trouble. Toby Curtis couldn't see Brenda for all the rest of the crowd. And so Brenda preferred—

Well, then, what was the matter with him?

He would see Brenda in a few minutes. There ought to have been joy bells in the tower, not bats in the—

Easy!

He was out in the open now, at sea level. Dan Fraser drove bumpingly along scrub grass, at the head of a few shallow terraces leading down to the private beach. Ahead of him, facing seaward, stood the overlarge, overdecorated bungalow which Brenda had rather grandly named "The King's House."

And there wasn't a light in it—not a light showing at only a quarter past ten.

Dan cut the engine, switched off the lights, and got out of the car. In the darkness he could hear the sea charge the beach as an army might have charged it.

Twisting open the handle of the car's trunk, he dragged out his suitcase. He closed the compartment with a slam which echoed out above the swirl of water. This part of the Cornish coast was too lonely, too desolate, but it was the first time such a thought had ever occurred to him.

He went to the house, round the side and toward the front. His footsteps clacked loudly on the crazy-paved path on the side. And even in a kind of luminous darkness from the white of the breakers ahead, he saw why the bungalow showed no lights.

All the curtains were drawn on the windows—on this side, at least.

When Dan hurried round to the front door, he was almost running. He banged the iron knocker on the door, then hammered it again. As he glanced over his shoulders, another flash of lightning paled the sky to the west.

It showed him the sweep of gray sand. It showed black water snakily edged with foam. In the middle of the beach, unearthly, stood the small natural rock formation—shaped like a low-backed armchair, eternally facing out to sea— which for centuries had been known as King Arthur's Chair.

The white eye of the lightning closed. Distantly there was a shock of thunder.

This whole bungalow couldn't be deserted! Even if Edmund Ireton and Toby Curtis were at the former's house some distance along the coast, Brenda herself must be here. And Joyce Ray. And the two maids.

Dan stopped hammering the knocker. He groped for and found the knob of the door.

The door was unlocked.

He opened it on brightness. In the hall, rather overdecorated like so many of Brenda's possessions, several lamps shone on gaudy furniture and a polished floor. But the hall was empty too.

With the wind whisking and whistling at his back Dan went in and kicked the door shut behind him. He had no time to give a hail. At the back of the hall a door opened. Joyce Ray, Brenda's cousin, walked toward him, her arms hanging limply at her sides and her enormous eyes like a sleepwalker's.

"Then you did get here," said Joyce, moistening dry lips. "You did get here, after all."

"I—"

Dan stopped. The sight of her brought a new realization. It didn't explain his uneasiness or his fear—but it did explain much.

Joyce was the quiet one, the dark one, the unobtrusive one, with her glossy black hair and her subdued elegance. But she was the poor relation, and Brenda never let her forget it. Dan merely stood and stared at her. Suddenly Joyce's eyes lost their sleepwalker's look. They were gray eyes, with very black lashes; they grew alive and vivid, as if she could read his mind.

"Joyce," he blurted, "I've just understood something. And I never understood it before. But I've got to tell—"

"Stop!" Joyce cried.

Her mouth twisted. She put up a hand as if to shade her eyes.

"I know what you want to say," she went on. "But you're not to say it! Do you hear me?"

"Joyce, I don't know why we're standing here yelling at each other. Anyway, I—I didn't mean to tell you. Not yet, anyway. I mean, I must tell Brenda—"

"You can't tell Brenda!" Joyce cried.

"What's that?"

"You can't tell her anything, ever again," said Joyce. "Brenda's dead."

There are some words which at first do not even shock or stun. You just don't believe them. They can't be true. Very carefully Dan Fraser put his suitcase down on the floor and straightened up again.

"The police," said Joyce, swallowing hard, "have been here since early this morning. They're not here now. They've taken her away to the mortuary. That's where she'll sleep tonight."

Still Dan said nothing.

"Mr.—Mr. Edmund Ireton," Joyce went on, "has been here ever since it happened. So has Toby Curtis. So, fortunately, has a man named Dr. Gideon Fell. Dr. Fell's a bumbling old duffer, a very learned man or something. He's a friend of the police; he's kind; he's helped soften things. All the same, Dan, if you'd been here last night—"

"I couldn't get away. I told Brenda so."

"Yes, I know all that talk about hard-working journalists. But if you'd only been here, Dan, it might not have happened at all."

"Joyce, for God's sake!"

Then there was a silence in the bright, quiet room. A stricken look crept into Joyce's eyes.

"Dan, I'm sorry. I'm terribly sorry. I was feeling dreadful and so, I suppose, I had to take it out on the first person handy."

"That's all right. But how did she die? Then desperately he began to surmise. "Wait, I've got it! She went out to swim early this morning, just as usual? She's been diving off those rocks on the headland again? And—"

"No," said Joyce. "She was strangled."

"Strangled?"

What Joyce tried to say was "murdered." Her mouth shook and faltered round the syllables; she couldn't say them; her thoughts, it seemed, shied back and ran from the very word. But she looked at Dan steadily.

"Brenda went out to swim early this morning, yes."

"Well?"

"At least, she must have. I didn't see her. I was still asleep in that back bedroom she always gives me. Anyway, she went down there in a red swim suit and a white beach robe."

Automatically Dan's eyes moved over to an oil painting above the fireplace. Painted by a famous R.A., it showed a scene from classical antiquity; it was called *The Lovers*, and left little to the imagination. It had always been Brenda's favorite because the female figure in the picture looked so much like her.

"Well!" said Joyce, throwing out her hands. "You know what Brenda always does. She takes off her beach robe and spreads it out over King Arthur's Chair. She sits down in the chair and smokes a cigarette and looks out at the sea before she goes into the water.

"The beach robe was still in that rock chair," Joyce continued with an effort, "when I came downstairs at half-past seven. But Brenda wasn't. She hadn't even put on her bathing cap. Somebody had strangled her with that silk scarf she wore with the beach robe. It was twisted so tightly into her neck they couldn't get it out. She was lying on the sand in front of the chair, on her back, in the red swim suit, with her face black and swollen. You could see her clearly from the terrace."

Dan glanced at the flesh tints of *The Lovers*, then quickly looked away.

Joyce, the cool and competent, was holding herself under restraint.

"I can only thank my lucky stars," she burst out, "I didn't run out there. I mean, from the flagstones of the lowest terrace out across the sand. They stopped me."

"They stopped you? Who?"

"Mr. Ireton and Toby. Or, rather, Mr. Ireton did; Toby wouldn't have thought of it."

"But—"

"Toby, you see, had come over here a little earlier. But he was at the back of the bungalow, practising with a .22 target rifle. I heard him once. Mr. Ireton had just got there. All three of us walked out on the terrace at once. And saw her."

"Listen, Joyce. What difference does it make whether or not you ran out across the sand? Why were you so lucky they stopped you?"

"Because if they hadn't, the police might have said I did it."

"Did it?"

"Killed Brenda," Joyce answered clearly. "In all that

stretch of sand, Dan, there weren't any footprints except Brenda's own."

"Now hold on!" he protested. "She—she was killed with that scarf of hers?"

"Oh, yes. The police and even Dr. Fell don't doubt that."

"Then how could anybody, anybody at all, go out across the sand and come back without leaving a footprint?"

"That's just it. The police don't know and they can't guess. That's why they're in a flat spin, and Dr. Fell will be here again tonight."

In her desperate attempt to speak lightly, as if all this didn't matter, Joyce failed. Her face was white. But again the expression of the dark-fringed eyes changed, and she hesitated.

"Dan—"

"Yes?"

"You do understand, don't you, why I was so upset when you came charging in and said what you did?"

"Yes, of course."

"Whatever you had to tell me, or thought you had to tell me—"

"About—us?"

"About anything! You do see that you must forget it and not mention it again? Not ever?"

"I see why I can't mention it now. With Brenda dead, it wouldn't even be decent to think of it." He could not keep his eyes off that mocking picture. "But is the future dead too? If I happen to have been an idiot and thought I was head over heels gone on Brenda when all the time it was really—"

"*Dan!*"

There were five doors opening into the gaudy hall, which had too many mirrors. Joyce whirled round to look at every door, as if she feared an ambush behind each.

"For heaven's sake keep your voice down," she begged. "Practically every word that's said can be heard all over the house. I said never, and I meant it. If you'd spoken a week ago, even twenty-four hours ago, it might have been different. Do you think I didn't want you to? But now it's too late!"

"Why?"

"May I answer that question?" interrupted a new, dry, rather quizzical voice.

Dan had taken a step toward her, intensely conscious of her attractiveness. He stopped, burned with embarrassment, as one of the five doors opened.

Mr. Edmund Ireton, shortish and thin and dandified in his middle fifties, emerged with his usual briskness. There was not much gray in his polished black hair. His face was a benevolent satyr's.

"Forgive me," he said.

Behind him towered Toby Curtis, heavy and handsome and fair-haired, in a bulky tweed jacket. Toby began to speak, but Mr. Ireton's gesture silenced him before he could utter a sound.

"Forgive me," he repeated. "but what Joyce says is quite true. Every word can be overheard here, even with the rain pouring down. If you go on shouting and Dr. Fell hears it, you will land that girl in serious danger.

"Danger?" demanded Toby Curtis. He had to clear his throat. "What danger could Dan get her into?"

Mr. Ireton, immaculate in flannels and shirt and thin pullover, stalked to the mantelpiece. He stared up hard at *The Lovers* before turning round.

"The Psalmist tell us," he said dryly, "that all is vanity. Has none of you ever noticed—God forgive me for saying so—that Brenda's most outstanding trait was her vanity?"

His glance flashed toward Joyce, who abruptly turned away and pressed her hands over her face.

"Appalling vanity. Scratch that vanity deeply enough and our dearest Brenda would have committed murder."

"Aren't you getting this backwards?" asked Dan. "Brenda didn't commit any murder. It was Brenda—"

"Ah!" Mr. Ireton pounced. "And there might be a lesson in that, don't you think?"

"Look here, you're not saying she strangled herself with her own scarf?"

"No—but hear what I do say. Our Brenda, no doubt, had many passions and many fancies. But there was only one man she loved or ever wanted to marry. It was not Mr. Dan Fraser."

"Then who was it?" asked Toby.

"You."

Toby's amazement was too genuine to be assumed. The color drained out of his face. Once more he had to clear his throat.

"So help me,"he said, "I never knew it! I never imagined—"

"No, of course you didn't,"Mr Ireton said even more dryly. A goatish amusement flashed across his face and was gone. "Brenda, as a rule, could get any man she chose. So she turned Mr. Fraser's head and became engaged to him. It was to sting you, Mr. Curtis, to make you jealous. And you never noticed. While all the time Joyce Ray and Dan Fraser were eating their hearts out for each other; and *he* never noticed either."

Edmund Ireton wheeled round.

"You may lament my bluntness, Mr. Fraser. You may want to wring my neck, as I see you do. But can you deny one word I say?"

"No." In honesty Dan could not deny it.

"Well! Then be very careful when you face the police, both of you, or they will see it too. Joyce already has a strong motive. She is Brenda's only relative, and inherits Brenda's money. If they learn she wanted Brenda's *fiancé,* they will have her in the dock for murder."

"That's enough!" blurted Dan, who dared not look at Joyce. "You've made it clear. All right, stop there!"

"Oh, I had intended to stop. If you are such fools that you won't help yourselves, I must help you. That's all."

It was Toby Curtis who strode forward.

"Dan, don't let him bluff you!" Toby said. "In the first place, they can't arrest anybody for this. You weren't here. I know—".

"I've heard about it, Toby."

"Look," insisted Toby. "When the police finished measuring and photographing and taking casts of Brenda's footprints, I did some measuring myself."

Edmund Ireton smiled. "Are you attempting to solve this mystery, Mr. Curtis?"

"I didn't say that." Toby spoke coolly. "But I might have a question or two for you. Why have you had your knife into me all day?"

"Frankly, Mr. Curtis, because I envy you."

"You—*what?*"

"So far as women are concerned, young man, I have not your advantages. *I* had no romantic boyhood on a veldt-farm in South Africa. *I* never learned to drive a span of oxen and flick a fly off the leader's ear with my whip. *I* was never taught to be a spectacular horseman and rifle shot."

"Oh, turn it up!"

"'Turn it up?' Ah, I see. And was that the sinister question you had for me?"

"No. Not yet. You're too tricky."

"My profoundest thanks."

"Look, Dan," Toby insisted. "You've seen that rock formation they call King Arthur's Chair?"

"Toby, I've seen it fifty times," Dan said. "But I still don't understand—"

"And I don't understand," suddenly interrupted Joyce, without turning round, "why they made me sit there where Brenda had been sitting. It was horrible."

"Oh, they were only reconstructing the crime." Toby spoke rather grandly. "But the question, Dan, is how anybody came near that chair without leaving a footprint?"

"Quite."

"Nobody could have," Toby said just as grandly. "The murderer, for instance, couldn't have come from the direction of the sea. Why? Because the highest point at high tide, where the water might have blotted out footprints, is more than twenty feet in front of the chair. More than twenty feet!"

"Er—one moment," said Mr. Ireton, twitching up a finger. "Surely Inspector Tregellis said the murderer must have crept up and caught her from the back? Before she knew it?"

"That won't do either. From the flagstones of the terrace to the back of the chair is at least twenty feet, too. Well, Dan? Do you see any way out of that one?"

Dan, not normally slow-witted, was so concentrating on Joyce that he could think of little else. She was cut off from him, drifting away from him, forever out of reach just when he had found her. But he tried to think.

"Well . . . could somebody have jumped there?"

"Ho!" scoffed Toby, who was himself a broad jumper and knew better. "That was the first thing they thought of."

"And that's out, too?"

"Definitely. An Olympic champion in good form might have done it, if he'd had any place for a running start and any place to land. But he hadn't. There was *no* mark in the sand. He couldn't have landed on the chair, strangled Brenda at his leisure, and then hopped back like a jumping bean. Now could he?"

"But somebody did it, Toby! It happened!"

"How?"

"I don't know."

"You seem rather proud of this, Mr. Curtis," Edmund Ireton said smoothly.

"Proud?" exclaimed Toby, losing color again.

"These romantic boyhoods—"

Toby did not lose his temper. But he had declared war.

"All right, gaffer. I've been very grateful for your hospitality, at that bungalow of yours, when we've come down here for weekends. All the same, you've been going on for hours about who I am and what I am. Who are *you*?"

"I beg your pardon?"

"For two or three years," Toby said, "you've been hanging about with us. Especially with Brenda and Joyce. Who are you? What are you?"

"I am an observer of life," Mr. Ireton answered tranquilly. "A student of human nature. And—shall I say?—a courtesy uncle to both young ladies."

"Is that all you were? To either of them?"

"Toby!" exclaimed Joyce, shocked out of her fear.

She whirled round, her gaze going instinctively to Dan, then back to Toby.

"Don't worry, old girl," said Toby, waving his hand at her. "This is no reflection on you." He kept looking steadily at Mr. Ireton.

"Continue," Mr. Ireton said politely.

"You claim Joyce is in danger. She isn't in any danger at all," said Toby, "as long as the police don't know how Brenda was strangled."

"They will discover it, Mr. Curtis. Be sure they will discover it!"

"You're trying to protect Joyce?"

"Naturally."

"And that's why you warned Dan not to say he was in love with her?"

"Of course. What else?"

Toby straightened up, his hand inside the bulky tweed jacket.

"Then why didn't you take him outside, rain or no, and tell him on the quiet? Why did you shout out that Dan was in love with Joyce, and she was in love with him, and give'em a motive for the whole house to hear?"

Edmund Ireton opened his mouth, and shut it again.

It was a blow under the guard, all the more unexpected because it came from Toby Curtis.

Mr. Ireton stood motionless under the painting of *The Lovers*. The expression of the pictured Brenda, elusive and mocking, no longer matched his own. Whereupon, while nerves were strained and still nobody spoke, Dan Fraser realized that there was a dead silence because the rain had stopped.

Small night-noises, the creak of woodwork or a drip of water from the eaves, intensified the stillness. Then they heard footsteps, as heavy as those of an elephant, slowly approaching behind another of the doors. The footfalls, heavy and slow and creaking, brought a note of doom.

Into the room, wheezing and leaning on a stick, lumbered a man so enormous that he had to maneuver himself sideways through the door.

His big mop of gray-streaked hair had tumbled over one ear. His eyeglasses, with a broad black ribbon, were stuck askew on his nose. His big face would ordinarily have been red and beaming, with chuckles animating several chins. Now it was only absentminded, his bandit's moustache outthrust.

"Aha!" he said in a rumbling voice. He blinked at Dan with an air of refreshed interest. "I think you must be Mr. Fraser, the last of this rather curious weekend party? H'm. Yes. Your obedient servant, sir. I am Gideon Fell."

Dr. Fell wore a black cloak as big as a tent and carried a shovel-hat in his other hand. He tried to bow and make a flourish with his stick, endangering all the furniture near him.

The others stood very still. Fear was as palpable as the scent after rain.

"Yes, I've heard of you," said Dan. His voice rose in spite of himself. "But you're rather far from home, aren't you? I suppose you had some—er—antiquarian interest in King Arthur's Chair?"

Still Dr. Fell blinked at him. For a second it seemed that chuckles would jiggle his chins and waistcoat, but he only shook his head.

"Antiquarian interest? My dear sir!" Dr. Fell wheezed gently. "If there were any association with a semi-legendary King Arthur, it would be at Tintagel much farther south. No, I was here on holiday. This morning Inspector Tregellis fascinated me with the story of a fantastic murder. I returned tonight for my own reasons."

Mr. Ireton, at ease again, matched the other's courtesy. "May I ask what these reasons were?"

"First, I wished to question the two maids. They have a room at the back, as Miss Ray has; and this afternoon, you may remember, they were still rather hysterical."

"And that is all?"

"H'mf. Well, no." Dr. Fell scowled. "Second, I wanted to detain all of you here for an hour or two. Third, I must make sure of the motive for this crime. And I am happy to say that I have made very sure."

Joyce could not control herself. "Then you did overhear everything!"

"Eh?"

"Every word that man said!"

Despite Dan's signals, Joyce nodded toward Mr. Ireton and poured out the words, "But I swear I hadn't anything to do with Brenda's death. What I told you today was perfectly true: I don't want her money and I won't touch it. As for my—my private affairs," and Joyce's face flamed, "everybody seems to know all about them except Dan and me. Please, please pay no attention to what that man has been saying."

Dr. Fell blinked at her in an astonishment which changed to vast distress.

"But, my dear young lady!" he rumbled. "We never for a moment believed you did. No, no! Archons of Athens, no!" exclaimed Dr. Fell, as though at incredible absurdity. "As for what your friend Mr. Ireton may have been saying, I did not hear it. I suspect it was only what he told me today, and it did supply the motive. But it was not your motive."

"Please, is this true? You're not trying to trap me?"

"Do I really strike you," Dr. Fell asked gently, "as being that sort of person? Nothing was more unlikely than that you killed your cousin, especially in the way she was killed."

"Do you know how she was killed?"

"Oh, *that,*" grunted Dr. Fell, waving the point away too. "That was the simplest part of the whole business."

He lumbered over, reflected in the mirrors, and put down stick and shovel-hat on a table. Afterward he faced them with a mixture of distress and apology.

"It may surprise you," he said, "that an old scatterbrain like myself can observe anything at all. But I have an unfair advantage over the police. I began life as a schoolmaster: I have had more experience with habitual liars. Hang it all, think!"

"Of what?"

"The facts!" said Dr. Fell, making a hideous face. "According to the maids, Sonia and Dolly, Miss Brenda Lestrange went down to swim at ten minutes to seven this morning. Both Dolly and Sonia were awake, but did not get up. Some eight or ten minutes later, Mr. Toby Curtis began practising with a target rifle some distance away behind the bungalow."

"Don't look at me!" exclaimed Toby. "That rifle has nothing to do with it. Brenda wasn't shot."

"Sir," said Dr. Fell with much patience. "I am aware of that."

"Then what are you hinting at?"

"Sir," said Dr. Fell, "you will oblige me if you don't regard every question as a trap. I have a trap for the murderer, and the murderer alone. You fired a number of shots—the maids heard you and saw you." He turned to Joyce. "I believe you heard too?"

"I heard one shot," answered the bewildered Joyce, "as I told Dan. About seven o'clock, when I got up and dressed."

"Did you look out of the windows?"

"No."

"What happened to that rifle afterwards? Is it here now?"

"No," Toby almost yelled. "I took it back to Ireton's after we found Brenda. But if the rifle had nothing to do with it, and I had nothing to do with it, then what the hell's the point?"

Dr. Fell did not reply for a moment. Then he made another hideous face. "We know," he rumbled, "that Brenda Lestrange wore a beach robe, a bathing suit, and a heavy silk scarf knotted round her neck. Miss Ray?"

"Y-yes?"

"I am not precisely an authority on women's clothes," said Dr. Fell. "As a rule I should notice nothing odd unless I passed Madge Wildfire or Lady Godiva. I have seen men wear a scarf with a beach robe, but is it customary for women to wear a scarf as well?"

There was a pause.

"No, of course it isn't," said Joyce. "I can't speak for everybody, but I never do. It was just one of Brenda's fancies. She always did."

"Aha!" said Dr. Fell. "The murderer was counting on that."

"On what?"

"On her known conduct. Let me show you rather a grisly picture of a murder."

Dr. Fell's eyes were squeezed shut. From inside his cloak and pocket he fished out an immense meerschaum pipe. Firmly under the impression that he had filled and lighted the pipe, he put the stem in his mouth and drew at it.

"Miss Lestrange," he said, "goes down to the beach. She takes off her robe. Remember that, it's very important. She spreads out the robe in King Arthur's Chair and sits down. She is still wearing the scarf, knotted tightly in a broad band round her neck. She is about the same height as you, Miss Ray. She is held there, at the height of her shoulders, by a curving rock formation deeply bedded in sand."

Dr. Fell paused and opened is eyes.

"The murderer, we believe, catches her from the back. She sees and hears nothing until she is seized. Intense pressure on the carotid arteries, here at either side of the neck under the chin, will strike her unconscious within seconds and dead within minutes. When her body is released, it should fall straight forward. Instead, what happens?"

To Dan, full of relief ever since danger had seemed to leave Joyce, it was as if a shutter had flown open in his brain.

"She was lying on her back," Dan said. "Joyce told me so. Brenda was lying flat on her back with her head towards the sea. And that means—"

"Yes?"

"It means she was twisted or spun round in some way when she fell. It has something to do with that infernal scarf—I've thought so from the first. Dr. Fell! Was Brenda killed with the scarf?"

"In one sense, yes. In another sense, no."

"You can't have it both ways! Either she was killed with the scarf, or she wasn't."

"Not necessarily," said Dr. Fell.

"Then let's all retire to a loony bin," Dan suggested, "because nothing makes any sense at all. The murderer still couldn't have walked out there without leaving tracks. Finally, I agree with Toby: what's the point of the rifle? How does a .22 rifle figure in all this?"

"Because of its sound."

Dr. Fell took the pipe out of his mouth. Dan wondered why he had ever thought the learned doctor's eyes were vague. Magnified behind the glasses on the broad black ribbon, they were not vague at all.

"A .22 rifle," he went on in his big voice, "has a distinctive noise. Fired in the open air or anywhere else, it sounds exactly like the noise made by the real instrument used in this crime."

"Real instrument? What noise?"

"The crack of a blacksnake whip," replied Dr. Fell.

Edmund Ireton, looking very tired and ten years older, went over and sat down in an easy chair. Toby Curtis took one step backward, then another.

"In South Africa," said Dr. Fell, "I have never seen the very long whip which drivers of long ox spans use. But in America I have seen the blacksnake whip, and it can be twenty-four feet long. You yourselves must have watched it used in a variety turn on the stage."

Dr. Fell pointed his pipe at them.

"Remember?" he asked. "The user of the whip stands some distance away facing his girl-assistant. There is a vicious crack. The end of the whip coils two or three times round the girl's neck. She is not hurt. But she would be in difficulties if he pulled the whip towards him. She would be in grave danger if she were held back and could not move.

"Somebody planned a murder with a whip like that. He came here early in the morning. The whip, coiled round his waist, was hidden by a loose and bulky tweed jacket. Please observe the jacket Toby Curtis is wearing now."

Toby's voice went high when he screeched out one word. It may have been protest, defiance, a jeer, or all three.

"Stop this!" cried Joyce, who had again turned away.

"Continue, I beg," Mr. Ireton said.

"In the dead hush of morning," said Dr. Fell, "he could not hide the loud crack of the whip. But what could he do?"

"He could mask it," said Edmund Ireton.

"Just that! He was always practising with a .22 rifle. So he fired several shots, behind the bungalow, to establish his presence. Afterwards nobody would notice when the crack of the whip—that single, isolated "shot" heard by Miss Ray—only seemed to come from behind the house."

"Then, actually, he was—?"

"On the terrace, twenty feet behind a victim held immovable in the curve of a stone chair. The end of the whip coiled round the scarf. Miss Lestrange's breath was cut off instantly. Under the pull of a powerful arm she died in seconds.

"On the stage, you recall, a lift and twist dislodges the whip from the girl-assistant's neck. Toby Curtis had a harder task; the scarf was so embedded in her neck that she seemed to have been strangled with it. He *could* dislodge it. But only with a powerful whirl and lift of the arm which spun her up and round, to fall face upwards. The whip snaked back to him with no trace in the sand. Afterwards he had only to take the whip back to Mr. Ireton's house, under pretext of returning the rifle. He had committed a murder which, in his vanity, he thought undetectable. That's all."

"But it can't be all!" said Dan. "Why should Toby have killed her? His motive—"

"His motive was offended vanity. Mr. Edmund Ireton as

good as told you so, I fancy. He had certainly hinted as much to me."

Edmund Ireton rose shakily from the chair.

"I am no judge or executioner," he said. "I—I am detached from life. I only observe. If I guessed why this was done—"

"You could never speak straight out?" Dr. Fell asked sardonically.

"No!"

"And yet that was the tragic irony of the whole affair. Miss Lestrange wanted Toby Curtis, as he wanted her. But, being a woman, her pretense of indifference and contempt was too good. He believed it. Scratch her vanity deeply enough and she would have committed murder. Scratch *his* vanity deeply enough—"

"Lies!" said Toby.

"Look at him, all of you!" said Dr. Fell. "Even when he's accused of murder, he can't take his eyes off a mirror."

"Lies!"

"She laughed at him," the big voice went on, "and so she had to die. Brutally and senselessly he killed a girl who would have been his for the asking. That is what I meant by tragic irony."

Toby had retreated across the room until his back bumped against a wall. Startled, he looked behind him; he had banged against another mirror.

"Lies!" he kept repeating. "You can talk and talk and talk. But there's not a single damned thing you can prove!"

"Sir," inquired Dr. Fell, "are you sure?"

"Yes!"

"I warned you," said Dr. Fell, "that I returned tonight partly to detain all of you for an hour or so. It gave Inspector Tregellis time to search Mr. Ireton's house, and the Inspector has since returned. I further warned you that I questioned the maids, Sonia and Dolly, who today were only incoherent. My dear sir, you underestimate your personal attractions."

Now it was Joyce who seemed to understand. But she did not speak.

"Sonia, it seems," and Dr. Fell looked hard at Toby, "has quite a fondness for you. When she heard that last isolated "shot" this morning, she looked out of the window again.

You weren't there. This was so strange that she ran out to the front terrace to discover where you were. She saw you."

The door by which Dr. Fell had entered was still open. His voice lifted and echoed through the hall.

"Come in, Sonia!" he called. "After all, you are a witness to the murder. You, Inspector, had better come in too."

Toby Curtis blundered back, but there was no way out. There was only a brief glimpse of Sonia's swollen, tear-stained face. Past her marched a massive figure in uniform, carrying what he had found hidden in the other house.

Inspector Tregellis was reflected everywhere in the mirrors, with the long coils of the whip over his arm. And he seemed to be carrying not a whip but a coil of rope—gallows rope.

THE X STREET MURDERS

By Joseph Commings (1913 -   )

Joseph Commings began writing short stories during World War II in a tent in Sardinia. They were written for the amusement of his companions, but back home he had no trouble finding magazines that would take them. Some appeared in the later pulps (which by then were a dying breed) but a lot more appeared in the singularly offbeat magazine Mystery Digest. *Perhaps this is why these stories, so much in the tradition of the Golden Age Carr with their ingenious impossible crimes and larger-than-life detective, Senator Brooks U. Banner, are so little known. Banner featured in about thirty stories but amazingly only two of them seem to have made it into anthologies. It is therefore with all the more pleasure that we present a third, as Banner, stogie at a provocative angle, tackles that most perplexing and ingenious series of criminal occasions, "The X Street Murders."*

CARROLL LOCKYEAR came out of the attache's private office at the New Zealand Legation on X Street, Washington, D.C. He was tall and skinny. The sallow skin of his gaunt face was drawn tight over his doorknob cheekbones like that of an Egyptian mummy. The resemblance to a mummy did not end with the tightness of his skin. Sticking out from his sharp chin, like a dejected paintbrush, was a russet-colored King Tut beard. He looked like a well-dressed beatnik. In his left hand he carried a brown cowhide briefcase, his long fingers curled under the bottom ot it.

The secretary in the reception room, Miss Gertrude Wagner, looked up at him. He approached her desk and laid his briefcase carefully down on it, then towered over it toward her.

"Yes, Mr. Lockyear?" she said.

"I have another appointment with Mr. Gosling on next Tuesday, Miss Wagner."

Gertrude penciled a line in an appointment pad.

"Good day," said Lockyear. He picked up his briefcase and walked out.

Gertrude smiled thinly at the Army officer waiting on the lounge. He was reading a copy of the *Ordnance Sergeant,* but it wasn't holding his attention as much as it should. He wore a green tunic with sharpshooter medals on the breast, and his legs, in pink slacks, were crossed. Gertrude stopped her professional smile and picked up the earpiece of the interphone and pressed a button.

"Mr. Gosling," she said, "Captain Cozzens is waiting to see you." She held the earpiece to her head for a moment, then lowered it. "Captain," she said. Cozzens looked up with bright expectancy from his magazine. "Mr. Gosling wants to know if you'd mind waiting a minute."

"Not at all," said Cozzens, eager to agree with such a goodlooking girl. No doubt, visions of dinners for two were dancing in his head.

Gertrude stood up suddenly and tugged her skirt straight. She had black hair cut in a Dutch bob and dark blue eyes. The austere lines of her blotter-green suit could not entirely disguise her big-boned femininity. She gathered up a steno pad and a mechanical pencil and started to walk toward the closed door of Mr. Gosling's private office. Glancing at the slim bagette watch on her wrist, she stopped short. It was as if she had almost forgotten something. She went back to her desk. On it lay a sealed large bulky manila mailing envelope. A slip of paper had been pasted on its side. Typed in red on the paper was the Legation address and:

Deliver to Mr. Kermit Gosling at 11:30 a.m. sharp.

Gertrude grasped the envelope by the top and proceeded into Gosling's office, leaving the door open. This private office, it was carefully noted later, was on the third floor of the building. It had two windows and both these windows were protected by old-fashioned iron bars. It was a room in which an attache might consider himself safe.

Captain Cozzens had been following Gertrude's flowing progress with admiring eyes. Those narrow skirts did a lot for a girl if she had the right kind of legs and hips. And Gertrude definitely had the right kind.

Another man sitting near Cozzens was watching her too. He was red-haired and young, with a square face and a pug nose. The jacket of his black suit was tight across his shoulders. He was Alvin Odell and it was his job to watch what went on in the office. He was an agent from the Federal Bureau of Investigation. But he too was watching Gertrude with more interest than his job called for.

From where Cozzens and Odell sat they could see the edge of Gosling's desk. They saw the closely-observed Gertrude stand before it, facing across it, and she held the bulky envelope up waist-high.

There was a slight pause.

Then three shots spat harshly.

Cozzens and Odell, shocked at the sudden ripping apart of their daydreams by gunfire, saw Gertrude flinch before the desk. Then the two men sprang up together and rushed in to her side.

Gosling, a heavy-featured man with limp blond hair, was tilted sideways in his desk chair. Blood stained his white shirt front, Odell stared at the three bullet holes under the left lapel of the grey business suit.

Captain Cozzen's voice was hoarse. "Those three shots— where did they come from?"

Gertrude's blue eyes, dazed, searched Cozzen's face as if she had never seen him before. Dumbly she lifted up the heavy envelope.

Before Cozzens could move, the FBI man was faster. Odell snatched the envelope out of her hand.

It was still tightly sealed. There were no holes or tears in it. Odell started to rip it along the top. A wisp of bluish smoke curled up in the still air.

Odell tore the envelope wide open and out of it onto the desktop spilled a freshly fired automatic pistol.

Heavy blunt-tipped fingers on speckled hands turned over the brown State Department envelope. It was addressed to *Honorable Brooks U. Banner, M. C., The Idle Hour Club, President Jefferson Avenue, Washington, D.C.*

The addressee was a big fat man with a mane of grizzled hair and a ruddy jowled face and the physique of a performing bear. He wore a motheaten frock coat with deep pockets bulging with junk and a greasy string tie and baggy-kneed grey britches. Under the open frock coat was a candy-striped shirt. On his feet were old house slippers whose frayed toes looked as if a pair of hungry field mice were trying to nibble their way out from inside. He was an overgrown Huck Finn. Physically he was more than one man—he was a gang. Socially and politically he didn't have to answer to anybody, so he acted and spoke any way he damned pleased.

He was sipping his eighth cup of black coffee as he read the letter.

It was from the Assistant Secretary of State. In painful mechanical detail, it reported the murder on X Street with as much passion as there is in a recipe for an upside-down cake. Toward the end of the letter, the Assistant Secretary became a little less like an automaton and a little more human. He confessed to Banner that both the State Department and the FBI were snagged. They couldn't find an answer. And considering the other harrowing murder cases that Banner had solved, perhaps he could be of some help in this extremity.

Banner crumpled the letter up into a ball and stuck it into his deep pocket. Thoughtfully his little frosty blue eyes rested on the white ceiling. He had read about the case in the newspapers, but the account had not been as full as the State Department's.

He pulled the napkin from under his chin, swabbed his lips, and started to surge up to his feet. He looked like a surfacing whale.

A waiter hurried up with a tray. On it were three more cups of black coffee. "Aren't you going to drink the rest of your coffee, sir?" asked the waiter in an injured tone.

"Huh?" said Banner absently. Already his mind was soaring out into space, grappling with the murder problem. "I never touch the stuff," he said and went lumbering out.

Jack McKitrick, who looked like a jockey trainer, was an FBI department chief. He stood near Captain Cozzens in the New Zealand Legation office. When Banner came trotting in the door McKitrick said sideways to Cozzens: "That's Senator Banner. They don't come much bigger."

Cozzens shook his head as he eyed the impressive hulk that rumbled forward.

"Morning, Senator," said McKitrick to Banner.

Banner grunted an answer, mumbling words around a long Pittsburgh stogie clamped in his teeth.

"Senator," continued McKitrick, "this is Captain Cozzens of the Ordnance Division, U.S. Army." The two men clasped hands. "Cozzens is a small firearms expert."

"Mighty fine," said Banner.

"You were an Army officer yourself, weren't you, Senator?" said Cozzens.

Banner truculently chewed on the stogie. "Yass. I never got above the rank of shavetail. We were the dogfaces who gave 'em hell at Chateau Thierry. But I'll tell you all about my war experiences later, Cap'n. We'll all work together on this. Not nice seeing our New Zealand friends getting bumped off. Not nice at all."

"No, certainly not," said Cozzens.

Banner struck an attitude of belligerent ease. "Waal, I'm lissening, Cap'n. You were one of the witnesses to this murder. What were you doing at the Legation?"

Cozzens frowned. "I was here by appointment, Senator.

Mr. Gosling wanted me to suggest a good handgun for his personal use and to give him instructions in how to handle it."

"Why?"

"I think," said Cozzens slowly, "he wanted to use it to protect himself."

"Against what?"

"He never had a chance to tell me. But I think *this* might supply part of the answer." He held up a wicked-looking pistol. "This is what did the trick, Senator. It's all right to handle it. No fingerprints were found on it."

Scowling, Banner took it from him. "So that's the Russian pop-pop."

"Right," said Cozzens. "A Tokarev, a standard Russian automatic. It's a 7.62-mm. with a Browning-Colt breech-locking system and it uses Nagant gas-check cartridges."

"This was the gun in the sealed envelope," said Banner. "Are you sure it wasn't some other gun you heard being fired?"

Cozzens slowly shook his head. "I've spent a lifetime with guns, Senator. I've got to know their 'voices' just the way you know people's. When you hear an accent, you know what part of the world the speaker comes from. That's the way I am with pistols and revolvers. So I'll stake my reputation that the shots we heard had a Russian accent, meaning they were fired from a Tokarev automatic, slightly muffled. Besides that, ballistics bears me out. The bullets found in Gosling's body were indisputably from that gun."

Banner grunted. "And all the while the gun was sealed up tight in an envelope and you could see the secretary holding the envelope while the shots were fired?"

"That's right," answered Cozzens.

"How d'you explain it, Cap'n? What's your theory?"

"Theory? I haven't any. I can't explain it. If I hadn't seen it with my own eyes, I wouldn't believe it."

"Anything else you have to offer?" asked Banner.

"Nothing. That's all."

The stogie in Banner's mouth was burning fiercely. He looked around the office where the murder had been committed. It was a completely equipped modern office. Nothing had been disturbed. He mumbled: *"Gosling knew his life was in danger!"*

Banner turned to McKirtrick. "I'll see Odell."

Cozzens left while Banner was being introduced to the FBI agent, Odell.

"You heard Cozzen's story about the shooting, Odell." said Banner. "Have you anything to add to it?"

Odell shook his red-haired head. "No, it happened just that way, Senator." His frank boyish face was grave.

"Why were you stationed here?"

"At a request from Mr. Gosling. He asked for our security."

"How long've you been hanging out here?"

"About a week, Senator."

McKitrick interrupted to say: "Odell asked for this assignment."

Banner studied the young man with the rusty hair. "What's the reason, Red?"

Odell hesitated, growing crimson around the ears. "Well, Senator—a—Miss Wagner—Well, you'll have to see her to appreciate her—"

Banner suddenly chuckled. He was thinking of his own misspent youth chasing the dolls.

Odell sobered. "She's a hard girl to make friends with," he admitted ruefully.

"It's tough, Red," grinned Banner. "Fetch in the li'l chickie and we'll see if I can't make better time with her than you did."

Odell went out of the office and returned with Gertrude. She looked scared at Banner. Big men in authority seemed to have given her a sudden fright. Her shoulders were hunched up as if she were cold. Odell held her solicitously by the elbow.

"Hello, Gertie," boomed Banner as familiarly as if he had helped to christen her. "Siddown."

She dropped gratefully on the leather lounge as if relieved to get the strain off her shaky knees.

"Gertie, there's no reason why you should think I'm gonna panic you. I'm your big Dutch uncle, remember?"

She smiled at him.

"Now, Gertie," he resumed, "you live with your people, don't you?"

"No," she said hoarsely, then she cleared her throat. "No, Senator. I have no relatives in America. They're all living in Germany."

Germany?" Banner make a quick pounce. "What part of Germany?"

"On a farm outside of Zerbst."

Banner's little frosty blue eyes looked shrewd. "That's in East Germany, ain't it, Gertie?"

"Yes."

"Tell me about 'em. And how you got out?"

It wasn't too complicated a story. Gertrude had been born just after the end of World War II. She grew up in a Communist dominated land, where everybody was schooled in the Russian language. She learned to speak English too—from an ex-Berlitz professor who ran a black market in *verboten* linguistics. Farm life had been stern, as she grew big enough to help her father and crippled mother with the chores, but Gertrude had become sturdy on plenty of fresh milk and vegetables, and she used to walk back from the haying fields with her rakehandle across her back and shoulders and her arms draped over it. It made her walk straight and developed strong chest muscles.

"Yass," muttered Banner at this point. "Like those Balinese gals carrying loads on their heads." He dwelt silently on Bali for a moment, then he said: "Go on. How'd you get outta East Germany?"

She had, she explained, visited East Berlin several times, helping to bring farm products to market. Each time she came an urge grew stronger in her to see all the things she had heard rumors about, the free and wealthy people of the West, the shops and cinemas along the Kurfurstendamm, and the opportunities for a better life. One day, at the Brandenburg Gate, the urge overcame her. She made a wild, reckless dash, eluding Soviet soldier guards, and made it, panting, falling into the arms of sympathetic West Berliners in the American Sector. She had thought that she would surely find somebody who could help to get her crippled mother and her father free too, but so far there was nobody who could perform that miracle.

Her good looks and quick-learning ability eventually got her sponsored for a trip to the United States. Mr. Gosling, of the New Zealand Legation, had proved kind to her and had got her the job.

She stopped talking, her brunette head with the Dutch bob bent low.

"Haaak!" Banner cleared this throat, making a sound like a sea lion. "Who're you living with now?"

"Nobody. I have a small apartment to myself. I have become an American citizen."

Banner sourly eyed the chewed wet end of the stogie in his hand. "Now about this envelope with the gun in it. When did it come to your desk?"

"Sometime near 11:00 o'clock in the morning, Senator."

"Who brought it?"

"A man from the special messenger service."

"Would you know him if you saw him again?"

"I think I would."

"Was your boss, Mr. Gosling, engaged at 11:00?"

"Yes, Mr. Lockyear was in there."

"What time did Cap'n Cozzens come into the reception room?"

"Around 11:15."

"Did anyone tamper with that envelope once it reached your desk, Gertie?"

"No, sir. No one."

"What time did Lockyear come outta the private office?"

"It was nearly 11:30."

"When he came out," said Banner carefully, "did he go straight out?"

"Yes—he stopped only to make an appointment for next Tuesday. I jotted it in my pad."

"Then what'd you do?"

"I spoke to Mr. Gosling on the interphone," she said in a low hushed voice. "I told him that Captain Cozzens was waiting to see him next. He told me to withhold him for a minute and for me to come in with my notebook. I started to go in, then remembered the envelope. The sticker on it had said: *Deliver to Mr. Kermit Gosling at 11:30 a.m. sharp.* I went back to my desk for it."

"It was now just about 11:30, eh? When you went into the private office, what was Gosling doing?"

"He was sitting at his desk."

"He was perfectly all right?"

"Yes, Senator."

"Did he say anything to you?"

She opened her mouth. She paused. "No, he didn't actually say anything. He just smiled and motioned me toward the chair I usually take dictation in. I held up the envelope. I was just about to tell him about it when the gun went off."

"And you saw Gosling being hit with the bullets?"

She nodded wretchedly. "He jerked back, then started to sag over. Then Captain Cozzens and Mr. Odell rushed in."

"Is that all?" rasped Banner.

She bowed her head again.

McKitrick, the FBI departmental head, stirred uneasily by the wall. "Now," he said, "you see what's got the wits of two organizations stymied!"

Banner was looking down at his stogie. It had gone out, but he wasn't even thinking about it. He said: "I'll tell you what I think about it."

McKitrick looked at him hopefully. "What?"

"It couldn't've happened! *It's too damned impossible!*"

Ramshaw must have been about forty-five. A cigarette dangled limply out of his slack lips as he sat on the bench at the special messenger service. He wore a weather-faded blue uniform with shrunken breeches and dusty leather leggings.

Banner loomed over him, his enveloping black wraprascal increasing his already Gargantuan size. "You remember the envelope you delivered to the New Zealand Legation yesterday?"

"That's easy, mister. I never handled one like that before. A 10-year-old kid came into our agency about 10:00 in the morning and said somebody told him to leave the envelope with us to be delivered immediately. We didn't ask too many questions, seeing as the kid had more than ample money to pay for the delivery."

"Did he say whether the *someone* was a man or a woman?"

"Nope."

"Did anyone tamper with the envelope while it was here?"

"Nope. I was assigned to do the job, mister. I kept the envelope right in front of me till I delivered it to the Legation at 11:00. It had written on it, *Deliver to Mr. Kermit Gosling at 11:30 a.m. sharp,* so I wanted to be sure it got there in plenty of time."

Banner glowered. "Didja know there was a gun in it?"

Ramshaw squirmed as if his shrunken breeches chafed him. "I—I thought there was. That's what it felt like through the heavy paper."

"Nobody stopped you on the way to the Legation? Tell me if someone even bumped into you."

"Nope, nope. Clear sailing all the way, mister."

Banner looked down at a pocket watch that must have been manufactured by the Baldwin Locomotive Works. He muttered: "I can still ketch Lockyear before lunch."

He went out of the agency, leaving behind him a grinning messenger. "Say, mister! Thanks for the tip!"

Lockyear, in his office on Pittsylvania Avenue, played with his King Tut beard as Banner made himself known to him.

"It's the strangest thing I ever heard of, Senator," said Lockyear. "But I'm afraid I can be of very little help. Gosling was far from dead when I left him."

"While you were in the office," said Banner, "did you notice anything threatening?"

"Threatening? No, not a thing, Senator."

"Perhaps you'd tell me what you were seeing Gosling about."

"Of course I have no objection, Senator. I'm an exporter-importer. I've been seeing Gosling about clearing some shipments that have been going in and out of New Zealand. Governments are touchy these days about cargoes."

"That's all?"

"That's all, Senator."

In a few minutes Banner was on his way back to the Idle Hour Club. As he entered the convivial surroundings and lumbered into the dining room, he found McKitrick waiting for him.

"The only thing about this case that's plain," said

McKitrick abruptly, "is the motive. We know why Gosling was killed."

"Do you?" Banner squeezed in behind a table and told a waiter he wanted some straight whiskey.

McKitrick said in a lower voice: "Gosling was collecting information on a spy who's been selling all our secrets to the Russian Government. Gosling didn't know exactly who it was, but he was getting dangerously close to that truth. Unfortunately the spy got to Gosling first. The Russian pistol is evidence of that."

McKitrick stopped talking long enough to allow the waiter to place Banner's whiskey before him.

"Yass?" Banner fired up another big stogie.

McKitrick continued: "I've been thinking about Gertrude Wagner. She admits she's from East Germany. Her sympathies might easily lie with the Commies. We have only her word that she'd broken with them. What's more to the point, Banner, she was in the room with Gosling when he was killed. The *only* person in the room with him. And she was holding the gun that killed him!"

"So?" muttered Banner. "Mebbe you can explain away the sealed envelope." When McKitrick didn't answer, Banner shrugged. "How was she able to shoot the gun through the envelope without making any holes in it?"

McKitrick sighed. "Times are getting brutal for us investigators when all a murderer has to do is send his victim a gun by mail and it does the killing for him."

The wind coming across the Potomac River that afternoon had the icy sting of early winter on its breath.

Gertrude Wagner, wrapped up in a cloth coat, walking on the park path, stopped suddenly. She stared nervously around her. A man in an oystercolord balmacaan, who had been following her, veered around a turn in the path. When he saw her looking straight at him he hesitated for a fraction of a second, then he kept on coming, his pace more deliberate. Under the slant brim of his hat Gertrude could see the bright red hair. The wide shoulders were familiar.

She stood there until Odell came up to her. He grinned

sheepishly. "Hello, Gertie. Mind if I walk the rest of the way with you?"

She drew back a pace as if she was afraid he might contaminate her. Her face looked pale and scared. "You've been following me," she accused him.

Odell was sober. "To tell the truth, Gertie—"

"Why do you have to hound me? Can't you leave me alone?"

"I'm not hounding you," he said, disheartening to know that she had interpreted his actions that way.

"You are, Mr. Odell. I haven't been able to make a move since you came to the Legation without having your eyes on me. You people are watching me all the time, waiting to pounce on me for the least slip I make. I thought America was a free country, but the police watch you here as much as they do over there . . . You think I killed Mr. Gosling!"

"Did it ever occur to you," he said through clenched teeth, "that I might have other reasons for wanting to be near you?"

"What?" she said, heardly believing her ears. "What did you say?"

"You're not hard to take, Gertie," he said.

"Take?" she said in confusion. "Oh but—"

"You never gave me much encouragement. You always seemed to have so much on your mind, Gertie."

"If that's really true, Mr. Odell, I'm sorry I—if I offended you just now."

"*If* it's really true! You don't think I'm telling you the truth?"

"I can't be sure of anything any more."

"I was in that office to protect Mr. Gosling—and you." He looked at her steadily. "You believe me, Gertie."

She looked back at him for a long moment, and he thought her eyes were watering.

She lowered her gaze. "Yes, Mr. Odell, I do. I do believe you."

"Well, then," smiled Odell, "I hope you're not doing anything tonight, as I want—"

"Oh," she said, "I'm sorry. Not tonight. I have an appointment I can't break. Shall we make it some other time?"

"Sure, Gertie. I'll see you tomorrow."

"Tomorrow." She smiled. "So long then." She had her right hand in her coat pocket. She took it out and held it toward him. He grasped her palm. And then he felt that she had something in her hand—a slip of paper. When she drew her hand away she left it in his palm. He felt, with a rush of intuition, that everything was wrong. He pretended not to notice what she'd left in his hand. As she turned on her high heels to walk swiftly away from him, he thrust his own hand into his pocket.

He watched her go out of sight along the path, then he walked out of the park in the opposite direction. He was curious about what she was trying to convey to him. He went into the first street corner phone booth he came to and took the slip of paper out of his pocket and unfolded it.

The wrinkles of perplexity increased on his forehead.

The paper was blank except for two circles, a small one inside a much larger one, drawn on it in pencil.

Gertrude, the cold night wind whipping the coat about her knees, went up the legation steps. All the windows were dark. X Street was dark. Fumbling in her handbag, she took out a key, unlocked the front door, and slipped into the vestibule. It was all cold marble, like a mausoleum. She left the front door unlocked behind her as she went in, as if she was expecting someone else to follow her.

She flicked on a cigarette lighter to light her way up the plush carpeted stairway to the third floor. This was the floor on which the murder had been committed. She went into the office, tiptoeing past her desk in the reception room, going into the private office.

She looked at Gosling's empty chair behind the desk. Gosling's bloodied ghost still seemed to occupy it. And she shuddered.

She remembered a line from one of the newspapers . . . *A nameless horror has stalked through the Legation . . .*

The watch on her wrist ticked away loudly. She was painfully conscious of time. Everything had depended on time.

She did not know anyone was in the room with her until she heard the door between the offices click softly closed.

She turned around with a violent start. The cigarette lighter flicked out when she released her thumb. A shadow moved against the closed door.

"Is that *you?*" she gasped.

A powerful flashlight blinded her.

"Yes," answered a voice. "Have you done all that was expected of you?"

She nodded miserably.

"Fine." She heard a heartless chuckle.

And that was all she heard, for it is doubtful if she heard the two quick coughs before the lead slugs tore into her breast.

She was dead before she hit the floor.

McKitrick was saying: "The patrolman on the X Street beat saw the door of the Legation swinging open in the wind. He thought something was up, so he took a prowl through the building. He was the one who found her."

Somberly Banner looked down at all that was left of Gertrude. "It's a crying shame," he muttered.

Odell sat gloomily on the edge of the desk. He roused himself up enough to say: "Well, this isn't as puzzling as the first shooting. I talked to Gertie in the park this afternoon, Senator. She said she was going to meet someone tonight. Whoever it was just followed her in here and shot her. If I had any inkling this would happen, I never would have left her alone."

Banner nodded. "It's not your fault, Red." He glared around. "What kinda gun this time? D'you know?"

McKitrick answered: "The medical examiner thinks it's a .38."

Banner snorted. "An American gun! This's striking closer to home."

Odell said: "There's something else I've got to tell you, Senator. It might help you. I confess it doesn't mean a thing to me. In the park today Gertie slipped this into my hand. She acted mighty secretive about it." He gave Banner the paper with the circles drawn on it.

"Whatzit mean?" snapped Banner.

"Circles within circles. Wheels within wheels. *You* tell me, Senator."

Banner looked at it front and back and held it up to the light to see if there were any pinpricks in it. Then, without saying anything, he crumpled it up and shoved it into his marsupial pocket. Plainly he could not make head or tail of it, but he wasn't going to say so.

Though they stayed there till dawn they found no other clue to point to Gertrude's murderer.

McKitrick woke up to find his phone ringing insistently and Banner on the other end of the wire.

"You never sleep, do you?" snorted McKitrick.

"Hardly ever, Mac. We ain't got time for that now. It's after breakfast. Come to the Legation and bring that small arms expert with you."

"Captain Cozzens?"

"Yaas. Him. I've figgered out what everything means."

"What put you on it?"

"Those circles."

"Suppose you quit being so damned mysterious, Banner, and—"

"Get cracking to the Legation," interrupted Banner. He hung up.

Banner was sitting in a leather chair, comfortably waiting for them to arrive. He bobbed his big grizzled head at McKitrick and Cozzens. His grizzled mane looked like a fright wig this morning, as if he had been trying to comb it with an eggbeater.

"Gennelmen," he said, "this won't take too much of your precious time. Lemme get on with it. First off, you will swear that there ain't any Tokarev pistols hidden in that private office."

"Of course not," responded McKitrick a little testily. His face bore the results of a very hasty shave. There was a nick on his chin. "There isn't as much as a needle hidden in there that we don't know of."

"And you can search me and find out I'm not packing a Russian pop-gun."

"We'll take your word for it, Senator," said McKitrick shortly.

"We get on together," chuckled Banner. He got up with a heave and a vast grunt. "You two sit here on the lounge, the way you were the other day with Odell, Cap'n." He watched them sharply as they followed his suggestion. "I'm going in there." He entered the private office, where Gosling and Gertrude had been killed, leaving the intervening door open. He was out of sight from the two watchers for about five minutes, then he reappeared and stood in the doorway, filling the frame with his bulk, his hands deep in the bulging frockcoat pockets. "Nothing up my sleeve, mates," he announced.

They both stared at him, not knowing what to expect. Then both of them leaped to their feet.

Three loud shots had crashed out in the empty office behind Banner's back!

Banner did not even take his hands out of his pockets. "And there you have it," he said.

"But, great Godfrey!" yipped McKitrick, pushing past Banner to see who else was hidden in the private office. "Who fired that pistol?"

"It was Tokarev automatic!" said Cozzens. "I'll swear to that!"

"But there isn't anyone here but you!" McKitrick glared helplessly around the room.

"Nevertheless—" began Banner. "But let it keep awhile. There're more important things like searches and seizures to be made."

"Confound you, Banner!" said McKitrick, but he was in good humor about it.

"You can begin by arresting—"

The search was fruitless until Banner suggested that what they were after might be on microfilm and if they could not find microfilm in all the obvious places, it might be hidden in the electric light sockets.

That was where they found it.

They had all the proof they needed to arrest their man for espionage and murder.

And Carroll Lockyear, the export-import man, almost pulled his King Tut beard out by the roots when they confronted him.

McKitrick and the Assistant Secretary of State made impressive members of Banner's small audience. Banner was prancing back and forth, gnawing a long stogie, as if he were holding a press conference. But he had not let the reporters in yet. They were all ganged up outside in the hall, waiting.

The Assistant Secretary of State fingered his chin reflectively. "The riddle of the sealed envelope—"

"Yaas, yaas!" Banner chuckled. "It's simple when you know the sorta thimblerrigging that went on behind the scenes. I said in the beginning that I thought the murder was too damned impossible cuz one person alone couldn't've accomplished it. Lockyear is the murderer and spy, all right, but he had forced poor Gertie to help him. Y'see, he was a Commie agent and Gertie told us that her crippled mother and her father are still stranded in East Germany. You can now see how easy it was for him to get her to agree to his scheme. He could tell her he'd get 'em outta East Germany if she played ball. If she still didn't agree, he could easily threaten to turn the old folks over to the untender mercies of the MVD agents."

He paused a moment before going on. "Gosling was getting onto Lockyear's trail. Some time before the murder, Lockyear used a standard tape recorder. Lockyear let the tape run silently for three minutes, then he fired his Tokarev pistol three times near the recorder. He now had a tape recording of three minutes of dead silence, followed by three quickly fired shots. He handed that roll of tape over to Gertie for her to put in Gosling's private office where he could get his hands on it later on. When he went into Gosling's office to commit the murder that morning he had in his briefcase the Tokarev pistol with a silencer on it, and also in the briefcase was a large manila mailing envelope that was a duplicate of the one to be delivered to Gertie's desk by the messenger service. The gun that was delivered to Gertie by the special messenger route was probably a toy pistol, so that if the envelope were opened prematurely the whole thing could be laughed off as a practical joke.

"It was all timed to the split second. Lockyear stalled with Gosling till almost 11:30, talking business, then swiftly he pulled the silenced automatic outta the briefcase and shot Gosling in the chest three times with it before his victim could blink or cry out. Naturally the shots were not heard outside the room with the door closed. He whipped out the prepared envelope, snatched the silencer off the pistol-barrel, and shoved the pistol, still smoking, into the envelope, sealing it immediately. Next he set the prepared reel of tape on the recorder alongside Gosling's desk—there's one in every office and you've noticed that Gosling's office had all the modern equipment—and then picked up the envelope and briefcase. It was now, according to his watch, 11:27. He flipped the tape recorder switch to *on*. Three minutes of dead silence, remember, then three shots. He put his arm around both the envelope and the briefcase so that the briefcase would entirely conceal the envelope to anyone waiting in the lounge. He came out of the private office and walked to Gertie's desk on which the second envelope with the toy gun in it was lying, waiting to be delivered at 11:30 sharp. He put his briefcase down on her desk, so that it covered both envelopes. After getting Gertie to jot down his phony appointment for next Tuesday, Lockyear picked up his brief again—*together with the envelope that had been lying on Gertie's desk!* In its place he left the one with the real murder weapon in it. He carried the other envelope out with him, still concealed behind his briefcase, and nobody was aware of the switch. So the gun that had just been used to commit the murder was now waiting for Gertie to carry it back in. She had been forced into it. She knew Gosling was already dead. She had to play out her part. She pretended to talk to Gosling on the interphone to give the illusion that Gosling was still alive after Lockyear left. Then she started to go into the private office, looked at her watch, knew the three minutes were almost up, then carried the sealed envelope in."

He stopped and glowered around the room. "The three shots that were heard by the two witnesses were the ones already on the tape recorder! Cozzens even remarked that were somewhat *muffled!*. . . The tape recorder ran itself out silently again, till Gertie, in the excitement that followed the discovery of Gosling's dead body, managed to flip the switch off."

"Good God!" muttered somebody in the room.

Banner cleared his throat with a big sea lion noise. "Haaak! Although Gertie had been terrorized into helping Lockyear remove a threat to his existence as a spy, she wanted desperately for one of us to know the truth. She knew she was being watched by everybody, their side as well as ours, so she couldn't come right out and tell us about it. She drew two circles, one inside the other, on a piece of paper. She didn't dare hint further. She was trying to call our attention to the reel of the tape recorder—circular. Yunnerstand? And she was trying to help us, boys. If she had completely obeyed the instructions of the murderer, I never would've found the tape still on the recorder in that office— she would've destroyed it. Last night the murderer killed her as a safety measure, thinking that his trail on tape had been completely wiped out."

THE MYSTERY OF ROOM NO. 11

By Nicholas Carter

John Dickson Carr once remarked that the impossible disappearance "is perhaps the most fascinating gambit in detective fiction." It is, therefore, somewhat surprising that one of the earliest and cleverest stories of a vanishing appeared in an 1890s dime novel featuring that master of improbable disguises and idol of our great-grandfathers, Nick Carter, who was not known for ingenuity. Probably, however, some of the cleverness should be credited to Arthur Conan Doyle, one of whose Sherlock Holmes stories was cribbed for part of the plot. The syndicate hiding behind the authorial "Nicholas Carter" turned Doyle's idea into a miracle problem, and wrote the whole thing in the marvelously declamatory language of the dime novels.

It has been said that great series characters never die: That certainly is the situation with Nick Carter. By the 1930s he had become a pulp magazine hero keeping the world safe from gangsters. During the next decade he starred in movies and on the radio, and for the past twenty years at the spry age of about 130 he has been saving civilization in a series of more than 200 "Killmaster" thrillers.

Willie Gray's Astonishing Adventure

WILLIE GRAY was a lucky youth. He had everything he wanted that was good for him, and a number of things that were not. All his father's pockets seemed to be full of money, and Willie never had to ask twice for any reasonable sum. He had once heard his father and mother discussing the propriety of giving him an unusually expensive present—a trick pony, that could do sums in addition, and stand on his forelegs.

"My son," said Mr. Gray, in settling the question, "is going to have all the things that I wanted and couldn't get when I was a boy; and there are a good many of them."

It is needless to say that Willie regarded this as sound doctrine, and hoped that his father would stick to it. He was gratified to note, also, that his mother had everything she desired. He believed she was the best-dressed woman in New York; and this was one of a hundred reasons why he was proud of her.

When Willie was seventeen he was a student in the College of the City of New York. One of his best friends there was a boy whose fortunes were the reverse of his own. He never had any money, or swell clothes; in fact, his parents could barely afford to keep him at school. One afternoon Willie was on his way to his friend's home—a tenement on the far East Side.

As he passed across Avenue B, he was greatly surprised to see his own mother coming up the avenue, and about halfway between the spot where he stood and the next street below. Though she was veiled and dressed in somber black, he knew her the instant that his eyes rested on her. It flashed across his mind at once that she must be making a visit of charity. He knew that she went regularly to the homes of poor people. But where was her carriage which she always used in making such calls? Probably she had left it in a neighboring street.

He was interested at once in the mission which had brought her there, and he hurried down the avenue to meet her, and ask her about it. He had taken only a few steps, however, when his mother suddenly disappeared in a narrow doorway, which led to one of the largest and most squalid of the tenements. Evidently she had not seen him.

He quickened his pace, and darted into the doorway on the run. The contrast with the bright day outside made the hall seem black as midnight. He hesitated a moment, then, perceiving a flight of stairs, he rushed up them, three steps at a time, regardless of the darkness. The next thing he knew, the gloom was illuminated by a vast number of stars, and he found himself sitting on the steps, with an indefinite notion that he had acquired three or four extra heads, and that all of them were very sore. He had run full tilt against an angle of the wall, with a violence that might have fractured his skull. For several minutes he sat there, dizzy and confused. At last the building stopped flying round and round, and he recovered full command of his senses.

"I've got a horrible lump on my head," he muttered: "A little cold water would be the best thing for it. If I can find my mother, she'll get me a chance to wash it."

He began to climb the stairs. Just at that moment somebody dashed in from the street, and went flying by him at a pace that made the rickety house shake. As the noise of the hurrying steps died in the regions above him, there came the sound of a loud whistle from the street.

"Police after somebody," muttered the boy. "This is a nice place for my mother to be in. I must find her."

Doors were opening in all the halls as he ascended, and women were thrusting their heads out to learn the cause of the disturbance. Willie halted before one of the doors and asked the woman standing there if she had seen anything of Mrs. Gray, using, of course, a description and not his mother's name.

"She'll be in number eleven, on the fourth floor," replied the woman. "I know her. She comes quite often to see Mrs. Manahan?"

"Who's Mrs. Manahan?"

"Ask herself," said the woman; and she shut the door.

Another flight of stairs brought Willie to the fourth floor. There he learned by inquiry that number eleven was the last tenement in the rear. As he walked quickly down the hall he saw that the door of number eleven was open, and that a woman was standing there. She drew back hastily as he approached, and seemed to be startled at the sight of him.

"It's the blood on my face," he muttered, drawing his handkerchief across his forehead, and glancing at the red stain on the linen. "I must be a tough-looking object. But mother'll patch me up in a jiffy."

He knocked at the door of number eleven, and again, for his first summons brought no response. Then the door was slowly opened by a short Irishwoman, with a large basket on her arm. It was she whom he had seen as he came down the hall; or, at least, he would have said so confidently, had he been asked.

"I'm looking for Mrs. Gray," he said. "She's my mother. You know her, don't you?"

"Shure, Oi know her," replied the woman; "and a good, kind lady she is. Well, well, so you're her son! an' a fine bye. Oi'll be bound."

"Thank you. Is my mother in your rooms?"

"No; she's just gone away."

"Is it possible? Why, I came right up the stairs, and I'm sure she didn't pass me."

"She went the other way." As she said this, Mrs. Manahan pointed to a narrow flight of stairs which led down from the hall at the rear."

"Where does that go?" asked Willie.

"To the alley that runs behind all these tinimints to the street beyant. Hurry, an' you'll catch her."

During most of this conversation, Mrs. Manahan had been fumbling with the lock of her door. At the last words she succeeded in turning the key; then, without another word, she hurried toward the stairs at the front of the building. Willie made the best speed possible by the other route.

"Hold on there!" exclaimed a man, with a particularly loud voice, as the lad was about to make his exit into the alley. It was too late for Willie to "hold on." He was going too fast; and the consequence was that he ran straight into the arms of the speaker, who was a large and strongly built man.

"I beg your pardon!" exclaimed the boy, attempting to free himself.

The man hung on to him. Willie lost his temper. He was an unusually big boy, and an artist in football tactics.

"Let go of me!" he yelled, and instantly performed the

elbow trick with such vigor that his antagonist narrowly
escaped falling headlong into the hall of the tenement
house.

Recovering himself, the man blew a shrill blast on a
whistle; and Willie, who was careering down the alley, found
himself confronted by a burly policeman. The lad had no
desire to resist the constituted authorities, and he surrendered at discretion. It seemed to him that he was having
more trouble in a quarter of an hour than he had had before
in all his life.

He was led back to the door, where he told his story to the
policeman and the other man, who proved to be a ward
officer in citizen's dress.

"That don't go," replied the latter. "Your mother hasn't
come out of this door."   .

"How long have you been here?" asked the boy.

"About four hours," was the reply.

"Four hours! Oh, I see. You've been on the watch for
somebody. Then my mother must be in the house."

"If she came in within twenty minutes she's there now.
Both doors and the roof are guarded. Nobody is allowed to
come out. There's a fellow inside that we want, and we're
going to have him." As he spoke, three more policemen
appeared in the alley.

"Now we're ready," said the ward man.

One of the policemen was left at the door, revolver in hand.
The remainder of the party went into the house. Willie made
a move to go with them; but they told him to remain at the
door.

"You'd better let me go," he said. "I was on the other stairs
when the man you want came in, and I believe I can tell you
what part of the house he's hidden in."

"Who is this chap?" asked one of the policemen.

"Says his name's William Gray," replied the ward man;
"and that he's looking for his mother, who came here on a
charitable visit. Seems to be a straight boy."

"Who split his head open?"

"Says he bumped it coming upstairs."

"Queer story."

"May be true, though. Come along, my lad; and if you can

give us any tip on Reddy Gallagher, we'll be much obliged to you."

"He's on the fourth floor," said Willie decidedly. "There's no use in looking for him lower down than that."

His straightforward manner produced an impression. The police proceeded at once to the fourth floor. They searched thoroughly till they came to Mrs. Manahan's door; but the criminal was not to be found. The ward man knocked, but there was no response from number eleven. A skeleton key was produced, and the door was opened.

When Willie Gray entered this tenement with the officers, he was in a state of excitement the like of which he had never known before. The strangeness of this affair was pressing upon him more and more strongly. He had begun to be a prey to a kind of panic terror. He knew that his mother had entered that house. Mrs. Manahan admitted having seen her, and said that she had gone away. That had been proved to be false. Then she must still be in the house. But, if so, where? And why did she not appear?

When Willie had been convinced that she had not gone out by the back way, he immediately concluded that she had visited some other person than Mrs. Manahan. But on his way up he had seen the occupants of all the tenements at their doors. They had been questioned by the police. If Mrs. Gray had been at that time with any family in that house, her presence would almost certainly have been discovered. There was a mystery here which frightened the lad, though he was possessed of splendid nerve.

Mrs. Manahan's rooms were very bare. There were three of them. One was evidently a workroom. It contained the things which a washerwoman would find necessary.

"Everybody takes in washing in this building," remarked one of the policemen. "That's why it's called 'Soapsuds Hall.'"

They glanced through the rooms. All seemed to be empty. The policemen opened the doors of three small closets, but discovered no one.

"Reddy isn't hidden here," said one of the officers, as he flung open the last of the closet doors.

Young Gray, who was just behind him, uttered a loud cry. "Those things are my mother's!" he exclaimed; and, darting by the officer, he snatched from the closet a lady's hat and cape.

"Well, they evidently don't belong to anybody who lives here," said the ward man. "They cost too much money."

Willie had taken them to the window, the ward man following. "They're hers!" cried the boy.

"Let me look at that cape," said the officer, in a peculiar tone.

He took it from the boy's hand. "What do you call this?" he said in a low tone to one of the policemen.

"Blood!" exclaimed the policeman, "and recently shed. Why, it's not dry yet!"

The Strange Conduct of Mr. Gray

"We've tumbled onto a queer case," said the ward man. "In the face of this, I can't fool away my time on Reddy Gallagher. Search the house thoroughly from top to bottom. If you find Gallagher, take him to the station; but don't stop the search. We must find out what's become of Mrs. Gray. If Mrs. Manahan has been stopped at the door, send her up; but not too soon. I want to look around here first."

Willie had been thunderstruck by the finding of his mother's garments in that room; and that later and most terrible discovery of the blood upon the cloak had, for the moment, deprived him of speech or motion. As the policemen hurried away to make their search, he recovered possession of his faculties. He sprang toward the ward officer who was still closely examining the cloak.

The blood stains were small and few in number, but they were perfectly distinct. There could be no doubt that several drops of blood had fallen upon the garment.

"She has been—hurt!" he cried. He would not speak the word that came into his mind. He could not bear even to think of his mother as the victim of an assassin.

The ward officer, Stephen Burke, laid the cloak down upon a chair carefully, so that the blood stains would not come in contact with anything. Then he hastily searched the room. There was scarcely anything of value in it; but in one of the drawers of a rude dressing table were some clothing of the washerwoman's. The policemen pulled it about without any definite object. Something clinked heavily on the bottom of the drawer. Burke plunged his hands under the clothing, and drew out a lady's gold watch, and a small purse with silver clasps.

"My mother's!" gasped the lad, with pallid lips.

"This looks mighty bad," said the officer.

He opened the purse. It contained over a hundred dollars. Burke put the articles into his pocket, and continued his search of the room. He discovered nothing else which seemed to have any bearing on the case. As he finished the search, Mrs. Manahan, accompanied by a policeman, appeared at the door. A second policeman followed, and announced to Burke, in a low voice, that Gallagher had been caught hiding in a room on the fifth floor, and had been sent to the station. The remainder of the house had been searched, but no trace of Mrs. Gray had been found.

"It's a certainty that she came in here, though," he whispered. "Our man on the avenue saw her. He corroborates the boy's story. There's a woman on this floor who saw Mrs. Gray come out along this hall, but didn't see her enter this tenement."

"But Mrs. Manahan admits that she came in here!" exclaimed Willie, who had pressed up behind Burke and overheard the policeman's report.

"Mrs. Manahan admits nothin'," said the washerwoman. "What's all this fuss about, Oi'd loike to know? Oi'm an honest, hard-workin' woman, Oi am, an' the loikes av yez ha no roight in me apartmints."

"Look here, Mrs. Manahan," said Burke, "this is a mighty serious matter, and you're very foolish to allow it to go any further without an explanation.

"This lady was seen to come to this house. It's known that she came to see you. She'd been here often before. Now she's disappeared as mysteriously as ever I knew any person to vanish. Some of her property has been found in your rooms. There's her cloak, with blood on it. Here's her purse, found hidden in that drawer. Catch her, Reardon! she's fainting."

Indeed, the sturdy washerwoman was tottering as if she would fall. But she recovered before the policeman could reach her side.

She put out a strong arm and repelled him. "Let me alone, ye brute!" she said. "Oi'm all roight. An' ye needn't question me, nayther. Oi know youse an' your ways. Ye'll testify ag'in me if Oi talks to ye. Not a word will Oi say till Oi've seen a lawyer."

"Well, this beats me," muttered the ward man. "I'll be hanged if I understand this business at all. Why, Mrs. Manahan," he continued, raising his voice, "you're crazy. Don't you know that I'll have to arrest you for murder?"

"Do it thin, ye loon!" cried the woman; "an' don't talk so much about it."

That was the last words she could be induced to speak. She maintained an absolute silence as she was led away.

Willie Gray turned to the ward man. "I must go to my father," he said; and was about to leave the room.

"Hold on," rejoined Burke. "I can't let you go. For all I can see, you're in it as deep as the woman."

"What do you mean?"

"Why, it's like this: I'm convinced that one of the most devilish and mysterious crimes on record has been committed in this house.

"There's been violence, and there's been blood shed. Now, you've been found here with a wound in your head. How did you get it? You tell a plausible story; but what do I know about it? I found you trying to get away, and you made a desperate push for it. You may be all right, and your story may be straight; but I don't know. Who was the woman who has disappeared? Are you her son? What were you both here for? I've only your word for any of it; and these questions have got to be answered by good evidence before I take my eyes off you, my young friend."

"Arrested for my mother's murder!" groaned the boy, and he sank into a chair.

It was a situation that might have frightened a timid boy out of his wits; but Willie Gray was not that kind of a boy. He was a lad of great nerve, and he proved it on this trying occasion. For a minute or more he sat with his face buried in his hands. When he raised his head, he looked the officer straight in the eye, with calmness and determination.

"You will take me to the station?" he said. "Very well. There are two things that must be done before that, and I think you will not object to either of them. The first is to send a message to my father."

"By all means," said Burke.

"The second is to secure the services of Nick Carter in this case."

"You can't do better than that. I'd be glad to see him take hold of it, and, when he knows the facts, I believe he'll come."

The two messages were sent while Burke and his prisoner were on the way to the station. The house where the mysterious affair had occurred, was left, meanwhile, under guard of the police.

The famous detective happened to be at home when Willie Gray's note was brought to the house. He lost no time in getting to the station, for the facts, as briefly stated, interested him. He found the boy in the police captain's room, undergoing examination. Nick was put in possession of all the facts known to the reader.

"What's been done?" he asked.

"Nothing," was the reply. "We have waited for you."

"Call Burke." The ward man was summoned.

"Where were you stationed," said Nick, "while you were watching for Gallagher to enter that house?"

"I was hidden in a jag of the wall of the alley, near the door of the tenement house."

"Could you see into the door?"

"Not far."

"There's a cellar under the house?"

"Yes."

"Could you see the head of the stairway leading down to the cellar?"

"No."

"Then a person might have gone down there unseen by you."

"Yes."

"What sort of floor has the cellar?"

"Earth."

"Was it examined?"

"Not carefully, as yet."

"I see your drift," said the captain. "You think that the

woman was decoyed to the house, murdered in Mrs. Manahan's room, and that her body was buried in the cellar."

"It's worth investigating. If such a crime was committed, it is certain that the body is now in the house; and it must be found."

"Attend to it, Burke, if Mr. Carter has no further questions."

"I have one. Mrs. Manahan was carrying a large basket when she attempted to leave the house. What was in it?"

"A gentleman's washing—clean clothes that she was returning."

"Whose clothes?"

"She refused to say."

"Weren't they marked?"

"That's one on me. I forgot to look. The point didn't seem to be important. But the basket, with the clothes, is here."

"Bring it."

It was brought. Nick looked at the clothes."Only initials," he said. "'M. P. B.'" Captain, have one of your men look through the B's in the directory for those initials. This man is rich and a bachelor. Note especially addresses of clubs or bachelor apartment buildings."

The necessary order was given.

"What is known of Mrs. Manahan in that house?"

"Almost nothing. She doesn't have much to do with her neighbors. She sticks to her rooms. Sometimes they don't see her for a fortnight at a time."

"Let me see the garments found in the room."

They were handed to him, and he spent some time in looking at them. The men who had been at work on the directory then made their report. To everybody's surprise, it was discovered that there was only one man mentioned in the directory who answered the conditions.

He was Merton P. Benedict, broker, with rooms in the Union Club building. Of course, the initials were repeated many times, but in every case but Benedict's, it was possible to exclude the person from the investigation in hand.

At this point, Nick's researches were interrupted by the arrival of Mr. Gray. He was greatly excited, as was natural under the circumstances. The note from his son had put him in possession of the essential facts in the case. Gray was a lean and nervous man, not much over forty, but seeming much older, with his scanty, grizzled hair, and deeply wrinkled forehead. He was expensively, but not correctly, dressed, and his manner, even making all allowances, was not quite that of a gentleman.

"This is all nonsense!" he exclaimed. "You've made a great fuss about nothing. Mrs. Gray is safe and well. This poor woman should be released."

"Where is Mrs. Gray?" asked Nick.

"Where is she? Well, it's nobody's business; but I don't mind telling you that she's in Brooklyn, visiting our relatives."

"How do you know?"

"By this, said Gray; and he took an envelope from his pocket.

Drawing a note from the envelope, he handed it to Nick, who read as follows:

> Friday, four o'clock.
>
> Dearest: I am going to Brooklyn to drive with Ned and Alice. Ned will come back with me in the evening. *Au revoir.*
>
> Charlotte.

"There; you see? This was written after this absurd affair was all over."

"William," said Nick to young Gray, who, of course, was overjoyed at this news of his mother's safety. "I wish you would go out into the other room and ask the sergeant to bring Mrs. Manahan from her cell. Tell him to wait till I call for her, and you wait with him."

Willie hurried away, and Nick, after the door was shut, turned to the captain. "This case gets darker at every step," he said. "It was bad enough before, but what can we think of it now?"

"I should think it was all cleared up."

"Not at all. We now have a new problem. It is this: Why does Mr. Gray come here and assert that his wife is in Brooklyn, with friends, when he knows she is not?"

Gray sprang to his feet. His face was pale. "I demand an explanation of this outrageous assertion!" he cried.

"Don't speak so loud. Your son may hear. I sent him away to spare him. And now to the point. Mr. Gray, we are not children. Why do you come and attempt to pass off such a note as this upon experienced men? You say it was written since your wife's mysterious disappearance. I tell you that it was not written this week, probably not this month. I am entirely familiar, sir, with the ink with which this is written. It does not assume this deep black color inside of three days. It is certain, then, that you have attempted to impose upon us with a note written by your wife on some other occasion, and happening to bear date on this day of the week. You have clumsily altered the hour, but that does not matter. I should have detected the fraud without that. And in view of all the facts in the case, I think that your conduct in attempting this imposition is sufficiently suspicious to warrant your arrest."

In The Rooms Of Broker Benedict

"I begin to see through this business," said the captain, sternly. "There's a conspiracy here for the removal of this woman. Gray, you are under arrest."

Gray ground his teeth with rage. "Cursed luck!" he muttered. "The devil himself is in this!"

"We do not wish to be harsh," said Nick. "For the present, we shall not permit the facts of this case to gain publicity. Your own conduct will determine our action. I shall ask you now to leave the room in charge of the captain, and to passively obey his orders. That is the way to avoid scandal, and to spare your boy—who, by the way, is a fine fellow, and worth the trouble."

As he spoke, Nick made a secret sign to the police captain. That officer instantly rose, and motioned Gray to accompany him out of the room.

Gray sullenly obeyed.

They went out into the main room of the station, where Mrs. Manahan was waiting to be sent into the private office where the great detective sat alone. The captain gave the order, and she was obliged to go in, though she protested, in her richest brogue, that it was no use asking her any more questions.

For nearly two hours they all awaited the result of Nick's examination.

Meanwhile a report came from Burke to the effect that traces of recent disturbance of the earthen floor of the tenement-house cellar had been discovered, and that there seemed to be every chance that their search would be grimly rewarded.

And then came a surprise, the most complete that could have overtaken the experienced captain of police; and it was not less overwhelming to Gray, if one might judge from the expression of his countenance. A carriage was driven rapidly up to the door. A woman alighted and entered the station. She raised the thick veil which covered her face.

"Charlotte!" exclaimed Gray.

"Mother!" cried the boy, and, overcome with joy, he threw his arms around her neck while the tears ran down his cheeks. It must be remembered that he had not seen the note which his father had brought. He had only his father's statement that Mrs. Gray was alive, and in his heart he had believed that his father was mistaken. He had the evidence of his own eyes that his mother had entered that tenement house, and he could not understand how it was possible for her to have left it.

"You have a woman here," said Mrs. Gray to the captain, "under arrest, on suspicion of having robbed and murdered me. You see that I have not been murdered, and I give you my word that I have not been robbed. Therefore, I ask her release."

"Well, this beats me!" exclaimed the captain, unconsciously repeating the words of his ward man. He opened the door of the private office, and called to Nick. "We can let Mrs. Manahan go," he said; "Mrs. Gray is here."

The detective was comfortably tilted back in a chair, smoking a cigar, and reading a newspaper. There was nobody else in the room.

"I have already released her." he said. "I learned the facts regarding Mrs. Gray, and so I gave the old woman her basket and let her go. She went out by the private way." He tossed his cigar into the grate, and followed the captain into the outer office.

"Mr. Gray," he said, "I want you and your son to go at once to the elevated station and get home as quickly as you can. You will follow my advice, if you are wise." He looked keenly into Gray's face. It was a glance which always secures obedience.

Then he turned to Mrs. Gray. "Allow me to see you to your carriage," he said.

"Wait for me at home," she said to her husband and her son; and then walked out of the station with Nick.

Half an hour later, the great detective sat in the rooms of broker M. P. Benedict. "I have been engaged in a case this afternoon and evening," he was saying, "which affects somebody you know. I refer to Mrs. Manahan."

"A very estimable woman," said the broker. "I hope no harm has come to her."

"As to that, you shall be the judge, after you have seen her. If I am not mistaken, she is at the door."

There was a knock. The broker called: "Come in."

The door opened, and Mrs. Gray entered. She was followed by a servant carrying a large basket. He set it down, and left the room.

"Here is your laundry, Mr. Benedict," said the woman, in a voice choked with embarrassment.

"I—I beg your pardon!" cried the broker, starting back. "I don't think I have the honor of your acquaintance."

"This is Mrs. Manahan," said the detective.

"Mr. Carter, upon my word, sir, what does this mean?" stammered Benedict.

"It means that I have stumbled upon a strange story. I will tell it to you. Pray be seated, Mrs. Gray. It is not new to you, but it is necessary that you should hear it. Years ago, Mr. Benedict, you employed a woman, named Mrs. Manahan, to do your washing. Mrs. Gray, whose husband was then a poor man, knew this Mrs. Manahan, and was kind to her. One day, Mrs. Manahan was ill, and Mrs. Gray, like the excellent woman that she is, volunteered to do the other's work. It consisted, principally, of your laundry, Mr. Benedict. When she went home that night, Mrs. Gray mentioned to her husband—who was then employed in a broker's office at a miserable salary—that a certain Mr. Benedict had a queer habit of making figures with a pencil all over his cuffs. Mr. Gray has an intelligence which is sharper than the point of a cambric needle. When he heard what his wife said, he saw what few other men would have seen; that those figures on your cuffs were a fortune to anybody who could read them aright. The next time Mrs. Manahan brought home your soiled clothes, Mrs. Gray was there. She cleverly abstracted the cuffs with the figures on them, and carried them to her husband, who made an accurate copy of them. He saw that they were calculations of the advance of certain stocks, and that they indicated the course of operations which you were about to make upon the exchange.

"Mrs. Gray succeeded in returning the cuffs to Mrs. Manahan's room, and neither she nor you knew that they had been seen by anybody else. Meanwhile, Mr. Gray raked and scraped all the money he could get together, and speculated on your tips. He won. This habit of figuring on your cuffs, as you ride up and down town, is an old one with you. I wonder if you borrowed it from that other well-known broker whose washerwoman died a dozen years ago, worth eighty thousand dollars, made in the same way as Mr. Gray's money has been made."

"I never heard of it," said Benedict.

"That's curious. It was in the papers. Well, to proceed, shortly after Gray's first operation, Mrs. Manahan died suddenly. Here was a great misfortune. The supply of tips threatened to be cut off. But the Grays were equal to the emergency. I need not tell you now that since that time, Mrs. Gray has personated Mrs. Manahan. She has done your washing every week. For the remainder of the time she has lived the life of a rich woman. Extremely cautious, she has always carried out the details of the plot. She has had a tenement in the so-called "Soapsuds Hall," and has actually spent a small part of her time there in order that the neighbors might be deceived. Of course, the two entrances to the house favored the work. Mrs. Gray was seen to arrive there. She was supposed to come on a charitable mission. The tenants who saw her come in, and didn't see her go out, supposed that she had used the other door. For years, this has been going on; but this afternoon, by an extraordinary series of coincidences, the secret was lost."

He then described the adventure of Willie Gray. "It certainly looked like a murder," he continued. "There was the blood, for instance, which, of course, really came from the boy's wound. He was so excited that he did not notice that it dripped upon the cape. I do not wonder that Burke was deceived. The only surprising thing—outside of the pure chance of the encounter with your son—was your extraordinary nerve, Mrs. Gray, and the skill with which you played your part. Of course, you were utterly desperate in your determination that he should not read your secret. It was that which carried you through. Well, I think he need not know it. When I discovered the secret of her disguise in the station house, Mr. Benedict, I stipulated only that you should be informed. She agreed; and I let her out by the private way. She hurried to her house, where she procured the necessary hat and outer garment, and then she appeared as Mrs. Gray at the station. Now, my duty is done. I shall make no disclosures."

"There is nothing that I can say," said Mrs. Gray, "except that this is all true. I can only ask your pardon."

Benedict was pacing the floor with a grim smile.

"Will you ask your husband to come and see me tomorrow?" he said, at last. "I have felt for some time that I needed a partner, but I have doubted whether there was a man on earth who was smart enough to fill the bill."

THE MAN WHO DISAPPEARED

By L. T. Meade (1854-1914) and Robert Eustace (1854-1943)

Elizabeth Thomasina Meade Smith, though now remembered only by specialists, was one of the most innovative of turn-of-the-century mystery mongers. Among her contributions were the first series of medical detective stories (Stories from the Diary of a Doctor), *the second or third collection of secret-service tales* (The Lost Square), *and early tales of female criminals* (The Brotherhood of the Seven Kings and *The Sorceress of the Strand*). *In 1898, she published* The Master of Mysteries, *the first collection of stories entirely dedicated to impossible crimes. All of these books have a strong strain of scientific gadgetry contributed by her co-authors, Clifford Halifax and Robert Eustace. One of her finest forays into the miracle problem, however, has never previously appeared in book form. "The Man Who Disappeared" is reprinted from a 1901 issue of* The Strand Magazine.

I AM a lawyer by profession, and have a snug set of chambers in Chancery Lane. My name is Charles Pleydell. I have many clients, and can already pronounce myself a rich man.

On a certain morning towards the end of September in the year 1897 I received the following letter:—

Sir,

I have been asked to call on you by a mutual friend, General Cornwallis, who accompanied my step-daughter and myself on board the *Osprey* to England. Availing myself of the General's introduction, I hope to call to see you or to send a representative about eleven o'clock today.

The General says that he thinks you can give me advice on a matter of some importance.

I am a Spanish lady. My home is in Brazil, and I know nothing of England or of English ways. I wish, however, to take a house near London and to settle down. This house must be situated in the neighborhood of a large moor or common. It must have grounds surrounding it, and must have extensive cellars or basements, as my wish is to furnish a laboratory in order to carry on scientific research. I am willing to pay any sum in reason for a desirable habitation, but one thing is essential: the house must be as near London as is possible under the above conditions.

Yours obediently,

Stella Scaiffe.

This letter was dated from the Carlton Hotel.

Now, it so happened that a client of mine had asked me a few months before to try and let his house—an old-fashioned and somewhat gruesome mansion, situated on a lonely part of Hampstead Heath. It occurred to me that this house would exactly suit the lady whose letter I had just read.

At eleven o'clock one of my clerks brought me in a card. On it were written the words, "Miss Muriel Scaiffe." I desired the man to show the lady in, and a moment later a slight, fair-haired English girl entered the room.

"Mrs. Scaiffe is not quite well and has sent me in her stead.

You have received a letter from my step-mother, have you not, Mr. Pleydell?"

"I have," I replied. "Will you sit down, Miss Scaiffe?"

She did so. I looked at her attentively. She was young and pretty. She also looked good, and although there was a certain anxiety about her face which she could not quite repress, her smile was very sweet.

"Your step-mother," I said, "requires a house with somewhat peculiar conditions?"

"Oh, yes," the girl answered. "She is very anxious on the subject. We want to be settled within a week."

"That is a very short time in which to take and furnish a house," I could not help remarking.

"Yes," she said, again. "But, all the same, in our case it is essential. My step-mother says that anything can be done if there is enough money."

"That is true in a sense," I replied, smilingly. "If I can help you I shall be pleased. You want a house on a common?"

"On a common or moor."

"It so happens, Miss Scaiffe, that there is a place called The Rosary at Hampstead which may suit you. Here are the particulars. Read them over for yourself and tell me if there is any use in my giving you an order to view."

She read the description eagerly, then she said:—

"I am sure Mrs. Scaiffe would like to see this house. When can we go?"

"To-day, if you like, and if you particularly wish it I can meet you at The Rosary at three o'clock."

"That will do nicely," she answered.

Soon afterwards she left me.

The rest of the morning passed as usual, and at the appointed hour I presented myself at the gates of The Rosary. A carriage was already drawn up there, and as I approached a tall lady with very dark eyes stepped out of it.

A glance showed me that the young lady had not accompanied her.

"You are Mr. Pleydell?" she said, holding out her hand to me, and speaking in excellent English.

"Yes," I answered.

"You saw my step-daughter this morning?"

"Yes," I said again.

"I have called to see the house," she continued. "Muriel tells me that it is likely to suit my requirements. Will you show it to me?"

I opened the gates, and we entered a wide carriage-drive. The Rosary had been unlet for some months, and weeds partly covered the avenue. The grounds had a desolate and gloomy appearance, leaves were falling thickly from the trees, and altogether the entire place looked undesirable and neglected.

The Spanish lady, however, seemed delighted with every-thing. She looked around her with sparkling glances. Flash-ing her dark eyes into my face, she praised the trees and avenue, the house, and all that the house contained.

She remarked that the rooms were spacious, the lobbies wide; above all things, the cellars numerous.

"I am particular about the cellars, Mr. Pleydell," she said.

"Indeed!" I answered. "At all events, there are plenty of them."

"Oh, yes! And this one is so large. It will quite suit our purpose. We will turn it into a laboratory.

"My brother and I— Oh, I have not told you about my brother. He is a Spaniard—Señor Merello—he joins us here next week. He and I are scientists, and I hope scientists of no mean order. We have come to England for the purpose of experimenting. In this land of the free we can do what we please. We feel, Mr. Pleydell—you look so sympathizing that I cannot help confiding in you—we feel that we are on the verge of a very great—a very astounding discovery, at which the world, yes, the whole world will wonder. This house is the one of all others for our purpose. When can we take posses-sion, Mr. Pleydell?"

I asked several questions, which were all answered to my satisfaction, and finally returned to town, prepared to draw up a lease by which the house and grounds known as The Rosary, Hampstead Heath, were to be handed over at a very high rent to Mrs. Scaiffe.

I felt pleased at the good stroke of business which I had done for a client, and had no apprehensions of any sort. Little did I guess what that afternoon's work would mean to me, and still more to one whom I had ever been proud to call my greatest friend.

Everything went off without a hitch. The Rosary passed into the hands of Mrs. Scaiffe, and also into the hands of her brother, Señor Merello, a tall, dark, very handsome man, bearing all over him the well-known characteristics of a Spanish don.

A week or two went by and the affair had well-nigh passed my memory, when one afternoon I heard eager, excited words in my clerks' room, and the next moment my head clerk entered, followed by the fair-haired English-looking girl who had called herself Muriel Scaiffe.

"I want to speak to you, Mr. Pleydell," she said, in great agitation. "Can I see you alone, and at once?"

"Certainly," I answered. I motioned to the clerk to leave us and helped the young lady to a chair.

"I cannot stay a moment," she began. "Even now I am followed. Mr. Pleydell, he has told me that he knows you; it was on that account I persuaded my step-mother to come to you about a house. You are his greatest friend, for he has said it."

"Of whom are you talking?" I asked, in a bewildered tone.

"Of Oscar Digby!" she replied. "The great traveller, the great discoverer, the greatest, most single-minded, the grandest man of his age. You know him? Yes—yes."

She paused for breath. Her eyes were full of tears.

"Indeed, I do know him," I answered. "He is my very oldest friend. Where is he? What is he doing? Tell me all about him."

She had risen. Her hands were clasped tightly together, her face was white as death.

"He is on his way to England," she answered. "Even now he may have landed. He brings great news, and the moment he sets foot in London he is in danger."

"What do you mean?"

"I cannot tell you what I mean. I dare not. He is your friend, and it is your province to save him."

"But from what, Miss Scaiffe? You have no right to come here and make ambiguous statements. If you come to me at all you ought to be more explicit."

She trembled and now, as though she could not stand any longer, dropped into a chair.

"I am not brave enough to explain things more fully," she said. "I can only repeat my words, 'Your friend is in danger.' Tell him—if you can, if you will—to have nothing to do with *us*. Keep him, at all risks, away from *us*. If he mentions us pretend that you do not know anything about us. I would not speak like this if I had not cause—the gravest. When we took The Rosary I did not believe that matters were so awful; indeed, then I was unaware that Mr. Digby was returning to London. But last night I overheard. . . . Oh! Mr. Pleydell, I can tell you no more. Pity me and do not question me. Keep Oscar Digby away from The Rosary and, if possible, do not betray me; but if in no other way you can insure his leaving us alone, tell him that I—yes, I, Muriel Scaiffe—wish it. There, I cannot do more."

She was trembling more terribly than ever. She took out her handkerchief to wipe the moisture from her brow.

"I must fly," she said. "If this visit is discovered my life is worth very little."

After she had gone I sat in absolute amazement. My first sensation was that the girl must be mad. Her pallor, her trembling, her vague innuendoes pointed surely to a condition of nerves the reverse of sane. But although the madness of Muriel Scaiffe seemed the most possible solution of her strange visit, I could not cast the thing from my memory. I felt almost needlessly disturbed by it. All day her extraordinary words haunted me, and when, on the next day, Digby, whom I had not seen for years, unexpectedly called, I remembered Miss Scaiffe's visit with a queer and ever-increasing sense of apprehension.

Digby had been away from London for several years. Before he went he and I had shared the same rooms, had gone about together, and had been chums in the fullest sense of the word. It was delightful to see him once again. His hearty, loud laugh fell refreshingly on my ears, and one or two glances into his face removed my fears. After all, it was impossible to associate danger with one so big, so burly, with such immense physical strength. His broad forehead, his keen, frank blue eyes, his smiling mouth, his strong and muscular hands, all denoted strength of mind and body. He looked as if he were muscle all over.

"Well," he said, "here I am, and I have a good deal to tell you. I want your help also, old man. It is your business to introduce me to the most promising and most enterprising financier of the day. I have it in my power, Pleydell, to make his fortune, and yours, and my own, and half-a-dozen other people's as well."

"Tell me all about it," I said. I sat back in my chair, prepared to enjoy myself.

Oscar was a very noted traveller and thought much of by the Geographical Society.

He came nearer to me and dropped his voice a trifle.

"I have made an amazing discovery," he said, "and that is one reason why I have hurried back to London. I do not know whether you are sufficiently conversant with extraordinary and out-of-the-way places on our globe. But anyhow, I may as well tell you that there is a wonderful region, as yet very little known, which lies on the watershed on the Essequibo and Amazon rivers. In that region are situated the old Montes de Cristes or Crystal Mountains, the disputed boundary between British Guiana and Brazil. There also, according to the legend, was supposed to be the wonderful lost city of Manos. Many expeditions were sent out to discover it in the seventeenth century, and it was the Eldorado of Sir Walter Raleigh's famous expediton in 1615, the failure of which cost him his head."

I could not help laughing.

"This sounds like an old geography lesson. What have you to do with this *terra incognita?*"

He leant forward and dropped his voice.

"Do not think me mad," he said, "for I speak in all sanity. I have found the lost Eldorado!"

"Nonsense!" I cried.

"It is true. I do not mean to say that I have found the mythical city of gold; that, of course, does not exist. But what I have discovered is a spot close to Lake Amacu that is simply laden with gold. The estimates computed on my specimens and reports make it out to be the richest place in the world. The whole thing is, as yet, a close secret, and I have come to

London now to put it into the hands of a big financier. A company must be formed with a captial of something like ten millions to work it."

"By Jove!" I cried. "You astonish me."

"The thing will create an enormous sensation," he went on, "and I shall be a millionaire; that is, if the secret does not leak out."

"The secret," I cried.

"Yes, the secret of its exact locality."

"Have you charts?"

"Yes; but those I would rather not disclose, even to you, old man, just yet."

I was silent for a moment, then I said:—

"Horace Lancaster is the biggest financier in the whole of London. He is undoubtedly your man. If you can satisfy him with your reports, charts, and specimens he can float the company. You must see him, Digby."

"Yes, that is what I want," he cried.

"I will telephone to his office at once."

I rang the bell for my clerk and gave him directions.

He left the room. In a few moments he returned with the information that Lancaster was in Paris.

"He won't be back for a week, sir," said the clerk.

He left the room, and I looked at Digby.

"Are you prepared to wait?" I asked.

He shrugged his great shoulders.

"I must, I suppose," he said. "But it is provoking. At any moment another may forestall me. Not that it is likely; but there is always the possibility. Shall we talk over matters tonight, Pleydell? Will you dine with me at my club?"

"With a heart and a half," I answered.

"By the way," continued Digby, "some friends of mine— Brazilians—ought to be in London now: a lady of the name of Scaiffe, with her pretty little step-daughter, an English girl. I should like to introduce you to them. They are remarkably nice people. I had a letter from Mrs. Scaiffe just as I was leaving Brazil telling me that they were *en route* for England and asking me to look her up in town. I wonder where they are? Her brother, too, Señor Merello, is a most charming man. Why, Pleydell, what is the matter?"

I was silent for a moment: then I said: "If I were you I would have nothing to do with these people. I happen to know their whereabouts, and—"

"Well?" he said, opening his eyes in amazement?

"The little girl does not want you to call on them, Digby. Take her advice. She looked true and good." To my astonishment I saw that the big fellow seemed quite upset at my remarks.

"True!" he said, beginning to pace the room. "Of course the little thing is true. I tell you, Pleydell, I am fond of her. Not engaged, or anything of that sort, but I like her. I was looking forward to meeting them. The mother—the step-mother, I mean—is a magnificent woman. I am great friends with her. I was staying at their Quinta last winter. I also know the brother, Señor Merello. Has little Muriel lost her head?"

"She is anxious and frightened. The whole thing seems absurd, of course, but she certainly did beg of me to keep you away from her step-mother, and I half promised to respect her secret and not to tell you the name of the locality where Mrs. Scaiffe and Señor Merello are at present living."

He tried not to look annoyed, but he evidently was so. A few moments later he left me.

That evening Digby and I dined together. We afterwards went exhaustively into the great subject of his discovery. He showed me his specimens and reports, and, in short, so completely fired my enthusiasm that I was all impatience for Lancaster's return. The thing was a big thing, one worth fighting for. We said no more about Mrs. Scaiffe, and I hoped that my friend would not fall into the hands of a woman who, I began to fear, was little better than an adventuress.

Three or four days passed. Lancaster was still detained in Paris, and Digby was evidently eating his heart out with impatience at the unavoidable delay in getting his great scheme floated.

One afternoon he burst noisily into my presence.

"Well," he cried. "The little girl has discovered herself. Talk of women and their pranks! She came to see me at my hotel. She declared that she could not keep away. I just took the little thing in my arms, and hugged her. We are going to have a honeymoon when the company is floated, and this evening, Pleydell, I dine at The Rosary. Ha! ha! my friend. I know all about the secret retreat of the Scaiffes by this time. Little Muriel told me herself. I dine there to-night, and they want you to come, too."

I was about to refuse when, as if in a vision, the strange, entreating, suffering face of Muriel Scaiffe, as I had seen it the day she implored me to save my friend, rose up before my eyes. Whatever her present inexplicable conduct might mean, I would go with Digby to-night.

We arrived at The Rosary between seven and eight o'clock. Mrs. Scaiffe received us in Oriental splendour. Her dress was a wonder of magnificence. Diamonds flashed in her raven black hair and glittered round her shapely neck. She was certainly one of the most splendid-looking women I had ever seen, and Digby was not many moments in her company before he was completely subjugated by her charms.

The pale little Muriel looked washed-out and insignificant beside this gorgeous creature. Señor Merello was a masculine edition of his handsome sister: his presence and her wonderful courtly grace of manner seemed but to enhance and accentuate her charms.

At dinner we were served by Spanish servants, and a repulsive-looking negro of the name of Samson stood behind Mrs. Scaiffe's chair.

She was in high spirits, drank freely of champagne, and openly alluded to the great discovery.

"You must show us the chart, my friend," she said.

"No!" he answered, in an emphatic voice. He smiled as he spoke and showed his strong, white teeth.

She bent towards him and whispered something. He glanced at Muriel, whose face was deadly white. Then he rose abruptly.

"As regards anything else, command me," he said, "but not the chart."

Mrs. Scaiffe did not press him further. The ladies went into the drawing-room, and by and by Digby and I found ourselves returning to London.

During the journey I mentioned to him that Lancaster had wired to say that he would be at his office and prepared for a meeting on Friday. This was Monday night.

"I am glad to hear that the thing will not be delayed much longer," he answered. "I may as well confess that I am devoured by impatience."

"Your mind will soon be at rest," I replied. "And now, one thing more, old man. I must talk frankly. I do not like Mrs. Scaiffe—I do not like Señor Merello. As you value all your future, keep that chart out of the hands of those people."

"Am I mad?" he questioned. "The chart is seen by no living soul until I place it in Lancaster's hands. But all the same, Pleydell," he added, "you are prejudiced, Mrs. Scaiffe is one of the best of women."

"Think her so, if you will," I replied; "but, whatever you do, keep your knowledge of your Eldorado to yourself. Remember that on Friday the whole thing will be safe in Lancaster's keeping."

He promised, and I left him.

On Tuesday I saw nothing of Digby.

On Wednesday evening, when I returned home late, I received the following letter:

I am not mad. I have heavily bribed the kitchenmaid, the only English woman in the whole house, to post this for me. I was forced to call on Mr. Digby and to engage myself to him at any cost. I am now strictly continued to my room under pretence of illness. In reality I am quite well, but a close prisoner. Mr. Digby dined here again last night and, under the influence of a certain drug introduced into his wine, has given away the whole of his discovery *except* the exact locality.

He is to take supper here late to-morrow night (Thursday) and to bring the chart. If he does, he will never leave The Rosary alive. All is prepared. *I speak who know.* Don't betray me, but save him.

The letter fell from my hands. What did it mean? Was Digby's life in danger, or had the girl who wrote to me really gone mad? The letter was without date, without any heading, and without signature. Nevertheless, as I picked it up and read it carefully over again, I was absolutely convinced beyond a shadow of doubt of its truth. Muriel Scaiffe was not mad. She was a victim, to how great an extent I did not dare to think. Another victim, one in even greater danger, was Oscar Digby. I must save him. I must do what the unhappy girl who was a prisoner in that awful house implored of me.

It was late, nearly midnight, but I knew that I had not a moment to lose. I had a friend, a certain Dr. Garland, who had been police surgeon for the Westminster Division for several years. I went immediately to his house in Eaton Square. As I had expected, he was up, and without any preamble I told him the whole long story of the last few weeks.

Finally, I showed him the letter. He heard me without once interrupting. He read the letter without comment. When he folded it up and returned it to me I saw that his keen, clean-shaven face was full of interest. He was silent for several minutes, then he said:

"I am glad you came to me. This story of yours may mean a very big thing. We have four *prima-facie* points. *One:* Your friend has this enormously valuable secret about the place in Guiana or on its boundary: a secret which may be worth anything. *Two:* He is very intimate with Mrs. Scaiffe, her step-daughter, and her brother. The intimacy started in Brazil. *Three:* He is engaged to the step-daughter, who evidently is being used as a sort of tool, and is herself in a state of absolute terror, and, so far as one can make out, is not specially in love with Digby nor Digby with her. *Four:* Mrs. Scaiffe and her brother are determined, at any risk, to secure the chart which Digby is to hand to them to-morrow evening. The girl thinks this so important that she has practically risked her life to give you due warning. By the way, when did you say Lancaster would return? Has he made an appointment to see Digby and yourself?"

"Yes: at eleven o'clock on Friday morning."

"Doubtless Mrs. Scaiffe and her brother know of this."

"Probably." I answered. "As far as I can make out they have such power over Digby that he confides everything to them."

"Just so. They have power over him, and they are not scrupulous as to the means they use to force his confidence. If Digby goes to The Rosary to-morrow evening the interview with Lancaster will, in all probability, never take place."

"What do you mean?" I cried, in horror.

"Why, this: Mrs. Scaiffe and Señor Merello are determined to learn Digby's secret. It is necesary for their purpose that they should know the secret and also that they should be the *sole possessors* of it. You see why they want Digby to call on them? They must get his secret from *before* he sees Lancaster. The chances are that if he gives it up he will never leave the house alive."

"Then, what are we to do?" I asked, for Garland's meaning stunned me and I felt incapable of thought or of any mode of action.

"Leave this matter in my hands. I am going immediately to see Inspector Frost. I will communicate with you directly anything serious occurs."

The next morning I called upon Digby and found him breakfasting at his club. He looked worried, and, when I came in, his greeting was scarcely cordial.

"What a solemn face, Pleydell!" he said. "Is anything wrong?" He motioned me to a seat near. I sank into it.

"I want you to come out of town with me," I said. "I can take a day off. Shall we both run down to Brighton? We can return in time for our interview with Lancaster to-morrow."

"It is impossible," he answered. "I should like to come with you, but I have an engagement for to-night."

"Are you going to The Rosary?" I asked.

"I am," he replied, after a moment's pause. "Why, what is the matter?" he added. "I suppose I may consider myself a free agent." There was marked irritation in his tone.

"I wish you would not go," I said.

"Why not?"

"I do not trust the people."

"Folly, Pleydell. In the old days you used not to be so prejudiced."

"I had not the same cause. Digby, if ever people are trying to get you into their hands, they are those people. Have you not already imparted your secret to them?"

"How do you know?" he exclaimed, springing up and turning crimson.

"Well, can you deny it?"

His face paled.

"I don't know that I want to," he said. "Mrs. Scaiffe and

Merello will join me in this matter. There is no reason why things should be kept dark from them."

"But is this fair or honourable to Lancaster? Remember, I have already written fully to him. Do, I beg of you, be careful."

"Lancaster cannot object to possible wealthy shareholders," was Digby's answer. "Anyhow," he added, laughing uneasily, "I object to being interfered with. Pray understand that, old man, if we are to continue friends; and now by-bye for the present. We meet at eleven o'clock to-morrow at Lancaster's."

His manner gave me no pretext for remaining longer with him, and I returned to my own work. About five o'clock on that same day a telegram was handed to me which ran as follows:

Come here at once.—Garland

I left the house, hailed a hansom, and in a quarter of an hour was shown into Garland's study. He was not alone. A rather tall, grey-haired, grey-moustached, middle-aged man was with him. This man was introduced as Inspector Frost.

"Now, Pleydell," said Garland, in his quick, incisive way, "listen to me carefully. The time is short. Inspector Frost and I have not ceased our inquiries since you called on me last night. I must tell you that we believe the affair to be of the most serious kind. Time is too pressing now to enter into all details, but the thing amounts to this. There is the gravest suspicion that Mrs. Scaiffe and her brother, Señor Merello, are employed by a notorious gang in Brazil to force Digby to disclose the exact positon of the gold mine. We also know for certain that Mrs. Scaiffe is in constant and close communication with some very suspicous people both in London and in Brazil."

"Now, listen. The crisis is to be to-night. Digby is to take supper at The Rosary, and there to give himself absolutely away. He will take his chart with him: that is the scheme. Digby must not go—that is, if we can possibly prevent him. We expect you to do what you can under the circumstances, but as the case is so serious, and as it is more than probable that Digby will not be persuaded, Inspector Frost and myself and a number of men of his division will surround the house as soon as it becomes dark, and if Digby should insist on going in every protection is case of difficulty will be given him. The presence of the police will also insure the capture of Mrs. Scaiffe and her brother."

"You mean," I said, "that you will, if necesary, search the house?"

"Yes."

"But how can you do so without a warrant?"

"We have thought of that," said Garland, with a smile. "A magistrate living at Hampstead has been already communicated with. If necessary, one of our men will ride over to his house and procure the requisite instrument to enforce our entrance."

"Very well," I answered: "then I will go at once to Digby's, but I may as well tell you plainly that I have very little hope of dissuading him."

I drove as fast as I could to my friend's rooms, but was greeted with the information that he had already left and was not expected back until late that evening. This was an unlooked for blow.

I went to his club—he was not there. I then returned to Dr. Garland.

"I failed to find him," I said. "What can be done? Is it possible that he has already gone to his fate?"

"That is scarcely likely," replied Garland, after a pause. "He was invited to supper at The Rosary, and according to your poor young friend's letter the time named was late. There is nothing for it but to waylay him on the grounds before he goes in. You will come with us to-night, will you not, Pleydell?"

"Certainly," I answered.

Garland and I dined together. At half-past nine we left Eaton Square and, punctually at ten o'clock, the hansom we had taken put us down at one of the roads on the north side of the Heath. The large house, which I knew so well loomed black in the moonlight.

The night was cold and fresh. The moon was in its second quarter and was shining brightly. Garland and I passed down the dimly-lit lane beside the wall. A tall, dark figure loomed from the darkness and, as it came forward, I saw that it was Inspector Frost.

"Mr. Digby has not arrived yet," he said. "Perhaps, sir," he added, looking at me, "you can even now dissuade him, for it is a bad business. All my men are ready," he continued, "and at a signal the house will be surrounded; but we must have one last try to prevent his entering it. Come this way, please sir," he added, beckoning to me to follow him.

We passed out into the road.

"I am absolutely bewildered, inspector," I said to him. "Do you mean to say there is really great danger?"

"The worst I ever knew," was his answer. "You cannot stop a man entering a house if he wishes to; but I can tell you, Mr. Pleydell, I do not believe his life is worth *that* if he goes in." And the inspector snapped his fingers.

He had scarcely ceased speaking when the jingling of the bells of a hansom sounded behind us. The cab drew up at the gates and Oscar Digby alighted close to us.

Inspector Frost touched him on the shoulder.

He swung round and recognised me.

"Halloa! Pleydell," he said, in no very cordial accents, "What in the name of Heaven are you doing here? What does this mean? Who is this man?"

"I am a police-officer, Mr. Digby, and I want to speak to you. Mr. Pleydell has asked you not to go into that house. You are, of course, free to do as you like, but I must tell you that you are running into great danger. Be advised by me and go away."

For answer Digby thrust his hand into his breastpocket. He pulled out a note which he gave me.

"Read that, Pleydell," he said; "and receive my answer." I tore the letter from its envelope and read in the moonlight:

> Come to me. I am in danger and suffering. Do not fail me.—Muriel.

"A hoax! A forgery!" I could not help crying. "For God's sake, Digby, don't be mad."

"Mad or sane, I go into that house," he said. His bright blue eyes flashed with passion and his breath came quickly.

"Hands off, sir. Don't keep me."

He swung himself away from me.

"One word," called the inspector after him. "How long do you expect to remain?"

"Perhaps an hour. I shall be home by midnight."

"And now, sir, please listen. You can be assured, in case of any trouble, that we are here, and I may further tell you that if you are not out of the house by one o'clock, we shall enter with a search warrant."

Digby stood still for a moment then he turned to me.

"I cannot but resent your interference, but I believe you mean well. Good-bye!" He wrung my hand and walked quickly up the drive.

We watched him ring the bell. The door was opened at once by the negro servant. Digby entered. The door closed silently. Inspector Frost gave a low whistle.

"I would not be that man for a good deal," he said.

Garland came up to us both.

"Is the house entirely surrounded, Frost?" I heard him whisper. Frost smiled, and I saw his white teeth gleam in the darkness. He waved his hand.

"There is not a space of six feet between man and man," I heard him say; "and now we have nothing to do but to wait and hope for at least an hour and a half. If in an hour's time Mr. Digby does not reappear I shall send a man for the warrant. At one o'clock we enter the house."

Garland and I stood beneath a large fir tree in a dense shade and within the enclosed garden. The minutes seemed to crawl. Our converstaion was limited to low whispers at long intervals.

Eleven o'clock chimed on the church clock near by; then half-past sounded on the night air. My ears were strained to catch the expected click on the front door-latch, but it did not come. The house remained wrapt in silence. Once Garland whispered:

"Hark!" We listened closely. It certainly seemed to me that a dull, muffled sound, as of pounding or hammering, was just audible; but whether it came from the house or not it was impossible to tell.

At a quarter to twelve the one remaining lighted window on the first floor became suddenly dark. Still there was no sign of Digby. Midnight chimed.

Frost said a word to Garland and disappeared, treading softly. He was absent for more than half an hour. When he returned I heard him say:—

"I have got it," and he touched his pocket with his hand as he spoke.

The remaining moments went by in intense anxiety, and, just as the deep boom of one o'clock was heard the inspector laid his hand on my shoulder.

"Come along quietly," he whispered.

Some sign, conveyed by a low whistle, passed from him to his men, and I heard the bushes rustle around us.

The next moment we had ascended the steps, and we could hear the deep whirr of the front door bell as Frost pressed the button.

In less time than we had expected we heard the bolts shot back. The door was opened on a chain and a black face appeared at the slit.

"Who are you and what do you want?" said a voice.

"I have called for Mr. Digby," said Frost. "Go and tell him that his friend, Mr. Pleydell, and also Doctor Garland want to see him immediately."

A look of blank surprise came over the negro's face. "But no one of the name of Digby lives here," he said.

"Mrs. Scaiffe lives here," replied the inspector, "and also a Spanish gentleman of the name of Señor Merello. Tell them that I wish to see them immediately, and that I am a police-officer."

A short conversation was evidently taking place within. The next moment the door was flung open, electric lights sprang into being, and my eyes fell upon Mrs Scaiffe.

She was dressed with her usual magnificence. She came forward with a stately calm and stood silently before us. Her large black eyes were gleaming.

"Well, Mr. Pleydell," she said, speaking in an easy voice, "what is the reason of this midnight disturbance? I am always glad to welcome you to my house, but is not the hour a little late?"

Her words were interrupted by Inspector Frost, who held up his hand.

"Your attitude, madam," he said, "is hopeless. We have all

come here with a definite object. Mr. Oscar Digby entered this house at a quarter past ten to-night. From that moment the house has been closely surrounded. He is therefore still here."

"Where is your authority for this unwarrantable intrusion?" she said. Her manner changed, her face grew hard as iron. Her whole attitude was one of insolence and defiance.

The inspector immediately produced his warrant.

She glanced over it and uttered a shrill laugh.

"Mr. Digby is not in the house," she said.

She had scarcely spoken before an adjoining door was opened, and Señor Merello, looking gaunt and very white about the face, approached. She looked up at him and smiled, then she said, carelessly:—

"Gentlemen, this is my brother, Señor Merello."

The Señor bowed slightly, but did not speak.

"Once more," said Frost, "where is Mr. Digby?"

"I repeat once more," said Mrs. Scaiffe, "that Mr. Digby is not in this house."

"But we saw him enter at a quarter past ten."

She shrugged her shoulders.

"He is not here now."

"He could not have gone, for the house has been surrounded."

Again she gave her shoulders a shrug. "You have your warrant, gentlemen," she said; "you can look for yourselves."

Frost came up to her.

"I regret to say, madam, that you, this gentleman, and all your servants must consider yourselves under arrest until we find Mr. Oscar Digby."

"That will be for ever, then," she replied; "but please yourselves."

My heart beat with an unwonted sense of terror. What could the woman mean? Digby, either dead or alive, must be in the house.

The operations which followed were conducted rapidly. The establishment, consisting of Mrs. Scaiffe, her brother, two Spanish men-servants, two maids, one of Spanish extraction, and the negro who had opened the door to us, were summoned and placed in the charge of a police-sergeant.

Muriel Scaiffe was nowhere to be seen.

Then our search of the house began. The rooms on the ground-floor, consisting of the drawing-room, dining-room, and two other big rooms, were fitted up in quite an everyday manner. We did not take much time going through them.

In the basement, the large cellar which had attracted Mrs. Scaiffe's pleased surprise on the day when I took her to see The Rosary had now been fitted up as a laboratory. I gazed at it in astonishment. It was evidently intended for the manufacture of chemicals on an almost commerical scale. All the latest chemical and electrical apparatus were to be found there, as well as several large machines, the purpose of which were not evident. One in particular I specially noticed. It was a big tank with a complicated equipment for the manufacture of liquid air in large quantities.

We had no time to give many thoughts to the laboratory just then. A foreboding sense of ever-increasing fear was upon each and all of us. It was sufficient to see that Digby was not there.

Our search in the upper regions was equally unsuccessful. We were just going down stairs again when Frost drew my attention to a door which we had not yet opened. We went to it and found it locked. Putting our strength to work, Garland and I between us burst it open. Within, we found a girl crouching by the bed. She was only partly dressed, and her head was buried in her hands. We went up to her. She turned, saw my face, and suddenly clung to me.

"Have you found him? Is he safe?"

"I do not know, my dear," I answered, trying to soothe her. "We are looking for him. God grant us success."

"Did he come to the house? I have been locked in here all day and heavily drugged. I have only just recovered consciousness and scarcely know what I am doing. Is he in the house?"

"He came in. We are searching for him; we hope to find him."

"That you will never do!" She gave a piercing cry and fell unconscious on the floor.

We placed the unhappy girl on the bed. Garland produced brandy and gave her a few drops; she came to in a couple of minutes and began to moan feebly. We left her, promising to return. We had no time to attend to her just then.

When we reached the hall Frost stood still.

"The man is not here," he muttered.

"But he is here," was Garland's incisive answer. "Inspector, you have got to tear the place to pieces."

The latter nodded.

The inspector's orders were given rapidly, and dawn was just breaking when ten policemen, ordered in from outside, began their systematic search of the entire house from roof to basement.

Pick and crowbar were ruthlessly applied, and never have I seen a house in such a mess. Floorings were torn up and rafters cut through. Broken plaster littered the rooms and lay about on the sumptuous furniture. Walls were pierced and bored through. Closets and cupboards were ransacked. The backs of the fireplaces were torn out and the chimneys explored.

Very little was said as our investigation proceeded, and room after room was checked off.

Finally, an exhaustive examination of the basement and cellars completed our search.

"Well, Dr. Garland, are you satisfied?" asked the inspector.

We had gone back to the garden, and Garland was leaning against a tree, his hands thrust in his pockets and his eyes fixed on the ground. Frost pulled his long moustache and breathed quickly.

"Are you satisfied?" he repeated.

"We must talk sense or we shall all go mad," was Garland's answer. "The thing is absurd, you know. Men don't disappear. Let us work this thing out logically. There are only three planes in space and we know matter is indestructible. If Digby left this house he went up, down, or horizontally. *Up is out of the question.* If he disappeared in a balloon or was shot off the roof he must have been seen by us, for the house was surrounded. He certainly did not pass through the cordon of men. *He did not go down*, for every cubic foot of basement and cellar has been accounted for, as well as every cubic foot of space in the house.

"So we come to the chemical change of matter, dissipation

into gas by heat. There are no furnaces, no ashes, no gas cylinders, nor dynamos, nor carbon points. The time when we lost sight of him to the time of entrance was exactly two hours and three-quarters. There is no way out of it. He is still there."

"He is not there," was the quiet retort of the inspector. "I have sent for the Assistant Commissioner to Scotland Yard, and will ask him to take over the case. It is too much for me."

The tension in all our minds had now reached such a state of strain that we began to fear our own shadows.

Oscar Digby, standing, as it were, on the threshold of a very great future, the hero of a legend worthy of old romance, has suddenly and inexplicably vanished. I could not get my reason to believe that he was not still in the house, for there was not the least doubt that he had not come out. What would happen in the next few hours?

"Is there no secret chamber or secret passage that we have overlooked?" I said, turning to the inspector.

"The walls have been tapped," he replied. "There is not the slightest indication of a hollow. There are no underground passages. The man is not within these walls."

He now spoke with a certain degree of irritation in his voice which the mystery of the case had evidently awakened in his mind. A few moments later the sound of approaching wheels caused us to turn our heads. A cab drew up at the gates, out of which alighted the well-known form of Sir George Freer.

Garland had already entered the house, and on Sir George appearing on the scene he and I followed him.

We had just advanced across the hall to the room where the members of the household, with the exception of poor Muriel Scaiffe, were still detained, when, to our utter amazement, a long, strange peal of laughter sounded from below. This was followed by another, and again by another. The laughter came from the lips of Garland. We glanced at each other. What on earth did it mean? Together we darted down the stone steps, but before we reached the laboratory another laugh rang out. All hope in me was suddenly changed to a chilling fear, for the laugh was not natural. It had a changing, metallic sound, without any mirth.

In the centre of the room stood Garland. His mouth was twitching and his breath jerked in and out convulsively.

"What is it? What is the matter?" I cried.

He made no reply, but, pointing to a machine with steel blocks, once more broke into a choking, gurgling laugh which made my flesh creep.

Had he gone mad? Sir George moved swiftly across to him and laid his hand on his shoulder.

"Come, what is all this, Garland?" he said, sternly, though his own face was full of fear.

I knew Garland to be a man of extraordinary self control, and I could see that he was now holding himself in with all the force at his command.

"It is no use—I cannot tell you," he burst out.

"What—you know what has become of him?"

"Yes."

"You can prove it?"

"Yes."

"Speak out, man."

"He is not here," said Garland.

"Then where is he?"

He flung his hand out towards the Heath, and I saw that the fit was taking him again, but once more he controlled himself. Then he said, in a clear, level voice:

"He is dead, Sir George, and you can never see his body. You cannot hold an inquest, for there is nothing to hold it on. The winds have taken him and scattered him in dust on the Heath. Don't look at me like that, Pleydell. I am sane, although it is a wonder we are not all mad over this business. Look and listen."

He pointed to the great metal tank.

"I arrived at my present conclusion by a process of elimination," he began. "Into that tank which contained liquid air Digby, gagged and bound, must have been placed violently, probably after he had given away the chart. Death would have been instantaneous, and he would have been frozen into complete solidity in something like forty minutes. The ordinary laboratory experiment is to freeze a rabbit, which can then be powdered into mortar like any other friable stone. The operation here has been the same. It is only a question of size. Remember, we are dealing with 12 deg. below zero Fahrenheit, and then, well, look at this and these."

He pointed to a large machine with steel blocks and to a bench littered with saws, chisels, pestles, and mortars.

"That machine is a stone-breaker," he said. "On the dust adhering to these blocks I found this."

He held up a test tube containing a blue liquid.

"The Guiacum test," he said. "In other words, blood. This fact taken with the facts we already know, that Digby never left the house; that the only other agent of destruction of a body, fire, is out of the question; that this tank is the receptacle of that enormous machine for making liquid air in very large quantities; and, above all, the practical possibility of the operation being conducted by the men who are at present in the house, afford me absolutely conclusive proof beyond a possibility of doubt as to what has happened. The body of that unfortunate man is as if it had never been, without a fragment of pin-point size for identification or evidence. It is beyond the annals of all the crimes that I have ever heard of. What law can help us? Can you hold an inquest on nothing? Can you charge a person with murder where no victim or trace of a victim can be produced?"

A sickly feeling came over me. Garland's words carried their own conviction, and we knew that we stood in the presence of a horror with a name. Nevertheless, to the police mind horror *per se* does not exist. To them there is always a mystery, a crime, and a solution. That is all. The men beside me were police once more. Sentiment might come later.

"Are there any reporters here?" asked Sir George.

"None," answered Frost.

"Good. Mr. Oscar Digby has disappeared. There is no doubt how. There can, of course, be no arrest, as Dr. Garland has just said. Our official position is this. We suspect that Mr. Digby has been murdered, but the search for the discovery of the body has failed. That is our position."

Before I left that awful house I made arrangements to have Muriel Scaiffe conveyed to a London hospital. I did not consult Mrs. Scaiffe on the subject. I could not get myself to say another word to the woman. In the hospital a private ward was secured for the unhappy girl, and there for many weeks she hovered between life and death.

Meanwhile, Mrs. Scaiffe and her brother were detained at The Rosary. They were closely watched by the police, and although they made many efforts to escape they found it impossible. Our hope was that when Muriel recovered her strength she would be able to substantiate a case against them. But, alas, this hope was unfounded, for, as the girl recovered, there remained a blank in her memory which no efforts on our part could fill. She had absolutely and completely forgotten Oscar Digby, and the house on Hampstead Heath was to her as though it had never existed. In all other respects she was well. Under these circumstances we were forced to allow the Spaniard and his sister to return to their own country, our one most earnest hope being that we might never see or hear of them again.

Meanwhile, Muriel grew better. I was interested in her from the first. When she was well enough I placed her with some friends of my own. A year ago she became my wife. I think she is happy. A past which is forgotten cannot trouble her. I have long ago come to regard her as the best and truest woman living.

THE INVISIBLE MAN

By G. K. Chesterton (1874-1936)

Essayist, short-story writer, artist, and creator of Father Brown, Gilbert Keith Chesterton was an expert on the impossible crime. He wrote about 25 stories about locked and guarded rooms, winged daggers, haunted castles, deadly curses, and strange vanishings. He loved paradoxes, statements and situations that seem inconsistent and perhaps impossible. Thus the circumstances of a Chestertonian crime may indicate to self-proclaimed modern observers that the supernatural is at work, but to Father Brown, who seems at first glance to be most unmodern, the problem of crime is one of sin and thus it must be human. He explains that "alone on earth, the Church makes reason really supreme. Alone on earth, the Church affirms that God himself is bound by reason." Chesterton admitted to "no pretensions to the scientific knowledge required to kill people," and Father Brown's solution to the problem of an invisible man is not based on H. G. Wellsian (or, for that matter, L. T. Meadeian) scientific speculation but on human perceptions.

IN THE cool blue twilight of two steep streets in Camden Town, the shop at the corner, a confectioner's, glowed like the butt of a cigar. One should rather say, perhaps, like the butt of a firework, for the light was of many colours and some complexity, broken up by many mirrors and dancing on many gilt and gaily-coloured cakes and sweetmeats. Against this one fiery glass were glued the noses of many gutter-snipes, for the chocolates were all wrapped in those red and gold and green metallic colours which are almost better than chocolate itself; and the huge white wedding-cake in the window was somehow at once remote and satisfying, just as if the whole North Pole were good to eat. Such rainbow provocations could naturally collect the youth of the neighbourhood up to the ages of ten or twelve. But this corner was also attractive to youth at a later stage; and a young man, not less than twenty-four, was staring into the same shop window. To him, also, the shop was of fiery charm, but this attraction was not wholly to be explained by chocolates; which, however, he was far from despising.

He was a tall, burly, red-haired young man, with a resolute face but a listless manner. He carried under his arm a flat, grey portfolio of black-and-white sketches, which he had sold with more or less success to publishers ever since his uncle (who was an admiral) had disinherited him for Socialism, because of a lecture which he had delivered against that economic theory. His name was John Turnbull Angus.

Entering at last, he walked through the confectioner's shop to the back room, which was a sort of pastry-cook restaurant, merely raising his hat to the young lady who was serving there. She was a dark, elegant, alert girl in black, with a high colour and very quick, dark eyes; and after the ordinary interval she followed him into the inner room to take his order.

His order was evidently a usual one. "I want, please," he said with precision, "one halfpenny bun and a small cup of black coffee." An instant before the girl could turn away he added, "Also, I want you to marry me."

The young lady of the shop stiffened suddenly and said, "Those are jokes I don't allow."

The red-haired young man lifted grey eyes of an unexpected gravity.

"Really and truly," he said, "it's as serious—as serious as the halfpenny bun. It is expensive, like the bun; one pays for it. It is indigestible, like the bun. It hurts."

The dark young lady had never taken her dark eyes off him, but seemed to be studying him with almost tragic exactitude. At the end of her scrutiny she had something like the shadow of a smile and she sat down in a chair.

"Don't you think," observed Angus, absently, "that it's rather cruel to eat these halfpenny buns? They might grow up into penny buns. I shall give up these brutal sports when we are married."

The dark young lady rose from her chair and walked to the window, evidently in a state of strong but not unsympathetic cogitation. When at last she swung round again with an air of resolution she was bewildered to observe that the young man was carefully laying out on the table various objects from the shop-window. They included a pyramid of highly coloured sweets, several plates of sandwiches, and the two decanters containing that mysterious port and sherry which are peculiar to pastry-cooks. In the middle of this neat arrangement he had carefully let down the enormous load of white sugared cake which had been the huge ornament of the window.

"What on earth are you doing?" she asked.

"Duty, my dear Laura," he began.

"Oh, for Lord's sake, stop a minute" she cried, "and don't talk to me in that way. I mean, what is all that?"

"A ceremonial meal, Miss Hope."

"And what is *that?*" she asked impatiently, pointing to the mountain of sugar.

"The wedding-cake, Mrs. Angus," he said.

The girl marched to that article, removed it with some clatter, and put it back in the shop window; she then returned, and, putting her elegant elbows on the table, regarded the young man not unfavourably but with considerable exasperation.

"You don't give me any time to think," she said.

"I'm not such a fool," he answered; "that's my Christian humility."

She was still looking at him; but she had grown considerably graver behind the smile.

"Mr. Angus," she said steadily, "before there is a minute more of this nonsense I must tell you something about myself as shortly as I can."

"Delighted," replied Angus gravely. "You might tell me something about myself, too, while you are about it,"

"Oh, do hold your tongue and listen," she said. "It's nothing that I'm ashamed of, and it isn't even anything that I'm specially sorry about. But what would you say if there were something that is no business of mine and yet is my nightmare?"

"In that case," said the man seriously, "I should suggest that you bring back the cake."

"Well, you must listen to the story first," said Laura, persistently. "To begin with, I must tell you that my father owned the inn called the 'Red Fish' at Ludbury, and I used to serve people in the bar."

"I have often wondered," he said, "why there was a kind of a Christian air about this one confectioner's shop."

"Ludbury is a sleepy, grassy little hole in the Eastern Counties, and the only kind of people who ever came to the 'Red Fish' were occasional commercial travellers, and for the rest, the most awful people you can see, only you've never seen them. I mean little, loungy men, who had just enough to live on and had nothing to do but lean about in bar-rooms and bet on horses, in bad clothes that were just too good for them. Even these wretched young rotters were not very common at our house; but there were two of them that were a lot too common—common in every sort of way. They both lived on money of their own, and were wearisomely idle and over-dressed. But yet I was a bit sorry for them, because I half believe they slunk into our little empty bar because each of them had a slight deformity; the sort of thing that some yokels laugh at. It wasn't exactly a deformity either; it was more an oddity. One of them was a surprisingly small man, something like a dwarf, or at least like a jockey. He was not at all jockeyish to look at, though; he had a round black head and a well-trimmed black beard, bright eyes like a bird's; he jingled money in his pockets; he jangled a great gold watch chain; and he never turned up except dressed just too much like a gentleman to be one. He was no fool though, though a futile idler; he was curiously clever at all kinds of things that couldn't be the slightest use; a sort of impromptu conjuring; making fifteen matches set fire to each other like a regular firework; or cutting a banana or some such thing into a dancing doll. His name was Isidore Smythe, and I can see him still, with his little dark face, just coming up to the counter, making a jumping kangaroo out of five cigars.

"The other fellow was more silent and more ordinary; but somehow he alarmed me much more than poor little Smythe. He was very tall and slight, and light-haired; his nose had a high bridge, and he might almost have been handsome in a spectral sort of way; but he had one of the most appalling squints I have ever seen or heard of. When he looked straight at you, you didn't know where you were yourself, let alone what he was looking at. I fancy this sort of disfigurement embittered the poor chap a little; for while Smythe was ready to show off his monkey tricks anywhere, James Welkin (that was the squinting man's name) never did anything except soak in our bar parlour, and go for great walks by himself in the flat, grey country all round. All the same, I think Smythe, too, was a little sensitive about being so small, though he carried it off more smartly. And so it was that I was really puzzled, as well as startled, and very sorry, when they both offered to marry me in the same week.

"Well, I did what I've since thought was perhaps a silly thing. But, after all, these freaks were my friends in a way; and I had a horror of their thinking I refused them for the real reason, which was that they were so impossibly ugly. So I made up some gas of another sort, about never meaning to marry anyone who hadn't carved his way in the world. I said it was a point of principle with me not to live on money that was just inherited like theirs. Two days after I had talked in this well-meaning sort of way, the whole trouble began. The first thing I heard was that both of them had gone off to seek their fortunes, as if they were in some silly fairy tale.

"Well, I've never seen either of them from that day to this. But I've had two letters from the little man called Smythe, and really they were rather exciting."

"Ever heard of the other man?" asked Angus.

"No, he never wrote," said the girl, after an instant's hesitation. "Smythe's first letter was simply to say that he had started out walking with Welkin to London; but Welkin was such a good walker that the little man dropped out of it, and took a rest by the roadside. He happened to be picked up by some travelling show, and, partly because he was nearly a dwarf, and partly because he was really a clever little wretch, he got on quite well in the show business, and was soon sent up to the Aquarium, to do some tricks that I forgot. That was his first letter. His second was much more of a startler, and I only got it last week."

The man called Angus emptied his coffee-cup and regarded her with mild and patient eyes. Her own mouth took a slight twist of laughter as she resumed, "I suppose you've seen on the hoardings all about this "Smythe's Silent Service"? Or you must be the only person that hasn't. Oh, I don't know much about it, it's some clockwork invention for doing all the housework by machinery. You know the sort of thing: 'Press a Button—A Butler who Never Drinks.' 'Turn a Handle—Ten Housemaids who Never Flirt.' You must have seen the advertisements. Well, whatever these machines are, they are making pots of money; and they are making it all for that little imp whom I knew down in Ludbury. I can't help feeling pleased the poor little chap has fallen on his feet; but the plain fact is, I'm in terror of his turning up any minute and telling me he's carved his way in the world—as he certainly has."

"And the other man?" repeated Angus with a sort of obstinate quietude.

Laura Hope got to her feet suddenly. "My friend," she said, "I think you are a witch. Yes, you are quite right. I have not seen a line of the other man's writing; and I have no more notion than the dead of what or where he is. But it is of him that I am frightened. It is he who is all about my path. It is he who has half driven me mad. Indeed, I think he has driven me mad; for I have felt him where he could not have been, and I have heard his voice when he could not have spoken."

"Well, my dear," said the young man, cheerfully, "if he were Satan himself, he is done for now you have told somebody. One goes mad all alone, old girl. But when was it you fancied you felt and heard our squinting friend?"

"I heard James Welkin laugh as plainly as I hear you

speak," said the girl, steadily. "There was nobody there, for I stood just outside the shop at the corner, and could see down both streets at once. I had forgotten how he laughed, though his laugh was as odd as his squint. I had not thought of him for nearly a year. But it's a solemn truth that a few seconds later the first letter came from his rival."

"Did you ever make the spectre speak or squeak, or anything?" asked Angus, with some interest.

Laura suddenly shuddered, and then said, with an unshaken voice, "Yes. Just when I had finished reading the second letter from Isidore Smythe announcing his success, just then, I heard Welkin say, 'He shan't have you, though.' It was quite plain, as if he were in the room. It is awful, I think I must be mad."

"If you really were mad," said the young man, "you would think you must be sane. But certainly there seems to me to be something a little rum about this unseen gentleman. Two heads are better than one—I spare you allusions to any other organs—and really, if you would allow me, as a sturdy, practical man, to bring back the wedding-cake out of the window—"

Even as he spoke, there was a sort of steely shriek in the street outside, and a small motor, driven at devilish speed, shot up to the door of the shop and stuck there. In the same flash of time a small man in a shiny top hat stood stamping in the outer room.

Angus, who had hitherto maintained hilarious ease from motives of mental hygiene, revealed the strain of his soul by striding abruptly out of the inner room and confronting the new-comer. A glance at him was quite sufficient to confirm the savage guesswork of a man in love. This very dapper but dwarfish figure, with the spike of black beard carried insolently forward, the clever unrestful eyes, the neat but very nervous fingers, could be none other than the man just described to him: Isidore Smythe, who made dolls out of banana skins and match-boxes; Isidore Smythe, who made millions out of undrinking butlers and unflirting housemaids of metal. For a moment the two men, instinctively understanding each other's air of possession, looked at each other with that curious cold generosity which is the soul of rivalry.

Mr. Smythe, however, made no allusion to the ultimate ground of their antagonism, but said simply and explosively, "Has Miss Hope seen that thing on the window?"

"On the window? repeated the staring Angus.

"There's no time to explain other things," said the small millionaire shortly. "There's some tomfoolery going on here that has to be investigated."

He pointed his polished walking-stick at the window, recently depleted by the bridal preparations of Mr. Angus; and that gentleman was astonished to see along the front of the glass a long strip of paper pasted, which had certainly not been on the window when he looked through it some time before. Following the energetic Smythe outside into the street, he found that some yard and a half of stamp paper had been carefully gummed along the glass outside, and on this was written in straggly characters, "If you marry Smythe, he will die."

"Laura," said Angus, putting his big red head into the shop, "you're not mad."

"It's the writing of that fellow Welkin," said Smythe gruffly. "I haven't seen him for years, but he's always bothering me. Five times in the last fortnight he's had threatening letters left at my flat, and I can't even find out who leaves them, let alone if it is Welkin himself. The porter of the flats swears that no suspicious characters have been seen, and here he has pasted up a sort of dado on a public shop window, while the people in the shop—"

"Quite so," said Angus modestly, "while the people in the shop were having tea. Well, sir, I can assure you I appreciate your common sense in dealing so directly with the matter. We can talk about other things afterwards. The fellow cannot be very far off yet, for I swear there was no paper there when I went last to the window, ten or fifteen minutes ago. On the other hand, he's too far off to be chased, as we don't even know the direction. If you'll take my advice, Mr. Smythe, you'll put this at once in the hands of some energetic inquiry man, private rather than public. I know an extremely clever fellow, who has set up in business five minutes from here in your car. His name's Flambeau, and though his youth was a bit stormy, he's a strictly honest man now, and his brains are worth money. He lives in Lucknow Mansions, Hampstead."

"That is odd," said the little man, arching his black eyebrows. "I live, myself, in Himylaya Mansions, round the corner. Perhaps you might care to come with me; I can go to my rooms and sort out these queer Welkin documents, while you run round and get our friend the detective."

"You are very good," said Angus politely. "Well, the sooner we act the better."

Both men, with a queer kind of impromptu fairness, took the same sort of formal farewell of the lady, and both jumped into the brisk little car. As Smythe took the handles and they turned the great corner of the street, Angus was amused to see a gigantesque poster of "Smythe's Silent Service," with a picture of a huge headless iron doll, carrying a saucepan with the legend, "A Cook Who is Never Cross."

"I use them in my own flat," said the little black-bearded man, laughing, "partly for advertisements, and partly for real convenience. Honestly, and all above board, those big clockwork dolls of mine do bring your coals or claret or a timetable quicker than any live servants I've ever known, if you know which knob to press. But I'll never deny, between ourselves, that such servants have their disadvantages, too."

"Indeed?" said Angus; "is there something they can't do?"

"Yes," replied Smythe coolly; "they can't tell me who left those threatening letters at my flat."

The man's motor was small and swift like himself; in fact, like his domestic service, it was of his own invention. If he was an advertising quack, he was one who believed in his own wares. The sense of something tiny and flying was accentuated as they swept up long white curves of road in the dead but open daylight of evening. Soon the white curves came sharper and dizzier; they were upon ascending spirals, as they say in the modern religions. For, indeed, they were cresting a corner of London which is almost as precipitous as Edinburgh, if not quite so picturesque. Terrace rose above terrace, and the special tower of flats they sought, rose above them all to almost Egyptian height, gilt by the level sunset. The change, as they turned the corner and entered the crescent known as Himylaya Mansions, was as abrupt as the opening of a window; for they found that pile of flats sitting above London as above a green sea of slate. Opposite to the mansions, on the other side of the gravel crescent, was a bushy enclosure more like a steep hedge or dyke than a garden, and some way below that ran a strip of artificial water, a sort of canal, like the moat of that embowered fortress. As the car swept round the crescent it passed, at one corner, the stray stall of a man selling chestnuts; and right away at the other end of the curve, Angus could see a dim blue policeman walking slowly. These were the only human shapes in that high suburban solitude; but he had an irrational sense that they expressed the speechless poetry of London. He felt as if they were figures in a story.

The little car shot up to the right house like a bullet, and shot out its owner like a bomb shell. He was immediately inquiring of a tall commissionaire in shining braid, and a short porter in shirt sleeves, whether anybody or anything had been seeking his apartments. He was assured that nobody and nothing had passed these officials since his last inquiries; whereupon he and the slightly bewildered Angus were shot up in the lift like a rocket, till they reached the top floor.

"Just come in for a minute," said the breathless Smythe. "I want to show you those Welkin letters. Then you might run round the corner and fetch our friend." He pressed a button concealed in the wall, and the door opened of itself.

It opened on a long, commodious ante-room, of which the only arresting features, ordinarily speaking, were the rows of tall half-human mechanical figures that stood up on both sides like tailors' dummies. Like tailors' dummies they were headless; and like tailors' dummies they had a handsome unnecessary humpiness in the shoulders, and a pigeon-breasted protuberance of chest; but barring this, they were not much more like a human figure than any automatic machine at a station that is about the human height. They had two great hooks like arms, for carrying trays; and they were painted pea-green, or vermilion, or black for convenience of distinction; in every other way they were only automatic machines and nobody would have looked twice at them. On this occasion, at least, nobody did. For between the two rows of these domestic dummies lay something more interesting than most of the mechanics of the world. It was a white, tattered scrap of paper scrawled with red ink; and the agile inventor had snatched it up almost as soon as the door flew open. He handed it to Angus without a word. The red ink on it actually was not dry, and the message ran, "If you have been to see her today, I shall kill you."

There was a short silence, and then Isidore Smythe said quietly, "Would you like a little whiskey? I rather feel as if I should."

"Thank you; I should like a little Flambeau," said Angus, gloomily. "This business seems to me to be getting rather grave. I'm going round at once to fetch him."

"Right you are," said the other, with admirable cheerfulness. "Bring him round here as quick as you can."

But as Angus closed the front door behind him he saw Smythe push back a button, and one of the clockwork images glided from its place and slid along a groove in the floor carrying a tray with syphon and decanter. There did seem something a trifle weird about leaving the little man alone among those dead servants, who were coming to life as the door closed.

Six steps down from Smythe's landing the man in shirt sleeves was doing something with a pail. Angus stopped to extract a promise, fortified with a prospective bribe, that he would remain in that place until the return with the detective, and would keep count of any kind of stranger coming up those stairs. Dashing down to the front hall he then laid similar charges of vigilance on the commissionaire at the front door, from whom he learned the simplifying circumstances that there was no back door. Not content with this, he captured the floating policeman and induced him to stand opposite the entrance and watch it; and finally paused an instant for a pennyworth of chestnuts, and an inquiry as to the probable length of the merchant's stay in the neighbourhood.

The chestnut seller, turning up the collar of his coat, told him he should probably be moving shortly, as he thought it was going to snow. Indeed, the evening was growing grey and bitter, but Angus, with all his eloquence, proceeded to nail the chestnut man to his post.

"Keep yourself warm on your own chestnuts," he said earnestly. "Eat up your whole stock; I'll make it worth your while. I'll give you a sovereign if you'll wait here till I come back, and then tell me whether any man, woman, or child has gone into that house where the commissionaire is standing."

He then walked away smartly, with a last look at the besieged tower.

"I've made a ring round that room, anyhow," he said. "They can't all four of them be Mr. Welkin's accomplices."

Lucknow Mansions were, so to speak, on a lower platform of that hill of houses, of which Himylaya Mansions might be called the peak. Mr. Flambeau's semi-official flat was on the ground floor, and presented in every way a marked contrast to the American machinery and cold hotel-like luxury of the flat of the Silent Service. Flambeau, who was a friend of Angus, received him in a rococo artistic den behind his office, of which the ornaments were sabres, harquebuses, Eastern curiosities, flasks of Italian wine, savage cooking-pots, a plumy Persian cat, and a small dusty-looking Roman Catholic priest, who looked particularly out of place.

"This is my friend Father Brown," said Flambeau. "I've often wanted you to meet him. Splendid weather, this; a little cold for Southerners like me."

"Yes, I think it will keep clear," said Angus, sitting down on a violet-striped Eastern ottoman.

"No," said the priest quietly, "it has begun to snow."

And, indeed, as he spoke, the first few flakes, foreseen by the man of chestnuts, began to drift across the darkening window-pane.

"Well," said Angus heavily. "I'm afraid I've come on business, and rather jumpy business at that. The fact is, Flambeau, within a stone's throw of your house is a fellow who badly wants your help; he's perpetually being haunted and threatened by an invisible enemy—a scoundrel whom nobody has even seen." As Angus proceeded to tell the whole tale of Smythe and Welkin, beginning with Laura's story, and going on with his own, the supernatural laugh at the corner of two empty streets, the strange distinct words spoken in an empty room, Flambeau grew more and more vividly concerned, and the little priest seemed to be left out of it, like a piece of furniture. When it came to the scribbled stamp-paper pasted on the window, Flambeau rose, seeming to fill the room with his huge shoulders.

"If you don't mind," he said. "I think you had better tell me the rest on the nearest road to this man's house. It strikes me, somehow, that there is no time to be lost."

"Delighted," said Angus, rising also, "though he's safe enough for the present, for I've set four men to watch the only hole to his burrow."

The turned out into the street, the small priest trundling after them with the docility of a small dog. He merely said, in a cheerful way, like one making conversation, "How quick the snow gets thick on the ground."

As they threaded the steep side streets already powdered with silver, Angus finished his story; and by the time they reached the crescent with the towering flats, he had leisure to turn his attention to the four sentinels. The chestnut seller, both before and after receiving a sovereign, swore stubbornly that he had watched the door and seen no visitor enter. The policeman was even more emphatic. He said he had had experience of crooks of all kinds, in top hats and in rags; he wasn't so green as to expect suspicious characters to look suspicious; he looked out for anybody, and, so help him, there had been nobody. And when all three men gathered round the gilded commissionaire, who still stood smiling astride of the porch, the verdict was more final still.

"I've got a right to ask any man, duke or dustman, what he wants in these flats," said the genial and gold-laced giant, "and I'll swear there's been nobody to ask since this gentleman went away."

The unimportant Father Brown, who stood back, looking modestly at the pavement, here ventured to say meekly, "Has nobody been up and down stairs, then, since the snow began to fall? It began while we were all round at Flambeau's."

"Nobody's been in here, sir, you can take it from me." said the official, with beaming authority.

"Then I wonder what that is?" said the priest, and stared at the ground blankly like a fish.

The others all looked down also; and Flambeau used a fierce exclamation and a French gesture. For it was unquestionably true that down the middle of the entrance guarded by the man in gold lace, actually between the arrogant, stretched legs of that colossus, ran a stringy pattern of grey footprints stamped upon the white snow.

"God!" cried Angus involuntarily, "the Invisible Man!"

Without another word he turned and dashed up the stairs, with Flambeau following; but Father Brown still stood looking about him in the snow-clad street as if he had lost interest in his query.

Flambeau was plainly in a mood to break down the door with his big shoulders; but the Scotchman, with more reason, if less intuition, fumbled about on the frame of the door till he found the invisible button; and the door swung slowly open.

It showed substantially the same serried interior; the hall had grown darker, though it was still struck here and there with the last crimson shafts of sunset, and one or two of the headless machines had been moved from their places for this or that purpose, and stood here and there about the twilit place. The green and red of their coats were all darkened in the dusk; and their likeness to human shapes slightly increased by their very shapelessness. But in the middle of them all, exactly where the paper with the red ink had lain, there lay something that looked like red ink spilt out of its bottle. But it was not red ink.

With a French combination of reason and violence Flambeau simply said "Murder!" and, plunging into the flat, had explored every corner and cupboard of it in five minutes. But if he expected to find a corpse he found none. Isidore Smythe was not in the place, either dead or alive. After the most tearing search the two men met each other in the outer hall, with streaming faces and staring eyes. "My friend," said Flambeau, talking French in his excitement, "not only is your murderer invisible, but he makes invisible also the murdered man."

Angus looked round at the dim room full of dummies, and in some Celtic corner of his Scotch soul a shudder started. One of the life-size dolls stood immediately overshadowing the blood stain, summoned, perhaps, by the slain man an instant before he fell. One of the high-shouldered hooks that served the thing for arms, was a little lifted, and Angus had suddenly the horrid fancy that poor Smythe's own iron child had struck him down. Matter had rebelled, and these machines had killed their master. But even so, what had they done with him?

"Eaten him?" said the nightmare at his ear; and he sickened for an instant at the idea of rent, human remains absorbed and crushed into all that acephalous clockwork.

He recovered his mental health by an emphatic effort, and said to Flambeau, "Well, there it is. The poor fellow has evaporated like a cloud and left a red streak on the floor. The tale does not belong to this world."

"There is only one thing to be done," said Flambeau, "whether it belongs to this world or the other. I must go down and talk to my friend."

They descended, passing the man with the pail, who again asseverated that he had let no intruder pass, down to the commissionaire and the hovering chestnut man, who rigidly reasserted their own watchfulness. But when Angus looked round for his fourth confirmation he could not see it, and called out with some nervousness, "Where is the policeman?"

"I beg your pardon," said Father Brown, "that is my fault. I just sent him down the road to investigate something—that I just thought worth investigating."

"Well, we want him back pretty soon," said Angus abruptly, "for the wretched man upstairs has not only been murdered, but wiped out."

"How?" asked the priest.

"Father," said Flambeau, after a pause, "upon my soul I believe it is more in your department than mine. No friend or foe has entered the house, but Smythe is gone, as if stolen by the fairies. If that is not supernatural, I—"

As he spoke they were all checked by an unusual sight; the big blue policeman came round the corner of the crescent, running. He came straight up to Brown.

"You're right, sir," he panted, "they've just found poor Mr. Smythe's body in the canal down below."

Angus put his hand wildly to his head, "Did he run down and drown himself?" he asked.

"He never came down, I'll swear," said the constable, "and he wasn't drowned either, for he died of a great stab over the heart."

"And yet you saw no one enter?" said Flambeau in a grave voice.

"Let us walk down the road a little," said the priest.

As they reached the other end of the crescent he observed abruptly, "Stupid of me! I forgot to ask the policeman something. I wonder if they found a light brown sack."

"Why a light brown sack?" asked Angus, astonished.

"Because if it was any other coloured sack, the case must begin over again," said Father Brown; "but if it was a light brown sack, why, the case is finished."

"I am pleased to hear it," said Angus with hearty irony. "It hasn't begun, so far as I am concerned."

"You must tell us all about it," said Flambeau with a strange heavy simplicity, like a child.

Unconsciously they were walking with quickening steps down the long sweep of road on the other side of the high crescent, Father Brown leading briskly, though in silence. At last he said with an almost touching vagueness, "Well, I'm afraid you'll think it so prosy. We always begin at the abstract end of things, and you can't begin this story anywhere else.

"Have you ever noticed this—that people never answer what you say? They answer what you mean—or what they think you mean. Suppose one lady says to another in a country house, 'Is anybody staying with you?' the lady doesn't answer 'Yes; the butler, the three footmen, the parlourmaid, and so on,' though the parlourmaid may be in the room, or the butler behind her chair. She says 'There is *nobody* staying with us,' meaning nobody of the sort you mean. But suppose a doctor inquiring into an epidemic asks, 'Who is staying in the house?' then the lady will remember the butler, the parlourmaid, and the rest. All language is used like that; you never get a question literally, even when you get it answered truly. When those four quite honest men said that no man had gone into the Mansions, they did not really mean that *no man* had gone into them.

They meant no man whom they could suspect of being your man. A man did go into the house, and did come out of it, but they never noticed him."

"An invisible man?" inquired Angus, raising his red eyebrows.

"A mentally invisible man," said Father Brown.

A minute or two after he resumed in the same unassuming voice, like a man thinking his way. "Of course you can't think of such a man, until you do think of him. That's where his cleverness comes in. But I came to think of him through two or three little things in the tale Mr. Angus told us. First, there was the fact that this Welkin went for long walks. And then there was the vast lot of stamp paper on the window. And then, most of all, there were the two things the young lady said—things that couldn't be true. Don't get annoyed," he added hastily, noting a sudden movement of the Scotchman's head; "she thought they were true. A person *can't* be quite alone in a street a second before she receives a letter. She can't be quite alone in a street when she starts reading a letter just received. There must be somebody pretty near her; he must be mentally invisible."

"Why must there be somebody near her?" asked Angus.

"Because," said Father Brown, "barring carrier-pigeons, somebody must have brought her the letter."

"Do you really mean to say," asked Flambeau, with energy, "that Welkin carried his rival's letters to his lady?"

"Yes," said the priest. "Welkin carried his rival's letters to his lady. You see, he had to."

"Oh, I can't stand much more of this," exploded Flambeau. "Who is this fellow? What does he look like? What is the usual get up of a mentally invisible man?"

"He is dressed rather handsomely in red, blue and gold," replied the priest promptly with precision, "and in this striking, and even showy, costume he entered Himylaya Mansions under eight human eyes; he killed Smythe in cold blood, and came down into the street again carrying the dead body in his arms—"

"Reverend sir," cried Angus, standing still, "are you raving mad, or am I?"

"You are not mad," said Brown, "only a little unobservant.

You have not noticed a man as this, for example."

He took three quick strides forward, and put his hand on the shoulder of an ordinary passing postman who had bustled by them unnoticed under the shade of the trees.

"Nobody ever notices postmen somehow," he said thoughtfully; "yet they have passions like other men, and even carry large bags where a small corpse can be stowed quite easily."

The postman, instead of turning naturally, had ducked and tumbled against the garden fence. He was a lean fair-bearded man of very ordinary appearance, but as he turned an alarmed face over his shoulder, all three men were fixed with an almost fiendish squint.

Flambeau went back to his sabres, purple rugs and Persian cat, having many things to attend to. John Turnbull Angus went back to the lady at the shop, with whom that imprudent young man contrives to be extremely comfortable. But Father Brown walked those snow-covered hills under the stars for many hours with a murderer, and what they said to each other will never be known.

THE ADVENTURE OF THE MAN WHO COULD DOUBLE THE SIZE OF DIAMONDS

By Ellery Queen (Manfred B. Lee, 1905—1971;
Frederic Dannay, 1905—1982)

Ellery Queen was, as most mystery fans know, the pseud-onym of Manfred B. Lee and Frederic Dannay, as well as the monicker of the detective in most of their books. Ellery also solved cases in the movies, in four different television series, in comic books, and for nine years on the radio. Like the early Queen novels, each episode of the radio Adventures of Ellery Queen *stopped just before the solution to issue a challenge to the audience to solve the crime. Quite a few of the radio plays, including "The Man Who Could Double the Size of Diamonds," involved the unraveling of an impossible crime. It is fair to give warning that the disappearance of the diamonds involves a cunning bit of misdirection, but even with that clue we doubt that you will be able to beat Ellery to the solution.*

The Characters

ELLERY QUEEN . . . . *the detective*
NIKKI PORTER . . . . *his secretary*
INSPECTOR QUEEN . . . . *his father*
SERGEANT VELIE . . . . *of Inspector Queen's staff*
PROFESSOR LAZARUS. . . . . *an inventor*
KENYON . . . . *an American diamond dealer*
VAN HOOTEN . . . . *a Dutch diamond dealer*
BRYCE . . . . *a British diamond dealer*
MASSET. . . . . *a French lapidary*
DR. COOK . . . . *the examining physician*

Setting

A Diamond Dealer's Office in New York—
The Queen Apartment—A Hotel Room

SCENE I: *Kenyon's Office, Maiden Lane*

(Kenyon is laughing very hard. He is a hard-headed business man. Professor Lazarus is an enthusiastic crackpot.)

LAZARUS: . . . and in my wonderful new diamond-manufacturing process—Why are you laughing, Mr. Kenyon?

KENYON: *(Stops and coughs)* Hrrrm! You're an inventor, you say, Professor Lazarus?

LAZARUS: Inventor, chemist, physicist, explorer into the hidden secrets of Nature . . . yes, Mr. Kenyon, a man of pure science, pure science! That's why I've come to you first, Mr. Kenyon. You're one of the leading diamond experts on Maiden Lane.

KENYON: *(Gravely)* Thank you, Professor. And you—uh—say you can *manufacture* diamonds? *(He suppresses a laugh.)*

LAZARUS: *(Excited)* It's a colossal discovery! Are you familiar with the experiments of Moissan—changing pure carbon into artificial diamonds?

KENYON: *(Tolerantly)* Oh, come, professor. Moissan's process has no commercial future. The cost of making the diamonds is considerably more than the diamonds are worth!

LAZARUS: True, Mr. Kenyon, true. But I've gone far beyond
Moisan! My new process will revolutionize the diamond
industry—change the financial structure of the world!

KENYON: *(Laughing)* Financial structure of the . . . *(Wiping
the tears away)* Sorry, Professor Lazarus. I . . . I've got a
tickle.

LAZARUS: *(Offended)* They laughed at Leeuwenhoek and
Pasteur and Galileo. Well, laugh! Let 'em all laugh! *(Mutters)* They always laugh at a genius. . . .

KENYON: *(Sharply)* See here, man. You expect me to believe
you've discovered a process by which you can manufacture diamonds at a cost that's not prohibitive? Fairy tales!

LAZARUS: Mr. Kenyon, give me a perfect diamond, and in
seven days I'll return it to you *twice as large!*

KENYON: The man who could double the size of diamonds!
(He laughs again.)

LAZARUS: *(Excited) Don't* laugh at me! I've done it, I tell you!

KENYON: *(With mock gravity)* Sort of scientific miracle, eh?

LAZARUS: Scientific fact! I've discovered one of Nature's
secrets, Mr. Kenyon!

KENYON: Professor Lazarus and Mother Nature, Incorporated. Uh . . . how do you accomplish this miracle?

LAZARUS: *(Slyly)* Aha! Wouldn't you like to know! But I'll tell
you this. It's a complex process based upon the introduction into the molecular structure of perfectly formed natural diamonds certain chemical elements—don't ask me
which ones, I won't tell you! But by this process I can
double the size and weight of the original diamond! I've
found a way to *grow diamonds chemically!*

KENYON: *(Amazed)* I believe you're really serious.

LAZARUS: Serious! I've devoted my whole life to it!

KENYON: *(Thoughtfully)* Perhaps I've been hasty, Professor.
But why come to me? Why not go it alone?

LAZARUS: Because I'm penniless. My life's savings have gone
into perfecting the formula and developing the apparatus.
I need financial backing, Mr. Kenyon!

KENYON: *(Dryly)* I should say you need raw material!—in this
case, perfect diamonds. Didn't you say you've got to start
with natural diamonds?

LAZARUS: Yes, Mr. Kenyon. Now look. I don't blame you for

being skeptical. You're a business man. So I don't expect you to take me on faith.

KENYON: *(Surprised)* You mean you're actually prepared to demonstrate your process, Professor?

LAZARUS: Of course, Mr. Kenyon!

KENYON: *Under any conditions I may impose on you?*

LAZARUS: Absolutely any conditions!

KENYON: *(Very serious—abruptly)* Professor Lazarus, be back here tomorrow!

SCENE 2: *The Same, Next Day*

(A slight argument is going on.)

VAN HOOTEN: *(He is a fat Dutch merchant)* Andt I say it is all poppycock!

KENYON: It won't hurt to look, will it, Van Hooten?

BRYCE: *(A slim London business man)* Kenyon's right, Van Hooten. You've been stuck away in that Amsterdam diamond-exchange of yours so long you've grown barnacles. Take a chance, old boy!

VAN HOOTEN: All righdt, I take a chance, Mr. Bryce. Doubling the size of diamonds! *(Short laugh)* I don't know whether it is to laugh, or to cry.

KENYON: Fine! Then you're with us, too, Bryce?

BRYCE: *(Chuckling)* Hard to convince, but open to proof. The true British spirit, Kenyon. Yes, I'm with you and Van Hooten. How about you, Monsieur Masset?

MASSET: *(A pudgy little French expert)* I am thinking.

VAN HOOTEN: *(Snort)* Masset is thinking! Do not breathe.

KENYON: We really need you in this little syndicate we're forming, Masset. As a lapidary you've no equal. You're better qualified than any of us to detect a possible fraud.

MASSET: Monsieur Kenyon, that is a bouquet I cannot resist smelling! Gentlemen, Masset enters the syndicate! Mynheer Van Hooten, Mr. Bryce—congratulate yourselves! *(They all laugh a little.)*

VAN HOOTEN: But to double the size of diamonds! This professor is a fraud. He must be.

BRYCE: I know it sounds like a fantastic idea. . . .

MASSET: *(Thoughtfully) Qui sait?* In the eighteenth century le comte Saint-Germain proved to King Louis the Fifteenth that not only could he remove flaws from diamonds but increase the size of pearls!

VAN HOOTEN: *(Scoffing)* A legend, Masset! Folklore!

BRYCE: Well, we'll soon see. Personally, I think the man's a quack, Kenyon.

KENYON: Judge for yourselves. Now we're all agreed on our conditions, gentlemen? *(As they agree a door opens off accompanied by a warning bell, which keeps ringing.)* Yes, Wolfe? He's here?

MAN: *(Entering)* Yes, Mr. Kenyon. It's Professor Lazarus.

KENYON: Send him in. And remember, Wolfe—no interruptions!

MAN: Yes, Mr. Kenyon. this way, Professor Lazarus.

LAZARUS: Thank you, thank you! *(The door closes and the bell stops.)*

KENYON: Come in, Professor! I want you to meet some business friends of mine. We've decided to form a little syndicate . . . just in case. Mynheer Van Hooten, the Amsterdam diamond merchant—Mr. Bryce, the London diamond-dealer—Monsieur Masset, the famous lapidary.

LAZARUS: A syndicate, eh? Excellent, excellent. Delighted!

VAN HOOTEN: Don't be too delighted, Professor Lazarus. We are a court of examination—no more!

BRYCE: Frankly, Professor, we don't know whether you're the genius you claim to be, or a lunatic.

MASSET: You will find us hard, Professor Lazarus. We do not believe you. But on the million-to-one chance that you have really stumbled on a new scientific principle . . .

KENYON: In a word, we're willing to be shown. *(They all murmur assent.)*

VAN HOOTEN: Providing, of course, thadt the conditions under which the experiment is conducted protecdt the syndicate against any possibility of loss, Mynheer!

LAZARUS: Naturally, naturally, Mr. Van Hooten. You would be fools not to protect yourselves!

KENYON: All right, then. Professor, do you see the steel safe-door in that wall of my office?

LAZARUS: Yes, Mr. Kenyon?

BRYCE: That safe-door leads into Mr. Kenyon's strong-room.
The strong-room is completely lined with steel and has
only one means of entrance and exit—the burglar-proof
safe-door you see there.

MASSET: In that strong-room, mon professeur, you will *try* to
double the size of diamonds!

LAZARUS: I understand. But air—I'll need air to breathe—

KENYON: My strong-room is air-conditioned. ("Ah!") Incidentally I'm having the door-combination changed. And only
Van Hooten, Bryce, Masset and I will know the new
combination!

VAN HOOTEN: You comprehend, Professor? Not you! You will
be admitted by one of us into the strong-room each morning, andt released each nighdt! *(Lazarus indicates that
he grasps the idea.)*

BRYCE: You may install your apparatus in the strong-room
and go to work on our diamonds, Lazarus!

LAZARUS: Very fair, very fair, gentlemen. But may I make one
condition? No one must disturb my work. I refuse to allow
anyone to enter that strong-room the entire week of my
experiment—either while I'm working there during the
day, or while it's locked up for the night!

VAN HOOTEN: *(Suspiciously)* Ah! Andt why is that, Professor?

LAZARUS: Obviously I must protect *myself.* I can't afford to let
anyone learn the secret of my process! *(Remarks of:
"that's fair," "Of course," etc.)*

MASSET: Agreed, then. But we warn you, monsieur le professeur! That room will be guarded as if it were the Bank of
France!

BRYCE: We should have experienced searchers to see that—
(Coughs)—the Professor doesn't carry off our diamonds
some night after his day's work.

KENYON: How about four detectives from Police Headquarters? Two to stand guard outside the strong-room all day,
two all night.

VAN HOOTEN: Andt each nighdt when you leave the strong-
room, Lazarus, you will be searched from headt to foot!

MASSET: *Mais certainement!* That I insist on!

BRYCE: *(Smoothly)* And to leave utterly nothing to chance,
gentlemen—I suggest we have a trustworthy physician in

attendance to—ah—complete the nightly search. *(Enthusiastic agreement from the others.)*

KENYON: *(Dryly)* You see, Professor, we're taking no chances. Since we're each lending you a valuable diamond to experiment on, take my word for it—you won't get the slightest opportunity to steal them!

LAZARUS: Steal! I'm a scientist, not a thief! Very well, we start tomorrow when I bring my apparatus in. But remember: Absolute secrecy! If the world learned of what we can do, the value of diamonds would be ruined forever! *(They agree)* Tomorrow each of you have a perfect diamond for me, in Mr. Kenyon's office, and I promise you—in one week your four diamonds will have grown to twice their present size! *(He laughs)* Like the Count of Monte Cristo—in one week you'll be able to cry: The world is mine!

SCENE 3: *The Queen Apartment, a Week Later*

(Kenyon is ending his story.)

KENYON: . . . and then, Mr. Queen, Professor Lazarus went to work in my strong-room at the office.

ELLERY QUEEN: *(Thoughtfully)* Amazing. Amazing story, Mr. Kenyon.

INSPECTOR QUEEN: So that's why you asked for the services of four of my detectives a week ago, Mr. Kenyon! *(Chuckles)* Weren't you gentlemen a little plastered when Lazarus turned on his highfalutin gas?

NIKKI PORTER: Why, it's fantastic! An Arabian Nights' story!

ELLERY: Why did you bring your friend Dr. Cook with you, Mr. Kenyon? No offense, Doctor; just curiosity.

KENYON: Dr. Cook is the physician who's been examining Lazarus every night when he quits the strong-room.

DR. COOK: *(He is a scientific robot)* Would have refused anyone but Kenyon, Mr. Queen. Old friends. But of all the nonsense! Wait till you hear the end of this!

KENYON: In the week that's passed since the Professor began his mysterious work in my strong-room, we've taken every precaution against fraud, Mr. Queen. Well, this afternoon at five we let the professor out, as usual, Seventh day—his time was up. "Well?" we demanded. "Show us our diamonds, twice as large!" The Professor was nervous . . .

INSPECTOR: *(Chuckling)* Doubling the size of diamonds!

NIKKI: Of course he failed, Mr. Kenyon?

ELLERY: And asked for more time? That would be the natural development.

KENYON: Exactly what happened! Well, the detectives and we five men—we searched him—Dr. Cook here examined him with special care—and then, satisfied the diamonds weren't on him, we let him go for the night.

DR. COOK: And the syndicate went into a huddle. *(Chuckles.)*

KENYON: After an argument, we decided to extend the Professor's time a few days. The others left, I went out for dinner . . . and started to worry. Suppose something *was* wrong! I'd got the other three into this; they'd contributed valuable diamonds as well as I. . . . Well, I ran back to my office. The two detectives on night-duty let me in—I unlocked the safe-door of the strong-room and went in. . . .

INSPECTOR: *(Sharply)* Don't tell me. . . .

NIKKI: The four diamonds you gave Lazarus to work on—

ELLERY: They were gone from the strong-room, Mr. Kenyon?

KENYON: *(Despairing)* Vanished! Not a sign of them! I turned that strong-room upside down! Tore his apparatus to pieces! Then I called the detectives in. They thought I was crazy, till they saw for themselves.

ELLERY: Seems simple enough, Mr. Kenyon. Professor Lazarus managed to smuggle the diamonds out with him during the past week, perhaps taking one diamond at a time, and your nightly searches just didn't turn up his hiding-place.

KENYON: Impossible, Mr. Queen! We didn't overlook even the most far-fetched hiding-place! That's why I stopped to pick up Dr. Cook on my way to see you tonight, after I left messages for Van Hooten, Bryce, and Masset that the diamonds were gone.

DR. COOK: I give you my word, Mr. Queen—I can't imagine where the fellow could have been hiding those diamonds when he took them out.

ELLERY: How about his clothing?

KENYON: We examined every stitch on his body every night— not only we four, but the detectives, too!

INSPECTOR: The men I put on this job, Ellery, wouldn't slip up on a body-search. They're perfectly reliable.

NIKKI: I know! Lazarus must have a hump on his back—a false hump! Or else he's got a hollow wooden leg, or something!

DR. COOK: No hump, false limb, finger . . . nothing like that.

ELLERY: How about his hair, Doctor? Has he a beard?

DR. COOK: No beard, and the man's as bald as an eagle.

ELLERY: His mouth, Doctor. Did you examine him there?

DR. COOK: Lazarus has no teeth of his own. He uses dental plates, which I examined carefully every night. No cavities of any kind. Nor could he have taken the diamonds out in his ears or nasal openings.

NIKKI: A glass eye! I'll bet that's it.

DR. COOK: No, Miss Porter. He has two very sound eyes.

ELLERY: Possibly he carried some *object* out of the strong-room in which a diamond might have been concealed. A watch—("No!")—cigaret case—("No . . .")

INSPECTOR: Wallet? ("It was examined.") Tobacco pouch? ("No, Inspector.") A finger-ring? ("No!")

NIKKI: A cane! A walking-stick that's hollow!

KENYON: *(Sighing)* The Professor has no stick. I tell you we examined everything. Even his pen and pencil.

ELLERY: Mr. Kenyon, is there a drain or water-tap in the strong-room?

KENYON: No opening of any kind except the air-conditioning vent and intake—and they were thoroughly searched.

NIKKI: Then couldn't he have hidden the diamonds *inside* of him, Dr. Cook?

ELLERY: *(Chuckling)* Excellent question, Nikki! Could he?

DR. COOK: I performed every conceivable test that would be conclusive, Mr. Queen—gastroscope, otoscope, nasal speculum, and so on. If X-Ray or fluoroscope would have helped, I'd have used those, too, because Mr. Kenyon and his associates told me to leave absolutely nothing to chance. I give you my word as a medical man, Mr. Queen—Professor Lazarus did *not* hide those four diamonds any-where *in* his body! *(The phone rings.)*

NIKKI: I'll answer it, Inspector.

INSPECTOR: No, I'll take it, Nikki. Probably Headquarters, with my men's report of the theft. . . .

ELLERY: Fascinating problem, gentlemen! *(The inspector an-*

swers the phone.) It appears we're dealing with the most ingenious thief of modern times. We'll have to see your Professor Lazarus . . .

INSPECTOR: Ellery, stop a minute. I can't hear . . . Hello! Who?

SERGEANT VELIE: *(On the other end)* This is Velie, Inspector!

INSPECTOR: Oh! Yes, Velie? Why aren't you home with your wife?

VELIE: I'm married to my job, ain't I? Inspector, you'll have to buzz downtown. A murder.

INSPECTOR: Why do they always pick out a man's bedtime! Well, well, Velie. Where is it?

VELIE: Some crummy hotel—the Jolly, or Jelly, or somepin', on East Twenty-fourth. Guy was found dead in his room by a chambermaid. Somebody's played chopsticks on his naked skull.

INSPECTOR: I'll be right down. Identify the corpse yet, Velie?

VELIE: Oh, sure. Some nut inventor, from the papers in his room . . .

INSPECTOR: Nut invent—! *(Hoarsely)* Velie! What was his name?

VELIE: Aw, you wouldn't know him, Inspector. A phony professor. Let's scc, now. Yeah . . . Lazarus—Professor Lazarus!

SCENE 4: *A Room in a New York Hotel, Later*

(A mean little hotel room filled with chattering detectives, police, etc.)

VELIE: *(Over the hubbub)* Say, Whitey! Inspector's yellin' for that fingerprint report! *(Whitey shouts)* What? That's nice! The old man'll love that! . . . Joe! Ain't you through muggin' the stiff? Get pictures of the struggle—bloody lamp, overturned chairs, torn clo'es . . . man, what a brawl this musta been!

INSPECTOR: *(Calling)* Velie! Where's Prouty? . . . Quiet, men!

VELIE: *(Bellowing)* Qui-et, you hyenas! *(The hubbub quiets)* Doc Prouty's gone already, Inspector. Nothin' sensational, he says. Guy just died from those blows on the head while he was fightin' with his killer. Happened tonight.

INSPECTOR: That's *very* helpful! Ellery, did you see this?

ELLERY: *(Absently)* What, dad? Oh, sorry.

NIKKI: Ellery Queen! You don't seem the least bit interested! What is it, Inspector? . . . Oh, what a *beautiful* diamond.

VELIE: My old woman'd give her right eye for a sparkler like that. Where'd you find it, Inspector?

INSPECTOR: In Lazarus's right hand, Mr. Kenyon!

VELIE: Kenyon! Over here, Mr. Kenyon! Watch it! Don't step on his hand!

KENYON: *(He is very upset)* Oh! Did I? I mean . . . For heaven's sake, this is awful! Awful!

ELLERY: *(Low)* Let's see the diamond, dad . . . Hmm . . .

INSPECTOR: Kenyon, do you recognize this diamond? *(Kenyon examines it.)*

KENYON: It's Bryce's! The diamond Bryce contributed to the syndicate for the Professor's experiment!

INSPECTOR: That settles it. Only Van Hooten, Bryce, Masset, and Kenyon knew about Lazarus's experiment—even the detectives on day and night duty didn't know what was going on!

VELIE: So it musta been one of the syndicate that bumped off the dead con man.

KENYON: One of *us?* Don't be—! *(Thoughtfully)* One of *us?*

INSPECTOR: One of you four men came to the professor's hotel room tonight, caught him with the stolen diamonds, and tried to take them away. Lazarus fought back and was beaten to death with this heavy metal table lamp. Murderer grabbed the diamonds and beat it.

NIKKI: But in the excitement he overlooked one of the diamonds—the one in the dead man's hand—

VELIE: Or maybe he thought he'd taken all four and didn't find out it was only three till he got away—then he was scared to come back.

NIKKI: But the big question is: Which of the four members of the syndicate killed Professor Lazarus?

INSPECTOR: What d'ye think, Ellery?

ELLERY: *(Thoughtfully)* Three secrets may have died with Lazarus. First, the secret of his diamond-doubling process—whose authenticity I doubt. Second, the secret of his murderer's identity—in this well-lighted room, after a considerable struggle, Lazarus must certainly have recognized his assailant. And third, the secret of how Lazarus managed to spirit those diamonds out of Kenyon's strongroom—past the suspicious eyes and searching hands of the four owners of the diamonds, two experienced detectives, and a medical doctor!

NIKKI: It's enough to make you dizzy. I can't *imagine!*

ELLERY: At the moment, neither can I, Nikki. I confess—I'd rather know how Lazarus accomplished the thefts than who murdered him!

VELIE: You would.

INSPECTOR: Velie!

VELIE: *(Hastily)* Yeah, Inspector?

INSPECTOR: Round up Van Hooten, Bryce, and that French lap—lap—whatever he is!—Masset. Get 'em down here on the double and we'll go over 'em—lightly!

VELIE: *(Fading)* Lemme slap on the hot towel . . . !

INSPECTOR: Ellery, *you* can play around with the mystery of how Professor Lazarus stole those diamonds—*I* want to know who beat him to death!

SCENE 5: *The Same, Later*

(Inspector Queen is grilling the suspects. Bryce is saying: "Yes, that is my diamond, Inspector." The others demand the return of their property.)

INSPECTOR: Murderer's got 'em! I want to know where you men were tonight. Bryce?

BRYCE: *(Nervously)* I was out strolling . . . returned to my hotel, found Kenyon's message that the diamonds had been stolen . . . thought it was a—a joke . . .

INSPECTOR: Mynheer Van Hooten? You were in the Park writing poetry, I suppose?

VAN HOOTEN: *(yelling)* I go back to my New York office! Later I go back to my hotel—find Kenyon's message—

INSPECTOR: *(Softly)* So you've no alibi, either. How about you, Monsieur Masset?

MASSET: I, too, Monsieur l'inspecteur—I return to my office on Maiden Lane. And I, too—I later find Monsieur Kenyon's message about the theft of the dimaonds . . .

VELIE: For a bunch of business men, these guys were sure pushovers for that con-man Lazarus!

NIKKI: Yes, Sergeant, and the Professor would have got away with it, too, if one of them hadn't gone to his hotel, killed him—and stolen the diamonds himself!

ELLERY: Hush, Nikki. Let dad handle this.

NIKKI: *(Indignantly)* I know, Ellery, but such *deceit*, such—such blood-thirstiness! They're all trying to look so innocent.

VAN HOOTEN: I want back my diamondt! Get it back, I say!

MASSET: *(Bitterly)* Mine, too. Bryce, you are fortunate. Your diamond was left behind. But mine—

BRYCE: But how did he *do* it? I can't understand it!

INSPECTOR: There's a lot of things I can't understand! Hold it, you four, Ellery, come here a minute.

ELLERY: *(Absently)* Yes, dad! *(They go to one side.)*

INSPECTOR: Any ideas?

ELLERY: Dad, I'm baffled. Baffled! It's an impossible crime!

INSPECTOR: What's impossible about it? No tricks to *this* murder. All we have to do is find the murderer—

ELLERY: I don't mean the murder, dad—I mean Lazarus's theft of the diamonds from Kenyon's strong-room! I shan't sleep till I find out how he smuggled them past seven searchers!

INSPECTOR: Hang it, son! This is a murder-case, not a puzzle!

ELLERY: This time *you* handle the murder, dad—I'll take the puzzle. *(Thoughtfully)* I've *got* to figure out how the Professor did it!

SCENE 6: *The Queen Apartment, Next Morning.*

INSPECTOR: And your check of the alibis, Velie?

VELIE: Whaddaya mean alibis? Van Hooten an' Masset claimin' they were workin' in Maiden Lane . . . but no one *saw* them! Bryce takin' a walk all by his lonely . . . *(The door opens)* Good mornin', Miss Porter.

INSPECTOR: *(Glumly)* Morning, Nikki.

NIKKI: *(Bouncing in) Good* morning! My, such gloomy faces. No luck on the murder, Inspector Queen?

INSPECTOR: I guess luck will be our only hope of solving it at that, Nikki. Ellery's no help.

NIKKI: He *has* been acting remote. Where is he this morning?

VELIE: Aw, the Master-Mind's in his bedroom poundin' the floor like an expectant papa.

INSPECTOR: Ellery didn't sleep a wink all night, Nikki.

VELIE: If y'ask me, for once in his life the Maestro's stumped. *(The bedroom door opens)* Aha! He enters!

ELLERY: *(Briskly entering)* Morning, everybody!

INSPECTOR: Come on, son—have some breakfast. You must be all tuckered out after last night.

VELIE: Forget it, Mr. Queen. You can't hit the jackpot every time. *(Ellery chuckles.)*

NIKKI: Ellery Queen! You're grinning! Inspector, Sergeant— he *knows* something!

ELLERY: Certainly I know something. I've spent ten sleepless hours figuring it out!

NIKKI: And just what is it you've been puzzling over, Mr. Queen?

ELLERY: How Lazarus managed to smuggle those diamonds past seven searchers. *(The Inspector and Velie groan.)* I've thought of every conceivable way in which he could have stolen the diamonds. Dad—I've solved the puzzle of the theft!

INSPECTOR: *(Sarcastically)* Fine! Now you can start solving the puzzle of the murder.

ELLERY: *(As if to himself)* Yes, I'm sure I'm right—it's the only possible answer. *I know how those diamonds got out of the strong-room!*

VELIE: Okay, Mr. Queen, so you win the puzzle champeen-ship of the world. But for cryin' out loud—

INSPECTOR: How about the *murder?* Ellery, we've got to know who *murdered* Lazarus!

ELLERY: *(Absently)* Oh, that? I know that, too!

ELLERY QUEEN *has just said that he knows how the dia-monds got out of* KENYON'S *strong-room, and also who murdered* PROFESSOR LAZARUS. *Do you? You can have some additional fun by stopping here and trying to solve the double mystery before* ELLERY *reveals the solution. Naming the criminal is not sufficient, if you play the game fairly. You must get the correct reasoning, too . . . Now go ahead and read* ELLERY QUEEN'S *own solution to*

"The Adventure of the Man Who Could Double the Size of Diamonds."

The Solution

SCENE 7: *The Same, Immediately After*

INSPECTOR: We're losing time, Ellery! Tell me who murdered Lazarus.

ELLERY: To do that, dad, I'll have to begin with the theft of the diamonds . . .

VELIE: *(Groaning)* There he goes again!

NIKKI: The man with the one-track mind!

ELLERY: *(Gently)* But it's the heart of this case, children. How did Professor Lazarus get those diamonds past seven searchers—the four owners, the two detectives, and the doctor? I saw no light until I asked myself one tremendously simple, one gigantically obvious question: *Was it really Professor Lazarus who took those diamonds out of the strong-room?*

NIKKI: Oh, dear. Oh, *dear!* That's the answer!

ELLERY: Yes, Nikki! A score of facts proved that not only *didn't* Lazarus take those diamonds out, he *couldn't.* It was *impossible* for Lazarus to have smuggled them past the seven men—and you can't find the answer to an impossibility. Therefore *Lazarus* wasn't the thief—someone *else* must have been!

INSPECTOR: But Ellery, only Professor Lazarus entered that strong-room all week—a condition he'd laid down himself before he began working there!

ELLERY: Yes, but is it *true* no one else entered that strong-room! It is *not* true. Because one other person *did* go in there before the diamonds were reported gone—and by his own admission was in there *alone!* And what's more, when he left the office, he knew he wouldn't be searched— because they were all protecting themselves against *Lazarus.* Therefore I knew that the only other person known to have been in the strong-room alone *must* be the thief! And who was that person?

NIKKI: Kenyon! It was Mr. Kenyon! *(Velie ad libs assent.)*

INSPECTOR: Sure! Kenyon himself told us he returned to his

office last night "worried" that something was wrong—that the detectives on guard let him in—that he went into the strong-room *alone*, and the detectives didn't rush in there until he yelled the diamonds were gone!

VELIE: Boy, that's masterful. Kenyon goes in, swipes the ice himself, then comes out, hollers he's been robbed, beats it over to the Professor's hotel room, kills the ol' guy, scrams, hides the di'monds, then picks up Dr. Cook an' brings him to you, Mr. Queen, to back up his story about how hard they searched Lazarus!

ELLERY: Yes, and in giving us that story, he brilliantly distracted our attention from himself and directed it towards Lazarus as the thief. Quite a psychologist, Kenyon! One of the cleverest rogues in my experience. He devised a theft of such colossal simplicity that I was nearly taken in by the complicated props.

NIKKI: Then Professor Lazarus wasn't a confidence man at all! *Could* he double the size of diamonds, Ellery?

ELLERY: *(Laughing)* Well, he didn't, Nikki, so I imagine the poor fellow was just an earnest crank who thought he'd solved one of the riddles of the universe.

NIKKI: Wasn't it foolish of Kenyon to overlook the diamond in the Professor's dead hand—Bryce's diamond?

ELLERY: Overlook it! Nikki, Kenyon left that diamond there *purposely.* For the same reason he *killed* Lazarus . . . to clinch the illusion that it was Professor Lazarus who'd stolen the diamonds in the first place.

INSPECTOR: Wait a minute, Ellery. Granting Kenyon was the only one who could have taken the diamonds out of the strong-room, how does that prove he also killed Lazarus?

VELIE: Yeah, why couldn't it 'a' been one o' of the other guys who bumped off the professor?

ELLERY: *(Laughing)* Kenyon's magic spell is still on you. Don't you see? The murderer planted one of the four diamonds in the victim's hand. To *leave* a diamond in the victim's hand meant that the murderer had to *have* the diamond. Who had the diamonds? The thief. Therefore the thief must have been the murderer. And who is the only possible thief? Kenyon. Conclusion. Kenyon is the murderer!

NIKKI: Q.—E.—D.!

VELIE: *(Awed)* Gosh! Inspector, why can't *we* figger 'em out so nice an' clean?

INSPECTOR: *(Sadly)* Velie, I've been trying to answer that question ever since I became a father!

(The music comes up.)

THE MYSTERY OF THE LOST SPECIAL

By A. Conan Doyle (1859-1930)

Debate continues about the name of "an amateur reasoner of some celebrity" who remarks that "when the impossible has been eliminated the residuum, however improbable, must contain the truth." Although he failed to solve "The Mystery of the Lost Special," some scholars have identified him with a more successful reasoner who was featured in nine of Sir Arthur Conan Doyle's books; on the other hand, the story appeared in an 1898 issue of The Strand *when Reichenbach Falls still guarded its secret. Whatever the case, "The Mystery of the Lost Special" was certainly one of the most challenging problems set before a detective, amateur or professional. How can a train vanish from a stretch of track with observers at either end?*

THE confession of Herbert de Lernac, now lying under sentence of death at Marseilles, has thrown a light upon one of the most inexplicable crimes of the century—an incident which is, I believe, absolutely unprecedented in the criminal annals of any country. Although there is a reluctance to discuss the matter in official circles, and little information has been given to the Press, there are still indications that the statement of this arch-criminal is corroborated by the facts, and that we have at last found a solution for a most astounding business. As the matter is eight years old, and as its importance was somewhat obscured by a political crisis which was engaging the public attention at the time, it may be as well to state the facts as far as we have been able to ascertain them. They are collated from the Liverpool papers of that date, from the proceedings at the inquest upon John Slater, the engine-driver, and from the records of the London and West Coast Railway Company, which have been courteously put at my disposal. Briefly, they are as follows.

On the 3rd of June, 1890, a gentleman, who gave his name as Monsieur Louis Caratal, desired an interview with Mr. James Bland, the superintendent of the Central London and West Coast Station in Liverpool. He was a small man, middle-aged and dark, with a stoop which was so marked that it suggested some deformity of the spine. He was accompanied by a friend, a man of imposing physique, whose deferential manner and constant attention was one of dependence. This friend or companion, whose name did not transpire, was certainly a foreigner, and probably, from his swarthy complexion, either a Spaniard or a South American. One peculiarity was observed in him. He carried in his left hand a small black leather despatch-box, and it was noticed by a sharp-eyed clerk in the Central office that this box was fastened to his wrist by a strap. No importance was attached to the fact at the time, but subsequent events endowed it with some significance. Monsieur Caratal was shown up to Mr. Bland's office, while his companion remained outside.

Monsieur Caratal's business was quickly dispatched. He had arrived that afternoon from Central America. Affairs of the utmost importance demanded that he should be in Paris without the loss of an unnecessary hour. He had missed the

London express. A special must be provided. Money was of no importance. Time was everything. If the company would speed him on his way, they might make their own terms.

Mr. Bland struck the electric bell, summoned Mr. Potter Hood, the traffic manager, and had the matter arranged in five minutes. The train would start in three-quarters of an hour. It would take that time to insure that the line should be clear. The powerful engine called Rochdale (No. 247 on the company's register) was attached to two carriages, with a guard's van behind. The first carriage was solely for the purpose of decreasing the inconvenience arising from the oscillation. The second was divided, as usual, into four compartments, a first-class, a first-class smoking, a second-class, and a second-class smoking. The first compartment, which was the nearest to the engine, was the one allotted to the travellers. The other three were empty. The guard of the special train was James McPherson, who had been some years in the service of the company. The stoker, William Smith, was a new hand.

Monsieur Caratal, upon leaving the superintendent's office, rejoined his companion, and both of them manifested extreme impatience to be off. Having paid the money asked, which amounted to fifty pounds five shillings, at the usual special rate of five shillings a mile, they demanded to be shown the carriage, and at once took their seats in it, although they were assured that the better part of an hour must elapse before the line could be cleared. In the meantime a singular coincidence has occurred in the office which Monsieur Caratal had just quitted.

A request for a special is not a very uncommon circumstance in a rich commercial centre, but that two should be required upon the same afternoon was most unusual. It so happened, however, that Mr. Bland had hardly dismissed the first traveller before a second entered with a similar request. This was a Mr. Horace Moore, a gentlemanly man of military appearance, who alleged that the sudden serious illness of his wife in London made it absolutely imperative that he should not lose an instant in starting upon the journey. His distress and anxiety were so evident that Mr. Bland did all that was possible to meet his wishes. A second special was out of the question, as the ordinary local service was already somewhat deranged by the first. There was the alternative, however, that Mr. Moore should share the expense of Monsieur Caratal's train, and should travel in the other empty first-class compartment, if Monsieur Caratal objected to having him in the one which he occupied. It was difficult to see any objection to such an arrangement, and yet Monsieur Caratal, upon the suggestion being made to him by Mr. Potter Hood, absolutely refused to consider it for an instant. The train was his, he said, and he would insist upon the exclusive use of it. All argument failed to overcome his ungracious objections, and finally the plan had to be abandoned. Mr. Horace Moore left the station in great distress, after learning that his only course was to take the ordinary slow train which leaves Liverpool at six o'clock. At four thirty-one exactly by the station clock the special train, containing the crippled Monsieur Caratal and his gigantic companion, steamed out of the Liverpool station. The line was at that time clear, and there should have been no stoppage before Manchester.

The trains of the London and West Coast Railway run over the lines of another company as far as this town, which should have been reached by the special rather before six o'clock. At a quarter after six considerable surprise and some consternation were caused amongst the officials at Liverpool by the receipt of a telegram from Manchester to say that it had not yet arrived. An inquiry directed to St. Helens, which is a third of the way between the two cities, eliciting the following reply:—

"To James Bland, Superintendent, Central L. & W. C., Liverpool.—Special passed here at 4.52, well up to time.— Dowser, St. Helena."

This telegram was received at 6.40. At 6.50 a second message was received from Manchester:—

"No sign of special as advised by you."

And then ten minutes later a third, more bewildering:—

"Presume some mistake as to proposed running of special. Local train from St. Helens timed to follow it has just arrived and has seen nothing of it. Kindly wire advices.— Manchester."

The matter was assuming a most amazing aspect, although in some respects the last telegram was a relief to the authorities at Liverpool. If an accident had occurred to the special, it seemed hardly possible that the local train could have passed down the same line without observing it. And yet, what was alternative? Where could the train be? Had it possibly been side-tracked for some reason in order to allow the slower train to go past? Such an explanation was possible if some small repair had to be effected. A telegram was dispatched to each of the stations between St. Helens and Manchester, and the superintendent and traffic manager waited in the utmost suspense at the instrument for the series of replies which would enable them to say for certain what had become of the missing train. The answers came back in the order of questions, which was the order of the stations beginning at the St. Helens end:—

"Special passed here five o'clock.—Collins Green."

"Special passed here six past five.—Earlestown."

"Special passed here 5.10.—Kenyon Junction."

"No special train has passed here.—Barton Moss."

The two officials stared at each other in amazement.

"This is unique in my thirty years of experience," said Mr. Bland.

"Absolutely unprecedented and inexplicable, sir. The special has gone wrong between Kenyon Junction and Barton Moss."

"And yet there is no siding, as far as my memory serves me, between the two stations. The special must have run off the metals."

"But how could the four-fifty parliamentary pass over the same line without observing it?"

"There's no alternative, Mr. Hood. It *must* be so. Possibly the local train may have observed something which may throw some light upon the matter. We will wire to Manchester for more information, and to Kenyon Junction with instructions that the line be examined instantly as far as Barton Moss."

The answer from Manchester came within a few minutes.

"No news of missing special. Driver and guard of slow train positive that no accident between Kenyon Junction and Barton Moss. Line quite clear, and no sign of anything unusual.—Manchester."

"That driver and guard will have to go," said Mr. Bland, grimly. "There has been a wreck and they have missed it. The special has obviously run off the metals without disturbing the line—how it could have done so passes my comprehension—but so it must be, and we shall have a wire from Kenyon or Barton Moss presently so say that they have found her at the bottom of an embankment."

But Mr. Bland's prophecy was not destined to be fulfilled. A half-hour passed, and then there arrived the following message from the station-master of Kenyon Junction:—

"There are no traces of the missing special. It is quite certain that she passed here, and that she did not arrive at Barton Moss. We have detached engine from goods train, and I have myself ridden down the line, but all is clear, and there is no sign of any accident."

Mr. Bland tore his hair in his perplexity.

"This is rank lunacy, Hood!" he cried. "Does a train vanish into thin air in England in broad daylight? The thing is preposterous. An engine, a tender, two carriages, a van, five human beings—and all lost on a straight line of railway! Unless we get something positive within the next hour I'll take Inspector Collins, and go down myself."

And then at last something positive did occur. It took the shape of another telegram from Kenyon Junction.

"Regret to report that the dead body of John Slater, driver of the special train, has just been found among the gorse bushes at a point two and a quarter miles from the Junction. Had fallen from his engine, pitched down the embankment, and rolled among bushes. Injuries to his head, from the fall, appear to be cause of death. Ground has now been carefully examined, and there is no trace of the missing train."

The country was, as has already been stated, in the throes of a political crisis, and the attention of the public was futher distracted by the important and sensational developments in Paris, where a huge scandal threatened to destroy the Government and to wreck the reputations of many leading men in France. The papers were full of these events, and the singular disappearance of the special train attracted less attention than would have been the case in more peaceful times. The grotesque nature of the event helped to detract from its importance, for the papers were disinclined to believe the facts as reported to them. More than one of the London journals treated the matter as an ingenious hoax, until the coroner's inquest upon the unfortunate driver (an inquest which elicited nothing of importance) convinced them of the tragedy of the incident.

Mr. Bland, accompanied by Inspector Collins, the senior detective officer in the service of the company, went down to Kenyon Junction the same evening, and their research lasted throughout the following day, but was attended with purely negative results. Not only was no trace of the missing train, but no conjecture could be put forward which could possibly explain the facts. At the same time, Inspector Collins's official report (which lies before me as I write) served to show that the possibilities were more numerous than might have been expected.

"In the stretch of railway between these two points," said he, "the country is dotted with ironworks and collieries. Of these, some are being worked and some have been abandoned. There are no fewer than twelve which have small guage lines which run trolly-cars down to the main line. These can, of course, be disregarded. Besides these, however, there are seven which have or have had proper lines running down and connecting with points to the main line, so as to convey their produce from the mouth of the mines to the great centres of distribution. In every case these lines are only a few miles in length. Out of seven, four belong to collieries which are worked out, or at least to shafts which are no longer used. These are the Redgauntlet, Hero, Slought of Despond, and Heartsease mines, the latter having ten years ago been one of the principal mines in Lancashire. These four side lines may be eliminted from our inquiry, for, to prevent possible accidents, the rails nearest to the main line have been taken up and there is no longer any connection. There remain three other lines leading

(a) to the Carnstock Iron Works;
(b) to the Big Ben Colliery;
(c) to the Perserverence Colliery.

Of these the Big Ben line is not more than a quarter of a mile long, and ends at a dead wall of coal waiting removal from the mouth of the mine. Nothing had been seen or heard there of any special. The Carnstock Iron Works line was blocked all day upon the 3rd of June by sixteen truckloads of hematite. It is a single line, and nothing could have passed. As to the Perserverence line, it is a large double line, which does a considerable traffic, for the output of the mine is very large. On the 3rd of June this traffic proceeded as usual; hundreds of men, including a gang of railway platelayers, were working along the two miles and a quarter which constitute the total length of the line, and it is inconceivable that an unexpected train could have come down there without attracting universal attention. It may be remarked in conclusion that this branch line is nearer to St. Helens than the point at which the engine-driver was discovered, so that we have every reason to believe that the train was past that point before misfortune overtook her.

"As to John Slater, there is no clue to be gathered from his appearance or injuries. We can only say that, as far as we can see, he met his end by falling off his engine, though why he fell, or what became of the engine after his fall, is a question upon which I do not feel qualified to offer an opinion." In conclusion, the inspector offered his resignation to the Board, being much nettled by an accusation of incompetence in the London papers.

A month elapsed, during which both the police and the company prosecuted their inquiries without the slightest success. A reward was offered and a pardon promised in case of crime, but they were both unclaimed. Every day the public opened their papers with the conviction that so grotesque a mystery would at last be solved, but week after week passed by, and a solution remained as far off as ever. In broad daylight, upon a June afternoon in the most thickly inhabited portion of England, a train with its occupants had disappeared as completely as if some master of subtle chemistry had volatilized it into gas. Indeed, among the various conjectures which were put forward in the public Press there were some which seriously asserted that supernatural, or, at least, preternatural, agencies had been at work, and that the deformed Monsieur Caratal was probably a person who was better known under a less polite name. Others fixed upon his swarthy companion as being the author of the mischief, but what it was exactly which he had done could never be clearly formulated in words.

Amongst the many suggestions put forward by various newspapers or private individuals, there were one or two which were feasible enough to attract the attention of the public. One which appeared in the *Times*, over the signature of an amateur reasoner of some celebrity at that date, attempted to deal with the matter in a critical and semi-scientific manner. An extract must suffice, although the curious can see the whole letter in the issue of the 3rd of July.

"It is one of the elementary principals of practical reasoning," he remarked, "that when the impossible has been eliminated the residuum, *however improbable*, must contain the truth. It is certain that the train left Kenyon Junction. It is certain that it did not reach Barton Moss. It is in the highest degree unlikely, but still possible, that it may have taken one of the seven available side lines. It is obviously impossible for a train to run where there are no rails, and, therefore, we may reduce our improbables to the three open lines, namely, the Carnstock Iron Works, the Big Ben, and the Perserverence. Is there a secret society of colliers, an English *camorra*, which is capable of destroying both train and passengers? It is improbable, but it is not impossible. I confess that I am unable to suggest any other solution. I should certainly advise the company to direct all their energies towards the observation of those three lines, and of the workmen at the end of them. A careful supervision of the pawnbrokers' shops of the district might possibly bring some suggestive facts to light."

The suggestion coming from a recognized authority upon such matters created considerable interest, and a fierce opposition from those who considered such a statement to be a preposterous libel upon an honest and deserving set of men. The only answer to this criticism was a challenge to the objectors to lay any more feasible explanation before the public. In reply to this two others were forthcoming (*Times*, July 7th and 9th). The first suggested that the train might have run off the metals and be lying submerged in the Lancashire and Staffordshire Canal, which runs parallel to the railway for some hundreds of yards. This suggestion was thrown out of court by the published depth of the canal, which was entirely insufficient to conceal so large an object. The second correspondent wrote calling attention to the bag which appeared to be the sole luggage which the travellers had brought with them, and suggesting that some novel explosive of immense and pulverizing power might have been concealed in it. The obvious absurdity, however, of supposing that the whole train might be blown to dust while the metals remained uninjured reduced any such explanation to a farce. The investigation had drifted into this hopeless position when a new and most unexpected incident occurred, which raised hopes never destined to be fulfilled.

This was nothing less than the receipt by Mrs. McPherson of a letter from her husband, James McPherson, who had been the guard of the missing train. The letter, which was dated July 5th, 1890, was dispatched from New York, and came to hand upon July 14th. Some doubts were expressed as to its genuine character, but Mrs. McPherson was positive as to the writing, and the fact that it contained a remittance of a hundred dollars in five-dollar notes was enough in itself to discount the idea of a hoax. No address was given in the letter, which ran in this way:

"My Dear Wife,

"I have been thinking a great deal, and I find it very hard to give you up. The same with Lizzie. I try to fight against it, but it will always come back to me. I send you some money which will change into twenty English pounds. This should be enough to bring both Lizzie and you across the Atlantic, and you will find the Hamburg boats which stop at Southampton very good boats, and cheaper than Liverpool. If you could come here and stop at the Johnson House I would try and send word how to meet, but things are very difficult with me at present, and I am not very happy, finding it hard to give you both up. So no more at present from your loving husband,

"James McPherson."

For a time it was confidently anticipated that this letter would lead to the clearing up of the whole matter, the more so as it was ascertained that a passenger who bore a close resemblance to the missing guard had travelled from Southampton under the name of Summers in the Hamburg and New York liner *Vistula*, which started upon the 7th of June. Mrs. McPherson and her sister Lizzie Dolton went across to New York as directed, and stayed for three weeks at the Johnston House, without hearing anything from the missing man. It is probable that some injudicious comments in the Press may have warned him that the police were using them as a bait. However this may be, it is certain that he neither wrote nor came, and the women were eventually compelled to return to Liverpool.

And so the matter stood, and has continued to stand up to the present year of 1898. Incredible as it may seem, nothing has transpired during these eight years which has shed the least light upon the extraordinary disappearance of the special train which contained Monsieur Caratal and his companion. Careful inquiries into the antecedents of the two travellers have only established the fact that Monsieur Caratal was well known as a financier and political agent in Central America, and that during his voyage to Europe he had betrayed extraordinary anxiety to reach Paris. His companion, whose name was entered upon the passenger lists as Eduardo Gomez, was a man whose record was a violent one, and whose reputation was that of a bravo and a bully. There was evidence to show, however, that he was honestly devoted to the interests of Monsieur Caratal, and that the latter, being a man of puny physique, employed the other as a guard and protector. It may be added that no information came from Paris as to what the objects of Monsieur Caratal's hurried journey may have been. This comprises all the facts of the case up to the publication in the Marseilles papers of the recent confession of Herbert de Lernac, now under sentence of death for the murder of a merchant named Bonvalot. This statement may be literally translated as follows:

"It is not out of mere pride or boasting that I give this information, for, if that were my object, I could tell a dozen actions of mine which are quite as splendid; but I do it in order that certain gentlemen in Paris may understand that I, who am able here to tell about the fate of Monsieur Caratal, can also tell in whose interests and at whose request the deed was done, unless the reprieve which I am awaiting comes to me very quickly. Take warning, messieurs, before it is too late! You know Herbert de Lernac, and you are aware that his deeds are as ready as his words. Hasten then, or you are lost!

"At present, I shall mention no names—if you only heard the names, what would you not think!—but I shall merely tell you how cleverly I did it. I was true to my employers then, and no doubt they will be true to me now. I hope so, and until I am convinced that they have betrayed me, these names, which would convulse Europe, shall not be divulged. But on that day . . . well, I say no more!

"In a word, then, there was a famous trial in Paris, in the year 1890, in connection with a monstrous scandal in politics and finance. How monstrous that scandal was can never be known save by such confidential agents as myself. The honour and careers of many of the chief men in France were at stake. You have seen a group of nine-pins standing, all so rigid, and prim, and unbending. Then there comes the ball from far away and pop, pop, pop—there are nine pins on the floor. Well, imagine some of the greatest men in France as these nine-pins, and then this Monsieur Caratal was the ball which could be seen coming from far away. If he arrived, then it was pop, pop, pop for all of them. It was determined that he should not arrive.

"I do not accuse them all of being conscious of what was to happen. There were, as I have said, great financial as well as political interests at stake, and a syndicate was formed to manage the business. Some subscribed to the syndicate who hardly understood what were its objects. But others understood very well, and they can rely upon it that I have not forgotten their names. They had ample warning that Monsieur Caratal was coming long before he left South America, and they knew that the evidence which he held would certainly mean ruin to all of them. The syndicate had the command of an unlimited amount of money—absolutely unlimited, you understand. They looked round for an agent who was capable of wielding this gigantic power. The man chosen must be inventive, resolute, adaptive—a man in a million. They chose Herbert de Lernac, and I admit that they were right.

"My duties were to choose my subordinates, to use freely the power which money gives, and to make certain that Monsieur Caratal should never arrive in Paris. With characteristic energy I set about my commission within an hour of receiving my instructions, and the steps which I took were the very best for the purposes which could possibly be devised.

"A man whom I could trust was dispatched instantly to South America to travel home with Monsieur Caratal. Had he arrived in time the ship would never have reached Liverpool; but, alas, it had already started before my agent could reach it. I fitted out a small armed brig to intercept it, but again I was unfortunate. Like all great organizers, I was, however, prepared for failure, and had a series of alternatives prepared, one or the other of which must succeed. You must not underrate the difficulties of my undertaking, or imagine that a mere commonplace assassination would meet the case. We must destroy not only Monsieur Caratal, but Monsieur Caratal's documents, and Monsieur Caratal's companions also, if we had reason to believe that he had communicated his secrets to them. And you must remember that they were on the alert, and keenly suspicious of any such attempt. It was a task which was in every way worthy of me, for I am always most masterful where another would be appalled.

"I was ready for Monsieur Caratal's reception in Liverpool, and I was the more eager because I had reason to believe that he had made arrangements by which he would have a considerable guard from the moment that he arrived in London. Anything which was to be done must be done between the moment of his setting foot upon the Liverpool quay and that of his arrival at the London and West Coast terminus in London. We prepared six plans, each more elaborate than the last; which plan would be used would depend upon his own movements. Do what he would, we were ready for him. If he had stayed in Liverpool, we were ready. If he took an ordinary train, an express, or a special, all was ready. Everything had been foreseen and provided for.

"You may imagine that I could not do all this myself. What could I know of the English railway lines? But money can procure willing agents all the world over, and I soon had one of the acutest brains in England to assist me. I will mention no names, but it would be unjust to claim all the credit for myself. My English ally was worthy of such an alliance. He knew the London and West Coast line thoroughly, and he had the command of a band of workers who were trustworthy and intelligent. The idea was his, and my own judgment was only required in the details. We bought over several officials, amongst whom the most important was James McPherson, whom we had ascertained to be the guard most likely to be employed upon a special train. Smith, the stoker, was also in our employ. John Slater, the engine-driver, had been approached, but had been found to be obstinate and dangerous, so we desisted. We had no certainty that Monsieur Caratal would take a special, but we thought it very probable, for it was of the utmost importance to him that he should reach Paris without delay. It was for this contingency, therefore, that we made special preparations—preparations which were complete down to the last detail long before his steamer had sighted the shores of England. You will be amused to learn that there was one of my agents in the pilot-boat which brought that steamer to its moorings.

"The moment that Caratal arrived in Liverpool we knew that he suspected danger and was on his guard. He had brought with him as an escort a dangerous fellow, named Gomez, a man who carried weapons, and was prepared to use them. This fellow carried Caratal's confidential papers for him, and was ready to protect either them or his master. The probability was that Caratal had taken him into his counsels, and that to remove Caratal without removing Gomez would be a mere waste of energy. It was necessary that they should be involved in a common fate, and our plans to that end were much facilitated by their request for a special train. On that special train you will understand that two out of the three servants of the company were really in our employ, at a price which would make them independent for a lifetime. I do not go so far as to say that the English are more honest than any other nation, but I have found them more expensive to buy.

"I have already spoken of my English agent—who is a man with a considerable future before him, unless some complaint of the throat carries him off before his time. He had charge of all arrangements at Liverpool, whilst I was stationed at the inn at Kenyon, where I awaited a cipher signal to act. When the special was arranged for, my agent instantly telegraphed to me and warned me how soon I should have everything ready. He himself under the name of Horace Moore applied immediately for a special also, in the hope that he would be sent down with Monsieur Caratal, which might under certain circumstances have been helpful to us. If, for example, our great *coup* had failed, it would then have become the duty of my agent to have shot them both and destroyed their papers. Caratal was on his guard, however, and refused to admit any other traveller. My agent then left the station, returned by another entrance, entered the guard's van on the side farthest from the platform, and travelled down with McPherson, the guard.

"In the meantime you will be interested to know what my own movements were. Everything had been prepared for days before, and only the finishing touches were needed. The side line which we had chosen had once joined the main line, but it had been disconnected. We had only to replace a few rails to connect it once more. These rails had been laid down as far as could be done without danger of attracting attention, and now it was merely a case of completing a juncture with the line, and arranging the points as they had been before. The sleepers had never been removed, and the rails, fish-plates, and rivets were all ready, for we had taken them from a siding on the abandoned portion of the line. With my small but competent band of workers, we had everything ready long before the special arrived. When it did arrive, it ran off upon the small side line so easily that the jolting of the points appears to have been entirely unnoticed by the two travellers.

"Our plan had been that Smith the stoker should chloroform John Slater the driver, and so that he should vanish with the others. In this respect, and in this respect only, our plans miscarried—I except the criminal folly of McPherson in writing home to his wife. Our stoker did his business so clumsily that Slater in his struggles fell off the engine, and though fortune was with us so far that he broke his neck in the fall, still he remained as a blot upon which would otherwise have been one of those complete masterpieces which are only to be contemplated in silent admiration. The criminal expert will find in John Slater the one flaw in all our admirable combinations. A man who has had as many triumphs as I can afford to be frank, and I therefore lay my finger upon John Slater, and I proclaim him to be a flaw.

"But now I have got our special train upon the small line two kilometres, or rather more than one mile in length, which leads, or rather used to lead, to the abandoned Heartsease mine, once one of the largest coal mines in England. You will ask how it is that no one saw the train upon this unused line. I answer that along its entire length it runs through a deep cutting, and that, unless someone had been on the edge of that cutting, he could not have seen it. There *was* someone on the edge of that cutting. I was there. And now I will tell you what I saw.

"My assistant had remained at the points in order that he might superintend the switching off of the train. He had four armed men with him, so that if the train ran off the line—we thought it probable, because the points were very rusty—we might still have resources to fall back upon. Having once seen it safely on the side line, he handed over the responsibility to me. I was waiting at a point which overlooks the mouth of the mine, and I was also armed, as were my two companions. Come what might, you see, I was always ready.

"The moment that the train was fairly on the side line, Smith, the stoker, slowed-down the engine, and then, having turned it on to the fullest speed again, he and McPherson, with my English lieutenant, sprang off before it was too late. It may be that it was this slowing-down which first attracted the attention of the travellers, but the train was running at full speed again before their heads appeared at the open window. It makes me smile to think how bewildered they must have been. Picture to yourself your own feelings if, on looking out of your luxurious carriage, you suddenly perceived that the lines upon which you ran were rusted and corroded, red and yellow with disuse and decay! What a catch must have come in their breath as in a second it flashed upon them that it was not Manchester, but Death which was waiting for them at the end of that sinister line. But the train was running with frantic speed, rolling and rocking over the rotten line, while the wheels made a frightful screaming sound upon the rusted surface. I was close to them, and could see their faces. Caratal was praying. I think—there was something like a rosary dangling out of his hand. The other roared like a bull who smells the blood of the slaughter-house. He saw us standing on the bank, and he beckoned to us like a madman. Then he tore at his wrist and threw his despatch-box out of the window in our direction. Of course, his meaning was obvious. Here was the evidence, and they would promise to be silent if their lives were spared. It would have been very agreeable if we could have done so, but business is business. Besides, the train was now as much beyond our control as theirs.

"He ceased howling when the train rattled round the curve and they saw the black mouth of the mine yawning before them. We had removed the boards which had covered it, and we had cleared the square entrance. The rails had formerly run very close to the shaft for the convenience of loading the coal, and we had only to add two or three lengths of rail in order to lead to the very brink of the shaft. In fact, as the lengths would not quite fit, our line projected about three feet over the edge. We saw the two heads at the window; Caratal below, Gomez above; but they had both been struck silent by what they saw. And yet they could not withdraw their heads. The sight seemed to have paralyzed them.

"I had wondered how the train running at a great speed would take the pit into which I had guided it, and I was much interested in watching it. One of my colleagues thought that it would actually jump it, and indeed it was not very far from doing so. Fortunately, however, it fell short, and the buffers of the engine struck the other lip of the shaft with a tremendous crash. The funnel flew off into the air. The tender, carriages, and van were all smashed into one jumble, which, with the remains of the engine, choked for a minute or so the mouth of the pit. Then something gave way in the middle, and the whole mass of green iron, smoking coals, brass fittings, wheels, woodwork, and cushions all crumbled together and crashed down into the mine. We heard the rattle, rattle, rattle, as the *débris* struck against the walls, and then quite a long time afterwards there came a deep roar as the remains of the train struck the bottom. The boiler may have burst, for a sharp crash came after the roar, and then a dense cloud of steam and smoke swirled up out of the black depths, falling in a spray as thick as rain all round us. Then the vapour shredded off into thin wisps, which floated away in the summer sunshine, and all was quiet again in the Heartsease mine.

"And now, having carried out our plans so successfully, it only remained to leave no trace behind us. Our little band of workers at the other end had already ripped up the rails and disconnected the side line, replacing everything as it had been before. The funnel and other fragments were thrown in, the shaft was planked over as it used to be, and the lines which led to it were torn up and taken away. Then, without flurry, but without delay, we all made our way out of the country, most of us to Paris, my English colleague to Manchester, and McPherson to Southampton, whence he emigrated to America. Let the English papers of that date tell how thoroughly we had thrown the cleverest of their detectives off our track.

"You will remember that Gomez threw his bag of papers out of the window, and I need not say that I secured that bag and brought them to my employers. It may interest my employers now, however, to learn that out of that bag I took one or two little papers as a souvenir of the occasion. I have no wish to publish these papers; but, still, it is every man for himself in this world, and what else can I do if my friends will not come to my aid when I want them? Messieurs, you may believe that Herbert de Lernac is quite as formidable when he is against you as when he is with you, and that he is not a man to go to the guillotine until he has seen that every one of you is *en route* for New Caledonia. For your own sake, if not for mine, make haste, Monsieur de——, and General——, and Baron—— (you can fill up the blanks for yourselves as you read this). I promise you that in the next edition there will be no blanks to fill.

"P.S.—As I look over my statement there is only one omission which I can see. It concerns the unfortunate man McPherson, who was foolish enough to write to his wife and to make an appointment with her in New York. It can be imagined that when interests like ours were at stake, we could not leave them to the chance of whether a man in that class of life would or would not give away his secrets to a woman. Having once broken his oath by writing to his wife, we could not trust him any more. We took steps therefore to insure that he should not see his wife. I have sometimes thought that it would be a kindness to write to her and to assure her that there is no impediment to her marrying again."

OFF THE FACE OF THE EARTH

By Clayton Rawson (1906-1971)

Clayton Rawson was an illustrator, a magazine editor, a professional magician, and the creator of the magician-detective, The Great Merlini. In Death from a Top Hat *(1938), one of the great first novels, Rawson paid a tribute to John Dickson Carr's analysis of locked-room methods. Soon Carr and Rawson, along with Anthony Boucher and Frederic Dannay (half of Ellery Queen), began discussing the care and feeding of miracle crimes, at first by correspondence and later in all-night sessions at the Westchester homes of Carr and Dannay. Early in their acquaintance, Carr set Rawson a challenge: "A man walks into a telephone booth to make an ordinary call, and vanishes. The booth is not prepared in any way. Work that one out." Work it out Rawson did in brilliant fashion in "Off the Face of the Earth."*

THE lettering in neat gilt script on the door read: *Miracles For Sale,* and beneath it was the familiar rabbit-from-a-hat trademark. Inside, behind the glass showcase counter, in which was displayed as unlikely an assortment of objects as could be got together in one spot, stood The Great Merlini.

He was wrapping up half a dozen billiard balls, several bouquets of feather flowers, a dove pan, a Talking Skull, and a dozen decks of cards for a customer who snapped his fingers and nonchalantly produced the needed number of five-dollar bills from thin air. Merlini rang up the sale, took half a carrot from the cash drawer, and gave it to the large white rabbit who watched proceedings with a pink skeptical eye from the top of a nearby escape trunk. Then he turned to me.

"Clairvoyance, mind-reading, extrasensory perception," he said. "We stock only the best grade. And it tells me that you came to pick up the two Annie Oakleys I promised to get you for the new hit musical. I have them right here."

But his occult powers slipped a bit. He looked in all his coat pockets one after another, found an egg, a three-foot length of rope, several brightly-colored silk handkerchiefs, and a crumpled telegram reading: NEED INVISIBLE MAN AT ONCE. SHIP UNIONTOWN BY MONDAY.—NEMO THE ENIGMA. Then he gave a surprised blink and scowled darkly at a sealed envelope that he had fished out of his inside breast pocket.

"That," I commented a bit sarcastically," doesn't look like a pair of theater tickets."

He shook his head sadly. "No. It's a letter my wife asked me to mail a week ago.".

I took it from him. "There's a mail chute by the elevators about fifteen feet outside your door. I'm no magician, but I can remember to put this in it on my way out." I indicated the telegram that lay on the counter. "Since when have you stocked a supply of invisible men? That I would like to see."

Merlini frowned at the framed slogan: *Nothing Is Impossible* which hung above the cash register. "You want real miracles, don't you? We guarantee that our invisible man can't be seen. But if you'd like to see how impossible it is to see him, step right this way."

In the back, beyond his office, there is a larger room that serves as workshop, shipping department and, of occasion, as a theater. I stood there a moment later and watched Merlini step into an upright coffin-shaped box in the center of the small stage. He faced me, smiled, and snapped his fingers. Two copper electrodes in the side walls of the cabinet spat flame, and a fat, green, electric spark jumped the gap just above his head, hissing and writhing. He lifted his arms; the angry stream of energy bent, split in two, fastened on his fingertips, and then disappeared as he grasped the gleaming spherical electrodes, one with each hand.

For a moment nothing happened; then, slowly, his body began to fade into transparency as the cabinet's back wall became increasingly visible through it. Clothes and flesh melted until only the bony skeletal structure remained. Suddenly, the jawbone moved and its grinning white teeth clicked as Merlini's voice said:

"You must try this, Ross. On a hot day like today, it's most comfortable."

As it spoke, the skeleton also wavered and grew dim. A moment later it was gone and the cabinet was, or seemed to be, empty. If Merlini still stood there, he was certainly invisible.

"Okay, Gypsy Rose Lee," I said. "I have now seen the last word in strip-tease performances." Behind me I heard the office door open and I looked over my shoulder to see Inspector Gavigan giving me a fishy stare. "You'd better get dressed again," I added. "We have company."

The Inspector looked around the room and at the empty stage, then at me again, cautiously this time. "If you said what I think you did—"

He stopped abruptly as Merlini's voice, issuing from nowhere, chuckled and said, "Don't jump to conclusions, Inspector. Appearances are deceptive. It's not an indecent performance, nor has Ross gone off his rocker and started talking to himself. I'm right here. On the stage."

Gavigan looked and saw the skeleton shape taking form within the cabinet. He closed his eyes, shook his head, then looked again. That didn't help. The grisly spectre was still there and twice as substantial. Then, wraithlike, Merlini's body began to form around it and, finally, grew opaque and solid. The magician grinned broadly, took his hands from the electrodes, and bowed as the spitting, green discharge of energy crackled once more above him. Then the stage curtains closed.

"You should be glad that's only an illusion," I told Gavigan. "If it were the McCoy and the underworld ever found out how it was done, you'd face an unparalleled crime wave and you'd never solve a single case."

"It's the Pepper's Ghost illusion brought up to date," Merlini said as he stepped out between the curtains and came toward us. "I've got more orders than I can fill. It's a sure-fire carnival draw." He frowned at Gavigan. "But *you* don't look very entertained."

"I'm not," the Inspector answered gloomily. "Vanishing into thin air may amuse some people. Not me. Especially when it really happens. Off stage in broad daylight. In Central Park."

"Oh," Merlini said. "I see. So that's what's eating you. Helen Hope, the chorus girl who went for a walk last week and never came back. She's still missing then, and there are still no clues?"

Gavigan nodded. "It's the Dorothy Arnold case all over again. Except for one thing we haven't let the newspapers know about—Bela Zyyzk."

"Bela what?" I asked.

Gavigan spelled it.

"Impossible," I said. "He must be a typographical error. A close relative of Etoain Shrdlu."

The Inspector wasn't amused. "Relatives," he growled. "I wish I could find some. He not only claims he doesn't have any—he swears he never has had any! And so far we haven't been able to prove different."

"Where does he come from?" Merlini asked. "Or won't he say?"

"Oh, he talks all right," Gavigan said disgustedly. "Too much. And none of it makes any sense. He says he's a momentary visitor to this planet—from the dark cloud of Antares. I've seen some high, wide, and fancy screwballs in my time, but this one takes the cake—candles and all."

"Helen Hope," Merlini said, "vanishes off the face of the

earth. And Zyyzk does just the opposite. This gets interesting. What else does he have to do with her disappearance?"

"Plenty," Gavigan replied. "A week ago Tuesday night she
went to a Park Avenue party at Mrs. James Dewitt-Smith's.
She's another candidate for Bellevue. Collects Tibetan statu-
ary, medieval relics, and crackpots like Zyyzk. He was there
that night—reading minds."

"A visitor from outer space," Merlini said, "and a mind-
reader to boot. I won't be happy until I've had a talk with that
gentleman."

"I have talked with him," the Inspector growled. "And I've
had indigestion ever since. He does something worse than
read minds. He makes predictions." Gavigan scowled at
Merlini. "I thought fortune tellers always kept their customers happy by predicting good luck?"

Merlini nodded. "That's usually standard operating pro-
cedure. Zyyzk does something else?"

"He certainly does. He's full of doom and disaster. A dozen
witnesses testify that he told Helen Hope she'd vanish off the
face of the earth. And three days later that's exactly what she
does do."

"I can see," Merlini said, "why you view him with suspicion. So you pulled him in for questioning and got a lot of
answers that weren't very helpful?"

"Helpful!" Gavigan jerked several typewritten pages from
his pocket and shook them angrily. "Listen to this. He's
asked: "What's your age?" and we get: 'According to which
time—solar, sidereal, galactic, or universal?' Murphy of
Missing Persons, who was questioning him, says: 'Any kind.
Just tell us how old you are.' And Zyyzk replies: 'I can't
answer that. The question, in that form, has no meaning,'"
The Inspector threw the papers down disgustedly.

Merlini picked them up, riffled through them, then read
some of the transcript aloud. "Question: How did you know
that Miss Hope would disappear? Answer: Do you understand the basic theory of the fifth law of interdimensional
reaction? Murphy: Huh? Zyyzk: Explanations are useless.
You obviously have no conception of what I am talking
about."

"He was right about that," Gavigan muttered. "Nobody
does."

Merlini continued. "Question: Where is Miss Hope now? Answer: Beyond recall. She was summoned by the Lords of the Outer Darkness." Merlini looked up from the papers. "After that, I suppose, you sent him over to Bellevue?"

The Inspector nodded. "They had him under observation a week. And they turned in a report full of eight-syllable jawbreakers all meaning he's crazy as a bedbug—but harmless. I don't believe it. Anybody who predicts in a loud voice that someone will disappear into thin air at twenty minutes after four on a Tuesday afternoon, just before it actually happens, knows plenty about it!"

Merlini is a hard man to surprise, but even he blinked at that. "Do you mean to say that he foretold the exact time, too?"

"Right on the nose," Gavigan answered. "The doorman of her apartment house saw her walk across the street and into Central Park at four-eighteen. We haven't been able to find anyone who has seen her since. And don't tell me his prediction was a long shot that paid off."

"I won't," Merlini agreed. "Whatever it is, it's not coincidence. Where's Zyyzk now? Could you hold him after that psychiatric report?"

"The D.A.," Gavigan replied, "took him into General Sessions before Judge Keeler and asked that he be held as a material witness." The Inspector looked unhappier than ever. "It would have to be Keeler."

"What did he do?" I asked. "Deny the request?"

"No. He granted it. That's when Zyyzk made his second prediction. Just as they start to take him out and throw him back in the can, he makes some funny motions with his hands and announces, in that confident manner he's got, that the Outer Darkness is going to swallow Judge Keeler up, too!"

"And what," Merlini wanted to know, "is wrong with that? Knowing how you've always felt about Francis X. Keeler, I should think that prospect would please you."

Gavigan exploded. "Look, blast it! I have wished dozens of times that Judge Keeler would vanish into thin air, but that's exactly what I don't want to happen right now. We've known at headquarters that he's been taking fix money from the Castelli mob ever since the day he was appointed to the

bench. But we couldn't do a thing. Politically he was dyna-
mite. One move in his direction and there'd be a new Commissioner the next morning, with demotions all down the
line. But three weeks ago the Big Guy and Keeler had a scrap,
and we get a tip straight from the feed box that Keeler is fair
game. So we start working overtime collecting the evidence
that will send him up the river for what I hope is a ninety-
nine year stretch. We've been afraid he might tumble and try
to pull another 'Judge Crater.' And now, just when we're
almost, but not quite, ready to nail him and make it stick,
this has to happen."

"Your friend, Zyyzk," Merlini said, "becomes more interesting by the minute. Keeler is being tailed, of course?"

"Twenty-four hours a day, ever since we got the word that
there'd be no kick-back." The phone on Merlini's desk rang
as Gavigan was speaking. "I get hourly reports on his movements. Chances are that's for me now."

It was. In the office, we both watched him as he took the
call. He listened a moment, then said, "Okay. Double the
number of men on him immediately. And report back every
fifteen minutes. If he shows any sign of going anywhere near
a railroad station or airport, notify me at once."

Gavigan hung up and turned to us. "Keeler made a stop
at the First National and spent fifteen minutes in the
safety-deposit vaults. He's carrying a suitcase, and you can
have one guess as to what's in it now. This looks like the
payoff."

"I take it," Merlini said, "that, this time, the Zyyzk forecast
did not include the exact hour and minute when the Outer
Darkness would swallow up the Judge?"

"Yeah. He sidestepped that. All he'll say is that it'll happen
before the week is out."

"And today," Merlini said, "is Friday. Tell me this. The
Judge seems to have good reasons for wanting to disappear
which Zyyzk may or may not know about. Did Miss Hope also
have reasons?"

"She had one," Gavigan replied. "But I don't see how Zyyzk
could have known it. We can't find a thing that shows he ever
set eyes on her before the night of that party. And her reason
is one that few people knew about." The phone rang again

and Gavigan reached for it. "Helen Hope is the girl friend Judge Keeler visits the nights he doesn't go home to his wife!"

Merlini and I both tried to assimilate that and take in what Gavigan was telling the telephone at the same time. "Okay, I'm coming. And grab him the minute he tries to go through a gate." He slammed the receiver down and started for the door.

"Keeler," he said over his shoulders, "is in Grand Central. There's room in my car if you want to come."

He didn't need to issue that invitation twice. On the way down in the elevator Merlini made one not very helpful comment.

"You know," he said thoughtfully, "if the Judge does have a reservation on the extra-terrestial express—destination: the Outer Darkness—we don't know what gate that train leaves from."

We found out soon enough. The Judge stepped through it just two minutes before we hurried into the station and found Lieutenant Malloy exhibiting all the symptoms of having been hit over the head with a sledge hammer. He was bewildered and dazed, and had difficulty talking coherently.

Sergeant Hicks, a beefy, unimaginative, elderly detective who had also seen the thing happen looked equally groggy.

Usually, Malloy's reports were as dispassionate, precise, and factual as a logarithmic table. But not today. His first paragraph bore a much closer resemblance to a first-person account of a dope-addict's dream.

"Malloy," Gavigan broke in icily. "Are you tight?"

The Lieutenant shook his head sadly. "No, but the minute I go off duty, I'm going to get so plas—"

Gavigan cut in again. "Are all the exits to this place covered?"

Hicks replied, "If they aren't, somebody is sure going to catch it."

Gavigan turned to the detective who had accompanied us in the inspector's car. "Make the rounds and double-check that, Brady. And tell headquarters to get more men over here fast."

"They're on the way now," Hicks said. "I phoned right after it happened. First thing I did."

Gavigan turned to Malloy. "All right. Take it easy. One thing at a time—and in order."

"It don't make sense that way either," Malloy said hopelessly. "Keeler took a cab from the bank and came straight here. Hicks and I were right on his tail. He comes down to the lower level and goes into the Oyster Bar and orders a double brandy. While he's working on that, Hicks phones in for reinforcements with orders to cover every exit. They had time to get here, too; Keeler had a second brandy. Then, when he starts to come out, I move out to the center of the station floor by the information booth so I'm ahead of him and all set to make the pinch no matter which gate he heads for. Hicks stands pat, ready to tail him if he heads upstairs again.

"At first, that's where I think he's going because he starts up the ramp. But he stops here by this line of phone booths, looks in a directory and then goes into a booth halfway down the line. And as soon as he closes the door, Hicks moves up and goes into the next booth to the left of Keeler's." Malloy pointed. "The one with the Out-of-Order sign on it."

Gavigan turned to the Sergeant. "All right. You take it."

Hicks scowled at the phone booth as he spoke. " The door was closed and somebody had written 'Out of Order' on a card and stuck it in the edge of the glass. I lifted the card so nobody'd wonder why I was trying to use a dead phone, went in, closed the door and tried to get a load of what the Judge was saying. But it's no good. He was talking, but so low I couldn't get it. I came out again, stuck the card back in the door and walked back toward the Oyster Bar so I'd be set to follow him either way when he came out. And I took a gander into the Judge's booth as I went past. He was talking with his mouth up close to the phone."

"And then," Malloy continued, "we wait. And we wait. He went into that booth at five ten. At five twenty I get itchy feet. I begin to think maybe he's passed out or died of suffocation or something. Nobody in his right mind stays in a phone booth for ten minutes when the temperature is ninety like today. So I start to move in just as Hicks gets the same idea. He's closer than I am, so I stay put.

"Hicks stops just in front of the booth and lights a cigarette, which gives him a chance to take another look inside. Then I figure I must be right about the Judge having passed out. I see the match Hicks is holding drop, still lighted, and he turns quick and plasters his face against the glass. I don't wait. I'm already on my way when he turns and motions for me."

Malloy hesitated briefly. Then, slowly and very precisely, he let us have it. "I don't care if the Commissioner himself has me up on the carpet, one thing I'm sure of—*I hadn't taken my eyes off that phone booth for one single split second since the Judge walked into it.*"

"And neither," Hicks said with equal emphasis, "did I. Not for one single second."

"I did some fancy open-field running through the commuters," Malloy went on, "skidded to a stop behind Hicks and looked over his shoulder."

Gavigan stepped forward to the closed door of the booth and looked in.

"And what you see," Malloy finished, "is just what I saw. You can ship me down to Bellevue for observation, too. It's impossible. It doesn't make sense. I don't believe it. But that's exactly what happened."

For a moment Gavigan didn't move. Then, slowly, he pulled the door open.

The booth was empty.

The phone receiver dangled off the hook, and on the floor there was a pair of horn-rimmed spectacles, one lens smashed.

"Keeler's glasses," Hicks said. "He went into that booth and I had my eyes on it every second. He never came out. And he's not in it."

"And that," Malloy added in a tone of utter dejection, "isn't the half of it. I stepped inside, picked up the phone receiver Keeler had been using, and said, 'Hello' into the mouthpiece. There was a chance the party he'd been talking to might still be on the other end." Malloy came to a full stop.

"Well?" Gavigan prodded him. "Let's have it. Somebody answered?"

"Yes. Somebody said: *'This is the end of the trail, Lieutenant.'* Then—hung up."

456 DEATH LOCKED IN

"You didn't recognize the voice?"

"Yeah, I recognized it. That's the trouble. It was—*Judge Keeler!*"

Silence.

Then, quietly, Merlini asked, "You are quite certain that it was his voice, Malloy?"

The Lieutenant exploded. "I'm not sure of anything any more. But if you've ever heard Keeler—he sounds like a bullfrog with a cold—you'd know it couldn't be anyone else."

Gavigan's voice, or rather, a hollow imitation of it, cut in. "Merlini. Either Malloy and Hicks have both gone completely off their chumps or this is the one phone booth in the world that has two exits. The back wall is sheet metal backed by solid marble, but if there's a loose panel in one of the side walls, Keeler could have moved over into the empty booth that is supposed to be out of order . . ."   .

"Is supposed to be . . ." Malloy repeated. "So, that's it! The sign's a phony. That phone isn't on the blink, and his voice—" Malloy took two swift steps into the booth. He lifted the receiver, dropped a nickel, and waited for the dial tone. He scowled. He jiggled the receiver. He repeated the whole operation.

This specimen of Mr. Bell's invention was definitely not working.

A moment or two later Merlini reported another flaw in the Inspector's theory. "There are," he stated after a quick but thorough inspection of both booths, "no sliding panels, hinged panels, removable sections, trapdoors, or any other form of secret exit. The sidewalls are single sheets of metal, thin but intact. The back wall is even more solid. There is one exit and one only—the door through which our vanishing man entered."

"He didn't come out," Sergeant Hicks insisted again, sounding like a cracked phonograph record endlessly repeating itself. "I was watching that door every single second. Even if he turned himself into an invisible man like in a movie I saw once, he'd still have had to open the door. And the door didn't budge. I was watching it every single—"

"And that," Merlini said thoughtfully, "leaves us with an invisible man who can also walk through closed doors. In short—a ghost. Which brings up another point. Have any of you noticed that there are a few spots of something on those smashed glasses that look very much like—blood?"

Malloy growled. "Yeah, but don't make any cracks about there being another guy in that booth who sapped Keeler— that'd mean *two* invisible men . . ."

"If there can be one invisible man," Merlini pointed out, "then there can be two."

Gavigan said, "Merlini, that vanishing gadget you were demonstrating when I arrived . . . It's just about the size and shape of this phone booth. I want to know—"

The magician shook his head. "Sorry, Inspector. That method wouldn't work here under these conditions. It's not the same trick. Keeler's miracle, in some respects, is even better. He should have been a magician; he's been wasting his time on the bench. Or has he? I wonder how much cash he carried into limbo with him in that suitcase?" He paused, then added, "More than enough, probably, to serve as a motive for murder."

And there, on that ominous note, the investigation stuck. It was as dead an end as I ever saw. And it got deader by the minute. Brady, returning a few minutes later, reported that all station exits had been covered by the time Keeler left the Oyster Bar and that none of the detectives had seen hide nor hair of him since.

"Those men stay there until further notice," Gavigan ordered. "Get more men—as many as you need—and start searching this place. I want every last inch of it covered. And every phone booth, too. If it was Keeler's voice Malloy heard, then he was in one of them, and—"

"You know, Inspector," Merlini interrupted, "this case not only takes the cake but the marbles, all the blue ribbons, and a truck load of loving cups too. That is another impossibility."

"What is?"

"The voice on the telephone. Look at it. If Keeler left the receiver in this booth off as Malloy and Hicks found it, vanished, then reappeared in another booth and tried to call this number, he'd get a busy signal. He couldn't have made a connection. And if he left the receiver on the hook, he could have called this number, but someone would have had to be here to lift the receiver and leave it off as it was found. It keeps adding up to two invisible men no matter how you look at it."

"I wish," Malloy said acidly, "that you'd disappear, too."

Merlini protested. "Don't. You sound like Zyyzk."

"That guy," Gavigan predicted darkly, "is going to wish he never heard of Judge Keeler."

Gavigan's batting average as a prophet was zero. When Zyyzk, whom the Inspector ordered brought to the scene and who was delivered by squad car twenty minutes later, discovered that Judge Keeler had vanished, he was as pleased as punch.

An insterstellar visitor from outer space should have three eyes, or at least green hair. Zyyzk, in that respect, was a disappointment. He was a pudgy little man in a wrinkled gray suit. His eyes, two only, were a pale, washed-out blue behind gold-rimmed bifocals, and his hair, the color of weak tea, failed miserably in its attempts to cover the top of his head.

His manner, however, was charged with an abundant and vital confidence, and there was a haughty, imperious quality in his high, thin voice which hinted that there was much more to Mr. Zyyzk than met the eye.

"I issued distinct orders," he told Gavigan in an icy tone, "that I was never, under any circumstances, to be disturbed between the sidereal hours of five and seven post-meridian. You know that quite well, Inspector. Explain why these idiots have disobeyed. At once!"

If there is any quicker way of bringing an inspector of police to a boil, I don't know what it is. The look Gavigan gave the little man would have wrecked a Geiger counter. He opened his mouth. But the searing blast of flame which I expected didn't issue forth. He closed his mouth and swallowed. The Inspector was speechless.

Zyyzk calmly threw more fuel on the fire. "Well," he said impatiently tapping his foot. "I'm waiting."

A subterranean rumble began deep in Gavigan's interior and then, a split second before he blew his top, Merlini said quietly, "I understand, Mr. Zyyzk, that you read minds?"

Zyyzk, still the Imperial Roman Emperor, gave Merlini a scathing look. "I do," he said. "And what of it?"

"For a mind-reader," Merlini told him, "you ask a lot of questions. I should think you'd know why you've been brought here."

That didn't bother the visitor from Outer Space. He stared intently at Merlini for a second, glanced once at Gavigan, then closed his eyes. The fingertips of one white hand pressed against his brow. Then he smiled.

"I see. Judge Keeler."

"Keeler?" Gavigan pretended surprise. "What about him?"

Zyyzk wasn't fooled. He shook his head. "Don't try to deceive me, Inspector. It's childish. The Judge has vanished. Into the Outer Darkness—as I foretold." He grinned broadly. "You will, of course, release me now."

"I'll—I'll *what?*"

Zyyzk spread his hands. "You have no choice. Not unless you want to admit that I could sit in a police cell surrounded on all sides by steel bars and cause Judge Keeler to vanish off the face of the earth by will power alone. Since that, to your limited, earthly intelligence, is impossible, I have an impregnable alibi. Good day, Inspector."

The little man actually started to walk off. The detectives who stood on either side were so dazed by his treatment of the Inspector that Zyyzk had gone six feet before they came to life again and grabbed him.

Whether the strange powers he claimed were real or not, his ability to render Gavigan speechless was certainly uncanny. The Inspector's mouth opened, but again nothing came out.

Merlini said, "You admit then that you are responsible for the Judge's disappearance?"

Zyyzk, still grinning, shook his head. "I predicted it. Beyond that I admit nothing."

"But you know how he vanished?"

The little man shrugged. "In the usual way, naturally. Only an adept of the seventh order would understand."

Merlini suddenly snapped his fingers and plucked a shiny silver dollar from thin air. He dropped it into his left hand, closed his fingers over it and held his fist out toward Zyyzk.

"Perhaps Judge Keeler vanished—like this." Slowly he opened his fingers. The coin was gone.

For the first time a faint crack appeared in the polished
surface of Zyyzk's composure. He blinked. "Who," he asked
slowly, "are you?"

"An adept," Merlini said solemnly, "of the eighth order.
One who is not yet satisfied that you are what you claim to
be." He snapped his fingers again, almost under Zyyzk's
nose, and the silver dollar reappeared. He offered it to Zyyzk.
"A test," he said. "Let me see you send that back into the
Outer Darkness from which I summoned it."

Zyyzk no longer grinned. He scowled and his eyes were
hard. "It will go," he said, lifting his hand and rapidly
tracing a cabalistic figure in the air. "And you with it!"

"Soon?" Merlini asked.

"Very soon. Before the hour of nine strikes again you will
appear before the Lords of the Outer Darkness in far Antares. And there—"

Gavigan had had enough. He passed a miracle of his own.
He pointed a cabalistic but slightly shaking finger at the
little man and roared an incantation that had instant effect.

"Get him out of here!"

In the small space of time that it took them to hurry down
the corridor and around a corner, Zyyzk and the two detectives who held him both vanished.

Gavigan turned on Merlini. "Isn't one lunatic enough
without you acting like one, too?"

The magician grinned. "Keep our eyes on me, Inspector. If I
vanish, as predicted, you may see how Keeler did it. If I don't,
Zyyzk is on the spot and he may begin to make more sense."

"That," Gavigan growled, "is impossible."

Zyyzk, as far as I was concerned, wasn't the only thing
that made no sense. The Inspector's men turned Grand
Central station inside out and the only trace of Judge Keeler
to be found were the smashed spectacles on the floor of that
phone booth. Gavigan was so completely at a loss that he
could think of nothing else to do but order the search made
again.

Merlini, as far as I could tell, didn't seem to have any better ideas. He leaned against the wall opposite the phone booth and scowled darkly at its empty interior. Malloy and Hicks looked so tired and dispirited that Gavigan told them both to go home and sleep it off. An hour later, when the second search had proved as fruitless as the first, Gavigan suddenly told Lieutenant Doran to take over, turned, and started to march off.

Then Merlini woke up. "Inspector," he asked, "where are you going?"

Gavigan turned, scowling, "Anywhere," he said, "where I don't have to look at telephone booths. Do you have any suggestions?"

Merlini moved forward. "One, yes. Let's eat."

Gavigan didn't look as if he could keep anything in his stomach stronger than weak chicken broth, but he nodded absently. We got into Gavigan's car and Brady drove us crosstown, stopping, at Merlini's direction, in front of the Williston building.

The Inspector objected. "There aren't any decent restaurants in this neighborhood. Why—"

"Don't argue," Merlini said as he got out. "If Zyyzk's latest prediction comes off, this will be my last meal on earth. I want to eat here. Come on." He crossed the pavement toward a flashing green and purple neon sign that blinked: *Johnson's Cafeteria. Open All Night.*

Merlini was suddenly acting almost as strangely as Zyyzk. I knew very well that this wasn't the sort of place he'd pick for his last meal and, although he claimed to be hungry, I noticed that all he put on his tray was crackers and a bowl of soup. Pea soup at that—something he heartily disliked.

Then, instead of going to a table off in a corner where we could talk, he chose one right in the center of the room. He even selected our places for us. "You sit there, Inspector. You there, Ross. And excuse me a moment. I'll be right back." With that he turned, crossed to the street door through which we had come, and vanished through it.

"I think," I told Gavigan, "that he's got a bee in his bonnet."

The Inspector grunted. "You mean bats. In his belfry." He gave the veal cutlet on his plate a glum look.

Merlini was gone perhaps five minutes. When he returned, he made no move to sit down. He leaned over the table and asked, "Either of you got a nickel?"

I found one and handed it to him. Suspiciously, Gavigan said, "I thought you wanted to eat?"

"I must make a phone call first," the magician answered. "And with Zyyzk's prediction hanging over me, I'd just as soon you both watched me do it. Look out the window behind me, watch that empty booth—the second from the right. And keep your eyes on it every second." He glanced at his wrist watch. "If I'm not back here in exactly three minutes, you'd better investigate."

I didn't like the sound of that. Neither did Gavigan. He started to object. "Now, wait a minute. You're not going—"

But Merlini had already gone. He moved with long strides toward the street door, and the Inspector half rose from his chair as if to go after him. Then, when Gavigan saw what lay beyond the window, he stopped. The window we both faced was in a side wall at right angles to the street, and it opened, not to the outside, but into the arcade that runs through the Williston building.

Through the glass we could see a twenty-foot stretch of the arcade's opposite wall and against it, running from side to side, was a row of half a dozen phone booths.

I took a quick look at the clock on the wall above the window just as Merlini vanished through the street door. He reappeared at once in the arcade beyond the window, went directly to the second booth from the right, and went inside. The door closed.

"I don't like this," I said. "In three minutes the time will be exactly—"

"Quiet!" Gavigan commanded.

"—exactly nine o'clock," I finished. "Zyyzk's deadline!"

"He's not going to pull this off," Gavigan said. "You keep your eyes on that booth. I'm going outside and watch it from the street entrance. When the time's up, join me."

I heard his chair scrape across the floor as he got up, but I kept my eyes glued to the scene beyond the window—more precisely to one section of it—the booth into which Merlini had gone. I could see the whole face of the door from top to bottom and the dim luminescence of the light inside.

Nothing happened.

The second hand on the wall clock moved steadily, but much too slowly. At five seconds to the hour I found myself on my feet. And when the hand hit twelve I moved fast. I went through the door, turned it, and found Gavigan just inside the arcade entrance, his eyes fixed on the booth.

"Okay," he said without turning his head. "Come on."

We hurried forward together. The Inspector jerked the door of the second booth open. The light inside blinked out.

Inside, the telephone receiver dangled, still swaying, by its cord.

The booth was empty.

Except for one thing, I bent down and picked it up off the floor—Merlini's shiny silver dollar.

Gavigan swore. Then he pushed me aside, stepped into the booth and lifted the receiver. His voice was none too steady. He said one word into the phone.

"Hello?"

Leaning in behind him, I heard the voice that replied— Merlini's voice making a statement that was twice as impossible as anything that had happened yet.

"Listen carefully," it said. "And don't ask questions now. I'm at 1462-12 Astoria Avenue, the Bronx. Got that? 1462-12 Astoria. Keeler's here—and a murderer! *Hurry!*"

The tense urgency of that last command sent a cold shiver down my spine. Then I heard the click as the connection was broken.

Gavigan stood motionless for a second, holding the dead phone. Then the surging flood of his emotions spilled over. He jiggled the receiver frantically and swore again.

"Blast it! This phone is dead!"

I pulled myself out of a mental tailspin, found a nickel, and dropped it in the slot. Gavigan's verbal fireworks died to a mutter as he heard the dial tone and he jabbed savagely at the dial.

A moment later the Telegraph Bureau was broadcasting a bowdlerized version of Gavigan's orders to the prowl cars in the Astoria Avenue neighborhood. And Gavigan and I were running for the street and his own car. Brady saw us coming, gunned his motor, and the instant we were aboard, took off as though jet-powered. He made a banked turn into Fifth Avenue against a red light, and we raced uptown, siren screaming.

If Zyyzk had been there beside us, handing out dire predictions that we were headed straight for the Pearly Gates, I wouldn't have doubted him for a moment. We came within inches of that destination half a dozen times as we roared swerving through the crosstown traffic.

The Astoria address wasn't hard to find. There were three prowl cars parked in front of it and two uniformed cops on the front porch. One sat on the floor, his back to the wall, holding a limp arm whose sleeve was stained with blood. There were two round bullet holes in the glass of the door above him. As we ran up the walk, the sound of gunfire came from the rear of the house and the second cop lifted his foot, kicked in a front window, and crawled in through the opening, gun in hand.

The wounded man made a brief report as we passed him. "Nobody answered the door," he said. "But when we tried to crash the joint, somebody started shooting."

Somebody was still shooting. Gavigan, Brady, and I went through the window and toward the sound. The officer who had preceded us was in the kitchen, firing around the jamb of the back door. An answering gun blazed in the dark outside and the cop fired at the flash.

"Got him, I think," the cop said. Then he slipped out through the door, moved quickly across the porch and down the steps. Brady followed him.

Gavigan's pocket-flash suddenly sent out a thin beam of light. It started a circuit of the kitchen, stopped for a moment as it picked up movement just outside the door, and we saw a third uniformed man pull himself to a sitting position on the porch floor, look at the bloodstain on his trouser leg, and swear.

Then the Inspector's flash found the open cellar door.

And down there, beside the beginning of a grave, we found Judge Keeler.

His head had been battered in.

But he couldn't find Merlini anywhere in the house. It wasn't until five minutes later, when we were opening Keeler's suitcase, that Merlini walked in.

He looked at the cash and negotiable securities that tumbled out. "You got here," he said, "before that vanished, too, I see."

Gavigan looked up at him. "But you just arrived this minute. I heard a cab out front."

Merlini nodded. "My driver refused to ignore the stop lights the way yours did. Did you find the Judge?"

"Yes, we found him. And I want to know how of all the addresses in Greater New York, you managed to pick this one out of your hat?"

Merlini's dark eyes twinkled. "That was the easy part. Keeler's disappearance, as I said once before, added up to *two* invisible men. As soon as I knew who the second one must be, I simply looked the name up in the phone book."

"And when you vanished," I asked, "was that done with two invisible men?"

Merlini grinned. "No. I improved on the Judge's miracle a bit. I made it a one-man operation."

Gavigan had had all the riddles he could digest. "We found Keeler's body," he growled ominously, "beside an open grave. And if *you* don't stop—"

"Sorry," Merlini said, as a lighted cigarette appeared mysteriously between his fingers. "As a magician I hate to have to blow the gaff on such a neatly contrived bit of hocus pocus as The Great Phone Booth Trick. But if I must—well, it began when Keeler realized he was going to have to take a runout powder. He knew he was being watched. It was obvious that if he and Helen Hope tried to leave town by any of the usual methods, they'd both be picked up at once. Their only chance was to vanish as abruptly and completely as Judge Crater and Dorothy Arnold once did. I suspect it was Zyyzk's first prediction that Miss Hope would disappear that gave Keeler the idea. At any rate, that was what set the wheels in motion."

"I thought so," Gavigan said. "Zyyzk was in on it."

Merlini shook his head. "I'm afraid you can't charge him

with a thing. He was in on it—but he didn't know it. One of the subtlest deceptive devices a magician uses is known as 'the principle of the impromptu stooge.' He so manages things that an unrehearsed spectator acts as a confederate, often without ever realizing it. That's how Keeler used Zyyzk. He built his vanishing trick on Zyyzk's predictions and used them as misdirection. But Zyyzk never knew that he was playing the part of a red herring."

"He's a fraud though," Gavigan insisted. "And he does know it."

Merlini contradicted that, too. "No. Oddly enough he's the one thing in this whole case that is on the level. As you, yourself, pointed out, no fake prophet would give such precisely detailed predictions. He actually does believe that Helen Hope and Judge Keeler vanished into the Outer Darkness."

"A loony," Gavigan muttered.

"And," Merlini added, "a real problem, at this point, for any psychiatrist. He's seen two of his prophecies come true with such complete and startling accuracy that he'll never believe what really happened. I egged him into predicting my disappearance in order to show him that he wasn't infallible. If he never discovers that I did vanish right on time, it may shake his belief in his occult powers. But if he does, the therapy will backfire; he'll be convinced when he sees me, that I'm a doppleganger or an astral double the police have conjured up to discredit him."

"If you don't stop trying to psychoanalyze Zyyzk," Gavigan growled impatiently, "the police are going to conjure up a charge of withholding information in a murder case. Get on with it. Helen Hope wasn't being tailed, so her disappearance was a cinch. She simply walked out, without even taking her toothbrush—to make Zyyzk's prediction look good—and grabbed a plane for Montana or Mexico or some such place where Keeler was to meet her later. But how did Keeler evaporate? And don't you give me any nonsense about two invisible men."

Merlini grinned. "Then we'd better take my disappearance first. That used only one invisible man—and, of course, too many phone booths."

Then, quickly, as Gavigan started to explode, Merlini stopped being cryptic. "In that restaurant you and Ross sat at a table and in the seats that I selected. You saw me, through the window, enter what I had been careful to refer to as the second booth from the right. Seen through the window. that is what it was. But the line of phone booths extended on either side beyond the window and your field of vision. Viewed from outside, there were nine—not six—booths, and the one I entered was actually the third in line."

"Do you mean," Gavigan said menacingly, "that when I was outside watching the second booth, Ross, inside, was watching the third—and we both thought we were watching the same one?"

"Yes. It isn't necessary to deceive the senses if the mind can be misdirected. You saw what you saw, but it wasn't what you thought you saw. And that—"

Then Gavigan did explode, in a muffled sort of way. "Are you saying that we searched the *wrong* phone booth? And that you were right there all the time, sitting in the next one?"

Merlini didn't need to answer. That was obviously just what he did mean.

"Then your silver dollar," I began, "and the phone receiver—"

"Were," Merlini grinned, "what confidence men call 'the convincer'—concocted evidence which seemed to prove that you had the right booth, prevented any skeptical second thoughts, and kept you from examining the other booths just to make sure you had the right one."

I got it then. "That first time you left the restaurant, before you came back with that phony request for the loan of a nickel—that's when you left the dollar in the second booth."

Merlini nodded. "I made a call, too. I dialed the number of the second booth. And when the phone rang, I stepped into the second booth, took the receiver off the hook, dropped the silver dollar on the floor, then hurried back to your table. Both receivers were off and the line was open."

"And when we looked into the second booth, you were sitting right next door, three feet away, telling Gavigan via the phone that you were in the Bronx?"

Merlini nodded. "And I came out after you had gone. It's a standard conjuring principle. The audience doesn't see the coin, the rabbit, or the girl vanish because they actually disappear either before or after the magician pretends to conjure them into thin air. The audience is watching most carefully at the wrong time."

"Now wait a minute," the Inspector objected. "That's just exactly the way you said Keeler couldn't have handled the phone business. What's more he couldn't. Ross and I weren't watching you the first time you left the restaurant. But we'd been watching Keeler for a week."

"And," I added, "Malloy and Hicks couldn't have miscounted the booths at the station and searched the wrong one. They could see both ends of that line of booths the whole time."

"They didn't miscount," Merlini said. "They just didn't count. The booth we examined was the fifth from the right end of the line, but neither Malloy nor Hicks ever referred to it in that way."

Gavigan scowled. "They said Keeler went into the booth *'to the right of the one that was out of order.'* And the phone in the next booth *was* out of order."

"I know, but Keeler didn't enter the booth next to the one we found out of order. He went into a booth next to one that was marked: Out Of Order. That's not quite the same."

Gavigan and I both said the same thing at the same time: "The sign had been moved!"

"Twice," Merlini said, nodding. "First, when Keeler was in the Oyster Bar. The second invisible man—invisible because no one was watching him—moved it one booth to the right. And when Keeler, a few minutes later, entered the booth to the right of the one bearing the sign, he was actually in the second booth from the one whose phone didn't work.

"And then our second invisible man went into action again. He walked into the booth marked out of order, smashed a duplicate pair of blood-smeared glasses on the floor, and dialed the Judge's phone. When Keeler answered, he walked out again, leaving the receiver off the hook. It was as neat a piece of misdirection as I've seen in a long time.

Who would suspect him of putting through a call from a phone booth that was plainly labeled out of order?"

Cautiously, as if afraid the answer would blow up in his face, the Inspector asked, "He did all this with Malloy and Hicks both watching? And he wasn't seen—because he was invisible?"

"No, that's not quite right. He was invisible—because he wasn't suspected."

I still didn't see it. "But," I objected, "the only person who went anywhere near the booth next to the one Keeler was in—"

Heavy footsteps sounded on the back porch and then Brady's voice from the doorway said, "We found him, Inspector. Behind some bushes the other side of the wall. Dead. And do you know who—"

"I do now," Gavigan cut in. "Sergeant Hicks."

Brady nodded.

Gavigan turned to Merlini. "Okay, so Hicks was a crooked cop and a liar. But not Malloy. He says he was watching that phone booth every second. How did Hicks switch that Out-of-Order sign back to the original booth again without being seen?"

"He did it when Malloy wasn't watching quite so closely—*after* Malloy thought Keeler had vanished. Malloy saw Hicks look into the booth, act surprised, then beckon hurriedly. Those actions, together with Hicks's later statement that the booth was already empty, made Malloy think the judge had vanished sooner than he really did. Actually Keeler was still right there, sitting in the booth into which Hicks stared. It's the same deception as to time that I used."

"Will you," Gavigan growled, "stop lecturing on the theory of deception and just explain when Hicks moved that sign."

"All right. Remember what Malloy did next? He was near the information booth in the center of the floor and he ran across toward the phones. Malloy said, 'I did some fancy open-field running through the commuters.' Of course he did. At five-twenty the station is full of them and he was in a hell of a hurry. He couldn't run fast and keep his eyes glued to Hicks and that phone booth every step of the way; he'd have had half a dozen head-on collisions. But he didn't think the fact that he had had to use his eyes to steer a course rather than continue to watch the booth was important. He thought the dirty work—Keeler's disappearance—had taken place.

"As Malloy ran toward him through the crowd, Hicks simply took two steps sideways to the left and stared into the phone booth that was tagged with the Out-of-Order card. And, behind his body, his left hand shifted the sign one booth to the left—back to the booth that was genuinely out of order. Both actions took no more than a second or two. When Malloy arrived, 'the booth next to the one that was out of order' was empty. Keeler had vanished into Zyyzk's Outer Darkness *by simply sitting still and not moving at all!*"

"And he really vanished," Gavigan said, finally convinced, "by walking out of the next booth as soon as he had spoken his piece to Malloy on the phone."

"While Malloy," Merlini added, "was still staring goggle-eyed at the phone. Even if he had turned to look out of the door, all he'd have seen was the beefy Hicks standing smack in front of him carefully blocking the view. And then Keeler walked right out of the station. Every exit was guarded—except one. An exit big enough to drive half a dozen trains through!"

"Okay," the Inspector growled. "You don't have to put it in words of one syllable. He went out through one of the train gates which Malloy himself had been covering, boarded a train a moment before it pulled out, and ten minutes later he was getting off again up at 125th Street."

"Which," Merlini added, "isn't far from Hicks's home where we are now and where Keeler intended to hide out until the cops, baffled by the dead-end he'd left, relaxed their vigilance a bit. The Judge was full of cute angles. Who'd ever think of looking for him in the home of one of the cops who was supposed to be hunting him?"

"After which," I added, "he'd change the cut of his whiskers or trim them off altogether, go to join Miss Hope, and they'd live happily ever after on his ill-gotten gains. Fadeout."

"That was the way the script read," Merlini said. "But Judge Keeler forgot one or two little things. He forgot that a man who has just vanished off the face of the earth, leaving a deadend trail, is a perfect prospective murder victim. And he forgot that a suitcase full of folding money is a temptation one should never set before a crooked cop."

"Forgetfulness seems to be dangerous," I said. "I'm glad I've got a good memory."

"I have a hunch that somebody is going to have both our scalps," Merlini said ominously. "I've just remembered that when we left the shop—"

He was right. I hadn't mailed Mrs. Merlini's letter.

THE GRINNING GOD

By May Futrelle (1876-?)

The phrase "tour de force" has been overused, but it accurately describes the two short stories that follow. In 1907 May Futrelle wrote a ghost story under the title "The Grinning God." The editor for Associated Sunday Newspapers, producer of Sunday supplements, suggested that it be published with a rational solution in a succeeding story to be written by Mrs. Futrelle's husband, Jacques, the author of the Thinking Machine detective stories. Jacques had written what is still one of the most anthologized of all mysteries, "The Problem of Cell 13," and until his death in the Titanic disaster he continued to produce superb tales, including "The Phantom Motor" about the disappearance of an automobile and "The Crystal Gazer" about a crystal ball's accurate prophecy of murder. But in many ways his most daring and successful story is the continuation of his wife's tale in which The Thinking Machine explains how a road and a house could have disappeared as though they had never existed.

PROFESSOR Augustus S. F. X. Van Dusen—The Thinking Machine—readjusted his thick spectacles, dropped back into the depths of the huge chair, and read from the manuscript in his hand: "A little less than three months ago I had a photograph taken. As I look upon it now, I see a man of about 30 years, clean-shaven, full-faced, and vigorous with health; eyes which are clear and calm, almost phlegmatic; a brow upon which sits the serenity of perfect physical and mental poise; a pleasant mouth with quizzical lines about the corners; a chin with determination and assurance in every line; hair brown and unmarked with age. I was red-blooded then, lusty, and buoyant with life, while now—

"Here is a hand mirror. It reflects back at me the gaunt, haggard face of a man who might be 60 years old; furtive, shifting eyes in which lies a perpetual, hideous fear; a brow ruffled over into spidery lines of suffering; a drooping, flabby mouth; hair dead white over the temples. My blood has become water; all things worthwhile are gone. I have nothing left.

"Fear, Webster says, is apprehension, dread, alarm—and yet it is more than that. It is a loss of the sense of proportion, an unseating of mental power; a vampire which saps hope and courage and common sense, and leaves a quivering shell of what was once a man. I know what fear is—no man better. I knew it that night in the forest, and I know it now, when I find myself sitting up in bed staring into nothingness, with the echo of screams in my ears; I knew it when that grim, silent old man moved about me, and I know it now when without conscious effort my imagination conjures up those dead, glassy eyes; I knew it when vicious little tongues of flame lapped at me that night, and I know it now when at times I still seem to feel their heat.

"Yes, I know what fear is. It is typified by a little ivory god which squats on my mantel as I write, squats there grinning. Perhaps there is some explanation for what happened that night, some single hidden fact which, if revealed, would make it all clear; but in seeking that explanation I have grown like this. When it will end, I don't know—I can only wait and listen . . .

"Here is my terrifying story. Impatient, half-famished,

and disgusted at a sudden failure of my gasoline supply, I ran my automobile off the main roadway and brought it to a standstill in a small open space before a little country store. I had barely been able to see the outlines of the building in the darkness—a darkness which was momentarily growing more dense. Black, threatening clouds swooped across the face of the heavens, first obscuring, then obliterating, the brilliant star-points.

"I knew where I was, although I had never been over the road before. Behind me lay Pelham, a quiet little village which had been sound asleep when I drove through, and somewhere vaguely ahead was the town of Millen. I had been due there about seven o'clock; but owing to unforeseeable delays, it was now about ten. I was exhausted from hours at the steering wheel, and had had nothing to eat since luncheon. I planned to spend the night in Millen, eat a big meal, store up a few hours' sleep, then on the morrow proceed on my way.

"This was what I had intended to do. But an empty gasoline tank brought me to a stop in front of the forbidding little store, and a little maneuvering back and forth cleared the road's fairway of the bulk of my machine. No light showed in the store; but as I had not passed another building for two or three miles back, it seemed not improbable that the keeper of the store slept on the premises. I put this hypothesis to a test by a loud helloing, which in the course of time brought a nightcapped head to a window just above the door.

"'Got any gasoline?' I asked.

"'I cal'late as how I might have a little,' came the answer in a man's voice.

"'Well, will you please let me have enough to get to Millen?'

"'It's ag'in' the law in these parts to draw gasoline at night,' said the man placidly. 'Cal'late as how you'll have to wait till mornin'.'

"'Wait till morning?' I complained. 'Why, man, there's a storm coming! I've got to get to Millen.'

"'Can't help that,' was the reply. 'Law's law, you know.'

"Here was another dilemma, unexpected as it was annoying. The tone of the voice left no room for argument, and I know the obstinacy of this man's type. I was prepared, therefore, to accept the inevitable.

"'Well, if you can't sell me any gasoline tonight, can you give me a bite to eat and put me up till morning? I can't stay out in this storm.'

"'Ain't got no room,' explained the man. 'Jus' enough space up here for me an' the dog, an' he kinder crowds.'

"'Well, something must be done,' I insisted. 'What is the price of your gasoline?'

"'Twenty-five cents a gallon in day time.'

"'Well, how about 50 cents a gallon at night?' I went on.

"The whitecapped head was withdrawn, and the window banged down suddenly. For a moment I thought I had hopelessly offended some puritanical old man of the woods; but then a light glowed inside the store, and the front door opened. I stepped inside. The light came from a safety lantern in the hands of a shrunken little old man, who proceeded to draw the gasoline.

"'How far is it to Millen?' I inquired casually.

"'Cal'late as how it's about five miles.'

"'Straight road?'

"'Straight 'cept where it bends,' he replied. 'They ain't no turn out nor nothin'. You can't go wrong 'less you climb a fence.'

"The gasoline was drawn and paid for, after which the old man accompanied me to the automobile with his safety lantern. He stood looking on curiously while I filled the tank.

"'Pears to be a right smart storm comin' up,' he remarked consolingly.

"I glanced upward. Every starpoint was lost now behind an impenetrable veil of black; there was a whispering, sighing sound of wind in the trees.

"'I think I can beat the storm into Millen,' I replied hopefully.

"'I cal'late as how you oughter,' responded the old man. 'Ain't no thunder an' lightnin' yet, an' I cal'late as how they'll be a pile of it before it rains.'

"I handed back the empty gasoline can, then got into my car.

"'If I should get caught before I get to Millen, is there any place I might stop?' I inquired.

"'I cal'late as how you might stop anywhere,' the old man

chuckled, 'but they ain't no houses nor nothin'. They ain't no turnouts, an' you can hit it up as fast as you want to. You'll be all right.'

"A sudden gust of wind brought a cloud of dust upon us, and the thinly clad old man scampered off into the house.

"I backed my car, then straightened out into the road, a wide yellow stretch as smooth as asphalt. Then I stepped hard on the accelerator, and went plunging off into the night.

"It might have been only my imagination, or it might have been, as the car swept on, that I thought I heard someone calling me; I'll never know which. But the lowering clouds and a quickened rush of wind did not make another stop inviting; so the car sped on.

"I knew an excellent little all-night restaurant in Millen, and was speculating pleasantly as to whether it should be a chop and a mug of ale, or a more substantial steak and potatoes. I was aroused from this dreaming when suddenly the glittering lamps of my car showed me, straight ahead, a fork in the road. Two roads! Here was another unexpected annoyance. I brought the automobile to a stop, in doubt and perplexity.

"To the right, one fork ran into the thickening forest, as far as the light gleams revealed; to the left, the fork seemed a little more marked, as if more traveled, and where the light melted into the enveloping blackness it appeared to widen. I leaped out of the car and went forward, seeking a guidepost or something to show my way. There was nothing.

"Then I remembered that I had a road map in my pocket. Of course that would tell me. A grumble of thunder came from far off as I drew near the car to examine the map in the light. Here was Pelham, and here was Millen; here was the little store where I stopped, marked with a star, which meant that gasoline was to be procured there. Now I was somewhere between that store and Millen. The map was a large one. It should show not only the main road, but every little bypath that cut away from it. Yet from the little store to Millen the road on the map was an unbroken line. There was no branching off, and yet here was an unmistakable fork in the road.

"I was perplexed, impatient, and incidentally starving; so hastily I made up my mind which road to take—the left, the more used one. Heaping maledictions upon the head of the man who drew that particular map. I started to get into the car again when the darkness was suddenly torn by a vivid flash of lightning. It startled me, blinded me almost, and was followed instantly by the crash and roar of thunder.

"Then came another sound—a curdling, nerve-racking scream—a scream of agony, of pain, of fear which seemed to stop my heart for one fearful instant, then was lost in the thunder of the approaching storm. Suddenly all was silent again, save for the wind as it whipped its way through the forest.

"I was not a nervous man; so after the first shock the blood rushed back to my heart, my head cleared, and I was perfectly calm. But I stood waiting—waiting and listening. I argued calmly. Someone was evidently in distress. But where? In what direction? The singing wind, the whirling dust, left me no guess. And then came that scream again, this time a series of quick, sharp shrieks ending in a wail which made me clench my hands.

"But now I had the direction. The cries had come apparently from the road, somewhere behind me. I walked to the rear of the car where the tail-light shot out a feeble ray, and stood peering off in the direction from which I had come. At first I could distinguish nothing; then a white, intangible something slowly grew out of the night—something hazy, floating, indistinct, yet unmistakably something. Fascinated, I stood still and continued to stare. The floating white figure seemed to grow larger and clearer. It was coming toward me; it would cross the path of the tail-light in another moment. I caught my breath and waited.

"Suddenly the reverberating crash of thunder sounded again, nearer and louder, but unaccompanied by lightning. Instantly, as if in echo, came that scream again. Obviously it was someone in distress—a woman perhaps, lost in the woods and in terror of the approaching storm. If this was true, there was only one thing to do: go to her relief.

"I took a flashlight from the car and started back along the road to where I had seen the figure. With the light thrust straight out in front of me at arm's length, I ran back ten yards, twenty, fifty—and saw nothing. I screened the light with my hand and peered about in the gloom, and saw—nothing.

"A panic was growing upon me. I flashed the light to the right, to the left, and it showed only the gaunt, silent trees, straight ahead of me along the yellow road, and behind me toward the automobile. But there was nothing else—absolutely nothing. I rushed back to the car; but no one was there. I called aloud; but the forest gave back only the sound of my own voice, mingled with the swishing of the wind.

"Then I stopped still once more, and listened. For a long time I stood there, light in hand, until the silence grew more terrifying than the screams had been. Finally I turned and walked back to the car. Somehow, the car gave me confidence. I struck the hood with my open palm, and laughed at my unreasoning terror. I had heard the screams, yes; I had seen a floating white figure. There was nothing very remarkable about it—it was a thing that could be explained, I was sure of that now.

"So, deliberately, I searched the road again, this time with the light turned toward the ground. I went along, stooping, seeking footprints. I found none. But I could explain even that: the wind must have covered them with dust.

"I straightened up suddenly. Something had sounded, something louder than the rustling of the leaves, louder even than the creaking of the trees. It was a crackling sound—a sound that might have been made by a foot pressing on dry twigs. It seemed to be to the left, and I turned the light in that direction. Grotesque shadows danced and swayed as the trees reeled about me. Then high up where the light straggled through the branches I saw something white—dead white!

"I cleared the road in a few strides and plunged into the forest with the light turned upward. I stumbled over rocks half-buried in the leaves; I slipped once into a ditch which I couldn't see. Finally my foot struck a fallen tree, and I went sprawling on my hands and knees. The flashlight rolled beyond my reach, and blackness swooped down as the light was smothered in the underbrush. As I groped for it I again heard that crackling sound, as of breaking twigs.

"At last, my frantic fingers closed on the light, and I shot the beam high above my head, seeking that white something up among the trees. It was gone. I paused to wipe the perspiration from my brow, and loosened my collar. A sudden shower of leaves came down upon my head; there was another zigzag of lightning, a nearby roll of thunder, and the sinister patter of raindrops falling about me like leaden bullets. The storm had burst.

"I stumbled back to the automobile, got in, and sent it forward headlong on the road to the left—the road which bore evidence of travel. The pace was furious; for somewhere behind me was a misty, floating figure of white, and somewhere a woman screaming. Suddenly the road widened where a path cut through the dense wood. A single sidelong glance at it as I rushed past told me it was not wide enough for my car. Again the road map was at fault. I remembered that grimly, even as the automobile went splashing along through growing pools of water and invisible ruts. I clung grimly to the steering wheel with only one idea in mind: to get to Millen.

"Gradually the road turned toward the left, or so it seemed to me. But that too might have been the effect of an overwrought imagination. The road did not look so much traveled now, despite the deceptive ruts into which my wheels kept sinking. Yet beneath its sheet of water the steadily gleaming lights showed that there was a road, plainly marked. For a minute or more I went straight on, desperately, recklessly; then an illuminating flash across the sky showed me that I was plunging into open country and that the forest was gradually receding.

"Finally, through the swirling, drenching rain, I saw a faint rosy point in the distance. Whatever it was—a lantern, I supposed—it indicated the presence of some fellow human being. I drove straight toward it. The gleam did not falter or fade. Another dazzling burst of lightning answered my question as to the nature of the light. It was in a farmhouse—a farmhouse out here where there weren't supposed to be any farmhouses! But at least it would serve to shelter me from the fury of the storm. I took it all in at one glance, even to a small shed in the rear where I could park the car.

"I didn't pause to call out as I drew near, but drove directly to the shed and ran my car in. Then, guided by the constant lightning flashes, I walked round to the front of the farm-house, passing through the stream of light from the window. It cheered me, that light. I knocked on the front door loudly, shaking the water from my dripping garments. I waited—waited patiently for half a minute. There was no answering sound of any sort, and again I knocked, this time more insistently. Still no answer. It was not difficult to imagine that the continuous roar of the elements had drowned my knocking, so I repeated the performance, thumping loudly. Still no answer.

"Even in this desperate strait I did not care to enter the house as a thief might, by forcing my way, and run the risk of being received as a thief, possibly with a bullet. So I stepped down from the veranda, and went to the lighted window, intending to attract attention by rapping on the glass. My first glimpse told me no one was there; but the room indicated every evidence of occupancy. A big cheerful log fire was burning, and its flickering light showed books here and there, inviting chairs, a table, and all the little knickknacks that make a comfortable living-room.

"I had no further scruples about it. I ran up the steps, and was just reaching out my hand to try the knob, when the latch clicked, and slowly, silently, the door swung open. Naturally, I expected to meet someone—someone who had anticipated me in lifting the latch—but I saw no one. The door had merely opened, revealing a long, broad hallway, with a stair in the distance, and unlighted save for the reflection from the living-room. I took just two steps across the threshold, enough to get out of the swirling rain, then stopped and called. No one answered. I called a second time. The thunder was silent just then, and there was no sound save that of my own voice. I ventured along the hall to the living-room door and looked in. It was cozy, warm, even more comfortable than I had imagined when I looked in through the window.

"All at once I was overcome by a guilty sense of intrusion. What right had I to enter a strange house at this time of night, even to get out of a storm? My personal safety seemed at stake, somehow. I turned and started back for the door by which I had entered, with the intention of remaining there till in some way I could attract the attention of the occupants of the house.

"But I didn't reach the door: for directly in front of me stood a man. He was tall, angular, aged, and a little bent. A straggling gray beard almost covered his face, and thick gray hair hung down limply from beneath the brim of an old slouch hat. He was beside me, almost within reach of my hand, almost treading upon my toes with his great boots, and yet I had not heard a single sound of his coming.

" 'I must apologize—' I began; but I got no further. He had not heard me, had not even seen me, to judge by the manner in which he walked slowly past me with his chin upon his breast, his hands clasped behind his back. I stepped back to avoid a collision.

" 'I beg your pardon—' I began again; but he had disappeared into the living-room, stalked away noiselessly without even a glance in my direction, leaving me overcome by that indefinable sense of impending danger.

"I paused there in the hall and considered the situation. Surely the old man must have seen me; yet—yet—

" 'I'm going in there, and I am going to stay until the storm is over!' I told myself.

"I removed my coat, hung it on a peg, walked along the hallway, and stepped into the living-room.

"*It was deserted!*

"There are moments in every man's life when the weight of a revolver in his hand is tremendously reassuring. This was mine. I drew the weapon from my hip pocket, examined it, and thrust it into my coat within easy reach of my right hand. Then I stood by the table, drumming my fingers on it idly, and debating with myself as to what I should do. I was looking toward the door by which I had entered. No one came in, and yet—

"Suddenly the gray-bearded old man was throwing a log on the fire. The flames shot up and the sparks flew; but there was not the crackle of fresh burning wood as there should have been—just this silent old man. My heart was in my throat, and I laughed sheepishly.

" 'You startled me,' I explained foolishly.

"He did not look at me, but busied himself about the room for a moment, and laid his hat upon a couch. Then he went out by the door into the hallway.

" 'Well, upon my soul!' I exclaimed.

"I sat down and deliberately waited for the old man to return. The uncanniness of it all was growing upon me—the silence of his great boots as he walked, the fire which didn't crackle as it burned, the lack of any sign or movement to indicate that he had recognized my presence. Was the old man real? I came to my feet with an exclamation. Or was it— was it some weird continuation of that horrible business in the forest?

"I put out a cold, clammy hand to the fire. That seemed real—at least, a warmth came to me, and gradually my fingers lost their numbness, and looking upon my own hand I fell to remembering the hands of my strange host. They were knotted, toil-worn, and the left forefinger was missing. That fact struck sharply upon my memory, and I remembered also a scar over one eye when he removed his hat. That seemed real too, as did these things on the mantel in front of me: an empty spool; an alabaster cat, glaringly red and white; a piece of crystal of peculiar shape on the farthermost corner. And near it, so close that at first it seemed a part of it, was a queer little ivory god, sitting on his haunches, grinning.

"I lifted the ivory image and examined it curiously. It was real enough. I had stepped back from the mantel a pace to let the firelight fall upon it, when suddenly I knew that the old man had returned. I didn't hear him, I hadn't seen him—I merely knew he was there. I felt it. I slipped the little image into my pocket involuntarily as I turned; for all my interest was instantly transferred to a tray of food which the old man carried. And I remembered I was hungry.

"He placed the things on the table in the same ghostly silence. There was a jug of milk, some jelly, a little pat of butter, and several biscuits. I went forward and thanked him. He was absolutely impassive, seeing nothing, hearing nothing, and seeming to have no connection with the things around him. He didn't invite me to eat—I assumed that privilege and gingerly poked a finger into a biscuit. It felt like a biscuit. I bit it. It tasted like a biscuit. In fact, I am convinced to this day that it was a biscuit. But against the reality of that biscuit was the silent old man and his ghostly tread.

"Real, or unreal, the food was refreshing and good, and I fell to with a will. The old man sat down in a rocker by the fire and folded his hands in his lap. I ventured a remark about the storm. He didn't answer. I really had not expected that he would. The modest supper brought a tingle back to my blood. My nerves were calmed, the room cozy, the fire comfortable. I was beginning to enjoy this singular experience; but an occasional glance at the swaying rocker where the old man sat by the fire kept me alert. The rocker swayed dismally, but without the slightest sound.

"The warmth, the food, and my utter exhaustion conspired to make me a little drowsy, and once at least I must have closed my eyes. Then I opened them with a start. From somewhere above me, below me, or from outside where the storm still growled, came that awful, heart-tearing scream again, ending in a wail that brought me to my feet. The old man did not heed the quick movement by the slightest sign— he was still comfortably rocking.

" 'What is it?' I demanded.

"Revolver in hand, I rushed toward the door leading into the hallway. The old man was there ahead of me. He didn't touch me, and yet imperceptibly I was forced aside. He crossed the hall and went up the stairs. After a moment I heard a door open and shut.

"Except for the noise of the storm, the scream, and my own voice, it was the only sound I had heard since I had entered the house.

"I went up those stairs; why I cannot say, except that something, a vague, undefined curiosity, seemed to impel me. And with this impulse came again, stronger than ever, that sense of personal danger—the feeling that had possessed me ever since I had entered the house.

"I groped my way through the darkness to the top of the stairs; then my hand ran along a wall till I came to an open door. I stood there a moment, undecided whether to investigate further or to retrace my steps. I was on the point of going back down the stairs, but the flare of a candle almost in my face stopped me. The old man held the candle, shading it with his left hand, from which the forefinger was missing. The wavering light gave the withered old face a strangely drawn expression.

"He was within three feet of me, gazing straight into my face, and yet I felt that he didn't see me. For one moment he stood there, staring; then passing me, he entered the room beyond, where he put down the candle. I followed him into the room as a moth follows a flame. It was the light, I think, that lured me in. Here, once and for all, I would make an end of the thing. The old man, still noiselessly, went out the door by which he had entered, off into the darkness. The door swung to. Like a madman I sprang forward and shot the bolt. I don't know why.

"I felt caged. Whatever was to come, was to come here! It was an intuition that stirred more strongly in me than the sense of danger. I sat down on a clean little bed and stared thoughtfully at the single door—the only way out save by one of two small windows which I imagined overlooked the yard. I examined my revolver carefully. Every chamber was loaded, and the cylinder whirled easily. Well and good. I waited. What for? I don't know.

"The candle burned with a straight, unwavering flame, while I crouched there on the bed for a long time. The grumble of the thunder was growing faint and far away; but the rain swished against the windows in sheets. Here was a vigil, it seemed, and a long one; for sleep seemed hopelessly out of the question despite the insistent drowsiness of exhaustion. I wondered if the candle would last throughout the night. It was not yet half-burned. I gazed at it with a certain returning sense of assurance, and as I gazed, it flickered, flared up suddenly, and went out.

"I don't know what happened then. It might have been ten minutes later, or it might have been a half a dozen hours, when strangling, choking fumes of smoke aroused me. My lungs were bursting for air. I struggled up on the bed, and was instantly conscious of the crackling sound of burning wood—of fire. *The house was on fire!* I rushed toward the bolted door, to find the flames already eating through the thin panels, and huge red tongues shooting out at me. I was cut off from the stairs.

"From there to one of the little windows! The glow far out through the rain told me that the whole house was aflame. I glanced downward. Sinuous forks were below me, on each side of me, above me. There was nothing to do but jump. I had only a moment to decide. I drew in my breath and pulled myself upon the ledge.

"And then again I heard that scream. Far across the open field, where the glow from the blaze dimmed off into the shadows, I saw a misty white figure with outstretched arms fleeing toward the forest. A little behind the floating white figure, and nearer to me, well within the range of the firelight, the old man was following. Even at the distance I could see his chin drooped upon his chest and his hands clasped behind his back.

"The next instant I had jumped . . .

"I found myself in my automobile skimming along a smooth, hard road that led through a forest. It was not familiar, and I didn't know in what direction I was headed; nor did it matter, so long as I got away from those things behind me. My ankle was badly sprained, my clothing torn and burned in spots, and my head throbbing with pain.

"Then I found myself in what seemed to be a street in a small city. A faint, rosy line was just tinging the eastern sky. Houses to the right and left of me were closed forbiddingly; but just ahead was the solitary figure of a man, walking slowly, swinging a stick. I ran the automobile alongside him, shouting some senseless question, then fell forward in a faint.

"When I recovered consciousness it was to find myself lying on a cot in a strange room, perhaps a hospital. A physician was bandaging my ankle. A thousand questions leaped to my lips and some burst out.

"'Don't talk!' commanded the physician.

"'But where am I?' I insisted.

"'Millen,' he responded tersely.

"It struck me as curious that I should be here—that I should have reached the point for which I was bound even after all that had happened to me. It seemed centuries since I had left Pelham somewhere behind. Perhaps it was all a dream. But those screams! That silent old man! After a while I dropped into a sleep of sheer exhaustion . . .

"On the following day I was calmer. The physician asked me some questions, and I answered them to the best of my ability. He did not smile at my fright, only shook his head and gave me something which made me sleep again. And so for a week I lay there, helpless. But one day I awoke to clear consciousness. Then the physician and I discussed the matter at length.

"He listened respectfully, and at the end shook his head.

"'There is no intersecting road between the small store of which you speak and the outskirts of Millen,' he said positively.

"'But, man, I was there!' I protested. 'I turned into the other road and drove till I saw the house in the open field. I tell you—'

"But he let me go no further. I knew why. He thought it was some mental vagary; for after a while he gave me a pill and went away. So I determined to solve the matter for myself. I would go back along that road by day, and find that silent old man, and, if not the house itself, the charred spot where it had stood. I would know that intersection; I would know even the path which led from the mysterious road off into the wood. When I found these I knew the maze would fade into some simple, plain explanation—perhaps even an absurd one.

"So I bided my time. In the course of another week I was able to leave my cot and hobble about with the aid of a crutch. It was then that I took the physician in my car and we went back along the highway toward Pelham. It was all unfamiliar ground to me; there was no road, and suddenly there ahead of me was the little store where I had bought gasoline that night. I would question the old man I had seen there; but there was no old man. The little store was unoccupied; it seemed to have been unoccupied for weeks.

"I turned back and traversed the road toward Millen again. I recognized nothing; I could find no trace whatever of a bypath from the highway, in any direction. And once more I went over the ground at night. Nothing! After that, the physician—a singularly patient man—accompanied me as I hobbled through the forest on each side of the road, seeking the house, or its ashes. But I never saw anything that even suggested a single incident of that awful night.

"'I know the country, every inch of it,' the physician told me. 'There isn't any such place as you mention.'

"And—well, that's all. I know the doctor's opinion—that my story was some sort of delusion—a dream. And in time I came to believe the entire experience an hallucination. I was growing content with this interpretation, even knowing it to be wrong, because it brought mental rest, and I was beginning to be myself again.

"Then one day I had occasion to look through the pockets of the coat I had worn that night. In the course of the search I thrust my hand into an outside pocket, and drew out—*a little ivory god, sitting on his haunches, grinning . . .*"

When he had finished reading, The Thinking Machine dropped back into the chair, with squint eyes turned steadily upward, and long slender fingers pressed tip to tip. Hutchinson Hatch, the reporter, sat staring in silence at the drawn, inscrutable face of the scientist.

"And the writer of this?" asked The Thinking Machine at last.

"His name is William Fairbanks," the reporter explained. "He was removed to an asylum yesterday, hopelessly insane."

THE HOUSE THAT WAS

By Jacques Futrelle (1875-1912)

THE Thinking Machine rose and walked the length of the room three times. Finally he stopped before the newspaperman. "And is there really such a thing as the grinning god that he describes?" he demanded.

"Certainly," Hatch responded, and his tone indicated surprise.

"Not necessarily certain," said the scientist sharply. "Do you *know* there is such a grinning god?"

"Yes," replied the newspaperman emphatically. "It was taken away from Fairbanks when he was locked up. He fought like a fiend for it."

"Naturally," was the terse comment. "You have seen it, have you?"

"Yes, I saw it. It's about six inches tall, seems to be cut from a solid piece of ivory, and—"

"And has shiny eyes?"

"Yes. The eyes are made of amethyst, highly polished."

Again The Thinking Machine walked the length of the room three times. "You came to me, of course, to see if it was possible, by throwing light on this affair, to restore Fairbanks's mind?" he inquired.

"Well, that was the idea," Hatch agreed. "Fairbanks was evidently driven to his present condition by the haunting mystery of this thing, by brooding over it, and by the tangible existence of that ivory god, which established a definite connection with an experience which might otherwise have been only a nightmare. It occurred to me that if he could be made to see just what had happened and the underlying causes for its happening, he might be brought back to a normal condition." The reporter was silent for a moment, with eyes set on the preoccupied face of The Thinking Machine. "Of course," he added, "I am assuming that the things he wrote down in his manuscript *did* happen, and if they did, that you won't believe they were due to other than natural causes."

"I don't disbelieve in anything, Mr. Hatch," and The Thinking Machine regarded the newspaperman quietly. "I don't even disbelieve in what is broadly termed the supernatural—I merely don't know. It is necessary, in the solution of material problems, to work from a material basis, and then the things which are conjured up by fear may be dissipated. That is done by logic, Mr. Hatch. Disregard the supernatural, so called, in our material problems, and logic is as inevitable as the fact that two and two make four, not sometimes, but all the time."

"You don't deny the possibility of the so-called supernatural, then?"

"I don't deny anything until I know," was the response. "I don't know that there is a supernatural force; therefore," and he shrugged his slender, stooping shoulders, "I work only from a material basis. If this manuscript states facts, then Fairbanks saw an old man, *not* a spook; he saw a woman, *not* a wraith; he jumped to escape a real fire, *not* a ghost fire. When we disregard the supernatural, we must admit that everything was real, unless it was pure invention, and the sprained ankle and burned clothing are against that. If these were real people, we can find them— that's all there is to it."

The Thinking Machine rose from the chair. "Now the first thing to do is to see Fairbanks in person. I think, if he can comprehend at all, that I may be able to help him."

The Thinking Machine was cordially, even deferentially, received by Dr. Pollock, physician-in-charge of the Westbrook Sanatorium.

"I should like to spend ten minutes in the padded cell with Fairbanks," Professor Van Dusen announced.

Dr. Pollock regarded him curiously, but without surprise. "It's dangerous," he remarked doubtfully. "I have no objection, of course, but I should advise that a couple of keepers go in with you."

"I'll go alone," announced the diminutive man of science. "By the way, you have that little ivory god here, haven't you? Let me see it, please."

It was produced and subjected to a searching scrutiny, after which the scientist set it up on a table, dropped into a seat facing it, leaned forward on his elbows, and sat staring straight into the amethyst eyes for a long time. A silence fell upon the watchers as he sat there immovable, minute after minute. Hatch absently glanced at his watch and went over and looked out the window. The thing was getting on his nerves.

At last the scientist rose and thrust the grinning god into his pocket. "Now, please," he directed curtly, "I shall go into the cell with Fairbanks alone. I want the door closed behind me, and I want that door to remain closed for ten minutes. Under no circumstances must there be any interruption." He turned upon Dr. Pollock. "Don't have any fears for me. I'm not a fool."

Dr. Pollock led the way along the corridor, down some stairs, and paused before a door.

"Just ten minutes—no more, no less," directed the scientist.

The key was inserted in the lock, and the door swung on its hinges. Instantly the ears of the three men were assailed by a torrent of screams. The maniac rushed for the door, and Hatch for an instant gazed straight into a distorted, pallid face in which there was no trace of intelligence, or even of humanity. He turned away with a shudder. Dr. Pollock thrust his arm forward to stay the swaying figure, and glanced round at The Thinking Machine doubtfully.

"Look at me! Look at me!" commanded the scientist sharply, and the squint blue eyes fearlessly met the glitter of madness in the eyes of Fairbanks. The Thinking Machine raised his right hand in front of his face, and instantly the incoherent ravings stopped, while some strange, sudden change came over the maniacal face. In the scientist's right hand was the grinning god. That was the magic which had stilled the ravings. Slowly, with his eyes fixed upon those of the maniac, the scientist edged his way into the cell, Fairbanks retreating almost imperceptibly. Never for an instant did the maniacal eyes leave the ivory image; yet he made no attempt to seize it, he seemed merely fascinated.

"Close the door," directed The Thinking Machine quietly, without so much as a glance back. "Ten minutes!"

Dr. Pollock closed the door and turned the key in the lock, after which he looked at the newspaperman with an expression of frank bewilderment on his face. Hatch said nothing, only glanced at his watch.

One minute, two minutes, three minutes . . . The second-hand of Hatch's watch moved at a snail's pace . . . Four minutes, five minutes, six minutes. Then through the heavy, padded wall came faintly the sound of hoarse cries, of screams, and finally the crash of something falling. Dr. Pollock's face paled a little and he began to turn the key in the lock.

"No!" and Hatch sprang forward to seize the physician's hand.

"But he's in danger," declared the doctor, "perhaps even killed!" Again he tugged at the door.

"No!" said Hatch again, and he shoved the physician aside. "He said ten minutes, and—and I know the man!"

Eight minutes . . . The screaming had stopped; there was dead silence. Nine minutes . . . Still they stood there, Hatch guarding the door, and his eyes unflinchingly fixed on the physician's face. Ten minutes—and Hatch opened the door.

Professor Augustus S. F. X. Van Dusen was sitting calmly on a padded seat beside Fairbanks, with one slender hand resting on his pulse. Fairbanks himself sat with the ivory image held close to his eyes, babbling and mumbling at it incoherently. An overturned table lay in the middle of the cell. So great had been the power used to upset it that an iron bolt which held the table fast to the floor had been broken off. The scientist rose and came toward them; and Hatch drew a deep breath of relief.

"I would advise that this man be placed in another cell," said the little scientist quietly. "There is no further need to keep him in a padded cell. Put him somewhere where he can see outside and find something to attract his attention. Meanwhile, let him keep that ivory image, and there'll be no more raving."

"What—what did you do to him?" demanded the physician, in perplexity.

"Nothing—yet," was the enigmatic response. "I'd like him to stay here a couple of days longer, under constant watch as to his physical condition—never mind his mental condition now—and then with your permission I'll make a little experiment.

William Fairbanks sat beside The Thinking Machine in a huge touring car, with the slender hand of the scientist resting lightly on his wrist. In front of them was the chauffeur, and behind them sat Hutchinson Hatch and Dr. Pollock. They were scudding along a smooth road, guided by the ribbons of light which shot out ahead from their forward lamps. The night was perfectly black, with not a light visible save those carried by their own car.

Behind them lay the quiet little village of Pelham, and miles away in front was the town of Millen. From time to time, as the car rushed on, The Thinking Machine peered inquisitively through the darkness into the face of the man beside him; but he could barely make out its general shape—a pallid splotch in the darkness. The hand lay quietly beside his own, and a voice mumbled—that was all. The newspaperman and the physician had nothing to say; they too were peering vainly at Fairbanks.

At last, the outlines of a small building loomed dimly in front of them, just off the road. The Thinking Machine leaned forward and touched the chauffeur on the arm.

"We'll stop here for gasoline."

"Gasoline—stop here for gasoline!" babbled the senseless voice beside him.

The Thinking Machine felt the hand he held move spasmodically as the huge car ran off the main roadway and maneuvered back and forth to clear the fairway of its bulk. Finally it stopped, within a few feet of the door of the building.

Hutchinson Hatch and Dr. Pollock rose and got out. Hatch went straight to the little building and rapped sharply on the door. The sound caused Fairbanks to turn vacant, wavering eyes in that direction. After a moment a nightcapped head appeared at the window above. The Thinking Machine shot the beam of a flashlight into Fairbank's face. The eyes, now fixed on the nightcapped head, were wide open, and a glint of childish curiosity lay in them. The babblings were silent for a moment—somewhere in a recess of the maddened brain a germ of intelligence was struggling.

Hatch began and concluded negotiations for five gallons of gasoline. A shrunken old man brought it out in a can, and scuttled back into the house with his safety lantern. Dr. Pollock and Hatch took their seats again, while The Thinking Machine got out and went round to the back, where he spoke to the chauffeur, who was busy at the tank. The chauffeur nodded as if he understood, and followed the scientist to his seat.

"Now for Millen," directed the scientist quietly.

"Millen!" Fairbanks repeated.

The chauffeur twisted his wheel, backed a little, then whirled his car straight to the road again, and shot out through the darkness. For two or three minutes there was complete silence, save for the whir of the engine and the whish of the tires on the road. Then The Thinking Machine spoke over his shoulder to Hatch and Dr. Pollock.

"Did either of you notice anything peculiar?" he inquired.

"No," was the simultaneous response. "Why?"

"Mr. Hatch, you have that automobile map," the scientist continued. "Take this electric light and examine it once more, to satisfy us that there is no road between the little store and Millen."

"I know there isn't," Hatch told him.

"Do as I say!" directed the other. "We can't afford to make mistakes."

Obediently enough, Hatch and Dr. Pollock studied the map. There was the road, straight away from the star indicating the gas station, and on to Millen. There was not a bypath or deviation of any kind marked on it.

"Straight as a string," Hatch announced.

"Now look!" directed The Thinking Machine.

The huge car slowed up and came to a standstill. The glittering lamps of the car showed a fork in the road—two roads, where there were not supposed to be two roads! Hatch glared at them for a moment, then fumbled awkwardly with the automobile map.

"Why, hang it! There can't be two roads!" he declared.

"But there they are," replied The Thinking Machine.

He felt Fairbank's hand flutter, and then it was raised suddenly. Again he threw the light on the pallid face. A strange expression was there; a set, incredible expression which might have meant anything. The eyes were turned ahead to where the road was split by a small clump of trees.

"Keep on to your left," The Thinking Machine directed the chauffeur, without, however, removing his eyes from the face of the man beside him. "A little more slowly."

The car started up again and swung off to the left, sharply. Every eye, save the squint, blue ones of the scientist, was turned ahead; he was still staring into the face of his patient. Only the chauffeur realized what a steady turn to the left the car made; but he said nothing, only felt his way along till suddenly the road widened a little where a path cut through the dense forest. The car slowed up.

"Don't stop!" commanded the scientist sharply. "Go ahead!"

With a sudden spurt the car rushed forward, skimming along easily for a time, and then the heavy jolting told them that the road was growing rougher, and here, dimly ahead of them, they saw an open patch of sky. It was evidently the edge of the forest. The car went steadily on, and out into the open, clear of the forest; then the chauffeur slowed down.

"There isn't any road here," he said.

"Go on!" directed The Thinking Machine. "Road or no road—straight ahead!"

The chauffeur took a new grip on his wheel and went straight ahead, over plowed ground, apparently, for the bumping and jolting were terrific, and the steering gear tore at the sockets of his arms. For two or three minutes they proceeded this way, while the scientist's light still played on Fairbank's face and the squint eyes unwaveringly watched every tiny change in it.

"There!" shrieked Fairbanks suddenly, and he struggled to rise.

"There!"

Hatch and Dr. Pollock saw it at the same instant—a faint, rosy point in the distance; The Thinking Machine didn't alter the direction of his gaze.

"Straight for the light!" he commanded.

. . . the room showed every evidence of occupancy . . . log fire was burning, and its flickering light showed books here and there . . . directly in front stood a man, tall, angular, aged, and a little bent . . . hands were knotted, toil-worn; and the left forefinger was missing . . . eyes white and glassy . . .

With a choking, guttural exclamation, Fairbanks darted forward and placed the grinning god on the mantel beside the piece of crystal, then turned back to The Thinking

Machine and seized him by the arm, as a child might have sought protection. Meanwhile, the strange old man, who seemed oblivious of their presence, stood beside the fire. The scientist moved toward the old man slowly, Fairbanks staring after him as if fascinated. Finally the scientist extended his hand and touched the old man on the shoulder. He started violently and stretched out both hands instinctively.

Then, while Hatch and Dr. Pollock looked on silently, The Thinking Machine stood motionless, while the strange old man's hands ran up his arm, and the fingers touched The Thinking Machine's face. The right forefinger paused for an instant at the scientist's eyes, then was placed lightly across Professor Van Dusen's thin lips. It remained there.

"You are blind?" asked the scientist.

The strange old man nodded.

"You are deaf?"

Again the old man nodded. His forefinger still rested lightly on The Thinking Machine's lips.

"You are dumb?" the scientist went on.

Again the nod.

"Deafness, dumbness, blindness, result of disease?"

The nod again.

The Thinking Machine turned, grasped Fairbank's hand, and lifted it to the old man's shoulder.

"Real, real!" said The Thinking Machine slowly to Fairbanks. "A man—you understand?"

Fairbanks merely stared back; but it was evident that some great struggle was going on in his mind. There was a growing interest in his face, his mouth was no longer flabby, and his eyes were fixed.

. . then came another sound . . . a curdling, nerveracking scream . . . a scream of agony, of pain . . .

At the first sound Fairbanks had straightened up, then slowly he started forward. Three steps, and he fell. Hatch and Dr. Pollock turned him over and found an expression of utter, cringing fear on his face. The eyes were glittering, and he was babbling again. Only his weakness had prevented flight.

"Stay there!" said The Thinking Machine, and ran out of the room.

Hatch heard him as he went up the steps; then after a moment there came more screams—rather, a sharp, intermittent wailing. Fairbanks struggled feebly, then lay still, flat on his back. A minute more, and The Thinking Machine returned, leading a woman by the hand—a woman in a gingham apron and with her hair flying loose about her face. He went straight to the old man, who had stood motionless through it all, and raised the toil-worn finger to his lips.

"This woman—your wife?" he asked.

The old man shook his head.

"Your sister?"

The old man nodded.

"She is insane?"

Again a nod.

The woman stood for an instant with roving eyes, then rushed toward the mantel with a peculiar sobbing cry. In another instant she had clasped the ugly ivory image to her withered breast, and was crooning to it softly, as a mother to her babe. Fairbanks raised himself from the floor, stared at her dully for a moment, then fell back into the arms of Dr. Pollock and Hatch. He had fainted.

"I think, gentlemen, that is all," remarked The Thinking Machine.

It was more than a month later that The Thinking Machine called on William Fairbanks at his home. The young man was sitting up in bed, weak but intelligently aware of everything about him. There was still an occasional restlessness in his eyes; but that was all.

"You remember me, Mr. Fairbanks?" began the scientist.

"Yes," was the reply.

"You remember the events of the night we spent together?"

"Everything, from the time the automobile left the road and the light appeared in the distance," said Fairbanks. "I remember seeing the old man again, and the woman. I know now that he was deaf and dumb and blind, and that she was insane. That seems to clear the situation a great deal." He passed a wasted hand across his brow. "But where is the place? I couldn't find it."

"Listen to me carefully, please," said The Thinking Machine. When you were placed in a sanitorium, the ivory image was taken away from you. I went into the room where you were confined and gave it back to you. It acted as I thought it would—it quieted you. To make certain that it was this and nothing else that had that effect, I took it away from you again, and you grew violent—as a matter of fact, you became so violent that you overturned a heavy table that was bolted to the floor.

"I left the image with you. That really was the tangible cause of your condition. If it hadn't been for that, and your constant brooding over the mystery, the events of that first night would in time have passed out of your mind. But what happened was that you superinduced self-hypnotism with that little image. You understand, of course, that self-hypnotism is possible only to persons of a certain temperament— and only when the object employed to induce self-hypnotism is polished and shiny.

"Although that image brought you to the condition you were in, I restored the little idol to you to quiet you physically. That was necessary before I could reproduce for you the events of the first night. You went with us in an automobile, from Pelham to the little store where you had stopped that first night for gasoline. We too stopped for gasoline, and saw the man you saw that first night. As a matter of fact, he had gone away only for a short time, and is now installed in the little store again.

"Well, from the little store we went as you went the night of your first trouble, until we came to the two roads, one leading by sharp turns to the left. Then we went straight to the farmhouse where the old man and the woman lived. There I wanted to convince you that they were real people— that there was nothing of the ghostly about them. As a matter of fact, the old man and the woman never even realized that you were in the house that night. The man had no means of knowing it, so long as you never touched him, nor he you. You say he brought in something to eat. In all probability that was intended for the woman. You assumed it was for yourself. The fire which compelled you to jump, and which resulted in your sprained ankle, did not destroy the house. There were still marks of the fire there; but the heavy rain extinguished it, and carpenters made the necessary repairs. Now all that is clear, isn't it?"

"Perfectly; but the white thing in the road—the screaming?"

"There is no mystery whatever about that," continued the scientist calmly. "The road that turns to the left turns more sharply than you imagine. After a little distance it goes almost parallel with the main road, so that following it at night you would, without any knowledge of it, pass within a few hundred feet of a point on the main road. Now the house where these people live is, say, five hundred feet from the road that turns to the left—therefore, not more than seven or eight hundred feet, we'll say, from the main road. Thus the screaming you heard on the main road was from the woman who lived in that house; the figure you saw was that woman. Just why she had left the house and was wandering through the wood, we do not know; it is certain that she was there, and was frightened by the storm. Also, she was probably aware that you were pursuing her, and took refuge on an overhanging limb, thus giving you the impression of her figure rising.

"It followed naturally that by the time you had taken the roundabout way with your automobile and reached the house, she had already reached it by going straight ahead through the wood—and again you heard her screams there. Many things happened in the house that night of no consequence in themselves, but which to your excited imagination were mysterious. One of these was the incident of the candle going out. It is obvious that a gust of wind did that, or else a leak in the roof."

Fairbanks was silent for several minutes as he lay back with his eyes closed. "But the vital thing, the thing that bewildered me most of all," he said slowly, "you haven't touched. Why was it that after all my searching I could never again find either the road to the left or the farmhouse?"

"Of course you don't remember," explained The Thinking Machine, "but the night we all went over the route I asked Dr. Pollock and Mr. Hatch just after we left the little store whether they had noticed anything peculiar. They replied in the negative. As a matter of fact," and the scientist was speaking very quietly, "our automobile went the same way yours had gone—not toward Millen, as you supposed and as they supposed, *but back toward Pelham!* You never again found the road to the left or the farmhouse for the simple reason that they were on the other side of the little store—toward Pelham, eight or ten miles away."

A great wave of relief swept over the young man, and he leaned forward eagerly. "But wouldn't I have known when I turned the wrong way?"

The Thinking Machine shrugged his shoulders. "You would have known in daylight, yes," was the reply, "but at night, in a hurry and confused by the flying dust, you simply turned the wrong way. You see how possible it is when I tell you that neither Dr. Pollock nor Mr. Hatch noticed that we had turned the wrong way, even when there was no storm and when I virtually called it to their attention."

There was a long silence. Fairbanks dropped back in the bed, silent.

"In your manuscript," resumed The Thinking Machine at last, "you mentioned that you seemed to hear someone calling you as you started away from the little store. This you attributed vaguely to imagination. As a matter of fact, you did hear someone call—it was the man who had sold you the gasoline. He knew you intended going to Millen, saw that you had turned the wrong way, and called to tell you so. You didn't wait to hear."

And that was all there was to the Mystery of the House That Was . . .

THIN AIR

By Bill Pronzini (1943-   )

Tales featuring impossible crimes have been around a long time and so for that matter have been stories featuring private eyes, but it hasn't been exactly the fashion to put both elements into the same stories. There have been exceptions of course, most notably and successfully Jonathan Latimer in the thirties, but it has not been common. In the last ten years, Bill Pronzini has changed all that. In a series of novels and short stories his downbeat "Nameless" p. i. has investigated a succession of cunningly wrought impossible mysteries, and the considerable reputation Pronzini already had has been further magnified. There is no doubt about it: Bill Pronzini has been the outstanding addition to the impossible canon in the last decade, and "Thin Air" is one of Nameless's most mystifying cases.

THE man I'd been hired to follow was named Lewis Horn-back. He was 43, had dark-brown hair and average features, drove a four-door Dodge Monaco, and lived in a fancy apartment building on Russian Hill. He was also cheating on his wife with an unknown woman and had misappropriated a large sum of money from the interior-design firm they co-owned. Or so Mrs. Hornback alleged. My job was to dig up evidence to support those allegations.

Mrs. Hornback had not told me what she intended to do with any such evidence. Have poor Lewis drawn and quartered, maybe—or at least locked away for the rest of his natural life. She was that kind of women—a thin, pinch-faced harridan ten years older than her husband with vindictive eyes and a desiccated look about her, as if all her vital juices had dried up a long time ago. If Hornback really was cheating on her, maybe he had justifiable cause. But that was not for me to say. It wasn't my job to make moral judgments—all I had to do was make an honest living for myself.

So I took Mrs. Hornback's retainer check, promised to make daily reports, and went to work that same afternoon. Hornback, it seemed, was in the habit of leaving their office at five o'clock most weekdays and not showing up at the Russian Hill apartment until well past midnight. At 4:30 I found a parking space near the garage where he kept his car, on Clay near Van Ness. It was a cold and windy November day, but the sky was clear, with no sign of fog above Twin Peaks or out near the Golden Gate. Which was a relief—tail jobs are tricky enough, especially at night, without the added difficulty of bad weather.

Hornback showed up promptly at five. Eight minutes later he drove his Dodge Monaco down the ramp and turned left on Clay. I gave him a block lead before I pulled out behind him.

He went straight to North Beach, to a little Italian restaurant not far from Washington Square. Meeting the girl friend for dinner, I figured, but it turned out I was wrong. After two drinks at the bar, while I nursed a beer, he took a table alone. I sat at an angle across the room from him, treated myself to *pollo al' diavolo*, and watched him pack away a three-course meal and half a liter of the house wine. Nobody came to talk to him except the waiter; he was just a man having a quiet dinner alone.

He polished off a brandy and three cigarettes for dessert, lingering the way you do after a heavy meal. When he finally left the restaurant it was almost 7:30. From there he walked over to upper Grant, where he gawked at the young counter-culture types who frequent the area, did a little window-shopping, and stopped at a newsstand and a drugstore. I stayed on the opposite side of the street, fifty yards or so behind him. That's about as close to a subject as you want to get on foot. But the walking tail got me nothing except exercise. Hornback was still alone when he led me back to where he had his car.

His next stop was a small branch library at the foot of Russian Hill, where he dropped off a couple of books. Then he headed south on Van Ness, north on Market out of the downtown area, and up the winding expanse of upper Market to the top of Twin Peaks. There was a little shopping area up there, a short distance beyond where Market blends into Portola Drive. He pulled into the parking area in front and went into a neighborhood tavern called Dewey's Place.

I parked down near the end of the lot. Maybe he was meeting the girl friend here or maybe he had just gone into the tavern for a drink; he seemed to like his liquor pretty well. I put on the grey cloth cap I keep in the car, shrugged out of my coat and turned it inside out—it's one of those reversible models—and put it on again that way, just in case Hornback had happened to notice me at the restaurant earlier. Then I stepped out into the cold wind blowing up from the ocean and crossed to Dewey's Place.

There were maybe a dozen customers inside, most of them at the bar. Hornback was down at the far end with a drink in one hand and a cigarette in the other, but the stools on both sides of him were empty. None of the three women in the place looked to be unescorted.

So maybe there wasn't a girl friend. Mrs. Hornback could have been wrong about that, even if she was right about the misappropriation of business funds. It was 9:45 now. If the man had a lady on the side, they would have been together by this time of night. And so far, Hornback had done nothing unusual or incriminating. Hell, he hadn't even done anything interesting.

I sat at the near end of the bar and sipped at a draft beer, watching Hornback in the mirror. He finished his drink, lit a fresh cigarette, and gestured to the bartender for a refill. I thought he looked a little tense, but in the dim lighting I couldn't be sure. He wasn't waiting for anybody, though. I could tell that: no glances at his watch or at the door. Just aimlessly killing time? It could be. For all I knew, this was how he spent each of his evenings out—eating alone, driving alone, drinking alone. And his reason might be the simplest and most innocent of all: he left the office at five and stayed out past midnight because he didn't want to go home to Mrs. Hornback.

When he had downed his second drink he stood up and reached for his wallet. I had already laid a dollar bill on the bar, so I slid off my stool and left ahead of him. I was already in my car when he came out.

Now where? I thought as he fired up the Dodge. Another bar somewhere? A late movie? Home early?

None of those. He surprised me by swinging back east on Portola and then getting into the left-turn lane for Twin Peaks Boulevard. The area up there is residential, at least on the lower part of the hills.de. The road itself winds upward at steep angles, makes a figure-eight loop through the empty wooded expanse of Twin Peaks, and curls down on the opposite side of the hill.

Hornback stayed on Twin Peaks Boulevard, climbing toward the park. So he was probably not going to visit anybody in the area; he had by-passed the only intersecting streets on this side, and there were easier ways to get to the residential sections below the park to the north. I wondered if he was just marking more time, if it was his habit to take a long solitary drive around the city before he headed home.

There was almost no traffic and I dropped back several hundred feet to keep my headlights out of his rear-vision mirror on the turns. The view from up there was spectacular; on a night like this you could see for miles in all directions—the ocean, the full-sweep of the Bay, both bridges, the intricate pattern of lights that was San Francisco and its surrounding communities. Inside the park we passed a couple of cars pulled off on the lookouts that dotted the area: people, maybe lovers, taking in the view.

Hornback went through half the figure-eight from the east to west, driving without hurry. Once I saw the brief, faint flare of a match as he lit another cigarette. When he came out on the far side of the park he surprised me again. Instead of continuing down the hill he slowed and turned to the right onto a short, hooked spur road leading to another of the lookouts.

I tapped my brakes as I neared the turn, trying to decide what to do. The spur was a dead end. I could follow him around it or pull off the road and wait for him to come out again. The latter seemed to be the best choice and I cut my headlights and started to glide off onto a turnaround. But then, over on the spur, Hornback swung past a row of cypress trees that lined the near edge of the lookout. The Dodge's brake lights flashed through the trees; then his headlights, too, winked out.

I kept on going, made the turn, and drifted onto a second, tree-shadowed turnaround just beyond the intersection. Diagonally in front of me I could see Hornback ease the Dodge across the flat surface of the lookout and bring it to a stop nose-up against a perimeter guard rail. The distance between us was maybe 75 yards.

What's he up to now? I thought. Well, he had probably stopped there to take in the view and maybe do a little brooding. The other possibility was that he was waiting for someone. A late-evening rendezvous with the alleged girl friend? The police patrol Twin Peaks Park at regular intervals because kids have been known to use it as a lover's lane, but it was hardly the kind of place two adults would pick for an assignation. Why meet up here when the city is full of hotels and motels?

The Dodge gleamed a dullish black in the straight. From where I was I could see all of the passenger side and the rear third of the driver's side; the interior was shrouded in darkness. Pretty soon another match flared, smearing the gloom for an instant with dim yellowish light. Hornback was not quite a chain smoker, but he was the next thing to it—at least a two-pack a day man. I felt a little sorry for him, and a little envious at the same time; I had smoked two packs a day myself until a year and a half ago, when a doctor discovered a benign lesion on one of my lungs. I hadn't had a cigarette since, though there were still times I craved one. Like right now, watching that dark car and waiting for something to happen or not happen.

I slouched down behind the wheel and tried to make myself comfortable. Five minutes passed, ten minutes, fifteen. Behind me, half a dozen sets of headlights came up or went down the hill on Twin Peaks Boulevard, but none of them turned in where we were. And nothing moved that I could see in or around the Dodge.

I occupied my mind by speculating again about Hornback. He was a puzzle, all right. Maybe a cheating husband and a thief, or maybe an innocent on both counts—the victim of a loveless marriage and a shrewish wife. He hadn't done anything of a guilty or furtive nature tonight, and yet here he was, parked alone at 10:40 P.M. on a lookout in Twin Peaks Park. It could go either way. So which way was it going to go?

Twenty minutes.

And I began to feel just a little uneasy. You get intimations like that when you've been a cop of one type or another as long as I have—vague flickers of wrongness that seem at first to have no foundation. The feeling made me fidgety. I sat up and rolled down my window and peered across at the Dodge. Darkness. Stillness. Nothing out of the ordinary.

Twenty-five minutes.

The wind was chill against my face and I rolled the window back up, but the coldness had got into the car. I drew my coat tight around my neck and kept staring at the Dodge and the bright mosaic of lights beyond, like luminous spangles on the black-velvet sky.

Thirty minutes.

The uneasiness grew and became acute. Something was wrong over there, damn it. A half hour was a long time for a man to sit alone on a lookout, whether he was brooding or not. It was even a long time to wait for a rendezvous. But that was only part of the sense of wrongness. There was something else.

Hornback had not lit another cigarette since that one nearly half an hour ago.

The realization made me sit up again. He had been smoking steadily all night long, even during his walk along upper Grant after dinner. When I was a heavy smoker I couldn't have gone half an hour without lighting up; it seemed funny that Hornback could or would, considering that there was nothing else for him to do in there. He might have run out, of course, yet I remembered seeing a full pack in front of him on the bar at Dewey's Place.

What could be wrong? He was alone up here in his car except for my watching eyes; nothing could have happened to him. Unless . . .

Suicide?

The word popped into my mind and made me feel even colder. Suppose Hornback was innocent of infidelity, but suppose he was also despondent over the state of his marriage. Suppose all the aimless wandering tonight had been a prelude to an attempt on his own life—a man trying to work up enough courage to kill himself on a lonely road high above the city. It was possible. I didn't know enough about Hornback to judge his mental stability.

I wrapped both my hands around the wheel, debating with myself. If I went over to his car and checked on him and he was all right, I would have blown not only the tail but my client's trust. But if I stayed here and Hornback had taken pills or done God knew what to himself, I might be sitting passively by while a man died.

Headlights appeared on Twin Peaks Boulevard behind me, then swung in a slow arc onto the spur road. I drifted lower in the seat and waited for them to pass.

Only they did not pass. The car drew abreast of mine and came to a halt. Police patrol. I sensed it even before I saw the darkened dome flasher on the roof. The passenger window was down and the cop on that side extended a flashlight through the opening and flicked it on. The light pinned me for three or four seconds, bright enough to make me squint, then shut off. The patrolman motioned for me to roll down my window.

I glanced past the cruiser to Hornback's Dodge. It remained dark and there was still no movement anywhere in the vicinity. Well, the decision whether or not to check on him was out of my hands now; the cops would want to have a look at the Dodge in any case. And in any case, my assignment was blown.

I let out a breath and wound down the glass. The patrolman, a young guy with a moustache, said, "What's going on here, fella?"

So I told him, keeping it brief, and let him have a look at the photostat of my investigator's license. He seemed half skeptical and half uncertain; he had me get out and stand to one side while he talked things over with his partner, a heavy-set older man with a beer belly larger than mine. After which the partner took out a second flashlight and trotted across the lookout to the Dodge.

The younger cop asked me some questions and I answered them, but my attention was on the older guy. I watched him reach the driver's door and shine his light through the window. A moment later he appeared to reach down for the door handle, but it must have been locked because I didn't see the door open or him lean inside. Instead he put his light up to the window again, slid it over to the window on the rear door, and then turned abruptly to make an urgent semaphoring gesture.

"Sam!" he shouted. "Get over here on the double!"

The young patrolman, Sam, had his right hand on the butt of his service revolver as we ran ahead to the Dodge. I was expecting the worst by this time, but I wasn't at all prepared for what I saw inside that car. I just stood there gaping while the cops' lights crawled through the interior.

There were spots of drying blood across the front seat.

But the seat was empty, and so was the back seat, and so were the floorboards.

Hornback had disappeared.

One of the two inspectors who arrived on the scene a half hour later was Ben Klein, an old-timer and a casual acquaintance from my own years on the San Francisco cops in the '40s and '50s. I had asked the patrolman to call in Lieutenant Eberhardt, probably my closest friend on or off the force, because I wanted an ally in case matters became dicey. Eb, though, was evidently still on the day shift. I hadn't asked for Klein, but I felt a little better when he showed up.

When he finished checking over the Dodge we went off to one side of it, near the guard rail. From there I could look down a steep slope dotted with stunted trees and underbrush. Search teams were moving along it with flashlights, looking for some sign of Hornback, but so far they didn't seem to be having any luck. Up here the area was swarming with men and vehicles, most but not all of them official. The usual rubberneckers and media types were in evidence along the spur and back on Twin Peaks Boulevard.

"Let me get this straight," Klein said when I had finished giving him my story. He had his hands jammed into his coat pockets and his body hunched against the wind, because the night had turned bitter cold now. "You followed Hornback here around ten-fifteen and you were in a position to watch his car from the time he parked it to the time the two patrolmen showed up."

"That's right."

"You were over on that turnaround?"

"Yes. The whole time."

"And you didn't see anything inside or outside the Dodge?"

"Nothing at all. I couldn't see inside it—too many shadows—but I could see most of the area around it."

"Did you take your eyes off it for any length of time?"

"No. A few seconds now and then, sure, but no more than that."

"Could you see all four doors?"

"Three of the four," I said. "Not the driver's door."

"That's how he disappeared, then."

I nodded. "But what about the dome light? Why didn't I see it go on?"

"It's not working. The bulb's defective. That was one of the first things I checked after we wired up the door lock."

"I also didn't see the door open. I might have missed that, I'll admit, but it's the kind of movement that would have attracted my attention." I paused, working my memory. "Hornback couldn't have gone away toward the road or down the embankment to the east or back into those trees over there. I would have seen him for sure if he had. The only other direction is down this slope, right in front of his car; but if that's it, why didn't I notice any movement when he climbed over the guard rail?"

"Maybe he didn't climb over it. Maybe he crawled under it."

"Why would he have done that?"

"I don't know. I'm only making suggestions."

"Well, I can think of one possibility."

"Which is?"

"The suicide angle," I said. "I told you I was worried about that. What if Hornback decided to do the Dutch, and while he was sitting in the car he used a pocketknife or something else sharp to slash his wrists? That would explain the blood on the front seat. Only he lost his nerve at the last second, panicked, opened the door, fell out of the car, and crawled under the guard rail."

I stopped. The idea was no good. I had realized that even as I laid it out.

Klein knew it too. He was shaking his head. "No blood outside the driver's door or along the side of the car or anywhere under the guard rail. A man with slashed wrists bleeds pretty heavily. Besides, if he'd cut his wrists and had second thoughts, why leave the car at all? Why not just start it up and drive to the nearest hospital?"

"Yeah," I said.

"There's another screwy angle—the locked doors. Who locked them? Hornback? His attacker, if there was one? Why lock them at all?"

I had no answer. I stood brooding out at the city lights.

"Assume he was attacked," Klein said. "By a mugger, say, who's decided to work up here because of the isolation. The attacker would have had to get to the car with you watching, which means coming up this slope, along the side of the car, and in through the driver's door—*if* it wasn't locked at that time. But I don't buy it. It's TV-commando stuff, too far-fetched."

"There's another explanation," I said musingly.

"What's that?"

"The attacker was in the car all along."

"Not a mugger, you mean?"

"Right. Somebody who had it in for Hornback."

Klein frowned; he had heavy jowls and it made him look like a bulldog. "I thought you said Hornback was alone the whole night. Didn't meet anybody."

"He didn't. But suppose he was in the habit of frequenting Dewey's Place and this somebody knew it. He or she could have been waiting in the parking lot, slipped inside the Dodge while Hornback and I were in the tavern, hidden on the floor in back, and stayed hidden until Hornback came up here and parked. Then maybe stuck a knife in him."

"Sounds a little melodramatic, but I guess it's possible. Still, what kind of motive fits that explanation?"

"One connected with the money his wife claims Hornback stole from their firm."

"You're not thinking the wife could've attacked him?"

"No. If she was going to do him in, it doesn't make sense she'd hire me to tail him around. Hornback might have had some accomplice in the theft. Maybe they had a falling-out and the accomplice wanted to keep all the money for himself."

"Maybe," Klein said, but he sounded dubious. "The main trouble with that theory is, what happened to Hornback's body? The attacker would have had to get both himself *and* Hornback out of the car, then drag the body down the slope. Now why in hell would somebody kill a man way up here, with nobody around so far as he knew, and take the corpse away with him instead of just leaving it in the car?"

"I don't know. But I can't figure it any other way."

"Neither can I right now. Let's see what the search teams and the forensic boys turn up."

What the searchers and the lab people turned up, however, was nothing—no sign of Hornback dead or alive, no sign of anybody else in the area, no bloodstains except for those inside the car, no other evidence of any kind. Hornback—or his body—and maybe an attacker as well had not only vanished from the Dodge while I was watching it; he had vanished completely and without a trace. As if into thin air.

It was 1:30 A.M. before Klein let me go home. He asked me to stop in later at the Hall of Justice to sign a statement, but aside from that he seemed satisfied that I had given him all the facts as I knew them. But I was not quite off the hook yet, nor would I be until Hornback turned up. *If* he turned up. My word was all the police had for what had happened on the lookout, and I was the first to admit that it was a pretty bizarre story.

When I got to my Pacific Heights flat I thought about calling Mrs. Hornback. But it was after two o'clock by then and I saw no point or advantage in phoning a report at this time of night; the police would already have told her about her husband's disappearance. So I drank a glass of milk and crawled into bed and tried to sort things into some kind of order.

How had Hornback vanished? Why? Was he dead or alive? An innocent man, or as guilty as his wife claimed? The victim of suicidal depression, the victim of circumstance, or the victim of premeditated murder?

No good. I was too tired to come up with fresh answers to any of those questions.

After a while I slept and dreamed a lot of nonsense about people dematerializing inside locked cars, vanishing in little puffs of smoke. A long time later the telephone woke me up. I keep the damned thing in the bedroom and it went off six inches from my ear and sat me up in bed, disoriented and grumbling. I pawed at my eyes and got them unstuck. There was grey morning light in the room; the nightstand clock said 6:55. Four hours' sleep and welcome to a new day.

The caller, not surprisingly, was Mrs. Hornback. She berated me for not getting in touch with her, then she demanded my version of last night. I gave it to her.

"I don't believe a word of it," she said.

"That's your privilege, ma'am. But it happens to be the truth."

"We'll see about that." Her voice sounded no different from the way it had when she'd hired me: cold, clipped, and coated with vitriol. There was not a whisper of compassion. "How could you let something like that happen? What kind of detective are you?"

A poor tired one, I thought. But I said, "I did what you

asked me to, Mrs. Hornback. What happened on the lookout was beyond my control."

"Yes? Well, if my husband isn't found, and if I don't recover the money I *know* he stole, you'll hear from my lawyer. You can count on that." There was a clattering sound and then the line began to buzz.

Nice lady. A real princess.

I lay back down. I was still half asleep and pretty soon I drifted off again. This time I dreamed I was in a room where half a dozen guys were playing poker. They were all private eyes from the pulp magazines I read and collected—Race Williams, Jim Bennett, Max Latin, some of the best of the bunch. Latin wanted to know what kind of detective I was; his voice sounded just like Mrs. Hornback's. I said I was a pulp detective. They kept saying, "No you're not, you can't play with us because you're not one of us," and I kept saying, "But I am, I'm the same kind of private eye you are."

The jangling of the phone ended that nonsense and sat me up the way it had before. I focused on the clock: 8:40. Conspiracy against my sleep, I thought, and fumbled up the handset.

"Wake you up, hotshot?" a familiar voice said. Eberhardt.

"What do you think?"

"Sorry about that. I've got news for you."

"What news?"

"That funny business up on Twin Peaks last night—your boy Hornback's been found."

I stopped feeling sleepy and the fuzziness cleared out of my mind. "Where?" I said. "Is he all right?"

"In Golden Gate Park," said Eberhardt. "And no, he's not all right. He's dead—been dead since last night. Stabbed in the chest, probably with a butcher knife."

I got down to the Hall of Justice at ten o'clock, showered, shaved, and full of coffee. Eberhardt was in his office in General Works, gnawing on one of his briar pipes and looking as sour as usual. The sourness was just a facade; he wasn't half as grim and grouchy as he liked people to think.

"I've been rereading Klein's report," he said as I sat down. "You get mixed up in the damnedest cases these days."

"Don't I know it. What have you got on Hornback?"

"Nothing much. Guy out jogging found the body at seven-fifteen in a clump of bushes along JFK Drive. Stabbed in the chest, like I told you on the phone—a single wound that penetrated the heart, the probable weapon a butcher knife. The medical examiner says death was instantaneous. I guess that takes care of the suicide theory."

"I guess it does."

"No other marks on the body," he said, "except for a few small scratches on the hands and on one cheek."

"What kind of scratches?"

"Just scratches. The kind you get crawling around in woods or underbrush, or the kind a body might get if it was dragged through the same type of terrain. The ME will have more on that when he finishes his post-mortem."

"What was the condition of Hornback's clothes?"

"Dirty, torn in a couple of places. The same thing applies."

"Anything among his effects?"

"No. The usual stuff—wallet, handkerchief, change, a pack of cigarettes, and a box of matches. Eighty-three dollars in the wallet and a bunch of credit cards. That seems to rule out the robbery motive."

"I don't suppose there was any evidence where he was found."

"None. Killed somewhere else, the way it figures. Like up on that Twin Peaks lookout. Hornback's blood type was AO; it matches the type found on the front seat of his car."

We were silent for a time. I watched Eberhardt break his briar in half and run a pipe-cleaner through the stem. Then I said, "Damn it, Eb, it doesn't make sense. What's the motive behind the whole business? Why would the killer take Hornback's body away and then dump it in Golden Gate Park later? How could he have got it and himself out of the car without me noticing that something was going on?"

"You tell me, mastermind. You were there. You ought to know what you saw or didn't see."

I opened my mouth, closed it again, and blinked at him. "What did you say?"

"You heard me. I said you were there and you ought to know what you saw or didn't see."

What I saw. And what I didn't see.

Eberhardt put his pipe back together and tamped tobacco into the bowl. "We'd better come up with some answers pretty soon," he said. Klein got back a little while ago from breaking the news to the widow. He says she blames you for letting Hornback get killed."

Two things I didn't see that I *should* have seen.

"She claims he siphoned off as much as a hundred thousand dollars from that interior-design company of theirs. According to her, he overcharged some customers, pocketed cash payments from others, and phonied up some records. She also figures he took kickbacks from suppliers."

Several things I *did* see.

"Evidently she accused him of it earlier this week. He denied everything. She's got an auditor going over the books, but that takes time. That's why she hired you."

Add them all up, put them all together—a pattern.

"The money is all she cares about, Klein says. She thinks Hornback spent part of it on the alleged girl friend, but she means to get back whatever's left. That kind of woman can stir up a lot of trouble. No telling what kind of accusations she's liable to—"

Sure. A pattern.

"Hey!" Eberhardt said. "Are you listening to me?"

"What?"

"What's the matter with you? I'm not just talking to hear the sound of my own voice."

I stood up and took a couple of turns around the office. "I think I've got something, Eb."

"Got something? You mean answers?"

"Maybe." I sat down again. "Did you see Hornback's body yourself this morning?"

"I saw it. Why?"

"Were there any marks on it besides the stab wound and the scratches? Any other sort of wound, no matter how small?"

He thought. "No. Except for a Band-Aid on one of his fingers, if that matters—"

"You bet it does." I said. "Get Klein in here, would you? I want to ask him a couple of questions."

Eberhardt gave me a narrow look, but he buzzed out to the

squad room and asked for Klein. Ben came in a few seconds later.

"When you checked over Hornback's car last night," I asked him, "was the emergency brake set?"

"No, I don't think so."

"What about the transmission? Was the lever in Park or Neutral?"

"Neutral."

"I thought so. That's the answer then."

Eberhardt said, "You know how Hornback's body disappeared from his car?"

"Yes. Only it *didn't* disappear from the car."

"Meaning what?"

"Meaning the body was never inside it," I said. "Hornback wasn't murdered on the lookout. He was killed later on, somewhere else."

"What about the blood on the front seat?"

"He put it there himself, deliberately—by cutting his finger with something sharp, like maybe a razor blade. That's the reason for the Band-Aid."

"Why would he do a crazy thing like that?"

"Because he was planning to disappear."

"Come on, you're talking in riddles."

"No, I'm not. If Mrs. Hornback is right about her husband stealing that money—and she has to be—he was wide open to criminal charges. And she's just the type who would press charges. He had no intention of hanging around to face them; his plan from the beginning had to be to stockpile as much money as he could and, when his wife began to tumble to what he was doing, to split with it. And with this girl friend of his, no doubt.

"But he didn't just want to hop a plane for somewhere; that would have made him an obvious fugitive. So he worked out a clever gimmick, or what he thought was clever anyway. He intended to vanish under mysterious circumstances so it would look like he'd met with foul play—abandon his car in an isolated spot with blood all over the front seat. It's been done before and he knew it probably wouldn't fool anybody but he had nothing to lose by trying."

"O.K. This disappearing act of his was in the works for last night—which is why he stopped at the drugstore in North Beach after dinner, to buy razor blades and Band-Aids. But something happened long before he headed up to Twin Peaks that altered the shape of his plan."

Both Eberhardt and Klein were watching me intently. Ed said, "What was that?"

"He spotted me," I said. "I guess I'm getting old and less careful on a tail job than I used to be; either that or he just tumbled to me by accident. I don't suppose it matters. Anyhow, he realized early in the evening that he had a tail—and it wouldn't have taken much effort for him to figure out I was a private detective hired by his wife to get the goods on him. That was when he shifted gears from a half-clever idea to a really clever one. He'd go through with his disappearing act all right, but he'd do it in front of a witness—and under a set of contrived circumstances that were *really* mysterious."

"It's a pretty good scenario so far," Eberhardt said. "But I'm still waiting to find out how he managed to disappear while you were sitting there watching his car."

"He didn't," I said.

"There you go with the riddles again."

"Follow me through. After he left Dewey's Place—while he was stopped at the traffic light on Portola or when he was driving up Twin Peaks Boulevard—he used the razor blade to slice open his finger and drip blood on the seat. Then he bandaged the cut. That took care of part of the trick. The next part came when he reached the lookout."

"There's a screen of cypress trees along the back edge of the lookout where you turn in off the spur road. They create a blind spot for anybody still on Twin Peaks Boulevard, as I was at the time; I couldn't see all of the lookout until after I'd turned onto the spur. As soon as Hornback came into that blind spot he jammed on his brakes and cut his headlights. I told Ben about that—seeing the brake lights flash through the trees and the headlights go dark. It didn't strike me at the time, but when you think about it it's a little odd somebody would switch off his lights on a lookout like that, with a steep slope at the far end, *before* he stops his car."

Eberhardt said, "I think I see the rest of it coming."

"Sure. He hit the brakes hard enough to bring the Dodge

almost, but not quite, to a full stop. At the same time he shoved the transmission into Neutral, shut off the engine, and opened the door. The bulb for the dome light was defective so he didn't have to worry about that. Then he slipped out, pushed down the lock button—a little added mystery—closed the door again, and ran a few steps into the trees where there were enough heavy shadows to hide him and conceal his escape from the area.

"Meanwhile, the car drifted forward nice and slow and came to a halt nose-up against the guard rail. I saw that much, but what I didn't see was the brake lights flash again. As they *should* have if Hornback was still inside the car and stopping it in the normal way."

"One thing," Klein said. "What about that match flare you saw after the car was stopped?"

"That was a nice convincing touch." I said. "When the match flamed, I naturally assumed it was Hornback lighting another cigarette. But I realize now I didn't see anything after that—no sign of a glowing cigarette in the darkness. What really happened is this: he fired a cigarette on his way up to the lookout; I noticed a match flare then too. Before he left the car he put the smoldering butt in the ashtray along with an unused match. As soon as the hot ash burned down far enough it touched off the match. Simple as that."

Eberhardt made chewing sounds an his pipe stem. "O.K.," he said, "you've explained the disappearance. Now explain the murder. Who killed Hornback? Not his wife?"

"No. The last place he would have gone was home and the last person he would have contacted was Mrs. Hornback. It has to be the girl friend. She would be the one who picked him up near the lookout. An argument over the money, maybe—something like that. You'll find out eventually why she did it."

"We won't find out anything unless we know who we're looking for. You got any more rabbits in your hat? Like the name of this girl friend?"

"I don't know her name," I said, "but I think I can tell you where to find her."

He stared at me. "Well?"

"I followed Hornback around to a lot of places last night," I said. "Restaurant, drugstore, newsstand for a pack of cigarette, Dewey's Place for a couple of drinks to shore up his courage—all reasonable stops. But why did he go to the branch library? Why would a man plotting his own disappearance bother to return a couple of library books? Unless the books were just a cover, you see? Unless he really went to the library to tell someone who worked there what he was going to do and where to come pick him up."

"A *librarian?*"

"Why not, Eb? Librarians aren't the stereotypes of fiction. This one figures to be young and attractive, whoever she is. You shouldn't have too much trouble picking out the right one."

He kept on staring at me. Then he shook his head and said, "You know something? You're getting to be a regular Sherlock Holmes in your old age."

"If I am," I said as I stood up, "you're getting to be a regular Lestrade."

That made him scowl. "Who the hell is Lestrade?"

The following day, while I was trying to find a better place to hang the blow-up of the 1932 *Black Mask* cover I keep in my office. Eberhardt called to fill in the final piece. Hornback's girl friend worked at the branch library, all right. Her name was Linda Fields, and she had broken down under police interrogation and confessed to the murder.

The motive behind it was stupid and childish, like a lot of motives behind crimes of passion: Hornback wanted to go to South America, and she wanted to stay in the U.S. They had argued about it on the way to her apartment, the argument had turned nasty after they arrived, Hornback had slapped her, she had picked up a butcher knife, and that was it for him. Afterward she had dragged his body back into her car, taken it to Golden Gate Park, and dumped it. What was left of the stolen money—$98,000 in cash—had been hidden in her apartment. That would make Mrs. Hornback happy—sweet lady that she was—and insure my getting paid for my services.

When Eberhardt finished telling me this, there was a long pause. "Listen," he said, "who's this Lestrade you mentioned yesterday?"

"That's still bothering you, is it?"

"Who is he, damn it? Some character in one of your pulps?"

"Nope. He's a cop in the Sherlock Holmes stories—the one Holmes keeps outwitting."

Eberhardt made a snorting noise, called me something uncomplimentary, and banged the phone down in my ear.

Laughing to myself, I went back to the *Black Mask* poster. Eb was no Lestrade, of course—and I was no Sherlock Holmes. I was the next best thing though. At least to my way of thinking, and in spite of my dream.

A good old-fashioned pulp private eye.

ELSEWHEN

By Anthony Boucher (1911-1968)

Most of the time it would be cheating to combine a locked-room murder with a science-fictional device like a time machine, but not when it's done by Anthony Boucher. Best known as a mystery critic and a science-fiction editor, Boucher began his career as a novelist. His Nine Times Nine, Rocket to the Morgue, *and* The Case of the Empty Key *handle the miracle crime in a manner similar to that of his friends Carr and Rawson, but he is at most delightful in such stories as "Elsewhen" in which locked rooms are scientifically acceptable but in practice disastrous.*

MY dear Agatha," Mr. Partridge announced at the breakfast table, "I have invented the world's first successful time machine."

His sister showed no sign of being impressed. "I suppose this will run the electric bill up even higher," she observed. "Have you ever stopped to consider, Harrison, what that workshop of yours costs us?"

Mr. Partridge listened meekly to the inevitable lecture. When it was over, he protested, "But, my dear, you have just listened to an announcement that no woman on earth has ever heard before. For ages man has dreamed of visiting the past and the future. Since the development of modern time-theory, he has even had some notion of how it might be accomplished. But never before in human history has any-one produced an actual working model of a time-traveling machine."

"Hm-m-m," said Agatha Partridge. "What good is it?"

"Its possibilities are untold." Mr. Partridge's pale little eyes lit up. "We can observe our pasts and perhaps even correct their errors. We can learn the secrets of the ancients. We can plot the uncharted course of the future—new con-quistadors invading brave new continents of unmapped time. We can—"

"Will anyone pay money for that?"

"They will flock to me to pay it," said Mr. Partridge smugly.

His sister began to look impressed. "And how far can you travel with your time machine?"

Mr. Partridge buttered a piece of toast with absorbed concentration, but it was no use. His sister repeated the question: "How far can you go?"

"Not very far," Mr. Partridge admitted reluctantly. "In fact," he added hastily as he saw a more specific question forming, "hardly at all. And only one way. But remember," he went on, gathering courage, "the Wright brothers did not cross the Atlantic in their first model. Marconi did not launch radio with a worldwide broadcast. This is only the beginning and from this seed—"

Agatha's brief interest had completely subsided. "I thought so," she said. "You'd still better watch the electric bill."

It would be that way, Mr. Partridge thought, wherever he went, whomever he saw. "How far can you go?" "Hardly at all." "Good day, sir." People have no imagination. They cannot be made to see that to move along the time line with free volitional motion, unconditioned by the relentless force that pushes mankind along at the unchanging rate of—how shall one put it—one second per second—that to do this for even one little fraction of a second was as great a miracle as to zoom spectacularly ahead to 5900 A.D. He had, he could remember, felt disappointed at first himself—

The discovery had been made by accident. An experiment which he was working on—part of his long and fruitless attempt to recreate by modern scientific method the supposed results described in ancient alchemical works—had necessitated the setting up of a powerful magnetic field. And part of the apparatus within this field was a chronometer.

Mr. Partridge noted the time when he began his experiment. It was exactly fourteen seconds after nine thirty-one. And it was precisely at that moment that the tremor came. It was not a serious shock. To one who, like Mr. Partridge, had spent the past twenty years in southern California it was hardly noticeable, beyond the bother of a broken glass tube which had rolled off a table. But when he looked back at the chronometer, the dial read ten thirteen.

Time can pass quickly when you are absorbed in your work, but not so quickly as all that. Mr. Partridge looked at his pocket watch. It said nine thirty-two. Suddenly, in a space of seconds, the best chronometer available had gained forty-two minutes.

The more Mr. Partridge considered the matter, the more irresistibly one chain of logic forced itself upon him. The chronometer was accurate; therefore it had registered those forty-two minutes correctly. It had not registered them here and now; therefore the shock had jarred it to where it could register them. It had not moved in any of the three dimensions of space; therefore—

The chronometer had gone back in time forty-two minutes, and had registered those minutes in reaching the present again. Or was it only a matter of minutes? The chronometer was an eight-day one. Might it have been twelve hours and forty-two minutes? Forty-eight hours? Ninety-six? A hundred and ninety-two?

And why and how and—the dominant question in Mr.

Partridge's mind—could the same device be made to work with a living being?

He had been musing for almost five minutes. It was now nine thirty-seven, and the dial read ten eighteen. Experimenting at random, he switched off the electromagnet, waited a moment, and turned it on again. The chronometer now read eleven o'clock.

Mr. Partridge remarked that he would be damned—a curiously prophetic remark in view of the fact that this great discovery was to turn him into a murderer.

It would be fruitless to relate in detail the many experiments which Mr. Partridge eagerly performed to verify and check his discovery. They were purely empirical in nature, for Mr. Partridge was that type of inventor which is short on theory but long on gadgetry. He did frame a very rough working hypothesis—that the sudden shock had caused the magnetic field to rotate into the temporal dimension, where it set up a certain—he groped for words—a certain negative potential of entropy, which drew things backward in time. But he would leave the doubtless highly debatable theory to the academicians. What he must do was perfect the machine, render it generally usable, and then burst forth upon an astonished world as Harrison Partridge, the first time traveler. His dry little ego glowed and expanded at the prospect.

There were the experiments in artificial shock which produced synthetically the earthquake effect. There were the experiments with the white mice which proved that the journey through time was harmless to life. There were the experiments with the chronometer which established that the time traversed varied directly as the square of the power expended on the electromagnet.

But these experiments also established that the time elapsed had not been twelve hours nor any multiple thereof, but simply forty-two minutes. And with the equipment at his disposal, it was impossible for Mr. Partridge to stretch that period any further than a trifle under two hours.

This, Mr. Partridge told himself, was ridiculous. Time travel at such short range, and only to the past, entailed no possible advantages. Oh, perhaps some piddling ones—

once, after the mice had convinced him that he could safely venture himself, he had a lengthy piece of calculation which he wished to finish before dinner. An hour was simply not time enough for it; so at six o'clock he moved himself back to five again, and by working two hours in the space from five to six finished his task easily by dinner time. And one evening when, in his preoccupation, he had forgotten his favorite radio quiz program until it was ending, it was simplicity itself to go back to the beginning and comfortably hear it through.

But though such trifling uses as this might be an important part of the work of the time machine once it was established—possibly the strongest commercial selling point for inexpensive home sets—they were not spectacular or startling enough to make the reputation of the machine and—more important—the reputation of Harrison Partridge.

The Great Harrison Partridge would have untold wealth. He could pension off his sister Agatha and never have to see her again. He would have untold prestige and glamour, despite his fat and his baldness, and the beautiful and aloof Faith Preston would fall into his arms like a ripe plum. He would—

It was while he was indulging in one of these dreams of power that Faith Preston herself entered his workshop. She was wearing a white sports dress and looking so fresh and immaculate that the whole room seemed to glow with her presence. She was all the youth and loveliness that had passed Mr. Partridge by, and his pulse galloped at her entrance.

"I came out here before I saw your sister," she said. Her voice was as cool and bright as her dress. "I wanted you to be the first to know. Simon and I are going to be married next month."

Mr. Partridge never remembered what was said after that. He imagined that she made her usual comments about the shocking disarray of his shop and her usual polite inquiries as to his current researches. He imagined that he offered the conventional good wishes and extended his congratulations, too, to that damned young whippersnapper Simon

Ash. But all his thoughts were that he wanted her and needed her and that the great, the irresistible Harrison Partridge must come into being before next month.

Money. That was it. Money. With money he could build the tremendous machinery necessary to carry a load of power— and money was needed for that power, too—that would produce truly impressive results. To travel back even so much as a quarter of a century would be enough to dazzle the world. To appear at the Versailles peace conference, say, and expound to the delegates the inevitable results of their too lenient—or too strict?—terms. Or with unlimited money to course down the centuries, down the millennia, bringing back lost arts, forgotten secrets—

Money—

"Hm-m-m!" said Agatha. "Still mooning after that girl? Don't be an old fool."

He had not seen Agatha come in. He did not quite see her now. He saw a sort of vision of a cornucopia that would give him money that would give him the apparatus that would give him his time machine that would give him success that would give him Faith.

"If you must moon instead of working—if indeed you call this work—you might at least turn off a few switches," Agatha snapped. "Do you think we're made of money?"

Mechanically he obeyed.

"It makes you sick," Agatha droned on, "when you think how some people spend their money. Cousin Stanley! Hiring this Simon Ash as a secretary for nothing on earth but to look after his library and his collections. So much money he can't do anything but waste it! And all Great-uncle Max's money coming to him too, when we could use it so nicely. If only it weren't for Cousin Stanley, I'd be an heiress. And then—"

Mr. Partridge was about to observe that even as an heiress Agatha would doubtless have been the same intolerant old maid. But two thoughts checked his tongue. One was the sudden surprising revelation that even Agatha had her inner yearnings, too. And the other was an overwhelming feeling of gratitude to her.

"Yes," Mr. Partridge repeated slowly. "If it weren't for Cousin Stanley—"

By means as simple as this, murderers are made.

The chain of logic was so strong that moral questions hardly entered into the situation.

Great-uncle Max was infinitely old. That he should live another year was out of the question. And if his son Stanley were to predecease him, then Harrison and Agatha Partridge would be his only living relatives. And Maxwell Harrison was as infinitely rich as he was infinitely old.

Therefore Stanley must die. His life served no good end. Mr. Partridge understood that there are economic theories according to which conspicuous waste serves its purpose, but he did not care to understand them. Stanley alive was worth nothing. Stanley dead cleared the way for the enriching of the world by one of the greatest discoveries of mankind, which incidentally entailed great wealth and prestige for Mr. Partridge. And—a side issue, perhaps, but nonetheless as influential—the death of Stanley would leave his secretary Simon Ash without a job and certainly postpone his marriage to Faith, leaving her time to realize the full worth of Mr. Partridge.

Stanley must die, and his death must be accomplished with a maximum of personal safety. The means for that safety were at hand. For the one completely practical purpose of a short-range time machine, Mr. Partridge had suddenly realized, was to provide an alibi for murder.

The chief difficulty was in contriving a portable version of the machine which would operate over any considerable period of time. The first model had a traveling range of two minutes. But by the end of a week, Mr. Partridge had constructed a portable time machine which was good for forty-five minutes. He needed nothing more save a sharp knife. There was, Mr. Partridge thought, something crudely horrifying about guns.

That Friday afternoon he entered Cousin Stanley's library at five o'clock. This was an hour when the eccentric man of wealth always devoted himself to quiet and scholarly contemplation of his treasures. The butler, Bracket, had been reluctant to announce him, but "Tell my cousin," Mr. Partridge said, "that I have discovered a new entry for is bibliography."

The most recent of Cousin Stanley's collecting manias was fiction based upon factual murders. He had already built up the definitive library on the subject. Soon he intended to publish the definitive bibliography. And the promise of a new item was an assured open-sesame.

The ponderous gruff joviality of Stanley Harrison's greeting took no heed of the odd apparatus he carried. Everyone knew that Mr. Partridge was a crackpot inventor. That he should be carrying a strange framework of wires and magnets occasioned no more surprise than that an author should carry a sheaf of manuscript.

"Bracket tells me you've got something for me," Cousin Stanley boomed. "Glad to hear it. Have a drink? What is it?"

"No thank you." Something in Mr. Partridge rebelled at accepting the hospitality of his victim. "A Hungarian friend of mine was mentioning a novel about one Bela Kiss."

"Kiss?" Cousin Stanley's face lit up with a broad beam. "Splendid! Never could see why no one used him before. Woman killer. Landru type. Always fascinating. Kept 'em in empty gasoline tins. Never would have been caught if there hadn't been a gasoline shortage. Constable thought he was hoarding, checked the tins, found corpses. Beautiful! Now if you'll give me the details—"

Cousin Stanley, pencil poised over a P-slip, leaned over the desk. And Mr. Partridge struck.

He had checked the anatomy of the blow, just as he had checked the name of an obscure but interesting murderer. The knife went truly home, and there was a gurgle and the terrible spastic twitch of dying flesh.

Mr. Partridge was now an heir and a murderer, but he had time to be conscious of neither fact. He went through his carefully rehearsed motions, his mind numb and blank. He latched the windows of the library and locked each door. This was to be an impossible crime, one that could never conceivably be proved on him or on any innocent.

Mr. Partridge stood beside the corpse in the midst of the perfectly locked room. It was four minutes past five. He screamed twice, very loudly, in an unrecognizably harsh voice. Then he plugged his portable instrument into a floor outlet and turned a switch.

It was four nineteen. Mr. Partridge unplugged his machine. The room was empty and the door open. Mr. Partridge's gaze went to the desk. He felt, against all reason and knowledge, that there should be blood—some trace at least of what he had already done, of what was not going to happen for three quarters of an hour yet.

Mr. Partridge knew his way reasonably well about his cousin's house. He got out without meeting anyone. He tucked the machine into the rumble seat of his car and drove off to Faith Preston's. Toward the end of his long journey across town he carefully drove through a traffic light and received a citation noting the time as four-fifty. He reached Faith's at four fifty-four, ten minutes before the murder he had just committed.

Simon Ash had been up all Thursday night cataloguing Stanley Harrison's latest acquisitions. Still he had risen at his usual hour that Friday to get through the morning's mail before his luncheon date with Faith. By four-thirty that afternoon he was asleep on his feet.

He knew that his employer would be coming into the library in half an hour. And Stanley Harrison liked solitude for his daily five o'clock gloating and meditation. But the secretary's work desk was hidden around a corner of the library's stacks, and no other physical hunger can be quite so dominantly compelling as the need for sleep.

.Simon Ash's shaggy blond head sank onto the desk. His sleep-heavy hand shoved a pile of cards to the floor, and his mind only faintly registered the thought that they would all have to be alphabetized again. He was too sleepy to think of anything but pleasant things, like the sailboat at Balboa which brightened his week ends, or the hiking trip in the Sierras planned for his next vacation, or above all Faith. Faith the fresh and lovely and perfect, who would be his next month—

There was a smile on Simon's rugged face as he slept. But he woke with a harsh scream ringing in his head. He sprang to his feet and looked out from the stacks into the library.

The dead hulk that slumped over the desk with the hilt protruding from its back was unbelievable, but even more incredible was the other spectacle. There was a man. His back was toward Simon, but he seemed faintly familiar. He stood close to a complicated piece of gadgetry. There was the click of a switch.

Then there was nothing.

Nothing in the room at all but Simon Ash and an infinity of books. And their dead owner.

Ash ran to the desk. He tried to lift Stanley Harrison, tried to draw out the knife, then realized how hopeless was any attempt to revive life in that body. He reached for the phone, then stopped as he heard the loud knocking on the door.

Over the raps came the butler's voice. "Mr. Harrison! Are you all right, sir?" A pause, more knocking, and then, "Mr. Harrison!

Let me in, sir! Are you all right?"

Simon raced to the door. It was locked, and he wasted almost a minute groping for the key at his feet, while the butler's entreaties became more urgent. At last Simon opened the door.

Bracket stared at him—stared at his sleep-red eyes, his blood-red hands, and beyond him at what sat at the desk. "Mr. Ash, sir," the butler gasped. "What have you done?"

Faith Preston was home, of course. No such essential element of Mr. Partridge's plan could have been left to chance. She worked best in the late afternoons, she said, when she was getting hungry for dinner; and she was working hard this week on some entries for a national contest in soap carving.

The late-afternoon sun was bright in her room, which you might call her studio if you were politely disposed, her garret if you were not. It picked out the few perfect touches of color in the scanty furnishings and converted them into bright aureoles surrounding the perfect form of Faith.

The radio was playing softly. She worked best to music, and that, too, was in integral portion of Mr. Partridge's plan.

Six minutes of unmemorable small talk—What are you working on? How lovely! And what have you been doing lately? Pottering around as usual. And the plans for the wedding?—and then Mr. Partridge held up a pleading hand for silence.

"When you hear the tone," the radio announced, "the time will be exactly five seconds before five o'clock."

"I forgot to wind my watch," Mr. Partridge observed casually. "I've been wondering all day exactly what time it was." He set his perfectly accurate watch.

He took a long breath. And now at last he knew that he was a new man. He was at last the Great Harrison Partridge. The last detail of his perfect plan had been checked off. His labors were over. In another four minutes Cousin Stanley would be dead. In another month or so Great-uncle Max would follow, more naturally. Then wealth and the new machine and power and glory and—

Mr. Partridge looked about the sun-bright garret as though he were a newborn infant with a miraculous power of vision and recognition. He was newborn. Not only had he made the greatest discovery of his generation; he had also committed its perfect crime. Nothing was impossible to this newborn Harrison Partridge.

"What's the matter?" Faith asked. "You look funny. Could I make you some tea?"

"No. Nothing. I'm all right." He walked around behind her and looked over her shoulder at the graceful nude emerging from her imprisonment in a cake of soap. "Exquisite, my dear," he observed. "Exquisite."

"I'm glad you like it. I'm never happy with female nudes; I don't think women sculptors ever are. But I wanted to try it."

Mr. Partridge ran a dry hot finger along the front of the soapen nymph. "A delightful texture," he remarked. "Almost as delightful as—" His tongue left the speech unfinished, but his hand rounded out the thought along Faith's cool neck and cheek.

"Why, Mr. Partridge!" She laughed.

The laugh was too much. One does not laugh at the Great Harrison Partridge, time traveler and perfect murderer. There was nothing in his plan that called for what followed. But something outside of any plans brought him to his knees, forced his arms around Faith's little body, pressed tumultuous words of incoherent ardor from his unwonted lips.

He saw fear growing in her eyes. He saw her hand dart out in instinctive defense and he wrested the knife from it. Then his own eyes glinted as he looked at the knife. It was little, ridiculously little. You could never plunge it through a man's back. But it was sharp—a throat, the artery of a wrist—

His muscles had relaxed for an instant. In that moment of nonvigilance, Faith had wrested herself free. She did not look backward. He heard the clatter of her steps down the stairs, and for a fraction of time the Great Harrison Partridge vanished and Mr. Partridge knew only fear. If he had aroused her hatred, if she should not swear to his alibi—

The fear was soon over. He knew that no motives of enmity could cause Faith to swear to anything but the truth. She was honest. And the enmity itself would vanish when she realized what manner of man had chosen her for his own.

It was not the butler who opened the door to Faith. It was a uniformed policeman, who said, "Whaddaya want here?"

"I've got to see Simon . . . Mr. Ash," she blurted out.

The officer's expression changed. "C'mon," and he beckoned her down the long hall.

Faith followed him, not perhaps so confused as she might ordinarily have been by such a reception. If the mild and repressed Mr. Partridge could suddenly change into a ravening wolf, anything was possible. The respectable Mr. Harrison might quite possibly be in some trouble with the police. But she had to see Simon. She needed reassuring, comforting—

The tall young man in plain clothes said, "My name is Jackson. Won't you sit down? Cigarette?" She waved the pack away nervously. "Hinkle says you wanted to speak to Mr. Ash?"

"Yes, I—"

"Are you Miss Preston? His fiancée?"

"Yes." Her eyes widened. "How did you—Oh, has something happened to Simon?"

The young officer looked unhappy. "I'm afraid something has. Though he's perfectly safe at the moment. You see, he—Damn it all, I never have been able to break such news gracefully."

The uniformed officer broke in. "They took him down to headquarters, miss. You see, it looks like he bumped off his boss."

Faith did not quite faint, but the world was uncertain for a few minutes. She hardly heard Lieutenant Jackson's explanations or the message of comfort that Simon had left for her. She simply held very tight to her chair until the ordinary outlines of things came back and she could swallow again.

"Simon is innocent," she said firmly.

"I hope he is." Jackson sounded sincere. "I've never enjoyed pinning a murder on as decent-seeming a fellow as your fiancé. But the case, I'm afraid, is too clear. If he is innocent, he'll have to tell us a more plausible story than his first one. Murderers that turn a switch and vanish into thin air are not highly regarded by most juries."

Faith rose. The world was firm again, and one fact was clear. "Simon is innocent," she repeated. "And I'm going to prove that. Will you please tell me where I can get a detective?"

The uniformed officer laughed. Jackson started to, but hesitated. The threatened guffaw turned into a not unsympathetic smile. "Of course, Miss Preston, the city's paying my salary under the impression that I'm one. But I see what you mean: You want a freer investigator, who won't be hampered by such considerations as the official viewpoint, or even the facts of the case. Well, it's your privilege."

"Thank you. And how do I go about finding one?"

"Acting as an employment agency's a little out of my line. But rather than see you tie up with some shyster shamus, I'll make a recommendation, a man I've worked with, or against, on a half dozen cases. And I think this set-up is just impossible enough to appeal to him. He likes lost causes."

"Lost?" It is a dismal word.

"And in fairness I should add they aren't always lost after he tackless them. The name's O'Breen—Fergus O'Breen."

Mr. Partridge dined out that night. He could not face the harshness of Agatha's tongue. Later he could dispose of her comfortably; in the meanwhile, he would avoid her as much as possible. After dinner he made a round of the bars on the Strip and played the pleasant game of "If only they knew who was sitting beside them." He felt like Harun-al-Rashid, and liked the glow of the feeling.

On his way home he bought the next morning's *Times* at an intersection and pulled over to the curb to examine it. He had expected sensational headlines on the mysterious murder which had the police completely baffled. Instead he read:

SECRETARY SLAYS EMPLOYER

After a moment of shock the Great Harrison Partridge was himself again. He had not intended this. He would not willingly cause unnecesary pain to anyone. But lesser individuals who obstruct the plans of the great must take their medicine. The weakling notion that had crossed his mind of confessing to save this innocent young man—that was dangerous nonsense that must be eradicated from his thoughts.

That another should pay for your murder makes the perfect crime even more perfect. And if the State chose to dispose of Simon Ash in the lethal-gas chamber—why, it was kind of the State to aid in the solution of the Faith problem.

Mr. Partridge drove home, contented. He could spend the night on the cot in his workshop and thus see that much the less of Agatha. He clicked on the workshop light and froze.

There was a man standing by the time machine. The original large machine. Mr. Partridge's feeling of superhuman selfconfidence was enormous but easily undermined, like a vast balloon that needs only the smallest pin prick to shatter it. For a moment he envisioned a scientific master mind of the police who had deduced his method, tracked him here, and discovered his invention.

Then the figure turned.

Mr. Partridge's terror was only slightly lessened. For the figure was that of Mr. Partridge. There was a nightmare instant when he thought of Doppelganger, of Poe's William Wilson, of dissociated personalities, of Dr. Jekyll and Mr. Hyde. Then this other Mr. Partridge cried aloud and hurried from the room, and the entering one collapsed.

A trough must follow a crest. And now blackness was the inexorable aftermath of Mr. Partridge's elation. His successful murder, his ardor with Faith, his evening as Harun-al-Rashid, all vanished, to leave him an abject crawling thing faced with the double fear of madness and detection. He heard horrible noises in the room, and realized only after minutes that they were his own sobs.

Finally he pulled himself to his feet. He bathed his face in cold water from the sink, but still terror gnawed at him. Only one thing could reassure him. Only one thing could still convince him that he was the Great Harrison Partridge. And that was his noble machine. He touched it, carassed it as one might a fine and dearly loved horse.

Mr. Partridge was nervous, and he had been drinking more than his frugal customs allowed. His hand brushed the switch. He looked up and saw himself entering the door. He cried aloud and hurried from the room.

In the cool night air he slowly understood. He had accidentally sent himself back to the time he entered the room, so that upon entering he had seen himself. There was nothing more to it than that. But he made a careful mental note: Always take care, when using the machine, to avoid returning to a time-and-place where you already are. Never meet yourself. The dangers of psychological shock are too great.

Mr. Partridge felt better now. He had frightened himself, had he? Well, he would not be the last to tremble in fear of the Great Harrison Partridge.

Fergus O'Breen, the detective recommended—if you could call it that—by the police lieutenant, had his office in a ramshackle old building at Second and Spring. There were two, she imagined they were clients, in the waiting room ahead of Faith. One looked like the most sodden type of Skid Row loafer, and the elegant disarray of the other could mean nothing but the lower reaches of the upper layers of Hollywood.

The detective, when Faith finally saw him, inclined in costume toward the latter, but he wore sports clothes as though they were pleasantly comfortable, rather than as the badge of a caste. He was a thin young man, with sharpish features and very red hair. What you noticed most were his eyes—intensely green and alive with a restless curiosity. They made you feel that his work would never end until that curiosity had been satisfied.

He listened in silence to Faith's story, not moving save to make an occasional note. He was attentive and curious, but Faith's spirits sank as she saw the curiosity in the green eyes deaden to hopelessness. When she was through, he rose, lit a cigarette, and began pacing about the narrow inner office.

"I think better this way," he apologized. "I hope you don't mind. But what have I got to think about? Look: This is what you've told me. Your young man, this Simon Ash, was alone in the library with his employer. The butler heard a scream. Knocked on the door, tried to get in, no go. Ash unlocks the door from the inside. Police search later shows all other doors and windows likewise locked on the inside. And Ash's prints are on the murder knife. My dear Miss Preston, all that's better than a signed confession for any jury."

"But Simon is innocent," Faith insisted. "I know him, Mr. O'Breen. It isn't possible that he could have done a thing like that."

"I understand how you feel. But what have we got to go on besides your feelings? I'm not saying they're wrong; I'm trying to show you how the police and the court would look at it."

"But there wasn't any reason for Simon to kill Mr. Harrison. He had a good job. He liked it. We were going to get married. Now he hasn't any job or . . . or anything."

"I know." The detective continued to pace. "That's the one point you've got—absence of motive. But they've convicted without motive before this. And rightly enough. Murderers don't always think like the rational man. Anything can be a motive. The most outrageous and fascinating French murder since Landru was committed because the electric toaster didn't work right that morning. But let's look at motives. Mr. Harrison was a wealthy man; where does all that money go?"

"Simon helped draft his will. It all goes to libraries and foundations and things. A little to the servants, of course—"

"A little can turn the trick. But no near relatives?"

"His father's still alive. He's terribly old. But he's so rich himself that it'd be silly to leave him anything."

Fergus snapped his fingers. "Max Harrison! Of course. The superannuated robber-baron, to put it politely, who's been due to die any time these past ten years. And leave a mere handful of millions. There's a motive for you."

"How so?"

"The murderer could profit from Stanley Harrison's death, not directly if all his money goes to foundations, but indirectly from his father. Combination of two classic motives—profit and elimination. Who's next in line for old man Harrison's fortune?"

"I'm not sure. But I do know two people who are sort of second cousins or something. I think they're the only living relatives. Agatha and Harrison Partridge." Her eyes clouded a little as she mentioned Mr. Partridge and remembered his strange behavior yesterday.

Fergus' eyes were brightening again. "At least it's a lead. Simon Ash had no motive and one Harrison Partridge had a honey. Which proves nothing, but gives you some place to start."

"Only—" Faith protested. "Only Mr. Partridge couldn't possibly have done it either."

Fergus stopped pacing. "Look, madam. I am willing to grant the unassailable innocence of one suspect on a client's word. Otherwise I'd never get clients. But if every individual who comes up is going to turn out to be someone in whose pureness of soul you have implicit faith and—"

"It isn't that. Not just that. Of course I can't imagine Mr. Partridge doing a thing like that—"

"You never can tell," said Fergus a little grimly. "Some of my best friends have been murderers."

"But the murder was just after five o'clock, the butler says. And Mr. Partridge was with me then, and I live way across town from Mr. Harrison's."

"You're sure of the time?"

"We heard the five-o'clock radio signal and he set his watch." Her voice was troubled and she tried not to remember the awful minutes afterward.

"Did he make a point of it?"

"Well . . . we were talking and he stopped and held up his hand and we listened to the bong."

"Hm-m-m." This statement seemed to strike the detective especially. "Well, there's still the sister. And anyway, the Partridges give me a point of departure, which is what I needed."

Faith looked at him hopefully. "Then you'll take the case?"

"I'll take it. God knows why. I don't want to raise your hopes, because if ever I saw an unpromising set-up it's this. But I'll take it. I think it's because I can't resist the pleasure of having a detective lieutenant shove a case into my lap."

"Bracket, was it usual for that door to be locked when Mr. Harrison was in the library?"

The butler's manner was imperfect; he could not decide whether a hired detective was a gentleman or a servant. "No," he said, politely enough but without a "sir." No, it was most unusual."

"Did you notice if it was locked earlier?"

"It was not. I showed a visitor in shortly before the . . . before this dreadful thing happened."

"A visitor?" Fergus' eyes glinted. He began to have visions of all the elaborate possibilities of locking doors from the outside so that they seem locked on the inside. "And when was this?"

"Just on five o'clock, I thought. But the gentleman called here today to offer his sympathy, and he remarked, when I mentioned the subject, that he believed it to have been earlier."

"And who was this gentleman?"

"Mr. Harrison Partridge."

Hell, thought Fergus. There goes another possibility. It must have been much earlier if he was at Faith Preston's by five. And you can't tamper with radio time signals as you might with a clock. However—"Notice anything odd about Mr. Partridge? Anything in his manner?"

"Yesterday? No, I did not. He was carrying some curious contraption—I hardly noticed what. I imagine it was some recent invention of his which he wished to show to Mr. Harrison."

"He's an inventor, this Partridge? But you said yesterday. Anything odd about him today?"

"I don't know. It's difficult to decribe. But there was something about him as though he had changed—grown, perhaps."

"Grown up?"

"No. Just grown."

"Now, Mr. Ash, this man you claim you saw—"

"Claim! Damn it, O'Breen, don't you believe me either?"

"Easy does it. The main thing for you is that Miss Preston believes you, and I'd say that's a lot. And I'm doing my damnedest to substantiate her belief. Now this man you saw, if that makes you any happier in this jail, did he remind you of anyone? Was there any suggestion—"

"I don't know. It's bothered me. I didn't get a good look, but there was something familiar—"

"You say he had some sort of machine beside him?"

Simon Ash was suddenly excited. "You've got it. That's it."

"That's what?"

"Who it was. Or who I thought it was. Mr. Partridge. He's some sort of a cousin of Mr. Harrison's. Screwball inventor."

"Miss Preston, I'll have to ask you more questions. Too many signposts keep pointing one way, and even if that way's a blind alley I've got to go up it. When Mr. Partridge called on you yesterday afternoon, what did he do to you?"

"Do to me?" Faith's voice wavered. "What on earth do you mean?"

"It was obvious from your manner earlier that there was something about that scene you wanted to forget. I'm afraid it'll have to be told. I want to know everything I can about Mr. Partridge, and particularly Mr. Partridge yesterday."

"He—Oh, no, I can't. Must I tell you, Mr. O'Breen?"

"Simon Ash says the jail is not bad after what he's heard of jails, but still—"

"All right. I'll tell you. But it was strange. I . . . I suppose I've known for a long time that Mr. Partridge was—well, you might say in love with me. But he's so much older than I am and he's very quiet and never said anything about it and—well, there it was, and I never gave it much thought one way or another. But yesterday—It was as though . . . as though he were possessed. All at once it seemed to burst out and there he was making love to me. Frightfully, horribly. I couldn't stand it. I ran away." Her slim body shuddered now with the memory. "That's all there was to it. But it was terrible."

"You pitched me a honey this time, Andy."

Lieutenant Jackson grinned. "Thought you'd appreciate it, Fergus."

"But look: What have you got against Ash but the physical set-up of a locked room? The oldest cliché in murderous fiction, and not unheard of in fact. 'Locked rooms' can be unlocked. Remember the Carruthers case?"

"Show me how to unlock this one and your Mr. Ash is a free man."

"Set that aside for the moment. But look at my suspect, whom we will call, for the sake of novelty, X. X is a mild-mannered, inoffensive man who stands to gain several million by Harrison's death. He shows up at the library just before the murder. He's a crackpot inventor, and he has one of his gadgets with him. He shows an alibi-conscious aware-ness of time. He tries to get the butler to think he called earlier. He calls a witness' attention ostentatiously to a radio time signal. And most important of all, psychologically, he changes. He stops being mild-mannered and inoffensive. He goes on the make for a girl with physical violence. The butler describes him as a different man; he's grown."

Jackson nodded. "It's a good case. And the inventor's gadget, I suppose, explains the locked room?"

"Probably, when we learn what it was. You've got a good mechanical mind, Andy. That's right up your alley."

Jackson drew a note pad toward him. "Your X sounds worth questioning, to say the least. But this reticence isn't like you, Fergus. Why all this innuendo? Why aren't you telling me to get out of here and arrest him?"

Fergus was not quite his cocky self. "Because you see, that alibi I mentioned—well, it's good. I can't crack it. It's perfect."

Lieutenant Jackson shoved the pad away. "Run away and play," he said wearily.

"It couldn't be phony at the other end?" Fergus urged. "Some gadget planted to produce those screams at five o'clock to give a fake time for the murder?"

Jackson shook his head. "Harrison finished tea around four-thirty. Stomach analysis shows the food had been di-gested just about a half-hour. No, he died at five o'clock, all right."

"X's alibi's perfect, then," Fergus repeated. "Unless . . . unless—" His green eyes blinked with amazed realization. "Oh, my dear God—" he said softly.

"Unless what?" Jackson demanded. There was no answer.

It was the first time in history that the lieutenant had ever seen The O'Breen speechless.

Mr. Partridge was finding life pleasant to lead. Of course this was only a transitional stage. At present he was merely the—what was the transitional stage between cocoon and fully developed insect? Larva? Imago? Pupa? Outside of his own electro-inventive field. Mr. Partridge was not a well-informed man. That must be remedied. But let the metaphor go. Say simply that he was now in the transition between the meek worm that had been Mr. Partridge and the Great Harrison Partridge who would emerge triumphant when Great-uncle Max died and Faith forgot that poor foolish doomed young man.

Even Agatha he could tolerate more easily in this pleasant state, although he had nonetheless established permanent living quarters in his workroom. She had felt her own pleasure at the prospect of being an heiress, but had expressed it most properly by buying sumptuous mourning for Cousin Stanley—the most expensive clothes that she had bought in the past decade. And her hard edges were possibly softening a little—or was that the pleasing haze, almost like that of drunkenness, which now tended to soften all hard edges for Mr. Partridge's delighted eyes?

Life possessed pleasures that he had never dreamed of before. The pleasure, for instance, of his visit to the dead man's house to pay his respects, and to make sure that the butler's memory of time was not too accurately fixed. Risky, you say? Incurring the danger that one might thereby only fix it all the more accurately? For a lesser man, perhaps yes; but for the newly nascent Great Harrison Partridge a joyous exercise of pure skill.

It was in the midst of some such reverie as this that Mr. Partridge, lolling idly in his workshop with an unaccustomed tray of whiskey, ice and siphon beside him, casually overheard the radio announce the result of the fourth race at Hialeah and noted abstractedly that a horse named Karabali had paid forty-eight dollars and sixty cents on a two-dollar ticket. He had almost forgotten the only half-registered fact when the phone rang.

He answered, and a grudging voice said, "You can sure

pick 'em. That's damned near five grand you made on Karabali."

Mr. Partridge fumbled with vocal noises.

The voice went on, "What shall I do with it? Want to pick it up tonight or—"

Mr. Partridge had been making incredibly rapid mental calculations. "Leave it in my account for the moment," he said firmly. "Oh, and—I'm afraid I've mislaid your telephone number."

"Trinity 2897. Got any more hunches now?"

"Not at the moment. I'll let you know."

Mr. Partridge replaced the receiver and poured himself a stiff drink. When he had downed it, he went to the machine and traveled two hours back. He returned to the telephone, dialed TR 2897, and said, "I wish to place a bet on the fourth race at Hialeah."

The same voice said, "And who're you?"

"Partridge. Harrison Partridge."

"Look, brother. I don't take bets by phone unless I see some cash first, see?"

Mr. Partridge hastily recalculated. As a result the next half hour was as packed with action as the final moments of his great plan. He learned about accounts, he ascertained the bookmaker's address, he hurried to his bank and drew out an impressive five hundred dollars which he could ill spare, and he opened his account and placed a two-hundred-dollar bet which excited nothing but a badly concealed derision.

Then he took a long walk and mused over the problem. He recalled happening on a story once in some magazine which proved that you could not use knowledge from the future of the outcome of races to make your fortune, because by interfering with your bet you would change the odds and alter the future. But he was not plucking from the future; he was going back into the past. The odds he had heard were already affected by what he had done. From his subjective point of view, he learned the result of his actions before he performed them. But in the objective physical temporospatial world, he performed those actions quite normally and correctly before their results.

It was perfect—for the time being. It could not, of course,

be claimed as one of the general commercial advantages of the time machine. Once the Partridge principle became common knowledge, all gambling would inevitably collapse. But for this transitional stage it was ideal. Now, while he was waiting for Great-uncle Max to die and finance his great researches, Mr. Partridge could pass his time waiting for the telephone to inform him of the brilliant coup he had made. He could quietly amass an enormous amount of money and—

Mr. Partridge stopped dead on the sidewalk and a strolling couple ran headlong into him. He scarcely noticed the collision. He had had a dreadful thought. The sole acknowledged motive for his murder of Cousin Stanley had been to secure money for his researches. Now he learned that this machine, even in its present imperfect form, could provide him with untold money.

He had never needed to murder at all.

"My dearest Maureen," Fergus announced at the breakfast table, "I have discovered the world's first successful time machine."

His sister showed no signs of being impressed. "Have some more tomato juice," she suggested. "Want some tabasco in it? I didn't know that the delusions could survive into the hangover."

"But Macushla," Fergus protested, "you've just listened to an announcement that no woman on earth has ever heard before."

"Fergus O'Breen, Mad Scientist." Maureen shook her head. "It isn't a role I'd cast you for. Sorry."

"If you'd listen before you crack wise, I said 'discovered.' Not 'invented.' It's the damnedest thing that's ever happened to me in business. It hit me in a flash while I was talking to Andy. It's the perfect and only possible solution to a case. And who will ever believe me? Do you wonder that I went out and saturated myself last night?"

Maureen frowned. "You mean this? Honest and truly?"

"Black and bluely, my sweeting, and all the rest of the childish rigmarole. It's the McCoy. Listen." And he briefly outlined the case. "Now what sticks out like a sore thumb is this: Harrison Partridge establishing an alibi. The radio time signal, the talk with the butler—I'll even lay odds that the murderer himself gave those screams so there'd be no question as to time of death. Then you rub up against the fact that the alibi, like the horrendous dream of the young girl from Peru, is perfectly true.

"But what does an alibi mean? It's my own nomination for the most misued word in the language. It's come to mean a disproof, an excuse. But strictly it means nothing, but *elsewhere*. You know the classic gag: 'I wasn't there, this isn't the woman, and, anyway, she gave in.' Well, of those three redundant excuses, only the first is an alibi, an *elsewhere* statement. Now Partridge's claim of being elsewhere is true enough. He hasn't been playing with space, like the usual alibi builder. And even if we could remove him from elsewhere and put him literally on the spot, he could say: 'I couldn't have left the room after the murder; the doors were all locked on the inside.' Sure he couldn't—not *at that time*. And his excuse is not an *elsewhere*, but an *elsewhen*."

Maureen refilled his coffee cup and her own. "Hush up a minute and let me think it over." At last she nodded slowly. "And he's an eccentric inventor and when the butler saw him he was carrying one of his gadgets."

"Which he still had when Simon Ash saw him vanish. He committed the murder, locked the doors, went back in time, walked out through them in their unlocked past, and went off to hear the five o'clock radio bong at Faith Preston's."

"But you can't try to sell the police on that. Not even Andy. He wouldn't listen to—"

"I know. Damn it, I know. And meanwhile that Ash, who seems a hell of a good guy—our kind of people, Maureen—sits there with the surest reserved booking for the lethal-gas chamber I've ever seen."

"What are you going to do?"

"I'm going to see Mr. Harrison Partridge. And I'm going to ask for an encore."

"Quite an establishment you've got here," Fergus observed to the plump bald little inventor.

Mr. Partridge smiled courteously. "I amuse myself with my small experiments," he admitted.

"I'm afraid I'm not much aware of the wonders of modern science. I'm looking forward to the more spectacular marvels, spaceships for instance, or time machines. But that wasn't what I came to talk about. Miss Preston tell me you're a friend of hers. I'm sure you're in sympathy with this attempt of hers to free young Ash."

"Oh, naturally. Most naturally. Anything that I can do to be of assistance—"

"It's just the most routine sort of question, but I'm groping for a lead. Anything that might point out a direction for me. Now, aside from Ash and the butler, you seem to have been the last person to see Harrison alive. Could you tell me anything about him? How was he?"

"Perfectly normal, so far as I could observe. We talked about a new item which I had unearthed for his bibliography, and he expressed some small dissatisfaction with Ash's cataloguing of late. I believe they had had words on the matter earlier."

"Nothing wrong with Harrison? No . . . no depression."

"You're thinking of suicide? My dear young man, that hare won't start, I'm afraid. My cousin was the last man on earth to contemplate such an act."

"Brackel says you had one of your inventions with you?"

"Yes, a new, I thought, and highly improved frame for photostating rare books. My cousin, however, pointed out that the same improvements had recently been made by an Austrian *emigré* manufacturer. I abandoned the idea and reluctantly took apart my model."

"A shame. But I suppose that's part of the inventor's life, isn't it?"

"All too true. Was there anything else you wished to ask me?"

"No. Nothing really." There was an awkward pause. The smell of whiskey was in the air, but Mr. Partridge proffered no hospitality. "Funny the results a murder will have, isn't it? To think how this frightful fact will benefit cancer research."

"Cancer research?" Mr. Partridge wrinkled his brows. "I did not know that that was among Stanley's beneficiaries."

"Not your cousin's no. But Miss Preston tells me that old Max Harrison has decided that since his only direct descendant is dead, his fortune might as well go to the world. He's planning to set up a medical foundation to rival Rockefeller's, and specializing in cancer. I know his lawyer slightly; he mentioned he's going out there tomorrow."

"Indeed," said Mr. Partridge evenly.

Fergus paced. "If you can think of anything, Mr. Partridge, let me know. I've got to clear Ash. I'm convinced he's innocent, but if he is, then this seems like the perfect crime at last. A magnificent piece of work, if you can look at it like that." He looked around the room. "Excellent small workshop you've got here. You can imagine almost anything coming out of it."

"Even," Mr. Partridge ventured, "your spaceships and time machines?"

"Hardly a spaceship," said Fergus.

Mr. Partridge smiled as the young detective departed. He had, he thought, carried off a difficult interview in a masterly fashion. How neatly he had slipped in that creative bit about Stanley's dissatisfaction with Ash! How brilliantly he had improvised a plausible excuse for the machine he was carrying!

Not that the young man could have suspected anything. It was patently the most routine visit. It was almost a pity that this was the case. How pleasant it would be to fence with a detective—master against master. To have a Javert, a Porfir, a Maigret on his trail and to admire the brilliance with which the Great Harrison Partridge should baffle him.

Perhaps the perfect criminal should be suspected, even known, and yet unattainable—

The pleasure of this parrying encounter confirmed him in the belief that had grown in him overnight. It is true that it was a pity that Stanley Harrison had died needlessly. Mr. Partridge's reasoning had slipped for once; murder for profit had not been an essential part of the plan.

And yet what great work had ever been accomplished without death? Does not the bell ring the truer for the blood of the hapless workmen? Did not the ancients wisely believe that greatness must be founded upon a sacrifice? Not self-sacrifice, in the stupid Christian perversion of that belief, but a true sacrifice of another's flesh and blood.

So Stanley Harrison was the needful sacrifice from which should arise the Great Harrison Partridge. And were its effects not already visible? Would he be what he was today, would he so much as have emerged from the cocoon, purely by virtue of his discovery?

No, it was his great and irretrievable deed, the perfection of his crime, that had molded him. In blood is greatness.

That ridiculous young man, prating of the perfection of the crime and never dreaming that—

Mr. Partridge paused and reviewed the conversation. There had twice been that curious insistence upon time machines. Then he had said—what was it?—"the crime was a magnificent piece of work," and then, "you can imagine almost anything coming out of this workshop." And the surprising news of Great-uncle Max's new will—

Mr. Partridge smiled happily. He had been unpardonably dense. Here was his Javert, his Porfir. The young detective did indeed suspect him. And the reference to Max had been a temptation, a trap. The detective could not know how unnecessary that fortune had now become. He had thought to lure him into giving away his hand by an attempt at another crime.

And yet, was any fortune ever unnecessary? And a challenge like that—so direct a challenge—could one resist it?

Mr. Partridge found himself considering all the difficulties. Great-uncle Max would have to be murdered today, if he planned on seeing his lawyer tomorrow. The sooner the better. Perhaps his habitual after-lunch siesta would be the best time. He was always alone then, dozing in his favorite corner of that large estate in the hills.

Bother! A snag. No electric plugs there. The portable model was out. And yet—Yes, of course. It could be done the other way. With Stanley, he had committed his crime, then gone back and prepared his alibi. But here he could just as well establish the alibi, then go back and commit the murder, sending himself back by the large machine here with wider range. No need for the locked-room effect. That was pleasing, but not essential.

An alibi for one o'clock in the afternoon. He did not care to use Faith again. He did not want to see her in his larval stage. He would let her suffer through her woes for that poor devil Ash, and then burst upon her in his glory as the Great Harrison Partridge. A perfectly reliable alibi. He might obtain another traffic ticket, though he had not yet been forced to produce his first one. Surely the police would be as good as—

The police. But how perfect. Ideal. To go to headquarters and ask to see the detective working on the Harrison case. Tell him, as a remembered afterthought, about Cousin Stanley's supposed quarrel with Ash. Be with him at the time Great-uncle Max is to be murdered.

At twelve-thirty Mr. Partridge left his house for the central police station.

There was now no practical need for him to murder Maxwell Harrison. He had, in fact, not completely made up his mind to do so. But he was taking the first step in his plan.

Fergus could hear the old man's snores from his coign of vigilance. Getting into Maxwell Harrison's hermitlike retreat had been a simple job. The newspapers had for years so thoroughly covered the old boy's peculiarities that you knew in advance all you needed to know—his daily habits, his loathing for bodyguards, his favorite spot for napping.

His lack of precautions had up till now been justified. Servants guarded whatever was of value in the house; and who would be so wanton as to assault a man nearing his century who carried nothing of value on his person? But now—

Fergus had sighed with more than ordinary relief when he reached the spot and found the quarry safe. It would have been possible, he supposed, for Mr. Partridge to have gone back from his interview with Fergus for the crime. But the detective had banked on the criminal's disposition to repeat himself—commit the crime, in this instance, first, and then frame the *elsewhen.*

The sun was warm and the hills were peaceful. There was a purling stream at the deep bottom of the gully beside Fergus. Old Maxwell Harrison did well to sleep in such perfect solitude.

Fergus was on his third cigarette before he heard a sound. It was a very little sound, the turning of a pebble, perhaps;

but here in this loneliness any sound that was not a snore or a stream seemed infinitely loud.

Fergus flipped his cigarette into the depths of the gully and moved, as noiselessly as was possible, toward the sound, screening himself behind scraggly bushes.

The sight, even though expected, was nonetheless startling in this quiet retreat: a plump bald man of middle age advancing on tiptoe with a long knife gleaming in his upraised hand.

Fergus flung himself forward. His left hand caught the knifebrandishing wrist and his right pinioned Mr. Partridge's other arm behind him. The face of Mr. Partridge, that had been so bland a mask of serene exaltation as he advanced to his prey, twisted itself into something between rage and terror.

His body twisted itself, too. It was an instinctive, untrained movement, but timed so nicely by accident that it tore his knife hand free from Fergus' grip and allowed it to plunge downward.

The twist of Fergus' body was deft and conscious, but it was not quite enough to avoid a stinging flesh wound in the shoulder. He felt warm blood trickling down his back. Involuntarily he released his grip on Mr. Partridge's other arm.

Mr. Partridge hesitated for a moment, as though uncertain whether his knife should taste of Great-uncle Max or first dispose of Fergus. The hesitation was understandable, but fatal. Fergus sprang forward in a flying tackle aimed at Mr. Partridge's knees. Mr. Partridge lifted his foot to kick that advancing green-eyed face. He swung and felt his balance going. Then the detective's shoulder struck him. He was toppling, falling over backward, falling, falling—

The old man was still snoring when Fergus returned from his climb down the gully. There was no doubt that Harrison Partridge was dead. No living head could loll so limply on its neck.

And Fergus had killed him. Call it an accident, call it self-defense, call it what you will. Fergus had brought him to a trap, and in that trap he had died.

The brand of Cain may be worn in varying manners. To

Mr. Partridge it had assumed the guise of inspiring pa-
nache, a banner with a strange device, but Fergus wore his
brand with a difference.

The shock of guilt did not bite too deeply into his conscience. He had brought about inadvertently and in person
what he had hoped to bring the State to perform with all due
ceremony. Human life, to be sure, is sacred; but believe too
strongly in that precept, and what becomes of capital pun-
ishment or of the noble duties of war?

He could not blame himself morally, perhaps, for Mr.
Partridge's death. But he could blame himself for professional failure in that death. He had no more proof than before to
free Simon Ash, and he had burdened himself with a killing.
A man killed at your hand in a trap of your devising—what
more sure reason could deprive you of your license as a
detective? Even supposing, hopefully, that you escaped a
murder rap.

For murder can spread in concentric circles, and Fergus
O'Breen, who had set out to trap a murderer, now found
himself being one.

Fergus hesitated in front of Mr. Partridge's workshop. It
was has last chance. There might be evidence here—the
machine itself or some document that could prove his theory
even to the skeptical eye of Detective Lieutenant A. Jackson.
Housebreaking would be a small offense to add to his record
now. The window on the left, he thought—

"Hi!" said Lieutenant Jackson cheerfully. "You on his trail,
too?"

Fergus tried to seem his usual jaunty self. "Hi, Andy. So
you've finally got around to suspecting Partridge?"

"Is he your mysterious X? I thought he might be."

"And that's what brings you out here?"

"No. He roused my professional suspicions all by himself.
Came into the office an hour ago with the damnedest cock-
and-bull story about some vital evidence he'd forgotten.
Stanley Harrison's last words, it seems, were about a quarrel
with Simon Ash. It didn't ring good—seemed like a deliberate effort to strengthen the case against Ash. As soon as I
could get free, I decided to come out and have a further chat
with the lad."

"I doubt if he's home," said Fergus.

"We can try." Jackson rapped on the door of the workshop. It was opened by Mr. Partridge.

Mr. Partridge held in one hand the remains of a large openface ham sandwich. When he had opened the door, he picked up with the other hand the remains of a large whiskey and soda. He needed sustenance before this bright new adventure, this greater-than-perfect crime, because it arose from no needful compulsion and knew no normal motive.

Fresh light gleamed in his eyes as he saw the two men standing there. His Javert! Two Javerts! The unofficial detective who had so brilliantly challenged him, and the official one who was to provide his alibi. Chance was happy to offer him this further opportunity for vivid daring.

He hardly heeded the opening words of the official detective nor the look of dazed bewilderment on the face of the other. He opened his lips and the Great Harrison Partridge, shedding the last vestigial vestments of the cocoon, spoke:

"You may know the truth for what good it will do you. The life of the man Ash means nothing to me. I can triumph over him even though he live. I killed Stanley Harrison. Take that statement and do with it what you can. I know that an uncorroborated confession is useless to you. If you can prove it, you may have me. And I shall soon commit another sacrifice, and you are powerless to stop me. Because, you see, you are already too late." He laughed softly.

Mr. Partridge closed the door and locked it. He finished the sandwich and the whiskey, hardly noticing the poundings on the door. He picked up the knife and went to his machine. His face was a bland mask of serene exaltation.

Fergus for the second time was speechless. But Lieutenant Jackson had hurled himself against the door, a second too late. It was a matter of minutes before he and a finally aroused Fergus had broken it down.

"He's gone," Jackson stated puzzledly. "There must be a trick exit somewhere."

" 'Locked room,' " Fergus murmured. His shoulder ached, and the charge against the door had set it bleeding again.

"What's that?"

"Nothing. Look, Andy. When do you go off duty?"

"Strictly speaking, I'm off now. I was making this checkup on my own time."

"Then let us, in the name of seventeen assorted demigods of drunkenness, go drown our confusions."

Fergus was still asleep when Lieutenant Jackson's phone call came the next morning. His sister woke him, and watched him come into acute and painful wakefulness as he listened, nodding and muttering, "Yes," or, "I'll be—"

Maureen waited till he had hung up, groped about, and found and lighted a cigarette. Then she said, "Well?"

"Remember that Harrison case I was telling you about yesterday?"

"The time-machine stuff? Yes."

"My murderer, Mr. Partridge—they found him in a gully out on his great-uncle's estate. Apparently slipped and killed himself while attempting his second murder—that's the way Andy sees it. Had a knife with him. So, in view of that and a sort of confession he made yesterday, Andy's turning Simon Ash loose. He still doesn't see how Partridge worked the first murder, but he doesn't have to bring it into court now."

"Well? What's the matter? Isn't that fine?"

"Matter? Look, Maureen Macushla. I killed Partridge. I didn't mean to, and maybe you could call it justifiable; but I did. I killed him at one o'clock yesterday afternoon. Andy and I saw him at two; he was then eating a ham sandwich and drinking whiskey. The stomach analysis proves that he died half an hour after that meal, when I was with Andy starting out on a bender of bewilderment. So you see?"

"You mean he went back afterward to kill his uncle and then you . . . you saw him after you'd killed him only before he went back to be killed? Oh, how awful."

"Not just that, my sweeting. This is the humor of it: The time alibi, the elsewhen that gave the perfect cover up for Partridge's murder—it gives exactly the same ideal alibi to his own murderer."

Maureen started to speak and stopped. "Oh!" she gasped. "What?"

"The time machine. It must still be there—somewhere—mustn't it? Shouldn't you—"

Fergus laughed, and not at comedy. "That's the payoff of perfection on this opus. I gather Partridge and his sister didn't love each other too dearly. You know what her first reaction was to the news of his death? After one official tear and one official sob, she went and smashed the hell out of his workshop."

On a workshop floor lay twisted, shattered coils and bus-bars. In the morgue lay a plump bald body with a broken neck. These remained of the Great Harrison Partridge.

THE EDITORS

Douglas G. Greene is by profession a university teacher and by avocation a dilettante. He graduated from the University of South Florida in 1966, and after obtaining the degrees of Master of Arts and Doctor of Philosophy from the University of Chicago he joined the faculty of Old Dominion University, Norfolk, Virginia, in 1971. Since 1983, he has been Professor of History and Director of the Institute of Humanities. He is author and/or editor of eight books, including two posthumous collections of stories and plays by John Dickson Carr: THE DOOR TO DOOM (1980) and THE DEAD SLEEP LIGHTLY (1983). He is married with two children.

Robert C. S. Adey has been collecting things since he could walk and books since he could read. He has amassed a large book collection which includes nearly all those volumes featured in his bibliography, LOCKED ROOM MURDERS and OTHER IMPOSSIBLE CRIMES (1979). He is married, with two dogs, and when not busy adding to his collection, is employed as a tax surveyor in Worcestershire in Her Majesty's Customs and Excise.

Greene and Adey are frequent contributors to various books and magazines, including *The Armchair Detective, The Poisoned Pen, The Mystery Fancier,* and *CADS: Crime and Detective Stories.*

LIBRARY OF CRIME CLASSICS®

NEW TITLES

ISBN	Author and Title	Price
0-930330-		
65-X	Baxt—Satan Is A Woman	$5.95
75-7	Greene & Adey—Death Locked In	$12.95*
72-2	Armstrong—Mischief	$4.95
66-8	Baxt—Topsy & Evil	$4.95
71-4	O'Farrell—Repeat Performance	$4.95
73-0	Brean—Wilders Walk Away	$4.95
74-9	Rawson—No Coffin for the Corpse	$4.95
68-4	Dickson—The Peacock Feather Murders	$4.95
69-2	Dickson—Nine—and Death Makes Ten	$4.95
70-6	Queen—Drury Lane's Last Case	$4.95
67-6	Millar—The Iron Gates	$4.95

*Special Offer: Pre-publication price $10.95 until Dec. 31, 1987.

MARGARET MILLAR TITLES

ISBN	Author and Title	Price
0-930330-23-4	Millar—An Air That Kills	Pa. $4.95
0-930330-15-3	Millar—Ask for Me Tomorrow	Pa. $4.95
0-930330-14-5	Millar—Banshee	Pa. $4.95
0-930330-07-2	Millar—Beast in View	Pa. $4.95
0-930330-31-5	Millar—Beyond This Point Are Monsters	Pa. $4.95
0-930330-32-3	Millar—The Cannibal Heart	Pa. $4.95
0-930330-10-2	Millar—The Fiend	Pa. $4.95
0-930330-59-5	Millar—Fire Will Freeze	Pa. $4.95
0-930330-04-8	Millar—How Like an Angel	Pa. $4.95
0-930330-52-8	Millar—The Listening Walls	Pa. $4.95
0-930330-26-9	Millar—Rose's Last Summer	Pa. $4.95
0-930330-06-4	Millar—A Stranger in my Grave	Pa. $4.95
0-930330-42-0	Millar—Wall of Eyes	Pa. $4.95

JOHN DICKSON CARR TITLES

ISBN	Author and Title	Price
0-930330-50-1	Carr—Below Suspicion	Pa. $4.95
0-930330-27-7	Carr—The Burning Court	Pa. $4.95
0-930330-22-6	Carr—Death Turns the Tables	Pa. $4.95
0-930330-28-5	Carr—Hag's Nook	Pa. $4.95
0-930330-38-2	Carr—He Who Whispers	Pa. $4.95
0-930330-61-7	Carr—The House at Satan's Elbow	Pa. $4.95
0-930330-51-X	Carr—The Problem of the Green Capsule	Pa. $4.95
0-930330-24-2	Carr—The Sleeping Sphinx	Pa. $4.95
0-930330-39-0	Carr—The Three Coffins	Pa. $4.95
0-930330-21-8	Carr—Till Death Do Us Part	Pa. $4.95
	WRITING AS CARTER DICKSON	
0-930330-62-5	Dickson—The Judas Window	Pa. $4.95

BACKLIST

ISBN	Author and Title	Price
0-930330-55-2	Baxt—The Alfred Hitchcock Murder Case	Pa. $5.95
0-930330-36-6	Baxt—The Dorothy Parker Murder Case	Pa. $4.95
0-930330-57-9	Baxt— ''I!'' Said the Demon	Pa. $4.95
0-930330-47-1	Baxt—A Parade of Cockeyed Creatures	Pa. $4.95
0-930330-46-3	Baxt—A Queer Kind of Death	Pa. $4.95
0-930330-56-0	Baxt—Swing Low, Sweet Harriet	Pa. $4.95
0-930330-37-4	Boucher—Nine Times Nine	Pa. $4.95
0-930330-12-9	Brahms & Simon—A Bullet in the Ballet*	Pa. $4.95
0-930330-33-1	Brahms & Simon—Murder A La Stroganoff*	Pa. $4.95
0-930330-49-8	Brahms & Simon—Six Curtains for Stroganova*	Pa. $4.95
0-930330-18-8	Brand, C.—Cat and Mouse	Pa. $4.95
0-930330-48-X	Brand, M.—The Night Flower	Pa. $4.95
0-930330-01-3	Daly—Murder From the East	Pa. $4.95

ISBN	Author and Title	Price
0-930330-08-0	De La Torre—Dr. Sam: Johnson, Detector	Pa. $4.95
0-930330-09-9	De La Torre—The Detections of Dr. Sam: Johnson	Pa. $4.95
0-930330-34-X	De La Torre—The Return of Dr. Sam: Johnson, Detector	Pa. $4.95
0-930330-63-3	De La Torre—The Exploits of Dr. Sam: Johnson, Detector	Pa. $5.95
0-930330-64-1	Gallico—The Abandoned	Pa. $5.95
0-930330-40-4	Gollin—The Philomel Foundation	Pa. $4.95
0-930330-54-4	Gollin—Eliza's Galiardo	Pa. $4.95
0-930330-05-6	Hammett & Raymond—Secret Agent X-9	Pa. $9.95
0-930330-02-1	Hull—The Murder of My Aunt	Pa. $4.95
0-930330-35-8	Lincoln—A Private Disgrace Lizzie Borden by Daylight	Pa. $5.95
0-930330-41-2	Malzberg—Underlay	Pa. $4.95
0-930330-20-X	Nolan—Look Out for Space	Pa. $4.95
0-930330-19-6	Nolan—Space for Hire	Pa. $4.95
0-930330-43-9	Queen—The Tragedy of X	Pa. $4.95
0-930330-53-6	Queen—The Tragedy of Y	Pa. $4.95
0-930330-58-7	Queen—The Tragedy of Z	Pa. $4.95
0-930330-11-0	Rafferty—Cork of the Colonies	Pa. $4.95
0-930330-16-1	Rafferty—Die Laughing	Pa. $4.95
0-930330-44-7	Rawson—Death From A Top Hat	Pa. $4.95
0-930330-45-5	Rawson—Footprints on the Ceiling	Pa. $4.95
0-930330-60-9	Rawson—The Headless Lady	Pa. $4.95
0-930330-25-0	Sherwood—A Shot in the Arm	Pa. $4.95
0-930330-30-7	Talbot—Rim of The Pit	Pa. $4.95
0-930330-29-3	Teilhet—The Talking Sparrow Murders	Pa. $4.95

Please add $1.00 to the retail price of the first book, 50¢ for each additional book to cover postage and handling.

INTERNATIONAL POLYGONICS, LTD.
540 Barnum Avenue, Bridgeport, Connecticut 06608